West of Guam:

The Complete Cases of Jo Gar

Raoul Whitfield

WEST OF GUAM: THE COMPLETE CASES OF JO GAR

FROM THE PAGES OF BLACK MASK

RAOUL WHITFIELD

Illustrations by

ARTHUR RODMAN BOWKER

Essays by

E.R. HAGEMANN

&

R.H. MILLER

Series Editor

KEITH ALAN DEUTSCH

Another Volume in the BLACK MASK LIBRARY

ALTUS PRESS

BLACK MASK PRESS

Boston · Philadelphia · New York

2013

DESIGNED AND PUBLISHED BY
Matthew Moring

BLACK MASK SERIES EDITOR
Keith Alan Deutsch

PUBLISHING HISTORY
Owing to limitations of space, permissions to reprint previously published material appear on pages 539-42.

Published by arrangement with Black Mask Press/Keith Alan Deutsch (keithdeutsch@mac.com).

THANKS TO
The editor would like to thank every fan, scholar, and collector who helped in assembling the original stories. In particular the publishers would like to thank Peter Ruber, who unearthed new and original biographical information about Raoul Whitfield during the production of this book; of particular help in supplying material was Mr. Daniel J. Slive, Rare Books Librarian and the rest of the staff in the Department of Special Collections at the UCLA Library; Mr. Bill Pronzini good friend and *Black Mask* scholar; Paul S. Herman; Jim Cavett, Hearst's Reprint Rights Editor at Reed Brennan Media Associates; Tom Roberts; Gene Christie; David Blyth; Boris Dralyuk; Larry Estep; John Locke; Mr. Otto Penzler, publisher of *The Armchair Detective;* Mr. Michael Chomko, publisher of the great pulp fanzine, *Purple Prose;* Professor R.H. Miller, colleague of Dr. Hagemann; and Mr. Rob Preston, a great collector of all pulp magazines.

Visit altuspress.com for more books like this.
Printed in the United States of America.

Another volume in the BLACK MASK LIBRARY.

Table of Contents

Raoul F. Whitfield, A Star with the Mask

E.R. Hagemann

The first machine-gun started a staccato clatter from an alley on the right. Almost instantly there was a drum of a second one—from a shuttered window on the left. Metal started to make a sound. The chauffeur ran a few feet and sprawled to the street. At that moment, the Chinese sprang from the car, doubled over and ran to a door nearest the car. He disappeared. The other occupants of the car were crouched, out of sight, below the metal sides.

—"Diamond of Dread"
Black Mask, 13 (February 1931), 89; a Jo Gar Story

CONSIDERED BY scholars of detective fiction to be a founder of the Hard-Boiled School, Raoul Fauconnier Whitfield today is little known; yet during his prolific albeit rather brief writing career, he was popular, well-paid, and a respected peer of Hammett & Co.[1] And he was a Star among editor Joseph Shaw's stable of *Black Mask* stars: W.T. Ballard, William D. Bray, Paul Cain, Raymond Chandler, George Harmon Coxe, Eugene Cunningham, Tom Curry, Carroll John Daly, Norbert Davis, Erle Stanley Gardner, Dashiell Hammett, Nels Leroy Jorgensen, Ed Lybeck, Horace McCoy, Frederick Nebel, J.J. des Ormeaux, Norvell Page, Earl and Marion Scott, Stewart Stirling, J. Paul Suter, Theodore A. Tinsley, Roger Torrey, and Thomas Walsh—to call the roll of known and unknown pulp writers; for the focus of this article is Whitfield and *Black Mask*. (His hardback novels require a separate article.)

Whitfield was born in New York City in 1897 (also given as 1898)

---

1 *The reader is forewarned that the above biographical sketch was often conjectural and second-hand, and the author apologizes therefor. Attempts were put forth to verify all data but this proved an impossible task. Conversely, the reader is assured that bibliographic and published data are accurate throughout.*

and educated there.[2] His family seems to have had some social position and money—Andrew Carnegie's wife was Louise Whitfield, whom he married in 1887. As a youth, Whitfield journeyed, stopping over in Honolulu, to the Philippines with his father, who was attached to the Territorial Government in Manila. The young man was later to put this experience to good use in some of his fiction. While out in the Islands, he also visited Japan and China. In 1916, there is a chance he had a fling in the movies upon his return from the Far East.[3]

With the advent of the Great War, he enlisted first in the ambulance corps and then in the Air Service. He trained and soloed at Kelly Field, San Antonio, Texas. After commission as second lieutenant with his wings, he went over to The Big Show on the U.S.S. *Louisville* in the summer of 1918. In France, he ferried unarmed American-built DH-4s from Romorantin to forward areas, towed targets at St. Jean de Monts, and briefly saw aerial combat before the Armistice. He was a good but not expert pilot. Aviation figures prominently in his early pulp fiction and his juveniles.

After discharge, he went to Pittsburgh to "learn" the steel business in 1919, the year his famed relative died. Tiring of laboring in the mills, Whitfield switched to a variety of jobs, chiefly newspaper work, before eventually turning to writing full time. It is said that he sold his first story in 1923. This is entirely possible, but there is no record.[4] An early story, probably his debut for Joe Shaw, appeared in *Black Mask* in March 1926. The editor later remembered (on one of two different occasions): "When we had the pleasure of first acquaintance, he was on his way to Florida to hole in away from interruption and settle down to the serious business of making a first-rate newspaper-

2 *The main biographical sources are Joseph T. Shaw's discarded introduction to* The Hard-Boiled Omnibus, *written in 1946, and in the Special collections, University of California, Los Angeles, to whom the author expresses thanks for permission to quote from; three issues of* Black Mask, *November, 1926, August, 1930, and June, 1932; dust jackets to Whitfield's* Death in a Bowl *and* The Virgin Kills; *and headnotes to four of Whitfield's stories reprinted in* Ellery Queen's Mystery Magazine, *hereafter* EQMM, *October 1947, May 1948, February 1949, and March 1949.*

3 *The movies surface several times in limning his career, but nothing is definite except a credit for an original story. Certainly he had the looks and physique. He was six feet tall and had a dark handsomeness with a pencil mustache. In his days this was known as the Latin look.*

4 *It may have appeared in* Black Mask *before Shaw took over the editorship in 1926.*

man into a better writer."[5]

Writer he became, and an astonishingly prolific one, during a period when prolificacy was the necessary lot of pulp and popular fiction writers—Gardner and Brand come to mind—in order to survive. From March 1926 through February 1934, Whitfield published at least eighty-seven pieces in *Black Mask,* sixty-three under his own name and twenty-four under his one known pseudonym, Ramon Decolta; three hard-boiled novels for Alfred A, Knopf, *Green Ice* (1930), *Death in a Bowl* (1931), and *The Virgin Kills* (1932); and four juveniles, *Wings of Gold* (1930), *Silver Wings* (1930), *Danger Zone* (1931), and *Danger Circus* (1933), all of which are concerned with aviation.[6] And during this time, 1928 to 1930, a Knopf dust-jacket blurb would have us believe that the man was also pursuing his acting career in the movies. Not for one moment do I believe this. But I can vouch that for at least two years, 1930 to 1932, he was in Europe with his wife, Prudence, and lived in Paris for part of his stay.

Back to his phenomenal output, however.

> [He] always wrote very easily and quickly, and with a minimum or corrections [states Queen], He had a particular talent for starting with a title and writing around it. His wife has said that once he had a title, he had the story. He would place neat stacks of chocolate bars (which he ate by the thousands) to the right of his typewriter, and a picket fence of cigarettes to his left. He wrote and chain-smoked and ate, all in one unified operation.[7]

Shaw had a somewhat different remembrance of Whitfield as a writer:

> He was a hard, patient, determined worker. His style from the first was hard and brittle and over-inclined to staccato. Later, he became more fluent and went along... with the best of them. Earlier, a newspaperman, he wrote from knowledge of men, and women, and their

5 Black Mask, *15 (June 1932), 123. Shaw adds that Whitfield's first story for* Black Mask *was in April 1926; he meant March.*

6 *There were twelve stories in* Silver Wings, *all but one of which appeared in* Boy's Life *beginning in 1927; five are set in World War I. This volume and* Danger Zone, *another war collection, are autobiographical. I have never seen a copy of* Danger Circus *nor a review, but I assume that it, too, concerns wartime flying.*

7 EQMM, *10 (October 1947). 16. Queen's source was correspondence from Mrs. Prudence Whitfield.*

ways... Whit was ambitious. He wanted to invade other fields than that of crime detection and criminal conflict.[8]

Let Queen conclude the discussion.

> The fact is, [he] needed very little to start him on a story. An incident which most people would consider trivial, a newspaper account buried on an inside page, a casual remark by a stranger—these were the fragile details out of which he wove flashing designs.[9]

Some time in the late 1920s, when is unclear, Whitfield began corresponding with Hammett, who was living in San Francisco. He allegedly became Dash's champion and wrote letters to editors asking that they take his stuff. Finally, the two writers met and talked shop. "It was terrifying," Mrs. Whitfield recalled some twenty years later, "to hear them seriously debate whether a particular story should have seven murders—or twenty-seven!" Seeing Hammett writing "laboriously, alone in a room, with dirty dishes strewn all over the kitchen floor," left an indelible impression.[10] Shaw was aware of and knew of the friendship.

> Long and fascinating were the discussions between Whit and Dash. Whit maintained that, given characters and a general plot, it was a cinch to write a detective story. When in a spot, all you need do, is use the well-known props. A good writer should produce a novel without any of these appurtenances to achieve effect. And Dash's comeback, "All right, if you want to make it the hard way, try writing a book omitting every word that has the letter 'f' for example." [11]

Apocryphal? I will pass. It hasn't made the canon of myriad tales about Hammett.

By February 1934, Whitfield's career was nearing the end. He had been credited with the authorship of a story for a movie called *Private Detective 62* (Warner Bros.) starring William Powell and Margaret Lindsay and released in July 1933—his one and only confirmed screen

8 *Discarded introduction to* The Hard-Boiled Omnibus.

9 EQMM, *13 (March 1949). 81.*

10 EQMM, *11 (May 1948). 40.*

11 *Discarded introduction to* Omnibus. *Shaw gives no source.*

job.[12] A little more than a year before, Shaw in his editor's page in *Black Mask* had proclaimed somewhat loudly, "As this number goes into print, Raoul Whitfield has hied himself hence to Hollywood on a long period contract with Paramount on terms that take all the press out of Depression." This is moot. *Film Daily Yearbook,* Hollywood's bible, does not list anything of his emanating out of the iron gates on Melrose Avenue.

By the mid-1930s, Whitfield was stricken with a long, mysterious illness that literally stopped him in his tracks. Speculation about it, although irresistible, is worthless. Shaw called it a "personal tragedy," and indeed it was, for Whitfield, at the peak of his career, other than two lesser Jo Gar stories for *Hearst's International-Cosmopolitan* in February 1935 and August 1937, seems not to have published another word before his death, place unknown in 1945. No obituary has been found.

They come and they go in any business, especially the detective fiction business, and he who falters is forgotten. Good old Joe Shaw hung in there and tried for old times sake. On 29 November 1945 he wrote Whitfield's wife:

> Dear Prue:
>
> In that Anthology *[The Hard-Boiled Omnibus]* I mentioned, I have included two of Raoul's, including one under the name Ramon Decolta.
>
> As you will note on the enclosed forms, you will get $100 for the longer one; $40 for the short. Please sign and return to me.
>
> Have you heard anything further from the Mercury-Ellery Queen people?

Three weeks short of one year later, 8 November 1946, Shaw sent her the $140. Meanwhile, she had been successful in negotiating with Queen to republish her husband's *Black Mask* stories. In the October 1947 *EQMM* appeared "Blue Murder" (September 1932); by then, Queen was able to call him "a much too neglected member of the Hammett-Daly-Chandler hardboiled school," and made a very decent effort to rectify the neglect by reprinting eight stories in all. Nothing, much in the way of posthumous recognition came of it. Shaw had tried, too, in *Omnibus,* with "Inside Job" (February 1932) and "Death

12 His name is consistently misspelled "Whitefield" in the credits; the original story was "Man Killer," Black Mask, *15 (April 1932). Rian James was the adaptor and dialoguer and Michael Curtiz directed.*

in the Pasig" (March 1930). Nothing came of that either. Except irony; the book is now a minor classic, but Whitfield is still buried in the ash heap. Ron Goulart included "China Man" (March 1932) in his *The Hardboiled Dicks.*[13] And nothing, *nothing.*

They come and they go and when they go they are buried—for good—more or less.

WHITFIELD'S EARLY years on *Mask* were spent writing series grouped about central heroes and geographical locales; they were typical action stories, the kind Shaw was inordinately fond of. They vary vastly in quality. His earliest (1926) concerned Bill Scott (Scotty), a pilot, and Bing Russell, his mechanic, who roam the Border in their dilapidated J.H. 6, looking for crooks, adventure, and air shows. In December, Whitfield began a similar series about Chuck Reddington, a detective, who flies a plane for the Center City police department with his sidekick, Jake Bailey. The stuff is run-of-the-mill, although Whitfield does well with the flying, and today seems downright silly. But incredible as it may seem, readers in those days "ate it up" issue after issue, as is evidenced in June 1928, when Shaw introduced Border Brand (six segments) with a hard-sell flourish, something else he was fond of.

> "First Blood" is the first of a series of amazing stories by Raoul F. Whitfield of a daring Federal officer, a man who knows how to fly a machine when necessary, and their [sic] desperate fight with a gang operating along the Border. There is everything in this yarn that men of action like to read about—thrills galore.[14]

MacLeod, a former wartime flyer, and Ben Breed carry on a running battle with The Wop, Antonio Flores, and in the final installment, "The Sky-Trap" (November 1928), engage him in a dogfight and shoot him down. He dies in the crash.[15]

No more had Border Brand ended than Whitfield launched into "Laughing Death" (nine parts), February-October 1929, wherein Gary Greer, another World War flyer and owner of an airfield in Center City, avenges the death of his prosecuting attorney father, Sanford

---

13 *L.A.: Sherbourne Press, 1965; New York: Pocket Books, 1967.*

14 *11 (June 1928).*

15 *Like most pulp writers, Whitfield had no qualms about using racial and ethnic epithets and slurs aboundingly; such was perfectly acceptable fifty years ago.*

Greer, rubbed out by gangsters who laughed as they killed—a good scene.

> [Greer] had somewhere to go, something to do. As he moved, his eyes were narrowed, staring straight ahead. Only his tight-pressed lips seemed to be laughing. And theirs was not a pleasant laughter—it was the cold laughter of death. Death to gangsters who had killed with laughter on their own lips.[16]

I believe that "Laughing Death" was originally planned as a novel, then abandoned in favor of its immediate and far superior successor, "The Crime Breeders," December 1929-April 1930, the first version of Whitfield's first novel, *Green Ice,* published by Knopf, 11 July 1930. Mal Ourney, an ex-con who has done a two-year stretch in Sing Sing for a girlfriend he felt responsible to, goes after what he calls Crime Breeders, the big-time hoods who prey on the small-timers.

Whitfield was now in full stride and would continue until the sudden "silence" in the mid-1930s. He bracketed the three-part serialization of "The Maestro Murder," September-November 1930, published as *Death in a Bowl,* 13 March 1931, with two good tough-guy stories. The first was "Murder by Mistake," August 1930, an initial shy at the private-eye agency-eye genre. Don Burney, a former NYPD dick, solves the murder of gambler-broker Roger Gratton by submachine-gun fire in front of a New York speak. The ending is a bit weak, but the dialogue is good and sprinkled with a wry humor. The second was "Murder in the Ring," December 1930, Whitfield's finest for *Mask,* a fight story crowded with crooks, killers, and hangers-on. Gus Monkly has a heavyweight, Giant Pardo, who is headed for a championship bout.[17] However, treachery prevails: Pardo is killed in the ring and Monkly is shot and dies alone (in another good scene) in a lunch wagon. The story is spare, fast-moving, with believable characters. Whitfield knew the fight game and could describe a match with the best of them. The dialogue is the best he ever attained to.

He took a breather and fiddled around with racketeer-crime stories and the trite Skyline Murders (six parts) with millionaire bachelor, sportsman, and clubman Alan Van Cleve as hero and his deadly enemy, Barney Ruys, a shyster, as heavy. Van Cleve explains to Dale Byrons,

---

16 *"The Carnival Kill,"* Black Mask, *12 (July 1929), 60.*

17 *Pardo bears an amazing resemblance to Primo Carnera two and one-half years before he beat Jack Sharkey for the title.*

his fiancée:

> That's what New York is for us, Dale—a sort of steel arena. Barney Ruys and I have money—enough to buy death for each other. And we both know that. I haven't any evidence against him, and he knows that.... He's shrewd, hard—a killer. I guess he's always been a killer at heart.... And now—we're at each other's throats.[18]

Once shed of this, Whitfield got himself back on the track again with three stories in 1932 about agency-detective Don Free in New York. The pace is uneven, but "Man Killer" keeps moving along. Tim Hammond, agency boss, and Free talk about the dead gambler, Tony Bandor.

> Hammond swore gently, then smiled. "How about taking five minutes out—and we'll both weep for dear old Tony Bandor," he said with sarcasm. "He'll be missed at church on Sunday. I don't imagine he spotted out more than eight or ten guys—and he only beat three stick-up indictments." [19]

For the remainder of his time with *Black Mask,* Whitfield experimented with both private-and cop-detective modes, using either New York or Hollywood settings and first-person narrators except for Ben Jardinn, the Hollywood shamus who named the killer of conductor Hans Reiner in *Death in a Bowl.* Jardinn appears in two stories, "Murder by Request," January 1933, and a most unusual one, "Dark Death," August 1933, because of Whitfield's version of the March 1933 earthquake in Los Angeles County. In "Request," somebody asks Ben:

> "How's business with you?"
> Jardinn frowned. "Terrible," he said. "All the wives are hanging on to their husbands because the lovers' jobs may not last. And all the husbands are hanging on to their wives because they can't afford two girls." [20]

---

18 *"Steel Arena,"* Black Mask, *14 (October 1931), 29.*

19 Black Mask, *15 (April 1932), 16; the other two stories are "Walking Dynamite," May 1932, and "Blue Murder," September 1932. Free now has his own agency—Hammond turned out to be a crook, and Free killed him —and, believe it or not, a Jewish secretary, Beth Liner.*

20 Black Mask, *15 (January 1933), 27. These are the only two stories with Jardinn.*

But, really, business is good and Jardinn has all he needs in the murder on the lot of director Dave Cameron. Not a bad story at all until the final three or four pages, when Jardinn confronts the reader suddenly with all kinds of dope only he has had access to. Judicious rewriting would have helped immensely.

Sudden death occurs in "Death" as the earthquake strikes. In his office, Jardinn is faced with a hood, gun drawn.

> The indirect lighting suddenly was less brilliant. Sound beat into the room. Crackling sound. The light died completely. Outside glass was crashing. There was an explosion. The office was swaying now. Jardinn staggered and then let his body fall sideways and downward. Carrow shouted hoarsely:
>
> "——! Earthquake—"
>
> His gun crashed and Jardinn felt stinging pain just above the right elbow. The gun made only sharp, faint sound against the greater sound of falling material. There were screams in the boulevard, and the shaking was more violent now.[21]

On the set, the cameras continue to grind and shoot the violent demise of director Alan McLean by human means. Ben orders a re-run and the murderer is apprehended; the same gimmick was used as a finale in *The Virgin Kills* to discover the killer of Babe Herron, the California stroke, who was put away during the rowing of the Poughkeepsie Regatta.

Whitfield knew his way around Hollywood, and his stories show it; they are of more than passing interest as I write in 1978.

His residence in the Philippines was put to good use when, under the name of Ramon Decolta, he wrote his most sustained series for Shaw: the twenty-four stories featuring Jo Gar, the Island Detective, who has a tiny office above Wong Ling's place just off the Escolta, Manila's main drag.[22] A veteran of the Manila police force, Gar solves murder after murder, most of which are committed with a variety of knives. He smokes brown-paper cigarettes, speaks in a "toneless" (one of Whitfield's overused words) voice, carries and uses a .45 Army

---

21 Black Mask, *16 (August 1933), 8. The quake struck 5:45p.m., 10 March 1933; the aftershocks continued for a long time; the seventh temblor hit at 7:55p.m. Damage was widespread.*

22 Under his own name, he published two more Gar stories in Hearst's International-Cosmopolitan *in February 1935 and August 1937.*

Colt automatic (he is also skilled with a knife), drinks claret warm or chilled, and prefers a pony-hauled *carromatta* for transportation.

> He was a young man, but he looked rather old. His hair was grey; he was medium in size, but because of the loose way he carried himself he appeared rather small. His face was brown—very brown. He had good teeth, a narrow lipped mouth, fine features. His eyes were slightly almond shaped, and they were seldom normally open. They held a peculiar squint.[23]

Upon occasion he teams with Lt. Arragon, his friend, former comrade, and now rival; together they make a good contrast:

> The lieutenant of Manila police preferred action to thought. He was often too anxious. Thus, he had often failed where Jo Gar, proceeding in an almost sleepy manner, had succeeded. Jo suited his action to the climate of the Islands. Manila was not New York, or San Francisco.[24]

Jo is not necessarily bound to Manila, however. Twice he goes aboard ship for extended voyages, once to Nagasaki to trap jewel thieves and murderers, once across the Pacific (in a "serial" of six "chapters") to San Francisco to regain the Rainbow diamonds and to avenge the murder-death of Arragon. At the end he muses, " 'I have all—all the Rainbow diamonds. Now I can go home, after the police come. I hope my friend Juan Arragon—knows.' "[25]

The Gar stories are worthy of a revival, as are the hard-boiled items, and either or both would be a reasonable publishing venture in paperback. At his best in *Mask,* Whitfield was very, very good; at his weakest, he was infuriatingly bad. The weaknesses can be laid to speed and pressure of deadlines. Fifteen times he appeared twice in the same issue as Raoul Whitfield and Ramon Decolta. In other words, he wrote too much too quickly, and when he was in a spot he fell back on what he had warned Hammett against—"the well-known props." He was what I have called him, a Pulpeteer, and a damned good one. Despite the passage of some forty years since he ceased writing, he is not embarrassing to read, which is certainly not so with some of the *Mask* contemporaries. It is a shame that he has been forgotten, for he deserves better.

---

23 *"West of Guam,"* Black Mask, *12 (February 1930), 52; this was the first Jo Gar story.*

24 *"Signals of Storm,"* Black Mask, *13 (June 1930), 49.*

25 *"Diamonds of Death,"* Black Mask, *14 (August 1931), 54.*

Ramon Decolta, AKA Raoul Whitfield, and His Diminutive Brown Man: Jo Gar, the Island Detective

E.R. Hagemann

HE IS Jo Gar, the Island detective—the Philippine Islands, that is. Chances are that he was baptized Jose Garcia, although the more common nickname would have been Joe.

> He was a young man, but he looked rather old. His hair was gray; he was medium in size, but because of the loose way he carried himself he appeared rather small. His face was brown—very brown. He had good teeth, a narrow lipped mouth, fine features. His eyes were slightly almond shaped, and they were seldom normally opened. They held a peculiar squint ("West of Guam," p. 52).[26]

This was the initial description of Señor Gar by Ramon Decolta (Raoul Whitfield) in the first of twenty-four stories in *Black Mask,* February 1930 through July, 1933. As the series progressed, Decolta/Whitfield perfected and modified the physical description and repeated, often unduly, certain salient features. His eyes are blue-gray and pronouncedly almond-shaped. His body is short and small; his shoulders, narrow; his arms, short; his feet small; and his fingers, stubby. He has a habit of running them through his gray hair. He has another habit: keeping his eyes nearly or almost closed. He speaks in a toneless voice as frequently as he smiles and shows his white, even teeth, for he is polite, above all else.

He chain-smokes brown-paper cigarettes which no one else cares for. He permits himself an occasional glass of warm or iced claret or iced lemonade. The *betel*-nut is not for him. He will wear sandals when the weather demands and he will wear either a pith helmet or a Panama hat and very suitable clothing, favoring white duck and

---

26 *For six of the stories, I used the text as reprinted in* Ellery Queen's Mystery Magazine; *for "Death in the Pasig," I used the text in* The Hard-Boiled Omnibus; *for the remainder of the stories, I followed the text in* Black Mask *and* Cosmopolitan.

pongee, not always as clean as they might be. He carries a .45 Army Colt automatic in right-hip pocket; he uses it quite frequently. He is right-handed. He is often the intended target of a knife, and he has been known to wield one himself in self-defense ("Nagasaki Knives"). He lives sensibly in the heat of the Western Pacific.

> [He] relaxed his short body, kept his almond-shaped eyes almost closed. Now and then he lifted his brown-paper cigarette, inhaled. It was almost as though he slept between puffs... ("The Man in White," p. 81)

He maintains a small, not particularly comfortable office "above Wong Ling's place," on a "narrow and curving" street, not far off the Escolta, the main business thoroughfare in Manila, and almost on the bank of the Pasig River ("Red Hemp," p. 33; "Diamonds of Dread," p. 83). He seldom locks it, for he keeps "little of importance" there and is seldom in it ("Signals of Storm," p. 43). A visitor who has climbed the narrow, creaking stairs is apt to see lizards crawling on the ceiling and be annoyed by flies. The three-bladed ceiling fan, whirling at a slow speed, merely moves the tepid air around ("The Magician Murder," p. 91). If it is not too hot, Jo will wave a palm-leaf fan. His proudest possession is a fan-backed wicker chair, and a small cabinet where he keeps his meager files. His one luxury is a latter-day obtained jade paper knife "many years old" ("The Mystery of the Fan-backed Chair," p. 58). When he is not carrying his Colt, he keeps it in a desk drawer. The office has one other occupant: Jo's Siamese cat, of whom he is inordinately fond. He has no secretary, no receptionist, no assistant.[27]

> Several times he had thought of moving into more desirable quarters, but there was something about his tiny, hot office in the old building that he liked. His fees were not big... and many of his clients were not rich. If he were to move... he would perhaps not be able to accept cases that interested him, and his contacts would be different.
>
> He had decided that he would lose more than he would gain, and he had remained... he liked the river sounds that reached him from the dark-watered Pasig, and the odors that drifted up from the small shops near the river—odors of spices and hemp and shell foods ("China Man," pp. 93-94).

27 It is interesting to note that in FBC he does have an assistant, Sidi Kalaa, half Malay, half Arab!

Only very late in the series do we discover that Jo Gar owns a house with "a Spanish gate" and keeps a houseboy named Vincente ("The Amber Fan"). He habitually rises early and therefore misses his *siesta* if on a case. He owns a small automobile but he "did not like machines [autos]; he preferred a pony hauled *carromatta* to the *cales[a]*. But a horse got along better in wind and rain" ("Signals of Storm," p. 46). He is a devotee of cockfights and magic performances. He knows a good deal about Siamese cats and pearls. "He thought of the [Randonn] pearls. They were the finest he had ever seen. He had looked at many, in the South Seas and the Orient. He was something of an authority on them" ("Nagasaki Bound," p. 104). It is too bad that we know nothing of his family, his education, his background.

He is a polyglot: he speaks English, Spanish, Tagalog, Chinese ("a tongue with which he had difficulty" ["The Blind Chinese," p. 44]), Japanese, and Malay ("softly and not perfectly" ["China Man," p. 101]), precisely what he needs in polyethnic Manila in the early 1930s, then a city of only some 350,000, over ten per cent of whom were Chinese. (The population now, by the way, is over one and one-quarter million.)

"In Manila—many people have tried to murder me," Jo calmly informs Benfield, a deadly antagonist ("The Blind Chinese," p. 38). And understandably so, for The Island Detective is an implacable foe.

The point was—there were many enemies. Almost always, when Jo Gar caught a man, there was a conviction. The caught one remembered, and his relatives and friends remembered. There were many enemies. Señor Gar had a reputation—criminals were afraid of him and hated him ("China Man," p. 96).

And his reputation precedes him and follows him wherever he may go. In "West of Guam," the first story, the Army officers and enlisted men aboard the transport U.S.S. *Thomas* have heard of him. Colonel Dunbar, the CO., testily requests that Jo set to and help solve the murder of Captain Jerry Lintwell, U.S.A., which of course he does. He approaches Private Burker, a suspect.

> "Don't rise," he stated. "I'm Mr. [sic] Gar—perhaps you know that."
> The private nodded. "Guess we all do," he stated.
> "You're that Manila soft-shoe—the guy that always gets his man."...
> Jo Gar shook his head.
> "Not always," he stated. "Two years ago I failed. China is a difficult country. A transport at sea has advantages" ("West of Guam," p. 55).

Incidentally, Jo is a passenger and is bringing back to Manila a criminal he apprehended in Honolulu.

Naturally, because of his work in The Pearl of the Orient, he brushes up against the local police force."[28] Five years ago, before he became a private detective, he had been on the police ("Death in the Pasig," p. 49). His friend and comrade was Lieutenant Juan Arragon, now his friendly but suspicious antagonist. Poor Arragon—he is rarely right in his "solutions."

> The lieutenant preferred action to thought. He was often too anxious. Thus, he had often failed where Jo Gar, proceeding in an almost sleepy manner, had succeeded. Jo suited his action to the climate of the Islands. Manila was not New York or San Francisco ("Signals of Storm," p. 49).

Nonetheless, Arragon is gracious in defeat, but there is Carlysle, who does not always appreciate the diminutive detective. There are times when solving a "crime, in Manila, [is] a delicate affair" ("Death in the Pasig," p. 104), and Arragon never completely trusts Jo, who might favor a client instead of justice.

The two of them argue amiably but acerbically. During an investigation, Arragon insists that Gary Landon, a second-rate theatrical performer, was a suicide. Gar insists that he was a murderer.

> Arragon grunted in disgust, "You have been right too often, perhaps," he said. "You wish to be different."
>
> Jo Gar said: "You have been wrong so much, Juan, but you still wish to be the same" ("Enough Rope," p. 31).

But when Arragon is killed pursuing jewel-robbers in Manila, Jo, shrugging off Carlysle's request for help, goes after the gang with only one thought in mind: revenge—but more on this later in the article.

Arragon is superseded by Lieutenant Sadi Ratan, immaculate, "very handsome and well built for a Filipino" ("Shooting Gallery"). For Jo, the situation is never the same again north and south of the Pasig.

> The Filipino [Ratan] looked hatred at the Island detective, and Jo Gar thought of the difference in this second-in-command to the American head (now Major Kelvey) of the Manila force—and the dead Juan Arragon. This man hated him. Arragon had disagreed with him, argued with him, but he had never hated ("The Javanese Mask,"

---

28 *Arnold Carlysle, an American, heads the Manila force, composed of Americans and Filipinos.*

p. 56).

Ratan is vindictive, insulting, nasty—and as consistently wrong as Arragon. "You have always chosen to oppose me," Jo rebukes. "It is a mistake to allow personal prejudice to enter matters of this sort, for in so doing you have often neglected important facts" ("The Man from Shanghai," p. 122). Ultimately, Ratan executes a 180-degree turn and concedes that Jo is "very clever." He says they should work together more closely. "I might even consider resigning in order to enter and strengthen your private agency." Jo has the last devastating word. "I fear that the loss to the Force would be too great, Lieutenant" ("The Amber Fan," p. 109).[29]

Jo's m.o. is as crafty as it is ruthless. He practices deceptiveness with gusto; indeed, his sleepy facade, his toneless voice, constitute a wile. Bluffing seldom pays, he admonishes Ratan ("The Man from Shanghai"), yet Jo will often bluff about his knowledge of testimony or evidence and ferret out the murderer or the information he wants, or both. He will lie; he will bargain, but only to his advantage. He will threaten to kill. I cannot resist quoting two fine moments when The Island Detective is in action.

He demands that a corrupted Chinese chauffeur who has driven him into an ambush and near-death outside Honolulu take him to Tan Ying, The Blind Chinese.

> "If I take you to the place—they will kill you."
> Jo Gar shrugged. "And if you do *not* take me—*I* will kill you," he said. "It is a difficult position."
> The driver said: "I am a poor man—"
> The Island detective nodded. "Then you have less to live for," he replied. "Let us start." ("The Blind Chinese," p. 45)

Don't lie—you are dying, Jo reproves a suspect, injured in a sampan explosion on the Pasig, having already promised that "the saints will be kind" if he talks. Santos Costios admits to killing a *calesa* driver, among other deeds. Thereupon, Gar cynically comments to Arragon that Costios only *thinks* he is going to die.

> The Filipino was staring at Jo Gar and cursing him in a stronger voice. He was accusing [him] of tricking him. He was not going to

29 Ratan does not resign. In "The Mystery of the Fan-backed Chair" and "The Great Black," he is very much around.

> die, after all.
>
> Jo Gar interrupted, sighing. "I should have said, you're not going to die yet," he corrected. "For the murder of the cales[a] driver—you will die, of course. You are pleased?"
>
> Costios cursed in a weaker tone ("The Caleso Murders," pp. 101-2).

In another case, Jo directs his client, Lemere, to summon the police. Damn the police! Replies the curio dealer. Damning the police does little good—call them, tell them the truth. " 'They will do interesting things.' " Lemere reluctantly assents and then asks Gar what *he* will do. " 'I shall talk and think. Counteracting a bad habit with a good one' " ("The Javanese Mask," p. 54). Clients can be testy. One acidly remarks that he would prefer to ask the questions and have Jo answer them. Tonelessly, The Island Detective reminds Señor Wall that " 'it is almost always simpler to ask questions than to answer them' " ("The Black Sampan," p. 97). And clients can be unacceptable: Miss Virginia Crale, for example. " 'Hysterical ladies are not pleasing in the tropics... [Her] life has been threatened so often, in her imagination, that her fees bored me beyond their value in cash' " ("The Man from Shanghai," p. 116). In this instance she was right—Jo wrong. She is brutally murdered.

Above all, Jo Gar is stubborn and a fighter, the more so the more his life is threatened. Arragon offers that maybe it would have been wiser if Jo *had* taken a sojourn from Manila.

> The Island Detective nodded. "I am like the cock Ramirez had at the Casa Club, two weeks ago," he said. "You remember—it was almost blind. It didn't seem to know just where to leap. But it would not be beaten" ("Signals of Storm," p. 44).

Jo's turf is Manila and its environs, although he sails to Nagasaki (Kyushu) on one venture, ends up in San Francisco on another, solves one up-country slaying, and one in Baguio ("Silence House"), the summer capital of the Philippines, 150 miles north of Manila, high in the mountains of western Luzon.

Manila, before World War II, was a place where racial and ethnic slurs and invectives abounded, or so Decolta/Whitfield would have us believe, and I think accurately so.[30] Distasteful as such reading may be today—and it is—derogatory remarks in print were perfectly acceptable in the 1930s, whatever the level of publication. We would be unwise to accuse Decolta/Whitfield of racial or ethnic prejudices; he presented Manila and its people as he saw them. In other words, his was an exercise in verisimilitude.[31]

To be blunt, using Decolta/Whitfield's language verbatim, Jo Gar is a half-breed; that is he has "'the blood of the Spanish and the Filipino'" in his veins ("Diamonds of Death," p. 90). Some half-dozen times in the *Black Mask* stories this comes up; twice Jo is called a half-breed, with modified adjectives, to his face ("Signals of Storm," p. 51; "Diamonds of Death," p. 90); twice Jo is obliquely disparaged ("Death in the Pasig," pp. 104-105; "The Caleso Murders," p. 98); twice Jo's momentary companion is embarrassed because he goes too far. The Island Detective, always polite, handles himself impeccably.

On a bridge over the Pasig, he talks about the apparent suicide of Gary Landon with an American, Dean Price, the actual murderer.

> "They've cut him down. White or—"
> The American checked himself; his eyes held a confused expression. Jo Gar said quietly, smiling a little:
> "Not brown like myself, Mr. Price. White—like yourself."
> Price reached for a cigar...
> "I meant no offense Señor Gar."
> Jo nodded, "it is all very well," he replied tonelessly. "I imagine the man is dead, just as both of us will be someday" ("Enough Rope," p. 26)

In "The Javanese Mask," Lemere mutters angrily about "'damned Chinks and Filipinos,'" then checks himself, "realizing that Jo Gar

30 *For all I know, this situation may pertain today. No one in this country can ever deny that the lot of Filipinos in California before 1941 was less than happy. They were considered below the Chinese and Japanese, and jokes about Filipino houseboys were standard nightclub routine. If one thinks there has been improvement, he is invited to tour the Filipino barrio along Temple Street in downtown Los Angeles.*

31 *No question about it, Decolta/Whitfield was an innovator in seriously using an Asian protagonist during this period. Sax Rohmer's Dr. Fu Manchu was an arch-villain; Earl Derr Biggers's Charlie Chan, while enormously popular, was essentially a comic figure. On 30 June 1934, Hugh Wiley introduced in Collier's James Lee Wong, a Yale-educated Chinese-American, who is a U.S. State Department secret agent. Wiley was followed by John P. Marquand, who introduced his Japanese detective, Mr. Moto, on 30 March 1935 in the* Saturday Evening Post.

was a half-breed, and that there was Filipino blood in his veins. The Island detective said nothing." (p. 50)

Paradoxically, Jo is accused of being Pro-American—too much so, for Lieutenant Ratan's liking. " 'You are protecting an American [Markden, his client]. You have always protected them. You like them.' " ("The Magician Murder," p. 92) Jo merely shrugs his narrow shoulders and says that he has not been paid *that* well, doubts he ever will be paid *that* well. But he does like Americans and he will distinguish, astringently, the Asians from them. Markden is a gambler; the Chinese do not trust him "and the Chinese were known as the wisest of the gamblers" ("The Magician Murder," p. 89) who cover bets on cockfights. He is accused of murdering with a knife a magician, Cardoro the Great, because he did not pay his debts. Observes Gar: "Markden is an American, and he would not kill and then boast about it as a Filipino or a Spaniard might do. He would not hate that much'" ("The Magician Murder," p. 96). To Jo's way of thinking, Americans would never strangle a victim with a rope—" 'that is not the way of an American in killing,' " referring to young Carmen Carejo's demise ("Red Hemp," p. 37). Nor would an American use a knife, while " 'here in the Islands,' " he explains, " 'it is most often the knife" ("The Amber Fan," p. 101).

His attitude toward the Overseas Chinese in Manila is ambiguous. He is friendly with some shopkeepers, yet can cruelly claim that all fat Chinese look alike and that there are many fat Chinese in Manila. After a knife has been thrown at him outside his office, he ruminates:

> Two thoughts were strong—the knife thrower had been a Chinese, and he had thrown very poorly. He had thrown like a Filipino would shoot, missing at even a short distance ("China Man," p. 94).

On more than one occasion, Chinese are murdered in Jo's cases, and they can be untrustworthy, wily, and dangerous. This does not prevent his defending them against Ratan's open scorn and contempt.

> Jo Gar said: "Lieutenant—you have learned a motive for the murder? His servant had reason to kill him [Delancey, a curio dealer]?"
>
> Lieutenant Ratan said sneeringly: "Chinese servants do not always need motives for murder. A sudden rage—"
>
> The Island Detective smiled. "You are correct, of course," he said ("The Javanese Mask," p. 54).

Lemere, companion and friend of the dead man, tells of the time that Gao, the Chinese houseboy, stole a carved Igorot spoon of little value.

> Jo said slowly: "The Chinese are usually quite honest.... They give the least trouble—"
> The police lieutenant said sharply: "There are some forty Chinese serving terms in Bilibid prison, Señor Gar."
> The Island detective bowed slightly. "You are undoubtedly correct, Lieutenant," he stated. ("The Javanese Mask," p. 55).

Ratan is insatiable in his desire to pin the murder of Delancey on Gao. He implies that he might also have stolen the wooden Javanese dance mask " 'to show his contempt—the Chinese are strange people.' " Jo Gar chuckles and says, " 'And the Manila police are strange people, also. Very strange' " ("The Javanese Mask," p. 55).

Then there are the women of the islands as Jo sees them. He has as little interest in them as he does in his Western women clients, for he leads an utterly sexless existence. The native women are susceptible, deceptive, sometimes murderous; and Gar is less than complimentary about their physical attractiveness. He just doesn't care for them. In "Red Hemp" he asks Carejo for a picture of his missing daughter, Carmen.

> It was a clear snapshot; it showed a dark-haired, slender girl of about eighteen. She was rather pretty, in a way of the islands, which was not a lasting way. She had large eyes and a rather thin face (p. 34).

In "Signals of Storm," the Island Detective interviews Rosa Castrone, who, it later turns out, is an accomplice in the kidnapping of Sam Ying, a wealthy, corrupt Chinese.

> [She] was a plump girl of perhaps twenty. She had blue eyes and blonde hair, but she was not the true Spanish type. She was half Filipino; her lips were too thick and her features too big (p. 45).

The nameless chambermaid in "The Siamese Cat" is involved in two murders. "She was dark haired, medium in size. She was good looking for a Filipino girl, slenderer than most of them. Her English was very good" (p. 37). When she is cornered, she spats obscenities at Jo "in a half Spanish, half Filipino dialect" (p. 38). Another nameless Island woman impersonates behind a veil the supposedly grieving widow, Clara Landon. Jo unceremoniously tears off the veil. "She was a *mestiz[a],* mostly Filipino. But Spanish or Anglo-Saxon blood had given her skin a white tint. She was small, very thin" ("Enough Rope," p. 32). Jo threatens her with Bilibid Prison if she doesn't talk, and points out that many prisoners die there. She confesses.

But enough of this.

Lieutenant Ratan gives *his* solution to John Mallison's violent end in "China Man." Naturally, he is dead wrong, by now a familiar bit, but Gar is polite and patient with the man he knows hates him.

> Jo Gar nodded. "It appears to be very simple," he agreed.
>
> The police lieutenant smiled broadly. "Very," he agreed. "You waste your time, Señor Gar."
>
> The Island detective shook his head (pp. 98-99).

To Jo Gar, like any good detective, nothing is ever as it appears. "Things," are never as they appear. In the teeth of seeming evidence, he will pursue a case with dogged tenacity until he solves it—correctly. Admittedly, too much of his legwork and sleuthing is accomplished outside the boundaries of a story; at the end, therefore, the reader is suddenly "handed" data out of reach to him. This is decidedly a weakness in the series.

Another failing is what I call the "shoot-out" ending when Jo unlimbers his .45 from his hip-pocket or his side-pocket and goes into action; but even as I say this, I realize that the Code of the Pulps, e.g., *Black Mask,* dictated such a zip-bang, crash-bam finale. In a word, dear readers, it was *de rigueur.* Decolta/Whitfield knew The Code; he was not stupid.

Somehow these weaknesses are not bothersome. Nor is Jo's bluffing. Nor his unerring hunches. He is too fascinating a man to be the butt of such quibbling.

After Jo's wrap-up of Benjamin Rannis's murder, Juan Aragon has a word or two.

> "Death in the Pasig," he said slowly, "is always difficult." He smiled at Jo. "Not being a fool, I congratulate you."
>
> Jo Gar fanned himself slowly with his pith helmet. He smiled in return.
>
> "Perhaps I had the better opportunity," he said quietly. "But not being too modest—I am pleased" ("Death in the Pasig," p. 111).

And so is the honest reader pleased. Pleased by him, pleased by his bearing and his conduct, pleased by his adventures.

Sixteen of them stand by themselves and range from death on a

U.S. Army transport ("West of Guam") to death in an airplane ("Climbing Death"). More likely than not, murders happen off-stage or before a story commences. Knifings—Decolta/Whitfield has a thing about knives—shootings, and stranglings are favored, not to mention five suicides by the guilty ones, not to mention the five "humans"—one of Decolta/Whitfield's pet words—Jo either kills or wounds.

There are two serials made up of eight segments total. The first, and less interesting, is a tandem, "Nagasaki Bound" and "Nagasaki Knives." Here the diminutive Jo tracks down both the murderers of Randonn, a wealthy Englishman, and his valuable pearls which Howker and Deming have heisted. Hard-boiled action is handled very well by Decolta/Whitfield.

Jo's longest and most violent caper (a sextet) takes him from the blood-spattered streets of Manila to the suburbs of San Francisco as he chases stolen diamonds and the killers of Juan Arragon.[32] The story deserves a re-telling, for it is the high point of Decolta/Whitfield's series in *Black Mask*. Some of his best tough-guy style flashes time and again, and there are narrative passages and dialogue set pieces which compare with the finest in Hammett, Paul Cain, and Chandler.

A daring and death-dealing daylight robbery (two killed) of Delgado's jewelry shop in downtown Manila nets the gunmen the ten fabled Rainbow Diamonds, owned by Von Loffler and worth about $200,000. Arragon is killed by the gang and his body deposited in Jo's upstairs office. There is a good scene when he finds his dead friend and swears to himself to get "them." Some $15,000 in reward money is posted. Jo is approached by Delgado (whose son was killed) and Von Loffler. The Dutchman asks if Jo will work for them.

> [He] smiled with his thin, colorless lips pressed together. He parted them and said:
>
> "Yes—but I feel it will be difficult. This was not an ordinary crime. It may mean that I must leave the Islands."
>
> Delgado said firmly: "I want my son's killers—no matter where you must go..."
>
> Von Loffler said:
>
> "It will be dangerous, Señor. But that is your business."
>
> The Island detective looked expressionlessly at the room's ceiling.

---

32 *"Diamonds of Dread," "The Man in White," "The Blind Chinese," "Red Dawn," "Blue Glass," and "Diamonds of Death."*

"It will be so," he agreed. "It is my business" ("Diamonds of Dread," p. 90)

From the dying Malay whom he has shot, Gar learns of "'the one who walks badly… always in white'" and follows Ferraro aboard a Japanese liner, *Cheyo Maru,* bound from Manila to Honolulu, kills him, and obtains one diamond ("The Man in White"). From The Man in White, Jo picks up the trail of " 'the blind—Chinese—Honolulu.' " Escaping an ambush in the Hawaiian countryside at night, he finally comes upon Tan Ying, The Blind Chinese; three deaths ensue in the finale but no diamonds ("The Blind Chinese"). A name, Mendez, was given Jo, and in "Red Dawn" the detective learns from the man that diamonds were divided among the gang members. Mendez is killed in his own trap which he had set for Jo.

Once again aboard the *Cheyo Maru* ("Blue Glass") now bound for San Francisco, Jo picks up five diamonds from gang member Eugene Tracy who is shot and killed by the mysterious Woman in Black (Rosa Jetmars), also a gang-member. She has the remaining four Rainbows. She slips them on to Raaker, the renegade Dutchman, mastermind of the caper, and whom Jo Gar had driven out of Manila some years before. Out near the Cliff House, outside of San Francisco, the two men face each other.

"You stayed out of Manila, Raaker—you couldn't risk coming back. You hired men. Some of them tricked you—and each other. The robbery as successful, but you lost slowly. All the way back from Manila, Raaker, you lost" ("Diamonds of Death," p. 89).

In the shoot-out, Jo kills him. He now has the "diamonds of death," as he has dubbed them. He is so right; at least fifteen people are dead because of them.

Jo Gar found a package in his pocket, lighted one of his brown-paper cigarettes.

He said softly to himself: "I have all—all the Rainbow diamonds. Now I can go home, after the police come. I hope my friend Juan Arragon knows."… And he thought… of the Philippines—and of Manila—and of his tiny office of the Escolta. It was good to forget other things, and to think of his returning ("Diamonds of Death," p. 91).

Returning to the Pasig River, where the Sampans moor, side by side; to the Bridge of Spain which spans its dark waters; to the *Luneta* where the Constabulary Band plays in the late afternoon; to the Escolta, with its *mélange* of peoples and a sprinkling of American soldiers on liberty; the *Intramuros,* its old walls dating back to the late sixteenth century; and the spectacle of the fan-shaped, blood-red sunset across the Bay, with Cavite always in sight from the *Luneta.*

Returning to where he belongs.

I have a question: Whatever happened to him when the Japanese invaded Luzon? He got along with them better than any Asians. Did he remain in the city? Did the Japanese throw him into Bilibid along with the others? Or did he join the American forces on Corregidor? Was he in Manila during the bitter fighting to liberate it in 1945?

He was last heard of in mid-1937. After that, silence. Before Arragon's death, he and Jo were talking and Jo said, contemplatively:

> "A poet once wrote: 'There is mystery in the black-watered Pasig.' I shall go towards the river, because the poet is accurate. It is so." ("Death in the Pasig," p. 105).

Maybe he did…

Whatever… whatever, Jo—*Paálam! Mabuhay!*

West of Guam

Introducing Jo Gar, Manhunter....

CORAL REEF and green cliff—one showing a jagged edge of white in the blue water; the other a rising splash of color—were falling astern of the Army transport *Thomas.* The heat was terrific; the breeze was a hot blast sweeping the decks of the heavily laden transport. Five days more, with favorable weather, and the boat would reach Manila. Five hot days and nights, west of Guam.

Colonel Dunbar, infantry officer in charge of troops aboard, sat in the wicker chair of his cabin, let the electric fan bathe his sticky skin with warm air and cursed. It was his second Island job—and he didn't look forward to the arrival with much enthusiasm. He was sore because the West Point assignment hadn't come his way. He was sore because the transport was crowded with troops and civilians. He was sore because it had been so infernally hot since they had put out from Honolulu. A rotten trip.

There was a sudden pounding of heavy shoes along the deck. Burker, his orderly, stiffened near the open door of the cabin. His face was strangely white; the muscles of his mouth were twitching.

"It's—Captain Lintwell sir!" he muttered. "Major Jones found him—"

The orderly broke off. He was breathing heavily. Evidently he had run up from a lower deck. The colonel was impatient.

"Captain Lintwell—what *about* him, Burker? Get on with it—"

"He's dead, sir!"

The orderly got the words out all bunched up, but the commanding officer understood them. He jerked himself out of the wicker chair.

"The hell you say!" he snapped "Lintwell—dead? How?"

The orderly was calmer now. He stood stiffly, as though he were reciting a section of the manual.

"Major Jones said he was murdered, sir. The major found him. Up front, on C Deck. A bullet through his head—the back of it—"

The colonel swore sharply. He swore because it irritated him to think that after twenty-five days aboard a transport his orderly could be stupid enough to designate a spot on the boat as "up front." His lips formed the word "forward," and he forgot about the orderly, and the orderly's stupidity. He moved out of the cabin, went forward. His lean, browned face held a frown.

There had been three deaths at sea, from natural causes. There had been one drowning. A civilian's wife had lost all of her hair and a portion of her scalp, through carelessness near an electric fan. A sergeant had run amuck because of heat and smuggled booze—and had put two of the transport's crew in the ship's hospital. And now—Captain Lintwell had been murdered!

The colonel descended the forward companionway. He hadn't particularly liked Lintwell. The captain had played too good a game of bridge, and had played too loose with other officers' wives. But murder—that was a rotten trick. It would have to be cleared up. Before the transport reached Manila. Five days, five nights. The colonel was on B Deck now. He swore savagely. Perhaps there had been some mistake. He'd get a different orderly, anyway. "Up front!"

He was descending the companionway between B and C Decks now. There was a circle of khaki clad figures below—ten feet or so from the bottom step. A voice called—" 'Tention!" in a husky tone. Men straightened up—most of them were officers.

" 'Ease!" Dunbar snapped. "Where's Major Jones?"

The adjutant moved up close—the others moved away. Major Jones was short and thickset. He had a bristling, gray mustache, and even the heat of the tropics failed to destroy his efficiency.

"Rotten business, Joe," he muttered in a low voice. "They got him—back of the head. I was going below, found him."

The colonel stared down at the handsome face of Captain Jerry Lintwell. The man had a half smile on his face; his lips were drawn back slightly over his white, even teeth. The deck boards were stained with red. The colonel swore grimly. He started to kneel beside the dead captain, changed his mind.

"Keep everyone off this section of the deck, Adjutant!" he ordered crisply. "Two M.P.s should be able to see to that. Send for Major

Vane—"

"I've done that," Jones stated quietly. "He sent word from the hospital that Private Bulking is having convulsions—that he'll get up here as soon as he can. Lieutenant Robards came along right after I found him here—he found there was no pulse. Dead ten minutes or so, he said."

"He *guessed,*" the commanding officer corrected. "Very good—come up above with me, Adjutant. See about the guard first."

Jones moved away and gave orders. The colonel glanced at his wrist watch. It was five minutes past four. He looked down at the murdered man again. Browned skin was becoming a bit yellow. He noted that Lintwell's uniform was immaculate, as usual. Then he moved towards the steps of the companionway, climbed. There was a mild swell now. The effort of the trip down below had soaked him in perspiration. He felt vexed and irritable.

"Have that killer—by dark!" he muttered. "Damned fool to think he could get away with—that sort of stuff!"

IT WAS almost midnight. The *Thomas* nosed her way through a phosphorescent sea, rocking lazily in a mild swell. Guam was behind—miles behind. The night was hot, filled with stars. The transport steamed to the westward. In the colonel's cabin five men were gathered. Four of them were officers—one was a civilian. The colonel was speaking.

"It stands like this: At precisely thirty seconds after the ship's bells had struck four o'clock, Major Jones came up from D Deck and found the body of Captain Lintwell. Lieutenant Robards was next on the scene—that medical officer pronounced the captain dead. He stated that he did not believe Lintwell had been dead more than ten minutes. There was no one about when Jones, here, came along. Major Vane probed—the bullet is regulation. Colt .45. Major Vane feels that death was instantaneous. The bullet entered the back of the head—and almost emerged back of the left eye. Major Vane and I both feel that suicide was extremely unlikely." The commanding officer smiled faintly. His eyes went to those of the transport captain—Hungerford. That gentleman said nothing. He merely shrugged his shoulders. Majors Jones and Vane merely nodded their heads. The civilian spoke:

"Not suicide," he stated tonelessly but with assurance. "Lintwell was left-handed. The entrance point of the bullet was slightly to the right of the head, just above the neck. The bullet traveled towards the left eye. Impossible for a left-handed man to shoot that way—couldn't bend the wrist that much. Death was instantaneous but we can't find the Colt. Very little chance that Lintwell could have shot—then flung the gun overboard."

The colonel grunted. His eyes were on the civilian. He rather disliked all civilians; Jo Gar was no exception. He didn't like the name, in the first place. He didn't like the lack of emotion that Gar exhibited. And he didn't like Gar's looks.

The civilian half closed his blue-gray eyes, relaxed in the uncomfortable chair. His body swayed slightly as the transport rolled. He was a young man, but he looked rather old. His hair was gray; he was medium in size, but because of the loose way he carried himself he appeared rather small. His face was brown—very brown. He had good teeth, a narrow lipped mouth, fine features. His eyes were slightly almond-shaped, and they were seldom normally opened. They held a peculiar squint. Jo Gar wore soiled white trousers and a white shirt. His shoes had once been white, but his quarters on D Deck had prevented them from remaining so. He had abandoned socks at the same time that the *Thomas* had abandoned Honolulu.

"Captain Hungerford tells me that you have done some fine crime detection work, in the Islands, Mr. Gar." The colonel smiled with his lips. "He suggested, when we were making no progress, our calling you up here. We shall go right along with our investigation, of course—but we thought you might work—say, under cover."

Jo Gar smiled with half closed eyes. He spoke tonelessly, as always.

"It is the better way—under cover. Your blundering will help me."

The colonel flushed. He tapped on the seat of his wicker chair with a couple of knuckles. Major Jones swore beneath his breath.

"I fail to see where we have blundered," he stated simply.

Jo Gar continued to smile with lazy, blue-gray eyes.

"You have not," he replied. "I spoke in the future tense."

The colonel grunted. Only Captain Hungerford was smiling, and he allowed his dark eyes to meet the eyes of Gar. The colonel became sarcastic.

"We have called *you* in, Mr. Gar. That was damn sensible, wasn't it?"

The toneless-voiced one smiled faintly. He shook his head.

"It was very stupid," he stated. "But it was not a blunder. I came up alone—and I made sure that no one knew I was coming. In fact, I planted an alibi for myself. But that isn't important—it's done. There is a civilian under guard below—and he has a tongue. I caught up with him in two months, Colonel. He didn't expect me to do that. He thinks he is fairly clever—therefore he thinks—*I* am extremely clever. If he is believed by the enlisted men—"

"An enlisted man didn't murder Captain Lintwell." The colonel was emphatic. "Only a few of them carry Colts."

"*One* of them—was sufficient," Jo Gar stated. "You blunder, Colonel. You are sure of something. That is bad—one should never be sure."

The colonel was holding back angry words. The civilian got to his feet.

"I'm going to talk with a certain lieutenant who told his wife she was a fool, two nights ago," he said slowly. "I want to know why he told her that."

The colonel stared at him. He spoke grimly.

"How do *you* know he told her she was a fool?" he demanded.

Jo Gar smiled without opening his eyes very far. He stood near the door.

"You are a truthful man, Colonel," he stated. "I overheard *you* telling Major Jones

that the lieutenant had done so."

He nodded good-night to the three other officers, smiled at the colonel. He went from the cabin very quietly. There were no footfall sounds. The colonel swore harshly.

"The man's a fool—or a genius!" he muttered.

Captain Hungerford lighted his pipe, got to his feet and stretched.

"It'll take one of the two—to get this killer," he stated quietly. "And Jo Gar has the genius of playing a fool, Colonel."

"No motive—no clues," Major Jones muttered. "Beats the devil, it does!"

Colonel Dunbar reached for his pitcher of ice water. Civilians aboard a transport annoyed him. Ship's bells. Midnight. Eight hours of work, and they had gotten nowhere. He looked out through the cabin door opening. The transport swung lazily towards the Islands. She was a slow boat. This trip she was a death boat. And aboard her was a killer.

"The men know of the murder, of course?" The colonel felt foolish when he asked that.

Jones replied. "Of course—and the roll call showed everybody was aboard, including all of the ship's crew."

The colonel shook his head slowly. He was hot, tired and irritated.

"We'll work out the report tomorrow, Adjutant," he said grimly. "For the present we'll just rate it murder—west of Guam!"

JO GAR lay stretched on a hatch cover, aft of the radio room. He appeared to be sleeping—the hot, tropical sun beat down on his body. He was not sleeping. And the sun did not dull his brain. Jo was thinking.

"So *many* motives," he murmured to himself. "The colonel no doubt is a fine soldier. In this matter he is the great blunderer."

Jo Gar thought best under circumstances which would have dulled most human's brains. But Jo had been born in the tropics, raised in the Islands. With his body slugged by heat—his brain was most active. It was almost noon now, and he had come from a chat with the colonel. He had read the colonel's report—even in it there was a blunder. Jo Gar detested errors.

"The murder," he had pointed out to the colonel, "was *not* committed *west* of Guam. You have it written so here. The transport was steaming beneath the cliffs, almost, when Captain Lintwell was shot down. Agana was not to the eastward."

The colonel had stared, then had sworn grimly.

"Find the *killer*—never mind such small details," he had gritted. "For example—why didn't someone hear the shot? A Colt makes a noise."

Jo Gar had only smiled. He felt that the commanding officer had little confidence in him. He had got away as soon as was possible. Now he stirred his baking limbs, chuckled.

"So does steam escaping—make a noise," he murmured. "There is the Marine post, atop the cliffs. And the flag that is dipped. And the salute by whistle. Three blasts. That is good!"

He sat up on the hatch, swung his legs over the edge. Up on A Deck he caught a flash of white. A woman was swinging along rather briskly. It was very hot—and the woman was Lieutenant Solter's wife. She was very young and very beautiful. The night before the transport had reached Guam her husband had told her, heatedly, that she was a fool. He had pointed out that Captain Lintwell's reputation was not an enviable one. He had suggested that his wife walk the deck less in the captain's company.

Jo Gar smiled faintly. Helen Solter was doing so, at the moment. It was she who had told him, with reluctance, that her husband had rather hated Captain Lintwell. The captain was owed much bridge money by Lieutenant Briggs. Charlie Briggs was her husband's best friend. Her husband disliked gamblers, anyway. Captain Lintwell had been a gambler. And Helen Solter had also assured Jo Gar that her husband had been at her side, watching the Island of Guam slide out of sight, for fully a half hour after the transport had started to steam out from her anchorage beyond the coral reefs.

As for Lieutenant Briggs, he had been below, with his company. Sergeant Walker had accompanied him during an inspection. The alibis of the two lieutenants were excellent.

"So many motives," Jo Gar murmured as he got to his feet, "and not a clue."

He went to his quarters and dressed rather immaculately in white. Outside the colonel's cabin he found a private with red hair and a cheerful grin. Privates were not allowed on A Deck, so Jo Gar guessed out loud.

"You are possibly the colonel's new orderly? He told me he contemplated a change."

The orderly nodded. "He fired Sam Burker—I'm the new orderly. My name's Tod Harraker, and at the time the murder was committed I was—"

Jo Gar smiled. "It doesn't matter *where* you were, Tod," he stated. "Where will I find Burker?"

The new orderly told Jo where he thought Burker might be found. The door of the colonel's cabin opened, and Dunbar frowned at him. The orderly stiffened.

"Why Burker?" the colonel demanded of Gar. "He's too dumb to know anything about a murder."

Jo smiled more broadly. But his voice was as toneless as ever.

"Stupidity is sometimes a virtue, Colonel," he philosophized. "I wanted to know something about music—I hear that Burker plays a mouth organ."

The colonel swore. Jo Gar moved forward along the deck. Near the starboard companionway he almost ran into Mrs. Solter. She was rather pale. She looked ill, despite the fact that the *Thomas* was navigating through a sea of glass.

"Have you learned anything, Mr. Gar?" she asked in a low tone.

Jo nodded. It seemed to him that Helen Solter was breathing heavily.

"Many things," he replied. "All unimportant."

He imagined there was a flickering expression of relief in her dark eyes. But he wasn't sure. He bowed and moved down the steps of the companionway. On C Deck, aft, he discovered the former orderly. Burker was lying in the shade of a ventilator, with his eyes closed. He was lying on his back. Jo moved up close, careful that his figure cast no shadow in the sunlight beyond the reclining private. His rubber-soled shoes allowed him to move quietly. From a pocket of his white trousers he drew an Army Colt. He squeezed the trigger.

There was a sharp click. Burker's body jerked—in a flash the man was sitting up. He twisted around, stared at Jo. There was fear in his eyes.

"Jeeze!" he muttered. "That gave me a jolt!"

He smiled sheepishly. His nose was crooked and he had slightly stooped shoulders. His eyes were dark, rather squinted.

"I noted that fact," Jo stated quietly. "*Why* did it?"

The former orderly smothered an oath. He shook his head.

"I dunno," he replied. "But it did."

Jo Gar slipped the Colt back into his pocket. Private Burker wet his lips with the tip of a sick looking tongue. He started to get up, but Jo shook his head.

"Don't rise," he stated. "I'm Mr. Gar—perhaps you—know that."

The private nodded. "Guess we all do," he stated. "You're that Manila soft-shoe—the guy that always gets his man."

He chuckled. It was a nervous chuckle. Jo Gar shook his head.

"Not always," he stated. "Two years ago I failed. China is a difficult country. A transport at sea has advantages."

Private Burker looked towards the rail. He kept a half smile on his face. Jo Gar spoke tonelessly.

"The colonel has been in a bad humor," he stated. "He replaced you with a new orderly. Why?"

Burker grunted. "I dunno," he replied. "Maybe he thinks I'm dumb. Guess it's the heat—I ain't used to this sort of thing."

Jo nodded. "You took word to the colonel, that Captain Lintwell was dead," he stated. "You happened to come along, just after Captain Jones found the body."

"*Major* Jones," Burker corrected. "I had a message from—Captain Drake. I was bringing it up to the colonel."

Jo Gar nodded again. His gray-blue eyes held the dark ones of the former orderly.

"Burker," he said slowly, "the colonel was right. You *are* stupid. But you have *tried* to be clever. Very clever. Get up and come with me."

The former orderly was staring at Jo Gar. He got to his feet.

"I don't get you," he muttered. "You're on the wrong track—"

Jo Gar smiled faintly. "Perhaps," he agreed. "Just walk ahead, please—aft of this spot—"

Burker stared blankly. "Which way?" he muttered. "I ain't wise to—"

"Back, towards the stern, the rear of the boat," Jo said slowly. "It isn't far. You'll find steps there—they lead down to the ship's brig, jail, or what-not. That's where we're going, Burker."

The private's body stiffened. Jo Gar slipped his right hand into the right pocket of his duck trousers.

"If I were to squeeze the trigger again it would not click, Burker," he warned. "Possibly you know why."

The former orderly's face was turned towards Gar's. His facial muscles were twitching. He smiled with an effort.

"You got me wrong," he stated. "I don't know what you're gettin' at."

Jo Gar smiled with his thin lips. He spoke in a low voice.

"You contradict yourself, Private," he advised. "However, I want your nerves to relax. I want you to have quiet. Please walk aft, Private. That's—fine."

IT WAS five minutes of four. The *Thomas* was steaming westward; a mild breeze was kicking up some white through the blue-green tropical water. The water, however, was not rough. It was very hot. Colonel Dunbar drank ice water, and cursed. Major Jones dabbed at his face with a damp handkerchief. He would have preferred to wipe his face, but his bristling mustache prevented that.

"The men are holding up well, all things considered," he stated. "This murder has given them something to talk about. I hear they are laying bets—"

"Hell!" The colonel snorted the word. "What sort of bets?"

"Three to one that this Jo Gar won't produce the killer before we reach port," the major stated. "And I don't see how the odds got that low."

The colonel snorted again. "From what I hear he's asked questions of about everybody on board," he stated. "And he's learned nothing of importance."

Jo Gar bowed slightly from the open door of the cabin. The colonel reddened. He muttered something about "gum-shoes."

Jo spoke cheerfully.

"I have located the murderer of Captain Lintwell, Colonel," he announced.

The commanding officer stared at Jo. Major Jones stared, too. He spoke crisply.

"Who, Mr. Gar?"

Jo seated himself in a chair. He smiled faintly at the colonel.

"I said that I had *located* him. But there are a few questions, first. He is aboard the transport."

Major Jones swore. The colonel looked disgusted.

"I dislike such humor, Mr. Gar," he muttered. "Of course he's aboard."

"He might have gone over the side," Jo pointed out. "He *might* have been someone not accounted for in the roll call check-ups. Someone who came aboard at Guam."

The colonel grunted. Major Jones smiled cynically.

"But he wasn't," Jo said quietly. "And therefore Private Burker is confined under guard—"

"Burker!" The colonel's face was red. "That dumb orderly? Are you sure, Gar?"

Jo fingered one of the peculiar, brown-papered cigarettes, of which he seemed to have an unlimited supply.

"The murderer of Captain Lintwell," he stated slowly, "was not dumb, Colonel. You may remember that sergeant who ran wild—Schaeffer. He injured two of the ship's crew. He is still in the ship's hospital, and in bad shape. Investigation showed me that his Service Colt had never been found. Lieutenant Grace, his immediate superior, felt that he had thrown it overboard.

"I had doubts. Particularly so, after my examination of all the .45s aboard, after the murder. None had been cleaned recently—and that was what I had thought I might be able to determine. Sergeant Schaeffer did not toss his Colt overboard, before he was calmed down. It was used to murder Captain Lintwell."

Colonel Dunbar stared at Jo Gar.

"Burker!" he muttered. "And I thought he was dumb—talking about going—'up front'—after being aboard three weeks!"

Jo Gar smiled. "That struck me as peculiar, when you told me about it, Colonel," he stated. "So I looked over his service records. He was a *seaman* for eight years, before he entered the army, some two years ago."

The colonel wiped his face. He grunted. Major Jones had his eyes on the cabin ceiling.

"He overdid it a bit," Jo stated quietly. "He wanted to appear very stupid, you see. But he wasn't stupid. He had an alert mind. I talked with him and referred to Major Jones as Captain Jones. He corrected me instantly. A stupid man would very likely not have noted my mistake. He wanted you to think that he knew very little about a ship, Colonel."

"But *why*—did he murder Captain Lintwell?" Colonel Dunbar muttered.

Jo Gar shook his head. "He *didn't* murder Lintwell," he stated. "You misunderstood me, Colonel. I merely said that Burker was confined under guard. He was the accomplice."

The commanding officer was stiff in his chair now. Jo Gar lighted his cigarette, inhaled.

"Your orderly delivered a false message to Captain Lintwell—a verbal message. It was to the effect that you wanted him at the foot of the starboard companionway, on Deck C. The transport was passing close to the cliffs at that moment—at the moment Burker delivered the message. She was nearing the Marine post—and there was a flag to be dipped, and to be saluted by the transport's whistle. It is a heavy whistle, as you no doubt know.

"Captain Lintwell was shot through the back of the head, at close range, as he turned his back on the killer. He was shot as the whistle boomed in salute—and the men were all at the rails. Deck C, near the spot where Lintwell was killed, is closed in except for a small space. No one was near—no one but the murderer. Burker was not present, but he was on the deck above. He heard the shot, but it was so faint that even the men beside him missed it. They were all cheering, you see."

The colonel swore softly. His eyes were narrowed now. Major Jones arose. His face was white, set grimly.

"The motive was revenge," Jo said slowly. "Burker's job was to get a Colt without any record being made of it, and to deliver a message at the right time. He was paid well for it. He did both jobs. The murderer was—"

He stopped. The colonel's eyes were staring into his. Jo Gar did not look away from the colonel. Major Jones stepped past him—his shadow was for a second in the open doorway. The colonel looked up, startled.

His eyes were staring out towards the deck now, towards the rail. Suddenly he jerked from the chair, crying hoarsely.

"Jones—stop!"

Jo Gar did not turn, did not look towards the deck. The muscles of his mouth twitched a little. He heard the cry from somewhere above.

"Man overboard!"

Seconds passed. Ship's bells jangled. The engines shuddered. Jo Gar got up, walked out on the deck. He went to the rail, stared towards the stern. The transport was swinging wide now. He could see the fins. The water was filled with sharks.

After a while the fins vanished from sight. The transport was coming around in a wide circle. On the bridge ship's officers were using glasses. The colonel turned towards Jo, his face white, twisted.

"It was—Major Jones?" he managed thickly.

Jo Gar nodded. His face was sober, but his voice was still toneless.

"A year ago—his wife killed herself," he reminded. "You know of that, of course. I got it from Major Vane. It happened up in Alaska. She was there on a visit to some friends—army friends. I looked up Captain Lintwell's service record—you gave me permission to examine all the men's records, you remember, Colonel. I discovered that Lintwell was in Nome at the same time that Mrs. Jones was there. He had a way with women, you see."

The colonel nodded; he looked very tired, much older. Jo Gar spoke on:

"I asked Captain Hungerford about the steam salute of the Marine post flag. He told me that Major Jones had seemed very interested about that. He had wanted to know how long after the transport started to move—it would take to reach the point of salute. Hungerford had told him not thinking much about it. I worked over Burker—his nerves—were breaking. He'd reached a point where he dreaded the thought of hearing the transport's whistle again. Finally, I bluffed—told him that Major Jones was already under arrest, charged with murder. And Burker broke down—he told the truth."

Death in the Pasig

The Island Detective takes up a trail of justice and vengeance....

THE CEILING fans stirred hot air and made faint creaking sounds as they turned slowly. Shrill, native voices reached the café from the blue-gray eyes on the tall glass of lemonade he was sipping at intervals. It was about as hot as he had ever remembered! Baguio would be better because of the altitude. Or perhaps an inter-Island trip would help.

He raised his eyes to the bulk of Ben Rannis, noted that the manager of the Manila Hotel was pale, very pale. As Rannis stood near the screened doors and searched the café with his dark eyes, Jo Gar raised his right hand slowly and moved it from side to side. It was a languid motion—that of one who has spent many years in the tropics and has learned to conserve energy.

Rannis saw him, moved swiftly towards the table. He weighed more than two hundred; he was a powerful man. There wasn't much stomach, but he had broad shoulders and a great chest. He was several inches over six feet. Perspiration streaked his heavy face; he pulled a chair from the table, set it down closer to the one Jo Gar occupied.

"You appear ill—and you hurry too much. What is it?"

The Island detective spoke almost tonelessly. His English was precise. He was small in size, and his gray hair contrasted his brown, young face strangely. His slightly almond-shaped eyes were only half opened.

Rannis muttered something that sounded like a curse. He was breathing hard; it was almost as though he had been running along the Escolta.

"The *Cleyo Maru's* in," he said in his husky voice. "Got in two hours ago. Craise was aboard. He sent me a message. It was given to me over the phone by a Filipino who acted damned cheerful about it. He said 'Meester Craise has arrived. He wishes me to tell you that information has come to him. You are in great danger. It is better to leave the city at once.' Then he hung up."

Jo Gar frowned. "It was Craise's brother you killed, two months ago, I think," he said steadily.

Rannis groaned. "You know damned well it was, Jo," he replied. "And you know damned well Howard Craise is out to get me for it. One way or another. And it was an accident."

The Island detective shrugged his shoulders slightly. He smiled with his thin lips.

"You had been drinking," he reminded. "John Craise was not strong. You struck him very hard."

"He'd been drinking, too. He called me a nasty name. That all came out at the trial. Howard Craise knows all that, even if he was in England at the time."

Jo Gar sipped more of his lemonade. He turned his browned face slightly away from the hotel manager.

"That is so," he agreed. "And now he is not in England. He is in Manila. You have been called and told your life is endangered. Recently you have killed John Craise and have been acquitted of the charge of murder."

The hotel manager turned narrowed eyes towards Gar's. He said hoarsely:

"He'll kill me, Jo. I can't shoot. I want you to go to him, tell him how it was. You'd just come in on that transport—you worked the case. He knows you—he'll believe you."

The Island detective smiled with faint mockery in his eyes.

"You did not intend to murder his brother," he said slowly, tonelessly. "I feel certain of that."

BEN RANNIS shoved back his chair and rose. His voice was shaken, uncertain. But he kept it fairly low.

"He's at his brother's place—fix it up, Jo. He'll get brooding—in this damned heat—"

His voice broke. Fear was gripping the big man, and Jo Gar hated to see fear in a man's eyes. He said slowly:

"I will go to him. Where will you go?"

Rannis swore. "Along the river—got to get a drink. Keep away from the hotel until you see him. The heat'll get him thinking—"

He turned, went slowly from the soft drink café. His fingers were twitching at his sides. Jo Gar shook his head very slowly. He finished his iced lemonade. His slitted eyes watched Rannis go through the screened doors, merge with the crowd on the Escolta; Filipinos, Chinese, Japanese, English, Spaniards—and a scattering of Americans, mostly Army men.

Jo Gar sighed. He was aware of the fact, now made definite, that Benjamin Rannis was a coward. He was afraid of death, and yet he had killed. And the Island detective had given him a promise.

There was difficulty in getting the connection, nothing was done hurriedly in the Islands. A Chinese servant answered the phone. He was not sure that his master would speak with Señor Gar. His master was sleeping. Yes, he knew it was past *siesta* hours, but his master was very weary. He would see about the matter.

Jo Gar held the receiver, waited. Several minutes passed. Then a voice came to him. It possessed a slightly English accent. It was a heavy-toned voice.

"Are you there? Howard Craise speaking."

The Island detective said slowly:

"It is Señor Gar. You perhaps remember me in matters of the Island police. I would like to come to you, talk with you. It is the matter of your brother's death."

He paused. There was silence at the other end. Then the voice sounded again. It seemed colder in tone.

"At six, say? Here, at the house?"

Jo Gar watched a *carromatta* pass, in the street. The pony was white. He said:

"At six, thank you. I will arrive."

He heard the click of the receiver at the other end. The Craise house was beyond the Walled City, perhaps a mile along the Bay. It was a fine old place. Spanish, built many years ago. The Craise brothers owned plantations, not on Luzon but further south.

The Island detective left the café. It was almost five, but the heat was still very severe. He turned off the Escolta, moved down a narrow, winding street towards the Pasig. Behind him there was the clatter of a pony's hoofs. A native voice shrilled at the animal, urging greater speed. Jo Gar stepped into an evil-smelling doorway, turned. The *carromatta* passed close to the broken curbing; he saw the driver clearly. Back of the little seat, in the interior of the small, two-wheeled carriage, he saw another figure. Then the *carromatta* was beyond him, going rapidly towards the river Pasig.

Jo Gar stepped from the doorway, looked for another conveyance. There was none in sight. He sighed heavily. One could not answer a telephone three miles from the Escolta—and yet arrive on a narrow street just off the Escolta two minutes later. For that reason Jo Gar was very anxious to keep track of the *carromatta* which had just passed him, bearing as a passenger Howard Craise.

In five minutes he obtained a *carromatta,* gave the driver instructions. There was no sign of the two-wheeled conveyance in which he had seen Howard Craise. After a half hour tour of the narrow streets running towards the Pasig from the Escolta, Jo Gar descended and paid the driver. It was slightly cooler; he would sip another iced drink, hire another *carromatta* and go out to the Craise house. Filipinos could gossip; he did not wish to give his last driver the opportunity to talk—not with some servant in the vicinity of the Craise home.

He had his drink, hailed a native driving a good sized pony, and was driven at fair speed to the Craise house on the Bay. The Island of Cavite could be plainly seen; Jo stood on the wide porch and frowned at it. When the Chinese servant opened the door, however, he was smiling.

He waited less than five minutes in a large room that was almost cool. Howard Craise came downstairs rather noisily; he was medium in size with blond hair and blue eyes. He was dressed in a suit of white duck, but he did not look so cool.

"I awakened you?" The Island detective smiled at him.

Craise shook his head. He seemed a little nervous. He had a peculiar way of blinking his eyes, as though he were in bright sunlight rather than in a dark room.

"I was reading—lying around and reading," he said. "Good to be ashore, we had a rough passage."

Jo Gar nodded. "I will arrive directly at the object of my call," he said. "Mister Benjamin Rannis has been murdered."

He watched Craise's body jerk—watched the right hand come upward, then relax. He saw the blue eyes widen, narrow again. And then Howard Craise spoke:

"But it's only been—"

He checked himself. The Island detective nodded, smiling pleasantly.

"A very short time since you had your Filipino boy call and threaten him," he finished. "That is true."

Craise was staring at him. His fists clenched; there was sudden anger in his eyes. He spoke in a hard tone:

"You're accusing me of killing Rannis? You mean to tell me—"

Jo Gar looked hurt. He moved his head from side to side, slowly.

"He was murdered while you were sleeping, or reading," he pointed out. "But it was unwise of you to have your servant threaten him. He has probably told several people of the matter."

Howard Craise wet his lips with the tip of his tongue. He smiled nastily.

"Of course no servant of mine called him and threatened him. That's absurd. If it's circumstantial evidence you are counting on—"

He checked himself again. Rage was in his eyes. Jo Gar bowed slightly.

"I admire the way you think, Señor," he said quietly. "Circumstantial evidence is quite unsatisfactory—in the Islands, of course. I merely wanted to inform you—"

The bell tinkled. Silently the Chinese servant went to the door. He opened it, stepped aside. Juan Arragon, of the City police, his fat face a brown mask, came toward them. He nodded towards Jo Gar, bowed to Howard Craise.

"Will you be so kind as to come with me to the City?" he asked.

"We have just taken the body of Mister Benjamin Rannis from the Pasig River. He is dead, perhaps murdered. You are, implicated. My superiors are anxious that you—"

Craise smiled with his lips. "Frame-up, eh?" he muttered. "Of course I'll come—Wong, my helmet!"

He moved towards the square reception hall. Juan Arragon let his eyes meet Jo Gar's.

"You do not seem surprised—to learn of Mister Rannis' death," he said slowly.

Jo Gar smiled. "I had just informed Señor Craise accordingly," he said simply.

He watched Arragon's eyes narrow in surprise. The Manila police officer was no fool. He said very quietly:

"I came here very rapidly. In a machine. The body was just discovered. Yet you already knew?"

Jo Gar said slowly: "Why did you come here so quickly?"

The fat-faced officer smiled a little. His voice was very smooth as he replied:

"There was certain evidence."

The Island detective nodded. "That was my reason for coming here without knowing that Señor Rannis *had* been murdered," he said very slowly. "There was certain evidence."

JO GAR sat in the fan-backed, wicker chair, made by prisoners in Bilibid, and smiled faintly into the eyes of Juan Arragon. It was much cooler—tropical night had dropped over Manila. He spoke in a soft, steady tone.

"Señor Rannis was a coward, plainly. He did, however, give me work at times. I had promised to help him. He came to me in the café, afraid of Howard Craise. He had reason to fear the brother of the man he had struck down so hard that his fist caused death. I agreed to intercede. I called the Craise house, and I was answered by a servant who informed me he did not like to disturb his master. That was an untruth, you say. You tell me that Howard Craise did not speak to me at the time I mention—that you saw him in a *carromatta* only a few minutes later, driving towards the Pasig."

The Manila police officer nodded, showed white teeth in a smile.

"Perhaps you saw him, also," he said softly. "You went to his home, informed him that Señor Rannis had been murdered, before you knew that. There was a reason. You are clever, yes?"

Jo Gar chuckled. "We are *both* clever," he qualified. "And so is Howard Craise."

Juan Arragon shrugged his shoulders. "I do not see in what manner," he said. "He has a servant threaten a man he is bound to hate. He has another talk over the telephone for him. And he allows both you and me to see him riding towards the spot where the body of the man he threatened is dragged from the Pasig. Is that clever?"

The Island detective gestured with his hands spreading out, palms up.

"He *allows* us both to see him, you say," he observed slowly. "Perhaps it is very, very clever!"

He rose slowly, reached for his pith helmet. Arragon was watching him curiously. They were friends of old. Five years ago, before he had become a private investigator, Jo Gar had worked on the Manila police force.

"We are handling Mister Craise with what the Americans call the gloves," Arragon said slowly. "He is friendly with many important personages. He dines at Señor Carlysle's home. We must be careful, but sincere."

Jo Gar nodded. Arnold Carlysle was the American who headed the police force, an organization combining Americans and Filipinos. There were times when the solution of crime, in Manila, was a delicate affair.

"There were two knife wounds," Arragon went on. "One in the back, almost between the shoulder blades. The other just over the heart. Chinos on the junk near the shore heard the splash. One of them went overboard for the body. Mister Rannis had taken drinks at Manuelo's—two or three. He had left, saying he was much in need of air. There are many river boats, junks and *sampans,* anchored side by side within a square of Manuelo's. I feel that Mister Craise could have reached the junk near which the splash was heard within three minutes after the time I saw him riding in the *carromatta.* I feel that murder was committed shortly after these three minutes. Señor Craise possessed a motive."

Jo Gar smiled faintly. It amused him to note the application of "Señor" and "mister" to an Englishman. Arragon had Spanish blood in his veins, as did the Island detective. Forms of address were confusing.

He stood near the door of Arragon's office, facing the police officer. He said slowly:

"Señor Craise had much time, before he arrived in Manila, to cool his anger. He is a shrewd man. Circumstantial evidence is all against him. I will be honest with you. I, too, saw him riding towards the Pasig. Ben Rannis came to me in fear of him. He had a reason for his fear. I was answered from the house—but Señor Craise could not have been two places at once. Much of our evidence rests on what we saw with our own eyes. Perhaps others saw him, too. Supposing then, with one twist he could destroy this evidence—"

He paused. Arragon nodded his head and made clicking sounds with his tongue.

"It is difficult," he agreed. "I, too, believe he might have desired us to see him. And others to see him. He has been questioned, released. He has returned to his home. Silbino is strolling near the house. What next?"

Jo Gar placed his pith helmet over his gray hair. He smiled almost cheerfully.

"A poet once wrote: 'There is mystery in the black-watered Pasig,'" he said. "I shall go towards the river, because the poet is accurate. It is so."

Juan Arragon fanned himself slowly with a stained palm leaf, and rolled his little eyes towards the ceiling of the office.

"It is damn so!" he said softly.

MANUELO'S WAS a shack not far from the river—perhaps a hundred feet up a narrow alley. It was frequented by coolies, half-breed Spaniards, low class Filipinos, and others of the river. Manuelo himself was a small, emaciated human. He had bad teeth and a scarred face. His fingers were long and bony.

He repeated a good many times that the *Americano* Rannis had come in for a drink. It had been sake, he thought. He could not remember. Many rivermen had crowded his place. He said that Rannis had looked very sick. He had not stayed long. Manuelo was not sure of the time. Señor Rannis had needed air. He had gone away. No, Manuelo did not know Señor Craise. He had never come to the place.

And that was about all. The Chinos on the junk had difficulty in talking with Gar. They were not sure where the body had struck the water. They pointed at the spot where Rannis' body had been seen—the one who had gone overboard said that he thought Rannis had moved his arms a little. But not after he had reached the *Americano.*

After two hours along the Pasig, Jo Gar sighed and muttered to himself.

"It is always so with the river Pasig. So little seen or heard. And it was not dark, even. Supposing, now, another than Howard Craise had been in that *carromatta?*"

It was a thought, but he did not care much about it. There would have to be a remarkable similarity of humans. He had been fooled. Juan Arragon had been fooled. No, he did not think that. They were both familiar with Craise.

He called Arragon's office from a little tobacco shop just off the Escolta. Juan's voice held an excited note.

"Come to me at once!" he urged. "Here in my office we have the murderer of Señor Rannis! He has confessed."

Ten minutes later Jo Gar entered the office. His eyes went from

the khaki colored uniforms of the two Filipino police to the figure slumped over the desk. Juan Arragon said sharply:

"Donnell—up!"

The man raised his head, turned slightly, stared at the Island detective. Jo Gar sucked in his breath, muttered to himself.

"Marie! But they—are alike!"

This man's hair was a dirtier blond color. His eyes were blood-shot, larger than Señor Craise's. He was more stooped—and looked older. But there was similarity—great similarity. In the *carromatta,* seated erect, they could have been easily mistaken.

"He is—one Donnell. A sort of beachcomber," Arrogan said slowly, a trace of excitement in his voice. "My men found him cowering across the Pasig from the scene of the crime. We have the knife—he tossed it away as they closed in. He has confessed. It was a terrible scheme—he knew of his resemblance to Howard Craise. For months he has awaited the Señor's return. He has threatened Señor Rannis, again and again. He got into the *carromatta* after *siesta* time today, drove towards Manuelo's. He knew that Señor Rannis went there. When Rannis came from the place he followed him to the river, knifed him, dragged him across the junks—threw him overboard. He made his escape. Later, when we were bringing Señor Craise to trial, he planned to give himself up, tell what he had done for sufficient money. Many thousands of dollars. He would force Señor Craise to pay—and then he intended to get away with the money. And not to confess. A tremendous scheme!"

The man who resembled Howard Craise dropped his head in his arms. He cried out hoarsely:

"Let me go—into the Bay! The sharks—"

He had a broken, husky voice. His body looked thinner than Craise's. Collapsed across Juan Arragon's desk he was a pitiful figure of a beaten man.

"Do they not look alike?" Arrogan asked grimly.

"You see, after the murder his nerve deserted him. He went to pieces. Is it not fortunate we were careful with Señor Craise? You see he *did* speak with you over the telephone.

Jo Gar nodded his head slowly. The phone bell rang. Arragon answered it. He smiled. His white teeth showed.

"I will come soon to your home, Señor Craise," he said into the mouthpiece. "I have news of importance. I will be there within the half hour."

He hung up the receiver, smiled faintly at Jo Gar.

"It was Señor Craise—asking for news," he said. His eyes fell on the collapsed figure. He spoke sharply to the Filipinos, telling them to take him to a cell.

They half dragged the man to the door. Jo Gar stood aside, frowning. Arragon was smiling broadly. He rubbed his browned hands together. There was the sound of clattering as the Filipinos dragged the prisoner down the narrow stairs that led to the corridor through which they would walk to the cells.

"It is well we were not too hasty with Señor—"

Arragon's voice died. A strangled scream sounded from below. There was a heavy thud—the sound of a body falling. Jo Gar jumped towards the door. The wooden stairs had a landing half way down—the remaining steps were slanted in the opposite direction, hidden from his sight. There was a low groan—another crash of a body going down. He could hear heavy breathing as he started down the stairs, Arragon at his heels. On the landing they turned, stared down.

One Filipino was on his knees, holding his head with both hands. Red stained the fingers. The other was lying motionless against the corridor wall, face downward. The screened door opening on the alley just off the Escolta.

THE *CALESO*, pulled by a sturdy horse, moved swiftly towards the Bay. It was a dark night; there was no moon. A hot breeze blew in from the direction of Cavite. The *Luneta,* flanked by the Manila Hotel and the Army and Navy Club, was behind now.

Jo Gar sat in the open carriage and fingered the Army Colt. His lips were pressed tightly together; he was frowning with narrowed eyes. The police search was being carried out along the big boat waterfront, not along the Pasig. Juan Arragon was thinking of the prisoner's word—"Let me go—into the Bay. The sharks—"

A broken man—a prisoner who had looked so much like an important citizen of Manila, had suddenly, savagely twisted himself from the grip of the two Filipinos supporting him along the corridor. With one blow he had knocked one Filipino unconscious. As the other had reached for his short club the prisoner had battered him against the wall of the corridor, had jerked the club from his grip—and had struck him heavily over the head with it. Then he had made his escape. He had possessed the strength of a madman, truly.

The *caleso* driver pulled up the horse, twisted his brown face. Jo Gar paid the man, slipped from the carriage, moved swiftly towards the Bay. He kept close to an old stone wall on his right.

There were lights in the Craise house on the Bay. But the Island detective did not enter through the scrolled iron gate. He went through a narrow passage in the wall, moved through the heavy, tropical growth of the garden.

He circled the big house at the rear, reached the Bay side. Stars gave faint light to the water. In the distance he heard the muffled exhaust of a power boat. He halted, listened. The boat was going away—but it was not so far distant. He smiled grimly, moved more rapidly around the house. And then, crouched low and moving swiftly, he saw the figure that had left the sand behind and was coming towards the growth near the house.

Jo Gar waited, the Colt gripped in his right hand fingers. He could see the figure now—the man was ten feet from him. The Island detective spoke quietly, sharply:

"Up—Donnell!"

The figure stiffened. Gar heard the quick intake of breath. And then the man leaped towards him.

Jo Gar stepped to one side. He struck outward and downward with the Colt. It battered heavily against the attacker's head, just over the left ear. The man dropped—rolled over on his back. He was motionless.

The Island detective drew a deep breath. He shifted the weapon, got a small flashlight from his pocket. When he looked down upon the figure there was a hard smile in his blue-gray eyes.

"Like many tremendous schemes, Señor Craise," he said very slowly, "it has failed."

JO GAR let his eyes move from the figure of Juan Arragon to that of Arnold Carlysle. He was smiling cheerfully in spite of the heat in the police head's office.

"Señor Craise was always shrewd, cold," he said slowly. "He was not one to forget that Ben Rannis had struck his brother down. I do not believe too much in the similarity of humans. But he did fool me, in Juan's office. Belladonna to enlarge the eye pupils, dirt-matted hair, no erectness like that of himself. And the changed voice. Neither Juan nor myself knew him too well, you see. And he'd been away for months. This English friend of his who has confessed to imitating Craise's voice—that was a clever touch. Calling up, pretending it was Craise—with Craise passing as a beachcomber, right in Juan's office at the time. And it was this Condon who answered my call to the house, of course."

Juan Arragon nodded his head slowly. "Had Craise got back to his house we would have been beaten," he said. "He could have received me, immaculately attired. He would have been clean, changed. In a dark room I would not have noticed his eyes. But of course, after the escape, he realized I would be busy—and that would give him more time."

Jo Gar nodded. "He murdered Rannis, just as he as Donnell told us. He got back to the house from the murder in time to receive me. Your Filipino guard was not too good, Juan, though it is a large place for one man to watch. Craise went out again, after you released him. There was sufficient time. He went to the Pasig, crouched along the bank—and when your men found him he threw the knife away. Said he was Donnell—and looked—a beachcomber. After his escape he got to the big boat piers where he hid and waited. After dark Condon met him in a power boat. He brought him to the Bay house."

Arnold Carlysle smiled faintly. "But for you Señor Gar, we would have assumed that a man resembling Craise had tried a pretty plan and had failed. And had then preferred drowning—and the sharks."

Jo Gar said nothing. He wondered if Arnold Carlysle would not have preferred it that way. But it was not for him to say.

"I was suspicious," he said slowly. "Before I knew Rannis had been murdered, when I told Craise that—he was very startled. I was almost too soon for him. He hadn't expected it this fast. And then, very suddenly, he was too cool. He was thinking too much of the future, of the circumstantial evidence that he knew he could beat."

Arragon shrugged. "Death in the Pasig," he said slowly, "is always difficult." He smiled at Jo. "Not being a fool, I congratulate you."

Jo Gar fanned himself slowly with his pith helmet. He smiled in return.

"Perhaps I had the better opportunity," he said quietly. "But not being too modest—I am pleased. Señor Craise is not an inferior actor."

Carlysle frowned down at the polished floor of his office. Juan Arragon nodded agreement. Jo Gar closed his eyes, stopped fanning his browned face, and drowsed. He suddenly felt very weary.

Red Hemp

The Island Detective hunts for a girl whom a man wants found—so that "he may beat her...."

VINCENTE CAREJO might have been an immaculate Island Englishman, so far as his dress was concerned. From his pith helmet to his white shoes he was spotless. But the *betel*-nut that he chewed betrayed him. And when his lips parted a little too much there was the red that stained his teeth and gums. He had a fat face and body; his darkish eyes held no expression. He said in a thick voice:

"My girl has left me. I wish her found, so that I may beat her."

Jo Gar smiled with his almond-shaped, blue-gray eyes half closed. The arms of the Island detective were folded; his body was relaxed.

"There are the police," he suggested. "On the Escolta is the Missing Persons Department."

Carejo made a grunting sound without parting his thick lips.

"Manila police are fools," he said. "You are not a fool. I have come to you. It is that pig of an American—that renegade Parker. But I do not seek trouble. It is my daughter I want."

The Island detective nodded. "So you may beat her," he suggested quietly.

Carejo showed his red-stained teeth in a nasty smile. He nodded his head.

"This Parker—he is a cheap gambler," he said slowly. "He bets on the cock-fights, and when he loses he does not always pay. My girl—she is too good for him."

Jo Gar rolled a thin cigarette between his short, browned fingers. He regarded the single lizard crawling upside-down across the ceiling of his tiny office above Wong Ling's place, on the Escolta. He said quietly:

"When did she go away—and how?"

Carejo swore through tight-pressed lips. He shrugged his shoulders.

"She was to go to Baguio this morning. She slept in the house. But she did not appear at the breakfast table. She has taken nothing with her—no clothes. A few dollars, perhaps. I have searched the city—she is not to be found. Nor is the American, Parker. I have come to you."

The Island detective frowned. "Manila is not a big city, neither is it small," he mused aloud. "It is Saturday evening—there will be cock-fights tomorrow. You have a picture of your girl?"

Carejo reached into a pocket of his white duck suit, produced a picture. It was a clear snapshot; it showed a dark-haired, slender girl of about eighteen. She was rather pretty, in the way of the Islands, which was not a lasting way. She had large eyes and a rather thin face.

"Her name is Carmen—she is a devil," Carejo said. "A bamboo stick does not frighten her."

Jo Gar smiled. "Love is not annoyed by beatings," he philosophized. "I think I have seen this American, this Parker. A tall, blond fellow, with blue eyes. And you say he is a renegade?"

Carejo shrugged his broad shoulders. He narrowed his eyes on Jo Gar's.

"He has been in Manila only a few months. He came over from Nagasaki with a few prize cocks—but the birds did not win much here. Then he was involved in some cheating affair, at the Casa Club. He is no good."

The Island detective tapped cigarette ash to the polished floor of his office. He said in an apologetic voice:

"It may be difficult. I require a retainer—"

Carejo placed five crisp bills on the wicker table beside his fan-backed chair.

"You know where I reside," he said. "You have Carmen's picture. You know something of this Parker, and you can easily learn more. But I would like it not made public. How will you go about it?"

Jo Gar reached for a palm-leaf fan, waved heated air against the brown skin of his face. He smiled pleasantly "That I do not know," he said. "But I shall walk about a bit. Perhaps I shall ask a few questions."

Carejo grunted. "*I've* walked about and *I've* asked questions," he muttered.

The Island detective nodded. He said cheerfully:

"Perhaps you have not walked in the right places, nor asked the correct questions."

Vincente Carejo rose. He muttered something that Jo Gar did not catch. Then he said, more clearly:

"I want my girl back!"

Jo Gar rose and bowed a little. After Carejo had departed the Island detective seated himself in the more comfortable fan-backed chair and half closed his eyes.

"He is half Spanish, half Filipino," he murmured. "It is a strange way he has—wanting his daughter back, so that he may beat her. Another of his type would use a knife on this Parker. But this Carejo—"

Jo Gar let his murmur trail away, closed his eyes. It was as though he were sleeping in the evening heat. But he wasn't sleeping. He was thinking of certain questions he would ask—and certain Manila streets he would walk. A beginning was always important.

AT BARRES' curio store, on the Calle Avida, he was told that the *Americano* Parker had been present an hour ago. It had taken Jo Gar three hours to come upon the Barres' store; the information was welcome. In the rear, down five stone steps, was a fair-sized cellar. Parker had been drinking. He had taken three cups of saké. He had been drinking, but he had not been drunk. He had not stated his destination, but had bragged much about Diablo, the cock he was fighting tomorrow at the Casa Club.

Jo Gar smiled and talked about other things. There had been an earthquake in Mindoro, the next island south of Luzon; some of Barres relatives were very frightened. A Malay sailor had run amuck along the *Luneta,* several hours ago. He had knifed a wealthy Chinese by the name of Lin. There would soon be some of the nuts in from China—the ones Jo Gar liked so well.

The Island detective lingered for a half hour or so. It was not yet ten o'clock; he hailed a *caleso* with a sturdy-looking horse, instructed the Filipino driver to take him to the Casa Club. The driver grinned, showing fine, white teeth. Jo Gar settled back on the cushion of the two-wheeled conveyance. It was in his mind that if Parker had taken several drinks, and had bragged about his fighting-cock Diablo, the American might go to the Casa Club. The entries were often kept near the pits, for several days before the Sunday fights.

It was a thirty-minute drive. Manila was left behind—for more than ten minutes they passed between rows of native thatch-roofed huts, dimly lighted. The road was narrow and of dirt; the sweet odor of tropical growth in variety filled the heated air. And then, suddenly, the driver called shrilly to the horse—the *caleso* was turned to the right. A circular thatch-roofed arena loomed faintly before them in the thick gloom. It was the Casa Club.

Jo Gar descended, instructed the driver to wait. He went directly to the entrance of the cock-fighting arena, walked inside. Two kerosene lamps dimly lighted the interior—there was the odor of dried blood, of earth—and of thatch. Tier after tier of wooden planks rose from the small, circular arena. Wind whistled the roof. There was no other human present.

Jo Gar murmured to himself: "It is an unpleasant place—"

The scream was terrible. It came from the silence, somewhere beyond the cockpit, but not very far distant, it was shrill, high pitched. A woman's cry—of terror and pain. And then, wailingly, he caught two words in Spanish—

"Madre—Madre!"

There was another scream—it was choked off. Voices—native voices—rose from the thatch-roofed huts near the cockpit. Jo Gar turned, went out through the main entrance. He circled the Club, keeping close to the bamboo side poles. At the rear he distinguished figures running—they were moving towards a thick growth of palmetto, a hundred yards from the Casa Club. There were few huts near the growth.

There were no more screams. A path led into the tangle of palmetto. The Island detective came to it. Brown figures—those of half-naked Filipinos—were moving about. There was much confusion. Jo Gar said, in the native tongue:

"What has happened?"

No one seemed to know. There were many paths now, leading through the small jungle to native huts on all sides. Jo Gar took one of them; he had a small flashlight which he used. Filipinos crowded close to him, followed him. He heard one mutter to another: "It is Señor Jo Gar—he is the prison man—"

And then a sudden wailing rose, across the thick growth of palmetto. It was a sustained wailing, and Jo Gar turned, moved towards the sound. It took him several minutes to thread the confusing paths and come upon the spot where the natives were grouped around a figure that lay on the ground. He spoke roughly, went through the group. The white beam from his flashlight slanted down on the motionless figure.

One glance at the white face was enough for him. The eyes were staring—the red lips were parted. The face was twisted, contorted. Fingers were clenched; the earth around the body showed signs of human struggle. A red mark showed across the white throat, but it was not the mark of a knife.

Jo Gar bent low. He breathed to himself:

"It is Carmen Carejo—she is dead."

There was no pulse. The body was warm; it seemed almost alive. The Island detective loosened the rope that had been drawn about the girl's throat. He was not a doctor, and even though he was sure she was dead, he tried crude methods to force air into her lungs, as he gave orders to several natives crowding about the body.

WHEN JUAN ARRAGON, lieutenant to Carlysle, American head of the Manila Police, arrived in the palmetto jungle, some thirty minutes later, Jo Gar was standing near the body of Carmen Carejo, hands at his sides, eyes half closed. Arragon stared down at the dead girl.

"Murder," he breathed softly. "What was the weapon—"

Jo Gar shifted the beam of his light towards the dark shawl the girl had worn. It lay on the earth near her head. Stretched across it was a four-foot strand of rope, of hemp. In spots it was stained scarlet. Arragon said slowly:

"She was strangled—by that hemp."

Jo Gar nodded. Arragon knelt beside the shawl, narrowed his eyes on the rope strand. He muttered to himself:

"It is stained—with her blood."

Jo Gar lighted one of his thin cigarettes. His eyes were on the mask-like face of Carmen Carejo.

"It is certainly—red hemp," he said steadily.

Arragon rose and looked at Jo Gar. He asked in a curious voice:

"You arrived here quickly—how was that so?"

The Island detective smiled a little. He looked Arragon in the eyes.

"I was nearby—when she was murdered. I heard her scream. She called twice for her mother. Then her next cry was choked off. It was more than five minutes before some native women found her in here. There are many paths."

Arragon looked around the circle of native faces. His eyes came to Jo Gar's again. He said softly:

"She is Carmen Carejo—Vincente's girl."

The Island detective nodded. He was thinking that Vincente Carejo had found his daughter, but that his purpose was defeated. He could not beat her now. He said quietly:

"Yes—it is Carejo's girl. He was searching for her. He had retained me only a few hours ago. And now she has been strangled to death."

Arragon kept his eyes narrowed on Jo Gar's. He asked, in a sharper tone:

"Why did you come here?"

The Island detective smiled with his lips. He looked towards the dark shawl and the red-stained length of Manila hemp. He evaded the question.

"He was a strong man—this strangler," he said. "See how the hemp cut into her skin. There was just a twist knot, Juan—the killer held the rope ends until she was dead, or very nearly dead. And we were all about the jungle here, trying to reach her."

Arragon swore hoarsely. "If you have suspicions, tell them," he pleaded. "The murderer cannot have got far away."

Jo Gar shook his head slowly. "It is too bad," he stated apologetically. "But I have no suspicions."

IT WAS midnight when Jo Gar went up the wooden stairs to Juan Arragon's office at the police department. He knocked, and was told to enter. Arragon was talking with Vincente Carejo; he frowned at the Island detective.

"You did not tell me about Parker, this American," he stated. "That was not right, Jo. That was very bad. It has given the murderer of Señor Carejo's daughter a chance to escape."

Vincente Carejo was perspiring freely. He nodded his head jerkily, wiped the skin of his neck near the collar with a large handkerchief. He was chewing *betel*-nut again; there was red about the corners of his thick lips. He spoke hoarsely with anger in his voice.

"Did I not retain you, Señor Gar? Were you not working for me? And why did you not tell what I had told you? This renegade has murdered my daughter."

His voice was broken as he finished speaking. He shook his head slowly, muttering the name of the girl.

Arragon said: "I asked you if you had suspicions—you said that you had none. It is strange to me—"

Jo Gar smiled. "Parker is an American," he said. "The girl was strangled by hemp—that is not the way of an American in killing."

Carejo straightened in his chair. There was rage in his dark eyes.

"Parker is a clever man. That is the way he would kill—my poor girl."

Jo Gar shrugged. Juan Arragon, a puzzled expression in his eyes, spoke in a hard voice:

"He will not get too far away. We have notified the Constabulary."

The Island detective stood near a window of the office. He shook his head.

"Parker is not beyond the city—the Constabulary will not find him," he said. "I am sure of that."

Carejo got heavily to his feet. He blinked at Jo Gar.

"If you are crossing me—I will make trouble for you," he breathed. "Parker is the murderer of my girl. The police can force you to tell what you know—"

Jo Gar said slowly: "The police can force me to tell nothing, Señor Carejo. They attempted such a thing, some years ago—and failed. I am not crossing you. You have retained me to find your daughter. I have found her. But I shall go farther—I shall find her murderer. Perhaps you would like to beat *him,* now that you cannot beat her."

Arragon's body tensed at his last words. His eyes went to those of the dead girl's father. Carejo's face was flushed beneath the tan. He said hoarsely:

"You mock me. It is cruel. I am sorry for those words. I go now to my *casa*—I wish to be alone. But the American Parker—he is the strangler of—"

His voice had risen shrilly. Now it died. He moved from the office of Juan Arragon without speaking to either man. He went slowly down the wooden steps. Jo Gar closed the door of the office, took a chair.

"The American Parker did not strangle the girl, Juan," he said quietly. "I have been very busy since leaving the vicinity of the Casa Club. I do not think that Parker, at this moment, knows Carmen is dead."

Arragon wet his lips with the tip of his tongue. His eyes were narrowed on Jo Gar's.

"Who did murder her, Jo?" he asked.

The Island detective shook his head. "I had thought it was Vincente," he said steadily, and smiled at the surprise in Arragon's eyes. "But that was wrong, and I did not think that way for much time. But I have learned some things. Carejo threatened to kill his daughter if she again saw Parker. The house-boy has told me that. She has seen Parker several times since the first threat was made. Two days ago Vincente told her that he would kill Parker and beat her—if she again saw the American. This morning, early, a note was given to the house-boy by Parker. He delivered it to the girl—she has been giving the boy money for such service. It was just before dawn—and it was still dark when the boy saw her creep from the house. She was next seen dead."

Arragon shrugged. "It does not look good for Parker," he said.

Jo Gar smiled with his eyes half closed. He spoke tonelessly.

"I do not say that Parker *could* not have strangled the girl—he is strong enough. He has lived long enough around the Islands to know how such things are done with rope. But I say he *did* not kill her. There were prints of naked feet—and of feet on which there were shoes—in the palmetto growth. There were too many footprints to be of use. But what was Parker's motive, Juan?"

The police lieutenant shrugged. "She searched for him all day—at evening she found him. She told him it was the end. They must not see each other. She was afraid of her father. It was a crime of passion. If Parker could not have her—no one else should have her. Perhaps he had been drinking. They were alone, on a path of the palmetto jungle. He acted quickly—got away. There are many such crimes."

Jo Gar lighted one of his thin, brown-papered cigarettes. He nodded.

"There are many such, but this was not one," he said. "Carmen has been motherless for more than a dozen years. She hated her father, Vincente. She would not tell Parker that she would never see him again. She loved him—and she must have known that he could take care of himself."

Arragon said: "Why do you say she hated Vincente?"

"I heard her screams," the Island detective replied quietly. "She has had no mother for many years—yet she cries out: *'Madre—Madre.'* She does not call for her father. Is not that strange?"

Arragon rose from his chair and moved slowly back and forth in the hot office. The circular fan creaked.

"It might be instinct—to call for her mother," the lieutenant said.

Jo Gar shook his head. "It was hatred of her father," he replied.

"But Señor Carejo did not strangle his daughter. He was very careful. He was too careful, Juan. He dined with three friends this evening—he was not out of their sight from seven o'clock until one of your men traced him to the Hermossa house and brought him here. That is strange for Vincente has led a lonely life. Señors Hermossa, Carno and Allisi—they had not spent an evening with him for months, until tonight."

Juan Arragon stopped pacing back and forth. He stared down at Jo Gar. There was faint admiration in his small eyes.

"While we have been seeking Parker—you have been seeking Vincente Carejo," he murmured. "Why were your suspicions turned that way?"

The Island detective listened to a *carromatta* driver shrilling at his pony in the street below. He replied quietly:

"Vincente is stupid. He came to me seeking help—he wanted me to find his girl. But what was his reason? It was so that he might beat her. She was 'a devil,' he told me. His anger was not directed toward this American, Parker. That was strange, for one of his breed. Carmen was pretty—not beautiful. I do not think Parker was in love with her. I gambled on my thoughts in the matter. Americans do not strangle with rope. Carejo does not often dine with three friends. It was a perfect alibi, Juan—very perfect."

The lieutenant of Manila police said very slowly:

"Very well—we know that Vincente did not murder his daughter. We assume that Parker did not commit the crime. Who, then, is the guilty one?"

Jo Gar rose from his chair. "There is a house on the Calle Ventner where the American Parker sleeps," he stated. "He had not arrived there a half hour ago. Will you come with me to the house?"

Arragon jerked his head downward. He smiled grimly.

"Shall I take a weapon?" he asked.

The Island detective placed his pith helmet over his grayish hair. He smiled cheerfully.

"I cannot see the harm in that," he replied in a mild tone.

THE HOUSE on Calle Ventner was a poor one. It was a rambling, two-story affair constructed along bastardized Spanish lines. There was some rusted grilled iron-work—and a patio with the screening broken in several places. Naked children slept on the small patio that fronted the place. Jo Gar and Arragon—left the *carromatta* at the roadside; Gar led the way in. There were voices inside—a baby cried. After the Island detective had called out a few times an aged Filipino came to the door. His eyes widened as he looked into the face of the police lieutenant.

"The *Americano,* Parker—he has returned?" Jo Gar asked.

The Filipino nodded. He said that the *Americano* had been drinking much; he had come in perhaps ten minutes ago. He had assisted him to his room, and had partially undressed him. There was a cut on the *Americano's* face, and scratches, also.

He led the way up creaking stairs. The house was filled with bad odors. Jo Gar was behind the old Filipino; behind him he heard Arragon muttering:

"Finger nails make scratches—on a man's face."

The Island detective said nothing. They reached the doorway of a room at the rear of the house. The door was opened; the white electric glare, as the Filipino pushed the button, showed up the cheapness of the room. The house was close enough to the heart of Manila to be supplied with power.

Arragon ordered the Filipino from the room; the man went, muttering to himself. Jo Gar moved to the cot across which the body of Parker slanted. He shook the American roughly. Arragon went to a pitcher that contained water—he dumped a portion of it on Parker's blond hair. It was warm water, but it helped. The American sat up stupidly, blinked at the two men. Arragon snapped words at him.

"Why did you murder—Carmen Carejo?"

Parker stared at Arragon. His face was scratched badly; there was a two-inch cut across his forehead. He was dressed in soiled duck; his shirt was torn in several places. He muttered thickly:

"Carmen—murdered! I don't understand—"

Arragon was frowning down at him. He spoke sharply:

"You strangled her—in that palmetto jungle back of the Casa Club. You—come with us. You talk—"

Parker got unsteadily to his feet. His head was clearing. He said grimly:

"To hell with you! You can't frame me for anything—"

He groaned, dropped down on the bed again. He muttered weakly:

"Carmen—dead! The poor, damn fool of a kid—"

Arragon jerked Parker to his feet again. The police lieutenant was short, but he had strength. He said:

"You shall talk, Señor Parker! You shall tell us why you strangled—"

Parker twisted his body to one side. He shoved hard with his right arm. There was rage in his blue eyes. He was a big man, strong. Arragon went back against a wall of the room, he reached for his gun. It was a long-muzzled weapon—a Luger. He was leveling it when Parker leaped at him. In a flash the American had battered it from Arragon's grip, had sent the Filipino spinning across the room.

"That is not good, Parker." Jo Gar spoke quietly. He stood near the bed, facing the American as he turned. He was smiling; his parted lips showed white teeth. In his right hand he held an Army Colt. He held it steadily. He spoke in a low, conversational tone. "That is not good, because you have nothing to fear."

Parker stood with his hands at his sides, frowning towards Jo Gar. Arragon picked himself up from the wood flooring of the room. He cursed in his native tongue. He came towards the American again. Jo Gar spoke:

"I do not think you are guilty!" he said. "Please raise your hands—allow Lieutenant Arragon to look into your pockets."

Parker raised his arms slowly. He said to Arragon:

"You can't third degree me. If that poor kid has been killed—I can guess who did it."

Arragon moved forward and slid his left hand into the right pocket of Parker's soiled duck coat. Jo Gar asked a question.

"I would like to know your guess, Señor Parker," he said.

Parker muttered his reply in a thick tone.

"The kid's father—he hated her enough to do it."

Jo Gar shook his head. "It is a bad guess, Señor," he returned. "Vincente Carejo was with three friends at the time the murder was committed."

Parker stared at the Island detective. Arragon took his hand from another pocket, smiling with his small eyes.

"Perhaps you were with friends, at the time of the murder, Señor," he suggested with sarcasm.

The American swayed a little as he stood by the cot.

"I don't remember," he said slowly. "I had a few drinks at—"

He checked himself. Jo Gar smiled and spoke.

"At Barres' place. We know of it. You drank saké—three cups of it. You were not so drunk when you left. You bragged about a bird you were planning to fight at the Casa Club tomorrow—Diablo. What else do you remember?"

Parker swore softly. "Everything was going badly, after I left Barres' cellar," he said. "I got a *carromatta*—told the driver to take me to the Casa Club. The bird was out there. I remember falling, after I left the *carromatta.* My head hit something hard. Then I don't remember anything—until just now—"

He sank down on the cot. Arragon held out his left hand, opened the fingers slowly. Something lay coiled against his brown palm. He said grimly:

You do not remember this, Señor?" Jo Gar narrowed his eyes on the coil.

Arragon said in a tone that was slightly shaken:

"I found it in a pocket, Señor—it is a piece of rope, of hemp."

Parker kept staring blankly at the hemp coiled in the police lieutenant's palm. He muttered thickly:

"A piece—of rope—"

Jo Gar spoke. His voice was very steady, very soft.

"Undoubtedly it matches the hemp with which Carmen Carejo was strangled," he said. "It is an end not used in the murder."

Juan Arragon said:

"Perhaps the rope was too long for convenience. You cut it—and being drunk with saké stuffed this piece in a pocket before you committed the crime. It was a crude murder—such as a drunken man would commit."

Parker shook his head slowly. The rage had died from his blue eyes. He said quietly:

"I never saw—the rope before. I didn't kill—the girl. I wanted to break off days ago. She was only a kid—not worth getting her mixed up with her father. She'd been beaten. I sent her a note last night—telling her I was through. I didn't kill her—"

Jo Gar said: "You sent her a note *last night?* You are sure?"

Parker spoke grimly. "I'm damned sure. I gave it to the house-boy, with a silver dollar, at about ten o'clock. He said he'd see that she got it."

Juan Arragon shrugged at Jo Gar.

"I do not believe him," he stated.

The Island detective reached for his packet of cigarettes. He gave Parker one; Arragon refused. Parker said brokenly:

"Why—I wouldn't know *how* to strangle—anyone—"

Arragon smiled with his lips parted. He shrugged again.

"It is very simple," he stated. "One could do it, I think, even after three cups of saké."

From his right hip pocket he drew forth a pair of thin steel handcuffs. They glistened in the white light of the heated room as he moved with them towards the American.

VINCENTE CAREJO sat in the fan-backed chair of Juan Arragon's office and glared towards the door. There had been the sound of footfalls on the wooden stairs; the door was suddenly shoved inward, opened. The American, Parker, stumbled into the light of the room. His shoulders were drooping, his chin sagged. His face was streaming with perspiration. The steel cuffs glittered on his wrists.

"Dog!" Carejo gritted the word at the American. "To kill—my girl—"

Arnold Carlysle, the American head of the Manila police, came into the room, followed by Juan Arragon. Arnold looked tired; his eyes were heavy-lidded, strained. Juan Arragon looked fresh, cool. He was smiling.

Arnold said wearily: "It's almost dawn, We were at it more than two hours."

Jo Gar came into the room. He seemed surprised to see Carejo. He smiled grimly.

"We got it—the confession," he said, "You were right, Señor Carejo. Parker has told us the truth."

Carejo stared at the prisoner. He rose from the chair, stood with his hands at his side. His voice was filled with rage.

"You will die for this—but it will not bring my Carmen back. I could take your throat in my fingers—"

"Steady!" Arnold Carlysle spoke in a sharp voice. "In order to complete the case against Parker we must have the statement of your house-boy, Malo. He is here?"

Carejo shrugged. "He is downstairs," he said. "In that police room. I do not see what more you need—the man has confessed."

Arragon said: "We must have everything—so that the prisoner

cannot retract his statements. It is only a matter of form."

He went to the wooden steps and called down in his native tongue. Carejo took his eyes away from those of Parker. He smiled nastily at Jo Gar.

"And you did not think it was this man who killed my girl!" he mocked. "It was not an American's way, you said."

Jo Gar went over and stood near a window that faced the Escolta, the main thoroughfare of Manila. Few humans were on the street—a warm breeze was blowing in from Cavite, and the Bay.

"I did not think Señor Parker strangled your girl." Jo Gar said slowly.

Vincente Carejo seated himself heavily in the fan-backed chair. He placed the palms of brown hands over his face. He muttered to himself. The American, Parker, stood with his head bent forward, his eyes on the polished floor.

Arragon said:

"It was as I thought. He believed we would think a strangling with hemp was a native crime. He had drinks, after buying the rope. When he pleaded with the girl to go away with him, and she refused, he was in a frenzy. It was a crude, terrible thing. And when he was suspected he tried to place the blame on Señor Carejo, not knowing that the Señor had dined with friends—and had remained with them all evening."

Carlysle shook his head. "It was fine work of Lieutenant Arragon's," he said. "You should have come to the police in the beginning, Señor Carejo."

Carejo took his hands away from his fat face and glared at Jo Gar.

"I was afraid of the publicity," he said.

"And Señor Gar"—his voice was mocking again—"has a reputation."

There were footfalls on the steps. They grew louder—a small, dark-haired, Filipino came into the room. He had a lean face, dark eyes. There was no expression in them. They moved from one to another of the group. He raised an arm, pointed two browned fingers towards Parker.

"That is the one," he said slowly, and in good English. "He gave me the note, this morning. I was rising early, to get breakfast and to wax the floors. The cook is in the provinces. He gave me the note and a silver dollar."

Arragon asked: "What did you do with the note?"

The house-boy smiled with his lips. He spoke with his eyes on the floor of the office.

"I took it to my master. I awakened him. For many days I have been doing this."

Jo Gar chuckled harshly. "But you kept the silver dollar, even though you did not take the note to the girl," he mocked.

The house-boy nodded. There was no expression in his dark eyes as they met the Island detective's.

"I took the silver dollar—it was not good that I should not protect the Señorita."

Arnold Carlysle said grimly: "You have the note that Parker gave you this morning?"

The house-boy reached into a pocket, handed Carlysle a folded slip of white paper. Carlysle opened it, shoved the writing before the prisoner's eyes.

"Your handwriting, Parker?" he demanded.

Parker nodded his head slowly.

"What's the good of—all this?" he muttered weakly. "I've told you—I did it."

Carlysle said grimly: "It is a matter of record. You told us first that you gave the house-boy a note last night. You told Lieutenant Arragon it was at ten o'clock. We want to make sure you do not change your mind again."

Parker turned his body slowly, raised his eyes. They were narrowed on the dark ones of Malo. He said thickly:

"You tricked me, Malo—you squealed on me."

The house-boy's eyes flickered in a swift change of expression. Then they were sullen again, almost expressionless.

"It was my duty to protect the Señorita," he said steadily.

Arnold Carlysle spoke in a low, hard voice.

"You did not give Malo a note for the girl last night. You gave him a note this morning, as he has said. It was not a note breaking with her. It was one asking her to meet you in the palmetto jungle near the Casa Club. You were afraid of trouble—you—feared Vincente Carejo. You wanted to end it all. And you had been drinking much. So you strangled her. I will read the note."

Jo Gar's gray-blue eyes went towards the figure of Carejo, tense in the fan-backed chair. The father of the dead girl was staring at the house-boy. The Island detective moved his eyes towards Malo, without moving his head. The house-boy was smiling with his lips—his eyes were on the note that Carlysle held in the fingers of his right hand. His body was bent forward a little.

Arnold read in a clear, steady voice. He spoke each word slowly; there was silence except for his words:

" 'Dear Carmen—meet me near the edge of the palmetto jungle, near the Casa Club, tonight at ten. We will go away. Leave the house when you receive this note—stay out of sight so you will not be traced. I love you—Dan.' "

Carejo swore hoarsely in Spanish. Arnold Carlysle turned slowly towards Parker. He said in a hard voice:

"You tricked the poor girl. You were not trying to break with her. You will go to Bilibid Prison for this, there to wait until—"

The lights suddenly died in the room. Jo Gar moved swiftly and silently towards the door. Carejo sucked his breath in sharply. The house-boy muttered something indistinct. The office was in blackness.

And then, from somewhere beyond the room, came the scream. It was a terrible cry—the scream of a woman. It was shrill, high-pitched. It died abruptly. There were two strangled words—

"Madre—Madre!"

Carejo was on his feet—he was crying huskily in a choked whisper:

"Lights—the lights!"

Jo Gar's hands went up, out. He was close behind the house-boy now. A faint light from the tropical night sky filtered into the room. Gar's hands came down—in his fingers was a length of rope. It was red in the faint light.

The rope was twisted about Malo's neck now. It was tightening. The house-boy's body was twisting; he was choking. Carlysle's voice sounded slowly:

"*You* are the murderer, Malo—you are strangling as you strangled Carmen Carejo—"

Malo screamed hoarsely. He cried out in choked English:

"No—no—"

Jo Gar twisted the hemp more tightly. The house-boy was strong, but the twist of the rope was too much for him. He went to his knees, gasping for air. A woman's cry reached the room, faintly, choked:

"Madre—Madre!"

Arnold said slowly, calmly: "You are a murderer, Malo—confess before you die as the girl died—"

Once again Jo Gar moved his hands. The house-boy swayed on his knees. His breath was coming in long gasps, weakly. He cried hoarsely:

"Yes—yes—let me—breathe—"

Jo Gar moved his hands towards each other. The house-boy got his left hand to his throat. He tore at the hemp. Arnold snapped the button—the lights flashed on. Malo had the rope in his hands. His eyes, wide with fear, stared at it. It was stained red. The red streaked his fingers.

He flung it from him. His eyes met the staring ones of Vincente Carejo. He cried shrilly, one hand clutching at his throat, the fingers of the other pointing towards his master.

"You—made me—do it! You paid me money—helped me—"

Vincente Carejo's face was white, twisted. His right hand went to a pocket of his duck suit. Jo Gar caught the color of a knife sheath, sewn in the slanted material. The blade flashed.

Arnold shouted a warning. But it was Juan Arragon who leaped at the bigger man, battered the blade from his grasp. The weight of his body carried Carejo back against the fan-shaped chair. He went down heavily. Arnold had his gun out. Jo Gar stood near the door. There was a little smile playing around his thin lips. The house-boy sank to the wooden floor, sobbing.

Dan Parker stood close to Arnold, staring down at the father of the dead girl. He spoke in a low, bitter tone:

"You almost framed me, Carejo. I was down on my luck—and drunk. The drinks were doped, at Barres' place and it was easy enough for Malo, here, to get the piece of hemp that matched the one he used on the girl—in my pocket. I never knew what happened. And you forged the note, of course—destroyed the one I really gave to Malo last night."

Carejo kept his arms over his face. His body was shaking as he lay on the floor. Jo Gar said quietly from his place near the door:

"You write an easy hand to imitate, Parker. They gave the poor girl the note they wanted her to have. She destroyed it. She—"

Carejo took his arms away from his white face. He said hoarsely:

"You read—that note—"

Jo Gar shook his head slowly. "You were clever, Señor," he said. "We talked with our prisoner. We arranged the sort of note we felt you *would* use as a substitute. I imagine we did well. But Malo was guilty, you see. We secured Señora Castonne, of the police, and rehearsed her to scream as I heard Carmen Carejo scream. That was good. And there was the hemp—"

Malo cried thickly: "It was red with—her blood—"

Jo Gar reached for one of his brown-papered cigarettes. He shook his head.

"It was red with *betel*-nut juice," he corrected. "But that does not matter now. You used Malo, Señor Carejo, because he was faithful and could be bought. He had friends who went to Barres' place and doped the saké Parker drank. They kept him out of sight until after the crime. Then he was taken to the house on the Calle Ventner. I do not know these friends—perhaps we will learn soon. It might go easier with you two."

Malo said brokenly: "I will—tell all."

Arnold Carlysle addressed Arragon. "Put cuffs on them," he ordered. "Parker—you are free, of course. It is bad to play with half-breed girls—in the tropics."

Jo Gar let his narrowed eyes meet those of the American, Parker. He spoke quietly.

"It is particularly bad—when a girl's father has married her mother for the wealth of several sugar plantations in the Islands—and then has learned that the mother has died leaving the estate to her daughter, when she becomes of age."

Vincente Carejo stared at the Island detective as the steel cuffs snapped over his thick wrists. He said heavily:

"You learned *that,* too—"

Jo Gar nodded. "Americans do not strangle with hemp," he said. "Señor Arragon was too much concerned with the crime of passion, I think. He was interested in the American, Parker. I was interested in *your* affairs, Señor. There was little enough time, but I have access to the Bureau of Philippine Island Records. My friend, Señor Burneu, helped me. We found your wife's will."

Carejo groaned. His pale face was streaked with perspiration. He stared dully at Jo Gar. The Island detective shrugged his narrow shoulders.

"You retained me to find your girl, Señor. Perhaps you thought that *after* she was found, even though she was found murdered, I would think you a loving father. Even though you desired to beat her. I did not reason that way."

Arnold Carlysle looked at Jo Gar. "It was rather fine work, Señor Gar," he said. "Carejo would have gotten the plantations, with the girl out of the way. He was using Parker to cover the crime."

Jo Gar gestured gracefully with spread, brown hands.

"The girl hated him," he said simply. "She called for her mother, as she died. Yet she had lived with her father for years. I based much on her last words."

He walked across the room and picked up the length of red-stained hemp. He smiled ironically at Vincente Carejo.

"You did not give yourself quite enough rope," he said mildly. "In Bilibid Prison they will undoubtedly remedy that fault."

Signals of Storm

A knife is thrown in the dark
and Jo Gar, the Island detective,
reads its message

HARNVILLE BRUSHED a bit of loose tobacco from his immaculate duck suiting, half closed his brown eyes and smiled. He sat in the most comfortable fan-backed chair in the Civilian Club, and that fact annoyed Jo Gar. His own wicker was not uncomfortable, but he much preferred the one on which the Englishman rested his long body. Harnville said in his precise, soft voice:

"Certainly I am offering you sufficient money. It is only a two-day journey—there is an inter-Island boat sailing tomorrow. You would be very comfortable."

Jo Gar nodded. "That is probably quite true," he agreed. "But you do not seem to care to give me the details. I do not like traveling about in the typhoon season—if you would tell me exactly what it is there would be for me to do, perhaps I might go. Otherwise—"

He shrugged. Harnville frowned at him. He said with impatience in his tone:

"I haven't been to the plantation for three months. Two men have been killed there. I do not like the looks of things—it would be good to have you go out there. I can't tell you what the exact trouble is. You need only be gone a week or so."

Jo Gar smiled pleasantly. But he shook his head. His slightly almond-shaped eyes were almost closed. He ran stubby brown fingers through his gray hair.

"It is starting to blow tonight," he said quietly. "The Number Three typhoon signal has been hoisted. I do not like the small inter-Island steamers in these storms. You are not definite enough, Mr. Harnville. These deaths might have been accidental. No, I prefer to remain in Manila."

The tall Englishman got slowly to his feet. He frowned down at the diminutive Island detective. He said nastily:

"You have had some luck—and you now can choose what to do. I congratulate you."

He bowed sardonically. Jo Gar continued to smile, but the expression in his gray-blue eyes was not so pleasant.

"It is nice to be congratulated, Mr. Harnville," he said. "But I feel unworthy."

Harnville turned away, went towards the screened doors of the Civilian Club. Jo Gar watched him go with narrowed eyes. He heard the man call loudly for his car; it seemed to him that Harnville was always shouting at the Filipino he had trained as a driver.

Wind, coming in rising gusts, rattled the windows of the Civilian Club. It was still warm, but it was growing cooler. This was the first typhoon of the season. Outside the Club he could see the shapes of palms bending in the wind that blew over the Bay. He had the feeling that the storm would be severe.

He smoked a brown-paper cigarette, rose slowly and strolled towards the patio. Outside the air was cool and filled with the sweetish odor of tropical growth. The water of the Bay, on which the Club patio fronted, was roughed up. Jo Gar could see the white-caps in the faint light that reached the sand from the Club. He stepped down from the porch, moved along the path. A gust of wind rocked his slight frame; he turned his head to the right. His keen eyes caught a faint movement beyond the palms that swayed close to the path, there was something white—a flash of it.

Jo Gar took one step forward. He called out, rather sharply, in English:

"Hello, there!"

Something white flashed again. The Island detective was rocking back on his heels now. He let the gust of the typhoon gale carry him backward. There was a faint hiss—his blown coat material ripped, jerked. With one movement he had the knife pulled from the cloth—it had slashed through the pongee until the hilt had caught.

He turned towards the swaying palms. For seconds he hesitated. Then he swung around, moved back towards the Club patio. The light was uncertain. He would be foolish to take chances in the fairly thick growth of palm.

Inside the Club he went to his favorite chair. He was calm enough, though he felt suddenly let-down. The blade of the knife had not even pricked his skin, but it had been a very narrow escape. There was no other human in the room; he inspected the weapon. It was small, with a tapered, thin blade. The handle of wood had been wrapped in native grass. The wrapping would make the matter of discovering fingerprints extremely difficult.

After a few minutes of examination he wrapped the knife carefully in a handkerchief, placed it in a pocket of his suit. He examined the tear in the material, smiling rather grimly. He finished one cigarette, lighted another. A small Filipino boy, very young, came into the room and called softly:

"Señor Gar."

The Island detective rose. It was the telephone. He recognized Harnville's voice. The Englishman spoke with something that approached a pleasantness of tone.

"I want to apologize for my hastiness in leaving you—and for my lack of politeness," Harnville said. "As my chauffeur was passing the Manila Hotel I realized that my feelings had got beyond control. So I had him stop—and I am calling to apologize. Affairs at the plantation have worried me. I am sorry for being so abrupt."

Jo Gar said: "I understand, Mr. Harnville. It is nothing—do not think more of it."

Outside the small booth Jo Gar glanced at his watch. It was nine-fifteen. It had been about ten minutes since the Englishman had left him. That would give Harnville just about time to reach the Manila Hotel, at the far end of the *Luneta.* Just about time. Perhaps his driver had sped along. One thing was certain—Harnville had wanted him to know he was calling from the Manila Hotel. Had wanted *someone* to know.

Jo Gar got his soft straw, went outside and called for a *carromatta.* He gave the address, just off the Escolta, of the frame building in which he had an office. He relaxed in the seat back of the driver. When they got to the *Luneta* the wind rocked the cab. The rain was starting. As yet it was hardly more than a wind driven mist. Jo Gar murmured to himself:

"It will be a storm, perhaps bad. Harnville has never been friendly with me. Yet he is extremely anxious for me to go to his plantation. Native help are cheap. Why does he care about two deaths?"

The Island detective was smiling almost gently when the *carromatta* reached the address just off the Escolta. He paid the fare, went up to his small office. It was not a particularly comfortable place, he was seldom in it. The door was unlocked—the office was in darkness. But Gar's ears were extremely sensitive; there was the breathing of a human. He snapped the switch—Juan Arragon was seated in the most comfortable of the two wicker chairs. He smiled at Gar.

"I have been seated in the dark, thinking," he said. "Your office was not locked."

The Island detective smiled. "It holds nothing of importance," he replied. "Until you arrived, Juan, it was unimportant."

The lieutenant of the Manila police grinned up at him. He said:

"You have torn your coat, Jo."

The Island detective nodded. "The wind is strong enough to blow one against things," he replied.

Arragon smiled with his lips. "Sharp things," he said. "Like knife blades."

Jo Gar placed his hat on a small wicker table, seated himself near Juan and took the wrapped weapon from his pocket. He said as Juan gazed at it:

"I have enemies, Juan. That is too bad. But I have friends, also. I was offered a trip to an Island plantation. Two natives have died there—suddenly. There was a pleasant fee; it is nice to know you are trusted. But I decided not to go. On a path near the patio of the Civilian Club this knife came in contact with my coat. That is not nice."

Juan Arragon widened his eyes. He said:

"You did not catch the one who tossed it?"

Jo Gar smiled. "I do not chase knife throwers among palms, at night," he replied. "You have been here long?"

The police lieutenant shook his head. "Not more than a half hour," he rated. "I thought you would come here, after the news reached you."

The Island detective said slowly: "The news has not reached me—what is it?"

Juan Arragon frowned. "I thought you had heard," he said. "Sam Ying departed suddenly on the *Toya Maru,* for China."

Jo Gar relaxed in his chair. Sam Ying was a wealthy Chinese, an extremely wealthy Oriental. For several years the police had been attempting to stop his traffic with various races in Manila. It was Sam Ying who furnished drink and dope to the poor, and accordingly became wealthy. It was Sam Ying who was to blame when a coolie went berserk and slashed other humans with a knife. But these facts the police had found it difficult to prove. And now Ying had gone away from the Islands.

"It is true—that is news," Jo Gar stated. "But it appears to be good news. And why do you feel it would bring me here?"

Juan Arragon leaned forward in his wicker. He said quietly:

"You have been working against Ying for a month or so. There was a subscription taken up by several good citizens of Manila. You were selected by them to investigate Sam Ying's affairs. So, I thought you would come to the office, after learning the news."

Juan Arragon smiled and relaxed in the wicker chair. Jo Gar smiled, too. He glanced at the blade of the knife resting on the table, touched it with his browned fingers.

"The police are observant," he said slowly. "It is so, of course. Perhaps, though, you do not *think* Sam Ying departed on the *Toya Maru.* Perhaps there was a Chinese aboard who somewhat resembled Ying, and who registered under Ying's name. Perhaps you sent a radio to the vessel, and received a reply saying that the man aboard did not answer to your very complete description. And perhaps you have come to tell me *that.*"

Arragon widened his dark eyes on the gray-blue ones of the Island detective. He said:

"You think of too many things. But, it is so. The Sam Ying the police have been interested in is not aboard. We were curious, though we have no charges against him. We knew that you were more interested than we—you have aided us—I come to you."

Jo Gar nodded. "It is good of you," he said politely. "Have you any idea why Ying should be registered—and not aboard?"

Arragon shook his head. But his eyes held a peculiar expression. He rose.

"There will be the usual storm troubles—I must go," he said.

Jo Gar rose, too. He said quietly: "It is fortunate I did not agree to sail from Manila. Perhaps I would have missed something."

Juan Arragon nodded. "It is fortunate the thrown knife did not strike your body," he observed.

Jo Gar stopped smiling. He said quietly:

"Typhoon winds all blow towards a moving center. The center is quite calm. Perhaps Sam Ying is now dozing comfortably, not thinking of knives or trips to remote islands."

Juan Arragon said: "Perhaps he will sleep a long time, Jo."

Jo Gar shook his head. "He is worth much more alive," he observed. "He will give much to remain so."

The police lieutenant nodded. "There might have been a mistake, aboard the *Toya Maru,* of course. But I do not think so."

Jo Gar smiled wearily. "Sam Ying was very much in love with that half-breed girl. I saw her on the Escolta, only a few hours ago. I do not think he would leave her so hurriedly, carelessly."

Juan Arragon frowned. "Her name is Castrone—Rosa Castrone. She lives on the *Avenida*—"

"I know," Jo Gar interrupted quietly. "Perhaps I shall go there first. It is a quiet street—there would be less danger from knives that fly through the air."

Arragon smiled with grim, small eyes. As he went out he said softly:

"A journey away from Manila might have been wiser, Jo."

The Island detective nodded. "I am like the cock Rameriz had at the Casa Club, two weeks ago," he said. "You remember—it was almost blind. It didn't seem to know just where to leap. But it would not be beaten."

Juan Arragon was at the head of the stairs now. He smiled at Jo Gar.

"You are not so blind, Jo," he stated.

The Island detective shrugged.

"I am not so blind as to make long journeys without knowing sufficient things," he said. "I am not so blind as to walk into the path of a thrown knife."

Arragon said: "Or to believe that our friend is really aboard the *Toya Maru.*"

Jo Gar chuckled. "That is where he would like to be, I think," he said, and went back into his tiny office.

ROSA CASTRONE was a plump girl of perhaps twenty. She had blue eyes and blonde hair, but she was not the true Spanish type. She was half Filipino; her lips were too thick and her features too big. The house on the *Avenida Mandiez* was small and simply furnished; the boy had taken Jo Gar into a room that was filled with storm sounds. Rosa had come after a few minutes. They had spoken first of the storm. Now Jo said:

"I was surprised to learn that Sam Ying had departed so suddenly. We are friends. He has spoken of you. I think he is much in love with you, and I think he is to be envied. Will he return soon, do you know?"

She said quietly: "He will be back within the month. It was a business trip. But you are mistaken—Sam Ying is not in love with me. We have been just friends."

Jo Gar widened his eyes. He decided that Rosa Castrone was lying. He said:

"I have money for him—quite a large amount. He has told me that should he suddenly go away you would act for him. He has no family in Manila, no relations."

The girl was staring at him. She started to speak, but her lips closed tightly. Jo said:

"It is not always easy to raise a large sum of money hurriedly. That is why Sam Ying came to me and made arrangements. Perhaps he left some word with you, some address."

Suspicion showed in her eyes. She shook her head.

"I do not understand," she said.

Jo Gar smiled. "I will be very definite," he told her. "Sam Ying saw much of you before he departed. He did not depart, however, on the *Toya Maru*. A Chinese answering his description in a general way, and registering as Sam Ying did depart. Sam Ying is very wealthy, but his wealth was not all obtained strictly according to Island law."

He stopped. He was still smiling, but Rosa Castrone had become sullen. Her eyes were narrowed on his. She shrugged.

"Sam Ying went to China," she said. "That is all I know."

Jo nodded.

"Sam Ying has been kidnapped," he stated quietly. "He is being held because he will not pay an amount of money. It is bad of you not to pay it."

She laughed harshly. She turned her back on him and walked towards a window, the shutters of which were drawn. The wind was singing through the palms beyond the house—the *avenida* was fringed with them. Suddenly she faced him.

"Why do you say that?" she flared. "Why is it bad of me not to pay it? You have just said that you have money for him—that he came to you and made arrangements. Why do *you* not—"

She stopped abruptly. The expression in Jo Gar's eyes stopped her.

He was smiling in a cold mocking way.

"So you do admit that someone must pay money?" he said in a quiet tone. "Ying is not then aboard the *Toya Maru?*"

There was hatred in her eyes. She was breathing heavily.

"I do not know what you are saying," she said. "You are not of the Island police—they do not want Sam Ying. You have not been sent for, Señor Gar. It is late in the evening—all I know is—"

She hesitated. Then she shrugged her rather thick shoulders.

"Sam Ying has gone to China," she said. "He sailed on the *Toya Maru.*"

Jo Gar bowed just a little. He was smiling almost pleasantly.

"I am sorry to have made you admit that he is being held for a large sum of money," he stated. "He is in an unfortunate position—he cannot call for the police. Perhaps he was himself forced to go to the steamship office and register for the journey he did not make. Sam Ying is himself beyond the law."

Rosa said sharply: "What do *you* care? What does it matter to you? You would be anxious to bring charges against him. He gave you no money—you are keeping none for him. He never went to you. You have lied to me!"

The Island detective smiled, shrugged his narrow shoulders. He said:

"You have lied to me." He moved close to her; his eyes were on hers. "So has Mr. Harnville."

For a second he was sure fear flickered in the blue of her eyes—and then she was staring at him almost stupidly. He moved away from her, but he did not turn his back.

"If Sam Ying was being held—and you were to blunder—he would be killed," she said suddenly.

Jo Gar frowned at her.

"That would be unfortunate," he replied, "for you."

She cried out shrilly, in a rage:

"What have I—to do with it?"

He smiled at her. He shrugged. At a sharp clap of his hands the house-boy came pattering into the room. Jo Gar beckoned to him. The boy came to his side. He was very small, with large, black eyes. He looked very innocent.

With a swift movement the Island detective slipped the wrapped knife from his pocket.

He unwrapped it—held it towards the house-boy.

"Yours?" he said.

The boy reached for the weapon. His face was expressionless. There was no fear in his eyes. His hands were steady. He said slowly:

"She not mine—mine out back."

Jo Gar grinned. Rosa Castrone was standing near a tall cabinet of dark wood. She had gained control of herself; her eyes met the Island detective's. They held a mocking expression. Jo said:

"But you do dress your house-boy in khaki colored clothes, not white?"

She straightened. "I dress him in khaki," she said defiantly. "He is a good boy. I dress him as I please. I do not want you here—"

Jo Gar took the knife from the boy's brown fingers. He said:

"I would have gone sooner had you not lied to me."

She made a clicking sound with her tongue and mouth. It denoted disgust. She motioned to the boy; he went into the small hall, stood near the door that led to the street. Jo Gar said, quietly: "The typhoon is growing more severe—it will be bad for the houses along the Bay."

She said nothing. Jo Gar went out and moved towards the *caleso* whose driver was huddled down in the seat trying to protect himself from wind and rain. The Island detective did not like machines; he preferred a pony hauled *carromatta* to the *caleso.* But a horse got along better in wind and rain.

He instructed the driver to take him back to the Escolta, to cross the Bridge of Spain, skirt the Walled City and drive towards the Bay. The Filipino grumbled; he did not like the wind. But he drove. Jo Gar leaned back in the seat behind. He murmured to himself:

"Sam Ying is no good. He has been kidnapped. Mr. Harnville, I think, is involved. He compliments me by seeking to have me leave Manila. I refuse—a knife is thrown. Very shortly after this Mr. Harnville phones me. Perhaps he is surprised to hear my voice. Perhaps he expected another to answer, in which case he would make sure that person knew he had called, and the exact hour. He felt that he might need an alibi."

The *caleso* rocked as a gust of wind caught it. The Filipino shrilled words at the horse. Rain slapped against the wood of the carriage. They were nearing the Escolta. Jo Gar lighted a cigarette with difficulty. He settled back in the seat.

"Sam Ying is being held for ransom but I do not think he will be released when it is paid. Rosa Castrone would like to talk, but she is afraid. I do not think she knows where Sam Ying is a prisoner. Perhaps Mr. Harnville does. Perhaps *he* is not afraid to talk—"

The Island detective hunched down in the seat, allowed his body to sway with the *caleso.* His thin lips were pressed tightly together. Twenty minutes later, as the *caleso* stopped before the palm fringed path of the Harnville house, he smiled at the driver and tipped generously. He was in a good humor. In the wind swayed *caleso* an idea had come to him—either a very good or a very bad idea.

A Spanish servant opened the door, showed him to a large room that faced the Bay. The house shook under the blasts of wind; Jo Gar was breathing heavily from his short walk up the path. He waited for almost ten minutes before Harnville entered. The Englishman was carefully dressed in duck; he was freshly shaven. But he frowned at Jo.

"A bit late, isn't it, Señor Gar?" he asked. "Getting along toward midnight."

Jo nodded. He smiled pleasantly. "I am sorry," he said. "I've come to ask you about Sam Ying."

Harnville looked puzzled. "Ying?" he muttered. "That fat chink who peddles the bad stuff around the Pasig?"

Jo nodded again. "It is the gentleman," he said. "He is extremely obese."

Harnville frowned. "You come to me at this hour of the night to talk about a chink!" he said, raising his voice. "What would I know about Ying?"

The Island detective shrugged. "Perhaps you know he left on the Toya Maru, for China," he said slowly.

A slow smile spread across Harnville's long face.

"That isn't a secret, is it?" he asked.

Jo Gar shook his head. He said in a very quiet tone.

"You are not surprised to learn that. I did not think you would be. But Sam Ying did not sail on the *Toya Maru.*" He smiled as Harnville stared at him. "He sailed on the *Parambigue,* a small steamer. She is now just making the Straits."

Harnville was blinking at the Island detective. He started to say something, stopped. His long fingers were working nervously. With an effort he made a gesture with spread hands.

"What has all this to do with me?" he muttered.

Jo Gar said:

"I will be very frank. You have little liking for Sam Ying. You own river boats—many of them. You did not think Ying paid enough for their use. There was a quarrel—and Ying got his boats elsewhere. You were losing money, and that did not suit you. You tried to prevent Sam Ying from using other river boats. A few *bancas* and *sampans* were sunk. These things are known."

Harnville had a sneer playing around his lips. He looked down at the diminutive detective.

"What of it?" he demanded. "It's a bit stiff—your coming here at this hour to tell me this."

Jo Gar smiled.

"You were anxious to get me away from Manila—and there would have been only an untruthful reason for my going. You left me—and very soon after, a knife was thrown at me. And very soon after that you telephoned me, establishing the fact that you were at the Manila Hotel and could not have been near me when the knife was thrown."

Harnville chuckled. "You traced my call—to make certain?" he asked mockingly.

Jo Gar shook his head. "I believed you," he said simply. "You do not believe me. You do not think Sam Ying is aboard the *Toya Maru.* You are right. The substitute you placed aboard is on that ship. But you *do* think Sam Ying is being held a prisoner, in Manila. You are wrong. Ying is a very ordinary appearing Chinese. Many resemble him. *You* had little difficulty finding one who resembled him. It was also simple for Ying to do the same."

Harnville stood motionless, his eyes on Jo's. It was evident that he wanted to speak. But he did not. Jo Gar said:

"It is difficult, isn't it? You want to tell me that I am very wrong. That you have kidnapped the right person. Your pride desires that. But you do not wish to admit that you are at all involved. That is foolish—Rosa Castrone has talked."

Fear showed in Harnville's eyes. He took a step towards the Island detective. The fear went from his eyes as he moved. Rage was gripping him. He said:

"I know Sam Ying—I know him better than you do—"

Jo Gar was smiling coldly. Harnville got control of himself. He smiled, too. It was a nasty, hating smile.

"I saw friends off on the *Toya Maru*—Sam Ying was aboard her. You are trying to frame me, Señor Gar."

Jo shook his head. "My interest is in Sam Ying," he said quietly. "He is safely away, sailing towards his native land. I merely wanted to advise you that you are holding for ransom a substitute. Kidnapping is a serious crime."

He bowed. He said slowly: "I do not think you have seen this man you hold. You have been too busy in other places. Sam Ying is a wise man. He knew that if you were to hold him for a large sum of money he could not call on the police. He is not anxious to expose the reason for such kidnapping—the boats were not used lawfully on the Pasig. So he went away. Last night several men broke into his house and took away a substitute, sleeping in Ying's bed. Sam had already sailed. This morning you put aboard a fat Chinese who somewhat resembled Ying. That was not a bad idea, but mine was better."

He moved away from the tall Englishman. Harnville was smiling. He said in a mocking tone:

"It's the most idiotic thing I've heard. Perhaps you accuse an accomplice of mine with throwing a knife at you from the palms?"

Jo Gar faced the taller man. He said in his toneless voice:

"Why do you say 'from the palms'? *I* did not designate the spot from which the knife was thrown."

Harnville's face was white. He said harshly:

"I heard about it—at the Club. I've been there—"

The Island detective nodded. "I see," he said. "I should be very careful, Mr. Harnville. Kidnapping is unwise—murder is more unwise."

He went towards the door. Harnville stared after him, followed him to the door. The wind was blowing fiercely. Harnville said:

"You are very wrong—I shall go to the Island police in the morning. The idea of your coming here at this hour—"

His words were lost as wind rushed into the house. Jo Gar pulled the door shut back of him, slanted his body into the typhoon gusts. He was smiling grimly. A half block from the Bay he found the *caleso*. The driver was standing in the shelter of the carriage, muttering to himself. Jo Gar smiled at him. He reached into a pocket of his light suit, now wet with the rain, gave the man a handful of silver. He said:

"I am of the police—turn your *caleso* and drive slowly towards the Bay. Swear at your horse loudly as you near the house on the right. If no one comes out, descend and work over the harness. I think someone will come and ask you to drive to some spot not many miles distant. Do so. If the man asks about such a person as me, say only that you passed another *caleso* going towards the Walled City as you drove out. Carry the person to the spot he wishes—attempt to see what house he enters. Then drive to Fernandez' café off the Escolta, and report to me. There will be more silver for you."

The driver's eyes brightened. He nodded. He looked fairly intelligent. As he turned his *caleso* Jo Gar went across the street to the grounds of the Church of the Sisters. Palms protected him from eyes of a human riding in a *caleso.* The wind sang through them. After a few minutes he heard the clatter of the horses shoes—the *caleso* came past. The horse was running swiftly, a match flared behind the driver. Jo could not see the passenger. But he smiled faintly.

"Perhaps Mr. Harnville is stupid," he murmured to himself. "He is wise to think that his machine would be recognized. But he is stupid to think that I would not think he would prefer a *caleso.*"

ARRAGON, CROUCHED beside Jo Gar, shook his head from side to side. The rain slapped against his ancient raincoat. He perspired, though it was not warm in the tangle of tropical growth across from the house in which only one light showed. He muttered:

"Harnville—the Englishman! Are you sure you are not mistaken, Jo?"

The Island detective shrugged.

"I am seldom sure of anything," he said. "The *caleso* driver has said this is the house. If he does not come out soon, we will go inside."

Arragon nodded. That was more to his liking. The lieutenant of Manila police preferred action to thought. He was often too anxious. Thus, he had often failed where Jo Gar, proceeding in an almost sleepy manner, had succeeded. Jo suited his action to the climate of the Islands. Manila was not New York, or San Francisco.

Rain dripped from the foliage—the wind sang a steady song. The street between their hiding place and the house with the one light showing in an upper window was one not far from the center of Manila. It was a bad district—low caste Chinese and Filipinos occupied the frame houses. They were small houses—strong gusts of the typhoon wind seemed almost to rock them.

Jo Gar said:

"I think we shall go inside. We will go openly—you stay in the rear. I will knock upon the door."

They moved across the dimly lighted street. Juan Arragon went around to rear—Jo knocked on the dark wood of the door. He stood with his right hand fingers touching the grip of his Colt lightly. His eyes moved constantly. No one came. He knocked again. When they broke open the door, five minutes later, there was no sound from within. The house was poorly furnished. There were crude toys scattered about—no humans were about. Juan Arragon said:

"I will ask questions, next door."

When he returned he said that a Chinese family rented the house. They had many children and had been in the provinces for several days. The neighbors knew little about them.

Jo Gar shrugged. "Harnville was clever—or the *caleso* driver lied," he said simply. "There is no typhoon cellar in the place."

Juan Arragon muttered to himself. They went outside the house, after bracing the broken door securely. Juan said:

"Perhaps you were wrong, Jo—perhaps Harnville did not leave his residence. Perhaps this time it is *you* who have worked too rapidly."

The Island detective smiled grimly. He replied: "More likely I have not worked rapidly enough, Juan."

The lieutenant shrugged. "Sam Ying is of little importance, in any case," he stated.

Jo Gar nodded.

"Others are of more importance," he agreed. "Others interest me."

Juan Arragon was frowning. "It is like seeking a ghost," he said. "The name of Sam Ying is registered aboard the *Toya Maru,* after all."

Jo Gar smiled. He pointed beyond the house near which they were standing.

"An eighth of a mile distant is the home of Rosa Castrone," he said. "With a key a man could let himself in the front of this house. He could then go out by the rear, cut across between other houses, and reach the Castrone home very quickly. Let us go there."

Juan Arragon sighed. "When one has blundered, it is better to start afresh," he said. "I do not think Rosa Castrone would like Harnville. She loves Sam Ying—and Harnville has long been Ying's enemy. Why would the Englishman go to her?"

Jo Gar smiled with his narrow lips pressed together.

"It is one of the facts we will perhaps learn," he said softly, and they turned their backs to the gusts of wind blowing in from the Bay.

THE BELL tinkled under pressure from Jo Gar's fingers. No lights showed in the house—the *Avenida Mandiez* was deserted. There were faint sounds inside now; they reached the two men on the porch against the shrill of the wind. A voice said in native tongue:

"Who is there?"

Juan Arragon replied, "Open quickly. It is the police."

The latch snapped. A light flashed on. They stepped inside. The Filipino boy that Jo had questioned blinked sleepily at them. Jo Gar said in a hurried, breathless tone:

"Quick—we have just received word! The center of the typhoon—is almost here. You have a cellar?"

Fear shone in the boy's eyes. He muttered to himself in his native tongue. He was calling upon the saints. A gust of wind rattled the windows, shook the house. Juan said:

"Hurry—there is little time. The storm is terrible—"

The boy was afraid. But he was fighting something. Jo Gar caught him by an arm.

"You have a typhoon cellar here!" he said grimly. "Take us there!"

The house-boy was shaking his head from side to side. He cried out in terror:

"There is no—typhoon cellar—"

The Island detective said fiercely to Arragon:

"He's hiding something. Rosa told me this was one of the few houses that has one, in this section. We will all be killed—the house isn't strongly built—"

Arragon drew his gun suddenly. The house trembled under a gust of the wind. The police lieutenant jammed the gun muzzle against the house-boy's right side.

"Quick!" he ordered. "Take us—down!"

Something was ripped loose, on the roof. It crashed against the side of the house. The wind was shrilling. The house-boy moved away swiftly—Jo Gar following. Arragon followed him. They went through a bedroom, into a closet. The house-boy pointed towards the flooring. Jo Gar whispered:

"You pull on the ring—you go down first—"

The house-boy glanced towards the gun Arragon was holding. He pulled on the ring—the square of wood came up. His body was vanishing from sight now. There was the crash of a gun. The house-boy screamed; his body slipped from the ladder.

Jo Gar dropped downward. He heard the gun crash again—cloth of his left coat sleeve jerked. His feet struck soft earth. He was up—his right hand gripped his gun. And then he heard the hiss of the knife. He caught a glimpse of the house-boy's right arm. A figure ten feet away uttered a choking cry. There was a whining cry from a woman.

Jo Gar got to his feet. He stared towards the figure of Harnville. The knife had caught him in the side; he was pressing his palms against his coat material, groaning. He said:

"You damn—half-breed!"

Jo Gar went over and kicked his gun to one side. Juan Arragon said:

"The house-boy's all right—you shot too soon, Harnville."

Jo Gar looked at the girl. Her face was white—there was terror in her blue eyes. The Island detective said:

"Where is Sam Ying, Rosa?"

She motioned with her head. The light in the typhoon cellar was dim. Jo Gar went past her and looked down at the bound figure of the Chinese. He removed the gag from Sam Ying's mouth—the man-made guttural sounds. Jo Gar looked at Harnville. He said slowly:

"You were right, Harnville. It isn't a substitute. You did get Sam Ying, at that."

The Englishman pressed his hands against his side and gritted out words. "You knew that damn well—when you tricked me into coming here to make *sure* I had him!"

Jo Gar smiled almost cheerfully. "I am glad you did not think of that until this moment," he said quietly.

JUAN ARRAGON and Jo Gar sat in the police lieutenant's office. The typhoon was less severe now; the center was not expected to pass over Manila. It would not be a tremendously damaging storm. It was almost three o'clock. Arragon was smoking a small cigar; Jo fingered one of his brown-paper cigarettes. He said slowly:

"Harnville was too anxious. He wanted to be sure. He wanted me away from Manila. That was because I have had some good fortune lately—and also because he knew I was watching Sam Ying. Ying had no use for me—he suspected that certain citizens had requested me to seek evidence against him. But Harnville's idea was to have me go away—in case it was suspected that Ying had not sailed on the *Toya Maru.*"

Arragon nodded. "He had sworn that house-boy to secrecy," he said. "When he dropped into the cellar Harnville didn't care if he was a boy who had done much for him. He'd given away the hiding place—so Harnville fired. And the boy used his knife, though neither of them is much hurt."

Jo Gar smiled. "Or perhaps he was afraid the boy might talk," he suggested. "It was almost a confession, when he threw that knife. I knew then that it was he who tried to knife me. But I suspected it, in any case. He was wearing a white house coat when he tossed the knife. I've seen the boy before this, marketing with Rosa. He has always been dressed in white. Suddenly he wears khaki. But I could not be sure. That was insufficient evidence. It is the cool season; khaki is worn now. It was Harnville who betrayed things. First in trying to get me away by an offer. And then, so soon after the attempted knifing, he called me to apologize. It was not a natural act. But when he mentioned throwing a knife '*from the palms*' I knew something was very wrong. I had not mentioned the palms to him or to anyone else."

Juan Arragon nodded. He pulled on his little cigar.

"And there was the light he left in the empty house," the police lieutenant said. "You did not speak of that."

Jo chuckled. "Again, we could not be sure. His idea was that if he were followed it would be natural for the light to appear. He immediately slipped out the rear way, went to Rosa. They intended to get a large sum of money for Sam Ying. She is tired of him, and besides, he is too obese. Harnville thought that her typhoon cellar was an excellent place to hold the Chinese. The substitution was not difficult—Ying was kidnapped first."

Arragon grinned. "As you say, most fat Chinese look alike," he agreed. "And here in Manila there are many fat Chinese."

Jo Gar shrugged. "My only chance was to cause him to betray himself—this Harnville," he said. "He is not a good character. He has never liked me. Had I gone to his plantation I doubt that I should have returned. But I did not go. There were too many signals of storm. I preferred to cause him to believe that his aides had kidnapped a man substituted for Sam Ying. He knew that my clients were trying to deport Ying—and when I told him that the Chinese had sailed on the *Parambigue* he was worried. There was the ransom money involved—the money he hoped to obtain. He had to go to Rosa's house, see for himself."

Juan Arragon said: "It will not go easy with him, or with Rosa and the house-boy."

Jo Gar shrugged his narrow shoulders. He rolled the brown-paper cigarette between his lips, said tonelessly:

"I think that this time Sam Ying will *really* sail for his native land. He is a sick and frightened man. My clients will be glad."

Juan Arragon smiled. "The typhoon helped us," he mused. "Signals of storm, you say. But you had eyes for them. Your clients are often glad, Jo."

The Island detective closed his eyes. There was a little smile showing on his lips.

"The saints are often good," he said simply, "to those who help themselves."

Enough Rope

The Island detective, finds it strange that a man should hang from a forty-foot rope.

JO GAR shrugged his narrow shoulders, let his grayish-blue, almond-shaped eyes stare down over the rail of the bridge. He could see the body dangling from the rope; the wind that blew a drizzling, cool rain in from the Bay rocked the dead shape. The white face was upturned; the chin pressed against the hemp. Below there were several *sampans;* Chinese looked up at the body and kept their lips closed. Rain struck the black water of the river quietly; long legged birds skimmed the surface, some distance from the *sampans* screaming shrilly at intervals. A launch streaked out from the docks; Jo could see the khaki colored uniforms of Filipino police.

The bridge was at least forty feet above the surface of the water at this point. One end of the rope was knotted around the rail support almost at the Island detective's feet. And the shape that dangled at the end of the rope was not many feet above the surface of the water. Jo Gar, shaking his head slowly, said:

"It is very curious. Such a long rope. The body hanging so far below the bridge."

He listened to the *putt-putt* of the official launch as it neared the water spot above which the body rocked and swung in the breeze. He recognized the figure of Lieutenant Juan Arragon; he smiled and waved a hand. Juan waved back.

Jo Gar said in his toneless voice, to himself:

"The launch deck is only a few feet above the water—they reach the body with ease. If it is suicide the neck has surely been broken. Such a drop from the bridge. Certainly thirty feet or more."

A voice from behind him said in the tone of an American:

"What is it, Señor Gar? Someone fall in?"

Jo Gar watched the slash of the knife—saw the body collapse into the arms of several native police, standing close to Juan Arragon on the launch deck. He straightened, turned and faced Dean Price. He said slowly:

"The body did not reach the water, Mr. Price. See—there is one end of the rope."

He pointed towards the rail support, around which the rope was wound and knotted. Price stared down at it. He was a tall, lean man of about forty-five. His slicker seemed to cling to his thin body. He had a sharp, hatchet-like face. Tropic sun had burned the skin almost black. His blue, watery eyes came up and met Jo Gar's squinted ones.

"Suicide, eh?" he muttered, and looked over the rail.

The Island detective smiled. He said slowly:

"A strange way to suicide, Mr. Price. And yet, a broken neck is very certain."

Dean Price straightened; he smiled with his thin lips. He said grimly:

"They've cut him down. White or—"

The American checked himself; his eyes held a confused expression. Jo Gar said quietly, smiling a little:

"Not brown like myself, Mr. Price. White—like yourself."

Price reached for a cigar and offered one to the Island detective. Jo shook his head. Price spoke in embarrassment: "I meant no offense, Señor Gar."

Jo nodded. "It is all very well," he replied tonelessly. "I imagine the man is dead, just as both of us will be some day."

Price frowned. He said in a slightly aggressive tone:

"Well, it was his doing, anyway."

Jo Gar looked down at the knotted rope and nodded very slowly.

"It is a possibility," he said. "Perhaps you are right."

SHE WAS small and dainty in appearance; her skin was very white. Her hair was almost a golden color, and her blue eyes were filled with tears as she spoke. She had a thin voice, but it was steady in tone.

"He did not kill himself, I know that, Señor Gar. If the police think so—they are fools. It was not suicide."

Jo Gar leaned back in his chair and looked at the fly-specked wall. He smiled. He did not speak, and the girl, after a few seconds of silence, went on.

"He was in good spirits. We had just received a contract to tour through the bigger cities of the Orient—and we were going to Australia. It was a nice booking, one of the few made in Manila. He was—murdered—oh, I know he was—"

Her voice broke. Jo Gar leaned forward in the chair and spoke quietly:

"You were married to him?"

She nodded. "Ten days ago, very quietly. We came here from England together, you see. On the same boat. I work on the wire—but my act wasn't going well. We met on the boat, and talked a great deal—talked theatrical business, I mean. After about ten days—I guess we were in love. We talked of working together, doing a double—"

Her voice broke again. Jo Gar said very gently.

"Gary Landon—he was a very strong man. Lieutenant Arragon has told me of some clippings he found in your rooms. He was an acrobat?"

The girl shook her head. "He was a crack shot," she said. "But he was strong—very strong. He closed his act by going up a—" She stopped, covered her white face with her fingers. Her body trembled.

The Island detective said softly:

"I know how difficult it is, Mrs. Landon. But it is necessary, too. He went up a rope, hand over hand?"

She took her hands away from her face. She said shakenly:

"Yes—and then he fired at the targets as he swung in the air, holding to the rope by one hand. It was a good finish for an act."

Jo Gar nodded. He said in a voice that held little expression:

"He had enemies?"

She shook her head. "Everyone liked Gary," she said quietly. "He hadn't an enemy."

Jo Gar frowned up at the ceiling of his tiny office. The girl dabbed at her eyes with a handkerchief. She said:

"We lived at the Orient Hotel. We were always together. We had started to pack. Gary left our room at about ten o'clock last night. He went out to get some special cigars he always smoked. He said he might take a little walk, perhaps to the *Luneta,* or along the Bay. I was tired and went to bed. I woke at about one; Gary hadn't returned. I was worried. At three I called the police. I called every hour after that, until just after dawn. Then they found—"

She checked herself. Jo Gar leaned forward and touched her

trembling hands with his own browned ones. He said:

"You hadn't quarreled?"

She shook her head. "Never," she said emphatically. "He kissed me, just before he left the hotel—"

The Island detective smiled a little. He got up and stood looking down on the narrow alley that ran between the Pasig and the Escolta. It was growing dark; the rain had ceased.

"He was a strong man," he said. "He could have fastened the rope to the railing, tossed the length over the bridge. He could have gone down in the darkness, hand over hand."

He stopped. The girl said. "He didn't. I know he didn't. Why would he?"

Jo Gar shrugged. "He could have used a boat—there was a slip knot at the lower end of the rope. The boat could have gone on. But finding that dangling rope, in the darkness—"

The girl said dully: "But why? Why would Gary do such a thing? He didn't. He was lowered from the bridge. He was unconscious. It was—murder."

Jo Gar turned towards the door of the office, which was closed. There was a soft knock. He said: "Come in, Juan."

The girl rose. She looked at Lieutenant Arragon once, then turned her eyes away. She said to Jo Gar:

"I haven't much money. But Gary Landon didn't kill himself. That's a reflection on him—and on me. I won't have it that way. I'll pay you as much as I can. Will you help me?"

The Island detective took her hands in his. He said simply:

"I do not work always for money. I will surely try to help you."

She smiled through her tears. "I am going to the Orient Hotel," she said. "If you wish to see me—I'll be there."

Jo Gar went to the door of the office with her. Juan Arragon, stepping to one side, said very slowly:

"The verdict of the coroner's jury is suicide, I have just been told. There is evidence of no violence other than strangulation. Mr. Landon was an expert with rope. Perhaps, fearing that he would fight, after the rope tightened, he made certain that the bridge was far above. Weakened from the effort of getting down, combined with the first strangulation he believed it would be impossible for him to save himself. Perhaps he did not try to do that, but he thought of it. That is my theory. The coroner's verdict is a good one."

The girl said very softly: "It was murder. You are wrong."

She went into the hall, moved slowly down the wooden steps towards the alley. Jo Gar turned back into the office, closed the door. Juan Arragon said grimly:

"You think we're wrong, again, Jo?"

The Island detective shrugged. He stood near the window and listened to the strange sounds of Manila traffic—the horns of automobiles, the shrilling voices of *caleso* and *carromatta* drivers, the clatter of the ponies' shoes against the street surfaces. And there were river sounds, too. From the Bay the deep-toned note of an ocean boat's whistle. He said after a few seconds:

"I am not satisfied. The girl says her husband was happy. They were booked for theatrical work and were leaving soon. He had no enemies. His neck was not broken; there were no bruises, wounds. It was a strange way to die, Juan."

The lieutenant of Manila police smiled with his dark eyes. He said:

"Not for one who is strong—who can climb a rope. He wanted *enough* of it. He wanted to be sure instinct for life would not defeat him. He did not want to have an easy climb to safety."

Jo Gar said: "There are many ways of killing oneself without using rope. He was also an expert shot."

Juan smiled. "I suggested you to his widow, when it was clear she was not satisfied with our investigation today. I think perhaps they had quarreled—we have traced the rope. It was bought from Manuel Locracia's store. Forty feet of it. Manuel's son sold it to Landon. He remembered the man because the boy had seen his act at the Spanish Theatre, a few days ago. Landon stated, he needed the rope for practice. He specified that it must be very strong."

Jo Gar said: "What hour was the rope bought—and what day?"

Juan made a chuckling noise. "It was bought at about ten-twenty, last night," he said. "Locracia's store is often open until eleven. He is a thrifty man. Señor Landon did not lose much time. The medical examiner stated the body had been hanging between four and eight hours. River men discovered it at five."

Jo Gar nodded. "It is a strange thing," he said slowly. "But then, death is often strange."

Juan Arragon smiled, showing his white teeth.

"And women are so often in love with more than one man," he said quietly.

Jo Gar widened his eyes a little; he went towards a wicker chair, lifted a slicker and a soiled straw hat. He said:

"You have not told me all you know, Juan. You have found Mr. Landon's widow to be in love with another man?"

Arragon bowed.

"It might be wise to talk with Señor Flores, manager of the Spanish Theatre," he said. "It was about the Señor that a man and his wife quarreled so loudly it was necessary for the clerk at the Orient Hotel to request quiet in their room."

Jo Gar frowned. "That is unfortunate," he said slowly. "Mrs. Landon did not mention it."

Juan Arragon bowed again. There was a broad grin on his round face.

"I did not think she would," he said, with soft grimness.

ALVEREZ FLORES was a short, heavy man with shaggy, gray eyebrows and fine teeth. He frowned at Jo Gar, shrugged his shoulders to question after question and did not at all favor the interview. He knew little about Gary Landon; the act was not too good, the man who shot at targets while swinging from a rope had not been talkative—and the rain brought dampness into Señor Alverez' chest. Perhaps it was the *dengue.*

Jo was sympathetic. He said, after a little silence:

"Clearly Landon was annoyed by his wife. That fool woman—"

He broke off as Flores showed anger in his eyes. The theatre manager sucked his breath in with a hissing sound; his arms stayed at the sides of his drill suiting, but the fists were clenched. Jo Gar said:

"It is always some street rat of a woman, picked up by a man, that—"

He shrugged, turned away from the theatre manager. He could hear the man's heavy breathing as he moved a few feet away. And then Flores laughed. It was a bitter, strange laugh. Jo Gar turned slowly, looked at the theatre man with surprise in his narrowed eyes. Flores said:

"It is—as you say, Señor Gar. Most always it is for women that men kill themselves."

The Island detective nodded. "The police are clearly correct; it is suicide," he said quietly. "But I am interested in such cases, and the manner in which Mr. Landon died was unusual. The long rope—"

Señor Flores shrugged. He glanced at photographs on the wall of his theatre office.

"He was a strong man, Señor Gar," he said. "So often men try to die—and fight against their desire. Half strangled, weakened from the effort of lowering himself, Landon would have had great difficulty in climbing to the bridge again. Perhaps he knew that."

Jo Gar said: "He could have dropped into the water, after loosening the noose about his neck. He could swim, you see."

Flores said sharply: "He could not—think of so many things as one trained in your fashion, Señor Gar."

The Island detective bowed slightly. He said softly:

"You flatter me, Señor Flores. But you are undoubtedly correct. I am going towards the Manila Hotel. Perhaps you are walking in that direction?"

The theatre manager appeared regretful. He shook his head. He smiled.

"There is theatre business," he said. "I am sorry."

Jo Gar made a pleasant gesture and went from the office. He reached the Escolta; the street was crowded. He turned towards the Bay. His lips moved very little as he murmured to himself:

"Señor Flores is a deft man. But he is quite aware of the fact that Gary Landon could not swim."

THE DESK clerk at the Orient Hotel was a suave Filipino; he had recently returned from the States, where he had studied law. His position at the hotel was only temporary; he made Jo Gar instantly aware of that. He was not unwilling to talk. He had his own theory.

"It was very much of an argument, Señor. And the walls of this establishment are not too thick. Also, there was a sick English lady in an adjoining room. Upon her complaint I was forced to ascend and speak to the occupants of Room C12. They were instantly regretful, as I have told the police."

Jo Gar nodded.

"Life is filled with quarrel sound," he philosophized.

"You caught perhaps some words of anger as you approached the room?"

The Filipino made a gesture with his immaculate hands. He said smilingly:

"Señor Landon was a strong man. It seemed plain to me that I must be diplomatic. So I hesitated—to formulate the method of my entrance."

To Gar grinned. "You are very wise," he said simply.

The clerk smiled broadly. Then the smile vanished. He lowered his voice, glanced around the small lobby of the hotel.

"The Señor was saying that he was finished. He had been made a fool, a goat, an ass. He was sick of it all. The lady did not love him. She loved another. He was going to do some terrible thing. He would perhaps jump from one of the bridges."

The Filipino stopped. He shrugged.

"It was not right for me to listen. I knocked, told of the English lady being ill, requested more quiet. Then I descended. A few minutes later Señor Landon descended. He was surely in a fierce mood. He looked neither to the right nor left, and hurried from the hotel. That is all, Señor Gar."

The Island detective nodded, a serious expression in his eyes. He said tonelessly, raising his narrow shoulders a little:

"A pity—to do such a terrible thing. A lovers' quarrel."

The Filipino looked sad. His dark hair was slicked so perfectly to his small head.

"It is good that I was able to tell of his words and actions, to the police. Much effort is saved."

Jo Gar closed his eyes and rubbed the lids gently with the tips of his third finger and thumb. His left hand fingers tapped lightly on the counter behind which the clerk stood. When he opened his eyes again he smiled pleasantly at the Filipino.

"The one who is now dead did not mention a name—the name of the one he suspected his wife of loving?"

The Filipino shook his head. He said thoughtfully:

"His wife was very handsome, Señor. Perhaps he was jealous of little smiles. They had only recently arrived from England. We appreciate the women more, in the Islands, I think. We smile oftener, and mean less."

Jo Gar grinned again. "I repeat, you are very wise," he said softly. "Undoubtedly it was simply a foolish act. One works with rope—and one instantly turns towards it—to die. An interesting affair."

The Filipino looked sad again. "It is unfortunate—she is quite left alone," he said slowly.

The Island detective offered a brown-paper cigarette. It was refused; he rolled one, between his lips, said quietly:

"She will soon learn to smile again. There are so many men."

The Filipino widened his eyes, made a chuckling sound in his throat.

"That is very true, I think," he replied, as Jo Gar moved away from the counter.

JUAN ARRAGON shifted papers about, on his desk. He said, without looking at Jo:

"There was a quarrel. Landon was temperamental. Regardless of what Clara Landon told you, I do not think their act was doing so well. The girl is very pretty. Many humans have used a rope in order to find death. Landon was familiar with a rope, but conscious of the fact that he must completely defeat any instinctive effort to fight for his life. Few use the bridge late at night. It was dark, rainy. He waited for an opportunity, fastened the rope, went down and let the noose tighten. I do not think he fought much. The neck was not broken—the skin was bruised only as much as one might expect. At dawn he was found. Clara Landon is like many women—she seeks to defend him, and herself. She wishes to create enemies. But it was suicide."

Jo Gar smiled. "He had no insurance?" he asked.

Juan shook his head. "It was expensive for him to carry it," he replied. "His widow informs me they were trying to save money for it. But his theatrical work meant that a high rate must be paid."

The Island detective said: "Clara Landon—she has told me the dead man had no enemies. If she were trying to create enemies—"

The police lieutenant chuckled. He said in a very sure tone:

"She is not a fool, Jo. Suppose she were in love with—well, Señor Flores, say. She would not want him involved."

Jo Gar made a clicking sound with his lips. He rolled his cigarette between them, inhaled deeply.

"If he had been unconscious when he was lowered over the water—there would have been some mark on his body, I should think," he mused aloud, "But there is none—I have seen for myself. It is very strange."

Juan Arragon stood up and smiled cheerfully at Jo.

"You want very much to believe this has been a murder, Jo," he said. "For once you are wrong. I am convinced this Gary Landon hanged himself. It is finished."

Jo Gar said: "I think it was murder. I do not agree that such a man as Landon would kill himself in such a fashion. Because you think so, and Señor Flores thinks so—and the Filipino clerk thinks so—I am even more doubtful."

Arragon grunted in disgust. "You have been right too often, perhaps," he said. "You wish to be different."

Jo Gar said: "You have been wrong so much, Juan—but you still wish to be the same."

He went to the street, moved along the Escolta. A *carromatta* pulled in close to the curb, after he had walked a square or so. He recognized the thin voice of Clara Landon.

"Señor Gar—"

He removed his straw hat, leaned towards the carriage. The widow of Gary Landon was dressed in black; she wore a thin veil. She said, smiling wanly:

"I think—I have been wrong, Señor. My grief has been—so great. I think perhaps poor Gary wanted to end everything. He was very temperamental. I do not think he was murdered. I wanted to—tell you."

Jo Gar bowed. He said in a gentle voice:

"Perhaps you are right. I have found no evidence of murder. You have told me your husband had no enemies. Perhaps, after all, there was a quarrel—a little one—"

He watched her lower her veil. Her body was suddenly tense. She said, with an effort:

"Yes, there was. I tried to hide it, Señor Gar. I did not think Gary had taken it so seriously. I am terribly sorry—but there was a quarrel. At the hotel. I must accept what happened—"

Her voice broke. Jo Gar said quietly:

"That is much different, then. It gives us a motive for suicide. I think that is sufficient."

She bowed her head. Jo Gar stepped back from the *carromatta.* The driver twisted in the little seat, grinned at him. Jo said quietly:

"Proceed."

The pony pulled the vehicle away. Jo Gar stared after it. He shrugged his shoulders.

"It is all very nice," he murmured to himself. "Who can say her reactions were not normal? Hiding the real cause—then becoming calmer, stronger. Admitting the truth. Admitting that her husband took his own life."

He waved to a *caleso* driver; when the larger carriage reached the curb beside him he pointed down the Escolta.

"The brown *carromatta*—a square distant. You see? Follow it, but do not go close. When it stops—you stop. That is clear?"

The driver was an aged, bulky man with teeth stained red from the constant chewing of *betel*-nut. He nodded. Jo Gar got inside the *caleso;* the driver spoke shrilly to the horse. The *caleso* jerked forward. It was after ten in the evening; the day had been a busy one. And in the many things Jo Gar had done he had missed his *siesta.* Always an early riser, he was now tired. But it was a physical weariness. His brain was alert.

His eyes watched the lights of the Escolta, some of them flaring strangely, the rain had ceased; it was warmer again. At intervals he caught glimpses of the brown-colored *carromatta* ahead. He nodded, murmured to himself:

"Yes, it is all very natural—the things these people have said. Señor Flores, Mrs. Landon—the clerk; at the Orient Hotel. And yet"—he smiled with his thin lips—"I am very certain that it was murder."

The *caleso* jerked onward. The brown *carromatta* was beyond the Orient Hotel now. Still it was moving along the Escolta. And Manila's main street was becoming an alley of Chinese now. It was swinging close to the river, the Pasig. The lights were fewer; many of them were flaring torches. Strange, discordant music reached the street. Jo Gar narrowed his eyes on the carriage that carried Clara Landon; he kept his small figure back of the bulk of the driver most of the time. He muttered softly:

"Perhaps, if there is enough rope—"

WHEN THE brown *carromatta* was lost from sight, near the market-place, Jo Gar ordered his driver to stop. He descended, was reaching for silver coins when the driver touched his left arm, pointed to the far side of the market square, to the right of the Escolta. The brown-colored vehicle was circling the market square; the pony was walking. Jo Gar got back into the *caleso,* slumped low in the seat. He said quietly:

"Follow."

When the *carromatta* had passed they followed along. The route led up the Escolta, to the Orient Hotel. At the hotel the figure in black descended. The *carromatta* driver was paid—it drew away from the entrance. Jo Gar, moving more swiftly than usual, got from the *caleso,* paid his driver and hurried into the hotel. He went directly to the clerk's counter, but the woman in black was already moving up the stairs. There was no elevator.

The Filipino smiled at him. Jo Gar said:

"Mrs. Landon has ascended?"

The Filipino nodded. "She has taken the key," he replied. "It is very sad—"

But Jo Gar was moving towards the stairs. He went up them rapidly. The clerk had spoken of Room C12. That would be the third floor.

He came upon the woman at the second floor. She was breathing heavily; he could hear her drawing in deep breaths. She moved on, started up the third flight. Jo Gar said sharply:

"Mrs. Landon!"

The figure kept climbing the stairs.

Jo moved quickly to the woman's side. He said:

"You are tired, perhaps ill—"

She turned away from him. He caught her by the right arm, swung her around. She said weakly:

"No—please!"

And then the fingers of his right hand were jerking the veil: he stared into the white, pinched face of a woman he had never seen before. Her eyes were dark, wide with fear or pain. There were red spots on her cheeks.

Jo Gar said quietly: "You are ill—the steps are bad for you. It is your lungs, I think."

The woman did not speak. The Island detective said:

"You were going to Mrs. Landon's room. You have her key. That is unlawful. It will be necessary for you to come with me. I am Señor Gar, and my friend, Lieutenant Arragon, is of the police."

There was terror in the woman's eyes. She was a *mestizo,* mostly Filipino. But Spanish or Anglo-Saxon blood had given her skin a white tint. She was small, very thin. She did not speak.

Jo Gar said:

"You are dressed as Mrs. Landon was dressed when she spoke to me minutes ago. You have stepped into her *carromatta* when she stepped out in the market-square. You did this because it was Mrs. Landon's wish that if she were followed it would only appear natural that she should come to her hotel. But she did not come. Where is she?"

The woman shook her head. She said in broken English:

"I do—not—know."

Jo Gar shrugged his shoulders. He smiled into the woman's dark eyes.

"We will go to the police," he said simply. "Perhaps there you will be I persuaded to think more clearly."

The woman started to speak, but her lips closed suddenly. She was breathing deeply and with an effort. The Island detective said:

"I do not like to take one who is ill to the police. It is not good for them. In Bilibid Prison much work is done. Many die there—"

The woman said: "I did not want to wear these clothes. I am not a bad woman."

Jo Gar half closed his eyes. He said slowly: "I have seen you—you are in the house of Señor Flores—"

She shook her head. She said in a quieter tone:

"No—that is not so."

Jo Gar smiled. "Where is Mrs. Landon?" he asked. "She left the brown *carromatta* at the market square. Where did she go?"

The woman in black coughed. She shook her head from side to side. She said weakly:

"I do not know. I was told to come here. I had not seen Señora Landon before this. Even now I do not know her face. I am not able to climb so many stairs. The doctor—he has said—"

Jo Gar interrupted in a soft, persuasive tone:

"You have done a wrong thing. There is a penalty for impersonating another. You must go to the police, unless you answer my questions truthfully. You do not know Mrs. Landon. Then perhaps you do not know that the police are searching for her. Her husband is dead—murdered."

The woman's eyes were wide with terror. She started to speak, choked. She said finally:

"I was sent to meet the brown-colored *carromatta.* It came on time. This woman, dressed much like myself, descended. I got inside. That is all I know. I gave to the driver the address given me—"

The Island detective said quietly: "It is not well to be connected with murder. It is much better to tell the truth. Who sent you to meet the *carromatta?*"

The woman hesitated. She closed her eyes, swayed a little. Jo Gar did not touch her. He said:

"We will go now to the police—"

She cried weakly, shrilly: "No—no, please!" She was silent for several seconds. Then she spoke very softly. "I was sent to the square by—"

Her words died. She closed her eyes; he caught her in his arms as she crumbled towards the hardwood floor of the landing. She was very light; he lifted her, carried her up the remaining flight, moved towards Room C12. There was no one about. Steadying her with one arm, he took from her open, lace bag the key, turned it in the lock. When he had laid the woman on the bed he opened the shutters wide, moved towards the water pitcher. He said softly to himself:

"She has only fainted. But it will not be wise to wait here until Mrs. Landon returns. She is a clever woman. Or an obedient one. I must learn where to find her. The element of surprise is often—an important factor."

He moved back towards the bed, and the motionless figure of the woman in black. He was smiling with his almond-shaped eyes.

JUAN ARRAGON was nervous as the small car followed the road that ran along the river's edge. The Pasig was narrower here than it was downstream near Manila. Caribou slept along the muddy banks; thatch-roofed huts were passed, from time to time. Arragon, working with the wheel, said:

"It is very strange—it seems incredible. And why you were suspicious—"

Jo Gar said, interrupting: "It is the weaklings who kill themselves over little love quarrels. Gary Landon was not a weakling. He was a strong man. But the woman, Clara—she was not strong. An actress, yes. But when she spoke to me an hour ago, on the Escolta, I was instantly more suspicious. She wanted me to think that now she, too, agreed that her husband had killed himself. But not until she had first cried of murder. She was very clever."

Juan Arragon frowned. The car was slowing down. He said:

"We do not know much yet. We have nothing but the word of a servant."

Jo Gar smiled. "That is much," he replied. "Mrs. Landon did not think anyone would address the woman who returned in her place to the hotel. Grief is a barrier many fear. But I did not think Mrs. Landon, in so much sorrow, would drive around the Escolta and the market-square, on such a night. And this half-breed woman did not sit at ease in the *carromatta,* or walk from it into the hotel as Mrs. Landon does."

Juan Arragon grunted. "This is the place," he said, gesturing towards the right. "There is the bay and the dock. The house, too."

Jo Gar nodded. "We will leave the car some distance away, and walk to the house," he said. "I think it will be a surprise."

"Or perhaps—a mistake," Arragon said grimly.

Jo Gar nodded. "There are many of each in life," he replied with faint amusement, "We must accept the chance."

THE HOUSE was low and rambling; it was not the home of a poor man. There were many trees in the ground that surrounded it—the slope that rose to the screened front porch was perfectly landscaped. Jo Gar led the way; Lieutenant Arragon was just back of him. He muttered in a low voice:

"He is a very wealthy man—a powerful man. If we are wrong there will be trouble."

Jo Gar said in a whisper: "If we are not wrong it will be good for you. Do not forget that."

They reached the porch—the outer screen door was not locked. Jo opened it; they tiptoed to the front door. There were lights inside, dim and well shaded. They could see the wicker furniture, the huge, fan-backed chairs. There was a bell; Jo pulled the knob. It tinkled faintly, somewhere within the house. After a short time there was the pad of sandaled feet on hardwood flooring; the door was opened cautiously.

Arragon said: "It is Lieutenant Arragon, of the police. We wish to enter quietly. Do not give warning. Open the door."

The door opened. The Filipino boy was small and wide-eyed. Jo Gar smiled at him.

"Your master is in—and with him is a lady. An English lady. You will tell us where we may find them."

The boy, fear in his eyes, said brokenly:

"They are in the back—in the curio room. They have just arrived from the boat."

Jo Gar smiled pleasantly. He said:

"Would they hear that bell—in the curio room?"

The boy swallowed hard. He replied in a strained voice:

"I do not think so."

Juan Arragon said: "Lead us to the door of the room—make no sound. It will be bad for you, if you fail to obey."

They followed the house-boy down a hall that was dimly lighted. There was a sharp turn to the right, they descended several steps. There was a door ahead. Voices reached them faintly. The boy lifted an arm, gestured towards the door. Jo Gar led the way.

He recognized Mrs. Landon's voice, though it was distorted as she spoke. Her words came to them clearly but without strength.

"...the risk of doing this. It was a terrible thing. If I had only known, before I sailed—"

Her voice died. There was silence. Jo Gar waited long seconds, then stepped close to the door. He nodded to Juan Arragon, who slipped his right hand into the pocket of his khaki uniform. Jo Gar turned the knob, shoved open the door.

He stepped inside. The woman was in the arms of a man whose back was turned to them. She twisted free, stared wildly at Jo Gar, screamed. Arragon stepped into the room, closed the door behind him. The man swung around. Jo Gar said quietly:

"We are sorry. Love is a beautiful thing. We have come to arrest Mr. Price—for the murder of Gary Landon."

Dean Price's hatchet-shaped face was twisted. He took several steps towards a divan above which hung *Igorote* shields and spears. He sank down on the divan, said bitterly:

"It's—a lie. You can't come in here—"

Jo Gar said quietly: "We *are* here." His eyes narrowed on the white face of Clara Landon. He smiled with his thin lips. "We are here because Mrs. Landon did as you instructed—went to the market square and then to the dock where your boat was waiting. I intercepted the woman who rode back to the Orient Hotel in Mrs. Landon's place. She told of working for you, Mr. Price. So we are here. There are other reasons."

Clara Landon sank into one of the fan-backed chairs. She moved her head from side to side. She said:

"There is a mistake—"

Jo Gar smiled a little with his blue-gray eyes. He said quietly:

"There were several. The motive for the strangling of Gary Landon was self-protection. He was a strong man, Price—you feared him. You feared him because you wanted his wife, and he had learned of that. He had told her that he would kill you if you persisted in seeing her. That was the quarrel the clerk overheard. It was after such a scene that Landon left the hotel last night. He was going to hunt you, Price. He bought no rope. You own most of the Filipino stores on the street where Locracia's place is located. You set Locracia up in business, and you have promised to back Manuel's son. We went to him tonight, after we learned your name. He has confessed to telling a story that was not true. You own thc Spanish Theatre—and your—manager—Señor Flores, has also talked. Often in the last ten days you have met Clara Landon there. You suggested the suicide thought to Señor Flores, and he felt it would be wise to think the same way. It was a simple matter, Mr. Price, after we had your name."

Dean Price said hoarsely: "It's—ridiculous. I was on the bridge, asking you questions, as they were cutting the body down. That was just chance, like a number of—"

Jo Gar smiled more broadly: "It was not chance, Mr. Price," he said. "It was deliberate. But it will do you no good. There is too much evidence against you. We have found the woman here. She is guilty, too."

Clara Landon said hysterically: "No—I did not—"

Price cut in. His voice was hoarse; his eyes were wide, staring at Jo Gar.

"I suppose she lowered the body. I suppose Landon didn't fight. He was out to get me, you say. You say I murdered him. Yet there isn't a mark—"

The expression in Jo Gar's eyes stopped him. The Island detective said:

"There isn't a mark—except the mark of the rope," he agreed. "And the medical examiner has stated death was due to strangulation. You strangled him, Mr. Price. But you *didn't* lower him over the bridge. He didn't die *dangling in the air.* A rope was twisted around his neck—the same one from which he was cut down. He was choked until death came. On your launch, Price. Then, late at night or in the early morning, the rope was fastened to the bridge. The launch brought the body down—he was lifted from the deck, slipped into the noose."

Dean Price was on his feet, swaying. He was breathing heavily. He cried:

"It's—not—true—"

Jo Gar said sharply: "It is true. We have talked with the ones who helped you—those on the boat. They have—talked—to save themselves. They accuse you—and this woman."

He gestured towards Clara Landon. She rose to her feet, her eyes wide with fear.

"I didn't—I didn't!" she screamed. "I begged—Dean—not to do it. I tell you—I wasn't there! I warned him that Gary was coming—to the dock—to the launch. I sent a boy. But I wasn't there! I swear it—I swear—"

Her voice died. She turned her back, walked slowly, unsteadily towards Dean Price. He said grimly:

"Well—that finishes—me."

He sat down on the divan again. The woman went over and leaned against a wall. She buried her face in her arms and started to cry. Juan Arragon said:

"I guess you were right, Jo."

Price stared stupidly at the Island detective. He muttered:

"That damned, squealing crew. I can forgive a woman. We couldn't keep away from each other. I knew he was going to take her away. And when I heard he was coming after me—"

He checked himself. Jo Gar said quietly:

"I think it would be wise for you to tell the whole truth, Mr. Price. The crew say it was you who held Landon—"

Dean Price cut in grimly: "That's a lie! He was coming to get me—that will be my defense. We caught him as he came along the deck. One of the boys dropped the rope over his neck, tightened it. I held one arm—others of the crew gripped him from behind. He tried to struggle. He was strong. But the rope was tight around his throat; he couldn't twist his head. It was only a matter of seconds. That damned, squealing crew—"

Jo Gar said: "The crew didn't squeal, Mr. Price. We haven't been aboard the launch. I was hitting in the dark, because I felt it had happened as you have said."

Dean Price swore grimly. The woman was sobbing. Juan Arragon said, with grudging admiration in his voice:

"You felt it was not suicide, from the beginning, Jo."

The Island detective looked towards the many weapons hanging on the walls of the room. He spoke in his toneless manner.

"They gave Landon—sufficient rope. I was giving *them* enough rope, Juan."

Nagasaki Bound

A yacht with a precious cargo,
a murderous gun and Jo Gar,
the Island detective.

WHEN JO GAR stepped from the caleso, on the sun-rotted planks of the dock near the Manila Hotel, he glanced towards the stern rail of the yacht and saw Vandeer, the Holland detective, leaning against it and smiling down at him. Jo removed his pith helmet, wiped his forehead with a large-sized handkerchief, and sighed.

"I thought so," he breathed wearily. "There is too much native blood in me. Randonn lacks the complete trust."

He attended to his baggage, saw that it was started aboard. When he had paid the caleso driver he moved slowly up the narrow gangplank and was met on the awninged deck by the chief steward. The man was tall and thin; he towered over the diminutive Island detective.

"Señor Gar?" he guessed. "I will see you directly to your cabin."

Jo smiled a little. "I trust there is a fan," he said.

The chief steward nodded. "There is," he replied. "It will be cooler when we steam off Formosa. Your luggage has gone ahead."

Jo Gar nodded. He followed the tall man astern; the yacht was not particularly trim or new; her decks, where there were no awnings, baked in the hot sun. Vandeer came along and smiled at Jo. He was a ruddy-faced Hollander who had been in the Islands only a short time. He had broad shoulders, slightly rounded, and wore shell glasses over his blue eyes.

"So you did come," he said in a voice that was pleasant but that held a hint of mockery. "It is good to see you, Señor."

Jo Gar narrowed his almond-shaped eyes on those of the Hollander, said languidly:

"I feel my presence is unnecessary, with you aboard, Mr. Vandeer. But I was urged. It will be a change."

The Hollander chuckled. "We will all feel safer, Señor," he said

with exaggerated politeness. "You have done much fine work in Manila, I hear."

Jo Gar bowed his head slightly and moved on. When the chief steward stood aside and he entered the deck cabin it was agreeably cool. A small fan whirled—the air was cooler than the breeze blowing over the Bay.

The chief steward said: "We have our own cooling system, you see. The air is iced."

Jo Gar sat in a small wicker chair and carefully set his helmet on the cabin flooring.

"I'm sure it will be—a most pleasant journey," he said thoughtfully.

The chief steward bowed and withdrew. The Island detective stowed his luggage away in leisurely fashion and was reclining on the berth when Sanford Randonn tapped on the closed door of the cabin.

He came in at Jo's call, smiled as the Island detective sat up. Randonn was lean-faced, quick in movement—an extremely active man for his fifty-odd years. He did not appear to notice heat. With his energy and fine organizing ability he had made millions in the Islands, in a period of some twenty years. He said in a thin, nervous tone:

"I hope you won't mind my having Vandeer along. He's done work for me many years, you know. I really hadn't intended to take him on this trip, until a few days ago. But he seemed terribly hurt, disturbed. So I altered my plans."

Jo Gar smiled. He made a slow, graceful gesture with his right hand. Lowering his voice, he asked softly:

"You have the pearls aboard?"

Randonn frowned. Then he shrugged, nodded his head. He said nervously:

"God—they are beautiful things, Gar. I hate to have them out of my sight. Sara loves to look at them. They are the most beautiful—"

The Island detective said quietly: "Your man Toyen will be able to reproduce them—the imitations will be just as beautiful. Toyen is the best workman on such matters, in the Orient."

Randonn nodded, smiled. The yacht whistle sounded a long-drawn wail. The millionaire got to his feet.

"Vandeer does not know the real purpose of the trip," he said. "You do. Sara, myself and you are the only three who know. Vandeer believes we are Nagasaki bound so that I may purchase some important altar jewels. I have done that before. There are so many shrines near Nagasaki. But I do not want Vandeer to know that the pearls are aboard."

Jo Gar bowed. He did not speak. Randonn opened the cabin door and stepped on deck. The engines of the yacht were turning over, there was slight vibration. The wealthy Englishman said:

"It was a lucky deal, Gar. But I will feel much more secure when—"

He checked himself. The whistle of the yacht wailed again. Jo Gar slipped his small feet into sandals and moved slowly to the deck. Randonn smiled at him and went forward. The Island detective looked towards the stern and saw the Hollander at the rail. He frowned.

"It was a lucky deal—" he repeated slowly. "Randonn has often been wise and correct. Perhaps he is wise now—"

He thought of the pearls. They were the finest he had ever seen. He had looked at many, in the South Seas and the Orient. He was something of an authority on them. Randonn had paid a big price for the small lot, but they were worth twice as much as he had paid. And Toyen could imitate them beautifully, so that Sara Randonn could roll them in her fingers, wear them. But first they must reach Nagasaki—and Toyen.

The yacht was swinging clear of the dock now. Friends were waving. Jo Gar saw Juan Arragon climb hurriedly from a *carromatta,* move towards the edge of the dock. Jo waved his short arms—and the Manila police lieutenant grinned and waved back. The city became drowned in a sea of heat waves as the yacht headed out past Cavite and the Rock. After a while Jo went back into his cabin and lay on the berth again.

He dozed and was awakened by a Filipino boy who told him lunch was being served. He dressed, went forward towards the gay-colored awning under which several tables had been placed. The breeze was warm. Randonn smiled at him and gestured towards a table.

"Better than the dining saloon," he said. "The captain tells me we're in for a calm trip."

Jo Gar looked beyond the millionaire; his eyes flickered on those of the Hollander. Vandeer was smiling. The Island detective said quietly:

"That is very—nice to know."

THE ISLAND of Formosa was a mile to port of the Eastern Star as the yacht rode steadily through a nasty swell. It was dark; dinner had been served in the saloon, but several of Randonn's guests had not appeared. During the day the sea had been rough—at dusk, when the rugged coast line of Formosa had been sighted, the yacht was rolling heavily.

Jo Gar walked from the smoking room, turned towards the bridge. The door of Randonn's cabin was suddenly opened—Randonn stepped to the deck. His face was white, twisted. He stared at the Island detective. Jo went to his side; Randonn shoved him into the cabin, closed the door. He said grimly:

"The pearls—they're gone!"

Jo Gar half closed his eyes. He said in a quiet tone:

"Where did you have them?"

The Englishman took from a small writing desk a camera. It was box-like, old. He opened one end of it. He said bitterly:

"They were in a small chamois bag—stuffed in here. The camera was on my desk. On top of it were two rolls of film. I was sure they would be safe. No one would think of looking in a camera—it was right there on the desk. And no one knew—"

Jo Gar said quietly: "Someone knew. Someone besides your wife, you—and myself. Almost always someone knows. You feared that, or you would not have come to me, asked me to accompany you on this trip."

Randonn said savagely: "That German, Bacherman—he made money on the pearls. He bought them up, one by one, matching them. It took years. When he lost his money he had to sell them. He knew I'd pay the best price, but he hated to sell them to me. And I knew that. That's why I came to you. Now—they're gone."

The Island detective leaned down and inspected the camera box carefully. He did not touch it.

"There will be no fingerprints," he said. "But I'll use powder on it. The camera is an old make—and a cheap thing. You would not use such a camera. You were very foolish."

Randonn said slowly: "The pearls are gone—but they are aboard the yacht. I thought the camera would be a good hiding place. If I had made elaborate plans there might have been a leak."

Jo Gar reached for his handkerchief, smiled. He said slowly:

"You do not trust Vandeer. You do not trust me. You have been foolish. Such an old camera. But the thief is clever. When did you see them last— the pearls?"

Randonn frowned. "I had my *siesta*—rose at four-thirty. The blinds were down—the cabin door closed and locked. I took the camera into my shower room. There is no window. I looked at the pearls. They were beautiful. Then I returned the camera to the desk. That was the last I saw of them. The cabin is always locked when I am not here."

Jo Gar narrowed his eyes and rubbed stubby, browned fingers across his lips. He said:

"Does your wife know the pearls are gone?"

Randonn shook his head. "I was afraid of it," he muttered. "I was afraid—something would happen. The German, Bacherman—he hated me to have them."

Jo Gar said: "I will take the camera to my cabin. But I do not think there will be anything learned from it. You have told Vandeer?"

Randonn shook his head. "I just discovered they were gone," he muttered.

The Island detective looked at his wrist-watch. It was twenty minutes after nine. He stood with his feet apart, bracing himself against the roll of the yacht. The millionaire dropped heavily into a wicker chair. He swore bitterly.

Jo Gar said slowly: "The pearls are of much value. As you say, they are aboard. They were taken from this cabin between four-thirty and—"

He looked questioningly at Randonn. The Englishman said:

"—and ten minutes ago."

Jo nodded. "Only you and I—and the person or persons who took them know that they are gone. We will not reach Nagasaki for three days."

Randonn said: "I think—Vandeer should know. That is what he is aboard for—to know such a thing."

The Island detective said slowly: "Perhaps he—already knows."

Randonn stared at him. He spoke in a hard voice, his eyes narrowed on Jo's.

"You are accusing Vandeer of—" Jo shook his head. "I said perhaps he already knows," he stated. "You did not have the greatest confidence in him, or you would not have included me on this journey."

Randonn said grimly: "I was afraid—from the beginning."

"Why—were you afraid?" Jo Gar asked the question quietly, very quietly.

The millionaire fumbled in a pocket of his suiting, got a cigarette between his thin lips. He spoke sharply:

"I've told you—the German hated me. He loved the pearls. He'd never have sold them if he hadn't needed money to pay his Filipinos, out on the plantations. He knew I had them, and he must have known I was taking them away—when he learned I was making the trip. I should have left secretly."

Jo Gar shook his head. "He would have known, in any case," he said, "Why did you come to me?"

Randonn kept his eyes narrowed on the eyes of the Island detective. He spoke in a low, hard tone.

"I'd heard you were an expert on pearls. I wanted your opinion on this Toyen. Vandeer doesn't know pearls. Once I'd told you about them, I wanted you to come along."

The Island detective smiled. "Very well," he said. "Do not inform Vandeer of the loss. I will see about the camera. Later I will meet you on deck. Be cheerful, and say nothing about what has happened."

Randonn looked uncertain. Jo Gar said:

"You should not have brought both Vandeer and Señor Gar aboard the ship. You see how difficult it now becomes. You trust neither of us."

The millionaire smiled. It was a hard, bitter smile.

"Very well, Gar," he said sullenly. "I will not tell Vandeer. You will handle the thing. I am aware of your reputation. I will do just as you say."

The Island detective got the camera wrapped inside his handkerchief. He placed it carefully under his left arm.

"That is very good," he said. "I will be near the smoking room in a short while."

He went outside and towards the stern of the yacht, walking carefully in the darkness. Several times he was forced to stop and brace himself. The swell was a heavy one. When he reached his cabin he closed and locked the door, pulled the blinds shut. He placed the camera on a small table, fixing it securely. The handkerchief he returned to his pocket.

Getting into his berth he lay on his back and smiled. He murmured softly:

"This Randonn—he is a shrewd gentleman. He says that he will not tell Vandeer of his loss. So many shrewd men—are liars."

THE FOUR guests of the Randonns were assembled in the smoking room of the yacht. It was not quite ten o'clock. Captain Howker, of the yacht, stood beside Mrs. Lealand, the wife of Harvey Lealand. The captain was a short, thick-set man, with brown-gray eyes. His white uniform was spotless. Mr. Lealand and John Carris sat together, their eyes on Randonn. Mrs. Carris talked in low tones with Sara Randonn, a fine-looking woman in her late forties. Randonn was talking with Jo Gar and Vandeer; he was saying that the captain thought they would run out of the swell very soon. It was a condition usually encountered off the coast line of Formosa.

There was a puzzled expression in the Hollander's eyes. As the yacht owner moved away from them and went to one end of the smoking room he said quietly to Jo:

"We are gathered here—for a reason?"

Jo Gar shrugged. Randonn raised a hand for silence, said in a low voice:

"There are aboard two dozen finely matched pearls. They are probably the finest I have seen. I am taking them to a man in Nagasaki, who can reproduce the jewels in excellent fashion. The crew has been carefully picked—many of the men have been with me for years. The captain has great faith in them. You are all my friends. Señor Gar is a man with a splendid Island reputation as a detective. Vandeer has handled my affairs in England for a long time."

Randonn paused. He said, frowning: "The pearls disappeared from my cabin this evening. They are gone."

There were exclamations from those present. Sara Randonn cried out in a low voice. The captain's face was set in a grim line. At Jo Gar's side, breathing heavily, Vandeer stared at Randonn. He said:

"But I didn't know—I wasn't informed that the pearls—"

Randonn interrupted, smiling apologetically. He said:

"I regret that, Vandeer. It was Señor Gar's wish that you should not know. As I said—the pearls are gone from my cabin." He smiled more broadly. "Fortunately—they were not the real jewels."

There was silence, then exclamations of relief. Sara Randonn laughed in her rather high-pitched manner. The captain swore softly. John Carris said:

"Good! You already have had them imitated."

Randonn nodded. "It was not a satisfactory job," he replied. "But perhaps it has been good enough. I doubt that."

Jo Gar said quietly: "This being the case, what is your object in betraying the fact that the thief has not obtained the real pearls, Mr. Randonn?"

The millionaire nodded, kept the smile on his lean face. He said in a steady voice:

"I am sure none of the crew did this thing. I am exempting them from suspicion. I feel very certain that the real jewels are quite safe. They are not resting in a chamois bag, in another camera. I regret very much that one among you—"

He stopped, shrugged. Captain Howker was letting his eyes move from one face to another. There was a grim expression in them. Harvey Lealand said in a protesting tone:

"That's pretty thick, isn't it, Randonn? You're accusing one of us of being a thief."

Randonn said in a hard voice: "Yes—that's what I'm doing. I'd like to know who took the imitation pearls. You see, I've got to know. This trip will take several weeks. We will return together. I am making an offer. If the one who took the jewels will come to me and confess—that person may simply depart—at Nagasaki. There will be no prosecution, no further talk."

The captain was frowning. John Carris spoke in an amused tone.

"And if there is no confession?"

Randonn said grimly: "We will go after the imitations just as though they were real pearls. We will prosecute. And let me remind you that Señor Gar and Henrik Vandeer are aboard. They have each had much experience."

Vandeer said: "We do not have to land at any certain hour. We can cruise for days."

Randonn nodded. "I am very curious," he stated grimly. "I have always played fair. We will investigate the crew also, of course. But I am reasonably certain—"

He checked himself again, shrugged. Then he smiled at those in the smoking room.

"The imitations are worth only a few hundred dollars," he reminded. "There is a good chance that we will recover them. I will prosecute. Until midnight I shall be strolling about the deck, or in my cabin. A confession will mean absolute secrecy—no prosecution. I give my word."

He bowed slightly, went from the smoking room. Jo Gar looked at Vandeer. The Hollander said in a low, puzzled tone:

"It's a strange way—to go at the thing."

Jo said lazily: "Why is it? The thief has got nothing of value. But he or she remains a thief. And consequently a threat. Mr. Random is a clever man. But you know that, of course."

Vandeer said softly, smiling a little:

"Of course."

He turned and went from the cabin. Jo Gar listened to the varied comments of the guests for a few minutes, then he went outside and to his own cabin. He looked at his wrist-watch. It was fifteen minutes past ten. The yacht was rolling badly. He went to the stern for a half hour, then moved forward. Randonn came along, moving cautiously. The Island detective gestured towards the rail. They moved to it—and stood watching the distant blur of the Formosa coast-line.

Randonn said in a soft voice: "You think it worked?"

Jo shrugged. "If the thief knows pearls—it didn't," he said. "If the thief isn't an expert, it may yet be successful."

Randonn said: "It's a fearful chance to take. Supposing the thief becomes afraid—believes that he has only fake jewels, decides not to confess—and tosses them overboard?"

Jo Gar said: "It is—a chance. But I do not think the thief will do that."

Randonn frowned. "I would—if I believed they were not real," he said. "I'd toss them overboard and sit tight."

Jo Gar smiled in the darkness. "Why did you agree to make such a statement as you made, then?" he asked in a mild voice.

Randonn swore. "Perhaps I was a fool," he breathed. "You have a reputation, you see."

The Island detective said softly: "That is kind of you, Mr. Randonn. I think that one of two things will happen. The false jewels will be returned, or there will be a confession."

Randonn straightened up. He said: "I hope so. I must leave you—so there will be an opportunity. But if you are wrong—"

Jo Gar tapped his fingers against the wood of the yacht rail. He said quietly:

"Then it will be more difficult, Mr. Randonn—much more difficult."

AT ELEVEN-THIRTY, as Jo was smoking a brown-paper cigarette in his cabin, there was a knock on the door. The Island detective rose and opened the door—Vandeer stood outside. He smiled at Jo, who stood aside as he entered.

Vandeer touched long fingers to his shell-rimmed glasses and said:

"I am inclined to think that this matter is a joke, Señor. Mr. Randonn has a peculiar sense of humor, I know that. Perhaps you are not aware of it."

Jo shrugged. "Perhaps you are right," he said after a little silence. "Men with much wealth often joke in strange fashion. Perhaps it is so."

Vandeer stood near the cabin door and kept his ruddy face towards the Island detective's.

"If imitation pearls had been stolen I do not think Mr. Randonn would have said anything," he stated.

Jo Gar said quietly: "It is not pleasant to know a thief is aboard the yacht one owns."

The Hollander frowned. "But such a statement informs the thief that he has not obtained the real thing. He might try again."

Jo Gar spread his brown hands in a gesture of admission.

"He might not succeed so well—the second time," he said simply.

Vandeer grunted. "I am sure it is a joke," he said. "I did not want you to take it too seriously."

Jo Gar smiled. "It is good of you—to think of me," he returned. "Perhaps you are right."

Vandeer opened the cabin door. He said in a cheerful tone:

"The swell isn't so bad. It's growing much calmer. I think that—"

His words died. Jo Gar took a swift step beyond the cabin as the shot sound echoed down the deck. Vandeer whirled, said fiercely:

"Randonn—"

Then he was running forward, followed by the Island detective. The scream of a woman reached Jo as he was amidships. He caught a glimpse of a figure coming down from the bridge. It looked like Captain Howker's figure. A heavy list of the yacht sent him towards the rail—but he kept moving forward. When he reached the millionaire's cabin the door was opened—light streamed on the deck wood.

The body of Randonn lay on the floor of the cabin. Captain Howker was bending over the owner. He straightened as Jo reached his side. He went to Sara Randonn and led her from the cabin. Jo Gar looked at the bullet wound, just over the right eye, touched the right wrist of Randonn.

His eyes moved over the floor of the cabin; he saw the pearls. There were four or five of them. They were perfectly matched. They gleamed dully in the light. The Island detective did not touch them. He went outside. The other guests were crowding around, white faced. The first officer said to Vandeer: "What's happened?"

Jo Gar turned and said quietly: "Randonn is done—shot through the head."

He heard Vandeer say grimly: "There are pearls—on the floor—"

The first officer was saying: "Any one seen running from here, moving away?"

Jo Gar stood motionlessly, looking forward and aft along the deck. He said to himself:

"No powder burns—the cabin is small. The shot came clearly

enough—"

Vandeer came to his side and spoke in a grim tone.

"I guess it wasn't—a joke, Señor Gar."

The Island detective said quietly: "Someone came to return the pearls. They are in there, spilled on the floor. Then something went wrong—and the thief killed."

Vandeer said: "He might not have believed that Randonn wouldn't prosecute. Perhaps Randonn changed his mind, and told the thief—"

Captain Howker came up and said in a strained voice:

"I'd like you two gentlemen to come inside Randonn's cabin. We've got—a killer aboard."

Jo Gar and Vandeer followed the captain into the owner's cabin. The first officer went outside, closed the door. The murmur of the guests' voices came inside faintly. Howker said in a harsh voice:

"Those the—fake pearls?"

He pointed towards the jewels scattered about the floor. Jo Gar said quietly:

"I'm not an expert on jewels—perhaps you are, Vandeer?"

Vandeer shook his head. "I don't know anything about them," he returned.

The captain said grimly: "That's a small caliber bullet, I'd say."

Vandeer leaned over the body of the millionaire. When he straightened up his eyes were frowning. He said:

"A .22, perhaps."

The captain said: "A woman's weapon."

Jo Gar said very gently: "A woman's weapon—but one that men can easily use."

IT WAS one o'clock. Howker and Jo Gar were in the map room. The captain said in a hard voice, as his eyes narrowed on those of Jo Gar:

"We're holding the course for Nagasaki. Only we're under full steam. You and this Vandeer—you're not getting anywhere."

The Island detective touched his grayish hair with his short, browned fingers. He said in an apologetic voice:

"No one was seen near Randonn's cabin. Several of the guests are unaccounted for—they were alone, at the time of the shooting. The gun could so easily have been thrown overboard. We must accept the word of the guests who were alone. Mrs. Carris was indisposed and had retired. Mr. and Mrs. Lealand were at bridge with Mr. Carris and Sara Randonn, in the card room. They heard the shot clearly. They saw no one. The crew below—they saw no one. It was quite dark, of course."

The captain swore. "The thief got yellow," he said. "He stole the fake pearls. He was afraid that if he didn't return them he'd be caught. You and Vandeer were aboard. He went to Randonn and confessed, bringing him the stones. Randonn may have said that he was going to prosecute. We don't know what happened. But the thief murdered Randonn—and he's aboard the ship."

Jo Gar said quietly: "One of the crew—"

The captain shook his head. "None of them knew about Randonn's personal affairs," he said. "It was—one of the guests. Perhaps a woman."

The Island detective smiled a little. "But you referred to the murderer using the word 'he'," he reminded. "You do not think it was a woman."

Captain Howker frowned. "I want that killer," he muttered grimly. "It's up to you and Vandeer to get him."

Jo Gar narrowed his eyes on the face of the yacht commander. He said slowly:

"I will tell you something. The pearls that were stolen were not imitations. They were real."

The captain stared at him.

The Island detective nodded. "In Vandeer's presence I told you that I was not an expert on pearls. I am. I suggested to Randonn that he make the statement he made. It was my feeling that if the thief did not know pearls—he might return them. That was what happened. But the pearls that I now have in my cabin are real. They are extremely valuable. There are twenty-four of them—I found them all in the owner's cabin, scattered about."

The captain was still staring at Gar. His short body was tense.

"Vandeer doesn't know this," he muttered. "Why?"

Jo Gar said slowly: "Randonn did not trust him—that was why he brought me on this trip. Because Randonn did not trust him—I am not sure."

The captain swore softly. "Where was he when the shot was fired?" he snapped.

Jo Gar smiled with his thin lips. "He was talking with me—just outside my cabin, astern," he said.

Captain Howker frowned. "God!" he muttered. "The thief returned the real pearls!"

The Island detective nodded slowly. He turned his sun browned face towards the bridge.

"Vandeer felt that Randonn was joking," he said slowly, lazily. "That is what he told me. He was wrong, you see."

The captain muttered something that the Island detective could not distinguish.

"But he was with you—when the shot was fired," he stated. "I was on the bridge."

Jo Gar said: "Yes, I know. I saw you come down, as I ran forward. The companionway faces astern."

Howker spoke grimly. "If the thief killed Randonn—why did he leave the pearls?" he asked.

Jo said in a steady tone: "We do not know what happened in the cabin, Captain. The thief might have demanded the real pearls. He believed the ones he had were imitations—they were of no use to him. When Randonn refused—he killed. That is a possibility."

The yacht captain shook his head slowly. He said in a harsh voice:

"I have talked with each man in the crew. You have talked with the guests. What can we do?"

The Island detective smiled with his almond shaped eyes looking beyond the captain.

"Things did not work out as I had anticipated," he said. "I am not sure just what we can do. But for the present, Captain, please inform no one of the fact that I have in my possession pearls worth a great deal of money. When we find the one who stole and returned these pearls—we will have Randonn's murderer."

Howker swore bitterly. "The Eastern Star is still Nagasaki bound," he breathed. "I'll hold her on the course. You have the pearls in a safe place?"

Jo Gar looked towards the bridge and nodded his head. He lighted a cigarette in a leisurely manner and said quietly:

"An extremely safe place. Captain. But I will turn them over to you—"

Howker shook his head. "Keep them," he said grimly. "I'm after the murderer of Randonn. No one is missing. I've got two men on the deck, watching the boats. Even if this sea is bad—"

Jo Gar nodded. "Formosa is not too far distant," he agreed. "A watch over the small boats is wise, Captain."

Howker said: "Better watch this fellow Vandeer. If Randonn didn't trust him—the very fact that he brought you on this trip—"

Jo Gar went towards the door that led to the bridge. He interrupted quietly.

"I am going to my cabin for a nap," he said. "But later I shall go about the boat a little. You have radioed Manila about Randonn's death?"

The captain nodded. He spoke bitterly.

"I'd like to be able to radio that we have the murderer," he said.

Jo Gar glanced at the wheelman. He said in a grim tone:

"I think we should all like that, Captain. All but—one of us."

THE FIRST light of dawn was showing in the eastern sky when Jo Gar left his cabin. He closed the door, snapped the key in the lock. The sea was calmer; there was no blur of mountain peaks to port now. The Island detective went to the stern of the yacht, moved to the starboard side. Then he went forward. He moved soundlessly.

The sea was smoother than it had been in twenty-four hours; as he neared the bridge he thought his eyes saw a movement in the darkness. He stopped. Faint light came through from the smoking room, streaked across the deck behind him.

There was no sound from the spot near the bridge, where he had seen the change of color. He went forward again.

Back of him there was a creaking sound—the swift intake of breath. Jo whirled, saw the raised arm, the downward movement of it. He twisted his head to one side, threw up his left arm. Something struck him a battering blow on the shoulder.

The deck was slippery from spray— he slipped, went to his knees. His right hand fingers gripped the Colt—he jerked it from his duck trouser pocket. A voice, hoarse and strained, gritted:

"Sneakin' around the deck—"

Jo Gar didn't squeeze the trigger. He ducked under a second blow from the blunt object the man held in his right hand. He said sharply:

"Deming! Steady—it's Gar!"

The man muttered an exclamation of surprise, straightened up. Jo Gar got to his feet. He faced the second officer, said grimly:

"I might have—squeezed the trigger! Deming—"

The man stared at him. He said in his husky voice:

"I'm sorry, sir—I saw someone creeping along the deck—I thought it might be—"

Jo Gar moved back a little. He held his weapon low, in his right hand. Deming took a step towards him. Gar said softly:

"Keep off—Deming!"

The second officer was a short man with red hair and a large head. In the darkness his eyes showed like pin points of light. He said huskily:

"I'm mighty—sorry, sir—"

Jo Gar moved back towards the light that made a thin line across the deck from the starboard side of the smoking room. The second officer followed him. He repeated that he was sorry. The light struck the officer's uniform; he was wearing dark blue. The material was a heavy looking cloth, though the night was warm.

Jo Gar said grimly: "I wasn't exactly sneaking along the deck, Deming. I'm dressed in white duck. You could have called to me first."

He spoke slowly, his eyes narrowed on the second officer's. The dawn light was growing brighter now. The Island detective said in a soft voice:

"You wear a heavy uniform—why?"

Deming's body stiffened a little. He spoke in a shaken tone.

"It was chilly—on the bridge—"

"And you couldn't be seen so easily—on the deck," Jo Gar interrupted in a low tone.

He saw Deming's eyes move away from his, go towards the stern of the boat. He said quietly:

"You can return to the bridge, Deming—you were fortunate I didn't squeeze the trigger."

He turned abruptly, moved towards the stern. But before he had taken two steps his body swung around. And as he swung Deming leaped at him.

Jo Gar brought the Colt up sharply. The barrel crashed through the second officer's protecting hand. It stung him heavily on the forehead. His body relaxed—as he dropped to the deck the Island detective gripped him by the left arm partially breaking the force of the fall.

For a second he bent over the man. A blackjack was gripped in the second officer's right fingers—Jo tore it loose. Then he moved rapidly towards the stern of the yacht.

He crossed the deck forward of his cabin, kept close to the wood of the superstructure. From somewhere forward he heard the voice of a man, calling hoarsely. The second officer's fall to deck had been heard.

He was several feet from the door of his cabin when it opened outward. The beam of a flashlight struck across the deck, was extinguished suddenly. A cry came down the deck from up forward—it sounded like Harvey Lealand's voice.

Jo Gar stood with his back against the cabin wood—raised his Colt slowly. A figure moved out from his cabin—the door closed. The man's back was to the Island detective, and then the figure swung around, faced forward. Jo said quietly: "Please—stand still, Captain!" Howker's body jerked erect—his breath was sucked in sharply. His right hand moved out from his side—in the faint light of the dawn sky Jo caught a glimpse of blue-black steel.

He aimed at the captain's right arm—squeezed the trigger of the Colt. The gun crashed.

Jo Gar moved his body to the left as the captain's gun cracked. Wood from the exterior of the cabin splintered across his right shoulder. Then the gun slipped from Howker's grip—he stood swaying before Jo.

Men were running down the deck now. From the stern came the Hollander. He was clad in his pajamas—a gun was gripped in his right hand.

Jo Gar moved forward a few feet and kicked the captain's weapon to one side. He said to Vandeer:

"Go forward—on the starboard side. The second officer—I have knocked him—unconscious. See that he is made a prisoner."

Vandeer stared at Howker. The first officer came running up, followed by several of the crew. Harvey Lealand came along. Jo Gar kept his gun leveled on the captain and said quietly:

"I think we have found—the murderer of Randonn. He is shot—in the arm. We will go to the smoking room."

Howker stood glaring at him, holding his right arm, just above the wrist. He breathed hoarsely:

"Deming—turned me up—"

Jo Gar shook his head. He smiled a little. He spoke in a tired voice.

"Mistakes—turned you up, Howker. It is often that way. Please walk—forward."

CAPTAIN HOWKER sat in the smoking room with bandages on his right arm, and steel cuffs on his wrists. His face was expressionless. The women guests were not present, but the others were in the room. Jo Gar spoke in a steady voice, his eyes half closed.

"You see, the captain had many advantages. He could easily gain admittance to the cabins—there were duplicate keys. The first officer has informed me that Randonn intended to dispose of the yacht shortly. Howker saw a chance. He knows only a little about pearls. Randonn had told me that only himself, his wife and myself knew the pearls were aboard. That wasn't so. He had informed Howker, because he wanted to be sure of the crew. I guessed that, when Randonn was so positive the crew was not involved in the theft. The captain would be the one Randonn would take into his confidence."

Howker scowled at Jo. The Island detective said quietly:

"Howker got into the cabin and found the pearls. It wasn't difficult. He had never seen Randonn using a camera. The second officer stayed outside and watched. But when Randonn announced that the pearls that had been taken were imitations—Howker believed him. The very fact that he had got them from the camera box, placed so conspicuously, helped him to believe. And perhaps he was becoming a little worried. Randonn was a determined man. Howker went to the cabin to replace the pearls—perhaps to search again. Deming was supposed to be watching Randonn, but the owner got away from him. He surprised Howker. The captain had a .22 caliber gun. He used it, ran to the companionway, went up a few steps towards the bridge, turned and came down. It was dark—and he moved rapidly. He tossed the weapon overboard. Randonn was silenced, and he had been shot by a bullet from the type of gun a sea captain does not carry.

Jo Gar smiled faintly. "But he made several mistakes. He thought up a logical story—and kept referring to the thief and murderer as 'he.' In spite of the woman's gun that was used. I was suspicious. So I told the captain that the pearls that had been stolen and returned were not imitations, but the real thing. I told him they were in my cabin. At dawn I left the cabin and gave the captain the chance to seek the pearls. When Deming attacked me on the deck, when I saw he was wearing a dark-colored uniform—I knew Howker was the man. It was so."

Howker swore hoarsely. Jo Gar smiled at him. He said:

"Six of the pearls in the group of twenty-four were real, Captain. Only six. But you had the six, along with the others. Toyen will make six more—and even an expert will have difficulty in distinguishing the real from the reproduced. You were not an expert, Captain."

Howker said hoarsely: "I figured you'd go after—Vandeer."

The Hollander smiled at Jo Gar. The Island detective said slowly:

"Vandeer was with me when you shot Randonn. That was unfortunate, for you."

The captain said nothing. The first officer looked at Jo Gar.

"I wasn't in—on this, Señor Gar," he said. "I didn't even suspect—"

Jo Gar nodded. "I believe that," he said. "Few of us suspected the captain. He said a short time ago that he would like to send a radio stating that we had Randonn's killer." The Island detective's voice was grim. "Send it, please."

The first officer nodded. He moved towards the door of the smoking room. Deming glared at him. Jo Gar rose to his feet and lighted a brown-paper cigarette. He said very quietly:

"The six pearls of value were not in my cabin, Captain. But they are aboard the ship. They are in a safe place."

Howker smiled mockingly. "You half-breeds are clever, he said hoarsely. "Or lucky."

Jo Gar bowed, his blue-gray, almond-shaped eyes looking beyond the murderer of Randonn.

"It would have been so easy to have been unlucky—bound for Nagasaki," he said simply.

Nagasaki Knives

Jo Gar, the Island detective, learns ways the knives of Nagasaki are used.

THERE WERE no other persons on the iron-railed porch of the Oriental Hotel; the air was chilly and there was no moon in the sky. Jo Gar stood with his short arms at his sides and shivered slightly. He was not accustomed to the coolness of Japan, but he liked it. In the afternoon he had walked through the streets of Nagasaki; he had sipped saké and had dined well. Now he stood on the ancient porch of the rambling hotel and watched the little lights that flickered in the hills beyond the city—lights in small houses built on the terraced rice fields.

The hotel was in a noisy section of the town—it was not the sort of place tourists visited. But Jo Gar felt more at home among the natives of a town or city; he did not particularly care for English or American food. And he felt that Toyen, the expert on pearls, would be more at ease when visiting him at the Oriental.

The Island detective lighted one of his brown-paper cigarettes and smiled a little. He was thinking of a yacht aboard which there had been a murder—and of the yacht's captain, Howker. He was thinking of the second officer, Deming.

From the street below the porch there came the shrilling voice of a rickshaw man. It was raised in the peculiar cry of warning common to Nagasaki. Jo Gar half closed his almond-shaped eyes. Captain Howker and Deming were under a special guard, aboard the Eastern Star. The yacht was anchored off the docks, less than a half mile from the Oriental Hotel, and the first officer was aboard, waiting to hear what was to be done with the murderer and his accomplice.

Jo Gar shook his head slowly. He turned slightly as the sound of pattering feet reached him. A short, slant-eyed Japanese came towards him. He smiled, showing even, white teeth. He spoke in stilted English.

"Señor Gar—I am the servant of Ichito Toyen. My master is

ill—he wishes you come to his home. I have come to guide you."

The Island detective made a clicking sound with his lips. The servant bowed a little.

"It is too bad—I am so sorry," Jo said softly. "Your master—does he live far from this hotel?"

The servant shook his head. He grinned. He gestured towards the street that wound below the porch.

"It is very little to go," he said. "There is the rickshaw—I will go beside it."

Jo Gar nodded slowly. "Your master is not very ill?" he said anxiously.

The servant continued to grin. "It is the little fish he has eaten," he said. "I think that they were not good."

The Island detective smiled. "Go to the rickshaw—I am chilly," he said. "I will obtain a coat and come down in a short time."

The servant bowed and moved to the steps that led down from the porch to the narrow street. He went lightly, very quickly. Jo Gar stood watching him, a small smile playing about his thin lips. He ran browned fingers lazily through his graying hair.

"It is very strange," he observed softly, as he moved towards the dark-wooded doors that led into the hotel. "In Manila there is much fish. Yet when Toyen was there he preferred meats and rice. He did not once dine upon crawfish. It is very strange."

When he reached the first floor of the hotel, ascending wide stairs with ceiling fans hanging motionless above them, he went directly towards his small room. It was at the end of a corridor, and there was a figure standing near the door. Jo Gar halted a few feet from the figure, then said in a pleased tone:

"Toyen! It is good to see you again."

The Japanese came towards him— they clasped hands. Toyen's little black eyes were shining brightly. He said in good English:

"Señor Gar—and you look splendid!"

Jo Gar nodded "I do well," he returned. "And you, too, appear in fine health."

Toyen chuckled happily. "I eat and drink—and feel nicely," he stated. "You have had a difficult journey here. Murder—on the yacht."

The Island detective nodded. He opened the door of his room and gestured for the pearl expert to enter. When they were inside, Jo said:

"Tell me—you have not been made ill by eating little fish?"

Toyen chuckled again. "I do not eat fish," he stated. "There has been sickness in Nagasaki because of that. But one does not suffer from what one does not do."

Jo Gar gestured towards a chair and stood frowning at the shuttered windows of the room. From the city came many sounds—among them the sound of gongs. The Island detective nodded his head slowly.

"That is a truth—one does not," he agreed. "A man has just come to me on the porch. He stated he was your servant, and that you were ill—from eating little fish. I was requested to come to you."

Toyen rose from the chair in which he had seated himself and widened his dark eyes on those of the Island detective.

"It is a matter for the police," he said slowly. "I have been absent—and just returned to my house. I was given your note. My servant is in the hospital—a woman is taking his place."

Jo Gar shrugged. "I was returning for my coat," he stated. "I am glad you arrived—to give me warning."

The pearl expert said: "It would be wise to descend and have the man who posed as my servant arrested. In that way—"

The Island detective shook his head very slowly from side to side. He spoke in a toneless voice.

"Sanford Randonn was murdered, aboard his yacht, Toyen. I was bringing him to you, because he had purchased six very fine pearls. I had told him that you could imitate them splendidly. He was murdered for the pearls, by the yacht captain—Howker. The second officer aided the captain. Fortunately, I was able to trick them—they are prisoners aboard the yacht for the present. But there are the six pearls—"

In the corridor beyond the door that Jo Gar had closed behind him there was the sound of footfalls—heavy footfalls. Toyen stared towards the door as they died suddenly. There was a loud tapping—a voice called:

"Señor Gar!"

The Island detective sighed a little. He called in a low voice:

"Yes, Mr. Vandeer—come in!"

The door opened. The man who entered had a ruddy complexion, broad shoulders and eyes over which he wore shell-rimmed glasses. He looked at Toyen, the Japanese—said jerkily:

"Can I talk—"

Jo Gar interrupted. "You are excited," he said quietly. "You may talk—what has happened?"

The Hollander said: "Howker and Deming—they've escaped. They must have bribed someone in the crew—they got overboard. They're gone!"

The Island detective let his diminutive body relax. Toyen muttered something in his own tongue. Jo Gar said tonelessly.

"Ichito Toyen, Mr. Vandeer. An expert on pearls, Vandeer. A detective employed by the late Sanford Randonn, Toyen."

The two men bowed. Vandeer muttered. "I'd been ashore—the first officer gave me the news when I returned to the yacht. They've been gone about an hour. Nagasaki police officials have been notified."

Jo Gar turned his eyes towards those of the Japanese. He smiled coldly.

"It is very fortunate that you reached me, Toyen," he said. "I am doubly warned."

The Japanese said slowly: "You will not go with the one who waits for you—"

The Island detective shrugged. "It would be foolish to go," he stated. "But I think it would be more foolish not to go."

Vandeer stared at Jo, a puzzled expression in his eyes. The Island detective explained briefly, and the Hollander swore beneath his breath.

"It is a trap, of course," he said. "They have moved swiftly. Perhaps it is the pearls they are after, or perhaps—"

Vandeer stopped speaking and narrowed his eyes on the browned face of Jo Gar. The Island detective nodded his head slowly.

"Or perhaps it is Jo Gar they seek," he anticipated. "I shall take my coat—it is chilly outside."

He moved towards the closet at one end of the room. Toyen said protestingly:

"It is very foolish to go with this man. In Nagasaki there are ways of using knives—"

Jo Gar slipped a light coat over his gray suiting.

"In many spots about the world— there are ways of using knives," he agreed. "I have the feeling that if I do not go to them—they will come to me. I would prefer to make it simple—for them."

Vandeer said grimly: "I could accompany you, Señor—as a friend."

Jo Gar shook his head. "I will go alone," he said quietly. "And please do not attempt to follow."

Vandeer was frowning. "The pearls are of great value—and you have them," he reminded. "They belong to Mrs. Randonn, of course. You not only risk your own life, but you—"

Jo Gar smiled slightly. He bowed towards the Hollander.

"I suspected you were more interested in the pearls than in Señor Gar," he said. "I will not take the jewels with me—is that better?"

Vandeer said slowly: "Sanford Randonn trusted me, Señor. I was for several years in his confidence. I should like to accompany you."

Toyen said quietly: "It is dangerous, Jo. I do not like it."

The Island detective smiled a little. "It is dangerous, but it is my business. I am forewarned. I shall go alone. Please do not follow."

He went to the door, said to Toyen: "I will come to your house in an hour or so. I have the address. We will discuss matters then."

Toyen bowed; his face was a mask without expression. Vandeer said nastily:

"You are responsible—for the pearls, Señor Gar."

Jo nodded. He showed his teeth in a lazy smile. He nodded his head very slowly.

"As I was responsible for discovering the murderer of your employer," he agreed, and moved into the corridor, followed by Vandeer and Toyen.

He closed the door of his room, locked it carefully. Vandeer frowned down at the ancient lock. Jo Gar regarded the Hollander with a peculiar smile in his almond-shaped eyes.

"The lock does not matter too much, Mr. Vandeer," he said softly, tonelessly. "The pearls are not in the room."

He bowed and went down the wide stairs ahead of the Hollander and Ichito Toyen.

THE SLANT-EYED Japanese stood beside a rickshaw that was neither new nor comfortable in appearance. The one between the shafts had a scarred face, broad, rounded shoulders and finely muscled legs. He looked at Gar without expression in his small eyes. The one who professed to be Toyen's servant grinned.

"It is five, ten minutes—very short time," he stated. "I will come behind."

The Island detective nodded. He climbed into the rickshaw, seated himself. His eyes went to the porch of the Oriental; he saw in the semi-darkness the figure of Vandeer, near the rail. Jo smiled at the man behind.

"It will be good to see your master again," he stated. "Let us go."

The one who had lied to him spoke in a shrill tone to the rickshaw man. They moved down the slope—the street was lighted dimly. The motion of the rickshaw was easy and steady—the one between the shafts held back his strength until they neared the foot of the winding street. Then he cried out, pulled hard and turned sharply to the right. Coolies scattered from his path—the street became darker as they progressed.

Jo Gar shoved his right hand into a pocket of his coat and gripped the weapon within. He turned his head slightly and watched the Japanese who was trotting along behind the rickshaw. The man moved gracefully; he kept his eyes on the store fronts which they were passing. The windows were filled with nuts, foods in variety. Charcoal fires gleamed in the burners; Jo could see the figures of squatted humans around the glowing coals.

The wind whipped down a street that had now become a road. Flaming torches showed ahead and to the right and left. The rickshaw seemed to be moving away from the river and towards the rising rice terraces. They passed what appeared to be a temple. The rickshaw man was moving more slowly now. But his pace was a steady one.

From the water there came the deep toned whistle of a big ship, and almost immediately, from some spot ahead, there were the distant tones of a gong. Jo Gar smiled with his lips pressed together.

"Strange city," he murmured. "The old—and the new." His fingers loosened, then tightened on the grip of the automatic in the right pocket of his overcoat. He breathed softly: "The new—and the old."

As he breathed the last word he was thinking of knives. Vandeer was right, of course. And Toyen, also. Captain Howker and Deming—they had escaped from the yacht. They hated him. They wanted the pearls they had killed to procure—and then had not obtained. And they had sent a Japanese to trick him. He was very sure of that.

The rickshaw rolled over a dirt road now. There were bamboo huts along the road, most of them set back a short distance. It was a squalid section, on the outskirts of the city. There was faint light from the stars—and torches along the route. The road swung sharply to the left; Jo Gar twisted in the rickshaw seat.

The Japanese was not trotting along behind the vehicle now. He had vanished!

The Island detective leaned forward, slipped to the spot where his feet had rested. The rickshaw man noticed the change in balance, started to turn. Jo let his body swing ahead of the right wheel, struck the dirt of the road on his feet. He fell forward, went to his knees.

There was a thud from the rickshaw—the faint hiss that preceded it, ended in that sound. It was a sound not unlike that of a knife hilt battering against the cushion. Jo swung to his feet, half turned. He heard the hiss a second time, twisted his body to one side. An object streaked close to his head, struck the dirt beyond him.

The rickshaw was off to one side of the road now, the shafts dragging in the dirt. Jo caught a glimpse of the broad-shouldered Japanese. He was running in bent-over fashion, towards a hut off the road. A torch catapulted flaming through the darkness, struck the road close to the Island detective. His figure was a target in the flames, but only for a second.

He leaped to his right. One knife struck his trailing coat material—the other fell short, clattered over the little stones of the road. Jo Gar moved with his head and shoulders bent low—moved in zig-zag fashion. His right hand held the automatic, but he did not use it. He was breathing heavily.

He kept moving, but his eyes could see only the faint shapes of figures—human figures—across the road. He ran to the left, towards a small house that was set back twenty feet or so. The place was dark; he moved towards the rear. There was a small bamboo structure not far behind the house—he ran towards it.

When he stood with his back against the poles that supported the little house, he sucked in deep breaths of air. His eyes stared towards the rear of the larger house, but no figures came into sight. It had been a very narrow escape. Perhaps he had been a fool. But he had felt that Howker and Deming would try to deal with him. He had thought that they would make a bargain for the pearls.

Instead, knives had been flung. Only the fact that he had noticed the vanishing of the Japanese who had posed as Toyen's servant had saved him. Perhaps they had intended to search him, after the knives had struck into his body.

Jo Gar shook his head slightly. He didn't think that Howker would believe he would bring the pearls to Toyen. And yet, the yacht captain might have thought that. And the man was a killer.

A shape moved faintly in the darkness, near the rear of the larger house. Jo Gar stood motionless; his diminutive body was tense. He held the automatic low in his right hand fingers. For several seconds the figure near the rear of the bamboo shack was motionless. And then it moved, directly towards Jo. A voice said shakily:

"Señor Gar—Señor Gar—"

It was the voice of the Japanese who had run along behind the rickshaw. Jo raised his right hand slightly, spoke in a low tone:

"I am here—I hold a gun in my right hand. Come forward, please."

The Japanese sucked in his breath sharply. He moved towards the Island detective. He said softly:

"The rickshaw was attacked—by thieves. I was pulled off the road. You are not hurt?"

Jo Gar smiled a little in the darkness. He said steadily:

"Stop there—do not come closer. I shall kill you—very soon."

The Japanese cried out thickly: "I am the servant of Ichito Toyen—I come to-"

"You are a liar," Jo Gar interrupted very softly. "Keep your voice low, and answer my questions. You have tricked me and I—"

Something rustled behind the little house of bamboo.

The Island detective hesitated, then went on.

"And I shall kill you, unless you talk the truth to me. You understand?"

The Japanese was breathing heavily. There was a faint sound from Jo Gar's right. Someone was moving from the rear of the small house—creeping around towards him. And the Japanese was talking again.

"I did not trick you—it was the thieves. They thought you were a wealthy American, perhaps—"

Jo Gar said: "Do I appear to be an American?"

The Japanese was silent for several seconds. The rustling sound had died. Jo Gar said:

"You have tricked me—I will kill you!"

He squeezed the trigger of the gun. There was a sharp crack!—the Japanese screamed shrilly. Jo whirled around, moved swiftly to the right, close to the bamboo poles of the small house. He saw the figure crouched close to the curve of the rear wall, five feet from him—saw the upraised arm. As he dropped to his knees he fired twice.

The human groaned, leaned against the poles beside him, slipped to the earth. Jo Gar turned his head and looked towards the spot where he had left the Japanese. He could see no dim figure.

He crawled towards the man who lay on the earth, then rose to his feet. A voice said huskily:

"You got me—in the stomach—damn Howker!"

Jo Gar said softly: "Deming—it is you. Where is—Howker?"

The man on the ground groaned. His face showed white in the darkness. He gritted out the words:

"He bribed that red-haired deckhand—to get us loose. We got ashore in a boat. He said we had to get—you. Or we'd go back to Manila—for murder."

Jo Gar stood motionless, looking down at the figure of the second officer. He said slowly:

"You helped him—on the yacht. He murdered Randonn. But he does not care—about you. Where is he—now?"

Deming started to say something, stopped. Jo Gar said softly:

"If you talk—I will send someone here to you. If you do not talk—I will use another bullet—"

The second officer swore thickly. He muttered in a voice that was barely audible:

"He's at—the hotel—the pearls—"

His voice broke. Faint light caught the blade of the knife that lay on the earth beside him. Voices were shrilling, towards the road.

Jo Gar leaned down and lifted the knife. It was long-bladed, with a short hilt. The voices were growing louder. He leaned towards the body of the second officer.

"Help will reach you—do not talk about—the pearls—"

He stopped. The second officer was unconscious. There was faint heart action. Jo straightened, moved towards the terraces beyond the small house, keeping the structure between him and the road. When he reached the first of the rice ditches he turned sharply to his right and moved forward slowly, his body bent low.

He heard voices, raised and borne to him on the wind. One sounded like that of the Jap who had posed as Toyen's servant. He had not fired at the man, but into the earth near the spot where he had stood. He moved on steadily. After a few minutes the voices did not reach him. Once, looking back, he saw the flare of many torches. He guessed that Deming had been discovered.

AFTER A short time he reached a dirt road. It converged with another, a quarter of a mile or so beyond. Jo turned his collar high, bent his head low. The streets were crowded; he came suddenly into a section where there was a celebration. Fire crackers were being set off—there were banners and serpent designs hung and streaming from long poles.

Jo Gar moved through the crowded streets of the section. He found a rickshaw, got into it. The driver grinned at him, showing yellow, broken teeth. Jo smiled wearily at him.

"Hotel Oriental," he instructed, and was forced to repeat the words twice before the man understood.

As the rickshaw moved slowly from the crowded section of the city the Island detective relaxed in the seat and touched the hilt of the knife he had found beside Deming, with his left hand fingers. He murmured to himself:

"Howker—he is not a fool. How difficult it would be for the officials to prove that he or Deming would murder a Filipino with—Nagasaki knives."

The one who pulled the rickshaw was not so young or so strong as the other man had been. It took almost ten minutes to reach the street on which the Oriental Hotel faced. There was a curio shop a half block from the steps that led to the hotel porch. Jo stopped the rickshaw in front of the shop, descended and paid the one with the yellow teeth.

When the man moved off Jo went slowly towards the hotel. He ascended the stairs to the porch and thought to himself: Seven more bullets—in the gun. That is good.

He went inside; the hotel was dimly lighted, though the hour was not late. The Island detective climbed the wide stairs almost silently. His muscles ached; he was tired. His body was not accustomed to such effort. As he approached the door of his room he moved slowly. He reached into his pocket for the key—tried the knob before he inserted it. The door opened under slight pressure.

Jo drew in a deep breath, sighed. He did not use the key, but opened the door cautiously. The room was dark—he snapped the switch near the door, his right hand holding the material of the pocket forward. The one electric bulb glowed not too brightly.

The Island detective moved forward, stared down at the figure lying on the floor, not far from the small bed. He said slowly:

"Toyen!"

The pearl expert was lying face downward, but his dress and clothing identified him. Jo moved rapidly to his side, turned him over. The dark eyes of Ichito Toyen stared at him unseeingly. One glance was sufficient. The Japanese was dead.

Jo Gar narrowed his eyes on the hilt of the knife, the blade of which was buried just below Toyen's heart. The hilt was crimson stained; it was of wood that looked old. The Island detective fingered Toyen's left wrist; he straightened, stared about the room. There was no disorder.

The shutters were drawn; the few chairs were in the same position as when he had left the room, locking the door after him. And yet Ichito Toyen had returned to that room—and was lying dead, knifed through the heart.

The Island detective went to the edge of the bed and seated himself. He faced the window. He said in a whisper:

"There was the Hollander, Vandeer. And there was a man who has murdered once—Howker. Which of the two—"

A voice said very quietly: "You will keep your hands at your sides—and you will not turn! You will make no sound, Gar. It is very important that you obey me—for you!"

Jo's body had tensed—it relaxed now. He narrowed his eyes on the shutters of the windows, listened to the distant crackling of fireworks. He said in a voice that was very soft:

"I am not a fool, Captain Howker— I shall do exactly as—you say."

The closet door closed with a faint clicking sound. There were light footfalls behind the Island detective. In the corridor beyond the room there was the patter of sandled feet. The murderer, Howker, whistled a little as he moved around to one side. The footfalls beyond the room died away.

After a few seconds Howker moved to a spot near the shutters. He stood with his back to them and smiled down at Jo Gar. His brown-gray eyes held little expression—the smile was on his lips. It was a hard smile. The man's short, thick-set body was relaxed. Howker wore no hat—he was dressed in a cheap suit of dark material. He spoke with little emotion.

"More than ever, now—I need the pearls. You have them. I did not expect you to return here—Deming has failed. That is done. You have returned. I came here to search the room. This Japanese surprised me. I suppose he was—Toyen."

Jo Gar said nothing. Howker narrowed his eyes a little and said:

"I killed Randonn for the pearls— and I'm not a fool. They will take me back to Bilibid, or perhaps to England—and hang me. That, is, they will if I'm caught."

He paused, and Jo Gar said slowly: "You did not have to murder Toyen. He was not involved in this. He was my friend—"

There was a weary tone in the Island detective's voice. Howker smiled with his eyes. He moved his right hand a little and Jo looked at the gun. It was an Army weapon—it looked like one of the Colts that Randonn had kept aboard the yacht.

Howker said grimly: "I turned my back on him for a second—he drew the knife you see there. I knocked it out of his hands, and used it on him. He cut me—"

With a quick movement he pulled back the sleeve of his left arm. The skin was stained with red. He said bitterly:

"I've got to get away—and I'll need money. The pearls will bring me the money. You have the pearls. I can kill you, Gar. You trapped me, on the yacht. But I will—make a bargain with you."

Jo Gar sat motionless, his eyes on the eyes of the one who had twice murdered. He said slowly:

"I am not a fool—I do not care to die. It was my business to find the murderer of Randonn. It it not my business to find the murderer of Toyen, even though he was my friend."

Howker slitted his brown-gray eyes on Jo's and said grimly:

"You are tricky—and cold. When a man born in the tropics is cold—he's dangerous. I hate to deal with you."

Jo Gar said quietly: "As you say, I have the pearls. There are six of them—and they are worth much money. If you kill me—you will not have them."

The murderer swore softly. "You are cold," he repeated. "Colder than death."

The Island detective said slowly: "I will show you that I am honest with you. My life is worth much to me. You are wasting time. I have shot Deming—and the police will find him. Perhaps there will be a description of me. Deming will not talk, perhaps—but the rickshaw man may. Or the one you sent to pose as Toyen's servant. If the police come here seeking me—"

He broke off, shrugged. Howker moved his gun hand a little and said grimly:

"You brought the pearls ashore—you would not leave them on the yacht. You wanted to get them to Toyen. If they are not on you, or in this room, they are somewhere near. I will give you your life—for them. That is my offer."

Jo said simply: "My life is of more value than the pearls. You have killed twice—"

Howker widened his eyes a little and smiled disagreeably.

"As you know, I am not an expert! You will bring the pearls to a man I know. He is Japanese and his judgment is quite good. For years he lived in the South Seas—I met him down there."

The Island detective said slowly: "There will be risk, for you. On the streets—"

Howker interrupted grimly. "There will be risk for you, too, Gar! They will want you before they want me, perhaps. You have shot Deming. If they have your description—"

Jo Gar nodded. "It is so," he agreed. "They do not care so much about murder that occurred on a yacht at sea. An English yacht. And they do not know as yet that you have killed a Japanese."

Howker swore softly, looking down at the body of Toyen.

"It was self defense," he stated harshly. "I took his own knife from him."

Jo Gar said nothing. Howker took his eyes away from the figure on the floor, lowered his gun arm a little.

"You have the pearls here?" he asked in a voice that was too calm to please the Island detective.

Jo nodded. Howker questioned him with his eyes. After a little silence he said:

"Raise your hands—and get up. Stand very still."

The Island detective obeyed. Howker pressed the muzzle of the gun against his left side and searched him carefully. He grunted as he took the knife and automatic from Jo. Backing towards the shutters of the windows again, he spoke in a steady voice.

"I don't think you'll be foolish. If anything goes wrong I'll use this gun. You know that. Get the pearls, but use your left hand doing it—and keep the right where I can see it."

Jo Gar nodded, lowered his left hand. He went to a small piece of luggage he had brought from the yacht, snapped the bag open. It was not locked. He fumbled among a few objects, lifted out a bottle containing a blue liquid. He said quietly:

"The pearls are here—the liquid is colored water."

Howker smiled grimly. "Yes?" he said. "All right—but let me see the pearls."

There was a small sink at one end of the room. Jo went towards it, with Howker following. The distant cracking of fireworks had ceased; at intervals there were gongs sounding. The interior of the hotel was quiet—very quiet.

The Island detective poured the liquid to a glass—strained the pearls into the palm of his left hand, on which was a towel from a rack, and wiped them. They gleamed dully in the poor light of the room. There were six of them. Back of him he heard Howker's breath sucked in sharply. Jo said slowly:

"They are worth killing for?"

Howker swore at him. He said sharply:

"Set them on the towel on the sink."

Jo did as he was instructed. Howker took up the pearls into a handkerchief, keeping the gun in his right hand, and his eyes on Jo. He said slowly:

"Turn your back."

Jo Gar turned. He stood motionlessly, his body relaxed. Then Howker was speaking again.

"We go out—you lock the door. We go down the stairs, but not out the front entrance. There are steps in the rear—into the tea garden. You will be at my right, and my gun will be ready for action. The place to which I'm taking the pearls is only a few squares. We will walk."

Jo Gar nodded. He moved towards the door, opened it, stepped into the corridor. Howker followed him. He said in a quiet voice:

"Snap the switch off!"

The Island detective obeyed. He closed the door, locked it. They moved towards the wide stairs, went down. A sleepy looking clerk was back of the big, dark-wooded desk. He smiled a little as they turned towards the rear of the hotel. They went down a corridor, reached narrow steps that led to a small tea garden. Howker chuckled a little. His body was pressed close to Jo's—they went through an alley, over an old arched bridge that spanned a bad odored stream.

Suddenly they reached a narrow street that was well lighted. Rickshaws were moving in both directions. Howker got his body close to the wood of a tea house and said sharply:

"Wait—stay here!"

They stood in a dark spot and watched the narrow street. Suddenly Howker's body stiffened at Jo's side. He swore softly. A rickshaw was moving slowly into sight; there was a jam of humans ahead of it.

The driver was shouting shrilly. In the rickshaw were two men. One was short and thick-set, brown-faced. He was in the uniform of a police official. The other man was the Hollander, Vandeer. Vandeer was talking, gesturing excitedly.

The humans moved away from the rickshaw—the vehicle went on. Howker said grimly:

"That might have been bad—yes?"

Jo shrugged. "I left Vandeer at the hotel, with Toyen," he said simply. "Toyen must have returned. But I don't see—"

"Perhaps he, too, was after the pearls," Howker said mockingly. "Anyway, he was in the room when I entered."

Jo said quietly: "I do not think he was outside the door—and you forced him to enter. You thought he might have the pearls."

Howker narrowed his eyes on Jo's. He said slowly:

"That doesn't matter—cross the street now. Keep your head low—and don't look in either direction."

They crossed the crowded street; Howker swearing harshly at a coolie who got in his path as they had almost reached the far side. They were in another alley; it wound to the right. The wooden houses on either side were in bad shape—rotted and broken down. Oriental music sounded from them; sharp odors reached the Island detective's nostrils.

Howker said sharply: "Here—to your right!"

They passed through swinging doors. Beyond was a charcoal burner. The place seemed to be a small curio store—near faded, jade curtains stood the squat figure of a Japanese. His face seemed like a mask in the dull light of the evil smelling store.

Howker said quietly: "I have brought a friend, Matu—there is something of value he has given me. Will you look at the objects for me?"

The Japanese made no sound. He bowed his head slightly, spread his hands in a gesture of consent. He turned, moved beyond the faded, jade curtain. Jo could hear his footfalls as he climbed stairs.

Howker said: "Follow him, señor. And be very careful of the steps."

There was mockery in the man's tone. Jo went towards the curtain, passed it, walked slowly up the stairs. There were not many steps—they creaked beneath his weight. Behind him Howker mounted the steps. At the top Jo paused, looked around. The Japanese was seated back of a small table over which hung a light—a kerosene lamp, from the odor of the room. He gestured towards chairs that were near the table—Jo moved towards one.

Howker came up and walked to the table. With a swift movement of his left hand he let the pearls roll across the surface. The Japanese drew a quick breath. He muttered a word that Jo did not understand. Howker said slowly, mockingly:

"I am told they are good pearls—and of great value. I hope that is true."

He faced the Island detective, his gun made a bulge in the right pocket of his dark coat. His brown-gray eyes glittered in the light of the lamp. The Japanese was bending his head low, touching the pearls with slender nippers, getting his wide eyes close to them. Muffled sounds reached the room from the street.

The Japanese was muttering to himself—Howker kept his eyes narrowed on the figure of Jo Gar. Several minutes passed. Howker said in a husky voice:

"Well, Matu? They are good?"

The Japanese raised his head and his eyes glittered on Jo Gar's momentarily. He turned his head towards Howker, said very quietly:

"The pearls—are very fine, Captain. I do not think I have ever—looked upon finer ones."

Howker's body stiffened a little. Surprise showed in his eyes. He swore hoarsely. The Japanese rose from the stool on which he had been seated. He said in broken English:

"If I may point out—"

The knife rested on the edge of the table—near the stool on which the Japanese had been seated. Howker's right hand came from his pocket as the Japanese stepped towards him, the pearls in a tray. Jo Gar moved swiftly—the knife was in his right hand before Howker knew that he had left the chair in which he had been seated.

The Japanese cried out a shrill warning—Howker whirled, dug his righthand fingers into the pocket of his coat.

The first shot sounded—as the Island detective struck at the murderer. The bullet battered into curtains across the room. Howker screamed as the knife blade ripped his right shoulder. His body swung around, off balance.

Jo Gar struck for the second time. And Howker squeezed the trigger of the gun again. He was aiming blindly—the Japanese drew his breath in with a hissing sound, staggered towards the stairs that led down to the curio store. Beneath the second stroke of Jo's knife the body of the captain slumped forward. As he fell, the Island detective jerked his right hand from the pocket.

Howker's grip relaxed on the gun—Jo twisted it from his fingers. He backed away. The Japanese stood near the top of the stairs, holding his left wrist muttering to himself. Jo Gar said grimly:

"Get over there—near Howker!"

The one who had judged the pearls moved slowly to Howker's side. The captain pulled himself to his knees and pressed his right hand under his left arm-pit. He gritted:

"That damn—knife—"

Jo Gar smiled with his lips. He looked at the Japanese.

"You were not wise," he said quietly. "You knew that the pearls were imitations. Yet you told Howker that they were very fine. That was foolish. He thought he had beaten me—and he grew careless—just for a second."

Howker stared at the Japanese. He muttered thickly:

"Not real—the pearls? You tricked me, Matu—"

Jo Gar shook his head. "I think he wanted to warn you—but not before me," he said. "So he lied—and then he was about to take you aside, tell you the truth. But I knew they were not real—those pearls."

Howker stared at Jo Gar. The Island detective said slowly:

"You hate me, Howker. But you love the pearls. And you needed money. You wanted to kill me—and have the pearls, too. You would have killed me, even if you had possessed the real ones. You were too greedy."

Howker swore bitterly. Joe Gar said in a quiet voice, holding the gun's muzzle towards the captain and the Japanese.

"The irony of it is, Howker—that you had the real pearls in your possession."

Howker's brown-gray eyes narrowed on the half closed ones of Jo Gar. He breathed hoarsely:

"I—had them—"

Jo nodded. "They were in the hilt of the knife with which you murdered Ichito Toyen," he said softly. "They are still there—in a little hollow place in the wood. The knife was Toyen's—it was brought to me before I left the yacht. I placed the pearls within the hilt. The knife went back to him. He knew there would be stones of some kind for him to examine. He did not have the time to speak to me of the pearls, at the hotel. The Hollander, Vandeer—he interrupted us. When I left, in my attempt to find you—Toyen returned to my room. Perhaps he was suspicious of Vandeer, and thought he might attempt a search. I think you found Toyen outside the door—you forced the old lock, and made Toyen enter."

Howker groaned. He said hoarsely:

"He wouldn't come through—with them. I was sure he knew where they were. He drew the knife—and I got him with it."

Jo Gar said very softly: "And the pearls were in the hilt—in your palm as you stabbed."

There was a little silence, broken by the shrilling of voices beyond the room. Then Jo said in a toneless voice:

"We will go to the street—to the police. You are wounded. There will be no escape, this time."

Howker swore beneath his breath, got to his feet. He stood with his body hunched forward, his face twisted. Jo Gar said quietly:

"Go towards the stairs, please."

The captain moved forward slowly. He muttered to himself:

"And I had them—in my fingers—"

The Island detective said in a cold voice:

"There are more uses than one—for the knives of Nagasaki."

The Caleso Murders

A murderer is at large and vengeance the reason for his escape.

JUAN ARRAGON stood before the Island detective, his dark eyes narrowed, perspiration streaking his brown face. He was breathing heavily—he had run up the wooden stairs to Jo Gar's office. Few natives of Manila run up stairs during the hot season, and the lieutenant of the Manila Police was not a fool. There had been a reason for his haste.

"Palerdo has escaped!" he said in his husky voice. "It is the first escape from Bilibid Prison in years. The guards at the Work Gate have become careless. Palerdo choked the driver of an ox cart into unconsciousness dragged him to a ditch the prisoners had been marched away from a few minutes before, and stripped him of his clothes. The ox cart driver wore a big sun helmet—Palerdo hunched beneath it and drove through the Work Gate. His escape was discovered almost immediately."

Juan Arragon stopped and drew a deep breath. Jo Gar half closed his gray eyes and smiled a little.

"Almost immediately," he repeated. "They did not find him?"

Juan swore in his native tongue. He shook his head.

"He has vanished," he said. "We were notified almost immediately. Palerdo is very strong—and very fierce. We sent men to Señora Mantiro's house—she was not there. A servant informed the men she was driving in her carriage, and might be found on the *Luneta.* Men were sent there—"

He paused, swore again in his native tongue. Jo Gar made a clicking sound with his colorless lips pressed together.

"Almost immediately?" he finished mockingly.

The lieutenant of police frowned. He wiped perspiration from his face with a large, soiled handkerchief.

"It is not too humorous, Jo," he stated. "You remember what Palerdo swore, when he was taken to Bilibid, after the trial?"

Jo Gar nodded, rose from his wicker chair. He moved his diminutive body so that warm air circulated by the ceiling fan got inside of his white shirt.

"Palerdo is strong—and desperate," he agreed. "You were wise in getting men directly to Señora Mantiro's establishment. If she is out riding—so much the better. I think Palerdo will wait for darkness. Perhaps he will not seek to harm her."

Juan Arragon smiled coldly. "He has never forgotten to hate her," he stated. "If he is not caught—he will kill her."

The Island detective nodded. "I think that is so," he agreed. "Before he worked in Señora Mantiro's house, as gardener, he did business bringing plants down the Pasig, from the high country. He sold them in a little store off the Escolta—yes?"

The lieutenant of police nodded. "While you were in Nagasaki half of that block burned," he said. "Señora Mantiro owned most of the buildings. It was strange."

Jo Gar widened his eyes. "Perhaps Palerdo did not at that time plan to escape," he said slowly. "He has always possessed many friends. Señora Mantiro had insured the property?"

Juan Arragon nodded. "And her life," he said in a peculiar tone. "But I'm worried, Jo. Palerdo hates her—"

Jo Gar nodded. "Protect her—that is the most important thing. I will go down along the Pasig and talk with some natives who have sharp eyes."

Juan shook his head. "They may have sharp eyes, but if they have sharp brains they will *not* have seen Palerdo, Jo,"

The Island detective spoke musingly. "It is one thing to murder a man—and another to murder a woman," he said.

Juan Arragon shook his head.

"Palerdo should have died for the killing of Carlos Mantiro," he stated. "The widow interfered, wanted mercy for him. But he hates her as much as a human can hate."

Jo Gar said slowly, as he reached lazily for his pith helmet:

"That case always puzzled me, Juan. Palerdo knifed Carlos Mantiro, in his garden, after the Señor had struck his wife. It is strange that he should hate her so much. His act was one of passion, you would think."

Juan Arragon smiled a little. "The Señora is very beautiful," he said. "Palerdo would never talk. He would never even state why he threatened to kill Señora Mantiro. But he *did* threaten. And now he has escaped."

Jo Gar moved towards the stairs that led down from his tiny office. The Manila police lieutenant followed him.

"I hope my men have found the Señora," he breathed, and sighed heavily.

Jo Gar turned his head slowly and half closed his almond-shaped eyes.

"I hope they have found her—*alive*," he said simply.

THE ISLAND detective was talking with Sansino, the dealer in crawfish, when he heard the screaming of the police car's siren. There were few police cars in Manila, and only two of them were equipped with sirens. Jo Gar hurried from the ill-smelling store, held up a hand as Juan Arragon's little machine swerved towards the curb to avoid hitting a *carromatta* whose driver was too excited to be of much help.

Brakes squealed—Arragon snapped open the rear door. Jo widened his eyes, questioned the police lieutenant. Arragon nodded.

"Hurry!" he urged.

"An overturned *caleso* has been found, near the beach, beyond the Rondo house!"

Jo Gar got inside, frowning. The police driver drove from the *Luneta*, towards the Army and Navy Club. The Manila Hotel lay in a haze near the Bay. It was terribly hot.

Jo Gar said above the shrilling of the siren:

"It was—only the overturned *caleso?*"

Juan Arragon nodded. "But it was Señora Mantiro's *caleso*," he said grimly.

The police car turned to the right, towards the Bay beach. The houses were scattered in this section; there was thick foliage between them. The driver of the car made a sharp turn—they were suddenly upon the overturned *caleso*. They descended. Filipinos made room for them. The horse that had drawn the carriage stood quietly, near the vehicle. A native policeman came to Juan's side. He said a few words in his native tongue—both Juan and Jo Gar followed him to the palms that fringed the beach, perhaps a hundred feet from the spot where the *caleso* was overturned.

The body lay with the eyes staring. The mouth was slightly opened; there was no color in the lips. A black lace shawl of fine workmanship lay a few feet from Señora Mantiro. A short, English looking man stood a little distance away. He spoke as Jo looked at him.

"I am Doctor Potter. The officer stopped me as I was driving past this spot, along the beach road. The woman is dead—she was strangled with the shawl. I loosened it, of course, but I should say I was ten minutes or so too late."

Juan Arragon looked down at the dead woman and muttered a prayer in his native tongue. When he finished Jo Gar said slowly:

"There has been no trace of Palerdo?"

Juan shook his head. "No trace" he said. "And he has murdered the Señora."

Jo Gar smiled a little. "You are always so sure—you police," he said. "What you mean is that Señora Mantiro has perhaps been murdered."

Juan Arragon stared at Jo Gar. "He threatened her—he hated her. He has great fingers, and was known as a strangler. It is said that he—"

Jo Gar frowned. "He did not strangle the Señora's husband," he interrupted gently. "He used a knife. Where is the *caleso* driver?"

The khaki uniformed police officer shook his head from side to side. His dark eyes looked stupid.

"I come this way," he said in stiff English, "and here is the *caleso.* I have seen him before—it is Señora Mantiro's. I go quick and telephone. I return—I think I go to beach. Find the body. I stop the doctor. Some others come—and then you. I do not see driver."

Jo Gar nodded. Juan Arragon said: "He was a Filipino—and is probably hiding."

Jo smiled with his gray eyes. "Or still running," he said. "He is important, Juan."

The police lieutenant frowned. "Palerdo—he is *more* important," he said slowly. "You learned something, Jo?"

The Island detective shook his small head. He narrowed his almond shaped eyes on the body of the dead woman.

"Nothing" he said steadily. "He has not been seen along the Pasig."

Juan Arraron shrugged. "Of course he has not been seen—"

He stopped. There was a shrill cry from a brown-faced native, beyond the spot where the body lay, in the palms. Juan Arragon led the way towards the one who had shouted; when Jo arrived at his side he was kneeling beside a form that lay motionless.

"The *caleso* driver!" he told Jo. His voice was excited. "Strangled—dead. His belt has been used. Palerdo is—a double murderer, this time!"

Jo Gar's eyes were expressionless. He spoke in a toneless voice.

"You are always so quick, Juan," he said quietly. "It is too bad you did not give the Señora protection more swiftly."

The police lieutenant rose from his knees and frowned at the Island detective.

"It is too bad Palerdo escaped!" he snapped.

Jo Gar looked down at the body of the dead *caleso* driver.

"This man—this woman—I do not think they were murdered by Palerdo," he said quietly.

Juan Arragon stared at him. The native policeman made a clicking sound.

Juan said: "You are mad, Jo Gar—it is the work of that strangler—"

The Island detective shrugged. "Perhaps you are right, Juan," he said softly. "But remember, Palerdo *knifed* the woman's husband. These are stranglings. There are other matters—"

Juan Arragon narrowed his dark eyes. He said fiercely:

"We will have Palerdo—and the murderer of these two. I must send all of the men—"

Jo Gar smiled with his lips pressed together. He looked down at the dead *caleso* driver again.

"After Palerdo?" he said calmly, mockingly. "That is very nice—for the *real* murderer, Juan!"

THE STREET wound from the Escolta, main business avenue of Manila, towards the Pasig. Jo Gar traveled very slowly along the narrow cobbles; he wiped his brown skin continually with the large handkerchief. He had been talking to only a few natives, but those few were important ones. They were ones who had known Palerdo before the big Filipino had stabbed the husband of Señora Mantiro to death. Jo Gar smiled a little, showing his white teeth, as he thought of that case. Palerdo had confessed. Señor Carlos Mantiro had beaten his wife. She had cried out—Palerdo had stabbed him three times. The defense had not been sufficient—he had been sentenced to life imprisonment. And in prison, during one of his outbursts, he had threatened the life of the Señora. After that, he had remained silent. He had great hands—

huge for a native. There were rumors of past stranglings. And now Palerdo was free—and the Señora and her *caleso* driver were dead, strangled.

Jo Gar narrowed his gray eyes, shrugged. He was thinking that for once Juan Arragon might be right. Palerdo had committed the crime. But there was no certainty. In an hour it would be dark—Palerdo was still free. It was as though he had vanished into the black water of the Pasig. Not once since his escape had he been seen.

The Island detective stood near the narrow entrance of a nut store and watched a short Filipino come to the street from a store a hundred yards distant. The man was nervous; he moved his head from side to side—watched people. A uniformed policeman was across the street. The short Filipino turned his back to the officer. When he was gone he hailed a *carromatta.* There were bags in the short one's hands—and he was poorly dressed. Yet he rode in a *carromatta.*

Jo Gar hailed one that came along behind the other. He ordered the driver to follow, not drawing too close. The ride was to a squalid part of the city—the short Filipino descended before a series of bamboo shacks close together. Jo Gar paid his driver, dismissed him. He pulled his soiled, pith helmet low over his eyes and followed the man. He was quite close when the short one stepped suddenly through the entrance of a shack that seemed ready to fall apart. Jo Gar hesitated—then acted quickly, almost blindly. He stepped inside the shack almost on the heels of the brown, short one. He heard breath sucked in sharply—heard a man say in hoarse English:

"Fool!"

The light was dim inside the shack, but the sun had been sinking and there had not been too much glare outside. Jo Gar stared past the short man—saw the figure half crouched in the far corner of the shack. The man's hands hung at his sides—they were big hands. The fingers of the right one held something that gleamed in the faint light of a smoking lamp.

Jo Gar smiled a little. He said slowly:

"Do not you be a fool, Palerdo. Your friend was anxious—but he did look around. And I am not of the police."

Palerdo straightened a little. His right hand came up slightly. Jo Gar turned the palms of his hands towards the man, spread his short fingers.

"I have no weapon," he said. "I do not come to take you back to prison. I am Jo Gar."

Palerdo muttered something that Jo did not quite catch. He spoke sharply to the short native, in the Filipino tongue. He told him that he was a fool—that he should not have come to the shack until after dark. Jo Gar said quietly:

"Señora Mantiro is dead, strangled. Her *caleso* driver is dead, also strangled."

Palerdo had a big head for a native. His dark eyes were expressionless. His grip on the knife was unrelaxed.

"That is not news to you," Jo said quietly. "I will be very honest. I do not think you strangled Señora Mantiro. You were waiting for darkness. Perhaps you *would* have strangled her. But there was another before you. I will make a bargain. Give me the murderer's name—I will go from here. You will have the chance to escape."

Palerdo laughed sharply. In the semi-darkness of the Filipino shack he looked like a giant, facing the diminutive detective. The short Filipino stood to one side, his eyes wide on Palerdo's face.

"How should I know—who murdered Señora Mantiro?" Palerdo asked huskily.

Jo Gar smiled a little. "You do know," he said quietly. "You have friends. But you have enemies, too."

Palerdo sucked in his breath sharply. He spoke in a low tone:

"How do you know *I* did not murder those two?" he demanded, after a little silence.

Jo Gar said quietly:

"If you had murdered Señora Mantiro you would not have killed the *caleso* driver. You would have been satisfied—and there would have been nothing to hide. Whoever strangled the woman—strangled the driver to prevent him from giving a description of himself, of the killer."

In the semi-darkness the Island detective caught the gleam of Palerdo's eyes.

"I did not murder her," the big man said slowly. "I did not kill the driver. The killer wants the police to think I did."

Jo Gar smiled again. "Yes," he said slowly. "You escaped to kill her—but one was ahead of you. An enemy. One who feared you—and wanted to be sure the police would hang you, this time. Who was it, Palerdo?"

The big native shook his head. He laughed in a throaty, grim way.

"Why should I say?" he asked. "If I do not escape—"

Jo Gar watched the knife in the big man's right hand fingers. He spoke slowly, calmly.

"I will make a bargain with you. Tell me the name of the enemy who murdered Señora Mantiro. You will have the chance to escape. I do not think you can do that. I will not aid the police. I will find the murderer and if you are caught you will not be blamed for these crimes. You will not hang."

He read indecision in Palerdo's eyes. The big man was breathing heavily. Filipino laughter, shrill and loud, reached the interior of the thatch-roofed shack. A baby cried. From the distant Pasig came the faint whistle of a river boat. The shack reeked with odor. It was very hot.

Palerdo shook his head. He raised the knife.

"I know of you," he said. "You are Señor Gar. You work with the police. You will trick me."

Jo Gar shook his head. "I would not have blundered in this way—unless I came to help you," he said simply. "I want the murderer of the woman and the driver—not you."

Palerdo drew his body erect. "It was—Mona Taloy—the Malay!" he breathed sharply. "She is strong—"

Jo Gar shook his head. "It was—not a woman," he said slowly. "You are not telling—"

There was a swift movement of Jo Gar's body to the right. The right hand of Palerdo came up—the knife hissed through the air. It struck with a thud against the inner wall of the shack.

Jo's right hand fingers tugged at the grip of his automatic. Out of the corners of his eyes he saw Palerdo leap towards him—he squeezed the trigger—the bullet ripped through the pocket of his palm beach suit. Palerdo's body jerked to one side—he fell heavily.

There were cries from beyond the shack. Jo Gar stared down at the body of the big man. He backed away from it, towards the doorway of the shack. The big man was tricking him—he had not been hit. Jo had seen that the bullet had struck across the room! And his aim had been too hurried.

The short Filipino cried out in a half wail. Jo Gar leveled the gun on the prostrate body of Palerdo.

"You are not hit," he said grimly. "But now—I shall kill you. I shall kill you, Palerdo, and say that you resisted arrest—"

Outside there were shouts. The shot sound had attracted the attention of natives. The baby was screaming.

Palerdo pulled himself to his knees. His dark eyes were wide on Jo Gar's almost colorless ones. There was fear in them.

"The Malay—Mona Taloy!" His voice was uncertain, hoarse. "I swear—it was—"

He collapsed suddenly. Jo Gar swore very softly, as he saw the red that streaked the soiled shirt the prisoner had taken from the ex-cart driver. Palerdo lay on his back, motionless. His eyes were half opened.

The Island detective leaned down and touched a wrist. There was no pulse. In the left hand fingers of the dead man was a short, curved knife. Jo Gar sighed a little. Palerdo had flung one knife—and when it had failed to strike the mark he had ripped his heart with the short, curved one. He was dead—and before he had died he had lied. The Island detective was sure of that. He had preferred death to a prison return. Señora Mantiro was dead. Palerdo had been sure he would be taken prisoner again. Yet he had lied.

Jo Gar kept the muzzle of his gun pointed towards the short Filipino. Perspiration streaked his face. He shrugged.

"We will go outside," he said to the short one. "I was wrong. Palerdo murdered the woman—and the driver. I have done well. We will go outside—and seek the police."

JUAN ARRAGON came into Gar's office at eleven o'clock. It was a bright night, with a moon and the sky filled with stars. But it was very hot. The lieutenant of police dropped into a wicker chair and frowned at the Island detective.

"That native swears that Palerdo did not murder the woman and the *caleso* driver. He swears by all the saints that Palerdo told *you* that, before he stabbed himself to death. He says that a Malay woman—one Mona Taloy—committed the double murder. He is lying, of course."

Jo Gar nodded. "Of course," he agreed. "I was wrong in thinking Palerdo did not strangle the two. I was trying to bluff him, in the shack—so I tried to bargain with him. The native lies."

Juan Arragon was watching the Island detective closely. He smiled.

"Then why—did *you* go to the Malay woman's hut—an hour ago, Jo?" he said suddenly.

Jo Gar narrowed his eyes a little. "Loose ends of the rope," he said casually.

Juan Arragon shook his head. "Under the third degree—Filipinos are all the same," he said slowly. "When you say that this native is lying I do not think you believe that, Jo. You were lucky—and he led you to Palerdo. But now it is I who have changed my mind. I do not think Palerdo murdered Señora Mantiro or the driver."

Jo Gar smiled. "You are becoming wise, Juan," he said slowly. "Well, I will be honest with you. I have never thought that he did. But I wanted the native who led me to him to think that I thought him the murderer."

Juan Arragon said: "Why?"

The Island detective chuckled. "So that he would swear to you that the Malay woman was guilty—and perhaps tell you more than Palerdo told me."

Juan Arragon looked puzzled. "And yet you were trying to throw me off the track a few minutes ago," he said softly.

Jo Gar lighted a brown-paper cigarette. He smiled with his eyes almost closed.

"I like to work alone," he said. "The Malay woman did not murder Señora Mantiro. Palerdo was lying to me, before he died. That short native—what is his name?"

"Santos Costios," the police lieutenant replied.

"Costios—he lied, also," Jo stated. "We have not found the murderer of the woman and the driver."

Juan Arragon frowned. "You have seen the Malay woman?" he said slowly, "You are sure *she* is not lying."

Jo Gar inhaled cigarette smoke and smiled with his thin lips.

"You do not pay much attention to native accidents, Juan," he said quietly. "Yes, I have seen the Malay woman, Mona Taloy. She lies in the morgue. Two hours before Palerdo escaped she fell and was crushed between *sampans,* while selling nuts on the river."

Juan Arragon swore softly. His eyes were wide on Jo Gar's.

"And Palerdo did not know that!" he breathed. "But why did he name her—"

Jo Gar sighed heavily. "Perhaps if we could learn *that* answer," he said simply, "it would be easier to find the killer of Señora Mantiro—and the *caleso* driver."

TORCHES AND lamps flared lights from the decks of the river boats. It was almost midnight, and for thirty minutes Jo Gar had been following the short form of the native, Santos Costios. It had taken much persuasion to have Juan Arragon release the man. But he had done so—and Jo Gar had been trailing along behind since Costios had strolled along the Escolta, had wandered carelessly along the curving streets near the Pasig—and then had come more rapidly to the docks near the market.

It had been difficult work. Costios was suspicious. He was constantly turning about, doubling in his tracks and retracing short distances. But the Island detective moved swiftly and quietly. He was a half-breed, and the instincts of a half-breed were his now. And he knew that Costios was not being careless, as he pretended. The short Filipino was going to a place of importance. This time he was making sure that he was not followed.

The *sampans* were tied one to another, near the market place. From the shadow of one Jo Gar watched Costios leap to the deck of a craft with a curved roof of thatch. He vanished from sight. Jo Gar waited a little, then followed. There were four *sampans,* side by side. He stood near the thatch roof of one, and smiled a little.

"The Malay woman—sold nuts—to *sampan* men," he breathed softly. "Perhaps Palerdo—"

He broke off, shrugged his narrow shoulders. There was the sound of a stringed instrument on the water—in the distance a man's voice sang huskily.

Jo Gar moved towards the flat deck of the second *sampan.* When he jumped from one craft to the other it was with a cat-like lightness. He pressed his body close to the roof of the craft, listened for several seconds. And while he was listening his eyes were moving about. In the distance he could see the Bridge of Spain, curving low across the black-watered river.

"It was near this spot—that the Malay woman—died," he murmured softly. "It is strange—"

Many things were strange. It was strange that Palerdo had hated Señora Mantiro. Men killed women's husbands because of love for the wife, not because of hatred. Jo Gar shook his head a little.

Voices reached him, very faintly. They did not come from the shore, the market—but from the last *sampan* in the line of four. One was guttural, louder now. The other had a flat sound that the Island detective recognized. It was pitched low, but it was the voice of Santos Costios.

Jo moved to the third *sampan.* It was uncovered, and he bent his body low as he went across the deck. He was straightening—ready for the leap to the last craft, when he heard the sound of faint movement behind him. His body swung around—he dropped flat on the deck. A figure moved slowly around the roof of the second *sampan*—jumped to the deck of the one on which Jo was lying. The Island detective gripped his gun with his right hand fingers, lay motionless. A voice said, in a whisper:

"Jo!"

The Island detective raised his head. He swore beneath his breath. The river water made gurgling sounds along the stern of the *sampan.*

The figure of Juan Arragon was crawling towards Jo now. The Island detective lay motionless, a frown on his face. Arragon reached his side, got his head close to Jo's. He spoke softly:

"This is the spot—the Malay woman—"

Jo Gar cut in very quietly. "You followed—me here—"

The Manila police lieutenant said: "You followed—Costios here. You may—need me—"

Jo Gar made a low, clicking sound. His face was very close to Arragon's.

"You are—thoughtful," he said with irony.

They lay in silence. In the craft beyond there was the murmur of voices. Juan said in a whisper:

"I released—Costios. I am responsible—for him."

The Island detective smiled faintly in the semi-darkness. He said in a very low voice:

"You do not trust me, Juan. Why?"

The Manila police lieutenant was silent for several seconds. Driftwood—a heavy piece of it—struck against the stern of the *sampan,* on which they were lying. It bumped along the side. Arragon said in a whisper:

"I do not know what happened—before Palerdo died."

Jo Gar sucked in his breath sharply. "You think that he told me more than I have told you," he said. "And that I desire credit—for myself."

Juan Arragon did not reply. Jo lay flat on the *sampan* deck, his eyes half closed.

"You came to me—in the first place," he reminded. "You come to me—so often. And you are always afraid—"

He broke off as a voice rose, from the last *sampan.* It was not the voice of the short Filipino, Costios. It had a deeper, throatier tone. The dialect Jo Gar did not understand. Beside him, Arragon lifted his head.

"Malay, I think," he said softly.

Jo Gar narrowed his eyes on those of the police lieutenant.

"It is you who have held back, this time, Juan," he breathed. "You left me in the dark—it is a wonder I got this far. But I was sure Palerdo would not have murdered the *caleso* driver, had he killed the woman. Why did Palerdo knife Carlos Mantiro?"

He asked the question sharply, heard Juan Arragon's breath sucked in. There was a little silence except for the raised tones of the man speaking in the fourth *sampan* from shore. Then Juan whispered:

"Mantiro struck his wife—Palerdo was present. He was hot tempered—"

Jo Gar said softly: "You do not lie well. Why did he *hate* Señora Mantiro?"

Juan Arragon said very slowly. "There was the Dutchman, Bucher. She loved him. She was clever—she led Palerdo to believe that she loved—"

Jo Gar sighed softly. "And you kept that from me, Juan. She used Palerdo, to murder her husband—so that she could have Bucher. And Palerdo learned of that—and hated her."

Juan Arragon said quietly: "And Bucher left the Islands. We got that much—but there was no evidence. The woman played on Palerdo's emotions. That is why he got off with life."

The Island detective listened to the droning voice that sounded from the last *sampan* now. It was the voice of Costios. The Island detective frowned.

"And why did you hold this back?" he asked softly.

"Palerdo had friends—and you have clients," Arragon said in a whisper. "I did not know—how you stood. You trapped Palerdo, but he *killed himself.* I could not—be sure."

Jo Gar swore softly. "It did not matter—your distrust," he said. "But Palerdo did not murder the woman—or the driver."

Arragon lifted his head higher, stared towards the thatch roof of the last *sampan.*

"Costios swears—that Malay woman—"

He broke off. A voice sounded shrilly from within the covered space of the last craft in the line of four. It died—then rose again. There was panic in the tone—shrilling fear!

Jo Gar got to his knees, pulled himself to his feet. He got his automatic in the fingers of his right hand, leaped to the deck of the covered *sampan.* Arragon was at his side as he made his way towards the opened end of the craft, at the stern. The *sampan* swayed slightly to the current of the Pasig.

They came to a narrow portion of the deck; Jo Gar led the way. The automatic was held slightly before him and low. His body was crouched. He was smiling a little at the thought of Juan Arragon fearing that he might be working for Palerdo's friends. The Manila police lieutenant never completely trusted him.

The voice that had shrilled fear was silent now. Jo Gar stopped smiling, moved towards the stern of the *sampan* more slowly. The sudden silence might mean one of two things—that Juan and he had been heard, or that one man had silenced another.

Jo muttered under his breath: "Under the roof of this *sampan* we will find the murderer of Señora Mantiro and the *caleso* driver. We will learn why Palerdo lied even as he was about to kill himself." Back of him he could hear the swift breathing of Arragon.

And then, suddenly, there was the roar of the explosion. The *sampan* seemed to lift from the water—the thatch roof shot into the darkness—red streaking through it!

Jo threw his left hand before his face, twisted his body to the right. He felt a force lift him from the deck—heard Juan Arragon cry out hoarsely in his native tongue. Then the warm water of the Pasig was closing over him—he went underneath the surface!

He came up slowly, fighting for air. He was not a strong swimmer, but he was calm. There was a numbing pain in his left arm and shoulder—where a section of the *sampan's* roof had battered him. Twisting his head, he saw the red flames licking through the remaining section of the *sampan's* roof. There were shouts—torches were moving along the other craft. They were trying to cut the burning boat loose.

Jo Gar sucked in deep breaths of air—struck out towards the bank on left. He heard Juan Arragon call out shrilly—from some spot nearer the bank. There were other shouts, from coolies and natives on the river craft.

The red flare of the flames lighted the dark-colored water. The *sampan* being shoved out in the river now—it was drifting away from the other craft. Flames streaked up from it—over almost the entire length. The bank was close to Jo now—he swam with his uninjured arm working—the other useless at his side. He was tiring rapidly.

Then feet from a low barge-like river boat, he saw the other figure. For a second he thought it was Juan—and then the man's face was twisted towards him. His hands were half closed—the fingers were clutching at air. It was Santos Costios!

The short Filipino went under as Jo got his own body close to him. The Island detective gripped him as he came up—the Filipino was drowning. He tried to grip Jo's throat, failed. The Island detective struck him heavily with his right fist. His own body went under. When he came up Costios was sinking—Jo saw two figures on the flat boat ahead. One man was stripped to the waist—a coolie. He tossed a rope.

Jo Gar got an arm around the sinking body of the Filipino. The rope struck him across the face. He moved his numbing left arm and wrapped it around his body. The flat boat was close now. Red flames danced before Jo's eyes. He felt hands gripping him, muttered hoarsely:

"Take—the Filipino—first—"

JO GAR was kneeling beside the form of Santos Costios—the coolies were bending over him. A lighted torch shone on the twisted face of the Filipino. The Island detective said slowly:

"The saints—will be kind—if you talk—before—"

He stopped, breathing heavily. The Filipino spoke in a barely audible, broken tone.

"I kill—the—*caleso* driver. I choke—with belt. I wait for—Palerdo—"

Jo Gar stared down at the twisted face of Costios. There was a puzzled expression in his gray eyes. He said grimly:

"Do not—lie! You are dying—"

Costios widened his dark eyes. He shook his head slowly from side to side.

"I tell—truth," he breathed weakly.

"The Señora—she love Dutchman. She get Palerdo to—kill her husband. He learn—hate her. He escape—come to me. We go to house—he kill her with shawl—"

Jo Gar narrowed his gray eyes. "At her house—Palerdo murdered her!" he breathed.

Costios said hoarsely: "I help him—Palerdo my half brother. I take her to *caleso*—ride with her. Make driver go—to Bay. Make him upset—*caleso.* He run—I catch him—choke—"

He stopped. Jo Gar swore softly.

"It was Palerdo, after all!" he breathed. "But why did he tell me the Malay woman—"

Costios said very softly: "Palerdo—he knew she was dead—he think you believe—not catch me—"

The Island detective looked down at the Filipino. Costios said slowly:

"Palerdo—he no care—after he kill. He no go back to—Bilibid. The *caleso* driver—he with Señora Mantiro long time. He bad—he know of Dutchman. And he know of Palerdo. I kill—"

Jo Gar said quietly: "What happened—on the *sampan?*"

Costios closed his eyes. "Police—let me free. I go to coolie—want him to take me—up river. He say, no. We fight—he have powder for make ditch in high country. Lamp fall down—"

He stopped talking. Jo Gar smiled with his lips. There were voices beyond the coolies bending over him—he looked up to see Juan Arragon standing close to him. The Manilla police lieutenant spoke in a breathless tone:

"Powder—in that—*sampan.* It let loose. You got—Costios?"

Jo Gar got to his feet. He looked down at the Filipino.

"He was bargaining for an escape," he said slowly. "Quarreled with the coolie who owned the *sampan.* He thinks he's going to die, but he isn't."

Juan Arragon stared at the Island detective. He looked down at Costios.

"The coolie's dead," he stated. "Badly burned. We were lucky to—"

The Filipino was staring at Jo Gar and cursing in a stronger voice. He was accusing the Island detective of tricking him. He was not going to die, after all.

Jo Gar interrupted, sighing. "I should have said, you're not going to die yet," he corrected. "For the murder of the *caleso* driver—you will die, of course. You are pleased?"

Costios cursed in a weaker tone. Juan Arragon turned puzzled eyes towards Jo Gar.

"*He* murdered the driver?" he breathed. "But who—murdered—Señora Mantiro?"

Jo Gar smiled. He narrowed his eyes on those of the police lieutenant.

"Congratulations. Juan," he said in an amused tone. "You see, you were correct. Palerdo murdered the Señora. In her home—before your men arrived. He had thoughts of escape, until I ran into him, and tried to throw the police off by having his half brother, Costios, drive with the body to the Bay. When he failed to knife me—he decided a return to prison was not worthwhile. Costios strangled the *caleso* driver when the poor devil ran."

Juan Arragon frowned. Then he smiled a little.

"I was certain it was Palerdo," he said simply.

Jo Gar felt his injured arm and smiled with his lips.

"You did very well," he said, "under all the circumstances. Several things happened—and in *one* of them you were right."

Silence House

Jo Gar is called to a
house of murder.

JO GAR descended from the fourth car of the train, removed his pith helmet and drew deep breaths of the mountain air. It had been months since he had visited Baguio, the mountain resort of Manila.

He saw Major Crawford coming towards him; half closed his almond-shaped eyes on the figure of the American officer. The major tried to smile as he came close to the Island detective, but Jo saw that his eyes were shot with red, that he was not a well man. He bowed, and the major said:

"I'm very glad you came, Señor Gar. I'm on the ragged edge—"

He broke off abruptly, turned and looked about him. Two Chinese servants came up and blinked at Jo. The Island detective said slowly:

"I've just the one piece of luggage, Major. I have not planned for much of a stay."

The major's lip corners jerked a little. He forced a smile, pointed to the piece of luggage at Jo's side. One of the servants lifted it. The major said very softly:

"That sounds too good to be true, Señor Gar. Unless you mean that you can only be with us a few days, in any event."

Jo Gar shook his head. The servants went ahead; he walked by the major's side.

"Baguio is a small place," Jo said. "You have the threatening notes. I felt that perhaps we could trace the guilty person rapidly—and I could return."

The major breathed something that Jo failed to catch. They went from the railway station, got into a khaki-colored Army car, marked with a large U.S.—and the serial number. It was driven by an enlisted man—the servants rode in a small truck. Jo Gar and the major sat in the rear seat.

The machine rolled away from the station; the streets of Baguio were not crowded. Jo Gar relaxed and offered the major one of his brown-paper cigarettes. It was refused. The officer sat erect in the seat, his body tense. Jo lighted the cigarette with difficulty, leaned back and said:

"Your wife—she is in good health?"

The major smiled bitterly. "No," he said. "She is not a fool. I try to pretend the notes are silly things, jokes. But last night—"

He stopped abruptly. The Island detective watched him with narrowed gray eyes. He said:

"Last night—an attempt on her life was made?"

The major nodded, his face grim. The car slid almost silently through streets faced by gardens; the houses were set back, half hidden. They were low, rambling houses, well screened.

The major sat back and spoke softly. His voice was steady and held little emotion. But he was very nervous.

"There have been three notes. The first came to us at the Post, in Manila, before I came up here on leave. It was dropped on the screened porch of our place. It was addressed in a child-like hand—the letters seemed almost labored. A yellowish piece of paper, folded. My wife's name written outside—Mary. It read: *'You have not kept the promise—and you must die.'* "

Jo Gar frowned. "A bit dramatic," he said slowly. "Who found the note?"

The major said: "I was with Mary at the time. She saw it on the grass mat of the porch—I picked it up, saw her name. I handed it to her. She opened it and read it."

Jo Gar nodded his small head very slowly. The major was frowning, his brown eyes were on Jo's almost colorless ones.

"What was her reaction?" the Island detective asked.

Major Crawford shrugged his broad shoulders. He was a man of almost fifty, well built, with a square-cut face.

"She laughed," he said. "She thought it was one of the Post children's jokes. We forgot it very soon. But I did mention it to you, that day we met at the Manila Hotel."

Jo Gar nodded. He had known the major slightly, for some six months. The man had always seemed to him a typical American Army officer.

"And the second note?" he said quietly. "How long after the first was it—"

"Exactly seven days," the officer cut in. "The servants were packing us up for the trip here. Mary went with them into another room. The packing was being done in a spare room with a porch that opened at the side of the house. When she returned to the room she found the second note. It was addressed in the same way—the writing appeared identical. It read: *'There is still time. Or do you prefer death?'* "

Gar nodded. "No signature?" he asked.

The major shook his head. "Not on one of the three," he said. "The second note my wife treated in the same manner as the first, though she was worried, I could see that. And it was growing very hot. We left for this place two days later. We've been here ten days today. After we'd been here five days, or seven from the time we found the second note—the third was in the house to which we are now going."

Jo Gar pulled on his brown-paper cigarette and watched the car turn from a street near the end of town, into a dirt, country road. Mountain slopes were ahead and to the left. The air was almost cold; it was growing dark.

"I found it," the major said slowly, "on my wife's writing desk. She was out riding horseback—but she had written letters only a half hour before. It was addressed as the other two had been—in the same handwriting. It read: *'There will be no more warnings—this is the last. You have promised.'* "

The Army machine was climbing a slight grade. Jo Gar said:

"You showed it to Mrs. Crawford?"

The major frowned. "Yes," he said. "But not until the next morning. I was afraid it might frighten her—we've only been in the Islands six months—the first hot season has been very difficult. Her nerves have been in bad shape—and I hesitated. But then—"

He checked himself. Jo Gar waited and then spoke quietly:

"But then you felt that perhaps there *might* have been some promise—and you wanted her to know—"

He saw Major Crawford's body grow rigid—anger showed in the officer's eyes. The Island detective made a slow gesture with his small hands.

"It is difficult for me to be of any value—unless you are honest with me, Major."

The major's clenched hands relaxed. He said apologetically:

"I'm on edge, Señor Gar, as I told you. Yes, you are right. I wanted her to be protected, if there was any promise. A foolish promise, perhaps."

Jo Gar nodded. "Yes," he said tonelessly. "A foolish promise. What did she say to the third note?"

Major Crawford looked beyond Jo, towards the dry bed of a river near which the car was moving. He said steadily:

"She was frightened. She felt that one of the servants had taken a dislike to trying to frighten her. She knew of no promise. It was a ridiculous thing. But she was worried. At the Post, after the second note, I had a guard near the house, the quarters. Here I can't do that. A friend, Lieutenant Avery, is the house now. It's a little distance from town, you see."

Jo Gar smiled. "The country up here is lovely," he said. "And last night—"

Major Crawford spoke grimly. His brown eyes were almost closed.

"I have asked her not to go outside the house without me, or Lieutenant Avery along. She went for a little walk in the garden—alone. I was questioning the servants, without letting them know about the notes. I've felt they shouldn't know—they are easily frightened. There was a scream. Ben—that's Lieutenant Avery—was upstairs cleaning up. We both reached the garden at the same time. Mary was lying in a path, unconscious. There was a bruise on her left temple—a knife lay a few feet from her. It had been thrown, had apparently turned in the air—the hilt, made of hardwood, had struck her forehead."

Jo Gar turned expressionless eyes towards the car driver's head. He said softly:

"So the notes were *not* jokes, you see."

Major Crawford swore bitterly. "Lieutenant Avery carried her into the house. I got my Service Colt—and went all over the garden, and the house. There are only two servants—and I was questioning them when Mary screamed. A cook and a house-boy. You saw them—I brought them both with me."

The Army car was gliding down a steep grade now. It turned abruptly to the right, started to climb again, in low gear. Thick, tropical foliage rimmed the narrow road. There was the dank, heavy odor of the jungle growth. It was cold. Jo Gar shivered a little.

"We're climbing to the house now," the major said. "It's a bit isolated—but lovely. That is, it *would* be lovely if—"

He broke off. Jo Gar leaned back in the machine seat and half closed his eyes. His lean, brown face was turned towards the face of the Army officer.

"When your wife regained consciousness, what did she have to say?" he asked above the hum of the car engine.

The major shook his head. "Very little," he replied. "She was bending over some flowers—there was a sound behind her, in the foliage. She straightened, turned. The knife struck her. She saw nothing, before losing consciousness."

Jo frowned. "And you were talking with the two servants—and Lieutenant Avery was upstairs," he murmured slowly.

Major Crawford nodded. The house was suddenly in sight—the road widened and became level. The driver pulled the machine to the left, stopped before a few steps of wood. There was a heavily screened porch. Major Crawford said bitterly:

"Welcome to *Silence House,* Señor. It was not named by me, but by the owner."

Jo Gar rose in the rear of the car. He widened his eyes a little.

"Silence House," he repeated softly. "I suppose it is quiet up here."

The major shrugged broad shoulders. "Almost too quiet," he said grimly. "Hello—there's Avery now. Sleeping—"

Jo Gar stepped down from the car, mounted the steps, went through the door of the porch that the major held open. He saw the figure of the lieutenant, seated in a small, fan-backed chair. The officer was in mufti—he was slumped low, his head hanging forward, chin against his chest. The major stopped a few feet from him.

"Ben"—he said sharply—"I asked you to stay near—"

His words died. His eyes were wide on the right hand of the lieutenant. It hung over the side of the wicker chair—the fingers were slightly spread. There was a limpness about the hand—

Jo Gar moved swiftly to the slumped figure. He reached down, touched the right wrist. His body stiffened a little. His small fingers closed over the blond hair of the lieutenant. Slowly he raised the head. Major Crawford said hoarsely:

"God—he's dead!"

The Island detective looked at the half-opened eyes, then at the hilt of the knife. There was a thin, red stain below the hilt, on the white shirt of the officer. Jo Gar lowered the head again, released his grip on the lieutenant's chair. The major said in a weak voice:

"That's the—same knife—that was thrown at—"

He sucked in his breath sharply, and Jo knew what he was thinking about. The Island detective did not move as the major went past him, into the house. He heard Crawford calling hoarsely: "Mary—Mary!" But still he did not move. The enlisted man who had driven the car was staring through the screening of the porch. He said shakily:

"Lieutenant Avery—is dead, sir?"

Jo Gar fumbled for another of his brown-paper cigarettes. When he found it he nodded his head. He lighted the cigarette.

"Quite," he said softly, and went slowly into the house.

CAPTAIN RAMLIN of the Constabulary stared down at the knife. Major Crawford sat in the chair beyond the table, staring straight ahead and seeing nothing. Jo Gar said slowly:

"The major is positive it is the same knife that was thrown at his wife."

The Constabulary captain was a short man, stockily built. He nodded. Light from the table lamp was faint.

"The attempt failed. The murderer or murderers came into the house to try again. The lieutenant defended Mrs. Crawford. He was murdered, carried to the porch. Mrs. Crawford was—"

The captain stopped, looked narrowly at the major. He said calmly:

"Mrs. Crawford perhaps is being held a prisoner. If we can pick up the trail—"

He broke off again. Major Crawford said in a flat, dead tone:

"She's dead. They've killed her—somewhere in the mountains. I shouldn't have left her—"

The Island detective shook his head. "Why did they not kill her in the house?" he asked. "It would have been simpler, safer. There was no one here, with Avery dead. It is difficult to carry a woman, dead or alive, and not leave traces. And why was Avery stabbed to death with the same knife thrown at Mrs. Crawford?

Major Crawford said in the same flat voice:

"I had the knife in the second drawer of my writing desk. The drawer was not locked. Only Avery saw me place it there."

The Constabulary captain drew in a sharp breath. He nodded his head briskly.

"Lieutenant Avery was not in his uniform. He was not armed. When the house was entered—he got the knife from the drawer. But it was taken away from him. It happened that way."

Jo Gar's face was expressionless. Major Crawford said huskily:

"You are doing everything—to find her, Captain?"

The captain nodded. "Of course," he replied gently. "I have fifty men searching—and there are many regular army men on the search. We are doing everything, Major. I doubt that even Señor Gar could do more."

There was sarcasm in his final words. But Jo Gar merely bowed his head slightly. He went across the room, looked down at the half-opened second drawer of the desk. Captain Ramlin was saying:

"House in perfect shape. No bruises on Lieutenant Avery's body. Servants were with you, Major and behind you coming back. Enlisted driver assigned to you was with you. No one at the house but Avery and your wife. Avery an old friend. Your wife's life had been threatened in three notes—you have not the slightest reason why. Her life had been attempted, and you had wired for Señor Gar. Doors not locked. Perhaps there will be fingerprints on the knife—perhaps not. And even if there are—it may not be of any help. We have the notes, of course."

Jo Gar turned away from the half-opened drawer. He said very quietly:

"Your wife—she had never been in love with Lieutenant Avery?"

Major Crawford replied in a hard voice: "She had never been in love with him."

Jo said: "He did not love *her?*"

The major got up from his chair heavily. He stood near it, his eyes narrowed on the Island detective's gray ones.

"He never—gave evidence of that," he said grimly.

Jo Gar nodded. The Constabulary captain spoke in a surprised voice:

"That's pretty thick, isn't it, Señor Gar? Avery and—"

The Island detective shrugged. "They were here together. Mary Crawford is gone—Lieutenant Avery is dead. There is little evidence of a struggle. The knife was in a drawer. If the lieutenant had been struck in self-defense—had staggered to the porch chair—"

The Constabulary captain was watching Major Crawford closely. Jo Gar did not seem to be aware of the fact that the major was in the room. The major said in a dull tone, without anger:

"It was Avery who knew where the knife was—not my wife. And could he stagger to the chair on the porch—with such a wound? Would the knife remain in—"

He broke off. Jo Gar spoke very calmly.

"The drawer wasn't locked. The knife might have been discovered. Avery might have been struck as he was standing directly in front of the chair—he simply fell back into it."

The major said in a very low voice: "I must get out of the house—I'll search around the place, not getting far away. I'll be within call—"

The Constabulary captain nodded. "I can come with you, Major—" he offered.

Crawford shook his head. He went out towards the front porch. After several seconds Captain Ramlin said:

"His wife had no enemies—she quarreled with no servants. Strange."

Jo Gar shrugged. Captain Ramlin turned his browned face towards the door that opened into the garden. He said slowly:

"I will look about—in the garden, Señor."

Jo nodded. Ramlin went from the room. Jo Gar looked towards the half-opened door and thought:

"Why was Lieutenant Avery allowed to see where the major placed the knife? Why was his wife *not* allowed to know it was in the drawer? Why was it that the major came to meet me, rather than Avery? And why did he bring with him *both* servants?"

The Island detective moved about the room, went slowly to the front porch. He looked down at the chair in which there had been the dead body of Lieutenant Avery. He thought:

"It would require much time to learn of Avery's past—and of Mrs. Crawford's past. He is dead—she has vanished. It would be simpler to find her—"

He smiled faintly, murmured aloud: "A knife thrown in the Islands seldom turns in the air and strikes hilt first. A fighting man is seldom stuck in the heart. And why was Mary Crawford taken from the house?"

He moved to the center table and looked at the knife. The hilt was black—of hardwood. It looked old, much used. The blade was long, narrow. It had required strength to drive that knife blade almost to the hilt. More strength, perhaps, than Major Crawford's wife had possessed.

Jo Gar shrugged. The major had said that he had known Avery for some five years. His wife had known the lieutenant the same length of time. He was a good friend, who had chanced to be spending his leave at the Island mountain resort, while the Crawfords had come up.

Jo thought: It could easily be so. I have talked with the servants, and in all Avery's actions they saw nothing but friendliness. The Chinese have good eyes, and threats of Bilibid frighten them. But the manner of Avery's death, if he were defending the vanished woman, is strange. Very strange. And there are notes—they are strange, too.

He went away from the center table, went out into the garden. It was a small garden, but beyond it the foliage was thick. A slope was less than an eighth of a mile in the rear of the house—a steep slope. There was heavy growth on the slope. Jo Gar shook his head slowly, thinking that it would be difficult to find a body, in the mountains. With only starlight it would be almost impossible. He was fifty yards from the house, with his back to it, when he heard the scream. It was sharp—high pitched. It came once—

And then it came again and again!—

Jo Gar swung around—his right hand got his automatic from a pocket of his suiting. He started towards the house—the screams still ringing in his ears. From some spot behind him he heard Captain Ramlin shout hoarsely! One of the Chinese servants cried out, from the kitchen side of the house. The screams seemed to come from the front of the place, and Jo Gar remembered that Major Crawford had left the house by way of the front porch.

Jo was inside the living-room now, glanced around the room. It was empty. His eyes swept the table—he halted suddenly. He held the gun low—and his body was bent forward slightly. He said very softly:

"It—is gone!"

There was no knife on the table. The weapon that the major had said had struck down his wife in the garden—the weapon whose blade had been buried in the flesh of Lieutenant Avery—it was gone. And seconds ago—hardly more than a minute ago—it had lain on the center, wicker table!

The Island detective moved swiftly towards the screened door that opened on the porch. Even before he had shoved the door open he saw Major Crawford. The officer was running along the road, towards the house. His Service Colt was gripped in his right hand. From the rear of the house Jo heard the Constabulary captain call again: "Major—Señor Gar!"

The Island detective stepped on the porch. It was lighted dully by the lamps from within the house. The wicker chair in which Avery's body had been found was turned slightly. Sprawled across it was the figure of a woman. Dark hair trailed downward from her head—her white dress was disarranged—her arms hung loosely at her sides.

Jo Gar started towards the figure—Stopped suddenly. He heard Major Crawford cry out; there was the sharp *crack!* of the Service Colt—once, twice. He saw the major swing around—run towards the left side of the house.

Captain Ramlin came pounding through the house—reached the porch. He was breathing heavily. He stared at Jo Gar—saw the body of the woman, across the wicker chair. He said:

"Good God! It's—Mary Crawford!"

Jo Gar stood stiffly as two more shots sounded. He spoke to Ramlin:

"Go out there—around to the left. Major Crawford's—seen something. I'll see what can be done here."

Ramlin nodded, went down the steps and to the left. Jo Gar went to the body across the chair. He leaned over the woman, and after a few seconds straightened up. He placed his automatic in his pocket, went away from the dead woman and the chair. Near

the edge of the lower step leading down from the porch, at the right side, he saw the knife. He stood and looked down at it, thinking. Five minutes later, when Captain Ramlin came up, breathing heavily, he was still standing near the knife. Ramlin said:

"I can't—find the major—he's crashing off in the woods—somewhere—"

Jo Gar said: "Perhaps he's close—to his wife's murderer."

There was a peculiar tone to his voice. The Constabulary captain said hoarsely: "She's—dead?"

The Island detective nodded slowly. He looked down at the knife. Ramlin stared at it, swore harshly.

"It was—on the table—in the living-room!" he breathed.

Jo nodded again. "And more recently," he said softly, in a grim tone, "it was in the body of Mary Crawford."

MAJOR CRAWFORD was lying on a broad, low divan. Doctor McCall finished bandaging his right arm, near the shoulder, stood up. The major said, in a voice choked with emotion:

"Looked like—one of the chinks. But I couldn't—be sure. Fired four times—ran into a tree and went down. He struck at me with the knife, while I was trying to get up. Then he was gone. The woods are thick, and it's dark in there. By God—if I could get—"

He stopped, closed his eyes. Doctor McCall said in a quiet voice:

"You moved around a lot, after he knifed you. You lost a lot of blood. You must rest."

Captain Ramlin, standing close to Jo, nodded his head. The major groaned and rolled over on his left side. His right fist was clenched.

The doctor went towards the center table of the living-room, from the divan on which Crawford was lying. He washed his hands slowly and carefully. Jo Gar went over to him, turned his back on the major and said in a very low voice:

"The wound is not serious, Doctor?"

The doctor shook his head. "Just a blade rip, but he moved around and lost blood," he said. "Too bad he didn't get that rotten killer."

"He might have made a mistake," the Island detective said slowly.

Doctor McCall straightened a little. He said:

"You don't think it was one of the servants? I suppose you have noted they have both vanished?"

Jo smiled with his eyes almost closed. "The Chinese do not care for mysterious death. Many times I have seen servants vanish, in the Islands."

"*I* have seen them use knives," McCall said.

"Yes," the Island detective said quietly. "And sometimes they *throw* knives. When they do—there is seldom a miss."

The doctor narrowed his eyes on those of the Island detective for a few seconds. Jo Gar was smiling with his lips; his own almond-shaped eyes were slitted. He nodded his head suddenly, as if he had just thought of something, turned away.

Captain Ramlin came to him on the porch. He said huskily:

"It's pretty bad, Señor Gar. First Avery—now Mary Crawford. Those damn chinks—"

Jo Gar shrugged. "Mary Crawford was a tall woman," he said slowly. She was very healthy. Both of the missing servants were small and they did not look too strong, either of them. There were five or six knife wounds in the woman's body. It requires strength to hold a struggling person."

Captain Ramlin said: "You don't think one of the chinks—"

He stopped. Jo Gar sighed. "I should like to find a motive," he said softly. "But then, it is what anyone would like."

Ramlin swore softly. "I don't trust the servants down here. The major says his wife was always good to them, but perhaps he was wrong."

The Island detective nodded. "Perhaps," he agreed. "But Lieutenant Avery is dead—murdered. And there are the notes. I do not think they were written by either of the servants."

The Constabulary captain frowned and stared up towards the distant sky. The night was bright with stars. Ramlin said:

"I've got to go out and keep my men on the job. They're searching the slopes—and I've got some of them looking around in town."

Jo Gar said: "What are they looking for?"

Ramlin grunted. "They *were* looking for Mary Crawford," he muttered. "Now I'll have them after the chinks."

He went down the front steps. The Island detective went back into the house, stood still as he heard the doctor call sharply from the left side. He went past Major Crawford, who called to him weakly, found the doctor facing one of the two servants, in the kitchen. The Chinese was frightened—his eyes were wide. The doctor said:

"Here's one of 'em—I caught him sneaking in here."

The doctor held a gun low in his left hand. Jo Gar looked at the servant, smiled. He spoke very quietly to the man, using a jargon of Chinese and Filipino. The doctor stood motionlessly, frowning. Jo talked for several minutes, then said to the doctor:

"He was frightened. There were the screams. He screamed and ran from the house. The other servant was outside, getting water. They both ran. They saw nothing—the other servant is hiding in one of the outhouses; he will not come in. He says there is death in this house—it is called *Silence House,* and death is silence."

The doctor swore grimly. "You believe that?" he asked.

Jo Gar shrugged. "I will tell him to bring his companion inside," he said. "You can talk with them—but you will not need the gun—it will only frighten them more."

He spoke again to the servant. He smiled as he talked, and his voice was pleasant. After a few minutes the Chinese went towards the door. The doctor was about to stop him, but Jo said sharply:

"Let him go—I know these people. I have lived very close to them for years. He will return—with the other one."

The doctor muttered something that Jo did not catch. But he allowed the servant to go. The Island detective stood in silence until the two Chinese returned. They stared at him with wide eyes. The doctor said to Jo:

"Keep them here—I want to show them something."

He went from the kitchen. Jo Gar half closed his eyes and smiled. He said in a low tone:

"The man is bringing with him a knife. He will show it to you suddenly—like this—"

He made a swift gesture from his right side, extending his right hand, fingers opened. He said, smiling:

"Do not be afraid. Be very truthful. Do not lie—"

His low words died as the doctor came into the room. He went close to the two servants, extended his left hand suddenly. The knife lay in his palm. Jo smiled a little. The doctor said:

"It is—yours? Yours?"

His eyes went from one servant to the other. The shorter of the two shook his head, looked at his companion. The taller one's eyes were wide with fear. He stared at Jo. The Island detective shrugged his shoulders very slightly.

"A fool is often one because he lies," he said very softly.

The taller servant stared at the knife in the doctor's palm. He nodded his head rapidly. He said in a voice filled with panic:

"She is mine—she is mine! I tell you I no use—she go away—"

He broke off into rapid jargon. Jo Gar slowed him down. The doctor was staring at the taller of the servants with narrowed eyes. His left hand held the knife, but his right went towards the pocket in which the gun rested.

The servant stopped talking, panting. He was breathing heavily, and his eyes held nothing but fear. Jo said to the doctor, very softly:

"He lost the knife, somewhere about the house, two days ago. He has been searching for it since. He did not kill."

The doctor said grimly: "I'd hate to have that story to tell, just the same. We'll turn them both over to the Constabulary. He did the jobs, all right. Dirty, yellow—"

Jo said quietly: "*White* men have killed—in the Islands, Doctor."

He turned, went from the room. Major Crawford, lying on the divan, said weakly:

"What is it—Señor Gar? For God's sake—what—"

Jo Gar spoke tonelessly. "The knife—it is owned by the taller of your two servants," he said simply.

Major Crawford got to a sitting position. His brown eyes were narrowed; rage showed in them. They were streaked with red. He swore fiercely.

"A chink—did in Avery! A damn, dirty chink got my—"

He got to his feet. Jo Gar stood watching him. He nodded his head slowly.

"But you must be calm, Major," he said. "There is the law—"

The major said hoarsely: "Damn the law—I'm a white man! Where's my gun?"

The Island detective shook his head. "That is—not right," he said quietly. "It will do no good. The servant is a prisoner—the Constabulary will take care of him."

The major sank back on the divan, groaned. He touched his bandaged right shoulder, rolled over on his left side. His body shook—smothered sounds came from his lips. Jo Gar said very gently:

"I am very—sorry for you."

For several seconds he stood looking at the officer. Then he went slowly towards the screened porch of *Silence House,* and out into the darkness.

IT WAS almost two in the morning. There was a storm in the mountains, distant now but nearing the slope on which *Silence House* had been built. Jo Gar stood on the screened porch, beside the doctor. McCall was medium in size, with a lean, browned face. He was frowning.

"I'll see if he's sleeping," he said suddenly. "I've given him some tablets, but not enough to induce heavy sleep. But if you're wrong—"

The Island detective shrugged. "You are not sure that I am wrong," he said softly. "The lightning is strong enough—it is a chance we must take. Tomorrow it may be too late."

The doctor shivered a little. Thunder rumbled in the distance—the woods were lighted by flashes of lightning that ran across the sky. They outlined the house. They were less vivid than the lightning flashes of the States—gave a wavering light that held for several seconds.

The doctor said: "All right—everything is ready, inside?"

Jo nodded, "It was a disagreeable work," he said. "But there is much we do not know."

Doctor McCall spoke very quietly. "It is only because you know the natives—and the chinks," he said. "You have a reputation. But if you're wrong—"

Jo Gar smiled with his thin lips pressed closely together.

"I agree," he said simply. "It is very easy to lose one's reputation."

The doctor led the way into the house. He went close to the divan. Major Crawford lay with his left arm thrown across his face—his head was turned towards the wicker chair several feet from the divan. He was breathing heavily.

Captain Ramlin was slumped in a chair across the room. He nodded as the two men entered the room, said nothing. Lightning yellowed the room, showing the furniture clearly. The shutters were opened.

Jo Gar stood close to the wall, in a spot not easily seen from the divan. Captain Ramlin rose from his chair, went silently into the next room. The doctor stood near the Island detective. Jo said softly, listening to a louder rumble of thunder:

"A fool is often one—because he speaks—the truth."

He held his right hand low—squeezed the trigger of the gun. It crashed, filling the room with sound. The body on the divan moved—

the head and shoulders of Major Crawford came up. He was facing the chair near the divan. The room was in darkness.

And then the lightning ran across the sky—and yellow light came into the room. Major Crawford's breath was sucked in raspingly. His body was rigid—his brown eyes were staring—staring at the figure in white, in the chair. For brief seconds he looked into the wide eyes of his wife—and then he screamed!

Again and again his screams filled the room. They were high pitched, shrill. They had a peculiar quality. They were the screams of a woman—a woman who was being hurt. They were the screams that Jo Gar had heard from the garden of the house—and that Captain Ramlin had heard.

Lightning ran the sky again—and the figure in white still sat slumped in the chair facing the divan, eyes wide—on the wild eyes of Major Crawford. And then the wounded man saw the gun. It lay almost at his wife's feet. His right hand reached for it—he raised it. Distorted words twisted from his lips.

Gun sound filled the room as he squeezed the trigger again and again. The rumble of thunder was drowned by the sound. Lightning came once more—and the figure in white had not moved. No bullets had struck the woman in the chair—her eyes still stared at Major Crawford.

It was then that he flung the gun from him and screamed again. It was then that Jo Gar said in a voice that shook a little:

"You can only kill a human being once, Crawford—and you have done that."

The doctor threw out an arm and tried to stop the major—as he flung himself towards them. But Major Crawford swung to one side—he was near the door now. His body crashed through the screening—he went down. He was up almost instantly—and down the steps. He ran wildly to the right of the house—arms above his head, mouthing words they failed to distinguish as they followed. Captain Ramlin breathed:

"It was Crawford—who screamed—on the porch—"

When they reached the rocky ledge and looked over it they saw the body of the major, thirty feet below. They went down the trail cautiously, with lightning flashes to show the way. The doctor bent over the figure of the army officer. After a short time he rose, faced Jo Gar.

"Dead," he said steadily. "Broken neck—I'd say. Came down head first."

Jo Gar said nothing for several seconds. When he spoke it was in a tired voice.

"He was not a fool in this—it was the simplest way."

THE STORM had passed, though thunder still rumbled in the distance. Rain dripped from the roof of *Silence House,* made sound on the foliage below the eaves. Jo Gar sat across the table from Captain Ramlin and Doctor McCall. He spoke steadily, in a low voice.

"He was half insane, with that cunning so often possessed at such a time. He did not write the notes—Avery wrote them. Or he had some other person write them. He wanted Mary Crawford—and she wanted Avery. I discovered only a few things—there was little time. But they were important. Avery was having a short leave—and then he was ordered to the States. He was to sail next week, on the Army transport. He thought that Major Crawford would be afraid, for his wife. He thought the notes would help—would make the major send her away from the Islands. Send her back to the States. Then it would be easy. So he wrote the notes—and *she* placed them where they would be found."

The doctor muttered beneath his breath. Captain Ramlin shook his head slowly. Jo Gar went on:

"I think Crawford suspected. He was physically sick—and perhaps he'd suspected for a long time. There was just one way—a certain way. He played along with Avery—sent for me. He made mistakes. He must have known I would not bring much luggage—yet he sent *both* servants to the train to meet me. They came *ahead* of him, because they were in a slower car. The enlisted man came from Baguio and picked him up. The Army car was at his disposal, but was not kept at the house. You know that, of course. I learned it from the driver. And I learned something the major did not expect me to learn. Had he been more sane, he would perhaps have thought of it. Perhaps not. The driver did not come to the house for him—this time. He was coming, but Crawford met him down the slope a short distance. And said that he was afraid they would be late to meet me. But there was plenty of time. The driver knew that, and it seemed strange to him."

Captain Ramlin said: "Good God—he murdered Avery and put him in the porch chair—*before* he left the house!"

Jo Gar nodded. "Perhaps he found Avery and his wife together, not far from the house. More likely he planned to get them together, because he had sent for me. He had found the knife the servant had lost—and he knew that I'd reason an Army man would use a gun, not a knife. He had the notes to show me. He knifed Avery to death—took him to the porch, propped him in the chair. He came to the train, met me. When we reached the house—he acted. In his room there is a scrapbook that shows pictures of him on the Post stage. He was in many shows. He forgot to destroy the book."

Captain Ramlin swore softly. The doctor said, nodding:

"Yes—he was a fair actor. At the Club one night he gave imitations."

Jo Gar smiled a little. "I think he knocked his wife unconscious, bound and gagged her, left her in the woods. I think he knew that she had placed the notes—and wanted Avery. He hated her. When we went into the garden he risked a lot. He brought her to the porch—got the knife from the table. There are wounds on her head—perhaps she was already dead. A rock in his hands—he was strong. Perhaps she was not dead. He used the knife—and screamed. Again and again. That scream did not sound like a woman's to me, though I could not be sure. He ran down the steps, turned and came back, gun in hand. He pretended he saw something—and ran into the woods, shooting."

Captain Ramlin said: "And he knifed himself!"

Jo Gar shrugged.

"*I* think so," he said. "It would be simple for him to hide a knife out there. One quick slash—and he was half mad, anyway. He moved around, lost blood—then came back. He was weak—and we'd heard the shots. But it seemed strange to me—the same knife had been used on Avery—and Mary Crawford. And yet the major was asking us to believe that the killer had dropped it, and had used *another* on him."

The doctor nodded. He spoke softly.

"And in the garden—when Mary Crawford was struck on the head, the first time—and knocked unconscious?"

Jo Gar frowned. "Perhaps that was her own trickery," he said. "Perhaps she or Lieutenant Avery found the knife, and arranged the thing. And Major Crawford, sure of their guilt, played along. Or perhaps it never happened. You see—I could talk with neither of them. Avery was dead—and the woman—"

He checked himself. Captain Ramlin said grimly:

"The screaming betrayed him—and the body you placed in the chair. When he tried to shoot her, with the blanks in the gun—"

Doctor McCall shook his head slowly. He listened to the rain on the eaves. Except for that sound and the very distant rumble of thunder, the house was quiet.

"The tropics does something to people—" McCall said softly. "They try to be cunning—but they do not always succeed."

Jo Gar rubbed closed eyelids with his small, browned fingers.

"I shall return to Manila early in the morning," he said slowly. "There is too much for me—in *Silence House.*"

Diamonds of Dread

Jo Gar, the Island detective, takes up a trail of justice and vengeance.

THE BROWN-FACED driver of the *carromatta* shrilled words at the skinny pony, tugged on the right rein. He stood up in front of his small seat and waved his left arm wildly. Jo Gar leaned forward and watched the approaching machine sway down the narrow street. It was a closed car, mud-stained. It swung from side to side, traveling at high speed. For a second its engine was pointed to the right of the *carromatta,* now crowded far to one side of the street. And then it careened straight towards the small vehicle.

The driver shrilled one word. His small, scantily clad body curved from the front seat. For a second Jo Gar had an unobstructed glance of the speeding car. He muttered a sharp "Dios!"—hunched his small figure forward and jumped.

His sandals had not touched the broken, narrow pavement at the right side of the street when his ears heard the splintering of wood. A woman screamed, in a high, short note, down the street. There was another splintering sound—then the cry of the pony. Jo Gar's diminutive body struck the pavement; he went to his knees, lost balance and rolled over on his back. His pith helmet snapped from his head, thudded like a drum lightly struck, away from him.

He wasn't hurt, and got slowly to his feet. There was a great deal of excitement in the street. The pony had been dragged to the curb and lay on one side, tangled in the *carromatta* shafts. It was vainly trying to rise. The vehicle was a wreck. But the machine was still swaying on its way—a horn sounding steadily.

Near the Pasig the street curved sharply to the left. Even as Jo Gar stared after the machine, it swung far to the right. For a second he thought it would crash into the awninged Chinese shop at the curve. But it did not—it swung back into the middle of the street, was lost from sight. The sound of the horn died. Voices all about the Island detective were raised, pitched high. Chinese, Spaniards, Filipinos—the street was suddenly filled with them.

Jo Gar recovered his helmet, placed it on his head. The sun was still hot, though it was sinking over the bay. He moved towards the struggling pony, speaking sharply to the driver, who was shouting wildly after the vanished car. Together they freed the pony from the shafts and harness—it struggled to its feet and stood trembling, nostrils wide. The driver cursed steadily.

A brown, open car came down the street from the direction the other had come, horn screaming. Jo Gar narrowed his gray-blue eyes on the brown uniforms of Manila police—saw the face of Juan Arragon turned momentarily towards him. The Manila lieutenant of police shouted something—then the car was beyond. A wheel lifted wreckage of the *carromatta,* deposited by the crash car fifty yards distant, and sent it skimming towards the pavement. A voice behind Jo said excitedly:

"What the devil, Señor Gar! That was a close one for you—"

A man dressed in white duck was running down the street towards the wreckage of the *carromatta.* He wore no helmet. He shouted hoarsely, but slowed down as he neared the spot where the crowd had gathered. Jo Gar said in an unhurried tone:

"What is it, Grassner?"

The man in white duck was short, thick-set. He had the squarish face of a German. He widened blue eyes on the Island detective's narrowed ones.

"Delgado's!" he breathed heavily. "Robbery—there were three cars—different directions!"

Jo Gar said slowly: "Delgado's—yes. Of course. And three cars—"

The *carromatta* driver was standing near the pony, cursing shrilly. Tears of rage ran down his brown cheeks. There was still much excitement. The Island detective said sharply to the driver:

"Please stop it! Your pony is not much hurt. You will be paid for the *carromatta.* That is enough!"

Grassner said thickly, breathing with difficulty:

"Herr Mattlien is dead. A bullet hit him."

Jo Gar frowned. He had little use for Herr Mattlien. But robbery had now become murder. He asked in a low, almost toneless voice:

"You saw—the robbery?"

Grassner blinked at him with his small, blue eyes. He shook his head. People were crowding around them.

"I was in the International Bank, around the corner," he said more calmly. "There were shots—and I ran out. Cars were moving away from Delgado's, and Mattlien was running towards them, a gun in his hand. There were more shots—he fell. I went to him—he was dead."

Jo Gar made a clicking sound. He shook his head, spoke to the *carromatta* driver.

"I am Señor Gar—come to my office later and I shall help you."

The driver said: "I am a very poor man—"

The Island detective nodded. "It is true," he agreed. "But you are also alive."

He moved along the street, towards the corner near the Escolta, occupied by Delgado's jewelry shop. A crowd was gathering; there were many police. A deadline had already been established, but Jo Gar was well-known; he went through the entrance, into the warm air stirred by the shop's ceiling fans.

Arnold Carlysle, the American chief of Manila police, had arrived and was listening to words from the short, black-mustached owner of the place. Liam Delgado's white hair was ruffled; he moved his hands nervously. Carlysle, listening, saw Jo Gar enter the shop. He beckoned to him.

Delgado was saying in his perfect English: "It was terrible! Ramon—my only son—dying as I came out from the vault—"

He turned away abruptly, covered his face with his long-fingered, brown hands. Carlysle spoke grimly to Jo:

"They used—American methods, Gar. Three cars—with license plates covered with dust. Four of the men came inside. Delgado's son resisted—they shot him down. Mattlien, the German guard at the International Bank—he was shot down, in the street. They escaped in all directions—but we'll get them, Gar!"

The Island detective nodded. He said in his toneless voice:

"One of the cars upset the *carromatta* in which I was approaching the Escolta. It was going towards the Pasig, and Juan Arragon was in close pursuit."

Carlysle nodded grimly. "We heard the shots—at the station," he said. "It was a daring robbery."

Delgado had dropped into a wicker chair, near a counter. Jo Gar said quietly:

"Three machines—a double murder. And robbery—how much did they get?"

Delgado said in a dull tone, softly: "The Von Loffler diamonds. All ten of them. Two hundred thousand dollars, at least. And some small stones—"

Jo Gar widened his gray-blue eyes. Carlysle went to the entrance of the store and gave orders in a steady, hard voice. There was the clang of an ambulance gong, in the distance.

The Island detective said: "The Von Loffler diamonds. But I thought they were in the bank vault—"

Delgado's tortured eyes met Jo's. He said in a broken voice:

"Von Loffler brought them here this morning. I was to set them into a comb for his wife."

Jo Gar narrowed his eyes and nodded his head slowly. Delgado got to his feet, hands suddenly clenched at his sides. He said in a terrible voice:

"They will pay—for this! By —— they will pay! My only son—"

Jo Gar spoke softly: "It is—very bad. You saw faces?"

The jewelry shop owner said: "They were masked—their whole faces. There were just the eye slits. Four of them were in here. They held guns, and the one who shot my son down was tall and well built.

He was standing over Ramon—when I ran in—"

He turned away from the Island detective. Carlysle was coming into the shop again. There was a great deal of excitement outside, but inside there was almost silence. One white-clad clerk was walking back and forth behind a long display counter, muttering softly to himself.

Carlysle came close to Jo and spoke in the same grim tone.

"I have sent word to all the Constabulary stations. We shall pick up the cars in which they escaped."

Jo said: "Have there been reports of stolen cars lately?"

The Manila Police head frowned. "Two reports—one yesterday—one this morning."

The Island detective shrugged his narrow shoulders.

"I do not think it will help greatly to find the machines," he observed.

Carlysle said: "Juan Arragon was in close pursuit. There is a possible chance."

The Island detective nodded slowly. "Yes," he agreed. "A chance."

Liam Delgado faced them suddenly. His eyes were shot with red. He ran trembling fingers through his white hair. He said fiercely:

"There were four of them. I will have them—every one! I am wealthy—and I will use my wealth—"

There was the staccato cough of a motorcycle—a brown-uniformed figure rode to the curb before the shop. He dismounted, hurried inside. He was breathing heavily. He spoke rapidly in Filipino dialect to Carlysle. The head of the Manila police interrupted him sharply, telling him to speak more slowly. Jo Gar said quietly:

"He says Arragon's car skidded, beyond the bridge. There was a crash into iron railing—the driver was hurt and the car disabled. Pedestrians have told him that Juan stopped another car, and continued the pursuit. The bandit machine was far ahead, running along the right bank of the Pasig."

Carlysle groaned. "It will get away," he muttered. "The bandits were masked—the drivers of the three machines may not have been noticed—"

Jo Gar looked towards the back of Liam Delgado. The jewelry shop owner was standing near a counter, his body rigid. Jo said slowly:

"One leaves the Island only by boat."

Carlysle half closed his eyes. "There are many American visitors here—and English, too. Three boats sail in the next three days. Two of them are big vessels. It will be very difficult—"

He broke off. There was a little silence. Then the police head said slowly:

"But they have the diamonds—the Von Loffler stones. We can search thoroughly, at the docks."

Jo Gar touched the tips of his stubby, brown fingers to almost colorless lips. His almond-shaped eyes were slitted, three-quarters closed.

"We can do many wise things," he observed with a grimness strange in him. "But unfortunately, *others* can do wise things, also."

AT SEVEN o'clock Jo Gar paused before the Manila *Times* office and read the large-lettered bulletin before which a small crowd had gathered. It told him that none of the bandits had been captured, that they had got away with diamonds valued in excess of two hundred thousand dollars—the "famous Von Loffler ten," and that they had murdered Ramon Delgado and Herr Mattlien. It further stated that one escaping machine had crashed into a *carromatta* from which Señor Jo Gar and the driver had barely escaped with their lives. Also Lieutenant of Manila Police Juan Arragon, in pursuit of this crash car, was missing. He had hailed another car, with a Chinese driver, after the one in which he had been riding had skidded and crashed.

The machine, the Chinese and Juan Arragon—all had vanished along the right bank of the Pasig. The whole police force, aided by Island Constabulary, were hunting down the bandits. The *Times* offered a reward of five thousand dollars, and it was rumored that Liam Delgado would announce an offer of a large sum—for the bandits' capture. Two of the machines used in the robbery had been found, abandoned. They had each been stolen. They were being examined for fingerprints. It was the most daring crime in the history of Manila.

The Island detective smiled grimly, and then he thought of Juan Arragon and the smile went from his face. He was fond of Arragon—the lieutenant of police had often blundered in the past, but he had always tried. And the item that mentioned his disappearance was not pleasant to read.

Jo turned his back to the bulletin and waited for a *caleso* to pass—one with a strong-looking horse. He waited only a few minutes.

Across the bridge, on the far side of the black-watered Pasig, there were several police cars. Along the road over which Juan Arragon was supposed to have pursued the car that had struck the *carromatta* in which Jo had been riding there were Constabulary officers. On the left were moored *sampans* and various other type craft—on the right of the road there were hundreds of native huts, thatch-roofed and similar.

From the main road other roads angled off—many of them. Relaxed in the *caleso,* Jo Gar frowned at the roads. Three miles along the river road and the country suddenly became deserted. There were fewer crossroads—native shacks were scattered. The ground was rolling; there were curves. A half dozen times Jo stopped the *caleso* and made inquiry of natives, but always the answer was the same—nothing had been seen of the pursued car, or of the one in pursuit.

It was growing dark when Jo ordered the *caleso* driver to turn back. He breathed softly to himself:

"The bandits inside the shop were not recognized. No attention has been paid to the machine drivers; even I would not recognize the man who drove the car that crashed into us. Some say it was a Chinese who was driving the car that Juan commandeered, others say it was a Jap. No one seems to be sure of the type of car. It is always so."

He shook his head slowly. The *caleso* reached the Escolta, chief business street of Manila, and proceeded slowly towards the police station. Jo descended, paid the driver and climbed the stairs to the office of Carlysle. The American frowned into his eyes, shook his head slowly:

"Nothing—not a thing!" he breathed. "I don't like the way things look, Señor Gar. Arragon has dropped from sight. He was alone with that driver of the car he picked up. One of the police officers with him was stunned in the crash—and Juan ordered the other one to look after him. And he's dropped out of sight."

Jo said very slowly, wiping his brown forehead with a handkerchief, and narrowing his eyes on a slowly revolving ceiling fan:

"The killers are very desperate. That is natural. They have valuable diamonds, and they have murdered two persons. They would not hesitate—"

He broke off, shrugged. Carlysle swore beneath his breath and watched the Island detective. He said, after a little silence:

"Juan Arragon thought very well of you, Señor Gar. You showed him up many times, but he always was good-natured about it. If you—"

He broke off. Jo Gar smiled a little and said in his toneless voice:

"Herr Mattlien is dead. Ramon Delgado is dead. Ten extremely valuable diamonds are missing. The method of the robbery was very modern. I am interested, of course."

Carlysle said: "Good. Of course you are. The method was American, I'd say."

The Island detective shrugged. "Perhaps," he agreed. "But it does not mean that Americans were the bandits."

Carlysle said bitterly: "I hope not—for *their* sakes."

Jo Gar lighted one of his brown-paper cigarettes and said very slowly:

"I shall try to find Juan Arragon—but it is important that the vessels are watched. Very important."

Carlysle said: "I've got everything working—we're trying to find someone who can identify a driver of one of the three cars. The descriptions are all vague—guesswork."

Jo Gar turned his small body slightly. He said in a tone touched with grimness:

"I will return for a few minutes to my office, then I shall move about."

Carlysle's eyes were narrowed. He said with a touch of eagerness:

"You will let me know—as soon as you learn something?"

Jo moved towards the door of the office. He nodded his head a little.

"*If* I learn something—I will let you know," he said quietly, and went down the stairs to the street.

His small office was not far off the Escolta; the street was narrow and curving. There were few people on it; the shops were small and most of them had closed for the night. It was almost dark when he turned in at the entrance and climbed the narrow, creaking stairs. He climbed slowly, conserving his energy.

At the landing before his office he paused a few seconds, stood in the faint light from a small, hanging bulb. Then he went towards the door and reached for the knob. His office was seldom locked; he kept little of importance there.

When he opened the door there was a faint breeze from the window. He reached for the switch—and white light filled the room. For a second he stood motionless, his shoulders and head slightly forward.

His eyes looked towards the wicker chair near the small table.

He recognized the uniform first. It was khaki in color. Next he recognized the figure. Juan Arragon's body was half turned away from him—head and shoulders rested on the table. The helmet was not in sight—Arragon was bareheaded. His dark hair glistened in the white light. There was a definite inertness about the position of the body.

Jo Gar said very steadily: "Juan—Juan Arragon!"

From the Pasig there was the shrill note of a river launch whistle. A driver called in a high-pitched voice in the street below.

Jo Gar sighed. Then he stepped into his office, closed the door. He went slowly to the side of Juan Arragon. He looked first at the head, with the half-opened eyes. Then he found the two bullet holes, not far from the heart. There was little blood.

There were books on the floor; they had fallen as though swept from the table with force. An ink bottle had crashed and broken. Near the right, outstretched fingers of the dead police lieutenant was a bit of white paper. A stubby pencil lay beyond it. There were scrawled words on the paper. Jo Gar leaned forward and read them. After a few seconds he reread them, aloud.

" 'Calle Padrone—house in palmetto thick—high porch—shutters—go at once—I am shot—French—' "

That was all. Jo Gar straightened and turned his back on his friend. He went to the window and looked down towards the street, unseeingly. He felt very badly. Juan Arragon was dead, shot to death. They had worked together on many crimes. Now that was finished. Often Juan had been wrong, but he had always been fair.

Jo Gar slowly lighted a cigarette. He drew a deep breath and moved his lips a little. He said:

"I will find them, of course. They have murdered him. And Ramon Delgado. And Mattlien. Because of diamonds—ten of them."

He stood motionless for several seconds. Then he shrugged, turned and went from the office. He did not look again at Juan Arragon. He walked, not too rapidly, the short distance to the police station.

CARLYSLE SAID, looking with wide eyes at the body of Juan Arragon:

"God—they got him! But he scrawled the address of the hide-out. We'll get out there—"

Jo Gar shook his head slowly: "If you send men there—be very careful," he said tonelessly. "The address was meant for *me.*"

Carlysle blinked. "Yes," he agreed, "but that doesn't make any difference—"

Jo Gar said softly: "You see the pencil—it is near the right-hand fingers. The writing—it is in English."

Carlysle frowned. "It's Arragon's writing," he breathed. "He could write English."

The Island detective nodded. "He wrote with his *left* hand," he said quietly. "If he were dying and wished to give me directions, I do not think he would write in English. And how did he get here?"

Carlysle stared at the dead police lieutenant. He muttered something the Island detective did not hear. Jo Gar said slowly:

"He was shot—and brought here. His handwriting was imitated. It is clever work. But they did not remember that Juan was left-handed. And I understand Filipino—he would have scrawled words to me in that language."

Carlysle said: "They wanted you—to go to Calle Padrone—to the house in the thicket—"

Jo Gar said very quietly: "I should be very careful how your men approach the house."

The American police head frowned. "They're afraid of you, Jo," he said grimly. "They planned this crime carefully. They know Juan has worked with you. They thought they'd get you—out of the way—"

He broke off. The muscles of the Island detective's mouth twitched. He said:

"It is possible."

Carlysle looked down at the scrawl. "They figured the shaky writing would get by—with you thinking Arragon was in bad shape when he wrote it. They didn't know—he was left-handed. And I'd forgotten—"

He checked himself. Jo Gar spoke very quietly:

"The killers know of Señor Gar," he said. "That is unfortunate."

Carlysle, his eyes still narrowed on the scrawl, spoke grimly.

"There is this word 'French,'" he said. "They wanted you to believe their nationality was French. That eliminates something—they're not French."

Jo Gar said nothing. He went to the window of his office and stood with his back to Carlysle and several of his men. The American police head gave orders. Then he spoke to the Island detective.

"The coroner will be here soon. I'm going to the Calle Padrone, with my men—"

Jo nodded. "I shall see you in a few hours," he said quietly, and added in a toneless voice: "I hope."

Carlysle frowned. "Delgado is offering a ten-thousand-dollar reward," he said. "I'm going to have the boat passengers carefully checked, the luggage searched."

He moved towards the door of the office. Jo Gar followed him. Carlysle said: "You going my way?"

The Island detective shook his head. His eyes were almost closed.

"I think it will be better for both of us," he said softly, "if I go alone."

VON LOFFLER sat across the table from Delgado and Jo Gar. He was a German who had lived many years in the Islands. His body was lean and he was not young. He looked at Delgado's white hair and said thickly:

"It is very bad. The diamonds are insured, of course. But in England. I sympathize with Señor Delgado, and I agree with him. You have done much good work in the Islands, Señor Gar. These bandits and killers must be caught."

Jo Gar said nothing. Delgado spoke in a firm, low voice.

"Señor Gar is more familiar with conditions here than other detectives might be. Lieutenant Arragon was his friend. I think we have much—the three of us—to work for, together. But Señor Gar—it is his business."

Von Loffler nodded. His face was grim. His blue eyes narrowed on Delgado's.

"Your son, Liam," he said. "Señor Gar's friend. And my diamonds." His eyes flickered to Jo's. "You will work for us, Señor?" he asked.

Jo Gar smiled with his thin, colorless lips pressed together. He parted them and said:

"Yes—but I feel it will be difficult. This was not an ordinary crime. It may mean that I must leave the Islands."

Delgado said firmly: "I want my son's killers—no matter where you must go."

Von Loffler nodded his head slowly. "It is right," he said. "You have the description of the stones—it is the best I can do."

The Island detective nodded. He said very quietly:

"Just the three of us must know what I am doing. Even the American, Carlysle—he must not know. I shall need funds. It may prove expensive."

Delgado shrugged. "That is simple," he said.

Jo Gar got to his feet. "When Carlysle took his men to the Calle Padrone address he found only a deserted shack. There was not a clue—nothing. But had *I* gone—"

He spread his stubby-fingered hands. Von Loffler said:

"It will be dangerous, Señor. But that is your business."

The Island detective looked expressionlessly at the room's ceiling.

"It is so," he agreed. "It is my business."

CARLYSLE WAS smiling when Jo Gar moved along the cell block of the old police station and reached his side. He spoke with enthusiasm.

"I sent for you—we've got one of them. It's just a matter of a few hours now, and we'll have the others."

Jo Gar made a clicking sound. He looked at the American head of police with widened eyes.

"That is very good," he said slowly. "But how—"

Carlysle cut in on his calm voice. "I didn't want you to waste time running around the city."

Jo lowered his lids slightly. The change in the manner of Carlysle was very evident. He was almost patronizing now. He had one of the bandits—he would shortly have the others. He had done it without Jo Gar's aid.

The Island detective was silent. Carlysle said with a narrow-lipped smile:

"Lieutenant Mallagin picked up the Chinese driver of the car Arragon commandeered, about an hour ago. Just after eleven. He was staggering along the Pasig road—on the other bank. He'd been badly beaten and was soaked. They had tried to drown him, but he regained consciousness and let his body float with the current. Then he crawled ashore. He recognized one of the bandits—a Filipino. We've traced the crime to Cantine, the half-breed that we turned loose from Bilibid three months ago. He ran the hold-up."

Jo Gar said, in a slightly puzzled tone: "But you said you had one of them—"

Carlysle was excited; he made gestures with his hands.

"We'll have the one he recognized," he stated. "I meant we had found the Chinese driver."

Jo Gar said slowly: "That is—good."

Carlysle said: "I've got all the men out for the pick-up, and I didn't want you going off at an angle."

The Island detective half closed his eyes and spoke softly:

"And what became of the machine of this Chinese?" he asked.

Carlysle said: "He doesn't know. A bullet hit Arragon as they were gaining on the other car. He collapsed. The Chinese used brakes—but the other car had stopped, and he was rushed. They knocked him unconscious—the road was deserted; it was around a curve."

Jo Gar said slowly: "And you think Cantine was the leader—the half-breed?"

Carlysle made a grunting sound. "Sure of it," he snapped. "The Filipino that this Chinese identified was one that served a term at Bilibid—he was one of Cantine's men. We'll have them all pretty quick."

The Island detective spoke in his toneless voice:

"That will be—very good."

The American head of police chuckled. "We won't have to worry about the boats that are sailing tomorrow," he said. "Didn't care much for that job, anyway. Passengers are easily insulted. It would have been difficult."

Jo Gar lighted a brown-paper cigarette and blew a thin stream of smoke above his head.

"I did not think this Cantine—possessed so much courage," he said slowly.

Carlysle grunted. "He learned something—and took a chance," he said. "He wasn't so smooth. There was too much killing."

The Island detective said: "May I talk—with the Chinese?"

Carlysle frowned a little. But he nodded his head.

"I'll go along with you," he replied.

Jo Gar smiled with his eyes. "I shall be honored," he said simply.

THE ISLAND detective rose from the small wicker chair and smiled at Carlysle. He narrowed his eyes on the brown, fat face of the Chinese.

"He is of good breed," he said slowly. "He speaks without becoming muddled, and clearly. You have been lucky."

Carlysle smiled expansively. The head of the Manila police was in a genial humor.

"Not lucky, but rather careful, Gar," he said.

Jo shrugged. "He staggered right into your hands," he pointed out. "I meant that it was fortunate he was not killed—shot or drowned."

Carlysle said nothing. He turned towards the door leading from the room in which Jo Gar had been questioning the Chinese. It opened as he faced it; Lieutenant Mallagin entered. He was breathing heavily, obviously excited.

He spoke in broken English. "I have captured—one of Cantine's men. He is hurt—very much. He fell from a *sampan* deck—but will not talk. The doctor—he say he may die quick—"

Carlysle frowned. Jo Gar was watching Mallagin with expressionless eyes. He glanced at the Chinese—the man's mouth was half opened; he was staring at the chunky-bodied Filipino.

The chief of police frowned. Mallagin said in a husky tone:

"I think it would be wise—to take this Chinese—to him—while he lives. He then might talk—"

Carlysle nodded. "Yes," he said decisively. We'll get him right there. Where is—this man?"

Mallagin said: "In the shop of Santoni, who deals in fruit—not far from the Spanish bridge. He is very bad."

Carlysle nodded. He looked towards the Chinese. He said sharply:

"You are going with us—you will identify a man who is hurt."

The fear that was in the eyes of the Chinese seemed to grow. He mumbled something that Jo Gar failed to understand; his hands were moving about strangely. The Island detective said:

"You think it is wise—"

The expression in the American's eyes checked him. He smiled slightly and bowed. Carlysle said slowly:

"I'm taking charge of this case myself. In the past Juan Arragon did much good, and much harm, poor devil!"

The Island detective said nothing. Carlysle spoke to Lieutenant Mallagin.

"We will use my private car. There will be the driver and myself, and the Chinese. Yourself, of course—and pick two men in whom you have confidence."

Mallagin nodded and turned away. Jo Gar said in a quiet voice:

"I should like to accompany you. Juan Arragon was my friend—"

There was a touch of coldness in Carlysle's voice.

"I'm sorry—there will not be enough room. But I shall keep you informed—"

The Island detective narrowed his almond-shaped eyes. He said softly:

"I might replace one of the two men you told Lieutenant Mallagin to choose."

Carlysle said steadily: "It is a police matter—and you are not of the police. Go ahead, Lieutenant—get your men."

Jo Gar bowed slightly. He said in a faintly amused voice:

"I would choose one who can make notes of what your injured man may say."

Carlysle frowned. "Of course," he said in a hard tone. "That is understood."

Mallagin looked stupidly at Carlysle. Jo Gar watched the Chinese with eyes that were almost closed. Carlysle glanced at the Island detective as he moved towards the door of the room. He said:

"I'm sorry, Gar—but this is a police case."

Jo smiled a little. "I am sure it is being handled very well," he said in a peculiar tone, and went through the doorway.

THE BLACK closed car of Carlysle pulled away from the police station, cut across the Escolta and headed towards the Pasig.

After a time they were close to the river on a street running to the Spanish bridge.

A half block behind, Jo Gar sat in a machine he had hired from Cormanda. His small body was not relaxed; in his right hand he gripped a Colt. Abruptly Cormanda jerked his head and said in a rising voice:

"Jo—they're slowing down—"

The Island detective leaned forward, caught a glimpse of two red lights, across the road. He said in a swift voice:

"They were not repairing—at dusk—"

The Carlysle machine had almost reached the two lights. It halted. Jo Gar said:

"Stop, Cormanda—"

The small, open car stopped. The chauffeur of the car ahead got to the street and looked back at the car in which Cormanda and Jo Gar sat. He gestured towards the two red lights. Jo Gar spoke softly to his own driver:

"Get down—Cormanda—it is not good—"

The first machine-gun started a staccato clatter from an alley on the right. Almost instantly there was the drum of a second one—from a shuttered window on the left. Metal started to make sound. The chauffeur ran a few feet and sprawled to the street. At that moment, the Chinese sprang from the car, doubled over and ran to a door nearest the car. He disappeared. The other occupants of the car were crouched, out of sight, below the metal sides.

Jo Gar slipped out the right side of the small car and bent his body forward. He ran back over the street, keeping his short arms close to his sides and his head low. Suddenly he turned and moved down a second alley. One machine-gun had stopped drumming, but the other was still beating sound against the quiet of the night.

In the darkness of the alley Jo Gar paused for a second. He breathed heavily as he got his head slightly exposed and looked towards the Carlysle machine:

"The Chinese—was lying—"

A door shot open—the figure of the Chinese was pitched into the alley. Almost instantly it jerked, half spun. Then the man dropped to the pavement. The second machine-gun started to clatter again.

Jo Gar muttered: "And yet—they murdered him!"

Cormanda was reversing the small car now. It whined back from the red lights and the drum of bullets. Jo Gar swung back into the alley, moved rapidly along it. At the far end he saw the Pasig water and the silhouette of a *sampan.*

The machine-gun fire died. No sound but the whine of the reversing car came from the street behind the Island detective. He thought: They got the diamonds, but they were forced to kill. Ramon Delgado, Mattlien—Juan Arragon. And now the Chinese, perhaps others. Why do they trap and kill? Is it because they must leave the Islands? He thought: It is because they are clever and must clear the way.

He reached the row of *sampans,* moored abreast. There was a narrow path between piled, rotted planks and empty fish baskets. It led towards the next alley. Jo Gar gripped his Colt firmly and moved along it. At intervals he stopped and listened. The street he had left was very quiet. Only the river sounds reached his ears.

He had almost reached the next alley when he saw faint shadow. It was directly ahead—moving slowly.

A machine made sound in the distance; the engine getting into a roar—and dying gradually. A voice reached the ears of the Island detective; it sounded much like Carlysle's, raised hoarsely.

And then the shadow ahead of him became a figure. Jo Gar lifted his automatic and said very quietly:

"Raise your arms!"

The figure swung towards him—he caught a glimpse, in the wavering, reflected light from a *sampan,* of a brown, lean face and wide, staring eyes. The man drew his breath in sharply—his hands swung upward. But the left one went up first, and the right brushed the belt of his soiled duck trousers as it moved.

Jo Gar said sharply: "No!"

The reflected light caught the gleam of the blade. Jo Gar steadied the muzzle of his automatic and squeezed the trigger. He rocked back on his heels, curved his body to one side. The other man's right wrist made swift movement, even as his body jerked convulsively. The knife dug its blade point into the wood of a basket within six inches of Jo's left arm.

The man sank to his knees and pressed both hands against his belt, at the stomach. He groaned. Jo Gar stepped out from the piled baskets and jerked a small flashlight from his pocket. For a second he stood close to the man who had fallen, and listened for sound from the alley ahead. There was none. But in the distance voices were calling.

He flashed the beam on the one hunched near his feet, widened his almond-shaped eyes. Then he moved the beam to the knife that had been thrown. He breathed very slowly:

"Malay—"

He kneeled beside the groaning man, held the gun close to him. He said quietly, in the Malay tongue:

"Why was the Chinese murdered?"

The man widened his eyes and shook his head. Jo Gar smiled coldly and pressed the muzzle against the man's right side.

"If I shoot again—you will die," he said. "You were with others—what were their names?"

The Malay shook his head. He was muttering to himself. Jo Gar said:

"The Chinese told the police that a man named Cantine committed the great robbery and murder. He was lying—and yet he was murdered. Why?"

The Malay was getting his breath with difficulty now. There were footfalls in the alley from which he had come. Jo Gar lifted his head, and heard the voice of Lieutenant Mallagin, cautioning one of his men. The Island detective spoke softly:

"Quickly—the police come. I am not of them. Why was the Chinese killed?"

The eyes of the man hunched beside him were staring. He said weakly, in his own tongue:

"His family—was given money. He was to lie—and then to die. He was—very poor."

Jo Gar straightened a little and sighed. Then he lowered his head again.

"Who made—the arrangement?" he asked quietly.

The Malay shook his head. His body relaxed a little; he rolled over on his back. He said very weakly:

"It was—the one who walks badly—always in white—"

His lips closed; he shivered—cried out a little. There was a convulsive movement of his body, then it was still. From the alley Mallagin called:

"Who—is that?"

Jo Gar narrowed his eyes and rose. He was thinking: The one who walks badly—always in white. But he said in a steady voice:

"It is Señor Gar—I have shot one of them."

He heard the surprised exclamation from Lieutenant Mallagin. The Filipino came in close, stared down at the dead man. Carlysle, breathing heavily, was behind the lieutenant.

"The Chinese is dead—the chauffeur is dead," he said. "One of my men is wounded. Mallagin and I escaped. You followed us?"

Jo Gar nodded. He said quietly: "This one tried to knife me—I was forced to shoot. He did not die instantly."

Carlysle's eyes widened. He said eagerly: "He talked?"

Jo nodded. His voice was almost toneless. "Cantine did not commit the robbery or murders," he said. "The Chinese was paid to lie to you—and then to die."

Carlysle stared at Jo. "The driver—paid to lie and then—"

Jo Gar shook his head. "He was not the driver," he said slowly. "I spoke to him about machines—he knew very little. I was suspicious, and followed when you got word that one of Cantine's men had been hurt."

Carlysle breathed heavily. "You think it was a plan—to throw us off—" Jo Gar smiled a little. He glanced down at the dead man.

"If this man had not talked—you would have been after Cantine and his men"—he said quietly, "a wrong scent."

Carlysle nodded his head very slowly. "He said nothing about who—"

Jo Gar shook his head slowly. "I have told you what he said," he replied, and closed his eyes.

When he opened them, Carlysle was looking down at the dead man and frowning.

"We shall have to watch the boats," he said grimly. "They have the diamonds—and they have killed many men." He looked narrowly at the Island detective. "They got away with their machine-guns—all but this man," he said. "You will help us, Señor Gar?"

Jo Gar smiled with his thin lips. His colorless eyes seemed to be looking beyond the American head of police. He shook his head very slowly.

"No," he said. "It is—a police matter."

Carlysle stiffened. "Juan Arragon was your friend," he reminded.

Jo Gar stopped smiling. "It is so," he agreed. "But I will not help you, Señor Carlysle."

The American turned away, muttering something that the Island detective did not hear. Lieutenant Mallagin moved after his chief. Jo Gar looked down at the figure of the Malay and breathed very softly:

" 'The one who walks badly—always in white.' "

He sighed, and his eyes half closed. He glanced towards the knife handle, protruding from the basket wood. River odors were in his nostrils—a pony whinnied in the distance. Jo Gar said very slowly, in a half whisper:

"For Juan Arragon—I will help—myself."

The Man in White

An adventure of Jo Gar, the little Island detective, in search of murderers and their loot.

THE *CHEYO MARU* took red color from the setting sun; her boat deck was soaked in it. The sea was calm; even the white wings of the gulls that rose and dipped astern were tinted red. Manila and the Island of Cavite were no longer to be seen astern. There were few people in the deck chairs; the first dinner gong had already sounded.

Jo Gar relaxed his short body, kept his almond-shaped eyes almost closed. Now and then he lifted his brown-paper cigarette, inhaled. It was almost as though he slept between puffs, but that was not so.

When the Japanese steward came rapidly towards his chair, the Island detective lifted his head slightly. The steward had been well tipped, and had been asked only a simple task. He reached Jo Gar's chair now, bowed jerkily.

"He has left his cabin," he said. "The man in white—the one who limps. He is coming."

He spoke in his native tongue, which was the tongue in which Jo had spoken to him. When the Island detective jerked his head in a gesture of dismissal, the steward moved towards the stern of the liner and vanished from sight. Jo turned his head a little and watched the man in white approach. He was of medium size; dressed in duck. He had a lean face, and it was as though the sun had not touched it. It was almost the color of the spotless suit he wore. He moved slowly, as Jo had seen him move at the dock, several hours before the boat had sailed. There was a very slight limp; it appeared that he stepped lightly when weight was on his left leg.

The man's face was turned away from him as he approached the spot opposite Jo's chair. But as he neared it he took his eyes from the water, looked at Jo in a swift, searching glance. The man in white had blue eyes; they were small and expressionless. His lips were thin, and without much color.

He stopped suddenly, his eyes still on Jo. He said, a slow smile on his face:

"Señor Gar, isn't it?"

Jo sat up and nodded. He even managed a little smile. He was very surprised, and tried not to let the other man know this.

The one in white nodded his head and seemed very pleased. His voice was soft, almost careless.

"Leaving the Islands?" he asked.

Jo Gar smiled pleasantly. "I have relatives in Honolulu," he said. "Leaving the Islands—for more islands."

The one in white chuckled a little. He said in an easy tone:

"I am Ferraro. For a time I was connected with the Constabulary. I have heard of you."

Jo Gar bowed. Ferraro's English was good though not perfect. There was a clipping of words, a cutting short, despite his leisurely manner of talking.

Ferraro said: "You leave at a bad time. A terrible crime—Delgado's son, that watchman at the bank. And Juan Arragon. All dead."

He shook his head. Jo Gar said: "You were acquainted with Señor Arragon?"

Ferraro frowned. "No," he said. "But I had heard of him."

Jo Gar relaxed again, inhaled. The one in white looked at the sea, shrugging.

"The murderers will be caught, of course. And the Von Loffler diamonds found. It is almost always so."

Jo Gar closed his eyes and nodded. "Of course," he agreed. "It is so—almost always."

Ferraro looked at him again. "There are few passengers aboard, who came on at Manila. But perhaps you do not care to be addressed as Señor Gar?"

Jo widened his gray-blue eyes. "Why should I object?" he asked in a puzzled voice.

The one in white said: "Well, there has been this robbery—these murders. Only two days ago. There was a thorough search at the dock. I was asked many questions, myself. It seemed amusing."

Jo Gar said: "And you were formerly with the Constabulary?"

They both smiled; then Jo Gar said: "No, there is no secrecy. I am not of the police—I rather dislike the American who heads the force."

Ferraro said: "But Juan Arragon—he was one of your countrymen—a good friend—"

He paused, shrugged narrow shoulders. "At least, so I have heard," he said. "Having been in the Constabulary—"

Jo Gar nodded. "It is not so," he said quietly. "Juan Arragon was of the Manila police. He was always fighting me."

Ferraro said: "Oh, so that was it, Señor?"

The Island detective nodded very slowly. The man in white looked towards the water; then his eyes came back to Jo's again.

"I am dining alone," he said. "Will you join me?"

Jo thanked him and declined. "I do not think I shall dine tonight," he said. "My stomach pains me."

Ferraro expressed regret. He spoke a few words more and moved aft. His limp was barely noticeable, but it existed. Jo Gar reclined in his chair and remembered several things. Diamonds worth two hundred thousand dollars had been stolen from Delgado's jewelry store, on the Escolta, in Manila. Delgado's son had been murdered. A watchman had been murdered. And Juan Arragon had been murdered, after he had vanished in pursuit of one of the fleeing machines. His body had been returned to Jo Gar's small office, with a forged note attached. And later in the night, while trailing a clue, the Island detective had been forced to shoot a Malay who had come at him with a knife. The Malay had talked. He had spoken of the leader of the diamond thieves as "the one who walks badly—always in white."

For Liam Delgado, whose son was dead— and Von Loffler, who wished to recover the ten diamonds, Jo Gar had left the Islands. He had left aboard the *Cheyo Maru* because another was leaving on the same boat—a man dressed in white, who limped when he moved.

Jo Gar shrugged his narrow shoulders. The sunset red was almost gone now. The Island detective thought:

When a man *is* a thief and a murderer he does not seek out one who hunts down thieves and murderers. And yet this Ferraro has approached me, has invited me to dine.

A little grimness came into the gray-blue eyes of the Island detective.

"Sometimes such a man is very confident," he half whispered. "And sometimes he has been of the police." He nodded his head a little and ceased to smile. "And sometimes," he murmured very softly, "a dying man lies." The Island detective sighed. "It is very difficult," he said softly. "Even my own thoughts contradict."

WHEN JO GAR turned his key in the lock of his cabin, stepped inside, he closed the door slowly behind him. He hummed a little Spanish tune, and his body was rigid. There were his two bags—and they were opened, the contents spilled about. The lock of his small trunk had been smashed; the tray lay crosswise. His clothes were scattered. The berth sheets had been ripped up—the cabin was almost a wreck.

Jo stood with his back to the door, stopped humming. He lighted one of his cigarettes, moved about the cabin carefully, using his eyes. He touched nothing. After a few minutes he pressed a button and waited for the Japanese steward. When the man came he was breathing heavily, and his black, round eyes were wide. They grew wider as he surveyed the cabin. The Island detective made a little gesture with his brown hands.

"You see," he said. "There has been a search."

The steward broke into his native tongue. He was very excited. He had just entered the cabin of Señor Ferraro, who was of the Philippine Constabulary. And it, too, had been entered. Luggage had been ransacked. An officer of the boat had been notified.

Jo Gar made a clicking sound and nodded his head slowly.

"A clumsy person—this thief," he said. "I have nothing of value here. I am a poor man. Yet see how he has thrown things about."

The steward shrilled words—apologetic words. He had been away from the section only a short time. He had come on deck to do as Señor Gar had asked—to tell him that Señor Ferraro had left his cabin. He had come quickly and had taken a shortcut to the spot in which Señor Gar's chair had been placed.

Jo Gar quieted the man. He narrowed his gray-blue eyes on the ransacked trunk, then turned abruptly. He said as he moved through the doorway to the narrow corridor:

"You do not think the cabin was entered— before you went above to tell me that Señor Ferraro had left his cabin?"

The steward was sure neither cabin had been entered before that time. Señor Ferraro's cabin was only fifty feet distant from Señor Gar's. And it was in the same condition.

Jo Gar said: "Perhaps there are others in similar state."

He went along the narrow corridor to a wider one. The steward followed. Two ship's officers, clad in white uniforms and gold braid,

approached. The Chief Steward came from another direction. There was much swift talk—the Japanese who had charge of Jo's cabin led the way to the one occupied by Señor Ferraro.

It was an outside cabin, much similar to Jo's. It was in the same sort of disorder. Jo looked in—the others went inside. The Third Officer said in English:

"And your cabin was entered, too, Señor?"

Jo nodded. "I was on deck," he said. "Señor Ferraro talked with me, about twenty minutes ago. Then he went to dine."

The Third Officer said: "You are friends?"

Jo shook his head. "Acquaintances," he corrected.

There was more talk. The Third Officer suggested that Señor Ferraro be notified, and while he was offering the suggestion the one with the limp came along the corridor. His blue eyes widened on the group. The Chief Steward said apologetically:

"Your cabin has been entered, Señor."

Ferraro looked at Jo Gar, went to the doorway of his cabin. His eyes moved over the opened bags, broken trunk locks. He drew in a deep breath and said slowly:

"But why? I am a poor man—"

Jo Gar chuckled a little. He said: "Those were my words, Señor. I, too, have been treated like this."

The one in white stared at Jo. Then he smiled a little with his thin lips. His face was bloodless; he had thin, yellowish hair.

His lips parted; he was about to speak, but he changed his mind.

He went into the cabin and poked around among the clothes of a large bag. The officers were speaking with Jo when Ferraro uttered an exclamation.

"Ah—a woman!" he said.

Turning, he held out a white hand. In his palm lay the pin. It was perhaps two inches long. It had a setting so cheap that it could be immediately seen. There were a half dozen stones in the pin—but one was missing. They were glass— the glitter was false; they had not the appearance of even a clever imitation of diamonds.

The Third Officer took the pin and inspected it carefully. Jo Gar noted the cheapness of the metal—the flat backing. The pin clasp was bent—the whole thing a cheap job.

Ferraro stood close to the Third Officer. He said slowly, in his clipped-word manner:

"The sort of thing you buy on the Escolta for a few *pesos.* Cheap stuff—it fell while she was ransacking the place."

The Third Officer nodded. "You have not suffered a loss?" he asked.

Señor Ferraro shrugged. "I have nothing of importance—to lose," he stated.

He took the bar pin from the officer's fingers. He juggled it carelessly about in the palm of his right hand, without looking at it.

The Chief Steward addressed Jo Gar.

"And you, Señor Gar? You have not lost anything of importance?"

Jo Gar smiled at Ferraro. "I am much in the position of Señor Ferraro," he said quietly.

The Third Officer spoke in a peculiar tone.

"Neither of you gentlemen possess anything of great value—and yet each of you has been robbed."

Ferraro smiled a little, his blue eyes on the half-closed ones of the Island detective.

"It is very strange," he said softly.

Jo Gar spoke tonelessly. "It *seems* very strange," he agreed. "I shall return to my cabin and try to get things in order."

The Chief Steward said grimly: "We will make an investigation, of course. Perhaps the pin—"

Ferraro handed it to the Chief Steward. He looked at Jo.

"Señor Gar is quite skilled in these matters," he said slowly. "He is an interested person, in this case."

The Island detective smiled. "And *you* were formerly with the Island Constabulary," he reminded. "You see with what little esteem the intruder has regarded us."

The Third Officer said: "Perhaps it has been just a blundering affair—an attempt at quick robbery."

Jo Gar nodded his head, and kept his brown face serious.

"That is very possible," he agreed, and moved along the corridor towards his own cabin.

He was interrupted several times while he was adjusting things. It was not easy to think clearly, with so many people about. At ten o'clock the Third Officer came into the cabin, shutting the door behind him. He said very quietly:

"In matters such as this we always are suspicious of the cabin steward. We have questioned him at length. He states that you have tipped him generously, and that you had him come to you, on deck this evening, and warn you that Señor Ferraro had left his cabin and was going above for a bit of air before dining."

The Third Officer paused. Jo Gar nodded, his brown face expressionless.

"It is so," he said. "You wish to know the reason?"

The officer spread his hands in a little gesture, half of apology, half of assent. Jo said:

"I am weary of discussing Island matters. I wished to be alone. With the cabin steward advising me in time, I hoped to avoid Señor Ferraro for a few days. Unfortunately, I was unable to rise from the deck chair in time. So we met."

The Third Officer frowned. Then he nodded his head, very slowly. He said:

"Thank you, Señor Gar."

Jo smiled pleasantly. He said in a careless voice:

"You are keeping that imitation thing—that bar pin?"

The officer shook his head. "There was no loss to Señor Ferraro," he said. "We shall make adjustment for any baggage damage. He asked me to leave the pin with him. He intends, I believe, to do some quiet investigating. He was with the Constabulary."

Jo Gar nodded pleasantly. "That is quite the wisest thing to do, I think," he said.

The Third Officer expressed regrets. The captain was disturbed.

Such things seldom happened aboard the *Cheyo Maru.*

Jo Gar sighed. The Third Officer went from the cabin, turning at the door and smiling pleasantly. When he had gone Jo removed his palm beach suiting and got into clothes that were of dark silk. He waited a short time, went to the deck quickly, carrying a light blanket that bulked over his arm. His face held a tight smile as he approached the spot where his deck chair had been.

The night was warm and there was no moon. Most of the deck chairs had been collected and were being stacked together. Jo moved towards the deck steward, a tall Jap with eyes that were very black. He said:

"Please return my chair. I wish to rest a while on deck—I am sleepy and my cabin is stuffy."

The deck steward bowed. Jo showed him the spot, one that was fairly secluded, aft of the second stack. When the chair had been set up he relaxed in it. The deck steward smiled and moved away.

After a short time Jo turned his head to one side and appeared to doze. The deck steward passed him, treading very softly. He halted, and through slitted eyes the Island detective saw that he was staring at him. Then the steward moved hurriedly forward.

Jo Gar lay motionless in the chair. There was the steady vibration of the engines, and the faint sound of steam reaching the air. From some spot below music reached the boat deck. Jo said very quietly:

"How calm the sea is!"

His lips held an ironical smile. He breathed evenly, closed his almond-shaped eyes.

FIVE MINUTES later there were three shots. The first one was a muffled, Maxim-silenced pop-cough. The second was smothered but had more sound. The third was a sharp *crack* sound.

Jo Gar, his small body tense, stepped out from behind the ventilator—caught sight of a black figure moving aft. He bent his body low, ran along the deck, his automatic gripped tightly in his right-hand fingers. From some spot forward a voice called with the shrill of the Jap tongue a word that sounded like:

"Hai!"

The dark figure ahead had reached the steps of the port companionway. It seemed almost to dive down them. Jo Gar slowed his pace, approached the steps carefully. When he reached the bottom of them he heard shouts. Men were coming up from the deck below.

He tried to get past them, but a short, chunky man caught him by the right arm and tried to get his gun away. Jo said sharply:

"Stop—a man came down here! I am after—him."

He was breathing heavily. The chunky one wore a white uniform. He said in bad English:

"I—ship police. I see no one—"

Other men were coming up. Several of them were in dinner clothes. Jo Gar watched the Third Officer come into the group. He shook off the grip of the ship policeman, said grimly:

"I was on deck. Three shots were fired. A figure in black ran towards this companionway. I followed."

A man in dinner clothes said: "I heard only two shots—from above."

The Third Officer was beside Jo. He spoke in a soft tone.

"You are dressed in black, also, Señor Gar."

Jo Gar nodded. "It is less conspicuous," he replied. "I was on deck—and wished to be inconspicuous."

The Third Officer said: "Why?"

Jo Gar raised his voice, but did not answer the question.

"And none of this group saw the man I was pursuing?" he asked.

None in the group had seen any person in black—but Jo. The Third Officer said:

"The shots were fired—at you?"

Jo Gar shook his head. "At my deck chair," he said quietly. "I was some distance away."

He read suspicion in the Third Officer's eyes. The one in dinner clothes, who had spoken before, said grimly:

"You say there were three shots—I heard only two."

Jo Gar shrugged. "The first was Maxim-silenced," he replied. "If you will come to the boat deck—"

He broke off, turning. He went up the steps of the companionway, closely followed by the Third Officer. The others trailed along behind. When they reached the boat deck there were several other people. Two stood near the spot in which the steward had placed Jo's chair.

The Third Officer used his flashlight; he muttered an exclamation as the beam fell across the chair. Jo Gar stood to one side, smiling a little. His eyes were on the brown mask that had rolled from the chair. He said: "That is a mask that Sebastino, the Spaniard in Manila, made for me. It is a good likeness."

He moved forward, lifted it. The others crowded around him. The plaster had been broken in two places. There was a hole in the left cheek—another in the forehead. The Island detective said very softly:

"You see—the one in black was an excellent shot. The third bullet—"

He leaned over the chair and moved the cloth of the palm beach coat he had wrapped around the light blanket. There was a hole in the left lapel. He said in a toneless voice:

"There is where it struck. It was like this—"

He adjusted the trousers and coat, rested the face mask above the coat, laying it with the right cheek against the canvas of the deck chair. He said quietly:

"Switch off the light—and move back here."

The Third Officer switched off the flashlight. The group moved away from the chair, towards the vessel's port rail. They stood looking towards the mask and the palm beach material. In the faint light it resembled Jo Gar—sleeping in the deck chair. The mask was very life-like.

The Third Officer sucked in his breath sharply. The man in dinner clothes, who had spoken before, swore.

He said grimly: "It was—attempted murder, all right!"

Jo Gar nodded. "And the one who attempted it has got away," he said. "Below that companionway—are there several avenues of escape?"

The Third Officer nodded slowly. "A corridor to the concert room. Another companionway, to the deck below. A narrow passageway to the radio room—"

Jo Gar said slowly: "That is enough."

The Third Officer made a clicking sound. "We shall talk with the captain—you and I, Señor Gar," he said.

Jo nodded. There was the sound of footfalls—of a man running. A Jap came into the group, clad in the uniform of a subordinate officer. He addressed the Third Officer.

"Deck Steward Kamogi, sir!" he breathed. "He lies up forward, near your cabin. He's—dead."

The Third Officer spoke in Japanese. "Dead?" he asked. "Shot?"

The subordinate shook his head. "It was—a knife, sir," he replied. "In the back!"

The Third Officer narrowed his eyes on the blue-gray ones of Jo

Gar. He said very softly:

"The deck steward, Señor Gar."

The Island detective looked towards the face mask in the chair. He said in a voice that held a suggestion of grimness:

"He *would* have been the first person I would have questioned."

CAPTAIN HAROYSAN sat across the table from Jo Gar, his moon face crinkled, his black eyes narrowed on those of the Island detective.

"You knew your life was in danger—you changed your attire, arranged a trap—"

Jo Gar spread his brown, chubby hands.

"I *sensed* my life was in danger," he corrected. "It was the deck steward—"

The captain of the *Cheyo Maru* frowned. He spoke slowly, shaking his head.

"It is very bad. The vessel has never had anything like this—"

Jo Gar smiled a little. "I have been very frank with you, Captain," he said. "The one responsible for the theft of the Von Loffler diamonds is aboard your ship, I am sure of that. He knows that I am aboard. That does not please him. I think that he bribed the deck steward to tell him when I was sleeping. Then he wished to be safe. So the deck steward was knifed."

The captain frowned. "And you bribed the steward of your cabin, to be told when Señor Ferraro was approaching you, on deck."

Jo Gar nodded. "I wished to evade him," he said.

The captain shrugged. "I do not believe that," he replied.

The Island detective smiled. "Señor Ferraro's cabin was broken into—so was mine," he said. "That is puzzling."

Captain Haroysan said sharply: "You are changing the point of the discussion."

Jo Gar rose from his chair. "The Von Loffler diamonds are valued in excess of two hundred thousand dollars, Captain," he said. "Already, more than a half dozen men have been murdered, because of them. One of those men was Juan Arragon, my friend. Another was Señor Delgado's son. Both Von Loffler and Delgado have commissioned me to hunt down the thief and murderer. I had evidence that he was aboard your ship."

The Japanese stood up also. He said grimly:

"If it satisfies me—I will take charge of him."

Jo Gar sighed. "It is weak evidence," he said quietly. "A Malay involved in an attempt to kill the American head of the Manila police gave it to me. He was dying at the time. It is not strong enough to make an arrest."

The captain said: "And you want the diamonds, Señor Gar?"

Jo Gar nodded. "Of course," he agreed.

The captain shrugged. "A murderer is aboard the *Cheyo Maru,*" he said. "In less than two weeks we shall be in Honolulu. But what is to happen—before we land—"

The Island detective said tonelessly:

"We will have the murderer of the deck steward. *Perhaps* we will have the Von Loffler diamonds."

Captain Haroysan made a guttural sound.

"I have radioed Manila—about you, Señor. And about Señor Ferraro."

Jo Gar said with a faint smile:

"And the information you received—it was good?"

Haroysan said with grim amusement: "It was even flattering. Señor Ferraro has seen honorable service with the Constabulary. You are much respected. And yet—"

The *Cheyo Maru* captain broke off abruptly. He shrugged. Jo Gar smiled sympathetically.

"And yet you are far from satisfied," he finished.

The captain said nothing. His eyes were narrow lines of blackness. Jo Gar bowed slightly.

"I can understand your feelings, Captain," he said softly. "I feel—much the same way."

ON THE fourth day out the sky clouded, and there was wind. It was wind that blew gently at first, but increased steadily in velocity. There were rumors of a typhoon; the *Cheyo Maru* rolled badly. Racks were on the tables, and things creaked and rattled in the cabins. At four in the afternoon, with the sea growing steadily rougher, Jo Gar moved cautiously towards the cabin of Señor Ferraro and rapped on the door.

Ferraro called out: "Who is it?" And Jo answered him. The door was opened almost immediately.

The Island detective smiled and said: "Does the roughness bother you, Señor?"

Ferraro's white face was a little twisted, but he managed a smile.

"I am not exactly a sailor," he said.

Jo stepped inside the cabin. Ferraro closed the door behind him. Jo said:

"For the last two days I have been moving around in second- and third-class quarters. I think you were doing something along the same lines, yes?"

Ferraro nodded. "I had no luck," he said.

Jo Gar smiled a little. "This morning I had a little," he said. "I came across this."

He placed a brown hand in a pocket of his palm beach suit and withdrew it again. In his palm was a pin. It was a bar pin, of cheap manufacture. It had four imitation diamonds in it—one hole was vacant. The glass was large in size, but not matched.

Ferraro stared at the pin. He took it in his fingers and inspected it. Then he looked towards the small table in his cabin. On an end of it was the pin he had found after his cabin had been ransacked. He went over and placed it beside the other.

"The same sort of junk!" he breathed. "It might mean something."

Jo Gar nodded. "It might, but I'm afraid not," he said. "There are always a lot of women traveling second and third class on these ships. Many of them like cheap jewelry. A lot of these women are the dregs of the Orient. Captain Haroysan has told me that often first-class cabins are robbed. Or rather, attempts are made to rob."

Ferraro said: "But in this case—it was your cabin—and mine. And an attempt was made on your life."

Jo Gar nodded. "Many attempts have been made—to murder me," he said. "I found this pin in an empty third-class cabin. It lay beneath a berth."

Ferraro said very steadily: "We were both in police matters. What if the person thought he could learn something, or she could learn something, by getting into our luggage?"

The Island detective nodded. "A possibility," he said. "I've thought of that, Señor Ferraro."

Ferraro looked down at the two cheap objects in his palm. He poked them over on their backs. Jo Gar said slowly:

"I don't think that cheap stuff means anything. However, it is good to be careful."

He smiled at Ferraro and lifted one of the pins in his fingers. He said:

"We each have one—now."

Ferraro's mouth muscles twitched. He started to say something quickly, but caught himself. Turning, he made a movement as though to toss the pin towards the table. The ship was rolling heavily: he was forced to brace himself. Jo Gar leaned against the door. Ferraro said, facing him, a smile on his face:

"Wait—this is the piece of junk *you* found, Señor Gar."

There was a half-careless tone to his voice, yet he spoke hurriedly. Jo Gar looked at the bar pin in his hand.

"Of course," he agreed. "I am sorry."

They exchanged pins, both smiling. Jo slipped his into a pocket. He said:

"I'm going to nap—it's getting steadily rougher. Sleeping helps."

Ferraro tossed the pin towards the table. It struck it, but rolled from the surface to the floor. The one in white made an instinctive motion towards it, checked himself. He yawned, faced Jo.

"I'll have a try at it," he said.

Jo smiled and went outside. It took him five minutes to get to the captain's quarters. In another ten minutes the cabin boy had been sent to Ferraro's cabin. The Third Officer and Jo Gar, five minutes later, watched the one with the pale face following the cabin boy towards the captain's quarters. He did not see them. They went swiftly to his cabin, and the Third Officer used the key. Inside, Jo Gar looked on the floor. The bar pin was not there. It lay on the small table, on its back, the cheap stones face downward.

Jo Gar picked it up and handed it to the Third Officer. They went silently from the cabin, locking the door behind them. The *Cheyo Maru* was rolling heavily.

The Third Officer said: "Getting a little rough, Señor."

The Island detective nodded. "I trust so," he said softly.

FALLIBAR, A diamond expert returning to the States, seated across from Jo Gar and Captain Haroysan, spoke quietly:

"The third stone is a fine diamond," he said. "The others in the pin are just glass. Even this real one has been painted, to give it false glitter. Painted on the back. And crudely mounted. But then, all of them are just stuck in holes of the metal."

There was silence. Fallibar studied the slip of paper Jo had given him. He nodded his head.

"It answers the description," he said slowly. "It's one of the Von Loffler stones. I've handled diamonds for thirty years, and I'd swear to that."

Jo Gar sighed. "And it was lost, while Señor Ferraro's cabin was being ransacked," he said slowly.

The Third Officer said in a hard voice:

"Two of us have gone through everything he has in there. The purser is still detaining him, telling him there is a mistake in his passage papers. But we're through—we have found nothing."

Captain Haroysan regarded Jo with narrowed, dark eyes.

"Señor Gar has traced this one diamond," he said. "I think it should be his affair."

Jo smiled. "That is good of you," he said. "I can think of only one way."

The captain of the *Cheyo Maru* said quietly:

"You will need assistance?"

The Island detective smiled with his thin lips pressed together. He ran brown fingers across the skin of his forehead, then shook his head.

"I do not think so," he said very softly. "It is difficult to tell."

Fallibar said grimly: "There has been a murder, and your life has been attempted—"

Jo Gar smiled at the diamond expert who was returning to the States. The *Cheyo Maru* rolled sluggishly in the seas kicked up by the tail end of the typhoon.

"I shall not need assistance," he said firmly. "If the captain will instruct the purser not to detain Señor Ferraro longer, I shall wait a little while, and then go to his cabin."

The Third Officer said: "But he will notice, perhaps, that the bar pin has vanished."

Jo Gar smiled with his almond-shaped eyes on the swaying walls of the Captain's office.

"I am very sure that he will," he agreed tonelessly.

WHEN JO GAR rapped lightly on the door of Ferraro's cabin it was almost six o'clock. The one in white called again:

"Who is it?"

Jo Gar said: "Señor Gar."

The door was opened and Jo went inside. He was smiling a little.

Señor Ferraro was dressed in white trousers and a white shirt. He wore slippers. He said in a rather sharp voice:

"I have been in the cabin only a few minutes. A mix-up in my passage papers, and the purser is very stupid. But when I returned here—that bar pin had disappeared."

Jo Gar stood with his back to the door and extended the palm of his right hand towards Ferraro. He said quietly:

"I have the honor—to return it."

Ferraro's face got hard. He took the pin, stared at it. He said, in a surprised tone:

"But now—there are *two* stones missing!"

His lips were twitching; he was breathing hard. Jo Gar nodded almost pleasantly. He put his right hand in a pocket of his palm beach coat.

"We removed one of them—one was already missing," he said.

Ferraro stared at the Island detective. He said nastily:

"'We' removed one?"

Jo nodded again. "Mr. Fallibar aided me," he said. "He is a diamond expert—an acquaintance of the captain."

He watched the little jerk of Ferraro's body. The man in white was fighting for control. But he said in a hard, rising voice.

"But *why*—did you remove one?"

Jo Gar shrugged. "It was one of the Von Loffler stones," he replied. "I noticed a difference in the color, when you showed me the bar pin. I had Mr. Fallibar inspect it. The stone we removed is one of the ten missing ones—and quite valuable."

Ferraro said hoarsely: "It's a mistake! How would that pin have been lost—in here—"

Jo Gar stopped smiling. He said patiently:

"It *wasn't* lost in here, Señor Ferraro."

He waited, watching the fear in Ferraro's eyes, watching the man's attempt at control. Then he said in an easy tone:

"A Malay that I shot in Manila was dying. He told me to find 'the one who walks badly—always in white.' I wanted to know who the leader was—of the ones that robbed Delgado's store. I came aboard this ship—when I learned *you* were coming aboard, Ferraro!"

Ferraro said hoarsely: "You're—mad, Gar! You think I—"

His voice broke. Jo Gar nodded and moved his right pocket material a little.

"I think the Malay made a mistake, Señor Ferraro," he said. "You were *not* the leader of the diamond thieves. But you had been with the Constabulary, and you could aid them. You were valuable, and for your services you received one diamond. A very valuable stone."

There was a sneer across Ferraro's face. Jo Gar said:

"You were not worried about me being aboard. Perhaps you were offered a bigger reward—for my death. You wanted to create a mystery, and to show me that you possessed nothing of value. You did not work alone. You thought that a safe way to carry your diamond was in the cheap pin. And you used it to attempt throwing me off the trail. But you wished to kill, also. You bribed the deck steward—and he told you I was asleep. You fired three shots at what you thought was Señor Gar, and you got away. You wore dark clothes—and threw them overboard. Then you were in white—a man in white."

Ferraro said hoarsely. "That is a lie! I did not—"

Jo Gar said: "It is not a lie. The dark coat did not get clear of the vessel. It caught over an open port, just above the waterline—"

Ferraro's voice was almost a scream. He cried:

"You lie—you lie!"

Jo Gar said grimly: "I think that the first shot knocked the mask to the deck—you knew you had failed. You were afraid—and you went forward and knifed the deck steward so that he could not talk—"

Ferraro made a swift movement of his right hand. Jo Gar squeezed the trigger of his automatic. The *Cheyo Maru* was rolling—the bullet struck the mirror above the wash basin. Ferraro's gun cracked—wood spurted from the door behind Gar.

The Island detective fired again. Ferraro's body jerked; his gun arm dropped. He slumped slowly to his knees, swayed for a minute, rolled to the left as the vessel tilted in the rough seas.

Jo Gar said slowly: "You were too sure—you were not suspected, Ferraro. Too certain."

The man in white turned his head a little. Jo Gar moved forward and got the gun away from him. He said in a steady voice:

"You tried to be careless—with that bar pin. But you showed it had value."

Ferraro groaned. "That—damned coat—" he breathed in a tearing voice.

Jo said: "I was bluffing, Ferraro—it didn't catch on the port. Who were the others? Who was the one who planned the diamond steal—"

Ferraro's face was splotched with red. Blood was on his lips. He said thickly:

"It was that—"

He was coughing, his face twisted. Jo bent over him. Ferraro's eyes were staring. He muttered thickly:

"The blind—Chinese—Honolulu—you can find—"

His muttering died. There was a convulsive shiver of his body. In the corridor there was the sound of foot-falls, voices. Jo Gar bent down, straightened again. He braced himself against the ship roll, opened the door. The Third Officer stared past him, at the body of Señor Ferraro.

He said: "He *was*—the one—you were searching for!"

Jo Gar shook his head. But he didn't speak. The words of the dying Malay had helped. He was wondering if the last words of Ferraro would help, too. And he was making certain that he would remember them.

The Blind Chinese

Jo Gar, the little Island detective, finds strange things happen at the house of the blind Chinese.

IT WAS just a little time after dusk. There was a crescent moon half-hidden by the jagged peak of the Pali; a cool breeze blew through the garden not far from the Royal Hawaiian Hotel. Jo Gar relaxed in the wicker chair in which his diminutive body rested. But his gray-blue eyes were alert; they watched the mild ones of Benfeld, the Honolulu representative of the Dutch Insurance Company. Benfeld sipped his cool drink and said with a slight English accent:

"Herr Von Loffler had cabled me. It was in code and therefore quite safe. We are interested, of course. My home company insured the diamonds. A terrible crime."

Jo nodded his head. "The murders were incidental," he said in his toneless voice. "The one who planned the robbery perhaps thought it could be accomplished without a killing. He was mistaken. Delgado's son was murdered in the jewelry store. There was the bank guard, who was killed outside. And then Juan Arragon, my friend, who was in pursuit. An attempt was made to murder the American chief of police. In Manila he is not too well liked. I was forced to shoot a Malay, and he spoke of a 'man in white—who walks badly.' I traced such a man aboard the *Cheyo Maru*."

Benfeld said grimly: "And you were forced to shoot him to death. But you learned something."

Jo Gar widened his eyes slightly. He had only told the insurance representative certain things, not too much.

"Very little," he corrected.

Benfeld shrugged. He was a tall man, with a long face and blond hair.

"You recovered one of the diamonds," he said.

Jo Gar sighed a little. He smiled and straightened in his wicker. Palm trees swayed beyond the garden, and yet Honolulu was not like

Manila. It was cooler, less tropical in a sense.

"Señor Ferraro was a fool," he said placidly. "The Malay who spoke of him might have thought he was the important one of the bandits. But he was not. Perhaps he talked with the Malay, who I think was one of the robbers. But Ferraro was given only one of the ten Von Loffler stones."

Benfeld relighted a thin cigar and nodded his long head very slowly.

"And you have said he tried to murder you, on the *Cheyo Maru,*" he said.

The Island detective nodded. "In Manila—many people have tried to murder me," he said simply. "The stolen diamonds are worth more than two hundred thousand dollars. There was a diamond expert on the boat, by chance. He has valued the diamond I recovered from this Ferraro at in excess of twenty thousand dollars. It is one of the Von Loffler stones, of course. I think, had Ferraro succeeded in murdering me, he would have received another."

There was a flickering light in Benfeld's eyes. He said very softly:

"Who would have given it to him, Señor Gar?"

Jo Gar got a brown-paper cigarette from a pocket of his light-colored suit coat. He smiled with his almond-shaped eyes almost closed.

"Ferraro died during the fourth day out from Manila," he said very softly. "I spent the remaining days in attempting to associate him with some other person on the boat. It was a failure."

Benfeld frowned. Gray smoke curled upward from his thin lips. He was silent for several seconds.

"Then, as it stands, Señor Gar—" he said thoughtfully—"you have recovered one of the Von Loffler stones. You are thousands of miles from Manila. And you have completely lost the trail of the others."

Jo Gar closed his eyes. It was peculiar—the way Benfeld regarded the situation. It was almost as though the Dutch insurance representative was pleased. He was certainly extremely inquisitive. He *had* received a cable from Von Loffler, there was no doubt about it. And Jo considered that the German owner of the nine missing diamonds had been foolish, even though he had sent the message in code. But then, this man seated across from him represented the company that had insured the diamonds. That company would suffer a severe loss if they were not recovered.

He had not answered Benfeld's question— the long-faced one said quietly:

"Of course, I understand that your friend was murdered. Juan Arragon. And also that Señor Delgado wishes to bring to justice the person that murdered his son. And already you have recovered one diamond. But the trail—"

His voice died away; he frowned and shrugged. Jo Gar opened his eyes and smiled at the Dutchman.

"The trail is lost," he said simply. "There are nine diamonds still missing. They are worth almost two hundred thousand dollars."

Benfeld cleared his throat and said in a tone that was so careless Jo noticed it:

"If this Ferraro—had only spoken, before he died!"

Jo Gar inhaled smoke from his brown-paper cigarette. He lifted his glass with stubby, brown fingers. He sipped a little of the cool liquid.

"It would have helped—very much," he said simply.

He looked towards the swaying palm trees and remembered the words that Señor Ferraro had used. Benfeld did not know of those words, and he would not know of them. The man was getting at something.

The Dutchman shook his head and sighed heavily. He said:

"The company will investigate, of course. But it will be very difficult, I fear. And what are *your* plans, Señor Gar?"

Jo Gar shrugged. "The *Cheyo Maru* remains in port until noon tomorrow," he said. "She will be in San Francisco within six days. I shall make the voyage aboard her. Only a few passengers disembarked here—and I have made quite certain they are not involved."

Benfeld said slowly: "Of course, you have had much time to learn who was landing."

Again there was the peculiar tone of his voice. It was almost as though he were slightly amused. But the next second he was frowning, shaking his long head.

"The nine Von Loffler stones!" he murmured. "And diamonds are so simple—to hide away."

Jo Gar nodded and said wearily: "It will be good to sleep on shore tonight. Ship travel tires me. I think I shall retire, after a brief drive about."

He waited for the obvious offer. But it did not come. Benfeld lived in Honolulu; he had brought Jo to this garden from the small hotel in which he had taken a room. Yet he was not offering to drive him about for a short time.

Jo Gar waited in silence. Finally Benfeld said:

"I was trying to think of some way—I have an engagement it will not be possible for me to break—"

The Island detective said protestingly: "Do not even consider it."

Benfeld said suddenly: "Of course, I have it! You will use my car. I shall get other conveyance. In the morning we shall meet again."

He smiled cheerfully. Jo Gar protested. But Benfeld would not listen to him.

"Better still—" he said, and his voice died away as he frowned thoughtfully. Then he said with a smile: "I have two cars. You will remain here, Señor Gar—and I will drive to my appointment. It is a monthly affair, an important one. I will then send my chauffeur to you, with the other car, the open one. I will drive my own, when I return home, which will be late. In the morning I will come to your hotel."

Jo Gar bowed a little. "You are very good," he said softly. "You are very kind."

Benfeld glanced at his wristwatch and rose to his feet. He called a Chinese waiter and insisted upon paying for the drinks. Jo Gar rose and they shook hands. Jo said:

"Of course you realize you must be discreet about this affair—"

Benfeld said sharply: "Of course, Señor Gar. I think you have done very well. I will have my chauffeur return here within twenty minutes, say. You will not be too chilled in an open car?"

The Island detective shook his head. "I would like an open machine," he replied. "It is very good of you."

Benfeld smiled. "You will be able to see more of the Island," he said. He bowed. "Until tomorrow, then."

Jo Gar bowed a little. "Until tomorrow," he agreed.

The Dutchman went slowly from the garden, towards the palm-studded street. He walked erectly, with his shoulders thrown back. He bowed to two men seated at a small table in the garden. Then he was lost from sight behind a high, tropical hedge. Jo Gar reseated himself and called the waiter.

"Iced claret," he ordered.

He slumped in the wicker and watched the crests of the palms sway in the breeze. It was true that he was many miles from Manila. But other things were not so true. Perhaps he had lost the trail of the remaining nine Von Loffler diamonds—perhaps not. The thing that Benfeld did not know was that Señor Ferraro had used a few words, lying on the floor of his cabin on the *Cheyo Maru.* Most men, when they felt death coming close, used words. And Ferraro had said: "The blind Chinese—Honolulu—you can find—"

That was all he had said. And in the city of Honolulu, with a tremendous Chinese population, there would be more than one Chinese who was blind. But that did not mean that the trail was lost.

The waiter brought the iced claret. Jo Gar sipped it and smoked another cigarette. He thought:

The Dutchman, he is well established here. He perhaps has a fine reputation. But why did he question me so? And he has not a poker face. He is not experienced in these things. There is much that he would like to know, yet he has an important engagement. And my boat is sailing at noon tomorrow.

Jo smiled a little, with his lips pressed together.

"And he feels I would enjoy riding in an open machine," he murmured softly.

Music from a stringed orchestra reached his ears. It was the soft, lazy music of the Hawaiians. The Manila detective nodded his head very slowly.

"There is a possibility"—he half whispered, looking down at his drink—"that he is correct. I shall very soon see."

SOME TWENTY minutes later a waiter came to Jo Gar's table and said that his car was just beyond the garden. Jo thanked him and paid for the drink. He went slowly to the street in which the palms rose. The car was a short distance from the garden entrance. It was a small car, well polished. It seemed of an old make. The driver was a short Chinese. He wore a white coat that was several sizes too large for him, no hat. His trousers were not so clean as his coat. He smiled, showing broken yellow teeth, and bowed awkwardly.

"Señor Gar?" he asked.

Jo frowned. He thought first that Benfeld was a fool, using his name to a servant. And then he smiled with his eyes. He nodded.

"Yes," he said in English. "You are Señor Benfeld's chauffeur?"

He spoke slowly and clearly. The Chinese nodded his head. He said:

"It is so—I am—chauffeur."

Jo Gar nodded. He looked into the rear of the open car. The seat was clean, but the floor mat was not so clean. The top was back, and the sides of the car were low. It was not unlike many other cars Jo had noticed—cars that were hired out to tourists on the Island.

He stepped inside as the driver held the door open. He said:

"I do not care to go far from the heart of the city. Along the beach, and past the old Palace of the—"

He checked himself. The chauffeur was trying desperately to understand his English. He had spoken fast, but not too fast. And this man had spoken first in English.

Jo Gar sighed a little. He said very slowly:

"We will go—where you wish. You have been told—where to take me?"

The driver's face lighted. He jerked his head up and down, showing his broken teeth again.

"Me told—what do," he said cheerfully. "Me know—where go."

Jo smiled and nodded. The driver got into the front seat. When the car moved forward it jerked and made much noise. It reminded Jo of the car owned by himself, back in Manila. And the chauffeur was hardly the sort one might expect Benfeld to have.

The Island detective sat back in the seat. The streets were not too well lighted; as the car moved along the lights grew fewer, and there were not so many hotels. The foliage was thicker. There was a cross-roads ahead, and Jo was sufficiently familiar with Honolulu to know that the beach was to the right. But the driver turned the car jerkily to the left. The road grew narrower, and the houses far apart. There was the sweet odor of the foliage, and in the distance the slopes of mountains.

Jo Gar leaned forward and said above the clatter of the machine:

"I would prefer—the beach road—"

The driver jerked his head a little and nodded. He said in a shrill, raised tone:

"Me come—back along beach. He tell me—go by mountain road first—"

Jo Gar sat back in the seat and got his Colt from the holster under his left thigh. He smiled a little, but it was a grim smile. Once he turned in the rear seat, raised himself slightly and glanced behind. There were no lights of another car, but he was not reassured. The road on which they were driving was growing narrower. It was rough, and there were no shoulders.

Suddenly the headlights went out. They came on again almost instantly, then were extinguished. Jo's body was rigid; he could see that the driver was leaning forward slightly, back of the wheel. The lights flashed on. The car was moving slowly up a fairly steep grade. Foliage was thick on both sides of the road.

The Island detective leaned forward and called sharply:

"You have trouble—with the lights?"

The Chinese jerked his head around, nodded. His almond-shaped eyes held a hard expression; they seemed to glitter. His lips were drawn back. The car slowed down, halted. The Chinese used the emergency brake gratingly. He turned his head all the way and said shrilly:

"Him go bad. You wait—me fix."

He slid from the seat back of the wheel, got to the left side of the car. He went swiftly towards the headlights, which seemed to be showing dimly. Jo Gar was leaning forward in the seat, his gray-blue eyes narrowed.

He heard the other machine before he saw it. There was the roar of an engine—the car seemed to be speeding up the far side of the slope on which the car in which Jo was seated was resting. There were no lights, but the engine roar was increasing in sound.

The Chinese heard the roar, too. He stood near the lights, his small body rigid. He called shrilly:

"Me need—stick. Me get—him!"

His body swung around; he moved towards the right side of the road, the thick foliage. As he neared it there was a flare of light beyond the crest of the slope. Headlights of the approaching car had been suddenly switched on. But they slanted high, above the standing car and above the road.

The Chinese driver's body crashed through the foliage; his back was turned to Jo as he went into it. The Island detective moved with surprising swiftness. In a flash he was out of the car. He ran, in darkness, his small body bent low, to the left side of the road, dived into the thick foliage. Branches and leaves struck against his outflung arms. He went to his knees, let his body drop flat. Back of him the road was suddenly yellow-white with the glare from headlights.

There was the increasing roar of the car engine. And then the staccato beat of the guns. Metal made sound, and there was the shattering sound of glass. The air was filled with the clatter—Jo Gar could hear the bullets pounding into the body of the car.

The engine roar had diminished momentarily. Now it increased in volume. The clatter of the guns died away. There had certainly been more than one gun, and they had been machine-guns. Few bullets had missed the car in which he had been seated.

The engine roar became a hum as the car from which the bullets had been loosed sped back towards the heart of Honolulu. Jo Gar lay motionless, listening to the decreasing sound. His Colt was gripped in the fingers of his out-flung right hand.

He moved about very quietly, pulling his body nearer the road and parting the foliage a little. He could see the machine now. There was light from the stars and crescent moon. The windshield was shattered, both headlights had been shot out. He could see bullet marks along the side facing him. The rear left tire was flat.

In the distance the engine of the departing car was making only a faint hum sound. Jo Gar smiled with his lips and kept narrowed eyes on the foliage ahead of the bullet-filled car, across the road. He half whispered:

"Machine-guns in Manila. And now here. Methods of the Western world, these are!"

There was faint sound from the foliage across the road. He saw the short figure of the Chinese chauffeur appear, crawling. The man glanced towards the car, then slowly straightened his body. For several seconds he stood motionlessly, looking towards the battered machine. Then his head turned; he glanced in each direction, along the road. He listened intently.

There was no sound of another car. The hum of the speeding one had died away. Jo Gar guessed that the spot was a deserted one, one from which the noise of the machine-guns would not reach habitation.

The Chinese chauffeur moved slowly into the rough-surfaced, dirt road. He stood for a few seconds in front of the car, then walked around it. He stood with his back to Jo as the Island detective rose and lifted his Colt a little. The Chinese moved closer to the car, getting up on his toes and peering towards the floor at the rear.

Jo Gar stepped from the foliage to the roadbed. There was crackling sound as he did so, and the driver's body swung around. His eyes went wide with fear as he stared at Jo. His breath made a whistling sound and he cried out shrilly in his native tongue.

Jo said quietly: "I was not—in the machine, you see."

He smiled a little. The Chinese was staring at the gun now. His lips were drawn back from his teeth; his face was a mask of fear. Jo said:

"I think—you must die—for what you have done."

He moved the gun up a little, and forward. The chauffeur started shrilling words in his native tongue. His body was shaking. Jo said:

"Stop it! You are not Benfeld's chauffeur. This is not Benfeld's car. It is a hired car. Perhaps your car. Will you answer my questions?"

The Chinese was staring at him. He jerked his head up and down.

The Island detective said slowly: "You will certainly die, if you do not answer me truthfully. Who were those in the machine that just passed? Those who used the guns?"

The Chinese shook his head. Jo Gar smiled with his almond-shaped eyes almost closed. He repeated the question in stilted Chinese, a tongue with which he had difficulty, in spite of his many years in Manila.

The driver said: "Me—not know!"

Jo Gar said, moving a little closer to the chauffeur:

"The Dutchman, Benfeld—he went to you and paid you money. Very good money. He told you that you were to act as his chauffeur. He furnished you with a new coat, though there was no time to make it fit. He told you where to drive me and how to signal with your headlights. He said you must then stop the car—and hide yourself. Is this not so?"

He had spoken very slowly and clearly. The chauffeur nodded his head. He said:

"He do not—tell me more."

Jo Gar nodded and smiled grimly. He was thinking that Benfeld had taken a big chance. And yet, he had almost succeeded. There had been only a few seconds' time between life and death—for Señor Gar.

The Island detective stopped smiling. He moved his gun hand a little.

"I think you must die," he said steadily. "You would have killed me—"

The Chinese shook his head and shrilled words. After a few seconds he spoke more slowly. He said that he did not know that the big guns were to fire into the car. He did not know what had been about to happen. He was a poor man, and Benfeld had offered him much money.

Jo Gar cut him off, after a little time.

"I will give you a chance," he said slowly. "There is a person I wish to see. He is Chinese. And he is—blind."

He saw instantly that the chauffeur knew of such a man. And he saw that the man was of importance. But the driver shook his head.

"There are—more than one—blind Chinese in—"

Jo Gar interrupted again. "There is one of some importance," he said. "Think carefully. Perhaps this one has a place where dishonest men go. Perhaps he is not a good person. Think well, for you are young to die."

He spoke very slowly, and with no smile on his face. He held his Colt low and slightly forward of his right side.

The Chinese driver stared at him wildly. But he did not speak. Jo Gar said:

"Very well—I shall find him alone. But first I must silence you, so that you do not again interfere with me."

The chauffeur threw out his hands. They were browned, and the fingers were jerking, twisting. He said:

"I know—him! I go—his place—"

Jo Gar lowered his Colt slightly. He nodded his head and smiled. His voice was almost toneless when he spoke.

"You are wise—we shall go there together. We shall walk to a spot where perhaps we may obtain a ride. You will do as I say, and if you make one, slight mistake—"

He moved the Colt a little. The Chinese driver's facial muscles were twisting. He was breathing quickly. He said:

"Tan Ying—he is very bad. Even if he does—not see—"

Jo Gar nodded. "Many men are very bad," he philosophized quietly. "But after they are *dead*—how do we know what then happens?"

The driver half closed his staring eyes. He said in a shrill, shaken tone:

"If I take you to the place—they will kill me."

Jo Gar shrugged. "And if you do *not* take me—*I* will kill you," he said. "It is a difficult position."

The driver said: "I am a poor man—"

The Island detective nodded. "Then you have less to live for," he replied. "Let us start."

THE HOUR was almost midnight when Jo Gar and the Chinese chauffeur moved through the teeming streets of the Honolulu Chinese quarter. There was the sound of discordant music—the shrill, reedy notes that came down from rooms beyond balconies. The section was well lighted in spots, very poorly lighted in others. Jo Gar kept his body close to that of the chauffeur, and his Colt within the right pocket of his light suit coat. At intervals he let the weapon press against the chauffeur's side.

They turned suddenly into a narrow alley that wound from the lighted street. There were few lights in the alley; the section was very quickly a poor one. The shops were squalid and dirty; no music came down from the rooms beyond the balconies.

The street curved more sharply at the far end. The Chinese at Jo's side said thickly:

"It is—there—"

He pointed towards a narrow entrance, an oblong cut in unpainted wood. Strips on which letters were scrawled in Chinese, hung on either side of the entrance. Streamers of painted beads hung from the bamboo pole at the top of the entrance; they obscured the store beyond.

Jo said softly: "You will go—first—"

The driver's face was twisted, but he forced a smile as his browned hands shoved aside the beads. They made a rattling sound; Jo followed into the shop. A kerosene light made odor and gave little flare. There was the usual musty, aged smell of such shops. Baskets were about, with nuts in them—and jars contained brightly colored candy. There were shelves with boxes marked with Chinese lettering.

No one was about, but at the rear of the store was another bead curtain. The Chinese driver glanced towards it. Jo Gar said in a half whisper:

"Do as you—were told."

The chauffeur raised his voice and called in a shrill voice:

"Tan Ying!"

A quavering voice replied, from the room beyond the second curtain. It said:

"Welcome, Dave Chang!"

Jo Gar smiled grimly. The Americanization of the Chinese never failed to amuse him. He touched Chang lightly and pointed towards the beads of the curtain.

The chauffeur said in Chinese: "You are alone, Tan Ying?"

Ying replied that he was alone. He asked that the driver would enter his humble abode. Chang moved towards the beaded curtain and Jo Gar followed him. He was very close to him as they passed through the beaded curtain into the rear room. Two kerosene lamps were burning, but there was a clutter of objects in the place. Buddha's figure was in a corner; the light from the nearer lamp struck the face from an angle, making the figure seem very life-like.

Tan Ying was an aged Chinese. He sat cross-legged, but there was some object against which his back rested. He was obese and fat faced. His eyes were open but sightless. They shone whitely as he stared towards Chang. It was almost as though he were inspecting the chauffeur.

Jo Gar stepped soundlessly to one side of the beaded curtain. He took his Colt from his right-hand pocket, held it low at his side. He breathed as quietly as possible. But it was not enough. Tan Ying said quietly, steadily.

"You are not alone, Dave Chang."

He spoke in his native tongue, and Chang sucked in his breath sharply. He twisted his head and looked at Jo. The Island detective smiled and nodded.

Chang said: "It is my Spanish friend, Mendez. He has arrived on the boat today."

The blind Chinese nodded his fat face. His face was expressionless, except that his sightless eyes gave it a strange intenseness. He said:

"Welcome, Señor Mendez!"

Jo Gar spoke in Spanish. "You are good to welcome me, Tan Ying."

The Chinese smiled; he was almost toothless. The wick in one of the kerosene lamps was low; it flickered now and then. There was a little silence. Then Jo Gar said to the chauffeur, in Chinese:

"Will you speak of the business?"

The chauffeur's body stiffened. He said very softly:

"You are expecting the Dutchman, Tan Ying?"

Tan Ying's fat body rocked a little from side to side. His lips tightened. He said:

"Why do you speak of him?"

Jo Gar said: "It is because I am to meet him— in Honolulu, Tan Ying. That is the reason."

The lips of the fat Chinese relaxed a little. A clock chimed, and Tan Ying listened to it. He said, after a little silence following the chimes:

"The Dutchman—he is already late."

Jo Gar sighed a little. He moved his body and turned so that when Benfeld came in he could easily cover him with his weapon. The driver was looking at him with tortured eyes; Chang was feeling fear.

The blind Chinese said suddenly, in very precise English:

"It has gone well, Dave Chang?"

Jo Gar felt his body stiffen. The driver nodded his head, and looked at Jo again. The Island detective nodded and smiled.

Chang said: "It has gone well, Tan Ying."

The blind Chinese smiled again. His body continued to rock from side to side. There was a small screen near the print-covered wall at Jo's back. It was perhaps four feet high, and as many long. It was within several feet of the wall. Jo Gar moved quietly to it, stood close to it. He raised his gun a little and nodded at Dave Chang.

The chauffeur hesitated. Jo Gar's face grew hard; he narrowed his gray-blue eyes. Chang said:

"Señor Mendez will be of use to the Dutchman, Tan Ying."

The blind Chinese stopped swaying. He said in his native tongue:

"It may be so."

There was the sound of beads rattling, at the entrance of the shop. The blind Chinese stiffened, and Dave Chang half turned his body. Jo Gar raised his weapon, leveled it at the chauffeur. Then he stepped behind the screen and bent downward. He got his right eye near a section crack. There was little light on the screen. From the outer room there was the sound of tapping. He counted a half dozen taps; they were soft and well spaced.

The blind Chinese raised his voice and said:

"It is the way of the Western lands—"

There was the sound of footfalls. The beads of the inner curtain rattled and Benfeld came into the room. He straightened, looked sharply about. He said in a hard tone, in English:

"You—Chang—what was it that happened?"

The blind Chinese said softly: "Dave Chang—he has told me it is well."

Benfeld said fiercely in English: "He lied! When we got back there, after ten minutes, there was no body in the car. You—Chang—"

The chauffeur said hoarsely, fear in his voice:

"I do not know—what happened! I did as I was told. I signaled with the lights, and when I saw the beam of your car—I ran to the foliage. When I returned, there was no sign of Señor Gar. I swear it."

Benfeld said grimly: "What did you do? Why didn't you stay near the car?"

Chang replied in a shrill tone: "I was frightened. One of the bullets from your machine—it almost struck me. I went into the foliage, wandered around. Then I remembered that we were to be here at twelve."

Benfeld drew a deep breath. He kept his right hand out of sight in the pocket of a light coat he was wearing. He had on a soft hat, pulled low over his face.

The blind Chinese was muttering to himself. He stopped it and said:

"Señor Mendez is here, you see."

There was a little silence. Jo Gar watched Benfeld stare about the room. There was a puzzled expression on the Dutchman's face.

The right pocket of his coat moved a little. There was fear in Chang's eyes, but he did not look towards the screen. Jo Gar's body was tense, but he waited. Benfeld said in English:

"What is this? What do you mean?"

The blind Chinese seemed to sense that something was wrong. His head did not move, but he spoke very softly and very calmly.

"Dave Chang—he brought with him Señor Mendez. I have spoken with him, but a few minutes ago. Chang said that he would be of use to you."

With his one eye back of the section crack, Jo Gar watched Benfeld move away from the chauffeur. He saw the glint of steel as the Dutchman's gun came out of his pocket. Chang was breathing rapidly; fear was gripping him. Benfeld's eyes went about the room in a swift glance. The low-wicked lamp sent light wavering over the walls.

Benfeld said: "By God, Chang—you've tricked us—"

The Chinese chauffeur said in a shrill voice:

"No—it is not so! I have not—"

Jo Gar raised his Colt and got the muzzle within a half inch of the section crack. Benfeld was in a line, but beyond the Chinese chauffeur. He had his long face lowered a little; his eyes were slitted on Chang's. He said:

"By God—you have. I've told you too much. I've been a fool. But I've got you—in here. Gar had those diamonds on him. He got them from Ferraro. He lied to me. You took them from him—"

The blind Chinese said in his native tongue, his voice calm:

"Be careful—there is this Mendez—"

Benfeld's eyes went around the room again. He said savagely:

"There's no one else in here. If Chang said there was—he was lying to you, Ying. Or else he was—"

The chauffeur said in a shrill voice:

"I did not—steal the diamonds! That is not so—do not shoot—"

A knife was suddenly in the right hand of the seated Chinese. He held it out, his sightless eyes gazing straight ahead. He said calmly:

"Be careful—is not a knife better?"

Benfeld said in a low, hoarse voice: "I tell you—Señor Gar had the diamonds. He lied to me. Was I not informed that Ferraro was bringing them? Gar lied. Either he was trying to get away with them, or he wants them for himself. And you—"

The chauffeur said shrilly: "When I reached my car—he was not there—"

Jo Gar watched Benfeld, with thoughts running through his brain.

Benfeld figured that he had the diamonds, had gotten them from Ferraro and had lied to him. But did that mean that Ferraro had had more than one stone? Did it mean that someone on the *Cheyo Maru* had received the others, after all? Had Ferraro lied to him, dying?

Benfeld was staring at Dave Chang. He said very quietly:

"Why did you say Mendez was here? Why did you tell Tan Ying that?"

Jo Gar held his breath. He expected Chang to break any second now, to fail under the strain. He was between two guns, and he knew it. Jo had already gotten information from him; he had spoken of Mendez, and Jo Gar had forced him to use the name. The chauffeur was in a tight spot, but surely he must realize that if Jo Gar were to go down under the lead from Benfeld's gun—he would have a better chance. He had talked, because Jo had forced him to talk. But with the Island detective dead—

Tan Ying said in the same passive voice:

"The knife—it is better."

The body of the blind Chinese was swaying again. Benfeld said in a harsh voice:

"Very well—throw it at my feet, Tan Ying."

The knife fell several feet from Benfeld, but the judgment of the blind man was not bad. Benfeld glanced down at it, but did not move.

"Why did you say that Mendez was here?" he asked again.

The blind Chinese said steadily:

"You do not hear me, Benfeld. I tell you someone—*was* here! I talked with him—"

The eyes of Benfeld were slitted on the screen now. Jo Gar held the muzzle of his gun steady. The chauffeur said weakly:

"It was Mendez—we met in the Street of the Lanterns. He was coming—"

Benfeld swore hoarsely. "Then where is he now?" he asked very slowly.

The Chinese driver made a little movement of his left hand. A browned finger pointed towards the screen. He said at the same instant:

"I do not know—he went out—"

The gun in the hand of Benfeld slanted a little. Jo Gar looked at it, squeezed the trigger of his Colt. When the gun jerked and the room filled with sound, he hurled his body to one side.

The bullet from Benfeld's gun struck the wood of the screen, and then the wall back of it. Jo Gar pulled himself to his feet and swung around. Benfeld was sinking to the floor—he half raised his weapon. The blind Chinese said in a high-pitched voice:

"Dog of a—"

Benfeld's gun crashed again. The aged Chinese screamed and pitched forward. The gun dropped from Benfeld's right hand. He said thickly:

"The dead—do not—talk—"

His right hand reached out and groped for the knife the blind Chinese had tossed near him. Jo Gar said sharply:

"No—"

But it was Dave Chang who suddenly moved forward, bent down. He was screaming shrill words that had little meaning. His right-hand fingers were almost on the hilt of the knife when Benfeld gripped him, pulled him down. With a sudden, last strength the Dutchman raised the knife and struck. Jo Gar fired again, as the Chinese chauffeur groaned and rolled on his back.

Benfeld sat up a little and stared at him. There was red on his lips.

"Dead men—do not—talk—" he repeated weakly.

He lowered his head into outstretched arms and shivered a little. Then his body was motionless.

Jo Gar went to him first. He was dead. The knife had struck into the chauffeur's throat. He was trying to mouth words, but they did not come. And Jo Gar knew that they would never come again. He turned towards the blind Chinese. But he knew before he touched him that the man was dead.

There was a babble of voices beyond the two curtains of painted beads. Jo Gar went swiftly into the outer room. He thought, for a second, of trying to get away, of merging into the crowd of Chinese.

But already the crowd was thick, and there would be police. He would be seen trying to get away, and there would be difficulties. It would be better to work *with* the police, to attempt explanation.

He lighted a brown-paper cigarette and leaned against the counter. Faces were beyond the beads that rattled from hands that swayed them. Benfeld had expected the diamonds to be brought to him. They had not come. He had thought that Jo possessed them. The blind Chinese had known things—and the driver of the car riddled with bullets had known something. Dying, Benfeld had silenced them both. Even at the end, he was protecting someone.

The Island detective moved his lips a little. He said questioningly: "Who is Mendez?"

When the first of the police entered the shop, Jo Gar had almost finished his brown-paper cigarette. The police officer was small and brown faced. He was breathing heavily. He said:

"What—is it?"

Jo Gar gestured towards the second beaded curtain, and the room beyond it. He said in a tone that was weary:

"It is—death."

The police officer said: "Robbery?"

Jo Gar smiled with his eyes looking towards the curtain, shrugged his narrow shoulders. "Perhaps," he said simply. "But very surely—it is death."

Red Dawn

Jo Gar, the little Island detective, waited with killers for the coming of the red dawn in Honolulu.

BARRINGTON REGARDED Jo Gar with frowning, dark eyes. He was tall, immaculately dressed, fresh-looking. He was the power and brains back of the native Hawaiian police force, and it was very evident that the Philippine Island detective's calm annoyed him.

"I strongly advise you to return to your ship, Señor Gar," he said slowly.

Jo Gar smiled with his thin, colorless lips. His almond-shaped eyes seemed sleepy, but were not sleepy. And Barrington sensed that. He stretched his long legs, rose from the wicker chair of his office. But he did not move about. He stared down at Jo.

"Ten extremely valuable diamonds—stolen in Manila," he said quietly. "You have got one back—but nine are missing. You were forced to kill the man from whom you recovered the one, on the *Cheyo Maru*. That was unfortunate."

Jo Gar nodded his head just a little. "Very unfortunate," he agreed. "But also—very necessary."

Barrington shrugged. "Perhaps you were too aggressive, Señor Gar," he suggested.

Jo Gar smiled a little more broadly. He shook his head very slowly.

"I am never aggressive, Señor Barrington," he returned very quietly. "Manila is a city of heat—heat breeds laziness."

The American made a peculiar, snorting sound. He turned towards his desk and glanced at the report of the Hawaiian police, made less than a half hour ago, at midnight.

"Benfeld, Tan Ying and Dave Chang—all dead. And you are not aggressive?"

Jo Gar shrugged almost casually. "Benfeld was the representative of the Dutch company that had insured the diamonds. For some reason he wished me to stop my search for them, and for the thieves who murdered to get them. He attempted to trap me. He used Chang for that purpose and Chang suffered. The blind Chinese, Tan Ying—I am not sure how he was involved. I think there was to have been a meeting at his place. More than one person was concerned in the Manila robbery and murders. Perhaps there was to be a meeting at Ying's place. But Benfeld thought I had been shot to death, on the road beyond the city. I upset his plans—and there was sudden death."

"Triple death," Barrington said steadily. "You are sure you learned nothing?"

Jo Gar rose from his straight-backed chair. He lied impassively.

"Nothing—that seems to lead me anywhere," he said. "It is like that Street of the Lanterns where Ying lived—much color and sound, and so difficult to see or hear beyond either color or sound."

Barrington half closed his dark eyes. He said very grimly:

"You are known to be in Honolulu, Señor Gar. It is known that you are after the Von Loffler diamonds, and that you seek the murderers of your friend Juan Arragon—and of that jeweler's son, Delgado. Already there has been death. And dawn is hours away. I should strongly advise—"

Jo Gar's lips made a clicking sound. "You have already suggested that I return to the *Cheyo Maru,*" he said calmly. "It is kind of you to think of my protection. Perhaps I shall accept your advice."

Barrington continued to frown. "I hope so," he said. "We will do everything possible, here. You will be in San Francisco in six days—and I wish you luck."

Jo Gar smiled and bowed. They did not shake hands. The Philippine Island detective reached the street and kept his brown right-hand fingers in the right pocket of his light coat. A cool breeze swept from the direction of Pearl Harbor. The streets were almost deserted.

The Island detective smiled with his almond-shaped eyes almost closed, moved slowly in the direction of the docks. They were not far from the building in which Barrington had his office. And as he walked, with his eyes glancing sharply from the corners, Jo Gar sighed. His stubby fingers tightened on the grip of the automatic in his right coat pocket.

"Señor Barrington does not wish more death—in Honolulu," he murmured very softly. "He is anxious for my departure—he thinks of my health."

Jo's white teeth showed in a swift grin. It faded, and he reached with his left-hand fingers for one of his brown-paper cigarettes. The street became suddenly an alley; his eyes caught the slanting masts of ships, their rigging beside the docks. He was ten feet along the alley when he halted, struck the match. But even as the flare dulled his vision, he saw the shape that slid from the doorway less than twenty yards distant. He heard the swift intake of the short man's breath, saw the right arm go upward and back!

The Island detective moved his left hand away from his face, let his short body fall forward. As he went down his right hand shoved the material of his coat pocket ahead of him—started to squeeze the trigger.

But there was no hiss of a knife hurled through the air, and no crack sound from his automatic. He relaxed his grip, rocking on his knees, as he watched the figure of the man who had slid from the doorway bend forward. The man's head was held low—his body was almost doubled as he pitched downward. He choked terribly but weakly—there was a sharp crack as his head battered against the broken pavement of the alley.

Jo Gar swayed to his feet. He moved back into the darkness of a narrow doorway on the opposite side of the alley from that where the short one had fallen. He waited, his back flattened against a wooden door that did not give, holding his breath.

The man who had collapsed made no movement. His head had struck heavily, but Jo knew that he had been unconscious before he had fallen. And yet, when he had slid from the doorway across the alley, his movements had been swift and sure. He had sucked in his breath, drawn back an arm. And Jo was sure there had been a knife in his hand.

Minutes passed. There were the faint sounds of machines, in the direction towards the city center, away from the docks. A cool wind rustled some paper down the alley. It was quite dark, and Jo could not see beyond the body of the man. Once he had heard foot-falls in the distance, and the sound of high-pitched voices. The alley was on the edge of the Chinese quarter, perhaps in it.

His right forefinger pressed the steel of the automatic trigger—the material of his right pocket was held clear of his side. But he made no movement. Five minutes passed. Jo Gar shivered a little. He was sure that death had come to the one across the alley from some spot directly behind him—and that the person who had caused the death was waiting silently, for some other movement in the narrow alley.

He breathed slowly, carefully. His right wrist was aching from the tensity of his grip on the automatic, and his eyes moved only from the motionless figure on the pavement to the blackness of the low doorway behind the figure. The shacks along the alley appeared to be closed, deserted. But the entrances existed—and in the one almost opposite him was the human cause of another person's death. Unless—and there did not seem much chance of that—there had been an escape through the shack beyond the motionless, sprawled figure.

The Island detective listened to the shrill whistle of a small boat, beyond the docks. He relaxed his body a little, but suddenly it was tense again. He had heard, very distinctly, a faint chuckle. It had not come from the doorway in darkness, beyond the collapsed figure, but from some spot above him.

He raised his head slightly. The shacks were low—less than fifteen feet high. Clouds were over a crescent moon; the night had become dark. But he could see nothing on the roof of the shack opposite.

And then, very softly and quietly, the voice sounded. It was low and throaty—and very calm.

"Señor Gar—you are comfortable?"

Jo Gar did not move his body. There was a quality to the voice, an accent of grim amusement. He had a definite feeling that he was trapped—that the death of the man across the alley had been a part of the trap. He did not speak. The voice sounded again—from above, and to the left. The roof of a shack on his left and on his side of the alley held the speaker, he guessed.

"You will kindly disarm yourself—step into the alley, Señor Gar."

The Island detective raised his automatic higher, withdrew it from the right pocket. He moved only his right arm. The voice said, after a short pause:

"Do not be a fool, Señor Gar!"

The accent was clear. He had heard the same accent of precise English in Manila. It was Spanish—this man's native language. And the speaker was calm—very calm. He was sure of himself.

Seconds passed. Then the voice said, a little more loudly:

"*Si,* but very low, and—now!"

Jo Gar heard the steely hiss of the knife. He drew his legs together. The left trouser material, just above his ankle, was jerked sharply. Wood made dull sound as the knife blade cut into the door at his left side. His body was rigid.

The voice somewhere above said with sharp amusement:

"Señor Gar—you are comfortable?"

The Island detective sighed. The cat played with the mouse, but more wisely than most cats. Jo Gar reached down, jerked the knife loose from wood and cloth. He tossed it into the alley. Straightening, he said as steadily as he could:

"What is it you wish, Señor Mendez?"

Again there was the chuckle. And then a short silence. Jo Gar was thinking: It is Mendez. Chang said, before dying in the shop: "It was Mendez. We met in the Street of the Lanterns. He was coming—" That was what Chang had said. Mendez coming to meet someone, in Honolulu. Perhaps the one in white. The one Jo had been forced to shoot to death, on the *Cheyo Maru,* and from whom he had got the one Von Loffler diamond. But Mendez knew that Jo had killed, and he had trapped him now, and was toying with him, grimly amused.

The Island detective stood motionless, looking at the body across the alley. The voice from above came quietly:

"Kindly disarm yourself—step into the alley, Señor Gar."

Jo sighed again. He bent forward and tossed the automatic into the alley. There was a flashlight beam that picked it up, then faded. Jo stepped from the doorway, moved out a few feet. The voice said:

"Face towards the docks."

The tone was hard now, sharp. Jo did as directed. He stood for seconds, his eyes slitted, his body slightly relaxed. He expected death at any moment, from behind. But it did not come. There were sounds on the roofs of the shacks, sounds behind him. But he did not turn. And then the same, hard voice sounded, directly behind him.

"Go to the alley end, walk slowly. There will be a closed car. Enter it. I shall be near you, and I advise you to be wise."

The Island detective moved slowly forward. The alley narrowed, then widened. At the dock end there was a small, dirty machine. It was closed, and there was the fat, brown-yellow face of a Chinese faintly lighted by the instrument board light. The man did not turn his head, but a rear door of the machine opened as Jo neared it. The voice, now close behind, said:

"Step inside."

Jo got into the car. A figure made room for him. The seat had space for three, back of the driver. Jo dropped heavily beside the one already seated. The one who had spoken got in and sat on his right. The interior of the car was very dark, but Jo saw that the man's features were sharp, his face long.

He said to the driver, in an easy tone:

"Yes—and do not go too fast."

It was as though everything had been carefully planned. Jo tightened his lips. He was sure that the one on his right was the man known as Mendez, and he was sure that Mendez was hard and extremely clever. He had been followed from the police station to the building in which Barrington had an office, and Mendez had waited. Perhaps something had gone wrong, and there had been a death in the alley, or perhaps nothing had gone wrong, and it had been part of the scheme of things.

The man on Jo's right said softly: "It will not take very long, I hope, Señor Gar."

Jo smiled a little. He nodded his head. "You are Señor Mendez?" he asked.

The man was tall and thin. He had long, slender-shaped hands and wore a dark coat. That much Jo could see as the car moved slowly along the street by the docks.

He said: "*Si*—Señor Mendez. There have been words about me?"

The Island detective turned his head towards Mendez. He spoke very steadily.

"Chang spoke of you—and Tan Ying."

The grim quality returned to Mendez' voice again. He spoke very slowly.

"And both Ying and Chang are dead. That is too bad."

Jo Gar smiled, showing his white, even teeth. Then his lips pressed together.

"So many people die—for diamonds," he observed.

Mendez nodded. His face was turned towards the driver's back. The machine was running slowly out of town; it was not going towards the beach, but through the poorer section of Honolulu.

"It is so," Mendez agreed. "But you are a curious one, Señor Gar. Even so—why should *you* die—for diamonds?"

The Island detective said nothing. He tried to keep his body relaxed, but there was a threat in Mendez' words. It was a question that Mendez asked, and yet only half a question.

The machine was out of the town now; it was running through the tropical growth, and there was suddenly a moon showing through the clouds.

Mendez made a gesture with his long right hand. He said almost cheerfully:

"It is pretty, Señor—these warm countries. They make one want to live."

The Island detective kept his eyes to the front. For almost five minutes the car moved at good speed over a road that was fairly smooth. Then it slowed, turned abruptly to the left. The road became narrower. It was of dirt now, and the country was rolling. The moon seemed strangely bright for its size—and the car passed through what appeared to be a pineapple plantation. The one on Jo's left let his body rock with the car motion, but he did not look at the Island detective.

Mendez made another gesture with his right hand.

"It is not unlike the Philippines," he said slowly. "You would like to return some day, Señor Gar?"

Again there was the mocking quality in his voice. Jo turned his head, and the two regarded one another. Mendez' skin was a light brown color; his eyes were dark. They were cruel eyes, and intelligent. The man's features were good, but his lips were very thin and the curve of his mouth was barely perceptible. He had a sensitive face—but it was also a brutal face.

Jo Gar said steadily: "Yes—I should like to return—some day."

Mendez nodded. "It will not be difficult for you," he returned. "You are not—a fool."

The car jerked suddenly off the road. It ran a short distance, scraping foliage, so narrow was the path it traveled. It stopped. The one on Jo's left leaned forward and looked at Mendez, but he did not speak. Mendez said:

"That is all—but stay."

The door on the left was opened. Mendez said pleasantly, as the one to whom he had spoken descended:

"We will leave the machine, Señor. I have a gun in my right hand. There is a small plantation house just beyond the car. Will you walk towards it?"

Jo Gar let his eyes widen a little on the dark eyes of the Spaniard. He said quietly:

"You can murder me here—just as well, Señor Mendez."

For a second he saw sardonic amusement creep into the thin-faced one's eyes. And then a puzzled expression showed. But he knew that Mendez was acting now.

"Murder you?" The Spaniard laughed in a chuckling way. "Why do you think of murder, Señor Gar?"

The Island detective smiled. "Does it seem so strange?" he replied. "After all—you are aware of the Von Loffler diamonds. For them there has been much murder."

Mendez nodded, his face suddenly serious. "That is so," he agreed. "But you were not satisfied."

Jo Gar's gray-blue eyes showed no expression. "Not satisfied?" he said very tonelessly.

Mendez frowned. "At the house we can talk more easily," he said. "Please descend."

Jo Gar shrugged. He got from the car, saw the thatch-roofed house through the thinned foliage, up a slope a short distance. There were windows, but no lights. The house was well protected from even the narrow path. The dirt road was a hundred yards or more distant, and the other road perhaps a half mile.

The Island detective moved slowly up a path that wound. He heard Mendez instruct the driver to turn the machine and take it down near the dirt road. As he walked slowly up the slope he heard the engine of the car changing speed. Twice the brakes made squealing sounds. There was no sign of the one who had been seated on his left.

He was certain of one thing—Mendez held death for him. Perhaps there was information that the Spaniard wanted first. Perhaps he would make promises. But in the end there would be death. He could read it in the dark eyes, feel it in the cold amusement of Mendez' voice. And it was in the mockery of the Spaniard's words, too.

Behind him he heard the Spaniard's footfalls, very close. He moved slowly, and he was thinking fast. There was a better chance outside, here on the path, than there would be within the thatch-roofed plantation house. If he could take Mendez by surprise—

The Spaniard said almost pleasantly: "It is the fine view that Señor Benfeld liked here. The dawn—it is all red. The sun rising from the water—"

He let his voice die. He was breathing a little heavily now. Jo Gar said, suddenly stopping and breathing as though with difficulty:

"Benfeld tried to kill me, Mendez. He was a representative of the insurance company handling the Von Loffler stones. He thought I would be off my guard, because of that. How much was he offered—for my death?"

Mendez said cheerfully: "Enough, Señor Gar. But he was a fool—and not careful enough. He knew that you were trained in hunting down people, yet he was careless."

Jo Gar moved slowly up the slope again. He was breathing very heavily, though he was not tired. Behind him he could hear Mendez. And he was sure that the Spaniard was not pretending. He slowed his pace just a little, spoke haltingly.

"I will make—a bargain with you—Señor Mendez. If you will let me—have the chance—"

He uttered the last word softly, easily. And then, like a cat, he let his body swing around— he leaped at the figure of the man behind and several feet below him on the path!

But even as his short body shot through the air—he knew that he had lost. He saw Mendez' body stiffen—the features of the long, sharp face were twisted into a mask of hate. The Spaniard's body swung to one side. His right hand went up and then came down. Something gleamed dully in it. The first time it struck Jo a glancing blow on the shoulder. But as his hands and knees hit the earth—it struck him again, in a second chopping motion. Pain streaked across the back of his head—the yellow light of the moon became a curtain of black. He lost consciousness.

THE ROOM held little furniture, and what there was of it was bamboo. There was a table and two chairs, and between the windows a small bookcase. Mendez stood near the bookcase, his back to the wall of the house that was little more than a shack. The lamp on the table had a faulty wick, or the oil was bad. The light was faint and uneven. Shadows were on the walls. Mendez said in a conversational tone:

"You are lying, Gar. You have been lying for an hour. And there are few hours left to you. You were successful, in the Islands—but the Philippines are not like these islands. They are hotter—and the brain of that breed is stupid. You killed a man, on the *Cheyo Maru.* And that man had with him ten diamonds. They were worth more than two hundred thousand dollars. You tell me you found only one of them. You are lying."

Jo Gar slumped in one of the bamboo chairs. Pains stabbed across his head. The gun that Mendez used was a heavy one, and the Spaniard had struck him with a savage motion. There was blood on the Island detective's face, and on the fingers of his right hand. He was tired. Three times in the last hour Mendez had struck him. Once the one who had sat on his left in the car had struck him—he was a Chinese with a stupid, typical face. He sat in a chair and watched the Island detective now, his eyes expressionless. The driver of the car was not in the plantation shack.

Jo said thickly: "I have told you the truth, Mendez. From the one in white—the one the Malay spoke of before he died, in Manila—I got only one diamond. It was he who told me of the blind Chinese. That was why I went there."

Mendez' sharp face held a dull hatred now. It was clear that he did not believe the man who had tried to trick him on the sloping path that led to the plantation shack. Jo Gar knew that he had lost much, in that attempt. But he also knew that from the beginning Mendez had determined to kill.

The Spaniard said in a toneless voice: "You are a fool, Gar. For years you have been lucky. But that was with Chinks and Island half-breeds. I will tell you something—because now it will not matter. Either you are lying—or two others are lying. On the *Cheyo Maru* were three persons who might have had the Von Loffler stones. The man you murdered was one of them. But the diamonds were not separated. One person had the ten of them. That was agreed upon. And you got one from the man you killed. Which means that you are lying. You got them all."

Jo Gar shook his head. "Only one," he said steadily. "How do you know the truth of what you say?"

Mendez smiled. "I was one of the three persons—aboard the *Cheyo Maru,*" he said steadily. "I did not travel first-class. I did not have the diamonds. The man you killed had them—all ten of them. And you have them now. You are a fool—because they will do you no good."

The Island detective pulled his short body up a little. He said very slowly:

"There was—the third man—"

He watched Mendez' eyes narrow. But the Spaniard shook his head.

"I said that either you lie, or two others lie," Mendez said grimly. "I am one of those two others, and I do not lie. And the other one—she is—"

His body stiffened; for a second rage showed in his eyes. And then suddenly, as though he remembered that it would not matter, he relaxed. He smiled grimly. Jo Gar widened his almost colorless eyes.

"A woman—" he said very slowly. "There was a woman who—"

His own voice died away. Mendez smiled coldly. He lighted a cigarette.

"It makes no difference to you," he said. "You have killed one of the three who might have had the diamonds. I tell you that I was one of the three, and I did not have them. A woman was the other. *You* say you have one of the stones. *I* say you have them all."

Jo Gar said thickly: "Then why did I go to the shop of the blind Chinese?"

Mendez continued to smile. "That is simple," he replied. "Benfeld, who had told us much about the diamonds because he was in Holland when they were insured, and because he needed money which we gave him, was desperate when told that if he did not help us he would be exposed. He attempted to have you murdered, but he worked crudely, and you were suspicious. You avoided our guns—but you knew that there was a blind Chinese in Honolulu who was important. You were curious. You had the diamonds, but you wanted the thieves, the killers. And you were lucky—until you left Barrington."

The Island detective shook his head. Mendez was about to bargain with him, to make an offer—a final offer. He knew that. But Mendez would not bargain honestly. He could not. There had been three persons on the *Cheyo Maru*—three who were important. And one had been a woman. One was Mendez. The other was dead. Jo Gar had recovered one diamond—nine were missing. Yet he believed Mendez in one thing—the Spaniard was convinced that the man he had killed had possessed all of the diamonds, and that the Island detective had them now.

Jo Gar said slowly: "I tell you the truth, Mendez. Ten diamonds were stolen in Manila. I have recovered only one of them. I do not think the man I killed had more than that one. I believe you—you have none of them. The woman has tricked you into thinking—"

The Spaniard moved across the room and struck him heavily over the face. He stepped back, rage in his eyes. The Island detective pressed his lips tightly together. Mendez backed across the room. He took his gun from a pocket, stared at Jo. His eyes flickered to those of the Chinese, and he suddenly became thoughtful.

Jo Gar's tongue touched his lips and tasted blood. His brain was working clearly, in spite of the blow. He had something to work on now. Benfeld had given information that had led to the thieves tracing the diamonds, learning where they were. Three had got away from Manila aboard the *Cheyo Maru,* and one was a woman. He had not thought about a woman.

He muttered very softly: "It is *she*—who has the other nine stones. In some way—she got them, leaving the man in white only one—"

His muttering stopped as he watched Mendez' eyes slit on his. The Spaniard was smiling with his thin, straight lips—but his eyes held a cold hatred. He looked at Jo Gar, but he spoke to the Chinese.

"You tell driver—no need him. You take rifle and go where I show. Driver go back to Honolulu— keep quiet or it be bad. You stay with rifle ready. You know what I tell—much gold for you. Good?"

The Chinese rose and grinned. He said in the same doggerel manner:

"Good."

He showed red gums as he grinned at Jo Gar. Then he went from the plantation shack, closing the door back of him. Mendez waited several minutes, and then glanced through one of the windows that faced the east. The shack was almost atop a rise—the moonlight seemed brighter now.

Mendez said tonelessly: "For you—it will be a—red dawn, Señor Gar. One way or the other. If you tell me the truth—you will watch the sun come up from the path and go back to town. If you refuse to do that—you will go out of this room—and the Chinese with the rifle—"

He broke off, shrugged. Jo Gar said wearily:

"I have told you—the truth."

The Spaniard walked to within a few feet of him, stared down at him.

"One of Tan Ying's men tried to knife you tonight, Gar," he said slowly. "That was hate. He did *not* knife you because he was knifed first. I used him—to help me. Two hundred thousand dollars is more money than I need. Half of that is sufficient—for me. The other half—that is for you."

Jo Gar stared at the Spaniard. "And—the woman?" he said slowly.

He watched Mendez' facial muscles twitch. But the thin-faced one showed his teeth in a smile.

"I will—see to her," he said slowly, softly.

Jo Gar shook his head. "You could not—run the risk of allowing me to go free, Mendez," he said steadily. "If I gave you five diamonds—you would kill me—very swiftly."

Eagerness showed in the Spaniard's dark eyes. He took a step nearer Jo.

"I swear to it—by the name of—"

His words died; rage replaced the eagerness in his eyes. Jo Gar was shaking his head slowly. The Island detective said:

"I have recovered—only one stone."

Mendez reached down and struck him across the left temple with his right fist. Jo pulled himself up from the chair, but was battered down again by a sharp blow. He slumped low, groaning. Mendez moved away from his chair.

There was the sound of a match striking, and a little later Jo smelled the odor of a cigarette. He rocked his head from side to side, but did not look up. Mendez said grimly, harshly:

"You will have—until dawn. And then you will go outside—walking. The Chinese is less than fifty yards distant, with the rifle. I will remain inside until the sound of the shots has died. The Chinese will go away—after he has seen you fall. It is all—very simple."

Jo Gar raised his head slightly. He wiped red from his face with the back of his right hand.

"That will not get you—the Von Loffler— diamonds," he breathed thickly.

Mendez pulled on his cigarette, leaned against a wall of the plantation shack and smiled.

"If you go to your death—that way—I will believe you," he said. "Then I will know where to look. But she has never—"

Jo Gar tried a grim smile. "She has never— lied before?" he muttered. "Women are often—like that. There must be—the first time. And white glass—worth thousands—is a reason for—lies."

Mendez pressed his lips tightly together. "You've tricked—too many men, Señor Gar," he breathed. "I hate you for that—and I do not believe you. You have the diamonds—ten of them."

Jo Gar raised his eyes. Suddenly his body stiffened. He said weakly:

"I do not think—they are worth it. But five— that is too many—to give. I will—give you—three—"

Mendez dropped his cigarette and crushed it with his shoe sole. He took rapid steps to Jo's side. His eyes were shining.

"You will give—five!" he snapped.

The Island detective stared at him stupidly. But he shook his head from side to side. Mendez swore and struck at him savagely. The Island detective let his head fall low; he closed his eyes. Mendez struck him again, then moved across the room.

"By dawn," he muttered hoarsely, "you will give me—the five!"

Jo Gar said weakly, his eyes expressionless:

"And what proof have I—that you will let me go away from here—safely?"

Mendez shrugged his shoulders. He was confident of winning. He felt that Jo was breaking down; it had been a long night. Ten diamonds—perfect and of large carat. Two hundred thousand dollars! The Island detective could read his thoughts. He was so sure of winning, so sure the man in the chair before him possessed the diamonds.

And Jo was thinking of a woman—of the third of the three who had held up the Delgado jewelry store in Manila, and one of those responsible for the death of his friend Juan Arragon. She would be one of many women aboard the *Cheyo Maru,* which would leave Honolulu for San Francisco at noon—but he knew that *he* would not be aboard the boat that had brought him from Manila.

Mendez would see to that. The Mendez who stood before him now, mocking and battering him. The Mendez who was convinced that he had the ten Von Loffler diamonds, and who had already told him too much.

"Red dawn"—the Spaniard had said. There had been a mockery in those words, too. His lips shaped themselves into a bitter smile as he remembered the advice that Barrington had given him—advice to return to the *Cheyo Maru.*

Mendez said very slowly: "Well—there is an end to this, Gar. I will give you five minutes. The sun is getting up. I have much to do. If you swear to me—"

Jo Gar got unsteadily to his feet. Mendez regarded him with a twisted smile. The Island detective was unarmed and very weak. And once before tonight he had failed to surprise the Spaniard. Mendez said grimly:

"Steady—you are not accustomed to being— knocked around—"

The Island detective said thickly: "I do not want to die, Mendez. I will tell you the truth. But you must swear to *me*—that I will go free."

Mendez' eyes showed eagerness again. But the next second they had narrowed, and held a hard expression.

"I swear to you—that you will go free—if you tell me where the diamonds are."

Jo Gar nodded his head. He knew that no matter what he said he would not go free. He raised his head and looked Mendez squarely in the eyes with his bloodshot ones.

"I *did* get them—from the one—on the boat," he said steadily, softly. "I have had them—with me—*on* me. But in the car—it seemed very bad. I was—afraid. I had them in one of my Manila cigarette packages, mixed with a few cigarettes—"

He paused, swayed a little. Mendez stepped in very close to him. His voice was shaking.

"In your—cigarette package!" he breathed fiercely. "You had them—"

Jo Gar nodded as Mendez' voice died. He said weakly, brokenly:

"The Chinese—on my left. He had a sacklike coat. I slipped the cigarette package—in a pocket—his right pocket."

Mendez swore sharply. He muttered angrily:

"The Chinese—"

His body swung away from Jo Gar instinctively. His fingers clutched at the knob of the door that opened on the path. And then, suddenly, he remembered. There was the rifle.

His body started to turn, but even as he threw up his arms in protection, Jo Gar swung outward and downward with the chair he had lifted from the floor. All his remaining strength was in the swing. Wood crackled as Mendez' arms were battered downward—the bamboo was not heavy, but Jo had found power for his final chance.

The Spaniard's arms swung loosely—his head fell sideways under the impact of the blow. He staggered back from the door, his eyes staring. And in a swift movement Jo Gar had the door opened.

Mendez struck at him weakly—the Island detective had little power in the blow that caught the Spaniard on the right shoulder, spinning him around. But it knocked Mendez off balance—he plunged towards the opened door. He was almost to his knees as his body angled beyond the plantation shack.

The first shot crashed. There was a second—and then two more. Jo Gar stood motionless, listened to two more shots from the repeating rifle. Then there was silence, and later a crashing in the foliage below the shack.

After a long minute the Island detective went outside and made certain that Mendez was dead. Then he went back into the room. It was all red with the rising sun. He sat in a chair for a few minutes. He got a package of Manila cigarettes from a pocket and lighted one. He thought of the woman a man who was now dead had spoken about. Five minutes later when he stepped over the body of Mendez to leave the plantation shack he did not look down. But as he went down the path towards the road he muttered thickly:

"He did not lie—about two things. The Chinese was waiting—with his rifle. And the dawn was—very—red."

Blue Glass

Jo Gar, the little Island detective, finds that bullets often come with diamonds-when the diamonds are stolen ones.

WHEN THE cabin phone made a buzzing sound, Jo Gar was dozing. A soft, warm breeze blew in through the port; the *Cheyo Maru* was some seven hours away from the Hawaiian Islands—and Honolulu. The diminutive detective sat up wearily and turned his bruised face towards the French phone. When he spoke his words were low and precise: "Yes—this is Señor Gar."

The voice at the other end of the wire was flat, almost expressionless. It was low and a bit throaty.

"You would give much, Señor—to recover the other nine Von Loffler diamonds?"

The questioning note was very faint, but the words had an immediate effect on Jo Gar. His small body stiffened; he sucked in his breath sharply. There was silence at the other end of the line. Jo said, finally:

"Yes—much."

There was another silence. Then the voice sounded again, with no more expression.

"How much, Señor Gar?"

The Philippine Island detective narrowed his gray-blue, slightly almond-shaped eyes. He said very quietly:

"I do not appreciate jokes. Many aboard this boat are naturally aware of my identity. Quite a few men have died because of the Von Loffler stones. If you are—"

"I am not joking." For the first time there was some tone in the other's voice. "I have information that will be of value to you."

Jo Gar said steadily: "Then pardon me. If you will allow me to talk with you in your cabin—"

For the second time there was an interruption. The other's words were sharp now—very sharp.

"I have asked you a question, Señor Gar. I am aware of many things concerning the Von Loffler stones. Ten were stolen from the jewelry shop in Manila. You have recovered one. Your friend Juan Arragon has been murdered. You have killed—and others have killed. You believe that the nine missing stones are aboard this vessel, and that a woman has them in her possession. Is it not so?"

The Island detective closed his eyes. "It is as you say," he said simply. His mind was working very fast; his head was clear enough.

The voice continued: "You very narrowly escaped death more than once—in Honolulu, Señor Gar. The missing stones are worth almost two hundred thousand dollars. I can tell you that the one who carried out the orders of Benfeld, and who was responsible for murders that included your friend Arragon—that person is aboard the *Cheyo Maru.*"

There was a pause. The voice said: "Speak, please, Señor Gar."

Jo Gar smiled with a touch of grimness. "I am still in my cabin, Señor," he replied.

The other said: "That is wise. You will be wiser not to attempt tracing this call. It will prove useless."

The Island detective said: "Perhaps that is so."

There was a short silence. Then the other said in the same, flat voice:

"You would be well rewarded if you were to return to Manila with the missing stones, and the murderer, Señor Gar. There would be rest for you. That is why I ask the amount you would be willing to pay."

Jo Gar said slowly: "I am a poor man."

The other's voice became sharp again. "You have been fortunate, Señor Gar. In the States it will be different. And the diamonds will not be difficult to sell."

The Island detective's voice held a grim note. "They are very fine stones, and perfectly matched. By this time they are very well known. Perhaps they would be extremely difficult to sell."

Impatience was evident in the voice that came from the other end of the wire.

"You are not a fool—you know the stones will not be difficult to dispose of, Señor Gar. You know they will be smuggled through the customs officers. And in San Francisco you will lose the trail you were lucky enough to pick up. Even if you should blunder on—"

The voice died. Jo Gar said grimly: "All this being so, why do you call me?"

The voice said: "I do not care what becomes of the nine diamonds, or of a certain murderer. I need money. I call you to give you the chance, the big chance. You have traveled many miles, Señor Gar."

The Island detective spoke in a low voice. "How do I know that you will direct me to the right person?"

The voice held a hard note. "I do not expect you to trust me, señor. You may pay after you are convinced."

The Island detective was silent. The other said:

"The question is—how *much* will you pay?"

Jo Gar replied steadily: "There is a reward of ten thousand dollars offered by the owner of the Manila jewelry shop, whose son was killed. I imagine the insurance company would pay twenty thousand dollars for the return of the stones."

"No—that will not do." The other's voice was steady. "That is all in the future. I must have payment now. If I do not have it—the murderer and the diamonds will vanish when the *Cheyo Maru* arrives at San Francisco. That is all."

Jo Gar spoke gently into the French phone mouthpiece. His eyes were almost closed.

"I do not carry thousands of dollars about with me. I am a poor man."

The voice said calmly: "You are known to the captain of the boat. I am not asking much. Five thousand dollars, and one half of your reward, when you receive it, Señor Gar. And I am not to be betrayed."

Jo Gar widened his eyes and smiled. "You are only to betray," he said grimly.

The other's voice was very low and hard. "That is—quite so," he said. "You agree?"

The Island detective stopped smiling. "I agree," he said simply. "I will pay five thousand dollars to you, in the manner you direct, after the stones are recovered and the murderer is under arrest. I will give you half of my reward when it is paid. I am very tired. Your identity will not be known, only to me."

"No," the other said. "It will not be known to you. I will trust you. If you do not pay, I will kill you. That will be very simple, since you will not know against whom to guard."

Jo Gar said tonelessly: "Yes—very simple."

There was a short pause. The other's voice was very flat when it reached Jo's ear again.

"In Cabin C. 15 there was a woman named Jetmars. She has with her a little girl of about eight. She got aboard at Manila, and dresses in black most of the time. Possibly you have seen her."

The Island detective said steadily: "Yes—I have noticed her, and the little girl."

The voice said: "In her cabin or on her person, or on the person of the little girl—are the diamonds. When you have obtained them I will communicate again with you. I will know the time."

Jo Gar said, "And she is also a murderess?"

The voice replied flatly: "Yes."

There was a clicking sound, and when Jo spoke again there was no answer. He hung up the receiver, threw a light robe about him and hurried from the cabin. When he reached the small cabin that held the *Cheyo Maru* switchboard, he was breathing swiftly. A Chinese boy stared at him with dark, long eyes.

"I am Señor Gar," Jo said softly. "An important call just reached me in Cabin B. 10. I would like very much to know where it came from— what part of the boat."

The Chinese boy said easily: "I remember making the connection. It came from one of the three phones in the men's smoking room."

The Island detective smiled a little wearily.

"Thank you," he said, and moved back towards his cabin. Inside, he removed his robe, lighted a brown-paper cigarette and lay flat on his back, blowing thin streams of smoke towards the cabin ceiling. There was very little motion to the boat.

"Curious," Jo murmured. "A woman who dresses in black. A little girl. And the one who gives me the name tells me the woman is a killer and possesses the stones. He would share a large reward with me, and he will kill me if I refuse to pay his share. He is very careful—"

The Island detective sat up slowly as the phone made a buzzing sound again.

"Señor Gar," he said.

The flat voice came clearly. "I told you it would be useless to attempt tracing the call, Señor. You have made a bargain. If you do not stick to it—"

Jo Gar said grimly: "You will kill me?"

The other replied: "Yes."

The Island detective was silent for a few seconds. Then he said:

"In that case you will be able to collect the diamonds and the reward. You will not have to share anything."

There was a tight-lipped smile on his face as he spoke. But the one at the other end of the wire said sharply:

"It is simpler for you to do—than for me. That is why I made an offer."

Jo Gar inhaled smoke from his cigarette. "Look about the smoking room," he suggested. "Is there a short man present—rather heavy? Smoking a cigar—very black?"

The man at the other end of the phone chuckled. It was a dry, rasping chuckle.

"Thinking, that such a person might be present, I am not making *this* call from the smoking room," he said almost pleasantly. The switchboard boy will tell you I am calling from the sun deck, port side."

Jo Gar said: "Pardon—I shall make no further effort to learn your identity."

The other chuckled again. "Thank you, Señor," he mocked. "But even should you change your mind—it will be of no use. A pleasant trip—and good fortune."

Again there was the clicking sound. Jo Gar went away from the cabin phone, frowning.

"I think the gentleman is a liar," he muttered very softly, "but I can not afford to simply think. As for this being a pleasant trip—"

He squeezed the brown paper of the cigarette with stubby fingers, raised his narrow shoulders very slowly in a half shrug.

"He is too wise for that," he said with finality. "It will be extremely unpleasant—for one of us."

ON THE third day out the *Cheyo Maru* was rolling a bit; spray was breaking over the prow and there were not too many passengers on the decks. Jo Gar stood near the starboard rail, well aft, and watched the woman in black and the little girl who accompanied her. The woman was middle-aged, had a rather sharp, sunburned face. The child was not very pretty. She was stringing beads. The woman paid little attention to her, and none to the other passengers. Jo had been watching her closely for two days, and yet he had not appeared to be watching. And he had listened to many voices of men, hearing none like the one that had come over the phone. He had not expected that.

He was working under a handicap; he felt that he was being watched and he did not know the person who watched him. He had learned that the woman who wore black much of the time was named Rosa Jetmars, that she had come aboard at Manila and that the child was her daughter. The purser volunteered the information that he understood Mrs. Jetmars was Spanish, had married an American in the Islands. Her husband had died very recently. His body was not aboard the vessel, but it was thought that his widow was going to the States and his family. That was all the Island detective had learned. It had little to do with the nine missing diamonds.

Someone near the rail called attention to a school of flying fish. It was a large one; the little girl jumped from her deck chair, started towards the rail. She tripped, fell awkwardly, crying out. Beads scattered and rolled across the deck. Jo Gar started forward, but an elderly man had already lifted the girl. Something blue rolled and struck against Jo's right shoe. The woman in black was bending over the girl. She seemed angry. She spoke in Spanish and very rapidly. Her back was turned to Jo.

He leaned down and picked up the bead. It was peculiarly cut, for a bead—touch told him that instantly. He glanced at it, his eyes narrowing. Several men were picking up other beads from the deck surface—much fuss was being made over the child. The woman in black had taken her back to her chair, was talking rapidly to her. Jo Gar slipped the bead in his pocket and stared at the vanishing school of flying fish.

When he glanced towards the woman in black again she was still talking to the child. Men were putting beads in the girl's lap. There was laughter now, and the woman in black did not seem so angry. After a few minutes Jo Gar went below, locked his cabin door and got the one Von Loffler diamond from its tiny pocket in the cork of one of his medicine bottles.

He compared it with the bead, which was blue. His lips parted and he said very softly:

"The cutting is—exactly the same!"

An hour later, in the captain's cabin, he had the diamond expert who had helped him earlier in the trip examine the bead. When the expert had finished his examination he said in a puzzled voice:

"It is exceptionally well cut—diamond cut. Nothing cheap about the cutting. A great deal of care has been taken—for a piece of blue glass."

Jo Gar said slowly: "There is no doubt but what it is glass?"

The expert smiled at him. "Not a bit—it is blue glass, cut as a fine diamond might be. A good-sized diamond. Like, say, one of the Von Loffler stones you—"

Jo Gar's frown stopped him. The captain raised his head and stared at Jo. But the Island detective simply reached for the bead, slipped it into a pocket of his light suiting. He reached for his packet of cigarettes.

The captain of the Japanese liner said in his stiff English:

"It is very curious, Señor Gar—"

The Island detective showed his white teeth in a lazy smile. He nodded his head very slowly.

"Very curious," he agreed cheerfully. "But many curious facts are not too important."

The captain said: "It will not be very long before we dock in San Francisco, Señor. It has been an exciting voyage for you, and not very successful. One diamond recovered—and nine still missing."

Jo Gar offered cigarettes, lighted one. The diamond expert spoke.

"But he has this bit of blue glass—it may be that it is important."

The Island detective smiled. "In what way?" he asked.

The two others looked at each other. The captain shrugged, smiled. The diamond expert muttered to himself. The captain said:

"Each of us has our profession—yours is a difficult one, Señor Gar."

The Island detective grinned. "Often I am given unexpected help," he said. "Perhaps it will be that way—before we land."

He went towards the door of the captain's cabin, still smiling. But when he had bowed to the two men and was outside, his smile faded. He went without too much haste to his cabin, and had been inside only a few minutes when the phone buzzed. The flat voice said:

"I have additional information for you, Señor. The diamonds are to be smuggled through the customs as the child's beads. Perhaps they will be dipped in ink, or painted blue."

Jo Gar said evenly: "Thank you. But the diamonds have no holes in them—how can they be strung?"

There was slight impatience in the other's tone.

"Perhaps there will be some beads cut somewhat like the diamonds, in a box the child has. Some will be strung, but others will not be strung. It is not likely the customs officers will examine each bead in the box."

Jo Gar was smiling grimly, but his voice was serious.

"That is so. It is a clever idea."

The other's voice said: "But do not work too fast, Señor. I do not think the child has the diamonds, at present."

The clicking sound followed. Jo hung up and looked out of the port, at the roughening water. He thought: Nor do *I* think the child has them at the present moment. The woman in black was not much concerned about the spilled beads, when the girl fell on the deck. If I were to get into the cabin occupied by the woman and child, find a box of beads—I would probably find no diamonds. And yet, if I wait until the customs inspection is made—

He turned away from the port, frowning. He breathed softly:

"This one who calls—he knows so much. And yet he would share much with me. He would lose a great deal of money by doing that. The whole reward would be his if he did not—"

He broke off, and his gray-blue eyes got very small and long. After a short time he inspected his Colt automatic, slipped it into a pocket of his light coat, stuffing a handkerchief over it. When he reached deck he walked slowly towards the bow, conscious, as usual, of the curious glances the passengers directed towards him.

He circled the deck twice; the second time he noted that the woman in black and the child had vacated their chairs. A middle-aged man approached, walking unsteadily as the boat rolled. He looked at Jo, but there was no expression in his blue eyes. He had flabby, pale skin and very thin lips. They were almost opposite each other when the boat rolled more sharply. The Island detective let his small body strike the left side of the thin-lipped one, knocking him off balance.

"Pardon," Jo said. "I'm very—sorry."

He stood close to the other man, watched anger show in the blue eyes. More than anger showed, he thought. It was as though the thin-lipped one hated him fiercely, and had hated him for more than seconds.

"It was very careless of me," Jo said.

The other man's lips parted. He started to speak, but did not. A faint smile showed in his eyes; slowly his face twisted with it. He jerked his head downward abruptly, in an awkward bow. He shrugged, moved away from the Island detective.

Jo Gar continued his walk around the deck. But he did not meet the thin-lipped one on the starboard side. He did not see him again in the next half hour, and when he did locate the man he was in the smoking room, seated at a small table and with his back turned to the entrance from the port side of the deck.

A steward strolled along and smiled amiably at Jo. He beckoned to him, handed him a dollar bill. He designated the chair occupied by the thin-lipped one.

"That gentleman I seem to know," he said. "I should like you to go to the far end of the smoking room, then turn and come back. You will be able to see him. I should like to know his name. You are the deck steward?"

The steward nodded. He went into the smoking room and Jo Gar went to the port rail. When the steward returned he was smiling cheerfully.

"I placed his chair for him," he said. "He is a Mr. Tracy. He came aboard at Honolulu."

Jo nodded. "Thank you," he said. "It is not the one with whom I am acquainted."

He did a few more turns on the deck, his face expressionless. Then he went below and talked to the purser. Mr. Eugene Tracy occupied Cabin C. 82. He had booked passage at the last moment and had been forced to take a cabin on the lower deck, though he had wanted better quarters.

Jo Gar went up above and saw that the thin-lipped one was still in the smoking room. He was reading a magazine, and was slumped low in a comfortable chair. The Island detective moved close to the chair, very quietly. No other person was near the two of them; Jo spoke sharply but low, his voice holding a faint questioning note.

"Mr. Tracy?"

His words were very clear, but the one in the chair did not move. Jo stepped directly in front of the chair and looked down at the magazine that hid the thin-lipped one's face.

"Mr. Tracy?" he said again.

The man in the chair lowered his magazine. He looked at the Island detective with his blue eyes wide and questioning. Jo stared at him stupidly, shook his head.

"I'm sorry—again," he stated. "It is another Mr. Tracy I'm looking for—and they pointed you out. Please pardon me."

The one in the chair smiled almost pleasantly. He nodded his head, raised his magazine. Jo said very quietly:

"Have you the time, by any chance?"

Anger edged into the eyes of the man in the chair. Then the forced smile showed again. He shook his head. Jo bowed and moved away. As he went towards his cabin there was a half smile on his browned face. He was thinking that the thin-lipped one was a very silent person.

AFTER DINNER Jo Gar watched the thin-lipped man take the same chair he had occupied hours before, in the smoking room. The Island detective went to his cabin and changed from his dinner clothes to a dark, lightweight suiting. He wore a dark-colored shirt and was knotting a black bow tie when there was a knock at the cabin door. At his call a tall, slender man entered, closing the door carefully behind him.

"The captain said you had something for me to do," he said cheerfully. "My name's Porter—I'm an American and traveling to Frisco from Honolulu through courtesy of the line. I do ship news for a San Diego paper, and this is sort of a vacation."

Jo Gar nodded. "It is very simple," he said. "In the smoking room at present there is a man named Tracy. I will go up with you and point him out. I would like you to stay as close to him as is possible, for the next few hours, and to remember what he does. That is all. I shall be glad to pay—"

Porter smiled, shaking his head. "Not necessary, Señor Gar," he interrupted. "I'm glad to help out. And I won't talk."

Jo Gar smiled back at the newspaper man. "You would be very foolish if you did," he said. "There wouldn't be anything to talk about."

They went on deck and after walking several times around it, Jo pointed out the thin-lipped man. There was a vacant chair near him; Porter said he would go in and use it. Jo nodded.

"Do not come to me and do not speak to me if we meet later. I will speak first to you."

The newspaper man went into the smoking room. Jo passed the woman in black and the child, on the way to his cabin. The boat was rolling quite a bit and the woman looked sick and tired. She wore no jewelry and she paid little attention to the child, who trailed along behind her.

When he reached the cabin his phone was making a buzz sound. Jo Gar closed the door behind him, locked it. He lifted the instrument, said slowly:

"This is Señor Gar."

The voice was flat and low. It said: "Mrs. Jetmars is having the child attract attention to itself. She is letting passengers see that the child has an interest in beads."

Jo Gar said nothing. The voice continued:

"I point this out to you, because perhaps you do not believe she has the diamonds for which you are searching."

The Island detective said with his almond-shaped eyes almost closed:

"Perhaps it would be wise for me to enter her cabin, with the ship's captain, while she is absent. A thorough search—"

"I do not think it would be wise," the voice cut in. "But that is up to you, of course."

There was the clicking sound. Jo hung up and went to the ship switchboard room again. When he had asked the question the operator smiled cheerfully.

"The call came from Cabin C. 80," he stated. "I have been paying attention to the calls since you first asked me—"

He had been looking at a small book as he was speaking. His voice died abruptly; he widened his dark eyes on Jo Gar's expressionless ones.

"Cabin C. 80 is vacant," he said stiffly. "It is one of the poorest cabins on the ship."

The Island detective nodded his head. "The doors of vacant cabins are not always locked, are they?" he asked.

The switchboard boy narrowed his eyes. "No, Señor Gar," he replied. "They are left half-opened, for ventilation."

Jo Gar moved towards the main saloon, frowning. Too many persons aboard the boat knew too much about him; even the Chinese boy at the switchboard was now addressing him by his name. He murmured to himself:

"It becomes—always more difficult."

In the smoking room the thin-lipped one was seated in the chair he had occupied before, still reading his magazine. The newspaper man was sprawled in a chair that faced the port-side entrance to the room. Jo Gar beckoned to him, watched him rise slowly, stroll towards the entrance. The Island detective walked slowly aft, and Porter followed in the same fashion. Behind a ventilator Jo halted and lighted a cigarette. Porter reached his side.

"Well?" The Island detective's voice was very low.

Peter grinned. "You didn't expect him to move around much in *that* length of time, did you?" he replied. "He only turned two pages of the magazine."

Jo said steadily: "He never left the chair?"

Porter grunted. "All he moved was his fingers," he replied.

Jo sighed heavily. Then he showed white teeth in a slow smile.

"You have been very kind—and I shall not need your help for the present, Señor Porter."

The newspaper man looked surprised. "He wasn't the right guy, maybe?"

The Island detective made the tip of his cigarette glow in the semidarkness.

"After I left you I went to my cabin. I received a phone call that I half expected. But I expected, also, that the gentleman you were watching would *make* the call."

Porter whistled softly. "He didn't," he said. "That's sure enough. He stuck right in his chair."

Jo Gar nodded. Porter said slowly: "I'm sorry it didn't work out the other way—the way you expected, Señor Gar."

The Island detective smiled with his lips tight against the paper of the cigarette. He stood with his short legs spread, swaying with the roll of the ship. He had picked the thin-lipped passenger as the one who had called him, using the flat, peculiar tone. He had listened to most of the others talk—those who had come aboard at Honolulu.

The others he had heard before; it had been a long trip from Manila. And the thin-lipped one had failed to answer quickly, naturally to the name of Tracy. He had not spoken to Jo—had not answered his question about the time. It was difficult to disguise a voice, and Jo felt that the thin-lipped one had not made the effort. Thus he had not spoken when addressed. And yet, there had been the phone call just received—and the thin-lipped one had not made it.

Jo frowned down at the cigarette glow. Then, suddenly, his small body straightened; he drew a deep breath. Porter was watching him closely.

"You got an idea—that time," he muttered.

The Island detective narrowed his eyes on Porter's.

He spoke very slowly and softly, and his eyes held little expression.

"That is so, Señor Porter—but it is so difficult to tell whether it is a *good* idea."

The newspaper man said grimly: "If it isn't— you'll probably find out quick enough."

Jo Gar smiled narrowly. "That is the trouble," he said simply.

THE DOOR of Cabin C. 82 was tightly closed, locked. Jo Gar took from his pocket the small, adjustable key, worked with it swiftly and expertly. It was after nine o'clock, but the thin-lipped man was still seated in his chair in the smoking room. The cabin steward for this section of the *Cheyo Maru* was on the opposite side of the boat; Jo had come to Cabin C. 82 slowly and carefully. When the lock made a faint clicking sound he returned the master key to his pocket, moved the knob and slowly opened the door. He stepped inside quickly, shut the door without sound but did not lock it from the inside. The cabin was small and held the odor of cigarettes. There was little baggage about, but what there was bore the initials E.T. Jo Gar smiled a little, went towards cool-colored curtains that formed a protection for hung clothes. There was only a coat of gray material hanging behind the curtains.

"Señor Tracy is traveling very lightly," Jo observed in a half whisper.

He got his small body back of the curtains, arranging them so that he had a slitted view of the room, where they met. For several minutes he remained motionless. Then he stepped from behind the curtains and started the search. He worked very slowly and thoroughly, placing each object that he touched in the same spot from which he had raised it. Twice there was sound in the corridor, but neither time did he lock the cabin door. Instead, he got his diminutive body behind the curtains that faced the door from the opposite end of the cabin, waited.

He finished his search in a little over ten minutes, straightened and sighed. The phone made a buzzing sound, three times. Jo got his right-hand fingers over the grip of his Colt, moved behind the curtains and was motionless. Several minutes passed, and then there were footfalls in the narrow corridor beyond the cabin. A key turned in the lock—there was muttering. The door opened with a small crashing sound, but the thin-lipped one did not immediately enter. He stood in the doorway—his eyes going about the room. Through the very thin slit where the curtains met Jo Gar watched him.

His body relaxed suddenly; he entered the cabin, closed the door behind him, locked it. His eyes kept moving about. He lifted the smaller of the bags, opened it, looked inside. When he placed it on the floor again he was frowning. But the frown became a grin—a slow grin that twisted his thin lips.

"He's been in here," he said in a peculiar, flat voice. "A lot of good *that* did him!"

Jo Gar half closed his almond-shaped eyes. This was the one who had called him; he knew that now. He moved the muzzle of the Colt slightly, so that it was pointed towards the body of the thin-lipped one.

After he had drawn a small curtain across the port, the thin-lipped man placed a towel over the knob of the door, draping it so that it covered the keyhole. Then he seated himself at a small table beneath the center light, and faced the port. His left side was turned towards Jo. From a vest pocket he took a red-colored, large-sized fountain pen. His face was grim as he unscrewed an end of it. The table at which he sat had a green surface; the thin-lipped one spilled the diamonds across it very carefully. He chuckled, staring at them and poking them with a long, white finger.

Jo Gar straightened his cramped body a little. He drew the Colt from his pocket, extended it through the slit in the curtains. His eyes could count five diamonds—he thought there was another on the table surface but he could not see it.

"A hundred—thousand!" The thin-lipped one's voice was not so flat now. "And with Gar chasing the Jetmars woman—"

He chuckled again, huskily. Jo Gar said in a cold, hard voice:

"—you might easily have got the stones through the customs—"

The man at the table jerked his body straight. His right-hand palm flattened over the diamonds; his white face turned towards the curtains. Jo parted them with his left hand, stepped away from them. His face was expressionless. He held the Colt very firmly.

"But you weren't so wise," Jo said calmly and softly. "You don't know how much I knew, how much I had been told. So you thought I might be watching you, rather than the woman in black. You didn't know that Mendez had told me a woman had the Von Loffler diamonds. You called me, after she had given you the diamonds, afraid of me. The two of you gave the child beads of blue glass, cut very much like the Von Loffler stones. You wanted me to *believe* what you had suggested—that the woman in black was smuggling the stones through the customs—so that *you* could get them through without trouble. But you played too strongly."

The thin-lipped man was staring at him, breathing slowly and heavily. His right palm was still flat over the diamonds; his left arm rested on the table. The ship rolled and his body swayed with it. Jo Gar said:

"You didn't disguise your voice—and you couldn't speak to me when I addressed you, for fear of detection. That worried you. You knew you were being watched by Porter, and you had a confederate call me while *you* were seated in the smoking room. You had worked well with him, but his voice was not exactly like yours. Even so, for a little time I thought that you were not the one who had called me. And then I realized what you had tried to do—to make me believe that very thing. And I knew that you *were* the one. So I came here—for the diamonds—nine of them."

There was a little silence. The thin-lipped man said in a harsh, strained tone:

"You got to Jetmars—you scared her and— she squealed."

The Island detective shook his head. "I haven't spoken a word to her," he said steadily. "You were too worried about yourself—and too greedy. You betrayed yourself."

The thin-lipped one took his palm away from the diamonds. Jo Gar said softly:

"Please keep both arms—on the table. How many stones—are there?"

The one at the table did not speak. Jo Gar moved the gun muzzle sharply.

"Many men have died because of the stones," he reminded. "One more thief—one murderer—it would not matter too much. How many stones—have you?"

The thin-lipped one said huskily, the peculiar flat note barely evident:

"Five—the woman has—the others. Four of them. *You* have one, Gar."

There was hatred in his voice as he used the Island detective's name. Jo said softly:

"I would not lie—where are the other four stones?"

The thin-lipped one said savagely: "I tell you—the woman in black—she has them. She would not give them all to me. She is the one who—"

The Island detective smiled coldly. His gray-blue eyes were almost closed.

"Raise your arms," he said slowly, "Keep them raised. If you do not—"

He made a swift—strangely swift movement for him, as the thin-lipped one obeyed. When he stepped away from the man at the table there were five diamonds in his left palm. They felt warm and very good. He said steadily:

"We will stay here until a certain diamond expert comes to the cabin, with the captain. When the stones have been inspected we will go to the woman in black. We will obtain the other four stones."

The lips of the man at the table were tightly pressed and thinner than ever. He parted them suddenly.

"It is she who—"

The phone buzzed. Jo Gar moved towards it, but did not take his eyes from the figure of the man in the chair. He spoke into the mouthpiece, as he slipped the diamonds into a pocket.

"Señor Gar—"

Porter's voice said: "Did the buzz catch you in time? He went from the smoking room pretty fast."

The Island detective kept his eyes on the thin-lipped one. He said:

"Yes—it reached me in time. I was prepared for Mr. Tracy. Will you please call the captain and tell him—"

His words died as the thin-lipped one hurled himself from the chair, slashing his right arm at the Colt. Jo squeezed the trigger of the gun as it was battered to one side. There was a crashing sound, and then the thin-lipped one's fingers were on his throat; his white face was close to Jo's.

He muttered hoarse, distorted words as his fingers tightened their grip. He was strong; the swinging arms of the detective failed to hurt him. Already Jo's breath was coming in short gasps; his efforts to get free of the man's grip were growing weaker.

His head was pulled close to the thin-lipped one's body; there was a mist in his eyes. Blackness was coming now; he was choking terribly. He felt his body swung to one side; his head was battered against the wall of the cabin. And then, once again, the room was filled with a crashing sound. The strangler's body jerked; he cried out hoarsely. His fingers went away from Jo's throat; he swung gropingly towards the cabin door. Jo stared towards it, his vision clearing. It was half opened.

Voices reached him faintly from the corridor; they grew louder. The thin-lipped one was down on his knees now; he sprawled at full length, his left-hand fingers pawing at the small of his back. Then, very suddenly, he was motionless.

Jo Gar stared towards the half-opened door. He breathed hoarsely, sucking in deep breaths of air:

"He would have killed me—and yet—he was murdered—the woman in black—"

He couldn't be sure, but he thought his eyes had seen dark color, just after the shot had crashed. And if the woman in black had thought that the thin-lipped one had said too much, if she had overheard, following him to his cabin—

Porter's voice was calling from the corridor:

"Señor Gar—Señor Gar!"

There were heavier footfalls now. Gar tapped the pocket into which he had slipped the diamonds. He was sure they were real. Five of them, and there was the one he already had recovered. Six stones—with four still missing. And the one who could have told many things—he was dead.

The Island detective knew that, even before he bent over the man, calling hoarsely:

"Yes—Porter—it is—all right—"

Porter came into the room, pulling up short at the sight of the man on the floor.

"Heard the crash sound—over the phone—" he muttered.

Jo Gar straightened and smiled a little. "I was forced to shoot," he said more clearly. "But he got me by the throat—"

Ship's officers were inside the room now. The second officer stared at the figure on the floor, then at Jo.

"You shot him?" he breathed. "You had to shoot him, Señor—"

Jo Gar shook his head. Porter leaned down suddenly and lifted something from the floor near the doorway. The Island detective said:

"He had five of the Von Loffler diamonds— I've got them now. I tried to shoot him, but I failed. He was shot in the back, from the corridor."

The second officer drew in a sharp breath. "You saw who it—"

Jo Gar shook his head. "I saw nothing," he said very slowly. He was sure that he had seen black color—the color of a woman's dress. "He was choking me—"

The newspaperman extended a palm. "What's this?" he muttered. "Just picked it up near the doorway."

Jo looked at the bead in Porter's palm. He shook his head very slowly.

"It looks very much," he said huskily but with little tone, "like a bit of blue glass."

Diamonds of Death

Jo Gar, the little Island detective, collects.

THE ROOM was in a cheap hotel, a few blocks from Market Street. The room had two windows, one of which faced the Bay. Jo Gar, his small body sprawled on the narrow bed, shivered a little. San Francisco was cold; he thought of the warm winds of Manila and the difference of the bays.

He sighed and said softly to himself:

"Four diamonds—if I had them I could return to the Islands. I do not belong away from them—"

The telephone bell on the wall jangled; Jo Gar stared towards the apparatus for several seconds, then rose slowly. He was dressed in a gray suit that did not fit him too well, and his graying hair was mussed. He unhooked the receiver and said:

"Yes."

A pleasant voice said: "Inspector Raines, of the customs office. I have information for you."

Jo Gar said: "That is good—please come up."

He hung up the receiver and stood for several seconds looking towards the door. One of his three bags had been opened, the other two he had not unlocked. The *Cheyo Maru,* bringing him from Honolulu, had arrived three hours ago, and there had been much for the Island detective to do. In the doing of it he had gained little. Perhaps, he thought, Inspector Raines had done better.

He took from one of his few remaining packages a brown-paper cigarette, lighted it. His gray-blue eyes held a faint smile as he inhaled. Down the hall beyond the room there was the slam of the elevator's door, and foot-falls. A man cleared his throat noisily. Jo Gar put his right hand in the pocket of his gray suit at his right side, went over and seated himself on the edge of the bed, facing the door. A knock sounded and the Philippine Island detective called flatly:

"Please—come in."

The door opened. A middle-aged man entered, dressed in a dark suit with a light coat thrown across his shoulders. The sleeves of the man's suit were not within the coat sleeves; it was worn as a cape. Raines had sharp features, pleasant blue eyes. His lips were thick; he was a big man. He said:

"Hello, Señor Gar."

Jo Gar rose and they shook hands. Raines' grip was loose and careless; he looked about the room, tossed a soft, gray hat on a chair. Jo Gar motioned towards the other chair in the room, and the inspector seated himself. He kept the coat slung across his shoulders.

Jo Gar said slowly, almost lazily:

"Something was found?"

The inspector frowned and shook his head. He took from his pocket a small card. His picture was at one corner of the card, which was quite soiled. There was the printing of the Customs Department, some insignia that Gar merely glanced at, a stamped seal—and the statement that Albert Raines was a member of the San Francisco customs office.

Raines said: "The chief thought I'd better show you that right away, as we hadn't seen each other."

The Island detective smiled. "Thank you," he replied, and handed the card back. "Something was found?"

Raines shook his head. "Not a thing," he said.

"We held her up for two hours, and we searched everything carefully. We even searched the child—the child's baggage. We gave her a pretty careful questioning. For that matter—everybody on the boat got about three times the attention we usually give. And we didn't turn up a stone."

Jo Gar sighed. Raines said grimly: "If the diamonds were on that boat—they got past us. And that means you're in a tough spot, yes?"

The Island detective said: "I think that is very much—what it means."

Raines said in a more cheerful tone: "Well, the chief said you recovered six of the stones, between Manila and San Francisco—that's not at all bad."

Jo Gar smiled gently: "I was—extremely fortunate," he said. "But the woman in black—I had hopes that the four diamonds—"

Raines said quickly: "So had we. When we got your coded wire telling us that you suspected her of the murder of the man you recovered five stones from, but that you couldn't prove a thing against her, we figured we might be able to help. We weren't. But we did as you requested—when she left the dock we had a man follow her."

The Island detective said: "Good—she went to a hotel?"

Raines shook his head. "Don't suppose you've ever been out around the Cliff House, Señor Gar. It's a spot out on a bunch of jagged rocks, about an hour from town. A sort of amusement park has grown up around it. Seals fool around in the rocks and the tourists go for it strong. The woman took a cab, and our man took another. She went to the amusement park near the Cliff House."

Jo Gar's gray-blue eyes widened slightly.

"She spent more than three weeks on the *Cheyo Maru,*" he breathed slowly. "And when she landed and had been cleared after an exhaustive customs examination, she went to an amusement park. Strange."

Raines made a grunting sound. "Damn' strange," he said. "Took all the baggage, which included a trunk we'd gone very carefully through. And the child."

Jo Gar narrowed his eyes and looked beyond the inspector. He said quietly:

"In Manila we have an amusement park that is quite large. After entering the main gate there are many places one can go."

Raines nodded. "It's like that here. Only this park has several entrances, and you can drive through a section of it. The cab went in one entrance, stopped for a while near a merry-go-round—went out another. Then it went to a house and stopped. The luggage was taken inside, and the woman and child went in. Our man stayed around a short time, but nothing else happened."

The Island detective said: "You have the address?"

Raines nodded. He took from his pocket a small slip of paper, on which were scrawled some words, handed it to Jo Gar.

The Island detective read: " 'One hundred and forty-one West Pacific Avenue.' "

Raines nodded. "That's it—Cary said it was a frame house, set back a short distance from the road. The section isn't much built up out there."

Jo Gar nodded. "It is very good of you to bring me this information," he stated.

Raines made a swift gesture with both hands. "That's all right," he said. "Cary has another job just now, or he'd have come along to tell you about it. Looks queer to me."

The Island detective spoke slowly. "It is not *necessary* to drive through the amusement park, in order to reach this address?" he asked.

Raines said: "Hell, no—that's what seems funny. That woman was trying to hide where she was going. Maybe she figured she *might* be followed."

Jo Gar nodded. "I think you are right," he said.

Raines got to his feet, held out his right hand.

"Sorry the office couldn't get something on her at the pier," he apologized. "But you know where she is—and you know she acted funny getting there."

Jo Gar smiled and shook the inspector's hand. He sat down on the bed again as Raines took his hat. When Raines reached the door, he said:

"Luck on those other four." He grinned and went out. Going along the corridor he whistled. The elevator door slammed.

Jo Gar got to his feet with remarkable speed for him. He got his coat and hat, was out of the room quickly. He used the stairs instead of the elevator. When he reached the small lobby he saw Raines light a cigar, go outside and raise a hand. A cab pulled close to the curb. When it started away the Island detective hailed another parked some feet from the hotel entrance. He said to the driver:

"Follow that machine, please—but do not move too close to it. When it halts, halt some distance away."

The driver looked at Jo curiously but nodded his head. The two cabs moved from one street to another. There was a great deal of traffic, but Jo's driver was skillful. For perhaps ten minutes the two cabs moved through the city, apparently keeping in the heart of it. Finally the leading cab curved close to a building that had a large clock set in granite stone. It halted. Unfamiliar as Jo was with San Francisco, he recognized the building as a railroad station of considerable importance. There were many porters about, and cabs were everywhere.

As his own cab pulled close to the curb Jo watched Raines alight and pay his driver. The inspector hurried into the station, and when he was out of sight Jo paid up and left his cab. He pulled his hat low over his eyes, straightened his small body a little, went into the station. Almost instantly he saw Raines. The man was at a luggage checking counter; as Jo watched from a safe distance he saw Raines handed two large-sized valises. A porter picked them up; Raines gestured towards another clock inside the station and said something. The porter hurried away, followed by the inspector.

Jo Gar followed, being careful not to be seen. When Raines and his porter went through a train gate, the Island detective halted near it, a peculiar smile on his face. After a few minutes the colored porter came back through the gate. Jo beckoned to him.

"The gentleman whose luggage you just carried to the train—I think he was a friend of mine. You saw his ticket?"

The porter shook his head slowly: "He tol' me his car and seat number—didn't show no ticket," he replied.

Jo Gar frowned. "How did you know what train to take him to?" he asked slowly.

The porter grinned. "That's right," he said. "He wanted the Chicago train."

The Island detective drew a sharp breath. He handed the porter a quarter, walked slowly back into the station's waiting room.

"Mr. Raines had barely time to make his train," he breathed softly. "Yet he was very kind to me—and said nothing about leaving on such a journey."

He took a cab back to his hotel, found everything in his room in perfect order. He called the customs office and after considerable inquiry was told that Inspector Raines had left for his hotel some hour or so ago. He said:

"Yes, he has been here. I wondered if he had returned."

There was a pause, questions were asked at the other end, and he was informed that Raines was not expected to return for special night work, but that he would be on duty in the morning. Jo Gar thanked his informant and hung up the receiver.

He sat on the edge of the small bed and watched a light sign flash in the distance. A ferry boat was a glow of moving light, on the Bay waters. The air seemed very cold. Jo Gar decided that the real Inspector Raines had met with injuries, and that a certain person had impersonated him, had told him an untrue story about a certain woman in black—and had then departed from the city of San Francisco. He decided that he was expected to go to the house at One hundred and forty-one, West Pacific Avenue, that he was supposed to believe the woman had acted suspiciously in going there.

He said softly and slowly: "I have the six diamonds—they have

the four. I am in a strange city, and a card with a seal on it was expected to make a great impression. But one man's picture can replace another's—very easily—"

He rose and looked at his wristwatch. It was almost eight o'clock. He inspected his Colt automatic, slipped it back into a pocket of his coat. The phone bell rang, and when he lifted the receiver and gave his name he was told that the customs office was calling, and that Inspector Raines had been found unconscious in an alley not far from the piers. He was still unconscious and it was not certain that he would live. He had apparently been struck over the head with a blunt instrument. The customs office felt that Señor Gar should know why he had failed to arrive, and also that all passengers on the *Cheyo Maru* had been passed through the office. One had been followed as requested, but her cab had been lost in traffic. The office was very sorry.

Jo Gar said: "I am very sorry to hear of Inspector Raines' injuries. I will call at the office tomorrow. Thank you for calling."

He hung up the receiver, went to the window that faced the Bay and the distant, lighted ferry boat. His gray-blue eyes were smiling coldly. He thought: They did *not* expect Inspector Raines to be found so soon. They *did* expect me to go immediately to the address the impostor gave me. They might easily have escaped with the four diamonds, but they chose to lead me to them. They wish the six in my possession, being very greedy. But I am warned, directly and indirectly.

The Island detective turned away from the window and moved towards the room door. He breathed very softly:

"Just the same—I shall go directly to the address given me."

JO GAR left his cab a square from One hundred and forty-one West Pacific Avenue. He had picked the driver with care; the man was husky in build and young. He had a good chin and clear eyes, and he said his name was O'Halohan. Somewhere in the Islands Jo had read that the Irish were fighters.

He said now: "I am a detective—and I'm going inside of the house at One hundred and forty-one. Here is a ten-dollar bill. In about five minutes I want you to drive to the front of the house and blow your horn twice. After that just stay in your seat. Wait about ten minutes—then blow your horn again, twice. If I do not come to a window or the door, and call to you—go to the police and tell them I went into the house and was prevented from coming out. That is all—is it clear?"

The driver nodded. "I got a gun," he said. "And a permit to carry it. Suppose, after the second time I blow my horn, you don't show. Why not let me come in and *get* you out?"

The Island detective smiled narrowly. "You are young and strong, but neither of those qualities might be of too great value. Neither of us might come out."

The driver said: "If it looks that bad—what you goin' in alone for?"

Jo Gar continued to smile. He said patiently:

"I have an idea it will be better that way. You must follow my instructions."

The driver nodded. "You're doing the job," he muttered. "I'll be down there in five minutes, and make the horn racket. I'll give it to you again in ten. Then if you don't show I'll head for the police."

The Island detective nodded. "That is the way," he said. "Don't get out of the car."

The driver said: "Supposing I hear you yelling for help—I still stick inside?"

Jo said grimly: "You will not hear me calling for help, Mister O'Halohan. My visit is not at all complicated. After you blow your horn twice—the second time, I will either give you instructions, or you will go for the police."

The driver said: "You win."

Jo Gar half closed his almond-shaped eyes. "It may be very important to me—that you do just as I have instructed. You are sure you understand?"

The driver nodded; his eyes met Jo Gar's squarely.

"It ain't anything tough," he stated.

Jo Gar spoke very quietly. "It is extremely simple."

He half turned away from the cab, and heard the driver say harshly: "Yeah—if it works."

The Island detective moved along the broken pavement of the sidewalk, a thin smile on his browned face.

"It will be just as simple," he said in a low tone, a half whisper, "if it *doesn't* work. But much more final—for me."

NUMBER ONE hundred and forty-one was a rambling one story house in not too good condition. There were no streetlights near it; tall trees rose on either side. The nearest house to it was almost a square distant; opposite was a lot filled with low brush. The section was quiet and pretty well deserted, but less than a half mile away there was the flare of colored lights in the sky. And at intervals Jo Gar could hear distant and faint staccato sounds—the noise of shooting gallery rifles.

He did not hesitate as he reached the front of the house. A yellowish light showed faintly beyond one of the side windows. The pavement that ran to a few steps was broken and not level.

Out of the corners of his gray-blue eyes, as he moved towards the steps, Jo saw that the lights of the cab had been dimmed—their color did not show on the street in front of the place. A cold wind made sound in the trees as he reached the steps, moved up them. His right hand was in the right pocket of his coat, gripping the butt of the automatic.

He stood for a few seconds, his eyes on the number plate, which seemed new and had been placed in a position easily seen. The house was old, the section of San Francisco was not too good— but the number plate was in excellent condition.

The Island detective's lips curved just a little. But the smile that showed momentarily on his face was not a pleasant one. He had a definite feeling that this house marked the end of the trail. He thought of the ones who had died in Manila, when Delgado's jewelry store had been robbed—he thought of the men who had died since then. A vision of Juan Arragon's brown face flashed before his eyes.

He touched the index finger of his left hand to a button near the number plate, heard no sound within the house. One hand at his side, the other in his right pocket—he stood in the cold wind and waited.

He had come to this house, but he had not been tricked. He was gambling—gambling his life, in a strange country, against his chances of recovering the four missing Von Loffler diamonds, against the final chance of facing the one who had planned the Manila crime.

He could not be positive of anything, but he sensed these things. This was to be the finish, one way or the other. He would return to Manila—or he would never leave this house alive. He felt it, and he was suddenly very calm. From somewhere within he heard foot-falls; there was the sound of a bolt being moved, the door opened very wide.

Jo Gar looked into the eyes of a man who had a smiling face. It was a thin, browned face, and the eyes were small and colorless. The man was dressed in a brown suit, almost the color of his skin. There was nothing striking about the one who had opened the door, unless it was the smallness of his colorless eyes.

The eyes looked beyond the Island detective, to the sidewalk and road. The man moved his head slightly and Jo Gar said:

"I am Señor Gar, a private detective who arrived only today in San Francisco. I arrived on the *Cheyo Maru*—and have come here in search of a woman who was on that boat. She had with her a child—"

He stopped and looked downward at the dull color of black that was the metal of the gun held by the man in the doorway. The man had made only a slight movement with his right hand; the gun's muzzle was less than three feet from Jo's body.

Jo Gar smiled into the smiling eyes of the one in the doorway.

"I have made a mistake?" he asked very quietly.

The one in the doorway shook his head. "On the contrary," he said in a voice that was very low and cold, "you have come to the correct place. I have been—expecting you."

He stepped to one side, and Jo Gar walked into a wide hall. The light was dim, and though there were electric bulbs about, it was furnished by a lamp whose wick was uneven. The place was very cold. It had the air of not having been lived in for a long time, and there was no evidence about showing that it would be lived in.

The thin-faced man said: "The first room on your right, please. Lift your hands slightly."

Jo Gar raised his hands slightly, went through a narrow doorway into a room that seemed even colder than the hall. The light in the room was better—there were two lamps. Blinds were drawn tightly.

Beside a small table was a stool that might have been made for a piano.

The one with the gun said in the same, cold voice:

"Sit on the stool, Gar—put your hands on the table. Keep them there."

Hatred crept into his voice as he uttered the last three words. Jo Gar did as instructed. He said quietly:

"I knew that the man you sent to me at my hotel lied. I followed him to the station, and watched him leave the city. I returned to the hotel and the customs office informed me that one of their men, who was coming to me with information of no great importance, had been knocked unconscious. I knew then how the card presented me had been obtained, and that I was expected to believe a story that pointed to suspicious action by a woman I was interested in— and that I was expected to come to this address."

There was hatred showing in the small, colorless eyes of the thin-faced one. He stood almost ten feet away from Jo Gar, facing him.

"But you came, knowing all this."

Jo Gar smiled a little. "When you made that movement and held that gun on me—my fingers were on the trigger of my own gun. I could have shot you down—I did not."

There was a flicker of expression in the standing one's eyes. He said:

"You are very kind, Señor Gar."

Mockery and hatred were in his tone. Jo Gar said slowly:

"No—not kind. I have six diamonds that you would like. I think that you have four I would like. You wanted me here to bargain with me. You wanted me here so that you could trap me, then offer me my life for the six diamonds. You have worked that way, with your accomplices, since the robbery was effected."

The thin-faced one smiled and showed white, even teeth.

"You would risk your life and six diamonds—for the four you say I have?"

Jo Gar smiled gently. "My life is not too important," he said. "I have never regarded it that way. I came here because I knew the one responsible for many deaths would be here."

The thin-faced one said mockingly: "And you were not trapped? You simply wanted to see that person who you hated because of Arragon's death, and because of things done to you?"

The Island detective kept his hands motionless on the table surface. He shook his head.

"No," he replied. "Not exactly. I wanted to see that one taken by the police. And that is practically assured, now."

He watched the facial muscles of the thin-faced one jerk, saw his colorless eyes shift towards the blinds of the windows. His gun hand moved a little, in towards his body. Rage twisted his face, and then he smiled. It was a grotesque, mask-like smile. The brown skin was drawn tightly over the face bones and the lips were pressed together. Jo Gar said:

"I remember you, Raaker. You were in the insurance business in Manila until a few years ago. There was about to be a prosecution, and you left the Islands."

The thin-faced one said with hoarseness in his voice:

"And I have never forgotten you, Señor Gar. You tell me you have come here, not caring about your life—and that the police are outside. Well—I didn't bring you here to get your six diamonds, Gar—Von Loffler's diamonds. I brought you here because I hate you. I want to watch your body squirm on the floor, beside that stool."

Jo Gar said quietly: "That was how you knew about the Von Loffler diamonds—that Dutch Insurance Company. You stayed out of Manila, Raaker—you couldn't risk coming back. You hired men. Some of them tricked you—and each other. The robbery was successful, but you lost slowly. All the way back from Manila, Raaker, you lost. You used men and women, and they tried to kill me—too many times. They were killed—there were many deaths. Those were diamonds of death, Raaker—and you only got four of them. The woman in black brought them to you—I think she was the only one who was faithful."

Raaker was breathing heavily. He made a sudden movement with his left hand, plunging it into a pocket. When it came out four stones spilled to the surface of the small table. Three of them only rolled a few inches, but one struck against a finger of the Island detective's left hand. Raaker said fiercely:

"I hate you, Gar. You drove me from the Islands, with your evidence. I hated Von Loffler, too. He took all his properties away from me, because he learned that I was gambling, because he was afraid of the insurance. So I learned about the stones, where they were. And I planned the robbery. I stayed here—and got reports. I tried to direct. But you were on that boat—"

He broke off, shrugged. "You are going to die, Gar. So I can talk. The woman came to me with the diamonds. Four of them. And by the time she brought them to me here—she hated me. She had seen too much death. She's gone away, with her child—and you'll never find her, Gar. She killed a man on the *Cheyo Maru,* and that made her hate me all the more. She had to kill him, before he could talk—to you!"

Jo Gar said steadily: "I don't think—I *want* to find her, Raaker. I know now who planned the crime, who caused the deaths. And you are caught, Raaker—"

There was the sound of brakes beyond the room, the low beat of an idling engine. Two sharp blasts from a horn came into the room. Raaker jerked his head sharply, then turned his eyes towards Jo Gar again. The Island detective made no movement. He smiled with his lips pressed together. Raaker said: "What's—that?"

His voice was hoarse. Jo Gar parted his lips. He said:

"A signal from the police—that the house is properly covered."

Raaker sucked in a deep breath. "I'll get more than one of them—as they come in!" he muttered.

Jo Gar shook his head. "I do not think you will, Raaker. They will not come in. It is easier to wait for *you*—to go *out.*"

Raaker smiled twistedly, but there was fear in his eyes.

"They'll come in, all right," he breathed. "I'll get you first—when they come. You won't see them come in, Gar."

Jo Gar smiled. "They will not come in," he said softly. "If I do not go out, within the next ten minutes, they will unload the sub-machine-guns and the smoke bombs. They will know I am dead—and that there is a killer in the house. The smoke bombs—and the tear gas bombs—*they* will come in."

Raaker said hoarsely. "——! How I hate you, you little half-breed—"

He jerked the gun slightly. The Island detective looked him in the eyes, still smiling.

"That is true," he said. "You *do* hate me—and there *is* the blood of the Spanish and the Filipino in my veins. But I am not a criminal—a thief and a killer."

Raaker turned his head slightly and listened to the steady beat of the cab engine. Then his eyes came back to the small figure of Gar, went to the four glittering diamonds on the table. He said thickly:

"With the others—over two hundred thousand dollars—I would

have been fixed—"

His voice broke. Jo Gar said quietly: "Yes, you could have had things easy, Raaker. If I had not taken the same boat that your accomplices took—if things had turned out differently in Honolulu—"

Raaker stared at him, his little eyes growing larger. He said slowly:

"Where are—the other six stones?"

Jo Gar smiled. "In the vaults of the customs office," he replied. "You did not think I would bring them here?"

Raaker's body swayed a little. The wind made noise in the trees beyond the house, and he stiffened. Jo Gar said in a voice that was hardly more than a whisper:

"If you had had even the courage of a certain type of criminal—and had gone to the Islands yourself, you might have had the diamonds now. If you had not used others—"

Raaker said fiercely: "Damn the diamonds—I've got *you!* They brought you here—"

Jo Gar half closed his almond-shaped eyes. "And they've brought the San Francisco police here," he said steadily. "They've brought tear gas and sub-machine-guns—and they're bringing death here, Raaker."

Raaker's eyes held rage again. He was losing control of himself. He made a swift motion with his left hand, shaking fingers pointing towards the four stones on the table.

"Look at them—damn you!" he gritted. "Look at the four you couldn't—reach! Look at them—"

Jo Gar looked into the eyes of Raaker. He shook his head.

"I've seen the *others,*" he stated quietly. "I've seen many diamonds, Raaker."

Raaker laughed wildly. He backed towards a wall of the room.

"You'll never see diamonds again," he said in a fierce tone. "Never, Gar!"

He raised his gun arm slowly. From the cab outside there came the sharp sound of a horn, silence—and then another blast.

Jo Gar never took his eyes from the eyes of Raaker. He was smiling grimly.

He said very slowly: "Machine-gun bullets, Raaker. And choking, blinding gas. They'll be waiting for *you*—after you get through squeezing that trigger."

Raaker cried out in a shrill tone: "Damn you—Gar—that won't

help *you* any—"

There was a sudden engine hum as the cab driver accelerated the motor. Yellow light flashed beyond the house, along the road. O'Halohan was going for the police, starting his cab. For a second Raaker twisted his head towards the sound and the light. He was thinking of machine-guns—and tear gas—

Jo Gar was on his feet in a flash. The table went forward, over. The Island detective leaped to the right as Raaker cried out hoarsely, and the first bullet from his gun crashed into the table wood.

The second bullet from the gun ripped the cloth of Gar's coat, and his right hand was coming up, with the Colt in it, when the cloth ripped.

He squeezed the trigger sharply but steadily. There was the third gun crash and Raaker screamed, took a step forward. His gun hand dropped; he went to his knees, stared at Gar for a second, swaying—then fell heavily to the floor.

Jo Gar went slowly to his side. He was dead— the bullet had caught him just above the heart. One diamond lay very close to his curved fingers; it was as though he were grasping for it, in death.

The other three Jo found after a five-minute search. Then he went from the room into the hall, and out of the house. The cab was out of sight; in the distance there was still colored light in the sky. The shooting gallery noise came at intervals. Jo Gar found a package in his pocket, lighted one of his brown-paper cigarettes.

He said very softly, to himself: "I have all— of the diamonds. Now I can go home, after the police come. I hope my friend Juan Arragon—knows."

He stood very motionless on the top step that led to the small porch, and waited for the police to come. And he thought, as he waited, of the Philippines—of Manila—and of his tiny office off the Escolta. It was good to forget other things, and to think of his returning.

Shooting Gallery

The little Island detective finds that a shooting gallery can be a handy place for a murder.

THE FAT man whose eyes were much more slanted than those of Jo Gar sat slumped in the fan-backed chair that had been made by Bilibid prison inmates and shook his round head from side to side. Between chubby fingers of his left hand he held a large palm leaf fan, with which he made faint but graceful motion. He spoke in precise English.

"It is good to have you back in Manila, Señor Gar. You were away a short time, yet it was much too long."

Jo Gar smiled a little with his slightly almond shaped eyes and said politely:

"You are kind, Señor Kanochi. I am glad to be back, even though I arrive in the midst of the hot season. It is always good to be home."

A ceiling fan that turned very slowly stirred warm air in the tiny office just off the Escolta, main business street of Manila. Two lizards crawled languidly beyond the arc of the fan, and there were several annoying flies in the room. Jo Gar's diminutive body rested passively in the wicker chair beside the desk; he looked beyond the half-breed Kanochi and seemed to be thinking of things not concerned with the man. Yet he was actually remembering all he heard of the fat one.

Kanochi said in a flat, thinnish voice, still moving the fan in his fingers:

"There is trouble in my *Park of the Moon.* I have come to you about it. If you are at liberty—"

He let his voice trail off; the questioning note gentle and polite. It was almost as though he regretted mentioning the matter to Jo Gar.

The Island detective said:

"I am at liberty, Señor. I have had a good rest since recovering the

Von Loffler diamonds. Your *Park of the Moon* has greatly enlarged this season, I have heard."

The fat one nodded his big head slowly. "I have spent much money, and I do not wish trouble," he stated in a grim tone. "But one does not obtain always what one wishes, Señor Gar."

Jo Gar smiled. "It is so," he agreed.

The fat one sighed heavily. He listened a few seconds to the shrill sound of a native argument, in the *calle* below. One of Manila's antiquated flivvers made a staccato sound. A tail of one of the two lizards on the ceiling dropped suddenly from the reptile's body and struck the matting of the floor with a faint sound. The lizard scurried towards a corner of the ceiling. The shrill argument below was suddenly stilled.

Kanochi said:

"In my *Park of the Moon* I have installed a shooting gallery. It is already very popular. The Filipinos like to shoot. Many of them come in from the ranches for gaiety; come in from the plantations. Some are excellent shots with the rifles. My new shooting gallery is an attraction."

Jo Gar said thoughtfully: "So many men have the desire to kill."

Kanochi's small, slanted eyes held a swift expression of surprise, which quickly vanished. He made a little gesture of agreement with his fat hands.

"It is unfortunately so," he said. "But in the *Park of the Moon* they destroy only figures of clay, many of which move from side to side. And thus they learn to defend themselves."

Jo Gar said quietly: "Very admirable is such a defense, Señor Kanochi."

Suspicion flickered in the fat one's eyes, but died almost instantly.

"In my shooting gallery my son-in-law works," Kanochi went on. "He is a Filipino of the name of Vincente Calleo. He is not a good son-in-law, Señor Gar, but I am a patient man. I wish to give him every opportunity. He gambles at the cock fights and drinks too much. He has lost several positions I obtained for him. Now he works for me. He is not too grateful and not too good a husband for my daughter. Yet there is much about him that I like. He is very young and perhaps will outgrow his faults. That is what I think to myself. I urge my daughter to be patient."

The Island detective offered brown-paper cigarettes that were politely refused, lighted one himself. Kanochi said very slowly, his slanted eyes almost closed:

"This morning I received a telephone call. The one who called said that Vincente owed him quite a sum of money, had owed it to him for some time. He did not give me his name, of course. He spoke Filipino, and many voices are alike. He said, 'that if I did not at once give to my son-in-law sufficient money for him to pay his gambling debt—Vincente would be killed.'"

Jo Gar widened his eyes slightly. The ceiling fan made faint squeaking sound and the Island detective said:

"I shall have to oil the fan—in my absence it has been neglected."

Kanochi frowned and made a little clicking sound. His eyes met Jo Gar's; he spoke more hurriedly.

"I do not intend to pay the sum demanded; I have told the one who spoke with me that. It is a large sum. Vincente admits that he owes it. He will not tell me the name of the one he has a lost the money to, and he is frightened."

There was a little silence. Jo Gar said slowly:

"It is Vincente's duty to load the rifles, at the shooting gallery?"

Kanochi shook his head. His

eyes were expressionless.

"It is Vincente's duty to look after the clay targets," he said tonelessly. "He replaces those that are shattered—the figures of ducks and such things, when the machinery carries them out of sight and below the level of fire. At intervals the shooting is stopped, and he works swiftly replacing pipes and the silver balls on the water that spouts. I think that he does very well. But this afternoon he was not steady. A Chinese by the name of Matoy loads the guns and cares for the customers. He reported that Vincente was very careless in replacing the targets."

Jo Gar said: "Yet when he is out of sight he could not be hit? He is protected? And before he comes into range to replace the targets that do not move out of sight—all shooting is stopped?"

Kanochi said, frowning: "Yes—that is so."

The Island detective inhaled and spoke slowly: "I should like to go to the *Park of the Moon,* and to talk with your son-in-law. What hour would be the most convenient?"

The fat man seemed thoughtful. "At eight it begins to cool—at eight-thirty or nine there are crowds. Between seven and eight the shooting gallery is not very busy."

Jo Gar smiled. "I shall be there at seven-thirty," he said.

Kanochi nodded. "Vincente starts his work at seven," he said. "I will tell him to expect you, and that perhaps you can help him. But I do not think he will give you the name of the one to whom he owes this money—and who has threatened his life."

Jo Gar rose as the fat one rose.

"If he will not—perhaps there will be some other way of learning this man's identity," he said.

Kanochi nodded. "I think that shooting gallery work is bad for one whose life has been threatened," he said tonelessly. "And yet—"

Jo Gar shrugged. "There are many ways of killing," he interrupted. "But we must try to learn the identity of the one to whom Vincente owes money. Having learned it, we can perhaps convince the man that an accident around the shooting gallery might prove inconvenient for him."

Kanochi's eyes held a grim expression. "That is it—that is what I am afraid of—an accident," he said very softly. "And it is good of you to take this case, Señor Gar."

Jo Gar smiled, his gray-blue eyes looking beyond the fat man.

"It is good of you to think of me, Señor Kanochi," he replied. "I shall be at the *Park of the Moon* at seven-thirty."

He bowed slightly and the fat man left the room. It seemed slightly cooler after he had departed, and the odor was better. His bulk made sound going down the wooden steps to the street.

Jo Gar seated himself and stretched his short legs. He ran browned fingers through his graying hair and murmured very slowly:

"Señor Kanochi has lied before. He is a potential murderer. He does not care for his son-in-law. He has much money. Even should the publicity of an 'accident' at his shooting gallery mean a loss of business, I do not think the half-breed would regret too much. Yet he fears the 'accident' theory might not be strong enough. So he has invented a story—"

Jo Gar closed his eyes and was silent for several seconds. When he opened them he glanced at his wrist-watch, saw that it was almost six o'clock. He rose from the wicker chair and said with a touch of grimness:

"If this Vincente were to be dead when I arrive at the *Park of the Moon* it would be extremely difficult for me. There would be only the voice that Señor Kanochi heard—"

The Island detective smiled with his colorless, thin lips pressed into a straight line. Then he parted them and corrected himself.

There would be only the voice that Señor Kanochi *says* he heard," he murmured. "I feel it would be very wise for me to go early—to the shooting gallery."

THE *PARK OF THE MOON* was a fairly large amusement place beyond a turn of the dark, sluggish watered Pasig, perhaps three miles from the curving Escolta. On all sides of the park but the river side were thatch-roofed houses of the Filipinos. It was not yet seven when Jo Gar arrived and paid off his *carromatta* driver, and there was still almost a bright light. And at once the Island detective knew that Señor Kanochi had lied to him. The park was well attended. It wasn't crowded as yet, but the various rides and shows were all doing business. And in the distance he could hear the staccato crack of the shooting gallery; it reminded him of the sound he had heard from the porch of the house in San Francisco, weeks ago. But there was a difference. This shooting gallery sound was sharper, steadier. He moved in the general direction of it.

The *Park of the Moon* was filled with laughter—the laughter of Filipinos, Chinese, Japanese, and Spaniards. And there the laughter of the half-breeds—the offspring of marriage between these races. A scattering of English and Germans were in the park, and Jo Gar saw the American, Condon, wandering around with a grin on his browned face. He passed a merry-go-round that squeaked ancient music in waltz time. The staccato-clatter from the shooting gallery was increasing in tone now. Down the lane between side shows and rides he caught sight of a greater flare of lights.

And then, very suddenly, the crackling rifle sound ceased. It ceased abruptly and Jo Gar halted, his small body stiffening. Young Filipinos and Chinese moved past him, laughing. He stood motionless, waiting. He muttered:

"It might be—that he is replacing the targets—"

A woman screamed—a shrill, long-drawn note. There was the figure of a short, brown-faced man running towards the Island detective now. His face was twisted.

The Island detective moved his body, blocked the path of the running one. Others made way for him, but Jo said sharply:

"What is the trouble?"

The small Filipino swerved to one side, throwing out his right hand and saying shortly:

"Accident—at the—shooting gallery! I go for—doctor—"

Jo Gar stood quietly for several seconds, his gray-blue eyes very small. People were staring after the running man. The Island detective moved forward, towards the shooting gallery's flare of light. Perspiration was on his face, and his lightweight shirt clung to the skin of his back. As he neared the lane opposite the shooting gallery he saw that a large crowd had gathered. It took him a half minute to fight his way through the crowd, to reach the counter of the shooting gallery.

Two of the park police, clad in white duck uniforms, were keeping the crowd back. Another came through the crowd as Jo reached the counter and looked across it. Clay ducks were moving from side to side—a silver ball was swinging in pendulum fashion. On the floor, near the line of moving ducks, lay a figure, two men bending over it.

Jo Gar reached the side of the nearest, white-clad policeman. He smiled at the man, said in Filipino:

"I am Señor Gar—Señor Kanochi asked me to come here. What has happened?"

The park guardian said grimly: "An accident, Señor. It is the son-in-law of Señor Kanochi—he has been shot."

Jo Gar moved towards a small door at one side of the counter, opened it and went beneath the slanting roof of the gallery. On a small wicker chair a woman sat, rocking from side to side and moaning. A taller woman stood beside her; both were Filipinos. Jo Gar went past them and reached the two who bent over the motionless figure.

One of them turned; he was Chinese. Jo said:

"You are the Matoy who loads the guns?"

The Chinese looked surprised. He nodded. He had a round face and a heavy body. His eyes were gray and small. The second man straightened and said in very good English:

"He is dead—there are two slugs in his brain. He died almost instantly."

The man turned and Jo recognized him as Doctor Seth Connings, a rather well known English physician of the city. A woman's voice asked a question in an uneven tone, and the Chinese, Matoy, moved away from the body. He went to the woman who was rocking back and forth on the wicker, and spoke. Almost instantly she screamed—again and again. The doctor sighed.

"I'll have to quiet her," he said. "She was his wife."

Jo Gar stood looking down at the lean face of Vincente Calleo. He was thinking: "This woman who is screaming now is the one who screamed before. She did not know until the Chinese, Matoy, told her—that her husband was dead. She appears hysterical, and yet she was not beside her husband—she was in the chair over there."

Her screams were attracting a greater crowd, but more park police were arriving now. The doctor was talking to the woman; her screams became wails. Jo Gar went to Matoy's side and said:

"I am Señor Gar. Señor Kanochi asked me to come here, because his son-in-law's life had been threatened. How did the accident occur?"

Matoy shook his head. He spoke Filipino, and swiftly.

"I do not know, Señor. I was having trouble with one of the guns, and took it into the small room at one side, to inspect it more carefully. Several were shooting. I heard suddenly a scream—and hurried from the room. Vincente's wife was at the counter, pointing across it at the fallen figure of her husband. There was suddenly a great crowd—the English doctor came, and the park police—and yourself—"

Jo Gar said steadily: "You remember those who were shooting?"

There were little wrinkles around the eyes of the Chinese. He seemed to be thinking hard. But he shook his head.

"There has been much business—so many have used the guns. I think one was tall and skinny, Señor. I think three were shooting when I left with the gun I wished to repair. But they might have stopped shooting—and others might have started. I left several loaded guns on the counter. The three were Filipinos, I think, Señor. But I could not be sure—"

Jo Gar went to the counter. There were two rifles in a line. He inspected both—each was completely loaded with the special, small caliber shot used for the range. Three other rifles lay in different positions—two were empty—all shot having been ejected. The third had three small caliber slugs ready for action.

The Island detective faced the milling crowd and said clearly in Filipino:

"Those of you who were shooting when this accident occurred—please call out."

No person called out. Jo Gar said more slowly:

"You who were shooting were not to blame—the dead one should not have been within range. It will help me if you will speak."

No person spoke. The Island detective went away from the counter and to the woman on the wicker chair. There was horror in her eyes as she looked up at him. He said quietly:

"I sympathize greatly with you—but I must ask questions. You know your husband's life had been threatened?"

The woman's eyes were dark and wide. Jo Gar spoke Filipino to her and Doctor Seth Connings did not understand his words. The woman said:

"Yes—he had told me—he was worried—"

Her voice was broken. Jo Gar said: "You saw—what happened?"

Horror showed more clearly in her eyes. She had a thin face, and was small, slight. She was pretty, but the tropics would not allow her to be pretty much longer.

She replied weakly: "I often come to the—shooting gallery. Several persons were shooting—I moved near the counter. Matoy, the Chinese, went through a small door as I called to him. He had a gun in his hand. I was very near the counter—the guns were making sounds. And then Vincente's head came in sight, his shoulders—"

Her voice broke. Jo Gar said quietly:

"Please go on."

She said: "He groaned and threw out a hand—he fell forward, across a row of clay targets. I screamed—and there was the crowd rushing—"

She covered her face with her hands. The English doctor frowned at Jo.

"She's in pretty bad shape," he said.

Jo Gar nodded. "These questions are necessary," he replied. "You were just passing, Doctor?"

The Englishman stiffened and said coldly: "I was just looking about the park. And sampling some of the cool drinks. There have been rumors of epidemic—"

Jo Gar smiled faintly and nodded. "Of course," he said. "You have the interest of the city at heart." He looked down at the woman again. Her eyes were staring into his. "You would remember any of those shooting?" he asked.

She shook her head. "I saw only their backs—I think they were Filipinos. There were many near the counter who were watching—not shooting."

Jo Gar sighed. He thought of making another appeal to the crowd beyond the counter, but sensed it would be useless. A man was dead—and Filipinos, Chinese and half-breeds could be very silent when they thought silence wise. They would think silence wise now, he knew that.

Moving away from the woman he said to Matoy:

"May I see the little room into which you carried the gun that did not work?"

The eyes of the Chinese held a faint flicker of light. He bowed slightly and led the way into a small room at the right side of the counter. The walls were of light wood—a small window faced the lane along which the crowd moved. There was a bamboo table in the room, a gun rack and a chair. On shelves along one of the walls were ammunition boxes and cleaning materials. The entrance from the spot near the counter was the only entrance to the room. On the bamboo table rested a range gun. It was very warm in the small room.

The Chinese stood close to Jo Gar, coughing dryly, as the Island detective inspected the weapon. It was jammed—the trigger would not squeeze. Jo Gar set it on the table again. The Chinese said:

"You are satisfied, Señor Gar?"

Jo Gar said slowly: "I did not doubt your word, be sure of that. These things are necessary."

The Chinese bowed. It seemed to Jo that there was faint mockery in his eyes. He said slowly:

"Why do you think Vincente rose from the rear of the range—rose among the clay targets? He knew there were persons shooting. Yet he placed his body within striking distance of the slugs. And he was killed. Why?"

Matoy shook his head from side to side, frowning. He said after several seconds:

"He has been worried—it was the gambling debts he owed. He has been careless. It was almost time for him to replace certain of the targets. Perhaps there was a pause for a second in the shooting—perhaps he thought he heard me ring the bell—"

Jo Gar said: "Ah—there is a bell that you ring?"

The Chinese nodded. "It is just outside the door," he said. "It rings loudly, in the rear of the range. It is the signal that shooting has stopped, that the guns are all in my possession."

Jo Gar said: "Let us go outside. It is very hot."

They went outside and Jo Gar looked at the small button of the signal bell. When he pressed it there was instant ringing sound, quite loud, at the rear of the shooting gallery. He looked towards the counter, and Matoy, reading his thought, said steadily:

"The button cannot be reached from beyond the counter. No playful youths could make it ring."

Jo Gar nodded. He saw the fat form of Señor Kanochi fighting through the crowd. The half-breed entered the shooting gallery, went directly to Vincente's widow. He bent over her and spoke for several minutes. Then he straightened, mopping his face with a big handkerchief. He looked around, caught sight of Jo.

He came towards the Island detective, his eyes holding a dull expression. His thinnish voice wavered.

"You were—too late, Señor Gar."

Jo nodded his head and said very softly: "Too late," he agreed. "I am very sorry."

Kanochi said in the same shaken voice: "He has murdered him—the one who threatened to do it—"

Jo Gar said nothing. The pupils of Kanochi's eyes moved about within the slant-shape. He said without looking at the Island detective:

"You have learned anything—of importance?"

Jo Gar hesitated, and was conscious of a sudden tenseness of Kanochi's body. But he shook his head.

"I have learned—nothing of importance," he replied softly.

The half-breed sucked in a deep breath, making hissing sound.

"I want this murderer, Señor Gar!" he said with a strange fierceness. "You must find him."

Jo Gar was silent for several seconds. When he spoke his voice was almost toneless.

"I know the motive, Señor Kanochi—and that will help, perhaps."

Kanochi nodded. "I will pay you well," he said, and moved toward Vicente's widow again.

Jo Gar stood motionless for several seconds. When he ran his handkerchief over the wet skin of his face he was smiling grimly. And he was thinking that Vincente's widow had lied to him, and that the Chinese, Matoy, had lied to him. And that Señor Kanochi had lied to him *again.*

LIEUTENANT SADI RATAN was very handsome and well built for a Filipino. He had dark eyes and good features, he was tall and erect. His white duck uniform fitted him exceedingly well. He stood near the chair into which Jo Gar had sunk rather wearily, after shaking hands with the visitor to his office.

"I have come at the request of Major Kelvey, Señor Gar," the Filipino lieutenant of police said in a tone that was so loud and assured that it annoyed Jo. "He is displeased because you took things in your hands, after arriving by chance at the shooting gallery directly after the accident."

The Island detective smiled a little. "I am sorry," he said. "A new police chief and a new police lieutenant. I must grow accustomed to the changes which have occurred since I left Manila."

Sadi Ratan stood more stiffly. He said in a cold tone, loudly:

"We are aware of your reputation, Señor Gar—but we do not wish interference. You are a private detective. You arrived by chance early on the scene of the accident—"

Jo Gar sighed and said quietly: "I did *not* arrive by chance, lieutenant. And I do *not* think the scene was one caused by accident."

There was faint amusement in the dark eyes of the well built Filipino. Jo Gar saw it and thought: This one will not be a Juan Arragon, but that does not mean he will be less shrewd. He dislikes me more than Arragon did, that is all. And the new head of police dislikes me also.

Lieutenant Ratan spoke in his loud tone. "I have done some hours of investigation. Vincente Calleo gambled and owed money. His life was threatened, but that was just a bluff. If he were killed he could not pay, and the one he owed the money to wished mostly for payment. So he was not murdered. He was frightened, worried. Perhaps he mistook the bell used on the new ride for the one that signals all clear at the shooting gallery. He rose from behind the protecting strip of bullet-proof steel, and he was struck twice by the slugs. The shooters vanished, afraid of something there was no need to be afraid of. It was an accident. I shall report it as such."

Jo Gar smiled. "The police will miss Lieutenant Arragon as much as I feared," he said simply. "Offer my apologies to Major Kelvey. I inspected the guns and asked questions because Señor Kanochi had engaged me on the case, and because I felt immediate action was necessary."

Lieutenant Ratan said, amusement in his dark eyes:

"But you did not know of the new ride—the cars that dip over tracks, which has a bell very much like the one in the shooting gallery?"

Jo Gar looked at his wrist-watch. It was after eleven and the night was very hot. He said, wearily:

"I know of it now."

The new police lieutenant smiled coldly. "I am pleased to have informed you, Señor Gar," he said. "You did not realize that the one who was owed money would gain nothing by murdering the man who owed it to him?"

Jo Gar's smile widened. He shrugged. "I realize it now, Lieutenant Ratan," he said simply.

The Police lieutenant stood very straight. There was mild contempt in his dark eyes.

"Perhaps you have been away from the Islands too long—on this last journey, Señor Gar," he suggested.

Jo Gar nodded. "Perhaps, Lieutenant," he agreed passively.

The lieutenant bowed slightly. "I go now to make my report," he said. "In it I shall include your opinions, which I do not think are worth much, Señor."

Jo Gar rose and bowed. "Undoubtedly they will make your own

opinion seem stronger," he said.

For a brief second their eyes met, then Lieutenant Ratan turned and went from the office. His footfalls sounded on the wooden steps very much like his voice—precise, loud—and very sure. Jo Gar smiled as he seated himself again. He lighted a brown-paper cigarette and puffed contentedly. The footfall died away.

The Island detective inspected his favorite Colt automatic, slipped it into a pocket of his white drill suit. He rose, after finishing the cigarette, drew a deep breath.

"In spite of the very splendid report that Lieutenant Ratan is about to make on the shooting galley accident—I think—I shall now go and talk with the murderer of Vincente Calleo," he said very softly.

THE CHINESE, Matoy, sat stiffly in the chair near a window of his house not far from the *Park of the Moon*. His eyes shifted about, went to the gleam of the Pasig, not far from the stilted house. Jo Gar stood in the doorway and said quietly:

"I know that the police of Manila believe that Vincente's death was an accident. But Señor Kanochi does not believe so. He wishes me to bring to justice the murderer."

Matoy's eyes held a peculiar expression. He said dully:

"Of course—it was the Señor's son-in-law who was killed. If he thinks Vincente was murdered, he would naturally wish the murderer to be caught."

Jo Gar said: "It was not an accident. The police are wrong in thinking so. It was murder."

Matoy's eyes became very small. He said in the same dull voice:

"What good does it do a murderer to kill the man who owes him gambling debts? One does not collect from a dead man."

Jo Gar smiled a little. "Lieutenant Ratan has asked the same question," he said slowly. "But have I said to you that the one to whom Vincente owed money was the one who killed him?"

Matoy's eyes widened; he coughed dryly, made short gasping sounds.

"You have not said that to me, Señor," he managed, after a few seconds.

Jo Gar nodded. The Chinese was watching him closely; there was fear in his eyes now. Perspiration streaked his face. Jo Gar said very quietly:

"I have gone to the new ride in the *Park of the Moon.* It did not start until tonight, at almost seven. As it did not start until then—the bell used for the signal that the cars were about to start was not used. Perhaps the bell was tested in the morning, but in the morning Vincente Calleo was not at work in the shooting gallery. He did not know of the bell."

The Chinese sat heavily in the wide chair, breathing quickly. He kept his eyes on those of the Island detective. Jo Gar said suddenly, more sharply:

"But *you* knew of the bell, Matoy! Why did not you warn Vincente?"

The Chinese rose a little from the chair, his hands gripping the wicker arms, said hoarsely:

"*I*—knew of—the bell?"

Jo nodded.

"It was you who spoke to the owner of the ride, Herr Schrenn, the German, about a suitable bell. You suggested a certain shop not far from the *Luneta.* Herr Schrenn went there and purchased the bell that was shown him first. But before he went to the shop you visited it, Matoy. And you told the shopkeeper the sort of bell you felt Herr Schrenn should purchase."

Fear was in the eyes of the Chinese clearly now. He started to say something, stopped. He coughed, and his face crimsoned with the effort. The coughing spell was sustained. When it was over Jo Gar said very softly and very quietly:

"The new ride is at the rear of shooting gallery, less than a hundred yards distant. There is much clatter in the *Park of the Moon,* and often the bell in the shooting gallery sounds more faintly than at other times. It is true that Vincente's life had been threatened and that he was frightened. His nerves were not good. He made a mistake, rose into the range of bullets when the bell of the new ride rang. He thought you had pressed the button of the shooting gallery bell."

The Chinese stared at Jo, saying nothing. The Island detective said:

"It would have been simpler if you *had* pressed the button of the shooting gallery bell, but you refused to do that. Still you have assisted a murderer, Matoy. And that is very bad, very serious."

Matoy said hoarsely: "No—Señor Gar it is not so—I did not think about the bell—"

Jo Gar said very quietly: "They will take you to Bilibid Prison, and if you do not die—"

The Chinese cried out, "No—it was accident. Three or four persons were shooting—"

Jo Gar shook his head. "It was not an accident," he said firmly. "If you are wise you will go at once to the office of Lieutenant Ratan, the new lieutenant of police. You will tell him that I sent you to him, and you will tell him who suggested to you that Herr Schrenn should purchase a certain sort of bell. If you do not go to the lieutenant—"

He shrugged, half turned his back on Chinese. Matoy cried out in a choked voice:

"I will tell—*you,* Señor—"

Jo Gar shook his head. "You do not *need* to tell me, Matoy," he said. "I know. You will go to Lieutenant Ratan, at the police station."

He went from the stilted, thatch-roofed house. The Chinese loader of shooting gallery guns was coughing terribly as he left. There was a small smile on the face of the Island detective.

"I will go now and talk to the murderer of Vincente Calleo," he murmured to himself.

Señor Kanochi fanned himself slowly with his palm leaf, his slanted eyes on the gray-blue ones of Jo Gar. The veranda of the Kanochi house was large and well furnished with wicker. In the distance were the colored lights of the *Park of the Moon,* and at intervals a faint, hot wind drifted tinny music to the veranda. Señor Kanochi watched Jo light a brown-paper cigarette. He spoke in his thinnish voice:

"Lieutenant Ratan, of the police, has convinced me that it was an accident, Señor Gar. It is a terrible thing. Vincente was often a fool, but he was young. And as I said, I have patience. He might have rid himself of his bad habits. But he was worried about the threat, and he mistook the bell of the new ride—"

Jo Gar interrupted quietly. "Does it not strike you as strange that the new ride used a similar bell?"

Kanochi widened his small eyes. For a few seconds he was silent, then he shook his big head.

"No," he said simply. "The Chinese, Matoy, bought the shooting gallery alarm for me. He is not too bright. I think he might have suggested a similar bell to the owner of the new ride, never thinking—"

Jo Gar said quietly: "You reason clearly, Señor Kanochi. That is exactly what the Chinese did."

He watched the flicker of light in Kanochi's eyes. The half-breed drew a deep breath and sighed. He spoke in a sad tone.

"Lieutenant Ratan has pointed out that the one to whom Vincente was indebted would not have killed him—it would have gained him nothing. It was just a threat. The death was an accident—a terrible accident."

The Island detective smiled very faintly. He wiped his face with a handkerchief; the heat seemed to be beating down on the veranda. He spoke very slowly and tonelessly.

"It was terrible, Señor Kanochi—but it was not an accident. It was murder."

The fat half-breed sat more stiffly in the chair. Jo Gar said with the same toneless quality in his voice:

"You would like to hear what actually happened, Señor?"

Kanochi's fat face was splotched with reddish color. His eyes were small and very slanted. His thinnish voice grated nastily.

"Lieutenant Ratan reports that it was an accident, Señor Gar—his word will do for me."

Jo Gar smiled.

"It will not do—for—*me,*" he replied simply. "Matoy, the Chinese, has confessed. He has told me many things. Even now he is at the police station."

Kanochi rose heavily from the chair, his eyes staring. Jo Gar said quietly:

"I have talked much at the *Park of the Moon.* In the theatre there—the Oriental Theatre—is a young man named Katayou. He is very handsome, Señor Kanochi. Often, lately, your daughter has walked through the *Wood of the Lanterns* with him. And he has taught her many things. He is an actor, and your daughter has acting talent. She is very much in love with this Katayou. She does not think he would strike her, as Vincente Calleo did. Nor would he gamble. And above all, she is in love. This has gone on for a time. As for you—you like money, and Vincente is causing you to lose money. For your daughter's sake you must pay some of his debts. You have come to hate Vincente—"

The fat man said hoarsely: "No—it is not—like that—"

Jo Gar nodded. "It *is*—like that," he contradicted. "You come to me and tell me a story that is not true. You go to Vincente and tell him another. You received no telephone call threatening his life. But you wished to break his nerve. You knew when the new ride would start operation, and *you* told Matoy to suggest to the new ride's owner the purchase of a certain sort of bell—"

The half-breed's eyes were very narrow. He was calm now, too calm. Jo Gar watched him closely, and after a brief pause, said:

"But even with the bell—and with persons shooting, you could not be sure that he would be hit. He might have risen—and escaped death. The shooters might have seen him in time. So Matoy fixed a gun in a manner that caused it to jam, and went into the little room. That removed him from the scene, and allowed him to say he could not know who was shooting. And one of those who was shooting was Katayou, who is a fine shot—"

The fat half-breed made a hissing sound, his body rigid near the chair. Jo Gar slipped his right hand into the right pocket of his drill coat. He said tonelessly:

"And your daughter screamed—not *after* Vincente was killed, Señor Kanochi, but *before.* She screamed when she heard the bell at the ride behind the shooting gallery ring—and as she saw Vincente's head appear. And Katayou used the repeating rifle several times—then slipped away in the crowd. Vincente was dead, and it was not an accident."

There was silence except for the heavy breathing of the fat half-breed. Then Kanochi said:

"You are guessing at these things."

Jo Gar said: "Some I know—from them I make what you call guesses. They are good guesses."

Kanochi said: "You are wrong. It was I who stood in the crowd and used the rifle! It was I who killed the weakling Vincente! He was a gambler, and brutal to his wife—my daughter. Katayou is a good man—a fine man. That is why I killed Vincente."

Jo Gar shook his head. "You are too fat and too well known—you were not in the crowd—"

Kanochi's eyes became a stare, beyond Jo. With a swift movement the Island detective swung around. But even as he was swinging he saw the half-breed's right hand come up. He checked his swing, jerked his body to one side and got his Colt clear of the pocket.

But Kanochi's hands were empty. Liquid dripped from his lower lip; he swayed a little. His right hand fell to his side, and the ring was held in the light, with the stone of red swung away from the lower half. Jo Gar stood quietly and said in a low tone:

"Poison."

Kanochi nodded, swaying. It was a jerky, broken nod. He said in a thinner voice than ever:

"I planned—the murder. I used the gun. My daughter has gone away—with Katayou—they must be happy. Vincente was bad—you know that, I did it—for them. Let them—go—"

Jo Gar said very gently: "You did not—use the repeating rifle. Katayou used it—"

The half-breed spoke with choking effort. His face was a graying, twisted mask.

"Let them—go—and be happy—"

He pitched forward and fell heavily to the polished wood of the floor. Jo Gar said suddenly and in a strange tone:

"Very well—it shall be as you wish—"

The half-breed pounded the floor with a clenched fist. He forced words from between his lips.

"It is—good. Go—and let me die alone—"

Jo Gar bowed slightly. He turned his back on the big man on the polished floor, went from the veranda. He walked slowly away from the house and the sound and color of the *Park of the Moon.* It was not pleasant to see a man die in convulsions. He was convinced that Katayou had actually murdered Vincente Calleo, but of that fact he could not be sure. And Señor Kanochi had planned the murder, of *that* he *was* sure. He decided, on the long walk back to his office just off the Escolta, that he would keep his word to the half-breed. He would report that Kanochi had murdered his son-in-law. It would be as the man who was now probably dead had wished. And in a sense it was justice—a life for a life.

The Javanese Mask

The Island detective
studies a murder mystery.

A CHINESE boy answered the veranda bell which had made a musical, clanging sound within the house. The house was on the outskirts of Manila; it faced Oriental Road, and the Pasig River was at its rear, beyond a garden of palms and jungle growth. The Chinese boy had slick, black hair and dark, wide eyes. Jo said:

"Señor Gar—Monsieur Lemere has sent for me."

The Chinese boy bowed and opened the polished door wide. His eyes held a frightened expression. As the Island detective stepped into a large, square room a deep-toned clock struck the hour of eight. The tones echoed and reechoed through the house.

From the distance, from some spot beyond the screened and shuttered windows, there came a low cry which graduated into a high wail and then fell again to the low note. Jo Gar removed his pith helmet and ran stubby, brown fingers through his gray hair. He looked questioningly at the houseboy.

"What is that?" he asked in his toneless voice.

The house-boy made the sign of the cross. His face showed fear—the whole, brown fatness of it.

"He weeps for Señor Delancey—it is the *Americano's* boy," he replied,

Jo Gar said: "Gerry Delancey?"

The Chinese boy nodded. "I am Monsieur Lemere's boy," he explained.

Thc Island detective smiled very slightly. "And for that reason you do not weep," he said.

A hoarse voice called out suddenly, from a room above:

"Tanyo, damn you! Show Señor Gar up here. Hurry, damn you—hurry! You're all the same—the whole stinking breed of you. Chatter,

chatter talk nonsense—all the time—day and night—"

The voice was shaken, uncertain. It was almost as though the speaker were damning the house-boy in order to hear his own voice. Jo Gar half closed his gray-blue eyes and glanced towards the broad stairs. The house-boy said:

"You come, please—"

He moved almost soundlessly across the waxed floor. Manila was hot, had been hot for weeks. Hot with the reek of the tropics. But this house was cool almost damp. There was an odor of incense. It was a good, well-built house, and the Island detective imagined that the typhoon winds did not rock it too much, in season. Not even so much as they rocked the building in which he had his small office, just off the Escolta, Manila's main business street.

There was a small room to the right of the stairs, and the house-boy halted in the doorway, stood to one side. He made a small but graceful gesture with his left hand and said softly:

"The Señor Gar."

Jo Gar smiled a little at the boy's use of the word "the." He went into the room and saw that Lemere was standing with his back to a large screened window. Lemere was a big man, over six feet tall and weighing more than two hundred pounds. He was supposed to be of French descent, but he had lived for some fifteen years in the islands. He had brown hair and eyes and high cheek bones, and a mouth that Jo Gar did not like. The lips were too thin and straight.

Lemere said in his hoarse voice, speaking in English and with little accent:

"These damned Chinks and Filipinos—"

He checked himself abruptly, realizing that Jo Gar was a half-breed, and that there was Filipino blood in his veins. The Island detective said nothing. From the jungle growth at the rear of the house, somewhere between it and the river, there came the wail of Delancey's house-boy. Lemere put large, brown hands to his ears and shook his head slowly from side to side. Then he took his hands away and shouted hoarsely:

"Tanyo—have that damned yelling stopped! Tell that boy I'll come down there and beat him—"

His voice trailed off. He stared at Jo Gar as though he were seeing him the first time. He said:

"Good—I'm glad you came. Delancey's dead. Murdered."

Jo Gar said: "Murdered?"

Lemere nodded. "I haven't sent for the police yet, haven't made any report. Wanted you to come here first. They bungle things so much. And you seem to get somewhere. So I sent for you. I'm glad you came."

Jo Gar's gray-blue eyes moved around the room. It was comfortably furnished in wicker; there were fan-back chairs made in the great Bilibid prison, several tables and wicker book shelves. From the large windows one looked over the garden to the Pasig; two hundred yards or so distant, and curving sharply at this point.

The Island detective looked at Lemere again. He recalled that the Frenchman had lived with Gerald Delancey for several years, in this house. That is, they had lived together during the six months or so they were in Manila. The rest of the time they spent in travel about the Islands, and around China and Japan. They collected for one of the biggest curio houses in the Orient—Rescelli. They were pretty well known in Manila; both were members of the English Club; each was a bachelor. They were together a great deal; Jo recalled that only a week or so ago he had seen them attending a soccer game, near the old Walled City.

Lemere said:

"This is pretty rotten, Señor Gar. Coming as it did—"

Jo Gar said: "The death occurred here—in this house?"

Lemere ran fingers across his forehead, shivered. He went to a small table and poured himself a drink of what appeared to be brandy. When he looked questioningly at the Island detective, Jo shook his head.

"No thanks," he said. "It would be well if I were to see—"

Lemere nodded. "That's what I took the drink for," he breathed. "Gerry was my—best friend—"

He moved past Jo, and the Island detective followed him. They went along a narrow hall, came to a closed door. Lemere opened it, went into a room that was becoming dark. Jo followed him in, halted near the door. The room was about ten feet wide and quite long. Thirty feet, perhaps. It had only two small windows; there was a heavy odor of incense. The windows were at each end of the room, which apparently ran from the front to the rear of the house. Each window was screened.

The wall space was almost covered by the objects hanging on it.

There were native shields and spears, head-dresses of various types, tribal, religious markings and poles, strings of beads—wooden and stone and metal. On the several tables of the room were small objects of all types, weapons and trinkets and cooking utensils—mostly tribal. The room was fairly dark; it had a somber feeling. At one end of one table there was a crude incense burner, and though the incense was only ash, the odor was still strong. There were two wicker chairs, and near the small window that faced towards the Pasig River there was a low couch covered with a brownish rug of some sort of rough material.

Lemere stood for several seconds looking towards the couch, then turned away from it. His eyes met Jo's briefly; he said:

"On the couch—where I found him. I haven't—touched a thing in here."

The Island detective moved towards the body on the couch. He was thinking, as he went towards it in the dusk, with the odor of the incense in his nostrils, of strange death—poison by incense or liquid. The room gave him that sort of feeling.

But the body of Gerald Delancey held nothing mysterious in the way of death. He lay flat on his back, his eyes staring at the ceiling, wide. There was a bullet wound in the left temple and another in the throat. Both wounds were small, and from the one in the temple little blood had flowed. The right fist was clenched; the left held the material of the couch cover in a tight grip. There was a half bitter, half sardonic smile on Delancey's rather sallow face. It was almost as though he had expected death, and had mocked it when it had come.

Delancey had been a small, rather slight man. He had sparse, blond hair and blue eyes. In death he seemed to have grown smaller.

Jo Gar turned slowly and looked about the room. Lemere sank into one of the wicker chairs and wiped his perspiring face with a handkerchief. The wailing in the growth back of the house had stopped. One of the small river tugs made a whistle sound. The Island detective's eyes came away from the curios on the walls. He moved nearer Lemere.

"You had quarreled," he said slowly.

Lemere took his handkerchief away from brown eyes swiftly. He sat erect in the chair, his lips working without making sound. Jo said:

"I did not say that you had killed Delancey. I said that you had quarreled."

Lemere was breathing heavily. "That damned Chink!" he muttered. "I hate the breed—"

Jo spoke with faint impatience. "Your nerves are not good. You sent for me before the police because you felt one whom you would pay would be more sympathetic. You have had recent trouble with Delancey, and you are a bit worried about the police."

Lemere did not speak. Jo said: "Your house-boy told me nothing. But you were foolish to have told him he must not speak of the quarrel you had with Delancey. That might cause trouble. Many humans quarrel, but few murder because of that fact."

THERE WAS a little silence. Lemere said heavily:

"We quarreled over business. I thought he was letting some of the stuff we got in Java go too cheaply. We've been doing badly lately. This depression has hurt our business, which is a luxury business. Our nerves were bad, too. We had a nasty scrap last night, and another just after *siesta* time, this afternoon. There are five of us living here—and I took the Chinese cook and my house-boy and went into the city, at four o'clock. I was angry and thought of finding another place. A place for myself and the servants."

He paused. Jo spoke softly:

"That left Delancey and his house-boy here."

The Frenchman shook his head. "His house-boy went away yesterday, to visit his parents. He returned here from north of the city at seven o'clock. I had come back, by that time and had found—the body. I returned with the servants at about six-forty. The cook went into his quarters to change his clothes. I called Delancey's name several times, then came up here. This is stuff we haven't sold to Rescelli for one reason or another. We use the room often. The door was half opened—and things were just as they are now."

Jo Gar seated himself in a straight backed wicker and looked around the room. His eyes went from one hanging object to another. As he used them he said:

"The house was locked?"

Lemere shook his head.

"The front door was not locked. The screen door was closed, on the veranda, and the rear door was locked. But the front door was not locked."

Jo Gar's eyes rested on a spear that looked as though the design was *Igorrote.*

"Just why did you take the cook and your houseboy along with you, Lemere?" he asked slowly.

Lemere swore. "I was sore—and the Chink cook was my find. I've had him for five years. He's good. My idea was to get out of here with my servants; I didn't intend coming back—they were mine and I wanted them out—"

The Island detective nodded. "But they would have been forced to return for their things."

Lemere said heavily: "You don't believe me, Señor Gar?"

Jo said: "Yes, I believe you, Monsieur Lemere."

The Frenchman wiped his face with the handkerchief. His left hand was shaking.

"I had a place in mind—one that I could get right into. I had the feeling that I'd show it to my servants and say: 'We move into here tonight.' But I cooled down on the way in. I was coming back to suggest to Gerry that we go into some cold weather for a change.

We've made a little money. And when I got here—"

He broke off and stared towards the lounge. Jo said:

"You looked for the gun—did not find it?"

Lemere said: "Nothing had been touched in here. I didn't see any gun. I thought at first he might have gone crazy, killed himself. We keep the guns downstairs in a closet. They're all there."

Jo said, "Delancey had perhaps—an enemy?"

Lemere shook his head. "He had few friends, and no enemies so far as I know."

The Island detective frowned. He rose suddenly and went to a corner of the room that was quite dark. He stood looking towards the wall and said quietly:

"Nothing was missing from this room?"

Lemere shook his head. "Not a thing," he replied. "I've looked around—"

"What was it that has hung here—and does not hang here now?" Jo asked steadily.

Lemere rose with swiftness for his size. He reached the Island detective's side, stared towards a small space on the wall that was a different color from the rest. It was cleaner—dust had not accumulated on the spot. Lemere drew in a deep breath.

"Good God!" he muttered. "There is something missing. I didn't notice it—in this corner—"

Jo Gar spoke softly: "What was here, Monsieur Lemere?"

Lemere said: "A mask—A Javanese mask. When we had the argument, after *siesta* time, I remember seeing it. I stood over here, and Delancey was at the other end of the room, shouting. I looked at the mask—"

He went close to the wall and said: "It hung on a nail. There was a mouthpiece in the back of it, of bamboo—it hung on that. The nail's still here."

Jo Gar nodded. "What about the mask?" he asked. "Was it valuable—and who got it? How and where?"

And for the second time the Island detective expected something touched and colored by the tropics, the jungle, tribal customs—and got nothing of the sort. Lemere said:

"It wasn't much. Ten years old, maybe. I got it for the equivalent of a couple of American dollars, at Bangkop, the capital of Java. It was a dance mask, made of wood. Pretty good sculpture, but not important. Painted red and black—and gold color. A demon mask."

The Island detective said: "A demon mask?"

Lemere frowned. "But that doesn't mean anything. It was a dance mask, but not a ceremonial dance mask. They use them in their plays—the good spirits wear masks and do sort of a fighting dance with the bad spirits, the demons. It usually ends up with the good spirits winning. This missing mask had staring eyes and a wide mouth with gold, long teeth. It was held between the teeth of the dancer, by the bamboo mouthpiece. There are many of them in Java. But where could it—"

He broke off. Jo Gar said: "If it wasn't important, why did you buy it?"

The Frenchman shrugged. "It was cheap—I got it just before we left. Had some Dutch money I didn't want to bother changing. And anyway, there's a nice profit in that stuff. I can sell it in the States for around fifty dollars."

Jo Gar said a little grimly: "You mean that you could sell it for that price, if you had it."

Lemere said hoarsely: "But where did it go?"

The Island detective smiled a little. "And why did it go?" he asked in return. "Was Señor Delancey with you when it was bought?"

Lemere shook his head. "No," he said. "He's never cared much about it—no reason why he should. He glanced at it when I showed it to him, that's all. I don't think he ever spoke of it."

Jo spoke quietly: "Is there any chance that you might be mistaken as to the mask's value? Any chance that someone might have demanded the mask and on being refused—"

The Frenchman said: "Not a bit," very decisively.

Jo Gar sighed. He went over and looked down at the body of Gerald Delancey. Then he turned away and said thoughtfully:

"You left Delancey after a quarrel, leaving him alone in this house. You were gone two hours and forty minutes, and the front door was not locked. When you returned Delancey was dead. Apparently from bullets in the brain and throat—the autopsy will clear that up. The gun used was missing, and also a Javanese dance mask that you had noticed hanging here on the wall during your last quarrel."

Lemere ran his tongue over moist lips and said:

"Yes—and the mask was of little value."

Jo Gar nodded slowly. "Of little value, apparently," he said. "Now, will you please send the three servants to me here? And then send for the police."

Lemere said softly: "Damn the police."

The Island detective went to the small window that faced the Pasig. It was growing quite dark. The screen was very securely fastened.

"I'm afraid damning the police would do little good," he suggested. "Please send for them and tell them the truth. They will do interesting things."

Lemere said grimly: "All right—and what will you do, Señor Gar?"

The Island detective spoke tonelessly: "I shall talk and think," he replied. "Counteracting a bad habit with a good one."

The Frenchman moved towards the door of the long, narrow room.

"You've got to help me, Señor Gar," he said huskily. "I will pay you well. This is a terrible thing."

The Island detective watched a banca move down-stream, lanterns lighted. He did not reply to the Frenchman and Lemere spoke again, hoarsely.

"I'll telephone the police."

He went from the room and his footfalls made sound on the stairs that led to the floor below. Jo Gar moved away from the small window and looked with half closed eyes at the nail which had held the object that was gone. He said very softly:

"A Javanese mask—of little value—"

SADI RATAN stood in the living room, downstairs, looking more handsome than ever. His drill uniform fit his fine figure very perfectly. He spoke in his usual, loud voice.

"Major Kelvey is at Baguio; I will handle this murder myself—I have the authority. Your cook and house-boy were with you during the time you were absent from this house—they are therefore exonerated. The murdered man's house-boy I am not through with. He is shifty and uncertain, and I have already caught him in one lie."

Jo Gar widened his eyes and Lemere said in a surprised tone:

"He lied, eh?" He was silent for several seconds, then spoke thoughtfully: "Well, he could have been here while we were away."

Jo Gar looked at the lieutenant of Manila police and then inhaled smoke from his brown-paper cigarette. Sadi Ratan frowned at him.

"Doctor Renan states that the bullet in the brain of the dead man would have caused instant death. There is no chance of this being suicide—because the gun has not been found. The screens of both windows are secure, and it would not have been possible for the *Americano* to have tossed the gun out, in any case."

Jo Gar said: "Lieutenant—you have learned a motive for the murder? His servant had reason to kill him?"

Lieutenant Ratan said sneeringly. "Chinese servants do not always need motives for murder. A sudden rage—"

The Island detective smiled. "You are correct, of course," he said.

The Frenchman spoke in an excited tone. "My ——! I'd almost forgotten that! Gerry struck this Chink Gao, several days ago. Struck him with his walking stick. Hit him twice."

Sadi Ratan said: "Ah! He did that, Monsieur Lemere?"

The big Frenchman frowned. "Of course, that doesn't mean—"

He broke off. Jo said: "In the Islands many masters strike their servants, unfortunately."

Sadi Ratan said loudly. "Why did he strike Gao?"

Lemere hesitated. He looked at Jo and then at the lieutenant of Manila police. He shrugged.

"I suppose you should know the truth," he said. "It doesn't mean that Gao is guilty of murder. He's been wailing ever since he learned that Delancey was dead. But he was caught in the curio room, upstairs—by Gerry. Or rather, he was caught just outside the room. He had one of those carved *Igorrote* spoons on him. The handle shaped into a head. Not very valuable, but Gerry was pretty sore. He called him a thief and hit him a few cracks."

Sadi Ratan said: "Ah! His servant was a thief. But why did he not inform the police?"

Lemere shrugged again. "The spoon had no great value. We've got a drawer full of them in one of those tables up there. You know how servants are-they take a fancy to something, and just want it. Gerry thought the cane blows would cure him from petty theft like that."

Jo said slowly: "The Chinese are usually quite honest, Monsieur Lemere. They give the least trouble—"

The police lieutenant said sharply: "There are some forty Chinese serving terms in Bilibid prison, Señor Gar."

The Island detective bowed slightly. "You are undoubtedly correct, Lieutenant," he stated.

The Frenchman spoke softly but hoarsely. "I don't think Gao did it," he said. "He may be a petty thief, but he isn't a killer. He's never had a gun, and I don't think he can shoot."

The lieutenant of police spoke grimly. "That can very easily be determined. But first we will go to his quarters and search for the mask that is missing. I think we will find it."

A clock struck ten. There was a breeze blowing across the Pasig, but it was not a very cool one. The Frenchman blinked at the police lieutenant.

"You think we will find—the Javanese mask?" he breathed. "You think—Gao stole it?"

Sadi Ratan shrugged, and his dark eyes met Jo Gar's with faint contempt.

"He is a thief and a liar. The mask and the spoon were worth little. But he was whipped and he hated the one who had whipped him. He knew that the *Americano* and you had quarreled, Monsieur Lemere. The bullets that killed Delancey were not fired at a great distance. And the fact that one entered the brain and another the throat proves that the murderer was not a fine shot. It would not have been difficult for this servant of his to have bought or stolen a gun. And after he had killed he stole the mask. He might have thought it had value, and we would be thrown off the track. Or he might have stolen it to show his contempt—the Chinese are strange people."

Jo Gar chuckled, and watched anger flare in the police lieutenant's eyes.

"And the Manila police are strange people, also," he said softly. "Very strange."

Sadi Ratan said loudly: "Because you were fortunate in the shooting gallery murder—"

Jo Gar chuckled again. "Go and search for the Javanese mask, Lieutenant Ratan. Do what you will with this servant, Gao. It will be all very foolish. He did not murder Delancey, and I do not think he stole the mask."

The lieutenant of police drew in a sharp breath. He stood very erect and glared at the Island detective. He started to speak, but did not. Lemere spoke wearily:

"Delancey is dead, murdered. The mask is the only thing missing from that room, so far as I know. The servants are witnesses to the fact that I was away when the murder occurred. It happens that we were together all of the time and there are others who saw me, of course—"

Sadi Ratan smiled. "You are not suspected, Monsieur Lemere. The only fault I have to find with you is that the police were not notified before Señor Gar."

Jo Gar smiled pleasantly. "The handicap of arriving after me is nothing to a man of your ability, Lieutenant," he stated.

The Filipino looked hatred at the Island detective, and Jo Gar thought of the difference in this second-in-command to the American head of the Manila force—and the dead Juan Arragon. This man hated him. Arragon had disagreed with him, argued with him, but he had never hated.

"And, too," Jo said quietly, "you might not have noticed that the mask was missing from the room. I am glad to be able to give you that information."

Sadi Ratan turned away. At the door of the living-room he turned.

"Will you please accompany me, Monsieur?" he asked Lemere.

Lemere glanced at Jo Gar, who nodded. The Frenchman said:

"Won't you come along, Señor Gar?"

Sadi Ratan frowned but Jo Gar smiled a little.

"You are kind," he replied. "But you wish me to search for the murderer even though the police are working to the same end?"

Lemere said hoarsely. "Of course, Señor Gar."

Jo Gar nodded. "Then I shall not bother with the servant, Gao," he said quietly. "I shall walk about the grounds a bit."

Sadi Ratan said with sarcasm: "Perhaps you will find the gun that was used, Señor."

The Island detective nodded. "In that event I will show it to you immediately, Lieutenant," he said very softly. "I will call to you."

The lieutenant of Manila police said nastily:

"And if I do not answer your call, it will be because I am busy talking with Delancey's murderer."

"Or because you are busy talking with the one you think is Delancey's murderer," Jo said gently.

THE SERVANTS were quartered in a small, wooden building in the growth behind the house; when Jo heard the voice of Ratan and Lemere grow faint, as they went towards the Pasig, he walked to a screened window and looked towards Oriental Road. It was a narrow dirt road, and there was little traffic on it. After a short time he went up the stairs and into the curio room again. He spent some time inspecting the wall surface where the mask had hung. The coroner had not yet arrived; even the act of handling the dead was not hurried in the tropics.

Jo Gar said very softly:

"Lemere has a good memory, but important thoughts occur to him only when he has been pushed. He did not notice the mask was gone until he was told of something being missing. He did not remember that this Gao was a thief or that he had been beaten, until he had been told by Ratan that the servant had lied. And yet, he says that he has a perfect alibi—and I believe him. Why then, does he attempt to throw suspicion—"

He stopped talking softly; his ears had caught the sound of a creaking board. It had been a very little sound, but he knew instantly that it had been made by a bare foot. Someone was coming up the stairs.

Jo moved swiftly and silently towards a large shield leaning against the wall near the couch on which the body rested. The shield was of wood, and appeared to be a tribal protection against spears. It was painted in gaudy colors, crudely, and was almost as tall as Jo. The room was dimly lighted—and the light was at the opposite end; little of it fell upon the spear shield behind which Jo crouched.

He could see the doorway, though his body was in shadow and his face was so brown that there was little danger of his being seen. He guessed that whoever was coming up the stairs had made a mistake—had thought the three of them had left the house.

Seconds passed, with Jo Gar breathing very quietly and holding his body motionless. He commenced to think that no human was coming up. The house was of wood, and all wood in the Islands was constantly attacked by ants and was rotting. The creaking sound might not have been caused by a footfall. But he remained quiet and waited. A minute passed, and the greater portion of another. Still Jo did not move.

And then a figure was in the doorway. It did not pause there or inspect the room. It passed swiftly inside and moved towards the shield.

Jo Gar recognized the house-boy when he was ten feet or so from the shield.

He was not Gao, the dead man's servant. He was Tanyo, the one who had greeted the Island detective, had let him into the house. Lemere's house-boy!

The Chinese was out of Jo's vision now, but Jo could hear his quick breathing. There was a little scraping sound, and then the sound of foot-falls, very light. The house-boy was moving rapidly towards the doorway; he went through it and vanished from sight. Going down the stairs he was very careful, but once again there was the creaking sound, fainter this time.

The Island detective remained quiet for perhaps thirty seconds. Then he moved from behind the spear shield, stood up straight. His eyes widened, then grew very narrow. He walked cross the room and stood looking at the Javanese mask.

It hung on the nail, and it was as Lemere had described it. A red, black, and gold, eye-staring demon mask. The sculpture was good; the wood looked soft. Jo did not touch it. He turned slowly and looked towards the covered body of Delancey. He was frowning.

After a few seconds he went very quietly from the room and down the stairs. He descended by using every other step, and he was lucky. There was no creaking sound beneath his weight. In the living-room he stood by a screened window that was at the front of the house and tried to reason it out.

He was sure that Lemere had wanted him to leave the house with them, for the talk with Gao. He did not leave and Lemere was not able to warn Tanyo. That was one idea—that Tanyo had obeyed the instructions of his master. But the reason for returning the mask was not clear, nor was the reason for removing it in the first place, if Lemere had done so.

The Island detective shook his head. He said: "No," very softly. After a few seconds he went to a screened door that led from the room to the patio at the rear, opened it and then slammed it shut, without leaving the room. He coughed several times, and lighted one of his brown-paper cigarettes. In another room he heard movement and the sound of water running.

He thought: Tanyo returned the mask for Gao. They are both Chinese. Tanyo realized that the other house-boy was suspected. Gao had stolen some things, among them the mask. Lemere may have known the mask was missing, or he may not have noticed it until I called his attention to it. That gave him the idea—and he stated that he had seen it on the wall during his quarrel with Delancey. But he really thought that Gao had it, and that Gao would be seriously involved.

The Island detective sighed and said again:

"No."

He did not think that Lemere had murdered Delancey, but he had a strong feeling that the Frenchman was hiding something. He heard a wailing voice in the distance and guessed that Sadi Ratan was using severe methods on the house-boy, Gao. Raising his voice, he called:

"Tanyo!"

After a few seconds there were light foot falls and Lemere's servant came into the room. His face was expressionless now; the fright had gone from his eyes. Jo Gar smiled at him, and spoke softly.

"A murder is a very serious thing, Tanyo," he said. "Many facts must be learned. When you left the house with Monsieur Lemere you saw the *Americano?*"

Lemere's house-boy said: "Yes—him very mad. Him stand at top of stairs and damn Monsieur. Monsieur—him say no talk. Him very mad, too, but him say no talk. We go."

The Island detective nodded. He asked questions about where they went and learned the places. They were away from the house two hours and forty minutes, but at all times they were together. Jo said:

"It was very hot, after *siesta* time. Monsieur Lemere—he had no drink?"

The Chinese boy nodded. "He had drink—with much ice. We all have same drink—him good."

Jo Gar smiled. "You had drinks together?" he asked. "Where?"

Tanyo said: "At the drink place of Montanya, off the Escolta, not long way from—"

The Island detective interrupted quietly. "I know the place," he said. "That is all."

Tanyo turned away from him. Voices sounded—the voices of Lemere and Sadi Ratan. Jo lighted another cigarette from the tip of the shortened one. Tanyo went from the room as a screen door slammed at the rear of the house. Ratan said loudly:

"He will talk much, and tell the truth—when we have taken him to the station. Major Kelvey would have it done that way. In his absence I will—"

He stopped talking as he entered the living-room and frowned at Jo Gar. The Island detective smiled pleasantly.

"You found the Javanese mask?" he asked.

Lemere shook his head. "But this Gao acts guilty," he breathed. "You know what this is likely to be—Gao did the killing, damn him—but we'll never be able to prove it. I doubt that he'll confess or break down. Poor Gerry."

The Island detective spoke very quietly. "I did not find the gun, Lieutenant Ratan."

Sadi Ratan smiled nastily. "Of course not," he muttered. "And as for the missing mask—"

Jo said: "It is missing no longer. It hangs on the nail in the curio room, from which it was taken."

Lemere's big body swung towards him; the Frenchman's eyes were wide, staring. He was breathing quickly and the fingers of his large hands were twitching. Sadi Ratan said:

"The Javanese mask—is back in the room?"

Jo said: "Yes—it was returned while you were questioning Gao."

Lemere breathed: "Good God! Why?"

Sadi Ratan went swiftly from the living-room and up the stairs. Lemere stood motionless except for the twitching of his fingers.

Jo said softly: "You would really like to know why the mask was removed, then returned, Monsieur Lemere?"

The Frenchman stared at him, then nodded. The Island detective said:

"The mask had not been hanging from the nail for perhaps a week. You did not see it there when you quarreled with Delancey. You did not even think of the mask, until I suggested that something had been taken. And when I said that—you thought I believed it. You saw an opportunity, and you did not tell me the truth. There was not so much dust on the spot from which the mask been taken as on the other uncovered spots of the wall, but there was some dust. Quite a bit. More than could possibly get there in a few hours' time. Or in a day's time."

Lemere said: "Nonsense."

Jo Gar spoke again, very softly. "You did not go from here to find another place to live, this afternoon, after the quarrel. You pretended that was the reason, and you took the servants with you. You kept them with you—even drinking with them at Montanya's place—a place not usually visited by one of your station. Nor does one of your position ordinarily drink with servants—he goes to one place and the servants to another. But you did it the other way because you were in need of a perfect alibi—you must not be alone during those two hours and forty minutes, Monsieur Lemere."

Lemere said in his hoarse voice "You are telling me that I murdered Gerry Delancey—"

Jo said: "You know that I am not telling you that. You were not in the house when the American was murdered. And I think that you are aware of the fact that this house-boy of his, Gao, will have as good an alibi as you and your house-boy and cook have. You do not want Gao to suffer for a crime you know he did not commit."

Lemere said sharply: "I know nothing of the sort. You're talking—"

The Island detective said gently: "You have just said that you did not believe this Gao would confess or be broken down. It is your idea that this murder should be unsolved, even though you have sent for me, and are apparently working with the police."

Lemere laughed harshly, bitterly. "I never heard such rot in my life. I never—"

Jo's gray-blue eyes were growing small. "Tanyo is your servant, and faithful to you. He returned the mask, which you had somewhere in the house. He thought I was with you and the lieutenant, as you had planned for me to be. I saw him return the mask. I think that you wanted Lieutenant Ratan and myself to believe that Gao had stolen it, had become frightened, and had returned it. You wanted to implicate Gao, but not to convict him—"

Lieutenant Ratan came into the room, holding the Javanese mask between two fingers that were handkerchief covered. He said to Lemere:

"This is the missing mask—the one that was missing?"

Lemere said unsteadily: "Yes."

Sadi Ratan smiled narrowly. "It will show the fingerprints of Gao, I think. He returned it, or had it returned by one of the other servants, because he was frightened. Delancey probably caught him in the act of stealing it, they fought, and the *Americano* was killed. Gao has hidden the gun, but he did not hide this. He thought that to return it would confuse us all the more. Or perhaps he did not think it had been missed and was afraid it might be."

Jo Gar smiled at Lemere. "You see?" he said. His voice was very calm. "You were correct when you told me you had sent for me because the police bungle so much."

Sadi Ratan swore in his native tongue. The Island detective said very slowly:

"I will tell you what you did, Lemere. You had quarreled much with Delancey lately. You felt that he was ruining the business in which you were partners. You did not murder him—nor did you have him murdered. But you knew that death was close to Delancey, and you made that death simpler. You left him alone, and he was murdered. You know who murdered him, but you have attempted to protect that murderer and to implicate a servant you did not think could be convicted. Death for Delancey means that you will control the business—where a separation would mean that one would have to buy the other out, or the business would be split up. You saw death coming—and you stood aside."

Lemere's eyes were slits. Sadi Ratan muttered something that the Island detective failed to catch. Lemere said shakily:

"You don't know anything about our business arrangements, Gar—you don't know that his death means control of all of it for me."

Jo smiled a little. "I can find out," he said simply. "I think that is just—what it means."

There was a little silence. Lemere's big body was swaying a little. He breathed heavily and kept his eyes on the gray-blue ones of Jo. The Island detective said:

"Who fired those two bullets—who murdered your partner, Lemere?"

The big Frenchman said heavily: "Damn you—I don't know!"

But fear showed in his eyes now. Jo Gar saw it, and Sadi Ratan saw it. The Island detective said:

"That is true, you do not know. You were not here to see. But who did you expect would kill Delancey, Lemere?"

The Frenchman shook his head savagely from side to side. His lips were wet and his nerve was breaking. He had done a terrible thing, in stepping aside, and he knew it. Jo Gar said quietly:

"I doubt that you would now be protecting a man. I think Delancey was murdered with a small caliber gun held in the hand of a woman—"

The big man screamed fiercely. "No—for ——'s sake, Gar—no! I'll tell you the truth. The servants lied, and I lied. I left them in town, across the Pasig. I came back here—"

Jo Gar said: "No, please. You have lied, but do not lie again. You did not murder Delancey. Who was the woman—"

The big man made a swift movement with his right hand. Sadi Ratan cried out: "Stop!" Jo Gar moved his body swiftly to the left and ripped his own automatic from a pocket of his duck trousers. There was crashing sound in the room—once, twice. Smoke curled from the gun as it slipped from Lemere's creased fingers, but the bullet had gone wide of the Island detective.

Sadi Ratan kicked the gun aside. Jo Gar went close to the big man.

"You are very foolish, Monsieur Lemere," he said quietly, "to let your temper get the best of you. You have now done something for which the police can exact a penalty. And perhaps, while they have you in custody, they can obtain from you the name of the murderer of your partner."

"I cannot tell," Lemere said between clenched teeth, "that which I do not know."

There was a little silence, then Sadi Ratan said in a less confident voice:

"We must find the woman."

Jo Gar shook his head.

"You must, perhaps," he replied. "I am a peculiar man, and I feel that I have done enough. You will find it difficult even if you get a name, though I do not think she will use a mask to throw you off. But I am finished with the affair."

Sadi Ratan said with a touch of nastiness: "Perhaps you think it would be too difficult."

Jo Gar smiled. "Perhaps," he agreed.

LESS THAN ten days later, in his hot office off the Escolta, Jo Gar read of the suicide of one Marie Saronocca. She had been a half-breed and she had loved well if not too wisely. She had loved one Gerald Delancey, but he had refused to continue loving her. So she had hated him and she had killed him. The Filipino paper in which Jo read the item stated that she was very beautiful, and that her small house in the old, Walled City, contained many curios of native, Island tribes—and from China and Java. She left a written confession of her crime, and in it she did not mention Monsieur Lemere. Another item, in the next column, stated that Lieutenant Sadi Ratan, of the Manila police, had suspected a woman of Delancey's murder, and been working hard on the case.

Jo Gar used a palm leaf fan to bring warm air on his brown face. He laid the paper aside, and smiled. He said a little wearily:

"It is so easy to work hard. So many people work hard—and accomplish practically nothing."

China Man

A knife is thrown in the dark for Jo Gar.

THE NUMBER five typhoon signal had been hoisted and was standing straight out against a gray sky when Jo Gar paid his *caleso* driver, patted the mangy pony on the head and moved from the Escolta towards his office. A hot wind was blowing in gusts; it had been dark for an hour or so. The Island detective reached the front of the frame building, looked towards the wooden steps that led to the first floor, moved a few feet to the entrance.

He remembered that he had only a few of his brown-paper cigarettes in his office, and none in his duck suit pockets. Since he had come to the office to talk with a client he would need cigarettes. He halted with his diminutive body almost framed in the entrance, half turned away from the semi-darkness within. The tobacco shop was two squares distant, and it was almost ten. He decided that he had better ascend to see if his client had arrived.

He went into the entrance of the building and moved up the creaking steps. Several times he had thought of moving into more desirable quarters, but there was something about his tiny, hot office in the old building that he liked. His fees were not big; he accepted almost any case that was interesting, and many of his clients were not rich. If he were to move into better quarters he would perhaps not be able to accept cases that interested him, and his contacts would be different.

He had decided that he would lose more than he would gain, and had remained in the building on one little street off the Escolta, Manila's main business street. He liked the river sounds that reached him from the dark watered Pasig, and the odors that drifted up from the small shops near the river—odors of spices and hemp and shell foods.

There was a swaying electric light bulb, on the floor above the one that held his office—the light on his floor gave no glow.

He remembered that after many months a new bulb had been placed at the end of the connection that dangled from the ceiling—only yesterday. Yet it was dark above.

He had almost reached the first floor when he heard the sound. It was very faint—and it seemed to the Island detective's keen ears to be a combination of two sounds. There was the slow sucking in of breath and the rustle of cloth. Someone was at the far end of the dark floor.

Jo Gar climbed the last few steps; the door of his office was on his right, and when he turned to open it his back would be to almost the entire floor. He reached in his pocket for the small key, faced the door. Almost instantly he heard the sound of cloth scraping cloth—and of breath expelled with an effort. And he let his body go downward, very quickly.

The knife made a sharp humming sound—there was a short crash as the blade struck wood, just above his head. But the knife did not stick in the door, making vibration sound. The blade point had not struck cleanly. The hilt battered against wood, and the knife dropped, the blade pricking Jo Gar's right ankle as he twisted his body around.

His right-hand fingers jerked his Colt from the hip pocket in which he carried it almost all of the time now. There was sound on the steps leading to the floor above—and his eyes caught the shape of a figure that seemed tall and thin. He *thought* he saw the outlines, above the figure, of such a head covering as the rivermen wore—the *sampan* men. A coolie hat, it looked like—round and rising to a shallow point—of dark bamboo.

He raised his gun, and the figure was gone. The stairs creaked under weight, but there was no sound of shoes or sandals. The one who had thrown the knife was bare-footed.

Jo Gar got to his feet, took a few steps towards the second flight of stairs, halted. He was breathing quietly. Very slowly he lowered his gun. The creaking sound had died—a door slammed. The electric bulb dangling from the wire, on the floor above, swayed less and less.

The Island detective bent down and lifted the knife. Without attempting to inspect it he wrapped it in a handkerchief, touching only the blade with his fingers. He listened for several seconds—there was no more sound from above. The light bulb on the next floor was not swaying now.

JO GAR sighed and went swiftly down the steps to the narrow street. Almost directly across from the office entrance the doorway of a small spice shop was dark, and Jo hurried the few feet to the entrance. With his back to the shop, he got his small body in such a position that he could see the street—and the entrances of a half dozen or so of the lower frame buildings similar to the one in which he had his office.

Two thoughts were strong—the knife thrower had been a Chinese, and he had thrown very poorly. He had thrown like a Filipino would shoot, missing at even a short distance.

Seconds passed and only one figure emerged from one of the frame buildings across the narrow street. That was the figure of a very heavy Filipino woman, and she stood for a time in the doorway before she waddled towards the Escolta.

The roofs of the buildings were almost all of the same height. The knife thrower had gone to the roof, and from here he would find many exits, many ways of escape. And yet, Jo had reasoned that if he had thought himself followed, the one who had thrown the knife would simply cross the roof to another building and come down the stairs to the street. It was only a short distance to the Escolta, which would be crowded. With a typhoon approaching—the band would not be playing at such time on the *Luneta*—Filipinos, Japanese, Chinese—they were moving along the Escolta. He could hear the babble of their tongues.

For almost ten minutes the Island detective remained in the shadow of the doorway across from his building. Then he sighed again and moved from it, went to his office. He switched on a single small bulb hanging above his battered desk, locked the door behind him. As he turned towards the desk again, he saw the sheet of white paper on the floor. There was a scrawl on it—without lifting the sheet which had been shoved beneath the door, he knelt down and read the message, written in English:

"I have called—you were not in—in case I do not return it is my China man, Tavar, that I suspect. J.M."

Jo Gar lifted the white sheet of paper and placed it on his desk. From a drawer he took a check he had received from John Mallison two days ago, as a retainer. He compared the writing and nodded his head slowly, with his gray-blue eyes narrowed. His wrist-watch showed him that he had not reached the office late. Mallison had come early, and he had gone away. But first he had left the note.

The Island detective inspected his Colt, returned it to the right hip pocket of his white duck trousers. He took the knife from his pocket and got the handkerchief away from it carefully. The knife had a very narrow, eight-inch blade. The handle was of wood, and the whole affair was very cheap. There were thousands of such knives about Manila; it was a common type used by rivermen. The blade had been carefully sharpened.

Jo Gar went to work on the knife, and when he had finished he sighed for the third time. There were no fingerprints on the hilt—none on the blade. Whatever method the thrower had used, he had left no mark. And because it was not easy to throw such a knife *without* leaving a mark, the Island detective frowned and murmured softly:

"I think that his hands were covered—"

He placed the knife in a drawer of his desk; and locked the drawer. He smoked a brown-paper cigarette and read the note that Mallison had left, very slowly. His frown went away, and there was a blank expression in his slightly almond-shaped eyes. Mallison had come to see him before the hour appointed. He suspected Tavar, his China man, and he had wanted Jo to know that. But why had he not waited until the appointed hour? And if there had been some good reason for him not waiting, why had he written the note? Was he afraid that he might not be able to return?

The Island detective sat in his fan-backed chair, which had come from Bilibid Prison—which perhaps had been ironically made there by humans he had trapped—and pulled on the brown-paper cigarette. John Mallison was an American—an importer of jade in carved forms. His finer pieces he shipped to England and the Americas. He had five men working for him, searching in Oriental countries. Tavar, his China man, was one of them. In the last month, during which Tavar had been in Manila most of the tine, some twenty-odd carved pieces had disappeared from the Mallison shop. He valued them at about five thousand dollars.

These things he had told Jo Gar, when he had given him the retainer. But he had also told the Island detective that he had no suspicions. He had told him this only yesterday, and this evening he had sent Jo a message setting an hour for a meeting. He had come early, and he had gone—leaving a note. He suspected his China man.

Jo Gar placed the note and check in another drawer of his battered desk, locked the drawer. He finished his cigarette, thinking about the one who had thrown a knife at him—the one who had failed to murder. He decided that the man had worn a coolie hat and had gone bare-footed. He said softly:

"But I do not think he was a coolie. I think he *dressed* as one because he wished to go bare-footed without attracting attention. He wore skin colored gloves, perhaps—he did not wish to leave prints on the knife he threw. A coolie would not worry about that."

The point was—there were many enemies. Almost always, when Jo Gar caught a man, there was a conviction. The caught one remembered, and his relatives and friends remembered. There were many enemies. Señor Gar had a reputation—criminals were afraid of him and hated him. And there was this China man that Mallison suspected, this Tavar.

Jo Gar stood up and said very tonelessly and softly:

"Perhaps Señor Mallison was right in his suspicions. Perhaps this Tavar followed him here, and guessed that Mallison suspected him and was coming to me. He worked with speed—obtained the knife—"

Jo Gar raised his head and chuckled, Then he said in an amused tone:

"A flattering thought, but I do not think it happened that way. Others have tried to murder me because they were afraid—several others. Others have tried to trick me into believing the wrong thing, even clients of mine. But now—"

He shook his head and his gray-blue eyes were almost closed. A gust of the wind ahead of the signaled typhoon rattled the screens of the office window, and something crashed to the street, in the direction of the river.

Jo Gar thought: An importer of jade carvings suspects one of his men, his China man. And a man has thrown a knife at me, and has missed. That is really *all* that I know. I must learn more. I will search first for Señor Mallison.

HE TOOK a newly cleaned Panama hat from a closet in the office, placed it over his graying hair. When he left the office he first opened the door and did not immediately go to the landing. The electric bulb he did not switch on, but he saw that it had been switched off. He did not bother about prints on the switch.

When he reached the street he thought that it had grown a little cooler. The gusts of wind seemed to be coming at shorter intervals, and they twisted at his small body as he went towards the Escolta. It was not so crowded as he had thought; the natives were hurrying, eyes on the sky. The last Number Five typhoon that had struck Manila—the center of it passing to the southward—had done serious damage. The Filipinos were anxious, worried.

Jo Gar tried two drinking places; Mallison was sucking liquid through a straw in neither. He thought of Kayil's Malay eating place, and remembered that Mallison had spoken of liking such food. Kayil's place was very near a twist of the Pasig; Jo lowered his head and moved against the gusts of wind on a narrow, curving street that cut away from the Escolta.

When he reached the eating place he stood for a few seconds, outside. A *carromatta* driver shrilled words at his pony, and the two-wheeled carriage rattled past. Jo went through swinging doors into the dull-lighted single room that was the café. It was a large room, with bamboo tables and chairs, and there were many angles to it. Some of the tables were in corners, and were almost in darkness. There was an odor of fish and spices, not very pleasant.

Kayil was a short, evil-faced man of middle age. He had served a term at Bilibid, not many years ago, for a knifing and when he came to Jo's side, with a smile on his pock-marked face, the Island detective thought of the knife that had been flung at him. He smiled, knowing that Kayil would never have missed at such a short distance.

Kayil said in Filipino: "I have not seen you in a long time, Señor Gar. It is good that you come again."

The Island detective nodded. He looked beyond the Malay, and as his eyes became accustomed to the bad light, he watched a man eating alone at a small table in a corner. Kayil spoke of the coming typhoon and said that he did not think it would be severe; he thought the Filipino in charge of the weather was no good.

At intervals Jo Gar nodded, but he watched the one in the corner. He was tall and thin, and he had a yellowish face. His cheek bones were high, and though there was much food before him and he was making motions with it, he was not eating. His gestures were quick and uncertain; he seemed nervous. He never turned his face directly towards Jo.

The Island detective turned his back on the one at the table.

"That one, facing my back. The tall, thin one with the face of a Chinese— his name?"

He spoke casually, and after he had spoken he yawned. Kayil looked over Jo's right shoulder, and his black eyes flickered with recognition, then grew blank. He shook his head.

"I do not think I have ever seen him before, Señor," he said slowly. "I think that he is a newcomer to my place."

Jo Gar continued to smile lazily. He said:

"I am searching for Señor Mallison."

Again light flickered in the Malay's dark eyes. Then he shook his head.

"For many days he has not come here," he said. "I trust that he is not ill."

The Island detective spoke with a touch of grimness in his voice.

"I trust—that he is not," he agreed.

Kayil smiled broadly and said:

"You will dine here, Señor Gar."

He spoke the name loudly, too loudly, but the faint smile did not go from Jo's face.

"I have already dined," he said, and turned very slowly so that he faced the corner table again.

His small body stiffened; his gray-blue eyes got very small. The chair had been shoved back from the table in the corner, and the tall, thin one with the yellow face was gone. Jo Gar's eyes moved to the left; a Malay was coming through a swinging door with food on a tray. The Island detective said:

"The one who was eating there—he has left."

Kayil looked towards the shoved-back chair and his eyes widened. He spoke to the waiter with the tray, in Malay, and the waiter answered that the tall one had paid for his food. Kayil shrugged.

"Through the kitchen one reaches the river street," he said. "Sometimes customers enter and leave in that manner."

Jo Gar smiled pleasantly. "But you had never seen this one before," he reminded. "And you see all who enter here. A stranger would not be likely to leave through your kitchen."

Kayil's eyes grew small and bright. Jo Gar said:

"It is wise to be honest. I search for Señor Mallison—and also for one named Tavar, who works for Mallison."

The Malay looked puzzled. "One named—Tavar?" he said thoughtfully.

Jo Gar said: "I think it was Tavar who just left, through your kitchen."

Kayil shrugged and said: "Perhaps—I do not know, Señor Gar."

Jo Gar smiled coldly. "I shall leave in the same manner," he said.

He watched the Malay's expression, without seeming to do so, but Kayil was being very careful now. His face was a brown mask and only his eyes seemed alive. The Island detective walked to the swinging door, pushed it aside and entered a small and not too clean kitchen. A cook blinked at him and muttered in Malay. Jo Gar went close to the cook and was feeling in his pocket for *pesos* when he heard footfalls behind him. He turned away from the cook, only glancing at Kayil. Through another doorway he reached an alley. It was very narrow, and beyond it he could see the river street and the *sampans* tied one alongside of another.

There was a low *adobé* wall running the left side length of the alley, and it was very dark. Jo Gar turned and went back into the kitchen. Kayil was smiling at him.

"I have changed my mind," Jo said quietly. "I will leave as I entered."

The Malay said: "That way is closer to the Escolta, Señor Gar."

His voice held a peculiar, grimly amused tone. The Island detective nodded. He went from the low-ceilinged room to the street, and turned away from the river. He said very softly:

"Twice this evening—I have not followed after—"

He broke off, shrugging his narrow shoulders. As he neared the Escolta, with the gusts of typhoon wind tearing at his duck suiting and eddies of dust whirling in the narrow street, he breathed again:

"A swift pursuit is not always wise—"

He turned back in the direction of his office, and as he neared the store front occupied by the chief Filipino paper he saw that a crowd had gathered before it.

At first he thought that the crowd was seeking news regarding the center of the approaching typhoon, but when he arrived in front of the pasted bulletin he saw that he had been mistaken. The bulletin was a brief one.

At nine-fifty the body of John Mallison had been pulled from the Pasig by two Filipino *sampan* men. Mallison had been alive before he was pulled out—the *sampan* men had heard his weak cries for help as his body had drifted down-stream. But he had been dead by the time a doctor reached the *sampan* to which he had been lifted, and he had not spoken after being pulled from the water. He had been stabbed twice in the throat and several times around the heart. The Manila police, working under Lieutenant Sadi Ratan, were seeking the criminal or criminals

IT WAS almost midnight. Sadi Ratan sat in a chair before his polished desk in the police office assigned to him, his well-built body facing Jo Gar. He looked very handsome; his brown face was carefully shaven and his dark eyes held a slightly amused expression.

"He was a fool," he said with assurance. "To go among rivermen after dusk, with a valuable piece of jade on his person—that is very foolish. He was murdered for the jade piece, that is all. It is very simple."

The Island detective said: "Who was it that saw this piece he was murdered for, Lieutenant?"

Sadi Ratan smiled. "A Malay by the name of Kayil, who has come to me to tell of it. A waiter in his eating place. And a Filipino by the name of Vincente Galo, who was dining there. The Malay owner of the place says that the American had been drinking."

Jo Gar nodded. "It appears to be very simple," he agreed.

The police lieutenant smiled broadly. "Very," he agreed. "You waste your time, Señor Gar."

The Island detective shook his head. He spoke pleasantly to the man he knew hated him.

"Mallison was taken from the river at nine-fifty," he said. "Shortly after ten I talked with the Malay, Kayil. I said that I was looking for Mallison and the Malay told me he had not been at his place for many days. He said he trusted Mallison was not ill."

The lieutenant of police nodded and continued to smile.

"So he has said," he replied calmly.

"He did not at the time he talked with you know that Mallison had been murdered, of course. He says that he makes a practice of giving very little information about his customers. He has found it is not good for his trade."

Jo Gar lighted a brown-paper cigarette. "He is very thoughtful," he said quietly.

Sadi Ratan nodded and showed even, white teeth.

"He has been of great help to us," he said simply. "We have heard from other sources that the American had been drinking heavily."

Jo Gar narrowed his almond-shaped eyes and ran browned, short fingers through his graying hair. There was a little silence, broken only by the sound wind made against screens. Then the Island detective said:

"I have been paid a retaining fee by the dead man. Some five thousand dollars' worth of carved jade had been stolen from him, and he suspected an employee. He wished me to meet him at my office tonight. He arrived early and left a note. When I arrived a knife was thrown at me."

Sadi Ratan sat up stiffly. He said:

"A knife was thrown at you?"

Jo nodded.

The police lieutenant relaxed. "It is good that it did not strike you," he said in a not too convincing tone. "But then, you have enemies in Manila."

The Island detective nodded. "That is so," he agreed. "But Mallison named the employee he felt had stolen his jade, in the note he left. It might have been that he was followed, and that this employee was afraid of me—and threw the knife."

Sadi Ratan said with a smile: "You mean that Mallison's China man, David Tavar, might have thrown the knife?"

Jo Gar's thin lips were pressed tightly together. He half closed his eyes, and tried not to show the surprise he felt.

Sadi Ratan was enjoying himself. "Tavar was the one Mallison wrote he suspected, I suppose," he said too calmly. "Tavar came to me days ago, telling me that Mallison was drinking heavily and that Mallison hated him. He said that he was afraid Mallison might attempt to trap him in some way, and that he was acting very foolish with his jade."

The police lieutenant inspected his fingernails, and yawned. Jo Gar said:

"Yes, Mallison wrote that he suspected Tavar. I have never seen Tavar. Is he tall and thin, with high cheek bones—"

The police lieutenant shook his head, chuckling. "On the contrary, he is short and rather fat. Black hair and a small mustache. A very jolly fellow."

The Island detective pulled on his cigarette. Wind made hissing noise against a screen. Lieutenant Ratan said in a pleased tone:

"The center of the typhoon will pass to the northward. That is good."

Jo Gar looked at the mat on which he was standing.

"You believe Mallison—or Tavar?" he asked.

Sadi Ratan shrugged. "Mallison made no complaint to the police. You are a private detective. He went to you. But Tavar came to me. He was with friends from seven until eleven tonight—I have their names."

Jo smiled a little grimly. "Friends are often kind," he said.

Sadi Ratan spoke in an irritated tone. "John Mallison had been drinking heavily. He had been foolish with his jade. He was foolish again tonight. He hated an employee, and he wished to hurt him. Tonight he talked too much, and he was murdered, knifed for the jade pieces he had with him and which several persons saw."

Jo Gar spoke thoughtfully. "And he was murdered at a time when the man he suspected or *said* he suspected of robbery, was with friends."

The police Lieutenant nodded. "Yes," he said.

Jo smiled. "*Why* did Mallison hate this China man of his?" he asked.

The lieutenant smiled back at the Island detective.

"Because of a woman," he said "You do not perhaps think the reason sufficient?"

Jo said: "Completely sufficient, Lieutenant. The woman is unnamed?"

Once again the amused expression showed in Sadi Ratan's eyes.

"I have her name," he said. "Sorry, Señor Gar."

Jo Gar bowed slightly. "And you will report the murder as one growing out of robbery—by rivermen, probably."

Sadi Ratan nodded. "Murder because the American was a drunken fool," he said. "Still—we shall try of course to find the murderer or murderers."

Jo said, nodding: "You place no importance on the note Mallison left for me, or the fact that he retained me? Or the fact that he named this Tavar?"

Sadi Ratan smiled. "Mallison hated his China man," he said shortly. "I am convinced of that."

Jo frowned. "You have released Tavar?" he asked.

The police lieutenant spoke with impatience.

"He was never arrested, detained. He came to me of his own accord."

Jo nodded. "Of course," he said thoughtfully, and turned towards the doorway of the office.

The police lieutenant spoke cheerfully. "Be careful, Señor Gar, I am sorry to hear of that knife that was thrown."

Jo faced the lieutenant, smiling. "You are kind," he said quietly. "I shall be very careful, Lieutenant."

He bowed and went from the office. In the street, not many feet from the Escolta, he breathed to himself:

"Very careful, Lieutenant—much more careful I think than you have been."

MUSIC SOUNDED in Kayil's place—the music of a thin-toned piano and a violin. It was a few minutes after one. Jo Gar stood at the end of the alley that led to the kitchen for several seconds, his expressionless eyes almost closed. The typhoon wind was making sound along the river behind him—*sampan* men were working to keep their craft from battering against each other, but there was no flare of torches.

The music died and the Island detective shrugged his narrow shoulders. He transferred his Colt to the right side pocket of his duck coat, kept fingers on the grip of the weapon. With his left hand he pushed open the kitchen door, went inside.

The Malay chef blinked at him in the glare of heaped coals. Jo Gar smiled and went across the dirty kitchen and into the room beyond. It was well filled with humans—Malay, Chinese, Japanese and Filipinos. They were men of the river, and some of them had women with them. They were poor men, and rough looking. One very tall Malay stood near the other entrance to the room, talking with Kayil whose back was turned to the Island detective.

Jo Gar let his eyes move about the room; he saw the one he had seen earlier, sitting in the same corner, alone. The man was watching him; the color of his cheekbones showed yellow in the dull light.

The Island detective moved to the table in the corner, smiling a little. When he reached the table he halted and looked down at the tall, thin one. He spoke first in Chinese, very softly and rapidly, and when he had finished the thin one shook his head.

Jo spoke in Filipino, saying: "I would like to sit with you and talk."

There was a stupid expression in the dark eyes of the seated one. He shook his head slowly from side to side.

Jo Gar said in English: "I wish to talk with you."

The seated one spoke very hoarsely yet softly. "What is it—that you want?"

Jo Gar moved aside, smiling, and pulled over a rough bamboo chair from another table. The piano and violin made sound again, from a far corner of the room. The Island detective sat down, keeping fingers on his gun. He leaned across the table, so that his head was not far from the yellow-faced one's.

"I will make a bargain with you," he said very slowly and softly.

The dark eyes of the thin one shifted away from Jo Gar, looked in the direction of the Malay, Kayil, then came back to the Island detective's eyes.

"I do not know you," he said hoarsely and slowly.

Jo Gar nodded.

"One does not always know the man he seeks to kill," he said steadily.

The yellow-faced one's eyes grew very narrow. His thin body was tense; and he sat erect. Jo said:

"My eyes are very good. Even when there is little light I see well. You threw a knife at my back this evening."

The one seated across from him said in Malay:

"You talk like a fool!"

Jo Gar continued to smile. "I do not see like a fool. You waited for me in my office building. And you threw a knife at me. You were bare-footed and you wore a coolie hat. You ran up the stairs and went over roofs. On a roof you waited for me, with another knife. If I had followed you—you would have thrown again. And you might not have missed when you found me behind you."

The one with the yellow face said nothing. He was breathing heavily, and his eyes moved away from Jo's again, going towards the spot where the Island detective had last seen Kayil.

Jo said: "You did not think you were seen—but I have eyes for the dark. I did not shoot at you, though my fingers held a gun, as they hold one now."

The yellow-faced one made swift, breathing sound. His eyes looked downward. Jo Gar nodded his head. The piano and the violin were wailing swift, fierce music and in the center of the floor a Filipino and a half-breed girl were dancing, whirling about. Jo Gar glanced at them, turning his head swiftly. And he saw that the Malay, Kayil, was not where he had been. Then his eyes were on the dark eyes of the man seated across from him.

One of the yellow-faced one's hands was on the table, but the other was out of sight. Jo said in a hard voice.

"Put both hands on the table."

The one across from him hesitated. Jo Gar smiled and said in Malay:

"If I shoot you in here it will not be bad for me—it will only be bad for you."

The left hand of the yellow-faced one came to the table surface. There were *betel*-nut stains on the fingers, red-brown on the yellowish skin. The man had long fingers, and the back of the hand was scarred.

Jo Gar smiled. "In Bilibid Prison you would work long hours, twisting bamboo. You would work for many years. It is very bad to throw a knife."

The eyes of the thin one showed faint fear. Jo Gar stopped smiling. He spoke again in Malay, softly and not perfectly.

"I will make a bargain with you. If you tell me the truth—you will not go to Bilibid."

The one across from him said very hoarsely: "You are a fool—I do not know what you speak about."

Jo Gar smiled with his gray-blue eyes almost closed. He said:

"The gun will make sound and the police will come in. You will not see them. You will be dead. I will have killed the one who tried to kill me."

He moved his right arm slightly and watched the fear show in the yellow one's eyes. Then he said softly:

"Or the gun will make no sound—and you will answer my questions. You will not go even to Bilibid. It is a bargain that I will make."

The one across from him spoke hoarsely. "I did not *try* to kill you." He spoke in English, and he accented the word "try." Jo's eyes widened a little. He was silent for several seconds, then he said:

"So—you threw the knife, but you did not throw well? You did not want to kill me?"

The yellow-faced one said:

"It is so." He was breathing shortly, and his eyes were shifting away from Jo Gar's.

Jo said: "You wished to frighten me—to make me *think* that an attempt had been made on my life. Who was it paid you to do that?"

The yellow-faced one hesitated. Jo Gar moved his right arm again, and his gray-blue eyes were suddenly hard.

The man across from him said:

"The *Americano*—Mallison."

THE ISLAND detective sat stiffly, staring at the yellow-faced one. Mallison had paid this man to miss him, with a knife. Mallison. Was Sadi Ratan right, after all? Had the American hated his China man, Tavar, so much that he had planned to trick the detective he had retained into believing Tavar was guilty? Had this yellow-faced one's act been the beginning—and then had something gone wrong? Or was the one opposite him lying?

The music died again.

Jo Gar was silent for several seconds, then he said softly:

"You did not throw a knife that belonged to you?"

The other shook his head. "The *Americano* gave me the knife," he said. "I held black cloth in my fingers when I threw it. That is all I know."

Jo Gar's eyes were slitted on the dark ones of the man across from him. He said suddenly:

"I think that you are lying."

The thin one lifted a hand from the table and pointed a thin finger across the room. There was a round target, not more than a foot in diameter, hanging on a wall across from their table. It was such a target as tiny darts were thrown against, for sport. It was painted brown and red and black. Smoke drifted before it, from cigarettes. The yellow-faced one said:

"I do not miss, with the knife. I am Kanya, of Malay blood. I have done no wrong. I will show you. For years I guarded an Englishman who had a plantation on Mindoro."

Jo Gar gripped his gun more tightly and said:

"Very well—show me that you do not miss—unless you wish to miss."

He moved his chair slightly. The Malay made a swift movement and a long bladed knife flashed in his left hand. The left arm came up as he half rose from his chair. His fingers held the knife by the blade. The arm jerked forward and the knife sped towards the target, turning.

At the same instant a gun crashed. Jo Gar heard the yellow-faced one's shrill cry as the bullet struck him. And very close to the target he saw the one who had used the gun. He was short and thick-set, and he had a small mustache. He had come suddenly from a corner thick with smoke, half backing from a table. But he had seen the yellow-faced one throw the knife, and he had seen Jo Gar. And he had *not* thought of the target.

Jo Gar realized, even as the knife blade quivered almost in the center of the target on the wall, what had happened. And he knew that the yellow-faced one had lied for Tavar, and that Tavar feared he had been crossed—and had thought that the yellow-faced one had intended the knife for him. Smoke drifted between the Island detective and Tavar. The short man's eyes were staring at the body of the man he had shot, half sprawled across the table. Jo Gar rose suddenly.

Kayil stood near the entrance of the café, swaying a little, both hands at his sides. Everyone was very quiet.

Jo Gar said:

"I want you, Tavar. You stole jade from the American, Mallison." His eyes never left the eyes of the short one. "You murdered him, tonight—knifed him. You went to the police and said he was drinking heavily, and that he was a fool with his jade. He was drinking, that is true, but he was not a fool. You said that he hated you, and you were afraid of him. You knew he was coming to me, and that he would tell me he suspected you. But you prepared for that, and you paid the Malay to throw a knife at me, but to miss me.

"I think that knife was one of *yours*—and you had intended to show that Mallison had it in his possession. You had friends lie for you about Mallison showing his jade tonight, and you had an alibi—you were with friends. And then, because you thought the yellow-faced one was trying to knife you—shot him. He was only throwing at the target—"

Tavar's head jerked towards the target. Someone near the yellow-faced one said thickly:

"He is—dead."

Jo Gar pulled his Colt from his pocket. Tavar's gun hand jerked up and both guns crashed at the same time. Tavar fell forward, and the left side of Jo's duck coat jerked as a bullet ripped it. Kayil moved his right hand downward and Jo fired for the second time. The Malay café owner swore, and gripped his right arm near the elbow. Jo backed against a wall and watched the rush for the doors. When it was over only four of them remained in the room. The dead yellow-faced one;

Tavar collapsed on the floor, Kayil—and himself.

Jo Gar watched Kayil closely. Then he said, after long seconds:

"You are an accomplice—it will be worse for you if you do not tell the truth."

Kayil shrugged. Jo said: "Move Tavar against that wall. See where my bullet hit him."

When it was done, Kayil said: "Just under the heart—"

Tavar held his eyes open with an effort and said in a weak voice:

"I wanted—money—to get away from these—damned Islands—I knifed him—and tried to fix it—as you said—I knew he'd go to you and say—he suspected me—and I wanted the police to laugh—at you—"

He closed his eyes. Jo Gar said steadily: "You and I, Kayil—we'll go to your telephone. A doctor—and the police."

Kayil shrugged. They went towards a telephone. Kayil breathed:

"That damned target—"

Jo Gar smiled very grimly as he looked at the target on the wall and said in a tired voice:

"It was a damned one, certainly—for Mallison's China man!"

The Siamese Cat

The little Island detective, hunts a cat—and finds a murderer.

SADI RATAN looked up from his desk and smiled at Jo Gar. The police office was hot, the streets of Manila were hot. Tropic heat had been fierce during the past few weeks; it would be fierce for many more. But the Filipino police lieutenant did not seem to mind heat. His brown face was handsome and his dark eyes seemed alert and unwearied. He said in an amused tone:

"You were surprised, Señor Gar, at my sending for you?"

Jo Gar dabbed at his face with a large handkerchief, put it in a pocket of his duck suit. His gray-blue eyes smiled a little.

"I was surprised at your *request* for me to come here, Lieutenant," he corrected quietly.

The police lieutenant waved his left hand a little airily.

"We are very busy," he said. "That escape of the Chinese from Bilibid Prison—the disappearance of the English woman. Several small but annoying robberies. Yes, we are very busy."

The Island detective got his stubby-fingered hands in the pockets of his duck coat and said nothing. Sadi Ratan inspected a fly-specked ceiling and the slowly swinging fan. Then he said:

"Knowing that you had not been retained by John Collings in the matter of the search for his wife, and knowing that you would not be interested in the search for the two escaped prisoners or these minor store hold-ups—I thought of you for another matter."

He paused and smiled. Jo Gar smiled back at him and lighted a brown-paper cigarette. He said:

"With your fine efficiency you will capture the escaped convicts quickly. The English woman has a habit of disappearing; she will return shortly. I am sure you can pick up the store thieves, Lieutenant."

Sadi Ratan frowned slightly, then smiled again.

"Of course," he said. "But I regret you have not been retained in any of these instances."

The Island detective inhaled and wondered what the lieutenant of the Manila police was getting at. There was very little good feeling between them; it was the first time Sadi Ratan had sent for him. Jo said:

"Business cannot always be good."

The police lieutenant made another gesture with his left hand.

"An American named Brail—Walter Brail—has been in to see me. He has been in Manila only a week or so. He is wealthy and wanders about the world. An unfortunate thing has occurred. He has lost a cat."

Sadi Ratan looked down at a paper before him and tried not to smile. Jo Gar's eyes were expressionless. He said nothing. The police lieutenant went on.

"It is a very unusual cat—he is much attached to it. A Siamese cat. He is very anxious to recover it, and that is not exactly a police matter. So I suggested you, Señor Gar."

Jo Gar bowed very slightly. "It was kind of you, Lieutenant," he said.

Sadi Ratan looked him in the eyes, smiling peculiarly.

"I told him that perhaps you would consider such an assignment below your dignity—"

Jo Gar shook his head. "On the contrary—I am a great lover of cats," he interrupted. "Where shall I find this American, Lieutenant?"

Sadi Ratan's eyes widened a little then narrowed. He said:

"He is staying on the Bay, at the Manila Hotel. The cat escaped from his screened porch there. There has been much searching, and he is advertising, of course. He will be glad to see you, Señor Gar."

The Island detective nodded, still smiling. "It was very good of you to think of me," he said. "I shall try to return the favor at some time."

Sadi Ratan gestured carelessly again. He looked at his wrist-watch.

"You will go to the hotel tonight, Señor?" he asked.

Jo Gar nodded. "I shall go there immediately," he said. "The name is Walter Brail—and the American has lost a Siamese cat."

The police lieutenant's eyes were serious. "That is so," he said. "And the best of luck, Señor Gar."

Jo smiled and bowed again. He went from the office and to the

Escolta, Manila's main business street. It was almost nine o'clock in the evening, and not too many people were about. The Island detective hailed a *carromatta,* climbed slowly inside. He spoke to the Filipino driver in his native tongue, settled back in the comfortable seat.

The driver shrilled at his pony. The distance was short, and though Jo Gar thought a great deal about Sadi Ratan's mocking tone, and the idea of sending for him—he reached only a half decision. The police lieutenant had thought it would be amusingly insulting, when he had not been retained by those concerned in more important matters, to call Jo over and suggest his search for a cat. And yet, he felt there was something beyond that. He doubted that Ratan, who was not a fool, would bother with such a childish sort of humor.

He was smiling a little as he left the *carromatta,* and entered the hotel. In his not uneventful career as a freelance detective he recalled that this was the first time he had ever been concerned with a Siamese cat.

THE SUAVE clerk behind the desk smiled and then looked serious. "Mr. Brail is very disturbed," he said. "He has created a great deal of worry in the hotel. He will be glad to see you Señor Gar. I will call him."

Jo Gar nodded and waited. The clerk spoke to the switchboard girl and then motioned towards an enclosed phone. Jo went to it and when a heavy voice said: "Yes?" he said: "Señor Gar speaking, Mr. Brail. Lieutenant Ratan of the local police has told me you were interested in finding a Siamese cat—"

The heavy voice interrupted: "Ah—good, Señor Gar. I am glad you have come. Please come right up."

The phone clicked. Jo went to the desk and the clerk smiled at him.

"It is two flights up, Number Twenty-eight—at the extreme north wing. Our finest suite. Shall I send a boy—"

Jo Gar shook his head. "I know the way—the opera singer who lost her bracelet occupied the same suite, about a year ago, I think."

The clerk nodded. Jo smiled and said: "Mr. Brail is traveling alone?"

The clerk said: "He has his valet—an English valet. There are just the two of them, and there was the cat."

The Island detective nodded. "A fine cat?" he asked.

The clerk nodded. "Very beautiful," he said. "I saw it in the basket.

Beautifully marked—very large."

Jo smiled and moved towards the broad stairs. The hotel was low and spread out, with fine gardens and a beach on the Bay. Ceiling fans circled silently, and stirred iced air. Jo climbed the stairs slowly, accustomed to the tropics and knowing the results of speed. The corridors were wide; on the second flight he moved along the north wing towards the suite that faced the Bay, hung almost over the waters of it.

When he reached the double doors he knocked. After a few seconds he rang a bell that made sound he could hear from the corridor. Out on the Bay there was the deep-toned whistle of a big boat. Jo rang the bell again.

Seconds passed. He rapped sharply on one of the wooden doors, with his knuckles. The padding footfalls of a hotel maid sounded from along the corridor, and the Island detective went towards the woman. He said:

"I have just talked with Mr. Brail, in Suite Twenty-eight, from downstairs. He asked me to come up. He does not answer the bell, or my knock."

He followed the Filipino maid back to the double doors. She rang the bell several times, tapped on the door. She called in a high-pitched voice: "Señor Brail—Señor Brail—"

There was no sound from within the suite. The maid jingled keys on a ring and turned one in a lock. She pushed open a door and called again: "Señor Brail!"

Jo Gar walked past her through a small foyer and into a large, wicker-chaired living-room. He was half way across the room when the Filipino maid screamed. She screamed terribly—and ran towards the corridor. Jo Gar went over and looked down at the figure of the man. The man was lying on his back, with his arms and legs spread. His eyes were opened. There was blood on his lips—and his hands showed long, jagged streaks of red scratches. He was dead.

Jo straightened and looked around the room. His body stiffened as he glanced towards a wicker divan near the screened porch that hung over the Bay. The Siamese cat crouched motionlessly on the divan, its eyes focused on his figure. It was a dusty gray, huge for a cat. The black marking of its face and ears and the blueness of its eyes stood out in the reflected light from a table lamp. In the corridor the Filipino maid was still screaming, and there were sharp voices coming from below. Everything in the room was very motionless—Jo Gar, the body on the floor—and the figure of the Siamese cat.

SADI RATAN stood just inside the living-room of the suite and frowned at Jo. The hotel clerk said:

"Mr. Brail left the hotel at about five o'clock. He returned at about eight-thirty—and a half hour before Señor Gar called. Perhaps not that long. He asked if his cat had been found, and said he'd sent his valet along the Bay front, to inquire at the houses. Then he went upstairs. Nobody called to see him, until Señor Gar arrived."

Jo said: "That is, nobody *announced* that he was calling."

The clerk shrugged. Sadi Ratan looked at the body, then at the medical man.

"Two knife wounds—one in the back of the neck—one to the heart. They caused the death."

The doctor nodded. "Apparently," he said. "The scratches on the hands and wrists look like cat scratches."

Sadi Ratan glanced towards the Siamese, sleeping on the divan. He frowned. Jo Gar said to the clerk:

"When did you last see Phelps, this valet?"

The clerk thought for several seconds. "Around four o'clock. He went out without stopping at the desk. He's tall and very thin. He has a sad face."

Sadi Ratan said: "It's after nine-thirty, and he left at about four. That's a long time to be walking around the Bay front, looking for the cat."

The clerk looked at the Siamese. "How did it—get back here?" he asked.

Jo Gar spoke grimly. "The cat didn't knife Brail in the neck and the heart. Brail spoke to me, say five minutes before I came into this room. That is, a heavy-voiced man spoke to me."

The clerk said: "Señor Brail had a heavy voice."

Sadi Ratan looked at Jo Gar narrowly. "He didn't tell you over the phone that his cat had been returned, or had returned. Yet the chances are the cat was here then."

Jo Gar shrugged. "Perhaps," he said. "It is possible for a person to go down from the screen porch. There are vines that are strong. The suite below is not occupied. There's another stairway and several ways out of the hotel. After I spoke to Brail, if it was Brail, I talked at the desk a bit. Brail might have been dying then."

Sadi Ratan said: "How about the cat?"

Jo Gar shrugged. "The clerk says the cat disappeared this morning at about ten o'clock. These Siamese can climb. It might have been wandering around on the roof. The roof was searched, but it might have been missed. The porch isn't completely screened—the cat might have come back after Brail was murdered."

Sadi Ratan said: "I want to see Phelps—I think Brail talked to you, and that the cat was here then. There is something very strange about this."

Jo Gar smiled narrowly. "There is something very strange about most murders," he said quietly.

The telephone at one end of the living-room made ringing sound. Jo Gar started towards it, but Lieutenant Ratan caught him by the arm.

"I will answer, if you do not object," he said. "This is my investigation."

The Island detective stood aside, shrugging. "I thought you had turned the case over to me," he said slowly.

Sadi Ratan frowned. "A lost cat is not a murder case," he stated. "This is a matter for the police."

Jo Gar smiled a little more broadly. "I think you are correct," he stated as the police lieutenant neared the telephone. "A very good matter, Lieutenant."

The police lieutenant lifted the receiver. He listened for several seconds after he said: "Lieutenant Ratan speaking." His body grew tense and he swore once, in Spanish. The Siamese cat uncurled itself and stood up. It jumped lightly from the divan and crossed the room, paying no attention to the body of Walter Brail. Jo Gar watched it closely, his eyes half closed. The room seemed to be growing hotter. Sadi Ratan said sharply:

"I will be there immediately—do not allow the body to be disturbed."

He hung up the receiver, faced Jo Gar. His handsome face held a grim expression.

"Phelps is dead," he said slowly. "His body has been found, along the Bay front, by some boys in swimming. He committed suicide and left a note. You will come with me, please, Doctor?"

The Island detective watched the doctor nod. Sadi Ratan looked at him thoughtfully.

"Would you care to come, also?" he asked.

Jo Gar sighed, shook his head. "I think not, Lieutenant," he said tonelessly. "A murder and a suicide—it is most certainly a matter for the police."

IT WAS almost midnight when the Island detective went into Sadi Ratan's office. The police lieutenant was slumped low in his chair, relaxed and smiling, he moved a palm leaf fan gracefully, so that wind struck his handsome face. Jo Gar closed the door behind him and stood near it.

"You appear pleased, Lieutenant," he said.

Sadi Ratan nodded and gestured with the fan. "My men have captured the two escaped Chinese. The English woman has been found wandering beyond the city. And we have the murderer of Walter Brail. Things become quiet again."

Jo Gar said: "You have Brail's murderer?"

The police lieutenant nodded and took time in speaking. He was enjoying himself.

"The valet, Phelps, was the murderer," he said in a satisfied tone. "It was all very simple."

Jo Gar looked at his stubby, browned fingers. "Most murders are very simple," he agreed.

Sadi Ratan continued to smile. "Phelps had been with Brail for almost ten years. He wrote in the note he left that he has hated Brail for the last three of them. He did not show his hatred. He hated Brail because he would not give him money, back him in a small business he wanted to start in London. Every year for the past three or four years Brail had promised to let him go, back him in this business. But he never did it. Phelps hated to travel, and Brail was traveling most of the time.

"A month or so ago Brail told the valet that he was leaving him ten thousand dollars, in his will, and that he could start his business after Brail's death. He joked about it, showed Phelps the clause in the will. And the valet knew that Brail would never back him in his business while he was alive. He hated him all the more—Brail was in good health and younger than Phelps. The valet thought about murder—he first thought about it in Shanghai. In the note he stated he almost went through with it ten days ago, in Nagasaki. He wanted that ten thousand dollars. Tonight he murdered Brail. And when he realized what he had done—he shot himself. He wasn't the type who could kill and live, that was all."

Jo Gar said very softly: "So?"

Sadi Ratan smiled a little. "He deliberately let the Siamese cat loose. He wanted to get Brail along the Bay front in some deserted spot. But he decided Brail was suspicious, would not go. He followed Brail here, knew that he had reported the loss of the cat to the police. At first he thought he would wait. Then he decided the missing cat would make things more difficult for the police. He returned from the supposed search and when Brail stepped away from the phone after talking to you, he stabbed him twice. He went down the vines, below the screened porch and was not seen. But he couldn't stand being a murderer. He wrote this note—and shot himself.

Jo Gar looked at the polished floor of the office.

"You've compared the handwriting with other writing of Phelps?" he said slowly.

Sadi Ratan nodded. "Naturally," he said, still smiling. "We went right back to the hotel and got to work. We found a copy of Brail's will, and the clause leaving the ten thousand to the valet was there. We compared handwriting of the last note—it was written hurriedly, of course, almost scrawled. But it is Phelps' handwriting. Simply a murder for money, of greed. And Phelps was too weak for such a thing. He used the cat to attempt getting Brail from the hotel, in some deserted spot, searching. But that didn't work."

The lieutenant of police smiled and shrugged "So—you won't have to worry about the Siamese cat, Señor Gar, after all."

Jo Gar smiled a little. "On the contrary," he said very quietly. "I think I shall have to worry very much about the Siamese cat."

Sadi Ratan straightened in his chair. He narrowed his dark eyes.

"Why?" he asked.

Jo Gar's eyes were expressionless. "Because the valet did not murder Brail. Because the valet did not leave the note you found—and because I do not think Phelps committed suicide," he said tonelessly.

Sadi Ratan stared at him, his mouth slightly opened. He rose from the chair grimly:

"I am aware that you have been right several times in the past, Señor Gar. You have also been fortunate. But when you say what you have just said, in the face of the evidence we have—"

He broke off, gesturing widely with his arms. Jo Gar said quietly:

"You wished to amuse yourself, Lieutenant—and you thought you were insulting me by suggesting that I should search for a lost cat. There have now been two deaths. And because one appears to explain another, you eagerly accept any evidence that comes along. *I* do not accept your evidence."

The police lieutenant said angrily: "The case is closed. We have the motive, the manner—and the confession. You have not been retained—"

The Island detective grinned. "I am retaining *myself,*" he interrupted. "My reward will be obtained in a way familiar to you, Lieutenant. I shall be amused at you."

Sadi Ratan swore in Spanish. A nasty smile twisted his handsome face.

"The press will be amused—Señor Gar does not agree with the police and will hunt down the murderers of *both* Walter Brail and his valet," he mocked.

The Island detective inhaled smoke from the Filipino cigarette.

"The press has been amused before," he said quietly. "But not at me."

Sadi Ratan shrugged. "Again—I wish you luck," he said. "A simple case has been closed. The cat has returned. You are not satisfied—shall I tell you why?"

Jo Gar said: "Please do."

The police lieutenant continued to smile. "You are disturbed because I suggested you hunt for the Siamese. When I suggested it you did not show it, Señor Gar. And the murder gave you the opportunity to be first on the scene. When it was cleared up so easily, by us—"

He smiled more broadly, bowed slightly. Jo Gar smiled back at him.

"By a pencil scrawl on paper," he corrected. "That is what bothers me, Lieutenant. It is cleared up so easily."

Sadi Ratan sighed. "You prefer the mysteries of the Siamese cat, perhaps," he said mockingly.

Jo Gar watched a thin curve of smoke from his cigarette, his eyes expressionless.

"Perhaps," he agreed, and went from the office to the quiet of the hot Escolta.

IN THE morning the Island detective read in papers printed in several languages that Winton Phelps, English valet of Walter Brail, wealthy and eccentric American, had murdered for money to be left him, and had then, half mad with regret for what he had done, shot himself to death. The police had his confession note—the facts checked with a will found in Brail's baggage, the handwriting was that of Phelps.

A Siamese cat had been lost by Phelps in an attempt to lure his master to a deserted spot, but Brail had been murdered in his hotel suite. Another item in all of the papers stated that it was believed by the police that Señor Gar had been engaged to search for the lost cat, which always traveled with the eccentric Brail, and that Señor Gar had stated he did not accept the police theory of murder and suicide.

Jo Gar smiled and breathed softly: "Always this Siamese cat—Sadi Ratan is much amused. He is not concerned with the fact that having murdered and escaped, having the ten thousand dollars left to him, this Phelps killed himself. And so quickly, after writing such a note. And Lieutenant Ratan is amused with the cat, yet he does not *think* too much about it."

It was a reeking hot day, but the Island detective spent the morning moving about Manila, on the outskirts. He talked with two Chinese, and with a Malay who had a savage appearing Siamese cat. He asked many questions. After a light lunch he went to his home and had a *siesta.* At four he rode to the police station and received permission from a Filipino sergeant to look at photographs. It was almost six when he had finished, and Sadi Ratan was coming in as he went out. The police lieutenant grinned at him.

"You called to see me?" he asked.

The Island detective shook his head. "I have been looking at pictures," he stated.

Sadi Ratan widened his dark eyes, brushed dust from his well-fitting khaki uniform.

"You found the one you sought?" he asked.

Jo Gar nodded. "I think that is so," he said.

Lieutenant Ratan chuckled. "Was it of a cat?" he said gently.

The Island detective smiled back at Ratan. The lieutenant of police continued to chuckle and went inside of the police building. Jo Gar walked slowly in the direction of the Manila Hotel. At the desk he asked for Cummings, the director. Cummings was a short, red-faced man; he came to Jo's side with a frown.

"I've been away—just got in this morning. Up at Baguio, keeping cool. Terrible thing—the valet killing Brail. Terrible for the hotel."

Jo Gar nodded. "Unfortunate for Brail also," he said quietly. "You heard that Brail had a Siamese cat he was very fond of, perhaps?"

Cummings nodded. "Of course," he replied.

The Island detective nodded. "Who is taking care of the cat now?" he asked.

Cummings frowned. "The floor maid," he said. "She said she wasn't afraid of it—I think she said she'd had one before at some time. So we turned it over to her until we get word from Brail's relatives in New York. Terrible thing."

The Island detective nodded his head thoughtfully. They moved towards some palms and Jo said very softly: "Sadi Ratan is easily convinced, Mr. Cummings. I do not believe that the valet murdered Brail, nor that he committed suicide."

The director blinked at Jo. "You don't think—that the police are correct—"

Jo Gar shook his head. "The theory of the valet losing the cat to get Brail away from the hotel is weak. He must have had many chances to murder Brail, in more or less deserted spots. And if Phelps *had* stabbed Brail to death—then he committed suicide too soon after the crime. Also, I cannot quite see a man with the courage to murder not going through with what he started. And then, there is the Siamese cat."

Cummings said: "What about it?"

Jo spoke tonelessly. "I have asked questions about the breed. They are savage, part monkey. At times they are very affectionate. Blood excites them—they are extremely nervous. Apparently I talked with Brail from downstairs here, within five minutes of the time he was stabbed. When we entered the suite he was dead. The Siamese cat was on the divan, and not the least bit disturbed. There were scratches on Brail's hands and wrists."

Cummings said: "Well?"

Jo Gar sighed. "I do not think Brail spoke to me on the telephone. I think he had been dead some little time—long enough for the cat to have gotten over its nervousness. If the cat had been in the room when Brail had been struck down it would have still been excited when I entered the room. If it had come in *after* the murder, the body and the blood would still have been having an effect."

Cummings sucked in a deep breath. Jo Gar said very quietly:

"But the Siamese was almost sleeping,—it was not at all excited."

The hotel director half closed his eyes. "Well?" he said again.

Jo Gar shrugged. "The one who spoke to me as Brail was Brail's murderer. Brail was dead at that time. He had been dead for some little time. As I went upstairs—the murderer escaped."

Cummings said: "How about the scratches on Brail's hands and wrists?"

The Island detective frowned. "According to the statements Lieutenant Ratan has been giving to the press they were caused in a struggle. Fingernail scratches—of Phelps. He states that Phelps' nails were quite long, and several were broken. I disagree with him, but I do not think they were cat scratches."

Cummings said again: "Well?"

Jo smiled faintly. "Phelps was shot through the mouth. The gun muzzle was very close—but that does not mean it was suicide. I think he was murdered by the same ones who murdered Walter Brail."

The hotel director said: "By the same *ones?*"

Jo nodded slowly "Ones," he repeated. "I do not know the motive. But I could make a guess. In my own way."

The hotel director looked at Jo Gar narrowly. They had known each other over a period of years, and there were things that Cummings remembered.

"If I can help, Señor Gar—"

Jo's eyes were slitted on the broad stairs beyond the palms. They were more almond-shaped than usual.

"I would like to look over the suite again more carefully," he said. "The Siamese cat is now in the hotel?"

Cummings nodded. "The maid has quarters here—the cat is in her place, at the rear of the hotel."

Jo took his eyes away from the broad stairs. "I would like the maid to bring the Siamese to the suite," he said. "But first I should like to call Lieutenant Ratan. He might be interested."

Cummings grunted. "He told me that you were a fool, and that the case was finished."

The Island detective smiled tightly. "It is very likely that what he meant was that if I *had* been a fool the case would now *be* finished," he said softly.

WHEN SADI RATAN came into the living-room of Suite Twenty-eight he stopped and stared at Jo Gar, then at Hernandez. Jo smiled and gestured towards Hernandez.

"I asked the Señor to come here so that the Spanish papers could have the story," he said. "You do not object?" His tone was expressionless.

Sadi Ratan grinned at the newspaperman. "Not if it is an amusing story," he replied.

The Island detective spoke a little grimly. "I think you will like it," he said. "There is a cat in it."

He nodded to the hotel director who went to the telephone. Jo Gar said:

"I have just one request—*I* should like to do the talking, and I shouldn't like anyone to show surprise at what I say. I think we'd better be sitting down and taking things easy, as the Americans say."

They seated themselves. Cummings came away from the phone and said:

"She will be right along."

Less than a minute later there was a rap on the half-closed door that led to the corridor. Jo said:

"Please come in."

He was smiling as the maid entered, holding the Siamese cat in her arms. The cat regarded them stolidly; the light was fading and its eyes were very blue. Jo Gar looked at the maid and said:

"Just set the cat down and let it wander around, please." She said: "*Si* Señor," and did as instructed. The Siamese did not move around much; it stayed close to her and watched the others in the room. Jo rose slowly, still smiling.

"You are not frightened of the cat?" he asked the maid.

She shook her head, a very faint smile on her lips. She was dark haired, medium in size. She was good looking for a Filipino girl, slenderer than most of them. Her English was very good.

The Island detective said: "You are not frightened—of *this* one?"

Her dark eyes widened. The smile had gone from Jo Gar's face.

"Of *this* one?" she repeated slowly.

The Island detective nodded. "This one has seen a man murdered," he said very steadily and softly. "It has seen blood on the man's—"

He stopped as the Filipino maid raised a hand towards her throat. She said in a choked voice:

"No—please—"

Jo Gar turned his head back to her and pointed towards the floor. He spoke loudly, huskily.

"Walter Brail's body was lying about there—when I came in. The cat was on the divan. Brail was dead—there was blood on his lips. A knife wound in the heart and in the neck—"

He let his words die, went towards the slot on the floor where Brail's body had lain. The room was very quiet; he could hear the swift breathing of the maid, behind him. Cummings was breathing heavily, too.

Jo Gar turned slowly. He walked a few feet towards the maid, then stopped. "You screamed last evening—when you saw the body. You did not go near the body. All you saw was a figure lying on the floor. Yet you screamed, again and again. You ran down the corridor screaming—"

The maid spoke in a broken voice. "I was—frightened. I felt—that he was dead—lying there—"

Jo Gar moved nearer her. "You are not afraid of a cat. A cat that belonged to a dead man. A cat that was in this room when the man was murdered, knifed—"

She said in a strangled voice: "I've had—Siamese cats—before—"

Sadi Ratan spoke in a protesting voice. "What is it that you want to know, Señor Gar?"

The Island detective paid no attention to Ratan. He moved closer to the maid, his gray-blue eyes very small and his lips pressed together in a straight line. When he parted them he said very grimly:

"You are the sort of woman who screams again and again when she sees a body lying on the floor—and yet you are not at all afraid of a dead man's cat. A strange breed of cat—"

There was fear in the girl's eyes. She raised her browned hands, pressed palms against her face. Jo stepped forward quickly, caught her wrists in his hands. He said sharply:

"Your fingernails are very short—I think a doctor would say they had been cut very recently."

The maid pulled herself away from him. She swore fiercely, in a half Spanish, half Filipino dialect. When she had finished Jo Gar slipped right-hand fingers in the right pocket of his duck suit.

"And I do not think—that your nails were clipped short, *last* evening," he said slowly.

The maid's eyes were staring into his. Sadi Ratan muttered something that was not distinguishable to Jo. The maid said brokenly:

"I didn't—do it—I didn't! I know you think—I killed him. I didn't! I knew when you sent for me—"

Her words trailed off. She turned and started towards the door that led to the corridor. Jo Gar said sharply:

"Wait!"

She stopped, faced him slowly. The Island detective took the Colt from his pocket, held it low at his side. He smiled coldly at her.

"I saw you ten days ago—a Sunday at a cock fight. You were not alone. The face of the one you were with interested me. I thought I had seen it before. I remembered that face—and a half hour ago I saw it again. Photographs of it have been sent around the world. You were with Pedro Savon—a very clever forger, thief and murderer—"

The maid screamed shrilly loudly—the one word: "Pedro!"

There was the crash of a gun from the corridor door, and as Jo's body swung to one side something crackled on a far wall. A figure came into the room, swaying from side to side. Jo Gar dropped to his knees, saw the Siamese cat streak across the floor. Savon's gun crashed again. The cat screamed and seemed to leap from the floor. Jo Gar squeezed the trigger slowly—his Colt crashed.

Pedro Savon fell forward, struck the floor heavily. His gun spun from nerveless fingers. The maid cried out and ran towards the motionless body, but Sadi Ratan blocked her way, gun in his right hand.

Jo Gar stood up, went over to Savon. The man was unconscious—

the bullet had clipped him over the right ear. It was not a deep wound. The maid was fighting to get to his side. Cummings said grimly:

"Is he dead, Gar?"

Jo shook his head. "A doctor can save him, but what is the use? He won't talk—we might just as well let him die here—"

The maid pulled herself free from Ratan's grip. She said bitterly:

"No—don't let him die—this way! I'll—talk!"

The Island detective said: "Good—fast, please."

She spoke hoarsely, in a strained voice. Her eyes were on the man on the floor.

"Pedro went to Phelps, the valet. They drank together. Phelps hated Brail because he would not give him money to back him in the business. The business he wanted to start, in London. Pedro knew Brail carried a large sum of money and jewels. He offered to share with the valet. I met Pedro here in the Islands—I love him. We wanted to get away from here, and Pedro swore no one would be hurt.

And then—Phelps lost his nerve. He said he would not rob Brail. He threatened to go to the police. Pedro said we must work fast—I let the Siamese cat out, hid it in my quarters. Pedro wanted Phelps out of the way and knew that Brail would make him hunt for the cat. We were searching Brail's luggage when he surprised us. He tried to fight, and I held his hands—while Pedro struck him—with the knife. The scratches—he got them-then-"

Her voice sank to a whisper. Jo Gar said quietly:

"And then—"

She said: "Pedro answered your telephone call. We got away—I had to work very quickly, washing my hands. I had brought the cat in when we came to search the rooms. We were going to leave quickly, on one of the big boats. The cat was excited, at first. But it grew calm before I let you in. Then I ran out, screaming. I couldn't stand the sight of the body. And I didn't know until hours later—that Pedro had murdered the valet. He was afraid he would go to the police. We had not taken anything, but Pedro knew Phelps would tell of the plans—"

She paused, and Jo Gar said: "Pedro forged the note?"

She nodded. "He knew about the will—and the clause in it. He said the police would find the will, and believe. Phelps had told Pedro many things, but he lost his nerve—"

Jo said: "Let her go, Lieutenant—"

Sadi Ratan stepped to one side and the maid dropped on her knees beside Savon. Cummings said:

"The cat's dead—one of this Pedro's bullets got it."

Jo Gar looked at Sadi Ratan with narrowed eyes. He smiled a little. Hernandez muttered:

"This is—a piece for the paper!"

The police lieutenant frowned. Jo Gar said slowly:

"It does not matter—but I was sure the Siamese would not have been so calm, if the murder had been committed as I was on my way up. Or unless it had been in the room—even longer than she says it was. But I was not far wrong."

Cummings grunted. "I'll call a doctor," he said.

"*I* would say you were just about right, Señor Gar." Sadi Ratan breathed softly: "The note—the gun beside Phelps' body—the clause in the will—"

Jo Gar sighed. "You were so willing to be convinced, Lieutenant," he said very quietly. "So willing that you could not, naturally become interested in such an amusing creature as—a Siamese cat."

The Black Sampan

Jo Gar hunts a murderer on the banks of the Pasig.

IT WAS nearing the hour of the swift tropic twilight; a warm breeze blew in from Manila Bay and stirred the palm trees in the fringe of almost jungle growth between the narrow white beach and the low, straggling Spanish house. There had been a pink, fan-shaped sunset in the sky, but most of the light had faded now. Gulls screamed over the water and somewhere on the opposite side of the house a parrot shrilled monotonously.

Jo Gar stood near the black shape of the *sampan,* which rested in a cleared space about fifty yards from the house and towards the fringe of jungle growth. His gray-blue eyes were frowning. The *sampan* was like hundreds of others drifting on the water of the Pasig, the narrow curve of water that twisted through the City of Manila and emptied into the Bay. That is, it was like others in size and shape. But there were differences. This particular *sampan* rested on earth. And all the wood of it was black. The mast was black, and the drooping canvas of the sail had been painted black. Not a dull color, but a rich, almost glossy black. There was something funereal in the appearance of the craft, resting on land, with the palm trees swaying slightly between it and the water of the Bay. The color was funereal, and even the shape added to the effect.

Beside him, Harvey Wall said slowly and in his deep voice:

"I heard one terrible, shrill cry—I was in my study. I got a gun and came right out. My Chinese cook was upstairs, in his quarters. He came out behind me. We found Vincente as you see him now, but not until we'd searched quite a bit. You see, we didn't think to look in the *sampan* immediately."

The Island detective moved closer to the *sampan,* and Wall moved almost silently behind him. The American was a tall, lean man with gray eyes and slightly gray hair. There was a stoop to his narrow shoulders and his face was well browned. His voice was extraordinarily deep for a man of his build.

The dead figure of Vincente was lying sprawled on the deck of the *sampan,* the left arm flung out so that the hand almost touched the base of the mast. In the breeze the rings of the sail made faint scraping sound against the mastwood. Vincente's dark eyes were opened wide—he seemed to be staring in painful surprise at the darkening sky, as he lay on his back. There was blood on his throat, and more on his white shirt, over the heart. He was a small, wiry Filipino, and even the pain of his death had not robbed him completely of a dark handsomeness.

Jo Gar said softly: "You were not aware that he had enemies?"

Wall said with decision: "I do not think Vincente had an enemy. I can't understand it, unless robbery was the motive, and he surprised thieves who were waiting in the palm growth, for darkness to come."

Jo Gar leaned down and his gray-blue eyes searched the deck of the *sampan,* which was fairly small, near the body. He moved around the craft slowly, examining the ground, which was hard and dry from months without rain. Then he came close to the *sampan* and looked at the dead man again. The swift, tropical twilight came and was gone—it was suddenly dark.

Wall said in a steady, low voice: "Vincente has been with me for five years. He was more than my house-boy. I trusted him completely. Sometimes he did business for me. I live more or less of a secluded life, since I sold out my plantations up the river and on the other side of Luzon. Only Vincente and the cook, Sarong, live with me."

Jo Gar nodded. "Sarong is not a Chinese name," he observed. "Malay, perhaps?"

Wall said: "There may be Malay blood, but the man is Chinese. He was upstairs in his quarters when I heard the one scream. My study is on the second floor, and the servants have small rooms above, in the one high portion of the house. I called to Sarong as I came down, and he answered me."

The Island detective used the beam of a small flashlight on the ground around the *sampan.*

"What did this Sarong answer, when you called, Señor Wall?" he asked quietly.

Wall said:

"He replied—'I come, Señor.' That was all. And I could hear him moving hurriedly."

Jo Gar nodded again. He snapped off the beam of the flash, so that they were in darkness. There was a short silence, then the parrot shrilled again. Jo spoke thoughtfully.

"If he had been knifed in the throat first—I do not think the scream would have been shrill. He was struck over the heart first, then in the throat. Filipino cry of surprise or pain is most always shrill. As it is in anger."

Harvey Wall swore very grimly.

"There was just the one scream, high—of pain. It was terrible. I'll hear it at night- forever."

Jo Gar said quietly: "I think not. One forgets these things in time. You have notified the police?"

Wall spoke a little huskily. "I told Sarong to notify them, after you had arrived. I wanted you here first. I think that perhaps you work more slowly and more thoughtfully."

The Island detective bowed a little. "You are kind," he replied.

There was the sound of a car arriving at the far side of the house. A car door slammed. Harvey Wall said:

"Sarong will bring them here."

Jo Gar looked towards the sky and his eyes were almost closed. He spoke in a gentle voice.

"I think I shall take a short walk through the palms and along the beach," he said very softly. "The *sampan* here—it has been painted recently?"

Harvey Wall spoke in a toneless voice. "I am a sentimental man. When I came to the Islands, fifteen years ago, I was broke. I had to borrow the money to start in business, and my first business was hauling stuff down the river. I had two *sampans*—this is the first one I bought. I have always kept it, and when I sold that fleet of mine—I brought it over here. That was about a year ago. The ants were getting at it—it's had several coats of paint."

Jo Gar nodded slowly. "The color is peculiar," he said quietly. "Any particular reason for the color?"

Harvey Wall turned so that he faced the house. There were the sounds of voices, growing louder.

"Vincente painted it, and this time he said he had bought a new kind of paint. It was supposed to be thick and it contained a great deal of lead. He thought that would do for the ants and protect the wood."

The Island detective spoke very softly. "You suggested the color?"

Harvey Wall shook his head. "I was away at the time. But I do not object to the color. Why?"

Jo Gar shrugged and moved away from the *sampan* and the dead man, towards the fringe of palm trees that swayed in the breeze.

"It is a strange color for a *sampan,*" he said.

There was irritation in Wall's voice. "It's a strange place for a *sampan,* too," he said. "But neither of those facts is helping us to find Vincente's murderer."

The Island detective paused for a few seconds: "Often one can never tell *what* is helping in the search for a murderer," he observed.

Harvey Wall said: "Well, you know more about this sort of thing than I do. But I think Vincente surprised thieves and they—or one of them—knifed him. Perhaps it was only one thief that he surprised."

The voice of Lieutenant Sadi Ratan sounded more clearly, and a flashlight beam cut through the darkness, near a side of the house. Jo Gar said:

"Why should Vincente have surprised a man lying in wait to enter the house, after darkness? Why should the man have been waiting? Why couldn't he come here after dark? But if he was here—why should he be surprised?"

Irritation was again evident in Harvey Wall's tone.

"I merely advanced my theory, Señor Gar. I would prefer to ask the questions and have *you* answer them."

The Island detective moved in the darkness. "I shall do my best Señor Wall," he said tonelessly. "But it is almost always simpler to ask questions than to answer them."

LIEUTENANT SADI RATAN straightened up and faced the door as Jo Gar entered the library of the Wall house. There was perspiration on Ratan's handsome face, his dark eyes were frowning.

"The Chinese is either a fool or a murderer," he announced in his loud, sure voice.

Jo Gar smiled a little and said: "Good evening, Lieutenant. It has been cooler today."

Harvey Wall was pouring himself a drink of whiskey from a decanter. He said suddenly:

"Good God! To think that my two servants hated each other! I never suspected—"

The Chinese sat impassively in a small wicker chair, and the light from a lamp struck full on his face. It was a round, brown face. His eyes were black and very small and they held no expression.

Sadi Ratan said: "He admits he hated Vincente, and he says Vincente hated him. The hatred was very strong. But he knows nothing whatever about the knifing of the house-boy."

Jo Gar inspected the brown paper of his cigarette. "What is it that makes him a fool, Lieutenant?" he asked slowly.

Sadi Ratan swore in Spanish. He wiped his forehead with a brown colored handkerchief.

"I said he was *either* a fool or a murderer," he corrected. "If he is not a murderer—he is a fool for telling me he hated the dead man."

The Chinese said in a flat voice: "I not a fool."

He said it as though he were patiently correcting some slight error. Jo Gar's blue-gray eyes were on the dark ones of the lieutenant of Manila police.

"Perhaps the Chinese believes that even if he does admit that he hated Vincente—that *does* not make him a murderer," he said gently.

Harvey Wall downed his whiskey and turned towards Sadi Ratan.

"How could Sarong have done this thing?" he demanded impatiently. "I told you he was in his room, above my study. I called to him, just after the scream, and he answered me. He came from the house behind me, and we searched together."

The Chinese closed his eyes. Ratan looked at him with a peculiar expression in his dark ones.

"His room has a small balcony—it faces the *sampan,*" he said simply.

Jo Gar smiled a little. "It would be remarkable knife throwing, Lieutenant," he said.

Sadi Ratan shrugged again, and Harvey Wall blinked at him.

"Good God! What stupidity!" he breathed. "You mean to tell me you think this cook killed Vincente by throwing a knife from his balcony? How about the two wounds? And where would the knives have gone? And how could any person throw so accurately at such a distance? And what—"

He groaned and broke off suddenly, appealing with his eyes to Jo. The Island detective was looking at a wicker floor lamp and the light it cast on the waxed floor of the library. He was thinking about Sadi Ratan. The man was not a fool—he was trying to get at something, and was using his apparent stupidity as a mask.

The Chinese said impassively: "I no—kill Vincente."

Sadi Ratan spoke in a rising voice, "You hated him, and he's dead, murdered. Señor Wall called to you, and he *thought* he heard you answer."

Harvey Wall sucked in a noisy breath. "You mean—Sarong wasn't in his quarters?" he muttered. "You mean—"

He checked himself. There was a little silence and then Jo Gar said quietly:

"If I cared to believe that the cook murdered Vincente—I would prefer the lieutenant's theory. That Sarong was not in his quarters. You did not actually see him leave the house behind you, Señor Wall?"

Harvey Wall's eyes were wide. "No," he admitted. "I was in too much of a hurry to get outside. I didn't wait for him. But I heard footfalls, and the voice that answered me sounded like Sarong's. When I got around the house near the *sampan,* he came around—"

Sadi Ratan kept his eyes on the half-closed ones of the Chinese.

"He could easily have done that—and still have murdered the man he hated," he said grimly.

Jo Gar nodded his head. "Quiet easily," he agreed. "And the one who answered for him and made the footfall sounds could have gone from the house and vanished."

Harvey Wall swore softly. The Island detective smiled.

"But it did not happen that way," he said quietly.

Sadi Ratan frowned at the diminutive detective, his fine figure very straight. The Chinese said slowly and with little tone in his voice:

"I in my room. I hear scream. Master—he call and me call back. I come down quick. It is so."

Sadi Ratan said in a hard voice: "It is so now, but I do not think it will be so in a short time. You are lying, Sarong, and it will not be easy for you to continue lying."

Jo Gar lighted another of his brown-paper cigarettes and spoke to Lieutenant Ratan.

"You have so often jumped at conclusions in the past, Lieutenant—and so often you have been mistaken. A man is dead, murdered, and a man that hated him is alive. Does that make him the murderer?"

Sadi Ratan smiled coldly at the Island detective. "It so happens that the Chinese is an expert with knives," he said evenly. "Perhaps you were not aware of that fact, Señor Gar?"

Jo Gar shrugged. "Many Chinese are experts with knives," he said.

The lieutenant of police continued to smile.

"While you were strolling about the beach my men have been busy. I think that Sarong is both a fool and a murderer. They have found a palm that is scarred by the blades of thrown knives. There is a cleared spot near it. In the next house there is a house-boy Carinto. He has seen the Chinese at practice."

Harvey Wall swore again, softly. Jo Gar said nothing.

The Chinese smiled impassively. "I know—Carinto see me," he said. "He no good. He hear knife strike tree. One time me miss."

Jo Gar grinned, showing his white teeth. He chuckled softly. Harvey Wall grunted. Sadi Ratan frowned at the Chinese.

Jo said: "You have an accommodating murderer, Lieutenant. He even admits that there are times when he misses a throw."

The Chinese smiled at the Island detective, then suddenly his eyes held a worried expression. He spoke very rapidly in Chinese, and Jo saw that even Sadi Ratan did not understand.

Jo replied to the cook, and Sarong smiled again. Ratan said in a cold voice:

"What did he say, Señor Gar?"

Jo said: "He said that he did not murder the man that he hated, and that he did not wish to die because some other one did murder him. He trusts that I will be able to find this other one, because he thinks that I am an honest man and he thinks that you do not like him."

Sadi Ratan scowled at the Chinese, whose eyes again held no expression. Jo Gar asked:

"Why, Sarong, did you hate Vincente?"

The Chinese started to speak in his native tongue, but Jo shook his head.

"In English, Sarong," he said. "Señor Wall should be able to understand."

The cook turned his eyes towards Harvey Wall, then looked at Jo.

"He want to kill me," he said simply. "He no like me. He talk to himself—I hear him say some day he kill me. And I no like him."

Jo Gar chuckled again. "That is a good reason for disliking a man," he agreed. "A very good reason."

Sadi Ratan muttered something under his breath, then said coldly:

"It is not even funny. He is lying. Why did you hate Vincente, Sarong? Why did you murder him with a knife—with one of your knives, and then hide the knife, perhaps throw it into the Bay? Why did you place the body in the black *sampan?* What was the real reason?"

Jo Gar said dryly: "And why did you spend all this time in *practicing* throwing knives when you are supposed to have murdered Vincente *without* throwing one?"

Sadi Ratan swung his body towards Jo Gar's. "You will please remain silent," he said grimly. "I am questioning this man."

JO GAR turned his back, shrugging slightly. Ratan spoke in a hard, loud tone:

"Was it because of a woman? Because he owed you money?"

The Chinese sighed heavily. He half closed his eyes again. One of Lieutenant Ratan's men came into the library, almost silently. He went to Ratan's side.

"We have found the woman, Lieutenant," he said in precise Spanish. "It is the kitchen maid of the Dutch family in the adjoining house—

Herr Saaden."

Lieutenant Ratan stood very erectly, and when Jo Gar faced him again he was smiling in a satisfied manner.

"A woman or money," he announced.

"It is almost always one or the other."

"Or both," Jo added. "What about the woman?"

Sadi Ratan looked at the khaki-clad police officer who had come in.

"What about the woman?" he asked. "Tell us."

The officer was short and chesty. He stood very stiffly and said that as ordered he had gone to the nearest house to make inquiries. He had talked with the house-boy, one named Carinto, and had learned that the Chinese and the Filipino of the American Señor, Harvey Wall, hated each other. He had learned that the house-boy of the Dutch family had watched the Chinese throwing knives at a palm tree. He had brought this information to Lieutenant Ratan and had then sought a reason for the hatred. And he had now learned that both Sarong and the dead Filipino had been in love with this Filipino maid of the family in the nearest house. Her name was Maria Tondo, and she was a half-breed of Spanish-Filipino parentage.

Sadi Ratan gestured with spread hands, brown palms upturned, when the policeman had finished.

"That is good," he said.

"We will go with the Chinese to the woman—"

The officer interrupted to state that the woman was now outside. Sadi Ratan said sharply:

"Bring her in."

He faced the Chinese and spoke coldly.

"You will be wise to confess. We know that you hated the dead man, and that you are an expert with knives. You will confess and tell us who it was that you sent to your room, in case your master should call. The one who was to answer in your tone of voice, while you crept through the palm growth and knifed Vincente to death, because you wanted this Maria Tondo, and because perhaps you feared that she preferred Vincente."

The Chinese said flatly: "I no kill Vincente—I no want Maria."

Lieutenant Ratan slapped a fist against a palm of his left hand, swore, and in Spanish. The policeman came in behind a slim, short girl of perhaps seventeen. She was pretty in a dark, graceful way. Her eyes were very black.

She stopped several feet from the Chinese, and her breath was drawn in in a sharp hiss. Then she raised both arms above her head and cried out shrilly. She moved towards Sarong, who was watching her with narrowed eyes. Sadi Ratan caught her by an arm, held her firmly. But he let her talk.

She said that Sarong was the son of a dog; she cursed him, waving her one free arm about. Her eyes were flashing and she was breathing heavily. She said that he had murdered the man she loved, and that he would die for it. He deserved to die for it, a thousand times. She had told Vincente only this very morning that she would marry him, and he had told Sarong, of course. And therefore the Chinese had murdered the man she loved.

When she quieted, Sadi Ratan looked at Harvey Wall and smiled a little proudly. Then he turned towards Jo Gar, who had been smoking and watching the Chinese.

"It is finished," he said. "We now have the motive."

The Island detective smiled back at Lieutenant Ratan, while Harvey Wall was repeating that he could hardly believe it—he had never noticed any hatred between his two servants. But then, he had been very busy with his monthly accounts of late. Perhaps he had not paid much attention to matters between the two.

Jo Gar said suddenly: "You do not find it strange, Lieutenant, that the body was found in the black *sampan?*"

The lieutenant shrugged. "He was murdered perhaps alongside of it," he suggested. "No—I do not find it strange."

The girl, still breathing heavily, said that she often met Vincente beside the *sampan.* Because Sarong was a devil, he had deliberately placed the body of the man she loved in it.

Sadi Ratan smiled more broadly. "You see?" he said. "It is all very simple."

There was a little silence and then the lieutenant went close to the seated Chinese.

"Who was the one you had in your room, to answer Señor Wall?" he demanded.

The Chinese raised his eyes and looked at the lieutenant of Manila police. He shook his head slowly from side to side, then looked at Jo Gar.

"I did not—kill him," he said very steadily and tonelessly. "This girl—she lie."

The girl shrilled words at him again, in native tongues—a mixture of Low Spanish and Filipino. Sadi Ratan interrupted her.

"In prison it will be different," he said. "We will have his confession there."

Jo Gar spoke softly. "I do not think it will be different. It is not easy for one to confess to a murder not committed."

Sadi Ratan smiled nastily, then sighed. "Confession will hardly be necessary," he said. "The evidence is very strong against the Chinese."

Harvey Wall came over near Jo Gar and looked at him with wide eyes.

"You are not satisfied that Sarong is guilty?" he asked.

Jo smiled a little. "I certainly am not," he replied. "On the contrary, I am quite sure he is innocent."

Sadi Ratan gestured towards the girl and then motioned for her to be taken out. Two more policemen came into the room, and the lieutenant pointed at Sarong.

"He is arrested for the murder of Señor Wall's house-boy Vincente," he said slowly. "Take him away, and guard him carefully."

The Chinese stood up, raised his hands slightly and let them fall at his sides. Jo Gar smiled at him.

"It will be for only a short time, Sarong," he said. "Perhaps only for hours."

The Chinese lifted his shoulders, let them fall, and was led from the room. Sadi Ratan went to a small wicker table and placed his pith helmet on his head, adjusting it carefully. Jo Gar spoke quietly.

"You have probably worked more rapidly on this case than on any other, Lieutenant," he said. "Unfortunately, I do not think you have the right person."

Sadi Ratan smiled at Harvey Wall, as though in sympathy.

"It was your wish to call in Señor Gar," he said. "I regret that he was of so little use to you."

Harvey Wall looked at Jo Gar. "I think the lieutenant is right, Señor Gar," he said. "It is a surprise—but I think Sarong killed Vincente. The girl is sure of it, and the evidence is all against him."

Jo Gar narrowed his blue-gray eyes on the gray ones of the American. He let his gaze flicker to Sadi Ratan, and then come back to the

American again.

"But you still wish to find the murderer of your house-boy?" he asked pleasantly.

Harvey Wall frowned. "Certainly," he said.

The Island detective nodded his head and looked towards the screened windows that faced in the direction of the Bay.

"In that case," he said very tonelessly, "I shall wander about a bit."

Sadi Ratan sighed again. "While I am getting a confession from the Chinese," he said.

Jo Gar bowed slightly. "While you are *attempting* to get a confession from the Chinese," he corrected placidly.

A HALF hour or so before dusk, on the next day, Jo Gar stood near the desk of Lieutenant Ratan, at police headquarters, just off the Escolta. The creak of carriage wheels and the chug-noise of small machines on Manila's main business street came through the screened windows of the room. Sadi Ratan sat behind his desk and seemed very pleased with himself.

"He has not confessed," he said, "but these things take some time, as you know. Because you are interested in the case, and appear to sympathize with this Chinese, I shall be severe but not at all brutal with him."

The Island detective nodded. "It is kind of you," he returned. "You are dealing with a very clever murderer. He could not have been at all certain that Señor Wall would call for him, nor could he have been certain that Vincente would cry out. Yet he went to great trouble in putting a substitute in his quarters, in case of such a circumstance."

The lieutenant frowned. He tapped the desk surface with his right-hand fingers.

"You think that Sarong would not have planned so carefully," he said slowly. "I disagree—the Chinese are very shrewd."

Jo Gar nodded. "Sarong was the cook," he said. "Ground glass in food would have been much more simple."

Sadi Ratan shook his head. "In the autopsy it would have been discovered. Instantly Sarong would have been caught—just because he—*was* the cook."

The Island detective was silent for several seconds. "In the tropics one can hardly help but notice servants," he said. "Yet Señor Wall failed to notice they hated each other. That is unnatural."

Sadi Ratan made a gesture that was broad and dismissing.

"He was busy with his monthly accounts. And it is very possible that Sarong and Vincente were careful."

Jo Gar frowned slightly. "There is the matter of the *sampan,*" he said. "The body being placed on the wooden deck would make sound. Or if it fell there it would make sound. And yet it was found there."

The police lieutenant smiled coldly. "You are growing old, Señor Gar," he observed viciously. "The *sampan* was the love spot of the house-boy and the girl. Sarong had discovered that—it pleased him to deposit Vincente's body there."

Jo Gar said: "This Maria has told you that Sarong loved her, as well as Vincente?" he asked.

Sadi Ratan nodded. "Naturally, and that she refused him, even laughed at him. There is no Chinese blood in her veins. She would not marry him. Vincente was a Filipino."

Jo Gar looked at the ceiling fan. "The girl is here?" he asked.

The police lieutenant shook his head.

"I released her this afternoon. She is needed at the Saaden house. She will not go away. She hates Sarong. She says there is bad Malay blood in him. She will stay, and if he does not confess—her word will be enough to convict him."

Jo Gar placed his soiled Panama on top of his head and turned towards the office door.

"The newspapers are complimenting you, Lieutenant," he stated pleasantly. "But then, they have done that before."

Sadi Ratan frowned. "I have made mistakes," he said. "They have complimented me too soon. But this time I am right. Sarong was the murderer. You arrived on the scene ahead of me, Señor Gar, but you reasoned poorly. I regret that, sincerely."

Jo Gar smiled and bowed. "I would regret it also, Lieutenant," he replied cheerfully, "if I believed it was so."

THE ISLAND detective drove through the *Luneta,* between the Manila Hotel and the Army and Navy Club while the Constabulary Band was playing its final number. The sun was very low, beyond the Island of Cavite, but tonight there were no clouds in the sky and the sunset was not beautiful. The driver of the *caleso* made low, clucking sounds to his thin horse, and Jo Gar smoked a brown-paper cigarette.

Near the Army and Navy Club he told the driver to stop, and

descended from the carriage. He walked slowly along the avenue that wound nearest the Bay and when he was within five hundred yards of the Wall house it was almost dark.

When he reached the gate on the avenue frontage of the place the twilight was rapidly fading; it was gone as he used the key he had obtained from Wall an hour ago, in the city. There were no lights showing; Harvey Wall was staying with friends for the night. Jo Gar moved very quietly through the foliage just off the cinder path, circled the house and approached the spot where the black *sampan* rested, from the far side.

He stood motionless for almost five minutes, listening carefully. Gulls were crying, over the water, but the parrot did not make sound. The Island detective raised his eyes and saw the dark shape of the house rising beyond the *sampan.* He smiled faintly, waited another five minutes. There were no alien sounds to be heard; his smile became a frown.

And then, as he bent down and got first on his knees, then flat on the ground, he heard the light noise of footfalls. They seemed to be coming from the direction of the Bay. At intervals they ceased completely, then he would hear them again. And they increased in sound—the one who was making them was coming nearer.

The light from the stars was brighter tonight, but Jo Gar did not move his head as the person who was making the footfall sounds passed within ten yards of him. He waited for almost a minute, and when the sounds were very light he looked up. The black *sampan* was only a shape in the semi-darkness—a coffin-like shape, with the mast a tombstone.

But near it stood a small figure—and as his eyes became accustomed to the light Jo saw that it was the girl, Maria Tondo. She was standing motionless near the *sampan,* but her head was thrown back. She was looking, Jo realized, not at the craft but at the house.

For several seconds she stood without making any movement. Then she turned and moved back towards the Bay, passing so close to him as he lay flat among the dried palm leaves and shrubbery that he could hear her even breathing.

After another thirty seconds or so he raised his head. He got very slowly to his feet, moved carefully through the fringe of palms towards the beach and the water of the Bay. When he reached the Bay side of the palm thicket he could see her walking along the beach. Near the end of the Wall property line there was an outrigger that Harvey Wall sometimes used for swimming. The girl went straight to it, seated herself on it. Her back was to Jo Gar—she was facing the beach of Herr Saaden.

Jo Gar straightened and smiled grimly. He worked his way slowly along the edge of the palm fringe, getting nearer the outrigger. It was slow work, and once he halted for seconds and fingered the Colt in the right-hand pocket of his lightweight suit, getting the safety lock off.

When he reached a spot almost opposite the beached outrigger he crouched low and waited. The figure of the girl was very still. And then, from some spot farther along the fringe of palms, he heard a long, low whistle.

The girl's body moved. She stood up, but did not go away from the outrigger. She turned her head slightly and whistled as the other had whistled—long and softly.

Jo Gar's gray-blue eyes were expressionless as he waited. When the figure of the man came along the sand he drew in a short breath. He slipped his right hand into the right pocket of his coat and closed his short fingers over the grip of the gun.

When the man reached the girl's side he took her in his arms. Their bodies were close together for seconds. They stood facing the water, after a time, and Jo could hear the low murmur of their voices.

He stepped out from the fringe of palms; moved as quietly as he could across the pebbles and sand of the narrow beach. His eyes were on the two figures; they had stopped talking now. When he was within twenty-five feet of them, directly behind them, his right shoe struck against a piece of driftwood. The sound was sharp, and they both swung around.

Jo Gar walked forward, a smile on his face. The sand gave light to the scene, and he watched their hands carefully. The man's breath was coming sharply. The girl's eyes were wide. She said in a half whisper:

"Señor—Gar!"

Jo Gar smiled more broadly. He nodded his head, and stopped within ten feet of them. The man was a Filipino—he had a sharp face and a small mustache. His hair was very black and clipped short. He wore a white shirt and white trousers, and his feet were bare. There was a red sash around his waist.

THE ISLAND detective said: "Yes, it is Señor Gar. And this is the house-boy, Carinto, I suppose? The house-boy of Herr Saaden."

The Filipino's thick lips parted; he half muttered something, nodding his head jerkily. Jo Gar continued to smile. His eyes flickered to the eyes of the girl.

"You do not grieve long," he said with faint mockery. "One love is dead—only a short time. Yet already you have another."

The girl's body stiffened, and the man made a slight movement with his left hand.

Jo Gar said sharply: "No! My fingers hold a gun!"

There was silence except for the short breathing of the two. Jo Gar looked at the Filipino and said softly:

"The house-boy of Herr Saaden—and the murderer of Vincente!"

The girl screamed and raised her hands to her face. The Filipino ripped at the left side of his red scarf and the blade of the knife shone in the beach light. But he did not throw it. Instead he leaped forward, the knife held low in his hand. His arm was moving upward as he leaped.

Jo Gar twisted to one side and squeezed the trigger of the Colt. The Filipino groaned as the shot crashed; he fell heavily to the sand near the feet of the Island detective. The girl screamed again, took her hands away from her face and rushed at him. Jo Gar lifted his gun again, let his hand drop. The girl was tearing at him with her fingers, when he got a grip on her throat. His skin was ripped twice before she was quiet, relaxed in his arms.

He let her slip to the sand, turned the house-boy over on his back. The knife he twisted from his weak grip. There were cries from the direction of the Saaden house, and the beams of flashlights were showing.

Jo Gar straightened up and looked down at the Filipino. The girl stirred in the sand and moaned. Jo Gar said heavily:

"The bullet is in your shoulder—you won't die—yet. Why did you—murder Vincente?"

Carinto cursed in his native tongue. The girl pulled herself to her knees and faced Jo.

"If we tell the truth—will it help?" she asked.

Jo Gar nodded. "The truth always helps," he said a little grimly. "How much, I cannot say."

The girl said: "We'd saved money—to get married. Vincente did not want it. He saw that Juan drank, and then he gambled with him. He won all of his money. Juan did not think it was honest, and he knew why Vincente had done it. He caught him near the black *sampan*—and killed him. Vincente screamed, but Juan did not care. He put him on the *sampan.* He said it looked like a coffin—and he got away. He thought that Sarong would be suspected, because he knew the Chinese hated Vincente. He had lost money to him also—and the two had quarreled much. Juan thought that Señor Wall knew that, but he did not. I went to the house tonight; it was dark and I thought we were safe—"

Her voice broke. The thick voice of Herr Saaden was calling, and Jo Gar answered him. On the sand Juan Carinto was groaning. Jo Gar held his Colt low at his side; his eyes were expressionless. He nodded his head very slowly.

"It will interest Lieutenant Ratan to know that he was correct in one thing," he murmured tonelessly. "He said that murder was almost always for a woman or money."

The flashlight beams were moving nearer and the voices were growing louder. Jo Gar looked out over the water and sighed.

"And Vincente spent so much time painting the spot where his body was to rest," he said with irony. "He even chose the proper color—"

Herr Saaden came limping up and asked questions. Jo Gar answered them, and after a short silence he said:

"We will take the wounded man to your house, and from there I will call Lieutenant Ratan."

The Dutchman nodded his head. "He will be pleased," he said seriously.

Jo Gar smiled a little grimly. "He will be delighted," he said. "When he realizes that he did not recognize what a poor actress your kitchen maid is, and that he thought Sarong was much more clever than I did, and that he failed to wonder why your house-boy, Carinto, was so eager to come forward and state that he had seen the Chinese practicing with knives—he will be delighted."

Herr Saaden looked puzzled, but Jo Gar only smiled very faintly. He was not very concerned—whether Herr Saaden understood or not.

Climbing Death

A story of a man who had sworn never to fly again.

A LWIN THREADED his way slowly between the table-crowded Pasig Café; his stubby fingers were moving the thin stem of a palm fan and his fat face was beaded with perspiration. Jo Gar looked up from his tall claret and widened his blue-gray eyes slightly. It was seldom anyone in Manila saw Alwin frown; the big man was exceedingly good-natured. Yet he was frowning now.

He turned sidewise and his bulk rocked a table as he squeezed between two of them. An empty glass crashed to the polished floor of the café, but Alwin did not even turn to look at it. He came on slowly until he reached the table at which Jo Gar sat. With his eyes on Jo he pulled out the other chair; it creaked under his weight.

The Island detective smiled faintly. "It is the curry that you eat that gives you such weight," he said.

Alwin paid no attention to him. He lighted what was left of the cold, twisted cigar between his thick lips His stubby fingers took it away from his teeth and he leaned towards Gar.

"I have just had a telegram from Rooder," he said. "Jack Branders is dead."

Jo Gar's eyes became less almond shaped as he widened them on the black ones of Roger Alwin.

"Branders dead," he said very slowly. "It was an—accident?"

Alwin's eyes grew hard. "He crashed in his airplane," he said softly and in a strange tone. "He was taking off from that field near his plantation house, if you want to call that fruit place of his a plantation. Something went wrong. The plane went over on a wing, crashed. Perhaps only one hundred feet. Branders was dead when Carter and Tate got to the ship, after hearing the crash. They were in the house taking a *siesta*. That's all that was in the telegram."

Jo Gar shook his head slowly. Alwin wiped perspiration from his face with a large handkerchief. The ceiling fans made faint tinkling sounds and from the *Calle Diaz* came the shrill cries of the native nut sellers. Heat came into the café in waves, and the ceiling fans distributed them.

The Island detective said: "It is too bad—I had heard that Branders intended to stop flying."

Alwin's black eyes seemed very small. "He called me this morning at ten o'clock and asked me to find a buyer for the plane," he said grimly. "He said he would never fly again. He wanted me to find a buyer quietly, and he said he didn't intend to tell anyone on the plantation that he was going to quit."

Jo Gar whistled very softly. His eyes read the thought back of Alwin's. That thought was that Branders was known as a man of decision. He took time in making decisions, but once made there was never any change. Drink had almost beaten him before he had decided never to touch liquor again. He had decided one evening at the Manila Club. So far as anyone the Island detective knew was concerned, he had never been seen to drink liquor again. His house-boy had stolen from him, after five years of service. Branders liked the house-boy, but he told him that if he ever stole again, he would send him to Bilibid. He caught the house-boy, almost a year later, in the act of stealing some small silver change. He had sent him to Bilibid—the boy was still in prison. There were other cases.

The Island detective spoke very softly: "Did he tell you *why* he intended never to fly again?"

The fat man nodded; his eyes were very grim. "He has wanted to marry a woman in England—for several years. She has refused again and again. This morning in his mail there was a letter saying she would marry him. He intended to take no more risk—lately he has had several narrow escapes. The country out there is not good for flying."

Jo Gar said steadily. "He did not say anything about having one last flight?"

Alwin pounded a fist on the wood of the table, and glasses jumped about. He got his big head nearer Jo's.

"Damn it—I tell you he said he was through! 'I'll never fly again!' he said. And he said it that way. I tell you he *meant* he was through."

Jo nodded and ran browned fingers through his graying hair. He shifted his small, slender body a little, and reached into a pocket of his duck suit for a loose, brown-paper cigarette. He did not speak.

The big man said: "I want you to go up there, Señor Gar. When can you start?"

The Island detective looked thoughtfully at the big clock on a bare wall of the café. It was almost four o'clock. He said:

"I can go by train to Carejo—and I think there is a train at six. I will be there almost at midnight, and someone from the plantation can meet me and drive me over."

Alwin nodded. "There are three white men there," he said very carefully. "Erich Rooder, the German, and Bill Carter and Harry Tate, both Americans. Know any of them?"

Jo Gar shook his head. "I've seen Rooder and Tate, at the Manila Hotel, but not for months."

Alwin spoke softly. "They haven't come in from the plantation for months. The last time Branders came in he didn't speak of them, or of Carter. Never mentioned them."

The Island detective lighted the cigarette he had placed between his thin lips.

"It is your idea that Branders did not intend to fly again, yet that he did fly. You think he might have been forced to fly?"

Alwin frowned. "Branders was a good business friend of mine. I think something went wrong at the plantation. Something that made him change his mind. I want to know what it was."

Jo Gar spread his browned hands in a gesture of acceptance. He smiled just a little.

"It is my business," he said quietly. "I shall be at the plantation by midnight. It is called Plantation Rosita, I believe."

Alwin nodded, his eyes still grim. "The woman he loved was named Rosita," he said. "He was mad about her. I know. And I know that when he said he would never fly again, I understood why. And I know he didn't intend to fly again."

Jo Gar looked narrowly at the glowing tip of his cigarette. He said nothing.

The big man frowned. "What do *you* think, from what I have told you?" he asked.

The Island detective shrugged. "It is strange," he said. "Yet, except for one thing I would say that Branders *had* changed his mind, had gone up for one I last flight. And had crashed."

Alwin spoke very quietly. "And what is the one thing?"

The Island detective raised his eyes and watched a ceiling fan as it slowly circled.

"It is the worst time of the hot season," he replied. "Since Branders called you at ten, and since you have already heard from Herr Rooder that he is dead, he must have made the flight at the worst time of day. Greater heat and more difficult air. And the ones who heard the crash were taking their *siesta.* It is very strange that Branders was not taking his, too. He is a veteran and should not be foolish."

Alwin said: "I can afford to pay a good fee, Señor Gar. But if I were you—I would not go up there unarmed. Personally—I think he was trying to escape from something—"

Jo Gar shrugged. "A crash while trying to escape from something—that is not murder," he said gently. "And it would be very difficult to prove."

Alwin swore thickly. "It might not be difficult to prove it to *me,*" he muttered. "I'll handle it in my own way."

The Island detective looked at the big clock again. He rose slowly from the chair.

"I will telegraph you from Carejo, as soon as I learn something of importance," he said. "If I think it was an accident—I will wire that it was an accident."

Alwin muttered to himself, then said more clearly: "Take a gun along—there might be *another* accident."

Jo Gar's eyes were very almond-shaped and small. "It is one of the simple reasons for carrying a gun," he said tonelessly. "The chance of an accident."

ERICH ROODER was a tall, lean man with blond hair and a blond mustache. His eyes were blue and his face round for his build. The sun had burned him brown; he wore a soiled khaki shirt, khaki trousers and a khaki sun helmet. He shook hands with Jo, after the Island detective had descended from the train. His face was serious.

"Hello, Señor Gar," he said. "I've seen you around Manila, of course. This is a bad business."

Jo Gar smiled a little. "Death is always bad," he said. "It has the feeling of finality."

Rooder's blue eyes narrowed a little. He led the way towards a battered flivver, behind the wheel of which sat a Filipino of middle age. He opened a rear door and Jo got in. The sky was cloudless and there was a crescent moon. It was very hot.

When the flivver jerked forward along the dirt road that led from the station Rooder spoke thoughtfully.

"I was a bit puzzled by Alwin's wire saying you were coming out here. Of course, Alwin was a good friend of Brander's. But I didn't know you were an expert on airplanes."

Jo Gar smiled. "I'm interested in them," he replied. "Alwin thought I might learn something from the wreckage."

Rooder's eyes remained half closed. He looked ahead, and not at Jo Gar. The headlights showed the white dirt of the road, and thick, tropic foliage on each side. The country was hilly, and the road rough. They traveled at fair speed.

"My idea is that the heat got Jack," Rooder said steadily. His voice had a faint, guttural quality. "The thing that beats me is why he went up when he did—a half hour after noon. The hottest time of the day."

Jo Gar frowned. "Has he ever done it before?" he asked.

Rooder shook his head. "Not that I know of," he replied. "Bill and Harry were doing *siesta.* I was taking a shower, and with the water making racket coming down, and a lot of it in my ears—I didn't hear the crash. The Filipinos were in their quarters, but a Chinese cook for the hands was getting some water outside, and saw the plane go up. It seemed to bank and fall sidewise, on a wing. The nose dropped and then the crash came. The engine was running all the time, apparently—that's why I think Jack fainted at the controls."

Jo Gar nodded. "He wasn't ill?" he asked.

Rooder said: "He had a touch of fever—*dengue.* But he was pretty strong, you know. He hadn't said anything about taking the ship up. I thought he was taking *siesta*—so did Bill and Harry. It was a bad smash and he was dead when they got him out of the wreckage. The plane didn't burn."

"The Chinese who saw the plane fall—what did he do?" Jo Gar asked.

Rooder frowned deeply. "He got scared, of course—and ran towards the plantation house. Harry and Bill met him, and the three of them went out to the wreck. Jack was pretty badly smashed up."

Jo offered Rooder one of his brown-paper cigarettes, and they both lighted up.

"No urgent business, or anything that would have caused Branders to fly anywhere in a hurry?" the Island detective asked.

Rooder shrugged. "Not that I know of—and I probably would have known. Personally, I think he had a stronger touch of the fever than he thought. Maybe he went a little off his head and thought he wanted to fly. He might have fainted, or the ship might have just hit a bad spot and side-slipped down."

Jo nodded. The flivver bumped along over the rough road, made a turn and started up a fairly steep grade. Rooder said slowly:

"We're all pretty upset about it, naturally. And we can't help thinking that Alwin seems to feel there is more to it than just an accident."

Jo Gar's gray-blue eyes stared blankly ahead. "Why?" he asked softly.

Rooder made a gesture with his lean hands. "You're a private detective," he said. "He sent you up here."

The Island detective smiled. "It is because of my knowledge of planes," he replied. "Naturally, Alwin would like to know what caused the accident, if possible."

Rooder looked straight ahead. "Naturally," he agreed. "He was a good friend. But I doubt that you'll learn anything more than I've told you."

Jo Gar continued to smile slightly. "It is quite certain that I will not," he said very slowly, "if there is nothing more than that to learn."

CARTER AND Tate were about the same size—tall, well-built Americans. Carter was dark and thin faced, with a good chin. Tate had brown hair and eyes; he walked with a slight limp. They sat now, in wicker chairs in the living-room of the rambling plantation house. Tate spoke in a flat, almost toneless voice.

"The last I saw of Jack was about twenty minutes before the crash. He was going into his room, and said he was going to try to get some sleep. The heat has been fierce—he had a touch of *dengue.* Not much of one. Bill saw him about ten minutes before I did. Neither of us heard him leave the house, though he must have gone within five minutes or so after I saw him. The field is about ten minutes away. The ship is kept under a canvas hangar, but she was always ready for the air—that is, loaded with gas and oil."

Jo Gar said slowly: "Always ready—why was that?"

Bill Carter spoke in his rather heavy tone. "Jack liked to feel he could always work the electric starter and get right off the ground. If he was out on a long flight he always fixed her for the air, before he left the hangar."

Jo Gar looked at the low ceiling of the room. "Why do you suppose he felt the ship must always be ready for flight?" he asked steadily.

Carter and Tate exchanged glances, with little expression in the eyes of either. Erich Rooder shrugged.

"There was no reason, Gar," he said a little sharply.

"It was just a habit with him. Time didn't mean anything—and no one was after him, if that's what you think."

Jo Gar smiled with his lips. "I do not think," he said pleasantly. "I ask questions."

There was a little silence. Then Jo said quietly:

"So far as you three men know Branders had no enemies."

Carter and Tate shook their heads. Rooder said in his guttural voice:

"Not an enemy. Everyone liked him."

Jo Gar nodded. "Yet he always kept his plane ready for the air, and today he flew at the worst possible time."

Carter stood up abruptly, his face twisted. "Look here, Señor Gar—" he started, but Rooder interrupted.

"Take it easy, Bill. Alwin has sent Gar up here to find out what happened. Gar is a detective, and he approaches death with the idea that it couldn't very well be caused by an accident—ever."

Jo Gar's eyes held little expression. "At the moment I am more curious about Branders' motive for the sudden flight, at such a time, than in the cause of the ship crash," he said calmly.

Tate said: "My theory is that he felt like flying—the fever made him restless. He went out and flew. There was an accident. You've seen his body—no bullet holes in it, are there?"

Jo shook his head. "No bullet holes," he agreed. "His head was badly battered and there are bones broken. I think he was killed instantly."

Rooder nodded. "We had Doctor Cordozo over from his place. He said death was instantaneous."

Jo Gar looked at his wrist-watch. It was almost three o'clock.

"I think I shall sleep in the room you have so kindly had prepared for me," he stated as he stood up. "In the morning, as soon as it is light, I shall want to see the plane wreckage. It has not been touched?"

Tate spoke nastily. "Certainly it's been touched—we had to pull things apart to get him out of the wreck."

Jo Gar nodded. "Naturally," he agreed.

Rooder spoke grimly. "But if there any bullet holes in the wings or wood—they'll still be there for you, Señor."

The Island detective let his eyes move from one face to another. He was smiling almost pleasantly.

"I do not expect to find any bullet holes," he said quietly. "That would be too much of a piece of luck."

Tate's eyes were very small and hard.

"Just what do you mean by that?" he demanded.

Jo Gar bowed slightly. "Nothing," he said very precisely. "Very often I mean nothing by what I say."

Rooder led the way from the room, and there was silence except for footfalls. Tate and Carter remained behind. At the room that had been prepared for the Island detective, Rooder stood aside.

"I am older than Bill and Harry," he said. "I've been in the Islands longer. The fact that Alwin sent a detective out here doesn't bother me so much. My feeling is that the crash was an accident."

Jo Gar smiled. "It would seem that way," he agreed. "Branders was a wealthy man?"

Rooder shrugged. "He wasn't poor," he replied.

A kerosene lamp gave wavering light to the room. Night tropical sounds reached the two men. A lizard moved across the ceiling, making a sound at intervals like soft kissing.

"There was a will?" Jo said slowly.

Rooder's voice was toneless. "Yes," he said. "I happen to know about it. Branders had only a few relatives, distant. He didn't care anything about them. He left most of his money—a couple of hundred thousand—to Roger Alwin. The plantation here was left to us."

Jo Gar said very quietly: "Us?"

Rooder said: "A half interest to me—and a quarter each to Harry and Bill. We got along very well together—Jack liked us enough to do that. He knew we'd keep things going."

Jo Gar said: "The fruit is good?"

He could hear Rooder breathing heavily. "Fine," the German replied. "About the best yield we've ever had."

The Island detective looked towards the screened windows of the room.

"How much would you say the plantation was worth—counting the fruit, of course?"

Rooder said instantly: "Around a hundred thousand—probably more than that."

There was silence, then the German spoke slowly: "And now you have your motive for this murder, Señor Gar."

The Island detective smiled and shook his head. He said in a gentle tone:

"No—now I have a *possible* motive for a *possible* murder."

Rooder bowed his head slightly. "Good night, Señor Gar," he said.

Jo stood very still.

"Good night, Herr Rooder," he said pleasantly.

Rooder went along the corridor; his sandals made faint slap sound. Jo Gar inspected his automatic, removed his duck coat and stretched out beneath the mosquito netting on the bed. He did not undress. At intervals he heard the murmur of voices in the living-room. Then he heard them no more. A door slammed, somewhere in the house. Jo Gar breathed very softly:

"Alwin gains several hundred thousand. Rooder fifty thousand. Tate and Carter twenty-five thousand apiece. Because there was an accident, and Branders was killed."

His gray-blue eyes were half closed in an ironical smile. He said very slowly:

"Branders might have lived many years—if there had been no accident."

After that he dozed for a while. At four o'clock he rose, pushed the mosquito netting aside, and got his small flashlight from a bag. He changed to duel trousers that were black and put on a black shirt. Then he removed a screen noiselessly from a window, waited a short time, climbed outside. The room was on the level with the patio. The crescent moon made light, and there were the stars. He moved very quietly away from the house, in the direction that Rooder had told him the field and the wrecked plane were. He moved slowly, carefully. He was less than five hundred yards from the house, in a fairly thick palm grove, when he noticed a red glow ahead. He moved more rapidly up a slope. The crackling sound reached his ears before he was at the crest of it. The glow was becoming steadily brighter. There was a sudden roar.

Jo Gar broke into a trot. When he reached the crest of the palm studded slope he got to his knees and crawled along. There was another explosion, and then he was looking down at the small, level field. At the far end of it the wreckage of the plane was making a bright blaze. Pieces of it, sections, had been flung some distance by the explosion. The sky was reflecting the glow. In the direction of the house, behind him, he heard shouts.

He smiled grimly, lying motionless and watching the plane burn. After a few minutes he parted his thin, colorless lips and said softly:

"So often when there is one accident—there is very quickly *another.*

DAWN LIGHT and the first heat that came with it was in the living-room when Jo Gar entered it. Rooder sat staring at the waxed floor; he looked up quickly when the Island detective came into the room.

"We were looking for you," he said sharply. "We went to your room, but you weren't there."

Jo Gar smiled slightly. "All three of you?" he asked pleasantly.

Rooder frowned. "As it happened, the three of us did go to your room together," he said. "The plane burned—I suppose you know that?"

The Island detective nodded. "I was restless—couldn't sleep. So I thought I'd go along and have a look at the wreckage. Cooler at night."

He watched a flickering expression in the German's blue eyes. Rooder said tonelessly.

"You get there before she burned?"

The Island detective shook his head. "I was on my way when the fire started," he replied. "What do you suppose caused it?"

Rooder swore. "I suppose the crash crossed up the electric system in some way. Short circuit—something burned out and the doped material went up. Takes some time for that to happen—a wire might have been sizzling since the crash."

The Island detective nodded. "It might have," he agreed quietly.

Rooder drew a deep breath. "You left your room through a window, Señor Gar. You didn't want any of us to know where you were going. And then the plane burned. I suppose you think she was set off, so that you couldn't find the bullet holes in the fabric?"

Jo Gar shook his head. "But all three of you came to my room to tell me that the plane was burning," he pointed out pleasantly. "I could hardly suspect any of you."

Rooder's blue eyes smiled coldly. He stretched out in the wicker chair and watched the detective. After a short silence Jo said:

"How about a woman, Rooder? Could there have been one interested in Branders—or could he have been interested in one?"

Rooder shrugged, then shook his head. "I never knew of one," he replied. "He never spoke of one—to any of us."

The Island detective sighed slowly "He had a touch of *dengue,*" he said tonelessly. "He felt like flying—and he took off. The worst time of the day. Something went wrong, and he crashed and was killed. A short circuit caused delayed fire, and the plane was destroyed."

Rooder shrugged. "That is what I think," he stated. "And Alwin simply meant that an investigation should be made—which I understand. He—and the three of us here gain material things by Branders' death, of course."

Jo Gar nodded. Tate came into the room, wiping his face with a handkerchief. He was frowning.

"Going to be another scorcher, as usual," he said. "Where's that damned Chink cook, Erich? I want something to eat, and I can't find him."

Rooder widened his eyes. Jo Gar inspected the brown-paper of a cigarette. Carter entered the room and sat down. He looked narrowly at Jo, but he did not speak.

Rooder said: "Won should be around—he's usually up at this time. Come to think of it—I didn't see him near the plane, when it was burning. Most of the Filipinos were there."

Tate said slowly: "He's a heavy sleeper. I'll send one of the boys over to his shack."

He turned towards the door that led out to the patio at the side of the living-room. But he stopped suddenly. There were shrill shouts and the sounds of someone running swiftly. A screen door slammed and a half naked Filipino boy came into the room. He spoke several words in his native tongue, then said rapidly:

"Tony Won—I find him—him dead—"

There was silence in the room, except for the rapid breathing of the Filipino boy. Rooder stood up. Carter stiffened in his chair, but did not speak. Tate broke the silence.

"Dead?" he said heavily. "Are you—sure?"

The Filipino boy's eyes were very wide and black. He nodded.

"Me sure—very much cut with knife," he jerked.

Jo Gar lighted the cigarette he had been inspecting. Carter swore very slowly. The Island detective spoke in a soft voice:

"That is too bad. I was thinking, just a few minutes ago, of talking to him. It was he who saw the airplane fall."

Rooder said sharply. "Take us to where you found him, Juan. You coming, Señor Gar?"

The Island detective nodded. "Yes," he said quietly. "It may be that the knifing was not an accident."

Tate swung around so that he faced Gar. His eyes were very small and the fingers of his hands, at his sides, were moving.

"Listen here, Gar—"

Rooder said sharply: "Stop that, Harry—it won't do any good. Señor Gar has been paid to make an investigation."

Jo smiled very faintly. "It is so," he said simply.

Tate turned away from him. "Go on," he ordered the boy.

THEY WENT from the room, crossed the patio, went around to the rear of the plantation house. The Filipino boy led them away from it, towards a single shack, small and dirty, near thick palm foliage. No other shacks were close to this one, which was the nearest one to the house.

The door of the shack was open; the Filipino boy stood aside. Rooder went in and Jo followed him. Carter and Tate came in slowly.

The Chinese cook was lying on his back. He was short and fat and his eyes stared at the ceiling of the shack. There was blood on his throat and face, and his hands were covered with it. He was naked.

Jo Gar moved close to the body, looked down. Rooder said in his slightly guttural voice:

"His hands are slashed; he put up a fight. Got him in the throat. Probably he couldn't scream much."

The Island detective moved around the body; his eyes narrowed and expressionless. Tate stood near the opened door, breathing heavily. Carter said:

"Doesn't look as if he's been dead very long. I'd better send for Doc Cordozo again."

Rooder's blue eyes were watching the small figure of Jo Gar. He spoke softly:

"Yes—get Cordozo here. And get all the servants outside. I think I know why this happened."

Jo Gar looked at the German. "Why did it happen?" he asked quietly.

Rooder shrugged. "Won didn't get along too well with the hands. There have been complaints. He's allowed so much for food, and it was complained that he has been putting some of the money aside for himself, cutting down the food."

The Island detective smiled just a little. "And for that reason he was murdered," he said.

Rooder frowned. "Men have been murdered for a less logical reason than that—in the Islands," he stated.

Jo nodded.

"And for a more logical reason," he said simply.

There was silence except for Carter, outside, calling several names, giving orders. Jo Gar moved about the shack, searching with his eyes. He touched nothing. Tate said:

"If we could find the knife—"

Rooder swore. "We won't," he interrupted. "A knife is too easy to hide, out here."

Jo Gar walked past both men, went through the doorway of the shack. There had been no rain for months—the ground was hard. He moved over it for a short distance, circled the shack. It was growing steadily hotter. Erich Rooder came from the shack and stopped close to him.

"I can see your side of it, Señor Gar," he said easily. "You think one of us shot down Branders, and then, when you arrived, got worried. The plane was burned by one of us, before you could see the bullet holes. Won murdered by one of us because one of us thought he might have seen something."

Jo Gar looked thoughtful. Rooder said: "You think the three of us are protecting each other—or the guilty one."

The Island detective frowned. "I think the plane crash was an accident," he said slowly. "I think the fire was caused by a short circuit. I think Won was knifed because he did not give so much food to the hands. Does that please you?"

Rooder's eyes held a hard expression. "It *would* please me, if I didn't think you were lying," he said sharply.

Jo Gar bowed very slightly. "I shall be glad to hear what the servants say, and what the doctor says," he replied. "I do not think you will find the knife."

He turned away, towards the plantation house, and Rooder spoke in a puzzled voice.

"Where can we get you—"

The Island detective stopped and faced Rooder. He was smiling with his lips, but his eyes held no expression.

"I am going to my room and sleep," he said. "Sleep allows me to think more clearly, when I awake. Perhaps there is something I have not thought about."

Rooder's lips parted, and Jo waited for him to speak. But he said nothing. The Island detective turned away and went slowly back to the house. In his room he undressed and lay naked on the bed, on his back, his eyes staring at the ceiling. At intervals he could hear shouts, and after a half hour or so he heard the sounds of a car arriving. It was apparently an ancient car—it made a great rattle and wheeze.

THE ISLAND detective dozed for a half hour or so, rose and dressed. The Colt he inspected fully, slipped into a hip pocket of his trousers. He adjusted his pith helmet carefully, went outside and towards the flying field and the wreckage. He was soaked with perspiration when he reached the house again, almost an hour later. Cordozo, Tate and Rooder were in the living-room, sipping cool drinks. Rooder clapped his hands and ordered one for Jo.

"Been to the field again?" he asked pleasantly.

Jo Gar nodded. He seated himself in a wicker chair, wiped his face with a handkerchief.

"Again," he agreed.

Rooder remained seated but gestured towards the doctor.

"Doctor Cordozo—Señor Gar," he said.

They both nodded. Cordozo was short and thick-set; he had a browned face with a spatulate nose. His eyes were very small and his arms long. He spoke thickly but decisively.

"I can report to you, Señor Gar, that Branders was instantly killed in the plane crash. The cook was knifed to death, and it is doubtful that he was able to cry out. He died more slowly, but he was quickly unconscious. I should say he had been dead several hours when discovered."

Jo nodded and said nothing. Rooder said:

"Carter's out seeing that the work goes on—it's got to, you know."

Jo nodded again. After a short silence Rooder spoke very slowly:

"We got nothing from any of the servants. None of them knew a thing, and they all protested that Won had given them very good food. They all say that they loved him like a brother."

The Island detective smiled a little. "Naturally," he said.

Rooder frowned at the waxed floor of the living-room. "It is what happened," he muttered. "They wanted a new cook—and they knew their complaints had caused no change. So they murdered Won—that is the way it is done out here."

Jo Gar looked at the ceiling. "I might agree with you, except for one thing," he said. "With Branders alive and not paying any attention to their complaints—they might have killed Won. But with Branders dead—they would wait. When things quieted down they would speak to you. If you refused they might kill. But they could not *know* that you would refuse."

Rooder smiled with his lips; his eyes were hard. "They *did* know," he contradicted. "They knew last night, before you arrived."

Jo Gar lighted a brown-paper cigarette. "They came to you, and you refused to let Won go?" he asked.

Rooder's smile went away. He shook his head.

"No, Won came to me," he said slowly. "He demanded more money for the commissary. He said that some of the hands were threatening him, and he was afraid. He refused to name those who threatened. I suspected that he had been stealing, and I refused to give him more. He undoubtedly told the hands."

The Island detective said: "Branders was already dead."

Rooder nodded. "Of course," he said.

Jo Gar inhaled and removed the cigarette from his lips. "And now Won is dead," he said quietly. "You would think that he would have told the hands the food would be better in the future, and would have stopped stealing for a while."

Rooder smiled grimly. "He was a fool," he said.

Jo Gar drew a deep breath, sighed. The doctor yawned and apologized.

"I will make my report to the Constabulary," he said. "It is murder, and they will be here soon. It will do no good."

Rooder shook his head. His eyes were on Jo's. "No good," he agreed. "Natives are natives."

Jo rose and smiled towards Rooder. "I shall not be here for lunch," he said. "Perhaps not for dinner. Do not wait for me, please. I hope to return before midnight."

He watched the flicker of expression in Rooder's eyes. The doctor yawned again. Rooder said:

"Would you like the flivver, Señor Gar?"

The Island detective shook his head. "You are kind," he replied. "I shall not need it."

He smiled and went from the room, conscious that the eyes of Rooder and Tate were following him. Outside he met Carter, coming towards the screened porch. Carter was frowning.

"They won't work the way they should," he breathed. "And they all know who knifed Won. Not that it'll do any good—we couldn't even beat it out of them. And the Constabulary won't try to do that."

The Island detective said: "The Constabulary is wise."

He went around the house and towards the flying field. When he reached the slope and the thick foliage he picked a spot which held less insects than most spots, and crouched down. After a few minutes he heard faint sounds that grew louder. He did not see the figure that passed on towards the field and the wreckage. When the sounds had died away he changed his original direction, walked northward for several miles until he reached a small, bamboo shack that held an ant-eaten cot and a chair. The shack was for the field hands, but it had evidently not been used for weeks. It was hot inside. There were insects. Jo Gar swore several times.

He searched the shack thoroughly. He found nothing, left the place and walked northward again, avoiding natives who were working. In a half hour he found a cool spot on the slope of a hill. He was tired. He lay on his back, smoked two cigarettes, slept. When he awoke the heat of the afternoon was reaching the shade, and he dozed for several hours more. Then he left the spot and walked slowly in a wide circle. It was after dark when he reached the plantation house. He was soaked with perspiration and very tired.

TATE AND Rooder were seated in the living room when he entered; Carter stood near the corridor that led to Jo's room. No one spoke for several seconds and then the Island detective said:

"The Constabulary have arrived?"

Rooder and Tate watched him narrowly. Carter spoke in a low tone.

"Two of them were here, but they're gone into Carejo for the night."

Jo nodded. Rooder said: "You've been moving around, Señor Gar."

The Island detective smiled a little. "Moving around," he agreed.

Rooder looked at the ceiling. "We've held dinner up—such as it is," he said. "Learn anything?"

Jo continued to smile.

"Good of you," he replied. "I shall have a swift shower. I have learned something."

Tate drew a quick breath. Rooder said: "What?"

Jo shrugged and went from the room. As he passed Carter the American said:

"The Constabulary members didn't find a thing."

Jo spoke without turning his head. "It does not matter."

He went along the corridor to his room. The shower was a crude affair, but the water made noise when it fell from the tank. He waited several minutes before turning it on, but did not change his clothes. He took off his shoes, got his Colt in the right pocket of his duck coat. When he went from the room and along the corridor the sound of the shower water drowned other noises in the house.

He walked into the living-room silently. Rooder stood near a kerosene lamp, inspecting something he held in his left hand. Jo Gar stopped ten feet from him. He was inspecting a gun. Tate and Carter had their backs turned; Tate was saying:

"It's the only—sure way—"

The Island detective stood motionless, his right hand in the right pocket, and the coat cloth slightly away from his side. Carter said grimly:

"If we knew what he's been doing—"

Rooder looked up from the gun; his body stiffened. Jo Gar smiled with his blue-gray eyes half closed. The two Americans swung around. Carter sucked in his breath sharply. Jo looked at Rooder's gun.

"Please place the gun on the table," he said quietly.

Rooder stared at him.

"What the hell do you mean—" he started, but the Island detective interrupted.

"On the table," he repeated.

Rooder's lean body relaxed. He shrugged, moved a foot or so and placed the gun on the table. Jo looked at the hands of the two Americans. He was still smiling a little.

"Which one of you murdered Won?" he asked calmly.

There was a little silence, then Rooder made chuckling sound that was not very pleasant.

"You mean which one of us murdered Branders," he said mockingly.

Jo Gar shook his head slowly. "No," he said softly. "I do not mean that. The Chinese cook murdered Branders."

Tate's breath made harsh sound. Carter swore hoarsely and swung his body towards Rooder. Rooder's teeth were clenched and his lips were parted. He kept his blue eyes on Jo's almond-shaped ones. The Island detective said:

"There were things you did not know. And there were things you did know. You did *not* know that Branders called Alwin a few hours before the plane crashed—and swore that he would never fly again. You *did* know that there was a woman in his life, and that he was going to her, that she would marry him. That meant that you three would have to stay on here, run the plantation—and wait. Wait until he died. It meant something else—the will would probably be changed. So Won murdered him."

Rooder said slowly and in his guttural voice: "God—what rot!"

Jo Gar shook his head. "Then one of you murdered Won—making it look like a native knifing. That was because I was here—you were becoming frightened. One of you burned the plane, but not because you were afraid I'd find bullet holes. There were none."

Rooder said: "Of course not—it was an accident."

The Island detective shook his head. "It was murder," he said quietly. "Branders was knocked unconscious on the field or near the hangar. He was put in the plane and the stick was fastened back against his body. The engine was opened up. The plane took off—and climbed. A few hundred feet in the air, perhaps more—it fell off on a wing. It crashed. Branders was killed. It was murder."

Tate swung his body away and moved blindly a few feet. He had a hand pressed over his mouth—the back of his right hand. His face was twisted. Carter stood motionless. Rooder was breathing heavily; his eyes went to the right pocket of Jo's duck coat.

The Island detective said: "You burned the plane because you wanted me to believe Branders might have been shot down, if I refused to believe it an accident. I had no proof that there were no bullet holes. You paid Won to knock Branders unconscious. Which of you murdered the Chinese?"

Tate stopped moving blindly towards a shuttered window and faced the Island detective. His eyes were wide. Carter was silent. Rooder said huskily:

"It's—damned rot—you can't talk that—"

Jo Gar said in a sharp tone: "You do not have to answer. I know." His eyes went to those of Tate. "*You* murdered Won, Tate."

Tate's lips parted. "No—" he breathed in a whisper. "That's—a lie! A lie!"

Jo Gar slipped his left hand into the left pocket of his coat. He drew out a knife. He held it so that Tate's staring eyes could see it, then bent downward, slid it across the waxed floor towards the American.

"That's the knife used on Won. I found it in your room. In the dirt of that plant pot. Rooder told me it was yours."

Tate turned his head towards Rooder. His face was twisted and his fingers were working jerkily. Rooder said:

"I never—"

Tate swore fiercely. He twisted his head, stared at the knife. When he reached for it Rooder said hoarsely:

"For God's sake, Harry—"

Tate screamed above Rooder's voice: "You tried to—frame me. You put the knife in my room. You dirty—killer—"

His hand went upward and backward. Rooder leaped towards the table and the gun he had placed there. The thrown knife missed his moving body and battered against a wall. Jo Gar said:

"Stop—Rooder!"

Rooder's right hand was lifting the gun when he squeezed the trigger of the Colt. Crash sound filled the room. Rooder half turned and fired one shot as Tate rushed at him. Tate's body doubled forward; he went down heavily. Jo squeezed the trigger the second time. Rooder let his gun slip from his fingers. He stumbled several feet, half fell into a wicker chair. Carter stood motionless, watching Jo's gun hand.

The Island detective said: "Look at Tate, Carter."

Carter moved towards the body. Jo Gar picked up the gun Rooder had used on the American. Carter straightened.

"He's dead," he said tonelessly.

Jo walked towards the chair in which Rooder was slumped. He

kept Carter ahead of him, motioning him back with the Colt. Rooder looked up at him dully.

"I picked—the wrong, man," he said thickly, weakly. "I might have had better luck—with Carter."

Carter shook his head. "You wouldn't have," he said grimly. "I wouldn't have helped. I suspected you, Rooder—but I thought you were too strong to be caught. Too sure of what you were doing."

Rooder smiled wearily at Jo Gar. "The knife trick—that got him, Gar," he said softly. "You picked the weakest of the three—and worked on him. But you'd never have found the knife I used on Won."

Jo Gar was silent. Rooder breathed slowly. "You were—wrong about Won knocking out Branders. I did that. I got him in the plane and used a strap to hold the stick back. After the crash I found only—part of the strap. That's why I burned her. And I thought Won might have seen me. So I—knifed him. I knew Branders was going back—to England. I wanted—the plantation share. I told Tate—he kept Carter—out of the way—we were sure it would seem an—accident—"

He closed his eyes, and his body slipped forward. When Jo Gar leaned down and looked at him his eyes were open again, and he was dead. He straightened up and looked at Carter. Carter said:

"Tate was losing his nerve all day. You were away, and he didn't know where. He was nearly crazy by dark. He was even saying strange things in front of me—something about—it being the only sure way. I think they meant to kill you, Señor Gar."

"I think so," Jo agreed. "And I had no proof. I spent the day walking—and sleeping. And thinking."

Carter drew a deep breath. "And Branders was strapped in the plane—she climbed until she fell off on a wing, crashed."

Jo Gar nodded his head. "Things like that are much more successfully done during a war," he said softly. "I must telephone Señor Alwin."

Carter wiped his browned face with a handkerchief. "I can drive you to Carejo—I suppose everything will be all right—here.

The Island detective looked at the two figures that were motionless in the room.

"I think so," he agreed tonelessly.

The Magician Murder

A baffling case—but not to Jo Gar.

FROM THE spot in which Jo Gar was seated the two fighting cocks were whirling, feathered forms bouncing from the dark earth of the pit. Filipinos, Japanese, Chinese, Malays and Portuguese filled the rising tiers of wooden benches; their shouts were shrill and fierce. The betting was good; already there had been several fights. The event now under way was the last fight of the evening; one of the cocks, a small bird named Riazo, was the champion of a distant Philippine province. Riazo seemed to be winning and the majority of the crowd liked it.

The Island detective rolled the brown-paper cigarette between two short brown fingers of his right hand. His face was expressionless; it was as though he were unconscious of the excitement around him. At intervals he raised his right hand so that it was before his brown face. The fingers of the hand were spread carelessly; his blue-gray eyes looked between them.

Cardoro sat on his right, some twenty feet away, in the small box reserved for persons of importance. Cardoro was a magician—Cardoro the Great. He was Spanish, but spoke several languages. Only five days ago he had reached Manila from Australia, and already he was the talk of the city. Crowds stormed the box office of the theatre at which he executed his magic. His name was on the lips of the mixed breeds of the Islands. He was a savage magician, working with knives and poisons. He made incisions on people and there was blood in evidence. Yet it was only a trick. The audience saw incisions that did not exist, and blood that was only colored water. But they liked it, and Cardoro was great. Therefore he occupied the box of honor.

The shrill shouts now became a scream. Jo Gar smiled slightly as the favorite sank on the dark ground. It rose and launched itself into another attack. The larger bird met the attack with a more vicious one. The silver spurs glittered in the light shooting down on them. Riazo was battered back, fell on its side. The larger bird was on top of it now, spurs working. Riazo's movements were convulsive. Suddenly there were no more movements. The shrill of the crowd hushed. Filipinos were in the pit—bending over the birds.

Jo Gar said very softly, "Another champion is dead."

He raised his right hand again, spreading the fingers. Cardoro was on his feet in the box. He was staring towards the ground of the pit. He had large black eyes and a face that seemed very pale among the brown ones about him. His body was straight; he was a big man. His face seemed strained.

A Filipino standing in the pit raised a short arm and said into the silence:

"Riazo is dead!"

He spoke in Spanish, and before he could repeat the announcement in another language Cardoro had cried out. His voice carried over the close-packed circular arena.

"No!" he cried in Spanish. "It cannot be!"

Heads were jerked in his direction. A jeering voice from somewhere below reached Jo Gar's ears.

"It is so—Riazo is even too dead for *your* magic, Señor Cardoro!"

Jo Gar narrowed his blue-gray eyes very little. There was the edge of a smile on his tight-pressed lips. He looked down at the one who had jeered up at the magician. It was Markden, an American who handled many bets. Many bets that were large. Markden was a gambler; it was rumored that he made good sums on the fighting cocks. It was also rumored that some of his bets were placed after he had advance knowledge of certain facts. The Chinese did not trust him, and the Chinese were known as the wisest of the gamblers.

Cardoro's big body was swaying a little from side to side. His arms were drawn upward, the elbows extended, and his fists were clenched. There were white gloves on his hands; he wore them to protect his fingers, which were long and extremely sensitive. He called above the murmur of the crowd:

"I will not—"

His voice ceased abruptly. Jo Gar watched him turn from the box, saw a rather pretty girl lift a hand as though to stop him. But the magician paid no attention to her. The Island detective watched Cardoro move down wooden steps to a narrow exit. When he looked at Markden again the gambler was facing the direction in which the magician had gone. He was a small, slight man—slighter even than Jo. There was a set expression on his face. His body was tense under the glare of the lights, but as Jo's eyes watched he saw the man relax. He shrugged his narrow shoulders, looked down at the form of the dead bird.

The Filipino official who had announced the defeat of the champion now lifted the live winner in his hands. He turned slowly with the fighting cock above his head.

"The new champion!" he called. *"Garcia the First!"*

There was shrill sound in the arena. A group of Portuguese sailors started down towards the pit. There was the odor of varied tobaccos and of heat of people. *Betel*-nut chewers passed Jo, and there were red stains on the planks. It was very hot.

The Island detective went slowly towards an exit from the cock fight arena. The crowd milled around the dry ground beyond the entrance, chattering excitedly. *Calesos* and noisy, battered cars were making sound. Cardoro was not in sight, but there was talk of him. A well-dressed Chinese near Jo stated to his companion that the great one had lost much money. He had backed Riazo to the limit. Such a bet had not been made in many Sundays.

Jo Gar moved slowly to his *caleso,* nodded to the driver, who drowsed on the seat. Señor Ronisa passed close to the *caleso,* spoke cheerfully to Jo.

"I was lucky," the fat one stated. "I have won many *pesos.* But most have lost."

Jo Gar's eyes were very small. He placed a Panama carefully over his gray hair.

"It is not good—when most lose," he said quietly.

The fat one shrugged. "It is good for the few who win," he replied. "The winning is greater."

Jo Gar smiled a little, climbed into the *caleso.* The driver lifted the reins and spoke shrilly to the ancient horse. Jo said in a toneless voice:

"And the hating of the losers is greater."

He closed his eyes and relaxed in the seat. The *caleso* jerked forward and the light wind fanned greater heat against his face. When he opened his blue-gray eyes they were smiling. But the smile was a hard one, and very thoughtful.

SADI RATAN frowned across the few feet of Jo Gar's office that separated the two. He looked cool despite the heat; his khaki uniform was spotless, well pressed. He said with a slight accent, speaking in English.

"You have perhaps seen that the magician, Cardoro, is dead, murdered?"

Jo Gar leaned back in the wicker chair. He nodded very slowly.

"Yes," he replied.

The Manila police lieutenant's frown deepened. There was a short silence broken by the whistle of small craft on the Pasig.

"The crime was committed by the American, Markden," Sadi Ratan announced. "The gambler, Markden. He has been in difficulty before this. He has vanished. The Constabulary has been notified."

Jo Gar smiled pleasantly. "Is that so?" he said thoughtfully. "So it was Markden who knifed Señor Cardoro?"

Lieutenant Ratan nodded again. He stood erect, but did not smile.

"That is the way it was," he stated. "He had been betting against Markden three nights since he has arrived here. Large sums. He had lost each time. Last evening he made a big bet. It was Sunday and he had little money. He agreed to cable his bank in Australia this morning, if he lost. He lost and he refused to pay. At dusk tonight he was knifed to death by Markden in his room at the Manila Hotel. Markden escaped, but he will be caught."

The Island detective continued to smile. "Of course," he said simply.

There was another silence, and during it Sadi Ratan watched Jo closely.

"The knife we have not found. Perhaps it was not a knife. Beside the body was a blood-stained spur such as the cocks fight with. A knife spur. The wounds were on the back of the neck—many of them. The spinal column was struck. Markden was seen drinking very much at six o'clock. He talked of what he would do to Cardoro if he failed to pay. Perhaps it was that he fastened the silver spur to wood, and used it that way. He entered the room while Cardoro was sleeping. There was no struggle. Cardoro was stunned with the first blow and before he staggered from the bed to die on the floor. Markden had struck many others. Then he fled."

Jo Gar lighted a brown-paper cigarette. "Why did Señor Cardoro refuse to pay his bet?" he asked, after a short time.

Lieutenant Ratan smiled a little.

"He had been told, before the cock fights, that the champion bird,

Riazo, had been drugged. The fight was not fair. Markden had bribed the Filipino who cared for Riazo."

Jo Gar smiled with his eyes almost closed. "Why did he not cancel his bet?" he asked.

Sadi Ratan shrugged. "Perhaps he was not sure. Perhaps Markden would not allow it. The fight was not a good one. Riazo did not attack. Cardoro refused to pay. Markden drank saké and thought about it. He murdered the magician."

Jo Gar looked at the ceiling fan that whirled at slow speed, spreading tepid air around the small office.

"A foolish man," he observed. "He knew that murdering Cardoro would not get him the money he had won. He knew that leaving the knife spur behind would betray him. He knew that running away would make matters worse. Yet he did all three of these things."

Sadi Ratan smiled narrowly. "He hated," he said simply. "It is a hot country. He drank and he brooded. Perhaps he did not *intend* to leave the spur behind. He fled when he discovered it was lost, or when he sobered. He knew the police would think of him."

"And they *did* think of him," Jo said pleasantly.

Lieutenant Ratan frowned again. "I attended the cock fights and was near Cardoro. I saw Markden mock him, jeer at him. And I heard the magician call out 'I will not—' I knew that he meant he would not pay his bet."

The Island detective nodded. "It was fortunate you were so near," he observed. "After the murder you thought instantly of Markden. You questioned the bird handlers and learned that Riazo had perhaps been drugged and was unfit to fight, and that Cardoro had been warned of this fact. You have had the red on the spur knife analyzed and you know that it is human blood. It is common knowledge that Cardoro was betting heavily. Markden has vanished. Thus, he is the murderer."

Sadi Ratan's dark eyes had widened. They narrowed now. He spoke in a tone of triumph.

"That is so."

Jo Gar inhaled deeply on his cigarette. He regarded the police lieutenant with faint interest, reached for the palm leaf fan that was on the desk near his chair.

"And it being so, why do you visit me?" he asked softly.

The police lieutenant smiled, his white teeth showing.

"The Señor Markden was seen with you, not long before the hour of the first cock fight," he said slowly and clearly. "You were walking along the bank of the Pasig, talking seriously. You were seen by the police."

Jo Gar chuckled. "One never knows who watches," he said half to himself. His blue-gray eyes narrowed on the dark ones of the younger man. "It is true. We walked and talked together."

Sadi Ratan smiled coldly. "I think I should know what you talked about," he said.

The Island detective said thoughtfully "I think you should. Señor Markden wished me to learn if the cock fight—the final one—was to be honest. He stated that he had a large sum of money involved."

He paused and after a few seconds Sadi Ratan said impatiently:

"Well—did you accept the commission?"

Jo Gar nodded. "I made inquiries. I did my best. And I reported to him during the cock fights."

Sadi Ratan said, "You learned that the bird Cardoro was betting on was unfit to fight?"

The Island detective shook his head. "I reported to Markden that I felt the birds were evenly matched physically. It would be a matter of skill."

Sadi Ratan's brown face showed red color. He swore in Filipino. He said thickly:

"I do not think—"

He checked himself. Jo Gar smiled. "That I tell you the truth?" he asked quietly.

The police lieutenant's body was tense.

"You are protecting an American. You have always protected them. You like them. He was your client."

Jo shrugged his narrow shoulders.

"I was not paid that well," he said with irony. "I doubt that I could ever be paid that well. Riazo was not drugged. You have no proof of it."

Sadi Ratan said hotly, "I stood over Juan Derigo when he told me—"

Jo chuckled again. "A Filipino does not like to be beaten," he said. "He preferred to let you think as you wished."

The police lieutenant said, "It will not be good for you to protect

Markden, Señor Gar. When we have caught him—"

The Island detective fanned himself. His smile was gone and he said slowly:

"The birds were in condition. Each of them. Riazo was defeated. That is all."

Sadi Ratan said excitedly, "It is not all. Markden was betting against Cardoro. Cardoro stood up and shouted that he would not pay. I saw Markden's face—there was hate in his eyes. And Cardoro was murdered. A spur knife was used. Markden has vanished. We have searched the city for him. He is the killer of the magician!"

Jo Gar sighed. "Then it is all very simple," he said quietly. "You will find him, and that will be the end."

His calmness infuriated the police lieutenant. He said fiercely:

"And you will be brought to trial for lying to me, a police officer!"

Jo Gar placed the palm leaf fan on the desk. It was almost midnight. He said thoughtfully:

"He was murdered at dusk—that would be about eight-thirty. You have been searching for the American for three hours. That would give the *real* murderer sufficient time to travel far."

Sadi Ratan swore again. He pointed a brown finger at Jo.

"We will not accept the alibi that you establish for the American," he said. "Remember that."

Jo Gar smiled pleasantly. "That is unfortunate," he said.

The police lieutenant went to the office door, turned and faced the Island detective.

"Markden was seen on the grounds of the Manila Hotel, at eight-fifteen," he stated grimly. "The sun was very low over the Bay. He was seen by several servants. And then he was not seen again. At the time he was seen the magician was in his room, sleeping. There is a porch through which one may enter."

Jo smiled cheerfully. "In a hot country the screened porch is desirable," he said softly.

Sadi Ratan pointed a finger at him again. His voice was rising as he spoke.

"It will be bad for you," he warned. "A murderer is a murderer."

Jo Gar leaned back in the wicker chair and closed his almond-shaped eyes.

"It is so," he agreed almost tonelessly. "And I think it would be wise for you to find this one."

SAM MARKDEN sat slumped on the bench that faced the door of the dully lighted hut. A faint, hot breeze rustled the thatch roof. Markden seemed smaller than ever; his eyes moved at every sound. He was perspiring heavily. He spoke in a thick voice, softly and unsteadily.

"I tell you—they'll get me. They hate me in Manila. The fight was on the level. Maybe some haven't been in the past. This one was. They'll get me and frame me. You've got to do something, Señor Gar."

Jo Gar shook his head. "I have not got to do something," he corrected. "But your position is unfortunate. The police will not even believe me when I tell them you wished me to learn if the cock fight was to be fair. They will laugh at that. If I told them Cardoro had asked me that—they would have believed. But *you*—"

He checked himself. Somewhere beyond the hut on the edge of Manila, a dog howled. Markden shivered. Jo Gar said slowly and firmly:

"You have sent for me—you trust me. Do not trick me. Did you murder Cardoro?"

Markden sat up straight and struck clenched hands together.

"No—no!" he said desperately. "I threatened him, yes. That was in the afternoon. But I didn't kill him. I went to the hotel grounds, to talk to him again, just before dusk. But I was afraid to trust myself. I didn't see him. I went away. Then word reached me of what had happened. I hid out here—and sent for you."

Jo nodded. "It was difficult for me to reach you without being followed," he said. "The police are watching me carefully."

The American groaned. "They'll get me," he breathed. "I'd won from Cardoro. So much that I wanted this last fight to be absolutely fair. It had to be, or I knew he'd squeal. That's why I went to you."

Jo frowned. "It's a bad alibi, in any case. In this case—it's impossible."

Markden covered his soaked face with both palms and rocked on the bench.

The dog howled again. Jo Gar said:

"You do not know of any enemies Cardoro might have had?"

Markden removed his hands, shook his head. "I didn't know him well. He was just a man with money, who wanted to bet."

The Island detective frowned. "You drank—and talked. Made

threats before others?"

Markden's eyes were staring beyond Jo. "I drank saké. But I didn't make any threats. Only to Cardoro, and we were alone. I was careful not to make threats."

Jo sighed. "It is difficult," he said. "It was a good thing for someone who hated him enough to kill—this hatred of yours. But if we do not know the one who could have made use of it—"

He broke off. Markden muttered "Bilibid—I'll hang for it! They won't believe me."

Jo Gar half closed his eyes. He said in a calm voice:

"If *you* hang for it—*I* will be forced to leave the Islands. I think you are telling the truth. I do not wish to leave Manila. You do not wish to hang. You will stay here and I will do what I can."

Markden stared at him with bloodshot eyes.

"But what can you do?" he muttered. "All the evidence is against me. All that they have."

Jo Gar rubbed moist fingers together and smiled grimly down at the gambler.

"Perhaps there will be some evidence they do *not* have," he said softly. "There is a chance."

The American said bitterly "It's a hell—of a chance!"

Jo Gar drew a deep breath, shrugged. "Even a *hell* of a chance is worth while," he observed steadily and softly, and went cautiously from the thatch-roofed hut.

THE GIRL said, "It seems to me it's pretty late for me to have to talk about—this terrible thing."

Jo Gar stepped inside the large, high-ceilinged room, smiled apologetically.

"It is so, Miss Rayne," he said. "It is almost one o'clock. I am sorry."

The girl stood aside as he moved to the center of the room. There was moonlight beyond the Manila Hotel, on the water of the Bay. The girl was pretty, but her mouth and eyes were hard. She said huskily:

"I've been questioned—by the police."

The Island detective nodded. "Yes," he replied. "I suppose so. I am not of the police."

She watched him very closely. "I know. You're Señor Gar, a private detective."

Jo bowed slightly. The girl said: "Markden did this terrible thing. I was to have—married—Dario—next week—"

The Island detective said gently, looking at the older woman seated in the room:

"You think Markden killed Dario Cardoro?"

The girl said: "Yes—yes, I do! I'm sure of it. I was with Dario at the cock fights. He was sure he had been tricked. He said he would never pay. Riazo had no life, no fight. Dario left me in the box, hurried away. He was terribly upset."

Jo gestured towards a chair. "Please sit down," he said.

The girl went slowly to the chair, sat down. She looked at the older woman, said:

"This is my companion—Señora Riggia."

The Spanish woman bowed, her eyes on Jo's. She was short and thick-set. Her body relaxed in the chair.

"It is terrible," she said with an accent.

Jo Gar nodded. "It is bad for Señor Markden, the American," he stated. "He was owed money by the dead man. It was refused him. He threatened the dead man. He was on the hotel grounds not long before the murder was committed. He has vanished."

The girl said, "They will find him—the police."

The Island detective nodded. "I think so," he agreed. "But he is not the murderer of the magician, Cardoro."

The girl's brown eyes widened. She said in a half whisper:

"Not the—murderer—"

Jo smiled gently. His eyes were on the older woman. Her hands were gripping the sides of the wicker chair. Far out in the Bay a big boat whistled. Jo spoke slowly.

"Markden has been in trouble with the police before. He has shot a man. He possesses a gun. He did not use it on Cardoro."

The older woman said sharply, "That was because he did not wish to give himself away. He wished the police to think it was some other person—not an American. Americans do not use knives."

Jo Gar said, "That is good reasoning, Señora. Almost *too* good." He looked at the girl again. There was a short silence. Then Jo said pleasantly:

"I have been looking at the body. Cardoro was killed by a strong person."

The girl said: "A strong person? That is not so. The doctors have said that the spur blade did not penetrate more than an inch. A blow to the base of the brain—"

The Island detective interrupted, but his tone was cold and his words unhurried.

"And Markden is not a strong person?" he suggested.

The girl said with scorn: "Of course not. He is smaller even than you."

Jo bowed slightly. "That is so," he agreed. "I felt that you were aware of the fact that Markden is not strong."

THERE WAS a knock at the door of the room. The girl rose. Before she reached the door it was opened. Sadi Ratan entered. He said quickly, looking at the Spanish woman:

"I felt that you should know, Señora—"

He stared at Jo, broke off. The Island detective smiled at him.

"I came to talk with Miss Rayne, Lieutenant," he said.

Sadi Ratan frowned. Then his eyes narrowed until they were slits in his brown face.

"We have captured the American, Markden," he said grimly. "He has admitted that Señor Gar visited him tonight. That is bad for you, Señor Gar. You were protecting a murderer, one wanted by the police."

Jo Gar said quietly, "One wanted by the police, but not a murderer."

The police lieutenant said in a hard tone, "He will confess very soon. And even if he does not—"

The Island detective smiled with his lips. "You will try to hang him, anyway," he finished.

Sadi Ratan let his right hand go back towards a hip pocket. He said in a hard tone:

"It will be necessary for me to place you under arrest, Señor Gar, for interfering with the police and for aiding a murderer."

Jo shook his head. "Señor Markden is not yet a murderer," he reminded. "He has not been found guilty."

The girl said with scorn: "His record is not good. He has shot a man. He is a gambler and he has been caught cheating, before this happened. He killed Dario—because Dario refused to pay him."

Jo shook his head. His eyes were very small.

"You know much about the American," he said calmly. "Almost *too* much."

Sadi Ratan was watching him closely. Jo looked at the girl, addressed the police lieutenant.

"The Great Cardoro has done his tricks here often—for a period of years. He is Spanish—there is a bond between him and the Spanish here. There is a Spanish paper in Manila. News of Spaniards all over the world reaches it and is printed or filed away in the paper morgue. I have been looking through the morgue files. I find that Cardoro was worth twice as much two years ago than he was six months ago. His losses were due to gambling. I found a later item stating that Cardoro the Great had become engaged to an American girl of the theatre, Miss Jessie Rayne. And I found one more item of three months ago. In Melbourne a gambling place was raided. One of the heaviest losers had been Cardoro. He had stated then that he was willing his money to Miss Rayne, his fiancée, and that on the day of their marriage he would never gamble again."

The girl was watching him narrowly—her breathing was heavy. The older woman was tense in her chair. Jo said, smiling a little:

"So there you are."

Sadi Ratan said sharply, "There you are—where? What of it?"

Jo Gar shrugged. "But Cardoro has continued gambling. Continued losing. His fortune is willed to Miss Rayne. But will there *be* any fortune—would there *have been* any fortune—if Cardoro had not been—"

The girl shrilled at him, "You are telling me that *I* killed—Dario! You dare—"

Jo Gar shook his head. "I am not," he said quietly. "You did not love him, but you did not kill him. You do not know so much about knives, and you are not strong enough."

The girl's eyes were wide; her face was pale. Sadi Ratan breathed something that the Island detective did not catch. He said softly:

"But you realized, Miss Rayne, that the money you had married Cardoro for would not be for you, unless something was done. And you decided that something should be—death."

The girl cried: "No—"

Jo Gar said steadily: "Yes. You waited for the opportunity. The American, Markden, offered it. He had reason to hate Cardoro. He had a record and you knew about it. He was a gambler on cock fights, and that was why the blood-stained knife spur was found beside the dead man. But you went too far. Markden is an American, and he would not kill and then boast about it as a Filipino or a Spaniard might do. He would not hate that much."

He paused and said very slowly: "Cardoro was killed with a knife—not a cock fight spur. He was killed by a strong man or woman, who knew how to handle a knife. He was killed by—"

He turned and looked at the girl's companion. He said quietly:

"You murdered Dario Cardoro. You did not throw the knife far enough into the Bay, in your hurry. And you were seen throwing it. I have the knife."

The woman sprang from the chair. She screamed in Spanish, terribly. From the folds of her dress steel color caught the light of the room. Her right arm was lifted.

Jo Gar said, "Stop—"

The woman's right hand went down into the folds of the black dress she wore. She said in a hysterical tone:

"You lie—"

Jo Gar's right hand made swift movement; his Colt was low at his right side.

"No," he said steadily. "I do not lie. You murdered Cardoro. Drop the knife you were about to throw—on the floor."

The woman was breathing heavily; her eyes held a wild expression. But her hand remained in the folds of her black dress.

Jo said: "Quickly—drop it!" He raised the gun slightly.

The knife made clattering sound as it struck the wood of the floor. The woman in black slipped downward, slowly, in a faint. Jo said:

"Well, I have the knife *now,* anyway." He went over and picked it up. "She did not throw it into the Bay—and she was not seen throwing it. But I was coming close—and her nerves—"

The Rayne girl was on the divan, rocking back and forth. Her eyes stared somewhere beyond the figure of Jo Gar. She spoke in a monotone.

"She made me—tell her when Dario slept. She used the knife and left the knife spur, touching it in his blood. She hated him. He loved her once, but he sent her away. He was losing, gambling away all the money he had willed to me. She made me help her—she was to have some of—the money. I didn't want—to do it."

Jo Gar looked at Sadi Ratan. "I thought at first that he had been murdered outside, carried in. That was wrong. And I thought that the knife had been thrown away. That was wrong, too. But when I saw the woman's eyes, saw her watching me—"

He shrugged. The woman on the floor stirred and moaned. The Rayne girl said:

"He was brutal—it was self-defense. He was brutal to both of us—"

Jo Gar smiled slightly. "Your defense is your own affair," he said gently. "I am very little interested."

Lieutenant Ratan frowned and swore. Jo Gar said:

"You were so sure of the American. So sure he was guilty. Now you must free him."

Sadi Ratan muttered:

"All the evidence we had—pointed to him."

Jo Gar sighed. "That is so," he agreed softly. "And that was why I had to go to a newspaper and seek the evidence—you *did not* have."

The Man From Shanghai

Jo Gar has forty minutes in which to solve a murder.

SADI RATAN, lieutenant of police, flicked Manila dust from his khaki uniform and smiled at the shine of his boots. He inspected the insignia of his office, striped on the left sleeve of his coat, lifted his dark eyes and continued to smile at Jo Gar.

"I thought it would please you to know that I have been ordered to go aboard the *China Maru* at Quarantine, Señor Gar," he said gently. "The person in whom I have interest is a client of yours, I am told."

Jo Gar lifted a stubby, brown hand to his thin lips. His diminutive body was sprawled in the fan-backed chair of his office, almost beneath the slightly squeaking ceiling fan. The Island detective parted his lips and tapped his palms against a yawn.

"Many times my clients have disturbed me," he said tonelessly, his gray-blue eyes looking somewhere beyond Lieutenant Ratan. "However, Miss Crale is no longer a client of mine, Lieutenant."

Sadi Ratan widened his eyes in faint surprise. Jo Gar smiled very slightly.

"Hysterical ladies are not pleasing—in the tropics," the Island detective murmured. "I received her radio requesting me to board the *China Maru* on Cavite, Lieutenant. My answer was a refusal. I presume she then radioed the police."

Sadi Ratan pressed his lips close together and frowned in the direction of Jo's knees. The ceiling fan stirred hot air about the small office.

"Strange," the lieutenant of Manila police said with faint sarcasm. "I had felt that you preferred wealthy clients to poor ones, Señor Gar."

He turned towards the door that led to the creaky, wooden stairs and the *calle* off the Escolta, Manila's main business street.

Jo Gar lighted a brown-paper cigarette, blew smoke thinly towards the slow whirling fan.

"You had felt correctly, Lieutenant," he said tonelessly. "But Virginia Crale's life has been threatened so often, in her imagination, that her fees bored me beyond their value in cash."

Sadi Ratan turned near the door, facing the chair in which Jo Gar was seated.

"You are kind to allow the police to work on the case," he stated grimly, a sneer on his handsome face.

The Island detective smiled gently. "It was kind of you to inform me that you were going aboard the boat. I am afraid your trip will be useless, but there is the advantage of a cool breeze off Cavite."

Sadi Ratan bowed his head jerkily and went from the room. Jo listened to the sound of his highly polished boots on the creaky steps. From the *calle* below came the shrill cries of drivers. Odors reached the room and there was the deeper noise of whistles on the Pasig river.

The Island detective rolled the brown-paper cigarette between his short fingers. After a little time he leaned forward, lifted the radio message from his battered cane desk. He slumped back in the wicker chair, read softly and tonelessly.

> MY LIFE IS AGAIN IN DANGER STOP I HAVE BEEN THREATENED TWICE SINCE BOARDING THE BOAT AT NAGASAKI STOP I THINK IT IS THE MAN FROM SHANGHAI STOP PLEASE BOARD THE CHINA MARU AT QUARANTINE AND COME DIRECTLY TO MY CABIN STOP CRALE

Jo Gar tossed the radio message to the surface of his desk. He sighed heavily, leaned back and closed his gray-blue eyes.

"The man from Shanghai," he breathed softly. "That would be Jacobi."

He rose languidly, moved to a small cabinet in a corner. It was early afternoon, only an hour beyond *siesta* time. That corner of the office was even hotter than the other portions. Jo slowly opened a drawer and thumbed through cards until he found the one he wanted. He raised it, looked down at it. He read the words written in his own careful hand very softly.

> "Baron Jacobi. Legitimacy of title uncertain. Store on the *Calle Real.* Collector of lacquer—red a specialty. Many trips to China. Reputed wealthy. Collection in Manila second only to that of Vir-

ginia Crale. Who suspects him of threatening her life for the reason he wants to buy her collection which she has repeatedly refused to sell. Jacobi known along the Escolta as *the Man from Shanghai.* Methods of obtaining pieces for his collection sometimes not legitimate. Considerable power here and in Shanghai."

JO GAR placed the card back in the drawer, nodding his gray-haired head slowly. A faint smile edged his thin lips. He turned his left palm downward and looked at his wrist-watch. The hands showed forty minutes after two.

He went across to another chair and lifted his pith helmet, placed it on his head. The white duck suit was less soiled than the helmet. Jo stood thinking for several seconds, then went to the desk and took from a drawer his Colt .45. He placed it carefully in the deep right pocket of his trousers. Leaving the room he went slowly down the wooden stairs.

At the foot of them, just within the doorway of the old frame building he encountered a messenger boy. The Filipino smiled at him and handed him an envelope. "It is a message of the radio," he stated in Tagalog.

The Island detective said: "No doubt then that it has importance."

The messenger smiled and nodded, and left him alone. Tearing open the envelope Jo looked down at the printed words.

> KINDLY MEET CHINA MARU AT QUARANTINE STOP SHOW THIS TO PROPER AUTHORITIES AND DO NOT FAIL ME STOP MY LIFE ENDANGERED BECAUSE OF VALUABLE POSSESSION STOP BARON JACOBI

Jo Gar narrowed his gray eyes as he refolded the slip of paper, placed it within the envelope again.

"So," he murmured meditatively. "A female suspects a male—and a male suspects—"

He hesitated, beckoning to the driver of a *caleso* as he reached the street.

"— and a male suspects, *perhaps,* a female," he half whispered.

When the *caleso* driver had shrilled his pony into the proper position near the curb, Jo Gar climbed inside the carriage.

"The dock of the Quarantine steamer," he instructed. "I realize that it is ten squares distant, but still I should like to arrive there within an hour."

The *caleso* driver informed him in Tagalog that his pony was very fast, perhaps the fastest in Manila. He elaborated on the speed of the animal for minutes, as the pony ambled towards the Escolta. But Jo Gar was thinking of the *China Maru,* and of Virginia Crale—and of the man from Shanghai. Once, he closed his slanted eyes and chuckled. Sadi Ratan would be surprised to see him board the Quarantine steamer.

Near the Manila Hotel the driver twisted his head and stated that the heat was not good for his cough. He would prefer to be in Baguio, where there was mountain coolness. Jo Gar lighted a brown-paper cigarette. The driver observed that he was afraid he would not live long. Jo Gar said tonelessley:

"Many people fear death—most of them are fools."

The driver said: "Most of them are poor, like myself."

Jo Gar did not reply. Neither Virginia Crale nor Baron Jacobi were poor. Each feared death. He wondered, as he pulled on the cigarette, if they were fools. He decided, as the Quarantine dock came into sight, that they were not.

THE LIEUTENANT of Manila police, Sadi Ratan, stood aft on the deck of the *Luzon* as Jo Gar strolled up the gangway. His back was to the Island detective. Jo went forward and seated himself. When the Quarantine steamer got under way he dozed in the shade of the superstructure. After about twenty minutes the sloping island of Cavite was to the port and the *China Maru* was a half mile ahead. She was a big boat, one of the newest in service. Jo lighted a brown-paper cigarette, rose and went aft.

Sadi Ratan turned, facing him suddenly. The lieutenant's perfectly uniformed figure stiffened.

"I thought that Miss Crale was no longer a client of yours, Señor Gar," he stated coldly.

"That is so," Jo replied quietly. "A different matter takes me aboard the *China Maru*."

Sadi Ratan smiled mockingly. "It is one thing to refuse a client's orders—and another to see the Manila police interested, perhaps."

The Island detective shook his head slowly. "I am not interested in Miss Crale, Lieutenant."

Sadi Ratan shrugged, turned away from Jo. The *Luzon* steamed on, nearing the big liner. She came around in a circle, astern of the *China Maru*. Quarantine officials and few newspapermen lined the port rail. Passengers on the big vessel looked down at the small one steaming in towards the boarding ladder. Jo Gar shaded his eyes with a brown palm and looked outward and upward.

He did not see Miss Crale. But the figure of Baron Jacobi was easily seen. The baron was waving his right arm slowly from side to side. He was hatless, and his blond hair was as ruffled as ever. As the *Luzon* steamed close to the big boat Jo's keen eyes spotted the red tie that Jacobi usually wore—it stood out clearly against the white of his shirt and suit.

The Island detective waved a hand slowly, but the baron turned aside and Jo saw the figure of a deck steward at the rail, beside Jacobi. He was evidently saying something; the baron vanished from the rail. The steward stood for a few seconds, looking down at the Quarantine steamer, then he, too, vanished.

A voice from behind Jo said: "You understand, of course, that the police have been called into this case."

Jo Gar turned slowly, looked into the dark eyes of Lieutenant Ratan.

"Case?" he said gently. "Oh—of course. Miss Crale's life has been threatened."

Sadi Ratan frowned. He drew a deep breath.

"I am not fooled, Señor Gar," he said nastily.

Jo smiled.

"It is good that you use the present tense," he replied. "Often one is wise to neglect thoughts of the past."

He bowed slightly and moved towards the group forward, waiting to board the big boat. The *Luzon* scraped against the *China Maru's* boarding deck. As Jo moved forward the form of Sadi Ratan reached his side. He was brushed back as the police lieutenant called: "Step aside, please—it is a police matter."

The Island detective chuckled. Hennigger, of the Manila *News,* grinned at him and pointed a thumb towards the back of Lieutenant Ratan.

"Murder or suicide?" he asked.

Jo Gar smiled. "A serious crime, clearly," he replied. "It is a police matter."

Hennigger grunted, regarded Jo with narrowed, blue eyes.

"What you doing here?" he asked.

Jo Gar shrugged. "The Bay is cooler than the Escolta," he replied.

The reporter swore. "The ear is quicker than the eye," he returned. "Maybe you've heard something I haven't seen."

They moved to the boarding deck and climbed the gangway to a lower deck of the big boat. Jo said:

"I must see if my third cousin, Rinaldo, is still a member of the crew."

He moved away from Hennigger, who nodded his head and said with sarcasm: "That's why I came aboard—my grandmother is bringing her father over from Nagasaki."

Jo Gar turned and said seriously: "I trust they have had an easy voyage."

He went upstairs to Deck B, reached the purser's desk. The dapper Chinese showed white teeth.

"The cabin of Baron Jacobi?" Jo said questioningly. "I have been asked to come to him."

The Chinese said: "It is A Deck—Room 17."

Jo Gar smiled, thanked the purser. He climbed a broader flight of steps, reached A Deck. Glancing into the Grand Saloon he did not see Jacobi. After some difficulty he reached the corridor leading to Room 17, an outside room. He moved along the corridor, halted, rapped on the door.

There was no answer. Jo Gar rapped again. The deep-toned whistle of the *China Maru* sounded in a short blast. There was engine vibration. Jo knocked a third time, then turned the knob of the door with his left hand. The door opened inward—he stepped into the cabin.

When he saw the body on the bed, Jo stood very still. Baron Jacobi was lying on his back—there was red on his lips and chin. His eyes were opened, staring up at the ceiling. One arm hung over the edge of the bed—the hand of the other, with the fingers curved, clutched at his red tie. A chair overturned—Jo's eyes moved about the cabin, found nothing else disturbed.

After a few seconds he moved nearer the bed. The cabin was large—the bed was a good-size one. Jo said softly:

"A little more than five minutes—from the time he left the rail—until I entered the room. Perhaps—"

His body straightened, grew tense as a scream from somewhere beyond the corridor reached him. It was the scream of a woman. It came into the cabin of the dead man once—then again. There were men's voices, and the sound of shoes beating against the corridor linoleum. The Island detective stood almost motionless, looking down at the body of Baron Jacobi. A voice reached him from the far end of the corridor.

"Steward—get a doctor! Cabin 29 hurry!"

Jo turned his body slowly, went to a small desk near a deck window. He looked down at a check; it was on the Bank of Manila. It had not been filled in. A corner was folded—on the back of the fold there was small handwriting. Jo leaned forward and read: "Crale—29—port."

A voice beyond the room said loudly: "Lieutenant Ratan came aboard—get him, Kyoshi!"

Jo Gar left the desk, went to the opposite side of the bed. He placed brown fingers carefully in the dead man's thick, blond hair, lifted the head. The wound was in the neck—it was not a large one.

Jo said softly: "Knife—nape of the neck, just above the spinal column. Very decent job."

He released his grip on the dead man's hair. The knife was not in the room. There were hurrying footfalls in the corridors beyond as Jo moved about, searching with his eyes, touching nothing.

After a few seconds he left the cabin, went along the narrow corridor to the main one, leaving the door of 17 half open. Several stewards stood near a corridor running off to the port side. Jo asked:

"Is Cabin 29 down there?"

One of the stewards nodded. The Island detective moved along the corridor. Twenty-nine was an outside cabin, located in the corridor as Jacobi's had been located in the other. Several men stood near the opened door; they stepped aside as Jo reached them.

AN OFFICER of the vessel came out. He was Chinese; short and deep-chested.

"It is very bad," he stated in stiff English.

"It is her head—she has been struck heavily."

Jo Gar said: "Miss Crale?"

The officer nodded and moved towards the main corridor. Jo Gar went into the cabin. Virginia Crale was lying on her bed; a stewardess held red stained cloths over her forehead. The room was in good order.

Jo looked at the frightened eyes of the stewardess, who was Chinese and pretty.

"It was you who screamed?" he asked quietly.

The stewardess nodded. "I very frightened," she said shakily. "I come here—door come open—I come in. She lying on floor—very hurt."

Jo nodded, smiled a little. "Why did you come here?" he asked steadily.

The stewardess ran the back of her right hand across her lips.

"She ring for me," she said, and made a gesture towards a wall near the cabin door.

Jo Gar went to the wall and looked at a white button. Red was on it, and the wall around it was dabbed with red. As he faced the stewardess again Sadi Ratan came into the cabin. He halted a few feet inside, stared at the figure on the bed.

"Dead?" he asked quickly.

Two men entered behind him, one in the uniform of the ship's doctor. He beckoned for the stewardess to move aside, lifted the cloths, bending over Virginia Crale. Sadi Ratan turned his trim figure, looked around the cabin. He straightened a little as he saw Jo.

"Life is filled with a number of things, Lieutenant," the Island detective stated pleasantly.

Sadi Ratan scowled. "How long have you been here?" he demanded.

Jo Gar shrugged.

"The screams of the stewardess attracted my attention," he replied. "I have been here perhaps a minute."

Sadi Ratan continued to scowl. "Where were you when the stewardess screamed?" he asked.

The ship's doctor straightened. "Unconscious—serious brain concussion, clearly. We must remove her to the ship's hospital immediately."

Lieutenant Ratan said: "She will be able to make a statement soon, Doctor?"

The doctor looked impassively at the lieutenant. "Who can say?" he replied. "She may be unconscious for hours—it may be necessary to operate. That must be done ashore. She may never regain consciousness. A heavy blow—a terrible blow."

He went swiftly from the cabin. Sadi Ratan looked around the floor. Jo Gar said:

"I looked for the weapon—it does not seem to be in the cabin."

The deep-chested officer came into the cabin again. Sadi Ratan said:

"I am Lieutenant Sadi Ratan, of the Manila police." He gestured towards Jo. "This is Señor Gar, a private detective. Miss Crale requested him to meet the boat, stating her life was in danger. Señor Gar refused. She then radioed the police and I have come."

Jo Gar said quietly: "Miss Crale has been worried often in the past. I considered her appeal merely the usual fear of danger."

Sadi Ratan said grimly: "You were wrong."

Jo Gar looked at the ship's officer. "We are steaming to the dock?"

The officer nodded. Sadi Ratan wiped his brown face with a handkerchief. The cabin was very hot.

"The passengers and crew will remain aboard until I have made inquiries," he stated. "Miss Crale's injuries may prove fatal."

The ship's doctor returned with stewards bearing a stretcher.

"Facilities are greater in the hospital," he stated. "The moving will not cause further injury."

Sadi Ratan looked narrowly at Jo Gar. "I will repeat a question you did not answer. Where were you when the stewardess screamed?"

Jo Gar stepped aside as the stretcher was carried out, the doctor following it.

"I was in the cabin of Baron Jacobi," he replied simply.

Sadi Ratan's dark eyes narrowed a little more. He moved nearer the Island detective.

"Baron Jacobi? He is aboard?"

Jo Gar said: "It is so—he is aboard."

Sadi Ratan said: "You were in his cabin when you heard the screams. You came here. The baron did not come with you?"

"He was unable to come with me," Jo Gar said softly.

Lieutenant Ratan spoke sharply. "And why was that, Señor Gar?"

Jo Gar placed a brown-paper cigarette between his lips, lighted the tip of it.

"Because Lieutenant Ratan," he said very gently, "Baron Jacobi was dead."

SADI RATAN paced back and forth, in the captain's quarters, stopping every few seconds at the desk on which lay a radiogram, the one to the police from Virginia Crale. The *China Maru* was less than a quarter mile from her berth and going in slowly. Lieutenant Ratan faced Jo.

"Miss Crale's radio to us states that she appealed to you and you refused to meet the vessel. It asks our aid. Your radio from Baron Jacobi states that his life is in danger—he asks your aid."

Jo Gar nodded slowly. "That is so," he said quietly.

Sadi Ratan stood still and frowned."You came out to the boat to see Baron Jacobi. When you reached his cabin—he was dead, murdered. While you were in his cabin the stewardess discovered the unconscious Miss Crale. Her screams did not interest you very much—you did not hurry to see what was the matter."

He paused and regarded Jo narrowly.

The Island detective said tonelessly:

"I seldom hurry. There was a dead man in the room."

Sadi Ratan made a grunting sound. "I do not accept your explanation," he stated coldly. "You are concealing facts from me, from the police."

Jo Gar said: "On the contrary, I have told you of the words in Jacobi's handwriting, that I found in his cabin. I have told you that the baron was almost a fanatic where Chinese lacquer was concerned. I have told you that he greatly desired Miss Crale's collection, and that she had several times refused to sell."

Sadi Ratan nodded. "You have told me what you wished me to know. I have spent almost an hour questioning persons who seem to know nothing. Miss Crale is still unconscious and the captain refuses to hold the boat away from the dock any longer. In spite of the precautions that I have taken—once the *China Maru* docks there is a fine chance for the murderer to escape."

"It is as you say."

Sadi Ratan frowned heavily. "In the radio to you from Miss Crale—did she state why she felt her life was in danger? Did she suspect some person aboard the vessel?"

The Island detective half closed his gray-blue eyes. He looked thoughtfully beyond Lieutenant Ratan.

"Her radio stated that her life had been threatened twice since leaving Nagasaki, where she came aboard. We know that Baron Jacobi boarded the vessel at Shanghai. A portion of her radio read: I think it is the man from Shanghai."

Sadi Ratan sucked in a swift breath. "You did not tell me of this before. It is very important. She was afraid of Baron Jacobi. He wanted her collection and she refused to sell. He was almost a fanatic in the matter, you admit."

"Miss Crale has suspected many persons of intended injury," Jo Gar said slowly.

Lieutenant Ratan said sharply: "She has been injured, Señor Gar—seriously injured. She suspected Baron Jacobi."

Jo Gar rolled a cigarette between his fingers. He sprawled his diminutive body lower in the chair.

"Very well, Lieutenant. Baron Jacobi attacked her in her cabin. He knew that such an attack would not gain him her collection, but he was furious at her continued refusals to sell. He struck her with something and she knifed him in the neck. He wandered back to his cabin and died. She rang for the stewardess and lost consciousness. Does that theory please you?"

Sadi Ratan kept his dark eyes narrowed. He did not speak. Jo Gar chuckled.

"Please, Lieutenant," he said softly, "do not think so seriously. The theory is what the Americans often term 'lousy.' Miss Crale's head is badly battered. She probably lost consciousness after the first blow. Her attacker left the cabin with the weapon. Her attacker was not Baron Jacobi, because had he been knifed in such a manner as he was he could not have returned to his cabin. And where is the knife, where is the weapon Miss Crale was attacked with?"

Sadi Ratan said thoughtfully. "There is blood on the button that was pressed to call the stewardess, so Miss Crale did *not* lose consciousness after the first blow. She touched fingers to her wound, rang for the stewardess. The stewardess has stated that she did not reach the cabin for several minutes—she was busy with another passenger. The ship doctor informs me that in isolated instances such a wound as the one that killed Baron Jacobi is not instantly fatal. Jacobi might have tossed the weapon he used on Miss Crale, and the knife with which she defended herself—from a porthole."

The whistle of the *China Maru* made hoarse sound and there was the faint sound of the welcoming band, on the dock.

"**YOU HAVE** always chosen to oppose me, Lieutenant," Jo Gar said quietly. "It is a mistake to allow personal prejudice to enter matters of this sort, for in so doing you have often neglected important facts. You have your gun?"

Sadi Ratan scowled at him. "Naturally," he replied.

Jo Gar smiled up, at the lieutenant. "It is good," he said. "You shall make the arrest."

Sadi Ratan widened his dark eyes. "You have been to the hospital, against my orders! Miss Crale has regained consciousness—she has told you—"

Jo Gar shook his head. "I regret to state that Miss Crale has not talked. I doubt that she will talk again. Ten minutes ago, on my way here, I met the doctor. Miss Crale is dead."

The police lieutenant swore sharply in Tagalog. His slender body was tense.

"*Dios!* A double murder—"

He stared at Jo, spoke rapidly. "You have the murderer—"

The Island detective leaned lack in the chair. He inhaled and blew a thin stream of smoke towards the nearest fan. The music from the band on the clock was louder now. Sadi Ratan said suddenly:

"You are not bluffing, Señor Gar—"

Jo spoke quietly. "It seldom pays to bluff. In the half hour during which you were talking with people—I have been doing the same thing. But in a different way. I do not think that Jacobi even spoke to Miss Crale, aboard this boat."

The police lieutenant blinked his dark eyes.

"Then why did she appeal for help—"

Jo Gar said: "Had Baron Jacobi lived you could have arrested him for the murder of Virginia Crale."

Sadi Ratan swore sharply. "But you have just said that they did not speak—"

"Virginia Crale had no relatives. She hated museums. I doubt that she left any provision for her collection. It would have been sold. I think that Jacobi knew that. He would have bought the collection. But first—she would have to be dead."

Sadi Ratan narrowed eyes on Jo Gar. The engines of the *China Maru* were vibrating—the vessel was near the dock. Jo Gar said:

"The words on the check—they showed me Jacobi was interested in the location of Virginia Crale's cabin. He always felt that she did not appreciate her collection, did not deserve it. He was a hard man. So he decided to murder her. I don't think that he ever actually threatened her, but she realized, felt that he hated her."

Sadi Ratan kept his eyes on Jo's.

"Why did he radio for you to meet the *China Maru?*"

Jo Gar shrugged. "Protecting himself. He wanted the police to believe his life was in danger, so that after Virginia Crale's murder he could say that *both* of them had been followed from China. Lacquer chests—ancient, Godlike affairs, he would have said. The Chinese resenting their purchase. He felt the radio to me would have thrown the police off his track."

The lieutenant looked puzzled. "He murdered her so that he would gain the collection. But then—"

Jo Gar said: "He *had* her murdered. It was almost a blundered affair. And because of that—Baron Jacobi lost his temper. And for losing his temper he was knifed. And the murderer—"

He broke off, rose slowly from the chair. The music of the band had ceased; the *China Maru* was swinging close to the long dock near the Manila Hotel. Jo drew a handkerchief from a pocket of his duck suit, wiped his face. His right hand went to his right trouser pocket, felt the grip of his automatic.

"If you wish," he said quietly, "we will go to the murderer of Virginia Crale—and of Baron Jacobi. He is clever with a knife—and less clever with a wooden club."

Sadi Ratan spoke slowly. "But Baron Jacobi was considered a fine collector of swords and knives, and skilled in the use of them. If he were hiring a killer—"

"He would *not* allow the killer to use a knife or a sword," Jo cut in grimly.

Lieutenant Ratan coughed nervously. Jo Gar walked towards the door of the captain's quarters, followed by the police officer. On the deck he moved to the nearest companionway, went down it. On Deck C he moved towards the stern, crossed to the second-class quarters. In a narrow corridor he stopped and said to Sadi Ratan:

"Having twice murdered—this man might not hesitate to kill again."

Lieutenant Ratan spoke grimly.

"My fingers are in the proper place—but I would like to know how—"

"I am not too secretive a person, Lieutenant," the Island detective said.

He moved on, turned down a narrow corridor and stopped opposite a cabin marked with the number 12. He rapped on the door. A voice said questioningly, from inside the cabin: "Well?"

Jo gripped his Colt with the fingers of his right hand. He said cheerfully:

"It is Señor Gar. Baron Jacobi has sent for me. I was informed that I should see you, if not able to locate the Baron."

There was a clicking sound; the door opened. Jo Gar stepped into the small cabin, followed by Sadi Ratan. He smiled into the almond-shaped eyes of a stocky Chinese. The man said in very good English:

"You have been unable to find Baron Jacobi?"

Jo Gar said: "Lieutenant Ratan—this is Sam Toya. He is the trusted servant of Baron Jacobi."

Sadi Ratan did not speak. Toya looked impassively at the Island detective.

"My master, perhaps, is on deck," he stated calmly.

Jo Gar shook his head. "No," he replied quietly. "He is not on deck. And Miss Crale is not on deck."

The Chinese pursed his lips. His eyes were expressionless.

Jo Gar said: "I presume you tossed the knife overboard, Toya. And the other weapon."

There was a faint flicker in the servant's eyes. He spoke softly:

"The knife?"

The Island detective smiled almost gently.

"The knife," he repeated. He turned his body slightly, but kept his eyes on the Chinese. "You see, Lieutenant Ratan—I was very sure Virginia Crale could not have pressed the button that called the stewardess, after being struck. But there was blood on the button. So I decided that the finger that smeared it there was not Miss Crale's. And I remember that five years ago Baron Jacobi had hired Sam Toya as his servant. In spite of the fact that Toya had just been released from Bilibid Prison, a fact of which he was aware."

Sadi Ratan drew a deep breath. The figure of the Chinese was tense. Jo kept his right hand within the cloth of the right trouser pocket. He said:

"Jacobi planned the murder—he wanted the collection. It had

become an obsession. Toya battered Virginia Crale down. The pressing of the button was clever. Toya did that, but he was careless. There was Virginia Crale's blood on his fingers, and it stained the button. The indicator worked by the button is not far from Baron Jacobi's cabin, and at the time the bell of the indicator sounded Jacobi was talking with the stewardess."

Sadi Ratan said: "So—he had planned that."

Jo Gar kept his eyes on the eyes of the Chinese. He smiled very faintly.

"Toya was supposed to return to his quarters, after disposing of the club with which he had struck down Miss Crale. The stewardess, excused by Jacobi, would go directly to the cabin of Miss Crale and discover the body." Jo Gar paused. "But things did not work out that way."

The Chinese was breathing heavily, evenly. Jo tightened his grip on the automatic, continued to smile.

"The stewardess left Jacobi, perhaps a half minute after the indicator bell sounded. She has told me that he detained her by asking many foolish questions. She went to the indicator and saw that Room 29 had called her. As she was on her way along the corridor she was called into Room 18. A valuable jewel had been misplaced and the owner was quite excited."

Jo Gar stopped smiling. "And Toya, instead of returning to his quarters as instructed, went to the cabin of Baron Jacobi. He had thrown away his club, or whatever he used."

Jo Gar raised the cloth of his gun pocket slightly. His eyes were narrowed on those of the Chinese.

"He knifed Baron Jacobi to death," he said simply.

The Chinese made a twisting movement; his left hand flashed upward past his right side. Jo Gar squeezed the trigger of the Colt. The gun sound vibrated in the small cabin. The Chinese fell to his knees and coughed. The knife slipped from his fingers and struck the floor as he pitched face downward.

Jo Gar stood motionlessly. Sadi Ratan moved a few feet and lifted the knife. There were shouts in the corridors beyond the cabin. Lieutenant Ratan said:

"Yes—this would have made such a wound as killed Jacobi."

Jo Gar said slowly: "Toya—you were a fool. There was blood on Jacobi that did not come from his wound. You had a record. Your name was on the passenger list. I knew Jacobi could not have been stabbed by Virginia Crale—and have reached his cabin. I knew she had fallen at the second or third blow, and could not have gotten to his cabin. So when I saw your name—"

He paused. Sam Toya moaned and rolled over on his left side. Jo Gar said:

"I know why you murdered Virginia Crale. But why did you knife the baron?"

The Chinese spoke in a weak whisper. "In Manila they called him—the man from Shanghai. But he was—hated there. He stole—made bad bargains. One Chinese—wanted many pieces back—Jacobi's and the woman's. I was paid well! Now they—are both dead—and the chests can be—bought back—"

He fell over on his back. Jo Gar walked to his side, leaned forward. When he straightened up he said:

"He is dead." He smiled grimly, half closing his eyes. "A killer who Jacobi used to gain something he failed to get—because another person used him to murder—" he paused and then went on softly—"the man from Shanghai."

Sadi Ratan said thickly. "Toya was Chinese—and blood is thicker than money."

Jo Gar sighed. "It was Toya's blood that betrayed him," he said quietly.

The Amber Fan

The little Island detective, pits a fan against a knife in a murder.

THE SMALL shop window of Yut Gen, whose tiny store sprawled less than a half square from the Pasig River, was almost in darkness as Jo Gar padded slowly along the narrow *Calle Vanisto.* The rice and chicken had been good, at the home of Rinaldo Darian, and there had been a plentiful supply of wine. At nine o'clock Rinaldo had spoken again of the typhoon. The wind was growing severe; the rain was coming more heavily in gusts. The Number Six typhoon signal was flying over Manila, and already much damage had been done in the native quarter.

At ten, against the wishes of his host, Jo Gar had departed. Over his white duck suit he wore a light Army rain-coat. His pith helmet was of khaki and the rain could damage it little. He wore the strap under his chin. The streets were wet, but sandals were not of importance; he had many pairs.

When he reached the shop of Yut Gen the flickering light at the rear of the store threw moving shadows on the display of the one window. This section of Manila was not well lighted, and stores were few. A gust of wind rocked the Island detective. He moved close to the fly-spotted glass and tightened the strap of his pith helmet.

The odor of spices made him sniff deeply; he stood near the window, facing it, and wiped warm rain from his face with the back of a stubby-fingered hand. His gray eyes watched the moving shadows in the small window, and with his back to water and wind his almond-shaped eyes wandered over the objects on display.

The jade pieces, even in the poor light, he could see were bad. The bead strings were the usual things. There were some wood carvings, some spoons done by the *Igorrote* tribe. In a corner of the window was an opium pipe, elaborate and not very graceful.

Jo Gar was about to turn away, to move on towards the river, when his eyes discovered the fan. For several seconds he stood motionless, then moved his brown face so that it almost touched the wet glass of the window.

It was a small fan. The flat portion of it was circular, six inches or less. The material was silk of a blue-green color. The handle was round, almost a foot in length. The material was the color of old, brown wood, but to the keen eye of Jo Gar it was more than wood.

"Amber," he said softly. "Not the vegetable—but sea amber."

The typhoon wind swayed his short figure; his eyes moved from the handle of the flat fan to the object beside it. The object was a small silver box. The lid was open, with a chain stretched behind. The interior of the box was of wood and was stained red.

Jo Gar murmured: "*Betel*-nut—and a cheap box. But the fan—"

He stood for several seconds, straining his eyes, looking at the heavy, rich, brown of the fan's handle. There was a grace in the carving of it, a distinction in the simplicity.

Turning away, he saw that the shutters of the shop were down over the entrance. For a few seconds more he paused. He might obtain entrance, bargain for the fan. But such an entrance might only antagonize Yut Gen, who was not too charming a character.

Jo Gar shrugged, lowered his head against the wind and rain, and moved towards the Pasig.

"Tomorrow," he breathed huskily, "will do."

At the Bridge of Spain, although the distance to his home was short, he hailed a *caleso* that was motionless, climbed inside. The horse was ancient and the two-wheeled carriage was wet inside as well as out. The Island detective gave the Filipino driver the address of his house and sat back against the cane seat. He was filled with chicken and rice, and the wine had made him drowsy. Closing his gray-blue eyes, he dozed. When he reached the Spanish gate of his home he had forgotten completely the amber fan.

AT MIDNIGHT Jo Gar was awakened by what he thought was a vase crashing to the floor. He sat up and swore in two languages at his house-boy Vincente. He had told the boy to be sure all the vases were in safe places. A second crash, and he sat up in bed. Vincente's voice called shrilly:

"Señor Gar—if you please—Señor Gar!"

The Island detective shook his head and stared towards the door of his bedroom.

"What is it?" he demanded sleepily.

The house-boy said: "Señor, the *Americano* Edmond Neblo is here. He say it is much important you come awake."

Jo Gar swung his short legs from the bed, shoving the mosquito netting to one side.

"And so you must pound my door to pieces," he muttered. "Tell him I will be down soon."

He threw cold water from the basin on his face, dressed rapidly and moved from the room. The house seemed to rock in the gusts of typhoon wind, and rain beat against the glass of the windows. It was very hot.

When he crossed the waxed floor of his small living-room Neblo was standing near the door that led to the patio. The American's drill suit was wet; his white face was soaked with rain. He moved towards Jo.

"Señor Gar," he said shakily, "I've notified the police, but I wanted you, too. A terrible thing has happened."

Jo Gar said: "What is it that has happened, Mr. Neblo?"

The American rubbed wet fingers across his eyes. He said tonelessly:

"My secretary, Howard Strett, has been murdered."

The Island detective narrowed his eyes. "Murdered?" he repeated. "You are sure?"

Edmond Neblo said bitterly: "God, yes. In my house. I called the police and then came here for you. I live only two squares away, you know."

Jo Gar nodded. The American was a six-foot, heavily built man. He had brown hair and eyes, and a small, brown mustache. He was an exporter to the United States of hemp, and owned several large properties on the smaller islands. More than once Jo had watched him play polo, on the field near the Walled City.

"I will come immediately," he said. "May I offer you a drink?"

Neblo shook his head. "I haven't touched the body. The police should be along soon, though they have a distance to come. I know of your reputation, of course."

Jo Gar clapped his hands, told Vincente to bring him his helmet and raincoat. He got a pocket flashlight from a drawer. He said as

Vincente helped him into his coat:

"It was a knife wound—that killed your secretary?"

Neblo looked surprised. "Yes, but how did—"

Jo Gar interrupted wearily: "It is most often the knife, here in the Islands."

He placed the dry pith helmet on his head, led the way to the patio and towards the *calle* beyond. Outside the iron gate, they turned towards the Bay. The typhoon wind swung palm leaves along the street, and they had to bend their bodies forward against the force of it.

Neblo, keeping his head low and twisted towards the lowered head of the Island detective, spoke jerkily:

"I turned in at ten—I hate this damned wind. I left Strett in the small room off my living-room, a sort of study. He was finishing up some business reports, and said he'd be through by midnight. He seemed—cheerful enough."

Rain made sharp sound against their lowered helmets. Neblo went on in a louder voice:

"I couldn't sleep. The damned Chink hadn't filled my whiskey decanter. The two servants were in their separate house, back of my place. A short while ago, I took the decanter and went down to fill it from a bottle of whiskey I knew was in the dining-room."

Neblo swore bitterly. "Then—I found Strett. He was lying—well, you'll see how that is—I didn't touch him except to try his pulse. He was dead."

Jo Gar twisted his head towards Neblo and said tonelessly, against the whine of the wind:

"How many servants do you employ?"

Neblo replied: "Two—a Filipino cook and a Chinese house-boy. We spend most of our time traveling through the Islands. Didn't make much fuss—with the house here in Manila."

They crossed a street that was within a short square of the Bay. Jo Gar said: "There would be, perhaps, a reason for one or both of the servants—to hate your secretary?"

Neblo shook his head, and water sprayed downward from his helmet.

"If there *was* any reason—I never knew it. The servants seldom spoke. The house-boy is stupid. Damned if I know why I kept him on."

Jo Gar smiled faintly. "Most house-boys are stupid," he philosophized. "That is why they are house-boys."

Neblo said: "Here we are." He turned to the right; they went through a half-opened gate and along a palm-lined gravel path. Lights of the house were beyond; the wind made much sound in the palms. All around the house, set in a tropical growth of foliage, the typhoon made racket.

They went through a door in the screening, crossed a porch and entered the living-room directly. Neblo said a little shakily:

"I didn't wake the servants—I called the police and then went right to you. He's—in there—"

He pointed beyond the living-room. Jo Gar removed his helmet and walked slowly across the polished floor. When he reached the entrance of the study he stood for a few seconds, looking around. Then he went past the desk, which was littered with papers, and looked down at the body of Howard Strett.

The secretary lay on his stomach, his head twisted sidewise so that it faced the room. His white shirt was stained with red. There were knife wounds in his back, and when Jo carefully lifted the upper part of his body he found more knife wounds around the heart. Some of them were slashes, but most of them deep and straight.

He lowered the body to the divan, faced the head towards the room. When he looked towards the living-room Edmond Neblo was standing motionless, his palms covering his face. The Island detective turned his small body slowly, using his gray-blue eyes on the floor, the few wicker chairs, the surface of the desk. Suddenly he drew in a sharp breath.

Walking a few feet, he leaned down and lifted the fan from the spot where it had rested, under a small, wicker cabinet. Only the blue silk of the flat portion had protruded; the cabinet rested on four knobs of wood which raised the lower shelf about an inch from the polished floor of the study.

Jo Gar held the fan by the rim of the blue silk's circle, half closed his eyes on the handle. It was the color of brown-black wood; there was a grace in the carving, a distinction in the workmanship. The flat surface of the fan was about six inches in diameter; the handle was almost a foot in length.

Neblo said huskily, from the other room: "It seems unbelievable—Howard murdered—like this!"

Jo Gar went slowly from the room, reached Neblo's side. He held the amber-handled fan so that light from the floor-lamps of the living-room struck it.

Neblo blinked at the fan. "What's that?" he demanded.

The Island detective said: "You have not seen it before?"

Neblo reached for the handle, but Jo moved it swiftly to one side.

"Pardon, Mr. Neblo. I found it under the wicker cabinet, in your study. You have not seen it before?"

Neblo frowned at the fan.

"Never," he said. "It's a fan—Chinese, looks like." He leaned forward, got his head close to the handle. His brown eyes widened. "Say—that handle looks like amber, to me! The real thing."

Jo Gar nodded his head slowly. He ran the stubby fingers of his left hand through his gray hair.

"I think it is amber," he said. "Perhaps your secretary owned it."

Neblo was frowning. "No, I'm sure he didn't," he said. "Strett wasn't interested in anything like that. Never picked up any curios. Didn't like Chinese—" He broke off and then went on in a puzzled tone. "You found it in the study—say, how the devil—"

Jo Gar said quietly: "You are very sure it is not something belonging—"

Neblo interrupted impatiently: "Certainly I'm sure. I'm sure that handle is amber—damn good amber. You know what that means, Señor Gar—there's a lot of it there. That's a valuable fan."

The Island detective shrugged. "It is worth many *pesos,*" he agreed. "But unpolished amber like this is not always detected. You do not think Mr. Strett might have picked it up somewhere, even found it? Might have regarded the fan carelessly, not informing you, telling you of it?"

Neblo shook his head. "Howard would have told me, all right. He might have laughed at it, or sneered at it, but he'd have showed it to me."

He narrowed his eyes on the almond-shaped ones of Jo Gar.

"That fan!" he breathed excitedly. "The murderer of Howard Strett—"

Jo Gar shrugged. "Perhaps," he said quietly. "It is not, however, the type of fan one would carry about. And in typhoon weather the natives or other races seldom carry any fans with them. Also, this fan is valuable, and not likely to be carried from one's home."

There were the sounds of footfalls and of voices, beyond the house. Neblo said:

"The police, I suppose."

Jo Gar faced Lieutenant Sadi Ratan as he came into the living-room. Sadi frowned at Jo. A uniformed policeman halted behind Sadi Ratan, near the door leading to the porch.

Neblo said: "I am Edmond Neblo. I telephoned for the police. My secretary has been—murdered. This is Señor Gar, or have you—"

Jo Gar said tonelessly: "The Lieutenant and myself are acquainted, Mr. Neblo."

Sadi Ratan nodded coldly. He removed his helmet and raincoat. His uniform was well fitted and spotless, and his slender figure showed it well.

"The body?" he said in accented English.

Jo Gar said:

"In the study beyond." He raised the fan slightly. "I found this fan beneath the wicker cabinet. Mr. Neblo has never seen it before, and is certain that his secretary did not have it in his possession. I think the handle is amber. I have not touched the handle—there may be fingerprints on it."

Neblo said: "I have called Señor Gar in—want him on the case."

Lieutenant Ratan bowed slightly. He extended fingers and took the fan on the circular rim of the flat part. His dark eyes examined the handle. He sniffed it.

Jo said: "There is no odor. When the police have determined the presence or absence of prints it will be simple to burn the handle or rub it. Then you can—"

Sadi Ratan said sharply: "I am familiar, Señor Gar, with the methods of discovering amber. But this is nothing. Let us look into the matter of the murder."

Jo Gar bowed. "If you will pardon me, Mr. Neblo," he said quietly, "I will return for a short time to my house. In our haste to reach your home I neglected to bring my automatic. I would feel more safe—"

Lieutenant Ratan smiled. "Perhaps you would take mine, Señor Gar?" he said mockingly. "The murderer might attack you during your return to your home."

"You are kind, Lieutenant," Jo Gar's voice was expressionless. He moved towards the door. "But I am sure that while *you* are so near my home—the murderer will not dare to strike again."

IT WAS almost one o'clock when the small car of the Island detective pulled into the curb a quarter square from the banks of the Pasig. Jo descended and walked through the rain, with the typhoon wind behind him, along the *Calle Vanisto.* The night was very dark; the typhoon had increased in velocity; few people were about. An old Chinese passed him as he neared the shop of Yut Gen, hunched forward against the gusts of wind and showers of rain.

Before the small window Jo Gar halted. There was no flickering light at the rear of the shop now, and something had gone wrong with the nearest street light. Jo drew the pocket flash from his raincoat, snapped the button. The yellow beam struck the wet glass, penetrated beyond. The Island detective sucked in a swift breath.

The *betel*-nut box was where it had been a few hours before. The jade, the beads and the carved spoons had not been moved. But the amber fan was not in the window.

Jo Gar stood with his browned face close to the glass of the small shop. His gray-blue eyes were almost closed. After a short time he turned towards the door of the shop, stood facing it. Then, slowly, he shook his head, walked past the door and towards his small car.

When he reached the house of Edmond Neblo he swore softly in Spanish. He did not enjoy driving his car, preferred the *caleso.* He went along the path as the wind rocked the palms, crossed the porch, entered the house.

In the living-room were Neblo and Lieutenant Ratan. The policeman who had accompanied Ratan was placing shining handcuffs on a small, fat-faced Chinese, who was protesting shrilly in his native tongue. He stared at Jo, broke into bad English:

"They take me away—I no do kill! I tell him truth. I no do this—"

Sadi Ratan smiled sarcastically at Jo. "You were not attacked by the murderer," he stated calmly. "Because the murderer was *here.*"

Jo Gar looked with narrowed eyes at the house-boy.

"So?" he said softly. "And the motive, Lieutenant?"

Sadi Ratan smiled in a superior manner. "He had been drinking saké. He hated Señor Strett. The secretary had called him a stupid fool. He had even struck him. I have found unfinished saké in his quarters. It was almost a half hour before he could talk to us. He has admitted that Señor Strett called him stupid and struck him. And, Señor Gar, regard his right hand."

Jo Gar moved near the Chinese. He spoke quietly:

"You hated Señor Strett?"

The house-boy spoke Chinese rapidly. Jo Gar reached down and caught the right wrist of the Chinese in strong right-hand fingers.

Across the palm and fingers was a long, deep cut. It was a cut such as the blade of a knife might have made.

Sadi Ratan said: "You see, Señor Gar. Unless one is very clever, when striking another person, the blade of the knife may turn. He was injured as he murdered Señor Strett."

The house-boy stopped his rapid talk. Jo Gar released the wrist. He shrugged.

"He says that it is true he hated Señor Strett," he informed Lieutenant Ratan and Edmond Neblo. "But he says that he did not kill him. He was often struck and called stupid because he did not fasten the screens, when told to do so. He was in his quarters and had drunk much saké when you came to him."

Sadi Ratan smiled. "And the cut on his hand, Señor Gar?"

Jo spoke in Chinese, to the house-boy. When the Chinese had finished his reply Jo said:

"His story is very plain. He says that he was awakened in the night by the wind. Somewhat tardily he recalled Señor Strett's instructions to make fast all the screens, and for this purpose he came silently to this room to repair his neglect.

"On entering, he says, above the wind noises he heard the gasping of struggling men. There was no light—when he entered—but he heard the voice of Strett cry out once in pain; a choked cry, as if he were being strangled. Then the men in their struggle were right upon him. He reached out, he says, and grasped an arm, a wrist. It was suddenly withdrawn and the knife sliced his palm.

"He jumped back; then heard Strett groan, and the thud of a falling body. He turned, he says, and fearing for his own life, fled into the gardens. A half-hour later, he made his way back to his room, bound his hand and drank deeply of saké. And thus you found him."

"A very likely story," murmured Sadi Ratan, "—for children."

"I do not find it so," Jo Gar said coldly.

The lieutenant of Manila Police shrugged elaborately, almost too elaborately.

"And does he describe this other man—who cut him? He started to tell me this same wild tale—but his guilt is too evident; the case against him too apparent." He shrugged again, but at the same time his eyes were watching the little Island detective.

Jo Gar spoke again in Chinese to the house-boy.

"He says," he said slowly, "that he could not see the man. He knows only that the wrist was large; the man was very strong. He could not hold him."

Sadi Ratan lifted both hands and shoulders in sardonic gesture. Yet his eyes were very keen, although he veiled their expression from Jo Gar.

"So you see? How is it possible to find such a man—the man who used the knife, if there was one—through a thick, strong wrist alone? It is much simpler as it is."

"Of course," Jo Gar said agreeably. "Much simpler—for everybody except the boy here, and he will have great difficulty in making the court believe his story unless such a man is found and made to appear the guilty one. As you present it, Lieutenant, the case against him is very simple."

Sadi Ratan swore.

"The police," he said hotly, "do not wish to punish the innocent."

"The police," Jo Gar said softly, "are sometimes lazy. They often prefer the easiest, the simple way."

Sadi Ratan swung towards him angrily, with a threatening gesture. He seemed on the point of striking the little detective.

"You cannot say that to me, damn you!" he stuttered.

Jo Gar smiled slightly.

"The observation," he said quietly, "was a generality. It shall not apply to Lieutenant Ratan unless he himself makes it applicable."

The lieutenant seemed very angry; but behind his anger his eyes were shrewd.

"Very well," he said with sudden dignity. "Let us look further into this matter. If the story he tells is true, why did he not at once cry for help, or at least, when he felt safe to return, inform Señor Neblo? Perhaps he can answer that to *your* satisfaction, Señor Gar!" he added triumphantly.

Jo Gar shrugged slightly.

"I think," he said, "that he can."

He spoke again to the boy.

"It is," he interpreted for Neblo and the lieutenant, "as he feared—that he would be implicated in the murder. You know the Chinese. This boy is also stupid. He believed Señor Strett dead and did not wish to say anything in the matter. It was, of course, very stupid."

"There remains then," Sadi Ratan said with a tone of finality, "the necessity to discover this other man. For, surely, without him one must believe my simple story, and the boy will hang."

"That is all very true," Jo Gar agreed, "and without the real murderer, the boy will surely hang. I think, however, this man can be readily found."

"What!" Sadi Ratan shouted, and Edmond Neblo echoed the exclamation. "You know the man—have known him all along, while we've had this senseless talk? Before God, Señor Gar, you try my patience; and, as you know, your license depends upon the agreeability of the police department. Who is this man? What is his name? I demand it."

Jo Gar raised a slender, browned hand.

"My words," he said slowly, "were, I think the man can be readily found. That means that he is yet to be found. First, however, it is necessary to discover a motive; for without a reason for the killing and its story, it would be useless to confront such a man. He would simply deny—we could do nothing."

Sadi Ratan glanced about him with an air of exasperation.

"Then let us make a beginning—" He left off, frowning.

Jo Gar passed a hand swiftly across his lips, to conceal their involuntary smile.

"I shall gladly save the Lieutenant," he said, "much labor that may in the end prove fruitless. You have a prisoner," he added, "a very plausible suspect. That should content you for tonight. Tomorrow, if you will meet me at my office, at nine. I shall take you to the murderer—or will leave the simple case as it stands entirely in your hands."

Sadi Ratan frowned darkly.

"But—if you have reason to suspect a man, he might escape meanwhile."

"He would scarcely, I think, give us so much evidence against himself," Jo Gar said softly.

"Very well," the lieutenant said gruffly, "we will leave it meanwhile at that. I have a prisoner, a very reasonable suspect—" he shrugged. "I have also a knife, such a knife as could have been used in the murder. It is stained with blood. I found it beside the boy—on his bed."

"And I," Jo Gar said softly, "have a fan, an amber fan, whose presence here has not yet been explained."

Sadi Ratan glanced at him keenly; then turned and signed to the man in uniform to lead out the trembling house-boy.

"Do you leave with me, Señor Gar?" he asked, with elaborate politeness.

"No, I shall talk a while with Señor Neblo."

Sadi Ratan nodded stiffly to both and left.

SADI RATAN and the little Island detective moved towards *Calle Vanisto.*

"It was only an accident," Jo Gar said, "that I happened to see it; that my curiosity was aroused."

"Perhaps you even stepped upon it," said the lieutenant of police slyly.

"It may be so," Jo Gar murmured. "Often people stumble over what lies right before their eyes."

"Still, we have yet to prove the story," the lieutenant said, in different tone.

"The information you have given me will be helpful. Besides, a man who is guilty will often incriminate himself if pressed adroitly."

"But you say the papers which Señor Neblo discovered only hinted at the person; did not give even his name or address?"

"It is so—But we shall soon see, for this is the place."

It was ten minutes after nine when they entered the curio shop of Yut Gen. Sadi Ratan paused near the door and set himself to examine the many objects displayed. Jo Gar advanced farther.

Yut Gen himself came from the rear of the shop, moved soft-footed behind the evil-smelling counter. He was a moon-faced, youthful Chinese; his eyes were small and slitted. He was medium in height and was very stout. His wrists were thick and round.

Jo Gar said: "I am Señor Gar. Last night there was in your window a fan of blue silk. I do not care for fans, but the handle of this one appeared to be of amber. I should like to see the fan."

Yut Gen placed a lighted cigarette between his lips, tilted his chin high and regarded Jo through almost closed eyes. Slowly he shook his head.

"Never in my shop have I possessed such a fan as you describe," he said in very good English. "Perhaps it was in some other shop—"

Jo Gar smiled patiently. "I stood before your window last night. It was not yet ten-fifteen. The amber fan was beside the silver *betel*-nut box."

Yut Gen's small eyes grew smaller. "You are mistaken," he said gently. "I have no amber in my shop."

Jo Gar said: "Perhaps you have not, at this minute. Between ten and ten-fifteen last evening I saw with my own eyes the amber-handled fan. At one o'clock last night I returned to your window. The fan was not there."

Yut Gen made clicking sounds and spread his browned hands.

"I think that you have seen the fan in some other shop, Señor," he stated calmly. "Then, returning to my shop, you failed to see it. A not uncommon mistake."

Jo Gar smiled, but his gray-blue eyes held a hard expression.

"In the home of Señor Edmond Neblo his secretary was murdered, last night. The murder occurred between ten o'clock and fifteen minutes of twelve, since he was seen alive at the earlier hour and his knifed body discovered at the later. The doctors have thought the crime was committed about eleven-thirty. Beneath a cabinet, and not far from the body of the murdered man, I have found a fan. Of blue silk, and with a long amber handle. Sea amber, unpolished. The fan is very unusual. I think it is the one I saw in your shop window last night."

Yut Gen widened his small eyes. "How could that be so?" he demanded. "You saw the fan somewhere at ten-thirty—"

Jo Gar smiled, shook his head. "I saw the fan here not long after ten. If it had been removed from the window a few minutes *after* I left the *Calle Vanisto*—it might have been in the dead man's possession *before* he was murdered. Or it might have been dropped *by* the murderer."

Yut Gen twisted a large ring on a finger of his right hand. He was standing with his back against the long counter, leaning partially against it. He seemed quite at his ease.

"I am the owner of my shop. I do not recall such a fan as you speak about. I am sorry."

There was a finality in his voice. Jo Gar placed his right hand in a pocket of his drill suit. His raincoat was opened.

"It is yet early in the morning. But I have talked to several persons. A Chinese house-boy is accused of the murder of Señor Strett. He is *not* the murderer."

Yut Gen shrugged. The Island detective smiled agreeably.

"You have lied to me," he said pleasantly. "And where there is death it is not well to lie."

Yut Gen stopped toying with his ring. His face became set, his eyes sullen. Jo Gar said softly:

"The soles of the dead man's sandals were wet, though he was supposed not to have left the house last evening. I did not think that the amber fan could have *fallen* to the floor and have been kicked beneath the cabinet, during a struggle. I do not think there was much of a struggle, because Señor Neblo was upstairs. He would have heard the sounds."

Yut Gen said quickly: "There was wind in the—"

He checked himself. Jo Gar smiled coldly.

"You *remember* that, the wind in the palms. You *thought* of that—when you struck with the knife—"

The Chinese said calmly: "There was a typhoon last night. There is always the sound of wind—"

Jo Gar narrowed his blue-gray eyes. "Señor Strett came to your shop last night. When he departed he had with him the amber fan. Why was that?"

Yut Gen shrugged slightly. "I know nothing of the fan of amber," he said slowly.

The Island detective nodded his head. "Yes, you know of it," he contradicted quietly. "You went to Señor Neblo's house *for* it. You surprised Señor Strett in the study, but he had sufficient time to place the fan beneath the cabinet. You killed by the knife, and made your escape."

Yut Gen's forehead had deep lines in it. His bared lips showed teeth that were not even.

"You make talk, Señor Gar," he breathed.

Jo Gar smiled pleasantly and his right hand fingers moved within the cloth of the coat pocket. Sadi Ratan, some feet away, was bent over the counter, eyes intent on a small carving of jade.

"It is so," Jo agreed. "You alone live behind your shop. You alone are the proprietor. You have no relatives, and few friends. In the window of the shop you have a valuable fan. An expert has this morning assured me it is worth many *pesos*—the amber is very old, and very good. The secretary of Señor Neblo visits you secretly, when he is thought to be working on reports. He leaves, taking with him this amber fan. You follow him, and murder him. And you lie to me. That is the talk I make."

The Chinese made a faint hissing sound as he drew in a deep breath.

"Because the soles of a man's shoes are wet—does that prove that this man has visited *me?*"

Jo Gar smiled calmly. "Last night I talked with Señor Neblo—we found letters—letters which Señor Strett would not have allowed others to see, and which he had concealed cleverly. One was a demand to pay a gambling debt—tomorrow; if not paid, the holder of his obligation would appeal to Señor Neblo, and explain—certain matters of his secretary.

"Other papers were memoranda of money advanced to you at different dates; demands for repayment, references to your refusal even so recently as last week, and, what is of most interest, a promise to call upon you last evening, with the threat of exposing your affairs if you did not make some settlement immediately. Shall I explain that to you?"

"It means nothing to me—If you wish to talk—"

Jo Gar said slowly, smiling with his thin lips:

"For weeks the Manila police have been suspicious of you. For such a small shop too many men leave here, during the night. Too many men enter."

The wind of the typhoon made rattling sounds, outside the shop. Between the blasts could be heard the shuffling of Sadi Ratan's feet as he moved nearer, along the counter. Jo kept his narrowed eyes on the small ones of Yut Gen.

"I was not concerned with your shop, until the fan vanished from your window. I then became interested. Señor Strett was also interested in your shop. It was he who furnished you the money to purchase the opium. So that men could come here—and go from here. And you did not repay him. You promised at first; then you refused outright. You relied on his fear that Señor Neblo and the officials would learn of his connection with the illicit traffic.

"But Strett was desperate. That demand of the gambling debt and danger of exposure through that source made him so. He came to you in the late evening, when the typhoon was blowing and—received no satisfaction; only a repetition of your threat."

Jo Gar spoke slowly, confidently; yet his eyes watched the slit eyes before him as if for confirmation.

"And he probably told you," he went on, steadily, "that an anonymous letter to the police would draw you into prison. Then he left hurriedly; but, in going; he snatched up a thing of ready value—the amber fan."

Yut Gen dropped his cigarette to the floor and set his heel upon it; then he glanced up impassively.

"It is possible," Jo Gar continued, "that you discovered the theft. It is more probable that you started to think of the anonymous letter which Señor Strett in his desperation would write—for revenge. His secret notes that we found hinted of it.

"You followed him shortly, gained entrance to the house and to the study. As you came, he switched off the light, tossed the fan beneath the cabinet."

Jo Gar paused a moment; then continued tonelessly:

"After you had killed him, you did not look for the fan. You feared the house-boy who had entered the struggle and then fled. Perhaps—"

Yut Gen interrupted him, with a glance towards Sadi Ratan, who was standing not far from them, but with his shoulder turned and apparently not listening.

"I do not think I wish to hear you any further, Señor Gar," the Chinese proprietor said. "It is only talk and means nothing to me. I know of no such fan as you describe. You have no possible way of connecting me with this murder you speak of. It is—"

"Fool!" Jo Gar hissed. "You were too confident, too careless. Why, you even neglected to change your clothing."

The stubby fingers of his left hand pointed with quick gesture.

"See—the blood spots still on the cuff—"

Involuntarily, with a start, the eyes of the Chinese snapped downward. Then his whole body tensed. His small black eyes blazed into the gray-blue ones of the little Island detective.

"Damn you!" he snarled in frantic rage.

Apparently forgetful of the lieutenant of police, his left hand flashed from behind him. Jo Gar saw the knife, and the fingers of his right hand in his pocket clenched.

The shop was filled with the sound of the explosion. The knife slipped from Yut Gen's mangled left hand.

Yut Gen lifted his right hand, but there was no knife in it. Red spread from the fingers of the left hand, resting on the counter. Yut Gen spread his lips and seemed to bite into the large ring with his teeth. Jo Gar stood very quietly as the Chinese made sucking sound.

After a few seconds Yut Gen's body slipped down beside the counter. When Sadi Ratan, with the Island detective, stooped over him the poison of the ring had brought death. Jo Gar straightened up.

"It might have been," Lieutenant Sadi Ratan said slowly, "as you said. I think it is enough on which to let the house-boy go."

"Suicide is often an admission of guilt," Jo Gar murmured.

"You were very clever," the lieutenant said, in the same tone. "We should work more closely together, Señor. I might even consider resigning in order to enter and strengthen your private agency."

"I fear," Jo Gar murmured, "that the loss to the Force would be too great, Lieutenant."

The Mystery of the Fan-backed Chair

Even in the far off Philippines there is no such thing as murder without a clue.

A LONG-TAILED lizard scurried across the ceiling toward the three-bladed, slow-turning fan. It made sound like dry leaves in a faint wind, and Baba arched his back, rising from the floor near the shuttered window. Jo Gar, paying no attention to the Siamese cat or the lizard, rolled a brown-paper cigarette between two brown slender fingers of his left hand, half closing his gray-blue eyes.

There were footfalls, light and unhurried, beyond the waxed floor of the office; a light tapping against the old wood of the door Jo Gar faced. The Island detective said almost tonelessly:

"Come, Sidi Kalaa."

River sound, drifting over a reeking-hot Manila from the Pasig, reached his ears as the door opened and Kalaa entered from the outer office. The little man, half Malay, half Arab, came to within a few feet of the desk. His face was a brown mask, a flat mask of dark eyes, lips parted slightly showing white, even teeth. He spoke in precise English.

"It is the Miss Samson of the appointment."

Jo Gar said: "She has been in Manila so short a time that she is prompt. Yes, Sidi Kalaa."

He suspected always that there was not so much Arab blood within the veins of his assistant as Kalaa would have wished him to believe, but it pleased him to address the man with the formal "Mister," and he knew it pleased Kalaa. As the door to the outer office was opened, his eyes went to the lizard scuttling away from the ceiling fan.

From the room beyond Kalaa said: "Señor Gar, it is Miss Samson."

She came into the room gracefully, as Jo Gar rose from the fan-backed chair. She was tall and slender, cool in thin white. Her face was oval and her eyes were blue. Her skin was very white.

She said nervously: "Señor Gar, it is good of you to see me. They told me you were a very busy man. But I—"

Something flickered slightly down from the ceiling; the lizard made dry sound as it zigzagged toward a wall. Baba crouched, leaped upward near an end of the desk. The girl shrank back, raised a white gloved hand to her lips, stifled a cry.

The Siamese landed quietly on his feet as Jo Gar said sharply: "Baba! No, it is not good for you to do that." He said in a softer tone, in Tagalog; *"Omalis ka!"*

The cat moved instantly to a far corner of the room. Jo Gar's thin lips parted in a smile; he gestured toward a wicker chair.

"Please be seated. I am sorry. It is the time when our lizards shed their tails. Lizards are a delicacy to my Siamese."

He watched some of the fear go from her blue eyes as she took her gloved hand away from her lips. She smiled a little, moved toward the chair.

"It's—silly of me, Señor Gar. But I'm—"

She seated herself, and Jo Gar eased his slim figure to the fan-backed chair. He ran browned fingers of his right hand over his gray hair, pushed a lacquer box of brown-paper cigarettes toward her.

"You are nervous. The heat, perhaps, Miss Samson. And the cat startled you."

Her blue eyes narrowed, and the muscles around her mouth tightened. She said suddenly: "I'm damned nervous! I've been nervous for days now; ever since we sailed from Honolulu. I can't stand it—not much longer. So I've"—she spread her hands in a swift gesture—"come to you."

The gray, slanted eyes of the detective smiled reassuringly into hers. "The manager of the Manoa Hotel is a good friend of mine. He has told me that you felt someone should know of a trouble—"

She interrupted, speaking hurriedly, with rising excitement. "You know that my name is Joan Samson. My brother was Conrad Samson, he lived here in Manila. Perhaps you—"

She paused, shivered slightly. The Siamese, in the far corner, lowered his black head, stretched. His nails made scraping sound on the waxed floor. Joan Samson bit her lower lip nervously.

Jo Gar said: "Baba has been with me many years. Do not be nervous. You were speaking of your brother. I remember that he was the victim of a Chinese who ran amok in the old Walled City."

She said slowly and more steadily: "Yes, he was stabbed to death.

That was a month ago. He loved to walk about, particularly in strange sections of cities. I haven't seen him in two years. At first, when I was notified in San Francisco of his death, I didn't think I would come here. His body was returned to the States, but before it arrived, I received a letter."

Her eyes widened suddenly; seemed to fix on something behind Jo Gar. She said in a husky voice: "That fan-backed chair you're sitting in—"

Jo Gar smiled. "It is a very fine one, Miss Samson. One of the finest ever made by the prisoners at Bilibid."

"Oh, my God!" Her voice was a whisper in the office.

The detective said tonelessly: "It is not good for your mind and eyes to be filled with fear. My fan-backed chair is exceedingly comfortable."

Her eyes were on his. "He wrote they would—kill him—that way," she said softly.

Jo Gar touched match flare to a new brown-paper cigarette. "Your brother wrote he would be murdered?" He rolled the cigarette between his fingers."

She said: "Yes. The letter came after he had been knifed to death, supposedly by that insane Chinese. He wrote he had been threatened; that his enemy was an Oriental, and that he had been told he would die seated in a fan-backed chair."

The detective inhaled deeply. "He wrote you he had been warned he would die in a fan-backed chair. He did not die in a fan-backed chair. The Chinese who knifed him was found dead in a narrow street not far from the place where he accosted your brother. He had struck a child and an old woman, before he killed your brother. There were many knife wounds in the body of the Chinese. He was dead when the police found him. The medical report was insanity from drink—and death by his own hand."

The girl touched a handkerchief to her lips. "I didn't want to come here, but somehow I felt that I should. There were only the two of us left. We weren't close; saw each other only every two or three years. But I felt something was wrong. I felt that perhaps Conrad hadn't just happened to cross an insane man's path. The last letter, his fear—"

She broke off and Jo Gar spoke quietly. "You have the letter?"

She shook her head. "No," she said slowly.

Faint surprise showed in the gray-blue eyes of the Manila detective.

The girl said:

"It was stolen from my cabin on the *Tayo Maru,* somewhere between Honolulu and Manila."

Jo Gar leaned forward, his eyes slitted on hers. His short-cropped gray hair gave age to the youth of his face; his lean left-hand fingers toyed with a jade paper cutter many years old.

"You were traveling to Manila alone?"

She shook her head. "A very good friend—Barbara Prentice—came with me. We travel together often. We both have sufficient income—" She paused.

"That was only one thing—Conrad's letter vanishing. Three days out of Manila I found this on the floor of our cabin."

She reached in her bag, handed him a slip of paper. On it were scrawled in pencil the words: "For you, it shall be death in the fan-backed chair! Do not leave the boat at Manila! The wise one leaves death alone as Conrad Samson did not."

Jo Gar said slowly, looking at the pencilled scrawl: "In what way did your brother not leave death alone?"

The girl shrugged. "He collected carved wood. Now and then he sent me a piece. An *Igorrote* image; a Chinese box. Cases of his collection were returned to me. He often left Manila; went to small islands."

The detective nodded. "There was the theft of his letter, then this note found on your cabin floor. And then—"

She said: "Then this—lying on the floor."

She placed on the surface of his desk a loop of cord. He lifted the loop, looked at the slipknot. When he spread the cord out, its length was about three feet.

He said softly, "Hemp—island hemp, I should say."

Her voice was a whisper again, hoarse. She lifted her hands to her throat. "A strangler's knot, Barbara said!"

"When did she say that?" he asked.

"When I first showed her the cord. She said she'd read about such a knot being used in the East. She begged me not to leave the boat at Manila. She won't leave the hotel. She thinks—"

He waited several seconds, then spoke. "*What* does she think, Miss Samson?"

She straightened her slender body. Her voice was calmer. "Barbara thinks that Conrad did something terrible in his collecting. Desecrated some tribal grave, perhaps. Took something that had to do with death. He was warned to replace it but didn't. So he was—killed. She read something like that, she says. He was to have been strangled in a fan-backed chair. But he was killed another way. Barbara thinks the Chinese who killed him wasn't mad. He pretended to be, and then he was killed by others of the tribe so that he could never talk."

Jo Gar smiled faintly. "Your friend is an amateur detective. She reads and has an imagination. I am a professional detective with little imagination. There *are* tribes on the islands decorating burial grounds with wooden images and objects. There might be a tribe whose chief would be so incensed that he would warn a collector thief, then murder. The murder might be accomplished in such a way as your friend suggests. It is possible but highly improbable....

"Who might have known that you were coming to Manila to investigate your brother's death? Who would have followed from the States, or met the boat at Honolulu? Have you any of the objects your brother collected with you?"

She spoke softly. "Two—an *Igorrote* spoon and an old fan. It's very old Chinese, Conrad wrote when he sent it. I haven't any of the things that were in the boxes shipped after he died. As for the other part, Barbara says someone either in San Francisco or on the boat knew I was Conrad's sister. He was assigned to frighten me. Someone feared I might prove Conrad was murdered. That person might be caught."

"She has been reading mystery tales of the Orient, I am afraid," said Jo Gar.

Joan Samson frowned at him, "Then why was his letter which stated he was afraid of being murdered stolen from me? Why did I find the note threatening me with death in a fan-backed chair? And why was the cord left in my cabin?"

The detective spoke tonelessly: "I should like you to return to the Manoa Hotel. In fifteen minutes I must confer with a plantation owner whose rice weighs less when it reaches Manila than when it is put aboard the *sampans* miles away. When I have finished I shall come to the hotel. I should like to talk with your friend, and also I may see the two objects your brother sent you."

Her eyes held fear. "I am almost afraid to—" She paused, rose.

Jo Gar looked up at her. "My assistant. Sidi Kalaa, will accompany you."

She seemed relieved. "You will wish a retaining fee, Señor Gar. I have—"

He rose, shaking his head slowly. "Later, I think. Do not be afraid. But please remain in the hotel until I have seen you." He clapped his hands and called, not too loudly: "Sidi Kalaa!"

The girl went slowly toward the door to the outer office as footfalls sounded; the Siamese cat moved like a small, dark tiger toward Jo Gar and the fan-backed chair.

IT WAS almost six when Jo Gar left the office. Near the outer door he stooped and patted the Siamese. When he closed the door behind him, he locked it with the key he had used for almost a dozen years. He went slowly down wooden steps, one flight to the street. Walking half a square, he reached the Escolta, main business street of Manila, hailed a *caleso* driver and instructed the Filipino to drive to the Manoa Hotel.

At the hotel he dismissed the *caleso,* went along a palm-fringed patio entrance into the foyer. At the desk he was requested to announce himself; he moved to a booth and was connected with Suite A-12. A masculine voice said:

"This is Doctor Van Caan speaking."

Jo Gar narrowed his eyes. "It is Señor Jo Gar, doctor," he replied. "Miss Samson is expecting me. I trust there is no illness—"

The doctor said: "Oh, yes, Señor Gar. She spoke of you. Won't you come up?"

The detective hung up the receiver, left the phone booth. As he walked toward the wide stairway rising to the first floor the English manager of the hotel John Balding, hurried toward him. There was a worried expression on his thin face.

He drew Jo Gar aside, "Señor Gar, I am glad you have arrived. This American—she is in some great trouble."

Jo Gar said softly, "Perhaps it is not so great as her imagination."

The hotel manager shook his head. "I sent her to you, and when she returned, about an hour ago, she entered her suite. Her companion, Miss Barbara Prentice, was not there. Miss Samson sent for me, and when we could not find her companion on the grounds of the hotel she became hysterical. I then called Doctor Van Caan. He found it necessary to give her a sleeping powder."

Jo Gar frowned. "I was on my way to the suite now. But if Miss

Samson is sleeping—"

The manager spread his hands. "Her screams were very disturbing. Doctor Van Caan, of course, is—"

"A very fine physician," the detective agreed. "No person about the hotel has seen Miss Prentice?"

The manager shook his head. "Not since she was seen returning to her suite with Miss Samson after lunch. And Miss Samson stated incoherently that she had left Miss Prentice in the suite when she went to see you."

Jo Gar nodded. "I will go up and talk with the doctor," he said.

He smiled at the manager; walked slowly up the wide stairs. When he reached the door of the suite Doctor Van Can stood just inside. They bowed to each other, went into the living room.

The doctor said: "She was highly hysterical. I was forced to give her a rather strong sleeping powder. It will be hours before she will regain consciousness. She spoke of you—and I regretted having to give her the powder, knowing she would be unable to talk to you. But she managed to tell Mr. Balding and myself that she felt something terrible had happened to her companion. Balding stated that he had sent Miss Samson to you, and he thought that perhaps she had told you of her fears and perhaps that would clear up the apparent mystery of her companion's absence. Her condition was such that I was forced to give her the powder."

Jo Gar spoke softly. "May I see her?"

The doctor led the way to a partially closed door, opened it. Joan Samson was lying on a divan, motionless. Her breathing was slow, regular. She was dressed in white pajamas.

The Doctor said: "I got her to undress, then gave her the powder. She refused an injection, and it was a bit of a job to get her to take the powder. But ten minutes later she was sleeping like a baby. She said you were coming, so we didn't call you."

Jo Gar nodded. They moved out of the room, closed the door behind them.

"I trust nothing has happened to her companion," said the doctor.

He looked narrowly at Jo Gar. He was a short, thick-set man of Dutch descent. His reputation was fine; he had been some twenty-odd years in the Islands.

"I shall make inquiries, doctor," said Jo Gar. "It will be what hour, do you think, before she is able to talk?"

The doctor shrugged. "I should say perhaps midnight. Perhaps later, it is a strong drug."

Jo Gar bowed to the doctor. "I shall remain awake and in the meantime do what I can about finding her companion. It is perhaps worry over things that seem more important than they really are. As for Miss Prentice she may have wished to walk about the town. It is cooler now."

The doctor said: "But Miss Samson stated that her friend was afraid and would never have left the hotel alone. She seemed to feel that her friend had been lured away—something like that." The detective moved toward the door, looking at his wrist watch. It was six-thirty precisely. "I will do all I can," he said. "And I will return here about eleven, unless I am called sooner."

The doctor nodded. "I will return in a few hours. She will be all right until then. But perhaps—"

The detective interrupted. "Yes, I will have my assistant in the corridor outside until I return."

He smiled, bowed, left the suite. In the foyer he telephoned Sidi Kalaa at his home, gave him the number of the suite, told him to remain in the corridor outside, when he arrived.

Balding came up to him, looking more worried than before. "Perhaps we should call the police."

Jo Gar shrugged. "There would be publicity," he said. "Miss Samson is sleeping. Her friend is not around the hotel, but there are many places of interest. It is a new city, a new atmosphere. A walk, perhaps, despite the fact that Miss Samson feels her friend would not have left the hotel."

Balding said: "You think we should wait, then, for a while?"

Jo Gar said tonelessly: "For a while, I think I will make inquiries."

He left the hotel. No more were the heat waves rising from the paving of the *Luneta,* where the Constabulary Band would play in a few hours, in the park between the Manoa Hotel and the Army and Navy Club. The sun was sinking over the Island of Cavite, over the Bay of Manila. There would be a fan-shaped sunset, blood-red, Jo Gar decided.

He frowned as he watched an elderly Chinese stooped beneath the light weight of a chair he was carrying strapped to his back. The Chinese was moving toward the rear of the hotel, and the chair he carried was a fan-back.

"Not a very good one," Jo Gar breathed in Spanish, He stood for a few seconds before the hotel, thinking. He was thinking of Joan Samson's widening eyes, filled with fear, as she had regarded *his* fan-backed chair.

After a few seconds he lighted a brown-paper cigarette and moved away from the hotel. Out in the bay there was the deep-toned note of a big vessel's whistle. A small Filipino boy ran past him with a fighting cock under an arm. It was still very hot, and Jo Gar moved with wise slowness toward the Escolta.

LIEUTENANT SADI RATAN, of the Manila police, sipped his claret and smiled at Señor Jo Gar.

"Conrad Samson?" He spoke in Tagalog, in a rather high-pitched voice. "Nonsense! We found the shop where his assassin had been drinking saké. Much of it. The Chinese was bad. Keroti, his name. First he stabbed a child, who was swift enough to escape being badly hurt. Then an old woman—she died. And Samson, he had no chance. The Chinese came upon him from behind; struck many times. Then he ran on, crept into a doorway, knifed himself to death. It is not the first time such a thing has happened. A plot? Nonsense. Murder, yes; but the murder of accident. The Chinese was crazed."

Jo Gar finished his cool drink. "So I thought."

Lieutenant Sadi Ratan regarded him with curiosity. "Why do you speak of Señor Samson?" he asked. "He has been dead many days. By now, no doubt, the girl to whom he was *engaged* is anticipating receiving his money. There was much of it, you know."

Jo Gar leaned forward across the table. "The girl to whom he was engaged— she was willed his wealth?" he asked.

Lieutenant Ratan nodded. "We made a complete investigation, of course. We found a copy of his will. All his money was left to the girl. To his sister went his collection. Carved woods. I do not think he was a good collector, Señor Gar."

"You recall the name of the one to whom he willed his money?"

Sadi Ratan frowned. He tapped on the table surface with browned fingers, his eyes puzzled. "It is difficult," he breathed. Light came into his dark eyes. "An American name. But wait! I have it—something of it. That cat of yours, the devil of a Siamese—"

Jo Gar said "Baba—could it be Barbara, lieutenant? Barbara Prentice?"

The lieutenant of Manila police struck a palm against the table surface. "It is so," he said. "It was the American woman, this Baba Prentice, who received the fortune of this Conrad Samson."

The detective rose suddenly. He looked at the watch on his wrist. The hour was seven. He bowed to Sadi Ratan. The lieutenant raised his eyebrows.

"You depart suddenly. You have obtained information that interests you?"

Jo Gar smiled thinly. "You are always kind to me, lieutenant. But, to be truthful, you know my feelings for fan-backed chairs."

Lieutenant Ratan nodded, smiling. "You have several in your home, a fine one in your office. Perhaps it is that you seek another?"

The detective said: "It is so, lieutenant. I seek another. And there is little time to find it."

HE DUCKED his head, went from the café to the Escolta. A gray-ponied *caleso* clattered by and he called to the driver, who shook his head.

"The day has been hot," he said. "I go to dine."

The detective said, "I am Señor Jo Gar. I go to prevent death. Your dining must wait."

The driver stared at him. "It is so," he agreed, his dark eyes wide. "It is the Island detective."

Jo Gar climbed into the *caleso.* "The Manoa Hotel—and very fast, please."

The driver frowned. "Speed will kill my pony," he stated in Tagalog.

Jo Gar swore at the driver. "Laziness will cause a human death. Let the pony die. I will buy another for you."

The whip crackled and the *caleso* jerked forward, the driver shrilling words. Filipinos and Japanese, Chinese and Italian—the mixed breeds of the Islands—stared at the racing pony of the *caleso* as it swayed along the Escolta.

As they neared the Manoa Hotel Jo Gar looked at the sunset over Cavite and the bay. It was blood-red and commencing to fan. Already it was not unlike the rising wicker curve, some five feet high, of his finest fan-backed chair.

BEFORE THE hotel the *caleso* halted; Jo Gar was out of it swiftly. He paid the driver generously. "May your rice taste well!" he called over a shoulder, hurrying into the hotel.

It required minutes to find Balding. When he appeared, Jo Gar spoke with speed unusual for him.

"When I left the hotel shortly after six-thirty I saw a Chinese—an elderly man—bearing a fan-backed chair on his back. He was moving toward the rear of the hotel."

He paused, watching the Englishman's eyes. Balding said:

"Yes, that would be for Mr. Veiller. He sailed this afternoon for an inter-island trip, but he returns in a week. He requested that the chair be placed in the room he occupied, awaiting his return. He purchased it yesterday and was much pleased with it. I was glad to have it placed—"

"In what room?" Jo Gar interrupted harshly.

The hotel manager stared at him. "Mr. Veiller occupied Room A-30. It overlooks—"

Jo Gar said: "Follow me quickly to the room. And get a key to the door, please!" He started toward the broad stairway leading to the first floor.

Balding called after him. "It was reported to me that Mr. Veiller forgot to leave his key, took it with him to the inter-island boat."

Jo Gar halted, turned. "There is no inter-island boat sailing today. He did not *forget* to leave his key. Get another—and hurry!"

Balding moved toward the desk of the hotel, and Jo Gar hurried up the stairs. Room A-30 was in an opposite wing from the suite occupied by Joan Samson and Barbara Prentice. The corridors which Jo Gar walked were wide and dark against the sun, silent. When he reached the shuttered door, he placed an ear against wood, listened. There was no sound. He rapped sharply.

He was rapping for the second time when Balding came along the corridor. He silently handed the detective a key. As it turned in the lock, lights in the corridor were dashed on from below.

Jo Gar opened the door, moved along a short hall faintly lighted from the corridor. At the doorway to the large room he halted, stood motionless.

Behind him Balding sucked in a swift breath. "God!" he said huskily. "Miss Prentice—in the fan-backed chair!"

The light that filtered into the room was red from the sunset. The curving back of the huge wicker chair rose several feet above the girl's head. Her white hands hung limply over the sides of the wicker; she was sitting erect—so erect her position was unnatural. The color of her face was ghastly.

Jo Gar hurried to the side of the chair. His slant eyes were little more than slits as they looked at the thin cord fastened through the wicker of the chair's fan-shaped back and tight against the throat of the girl.

Quickly he opened his penknife, carefully forced the blade point between the skin and the cord, cut its strong loop.

The girl's head fell forward. Jo Gar caught her by the shoulders. He said to the hotel manager:

"Get a doctor—quickly."

He carried the girl to a divan as Balding's footfalls died in the corridor, rubbed her throat with practiced fingers, felt no beat from her pulse. Ten minutes later when Balding came in with Van Caan he was still working over her.

While the doctor examined her, Jo Gar went back to the chair to inspect the cut rope which had fallen to the waxed floor. It was similar to the piece of hemp Joan Samson had shown him, and about the same length. He was holding it in his fingers, looking down at it, when he heard the words of Doctor Van Caan:

"She is—dead."

SIDI KALAA stood near the door of the suite at the far end of the hotel, as Jo Gar, Balding and Doctor Van Caan approached it. Jo Gar said quietly to him: "Good evening, Sidi Kalaa. No one has entered or left this suite since you arrived?"

Sidi Kalaa nodded. "No person has entered or departed through this door since I arrived, Señor Gar."

"It is well," the detective said. "Please remain here a short time, Sidi Kalaa."

He led the way to the living room of Joan Samson's suite, followed by the hotel manager and the doctor. As Jo Gar lighted a brown-paper cigarette, the doctor spoke slowly.

"A case of mistaken identity, Señor Gar, That is my theory, from what you have told us Miss Samson told you. The murderer or murderers mistook Barbara Prentice for Joan Samson. They got her into that room on some pretext—strangled her. Perhaps Joan Samson's brother was murdered, after all and was not the victim of a crazed Chinese. In Manila there was fear of the sister, and a terrible mistake was made."

Balding nodded his head. "Miss Samson's fears were justified, you see. It is a terrible thing to have to tell her of this."

"The shock will be great," Doctor Van Caan said. "It might even—kill her."

The detective's eyes held a distant expression. He faced the doorway of the room in which he had looked down at Joan Samson. "It might—even kill her," he repeated softly.

He stood motionless, eyes almost closed. Then, suddenly, he drew a deep breath.

"Will you gentlemen please accompany me?" he asked.

He led the way into the bedroom. When he reached the motionless form of Joan Samson he stood beside her for long seconds. She was lying on her right side, arms relaxed, her face pale. Her profile was very beautiful.

Doctor Van Caan said thoughtfully: "She will sleep for several hours yet. It'll be damned tough telling her."

Balding said: "I must call the police, Señor Gar, much as I hate the publicity."

The detective raised his right hand in a halting gesture. "Please," he said. "Listen to me for a few minutes. After that, you may call the police."

Balding shrugged and seated himself on the arm of a chair facing the bed on which Joan Samson was lying.

The doctor moved closer to the girl touched her right wrist. After a half minute or so he said: "Good! Quite strong."

Jo Gar spoke evenly. "Joan Samson came to me, stated she was in trouble. She said her traveling companion believed she would be murdered. She had received a threatening note; a letter had been stolen; a coil of rope had been placed in her steamship cabin. She was to be strangled in a fan-back chair, which was the manner of death intended for her brother."

The doctor nodded. "The letter that was stolen had been from her brother to her, stating that he had been warned he would be strangled to death—in a fan-backed chair."

Jo Gar smiled faintly. "Rather elaborate idea, I think. It would have been much simpler to knife."

Balding said shortly: "They *did* knife him. But the Oriental mind is a colorful one. The strangling idea pleased the murderer more."

The detective watched the doctor nod again, in confirmation of the manager's words. The smile went from his face.

"Supposing that, for reasons unknown to us, Conrad Samson left all his money to a woman," he said slowly. "A woman who was *not* his sister—not Joan Samson. And supposing that, in the event of this other woman's death, the money would revert to the sister. That is the motive for a crime on the sister's part, is it not?"

The manager and doctor were staring at him. Neither of them spoke. A hot wind rustled palm trees beyond the room, beyond the balcony.

"I have some reputation as a detective." Jo Gar smiled faintly, almost sardonically. "If Joan Samson came to me, made me believe she was in danger, was to be strangled in a fan-backed chair—"

He broke off, shrugged. His eyes went to the motionless form of Joan Samson. Her breathing was slow, regular.

"I would, as I did, take the case," the detective went on. "And then what happens? Joan Samson cannot find her companion, Barbara Prentice, who was so worried about Joan. She is afraid something may have happened to Barbara Prentice. She becomes hysterical; is given a sleeping powder. A search is made for her companion, who is found strangled to death in a fan-backed chair. Doctor Van Caan believes the murder a case of mistaken identity. So does Mr. Balding. Señor Gar tells the police what has been told him. And what do the police think?"

The doctor said swiftly: "Murder; mistaken identity. And evidently Conrad Samson was murdered deliberately."

"It is possible," Jo Gar said slowly.

Balding's eyes had narrowed on his. "But Señor Gar would not agree with us or with the police, eh? Señor Gar thinks that Joan Samson was trying for a perfect crime—and that she murdered Barbara Prentice so she could get her brother's money!"

Jo Gar moved away from the sleeping girl, turned and faced her. "That is so," he said quietly.

The breathing of Joan Samson was unchanged, slow and quiet.

Doctor Van Caan said huskily: "Impossible! She has been unconscious for hours. The sleeping powder—"

Jo Gar coughed dryly. I believe you told me she refused to have an injection, doctor. How was the sleeping powder administered?"

Van Caan frowned. "She did refuse an injection. I gave her the glass containing the powder and water. She went into the bathroom—"

The detective nodded. "You did not actually see her swallow the drug?"

Van Caan's frown deepened. "No," he said.

Jo Gar smiled almost sadly. "You did not wait for Sidi Kalaa to arrive at the hotel, to watch outside Miss Samson's suite, did you, doctor?"

Van Caan shook his head. "*You* did not seem much worried about her being in danger. It was only a matter of ten or fifteen minutes. It was the other woman, Barbara Prentice, who appeared to be in danger."

The detective's voice was calm. "She was," he said. "It was after I left you, doctor, and you left the hotel—it was then that Joan Samson strangled Barbara Prentice to death in the fan-backed chair."

Balding stood up stiffly. "By God, Señor Gar, that's a hard one to believe!"

Jo Gar looked down at the evenly breathing girl. "There was this man Veiller—the one who left the room in which we found Miss Prentice strangled. He expected a fan-backed chair. He vacated the room saying he was taking an inter-island boat. That was a mistake. No boat sailed; the next sails tomorrow. He wanted his room held. When was the fan-backed chair placed in it, Mr. Balding?"

"This morning," said the manager.

Jo Gar nodded. "This Veiller neglected to turn in his key."

Balding spoke quickly. "No reason why he should have turned it in—he retained the room."

"There was a better reason than *that* for not turning it in," the detective said. "He gave that key to Joan Samson."

"How do you know that?" the doctor demanded.

Jo Gar did not answer the question. "When I left you, doctor, after you told me she would be unconscious for hours, I passed a carrier of a fan-backed chair. He was moving toward the hotel."

Balding said: "But the fan-backed chair in which we found Miss Prentice dead—*that* was put in the room this morning."

The detective nodded. "There is a fountain between the hotel grounds and the Escolta. The carrier of the chair was hot, thirsty. That chair did not come to the hotel, the bearer was only taking a short cut. But the sight of it being carried toward the hotel gave me an idea. And when Sadi Ratan told me that Conrad Samson's money had been left to Barbara Prentice—"

He broke off as Balding muttered sharply. The doctor's eyes narrowed:

"I insist Miss Samson is under the influence—"

There was the jangle of a telephone bell. Balding started toward a small table near the bed. But Jo Gar, moving swiftly, caught him by the arm. He raised a finger to his thin lips, pressed it against them in signal for silence. He went to the telephone, lifted the receiver, pressed it tight against his left ear. A voice said: "Is Mr. Balding there please? He is wanted at the desk."

Jo Gar said sharply: "My God! They have him, you say? Veiller? Where? On his way toward Baguio? And he has confessed! What's that? Please take it slowly—"

He paused, watched the sudden heavier breathing of Joan Samson.

"Yes," he went on. "Joan Samson strangled the Prentice girl? She wanted money. She was in love with Veiller and they needed her brother's money. It is a written confession, and you—"

The sound Joan Samson made was half scream, half moan. She sat up as Jo Gar replaced the receiver, rocking from side to side, staring at him wildly.

"Yes, yes!" she half shouted. "I did it! I strangled her. I hated her, hated her! She hated Gordon Veiller, she made my brother hate him. And I love him! She made my brother leave her all his money; all I got was wooden images, idols he collected! I strangled her, I tell you!"

Her eyes were savage lights in her white face. Her lips twisted, and she beat on the bed with her clenched fists.

"I told you lies about the letter stolen from me; the threatening note was a fake; the noose was, too! Gordon left me his room key. I got Barbara to go over to the room late this morning. The fan-backed chair was there. I told her the room was cooler, and that I wanted to be alone. She slept, and I pretended she was missing. I didn't take the powder. When you and the doctor left, I went to the other corridor. No one saw me. I got Barbara to sit in the chair told her it was a beautiful one. Then I tightened the—"

She broke off, covered her face with her shaking hands. After a few seconds she said in a smothered tone: "After she was—still, I came back here. I was an actress once, and pretending to be drugged wasn't hard." She stopped her rocking, fell backward on the bed.

The doctor said in a dull tone: "Well, Señor Gar—"

Joan Samson breathed from the bed, brokenly: "I thought he'd stick by me. I didn't think he'd tell them."

Jo Gar looked at Balding. "It wasn't a call for me," he said quietly. "It wasn't about this Veiller. I have no idea where he is. That was just a bluff to make her confess. You are wanted at the desk."

Balding regarded Jo Gar with admiration. "Good Lord!" he said slowly.

The girl pulled herself up, stared at the detective with wide eyes. "They said you were the best detective in the Islands," she said. "I wanted you on my side."

Jo Gar said steadily, "I think it was the wrong side."

She smiled desperately, bitterly. "I guess you were—too much the best detective." There was a touch of bravado in her voice. "And the fee, Señor Gar?"

The detective's eyes held little expression. He shook his head. When she had fallen backward again, and her hair was spread over outstretched arms on the bed, he said to the doctor and the manager: "It would now be wise to call the police."

As Balding went toward the phone, Jo Gar lighted a brown-paper cigarette. His fingers were trembling just a little. The wind made a higher sound in the palms beyond the room; dry leaves ran over the patio. The detective thought of Baba; wished that he might return to his office—and to the Siamese. He would be curled, Jo Gar knew, like a dark tiger, in the fan-backed chair.

The Great Black

A dusty lacquered box holds the key
for the little Island detective.

THE MOON-FACED Chinese sitting on Jo Gar's right made cheerful gurgling sounds as he slapped yellow palms together. The racially mixed audience in the heat-soaked Manila Theater was enthusiastic; on the stage the famous English magician Hugh Black—The Great Black—bowed gracefully to the clatter of applause and the hum of many tongues.

The ancient curtain of the theater descended slowly, rose with the famous magician still in the center of the stage, bowing. He was a tall, broad-shouldered man, with black, wavy hair. He had poise, dignity. His movements were rapid and filled with grace.

Gesturing toward a small table near him, he stamped a foot heavily. Smoke rose from the table, there was a flutter of wings. Dozens of pigeons winged out over the audience, circling back to the stage as the curtain again descended.

There were wrinkles of fat in the neck of the aged Chinese seated beside the Island detective. He gurgled up at the winging birds.

The last one circled, dived back toward the lowering curtain, flashed under it. Jo Gar reached for one of his brown-paper cigarettes. The curtain rose again, and The Great Black raised his arms above his head. Still the applause continued.

Jo Gar's gray-blue eyes smiled; he ran brown fingers through his gray hair, half raised his tall, lean body from the uncomfortable seat. And as he lifted himself, he was conscious of the fact that the figure of the magician no longer possessed grace. The Great Black was slumping—slumping downward toward the stage floor, sprawling forward now, toward the footlights!

There was a hush in the theater, and then a sudden babble. Jo Gar stood erect, staring at the motionless lure of the great magician. Two of his assistants were kneeling beside him; they lifted him from the stage floor, moved backstage as the curtain came down. The babble of excitement in the theatre continued. A voice spoke to the Island detective in Tagalog, the native tongue.

"Señor Gar! You saw that. He was struck—" Sadi Ratan, Lieutenant in the Manila police, was in the aisle beside Jo Gar's seat.

The detective said calmly: "You *saw* something strike the magician, Lieutenant Ratan?"

Sadi Ratan's lips curved downward. His dark eyes were narrow, aggressive. "You think it was a faint, perhaps. Señor?" There was contempt in his tone. "You observed the way he fell? I must hurry to the rear of the theater." He moved along the aisle.

The moon-faced Chinese plucked at Jo Gar's coat. "You see?" he muttered. "The Great Black—he is ill, very ill!"

Jo Gar smiled. "It is so, " he said. "The performer is either very ill, or he has already—ceased to be ill."

A small Filipino attired in dinner clothes appeared before the curtain. He raised a hand and when there was quiet spoke in a shrill, shaken voice.

"The Great Black—the management regrets—it is that the famous one—he is sick. Please—it is regrettable—you will now leave quietly."

Jo Gar sighed. He spoke half to the moon-faced Chinese, half to himself. "I think it is that the famous one—has *ceased* to be ill."

A BRIGHT-EYED *mestizo* winked at Jo Gar as he moved slowly along the Escolta, main business street of Manila, from the lobby of the theater toward the stage-entrance alley. Behind him the audience spilled into the street. At the stage door an elderly Filipino looked into the detective's slant eyes, frightened.

"Señor Gar, " he breathed, and stepped aside.

"I have come to see Señor Hugh Black. He is in the dressing room?"

The elderly Filipino shivered. "It is so, Señor. If you will go to the light..."

Along a dimly lighted corridor there was an electric bulb over one of the doors. When Jo Gar reached it, he heard the sharp voice of Lieutenant Ratan within the room, which was small and hot. The detective entered; his gray-blue eyes went to the lighted mirror of the dressing table, past photographs of actors and actresses hanging on the walls to the figure stretched on a Spanish-shawled couch.

As he noted the limpness of a dangling hand, he heard Sadi Ratan say, "You are the Princess Vlatchnoff? That is your stage name?"

Jo Gar looked at the woman. She was seated on a small chair at the right of the entrance door. She was very beautiful: her face was oval; her features were delicate, her eyes and hair dark.

"I *am* the Princess Vlatchnoff—Sonya Vlatchnoff." Her voice was soft and husky. Jo Gar said quietly: "Señor Black—he is dead."

SADI RATAN smiled, his dark eyes half closed. "I felt that you would come here, Señor Gar. It is good of you. You have often aided the Manila police. This is Doctor Montaloupe." He gestured toward a small dark-faced man. "He was in the audience and came to the stage by way of an entrance behind the boxes. Señor Black was dead when he reached his side. A knife wound in his neck—the base of the brain."

The doctor said: "It is a wound that *might* have been made by a knife."

The detective looked toward the body. "A thrown knife, doctor?"

The doctor shrugged. "There has been such impact. When I reached the magician's side, he had been carried in here. The weapon is missing."

Sadi Ratan spoke sharply, "You recall the Princess Vlatchnoff, Señor Gar? It was she who performed the knife-throwing act just after the intermission."

The detective nodded. His eyes went to the woman's white face, ran over her colorful costume. It was the same costume she had worn on the stage.

The husky voice of the princess broke the silence of the dressing room. "This police lieutenant suspects me of murder, Señor Gar." There was a strange flicker in her eyes, and then they were cold again. "I have heard of you in Shanghai. I should like you to help me."

Sadi Ratan said: "That is very well, but I should like Señor Gar to know that Mr. Hugh Black came to the police two days ago. He feared for his life. He stated that a woman hated him, and that if death came to him it would be by a knife."

The Princess Vlatchnoff's hands were clenched; she was breathing quickly. The police lieutenant went on: "The knife was thrown from behind the magician. He was facing the audience. There were cabinets and mirrors on the stage for the purpose of illusion. The two assistants of The Great Black and two men who work the lights did not see the knife thrown. When I came in here Madame Vlatchnoff was alone with Mr. Black."

The woman looked at Jo Gar and spoke huskily. "My husband was a sportsman who loved swords, knives. It was with him I learned—" She broke off.

Sadi Ratan said: "To throw a knife excellently!"

Her eyes appealed to Jo Gar. "I have not yet been accused of murder, but I am suspected of it. I should like to retain you, Señor Gar. I am not guilty of murdering this man."

"I am not a lawyer, princess," Jo Gar told her, "but if you wish to retain me—if you wish me to seek the murderer—"

She said firmly: "I do."

The detective bowed. Sadi Ratan moved toward the figure on the couch.

"The coroner will be here immediately—and two of my men. Poor devil—he was a great magician, this Black."

"He is a great magician, lieutenant," Sonya Vlatchnoff said quietly.

Sadi Ratan faced her. His voice was hard. "The princess chooses to doubt that Hugh Black is dead?"

Her dark eyes met Jo Gar's. She spoke in a husky, even tone. "Yes. I choose to doubt that The Great Black is dead."

The detective said softly, "And your reason for the doubt, Princess Vlatchnoff?"

There was silence. Then the woman said, "The dead man lying there, Señor Gar, is *not* The Great Black."

JO GAR pulled on a brown-paper cigarette, his figure lolling in a chair near the dead man. Don Castana, the coroner, was examining the wound; two of the police lieutenant's men stood near the door. Sadi Ratan paced back and forth, talking in a low voice.

"And you say, Madame Vlatchnoff, that after the trick performed by The Great Black about five minutes before the end of the show—the vanishing of a girl from a tank of water—it was the magician's habit to have himself impersonated by this dead man, unknown to the audience. This Richard Janisohn took the applause and did a few simple encore tricks. In the meantime, The Great Black was dressing for the street."

Princess Vlatchnoff nodded. "Yes," she said. "He started it as a whim—he told me once how simple it was to fool an audience. Of course the impersonating make-up is very good. When it worked well, Hugh decided to continue the trick. It allowed him to leave the stage sooner, rest from the strain of his performance."

Jo Gar said: "The entire company knew The Great Black was replaced by Richard Janisohn just before the end of the performance?"

The woman shrugged. "Some of us knew—I'm not sure how many. Janisohn stood in the wings for a few seconds. After the water illusion there was usually much applause. Hugh bowed from the side of the stage, walked off. Janisohn walked on in his place. That was all."

Sadi Ratan frowned. "But not all the persons backstage knew this?"

"Very likely not." The princess' voice was low and calm. "We carry our own lights and operators with us—it is necessary in a performance of illusions. Some of them may never have known; certainly none of the local staff did."

Ratan said: "But you did, Madame?"

She nodded. "To an extent."

Jo Gar stared at his cigarette. "You mean that at times The Great Black did finish the performance?"

She said: "That is so, Señor Gar."

Sadi Ratan swore in Tagalog. The coroner straightened up.

"The death was apparently instantaneous," he said. "At the impact of the weapon—a knife or a dagger. The impact point was the base of the brain; the weapon drove in with much force."

Ratan spoke swiftly. "The weapon might have been a thrown knife or dagger?"

Don Castana nodded. "Thrown or in the grip of the murderer, I should say."

The police lieutenant regarded the Princess Vlatchnoff with narrowed eyes. "When this Richard Janisohn substituted for The Great Black tonight he took the bows, made a gesture toward a small table, stamped a foot. Smoke was released. Pigeons flew out over the audience, circled back as the curtain descended. The curtain rose again and Janisohn bowed. Then he fell forward toward the footlights. Where were you, Madame Vlatchnoff, at that time?"

"I was here in this dressing room, seated there." She gestured toward the couch on which the body was lying.

Jo Gar smiled. "You were alone in this room at the time the dead man fell, princess?" he asked.

She said slowly "No, I was not alone. I was there on the couch. Hugh Black was holding me in his arms."

The lieutenant of police stared at her. "You did not tell us this before."

"You did not ask me where I was or who was with me."

A BROWN-FACED policeman appeared in the dressing-room doorway, spoke to Sadi Ratan in the native tongue.

When the policeman had finished, Ratan turned to the princess. "Mr. Hugh Black has not returned to the Manila Hotel. His clothes are in the closet, and his toilet articles are still there."

For the first time there was fear in the woman's eyes. Ratan's voice crackled at her.

"Why does *that* frighten you, Madame?"

Her eyes met the police lieutenant's squarely. "Because I think perhaps whoever murdered Richard Janisohn may have discovered the mistake, followed Hugh Black—" Her voice broke.

Jo Gar stood up. *"Followed,* you say, princess? He left you here, then?"

Her voice was steadier now. "Yes; we quarreled. He left me here. I was here when Crandon and Foxe carried Janisohn in. I was terribly shocked."

Sadi Ratan said: "Crandon and Foxe are The Great Black's assistants?"

She nodded. "Yes. They are English. They ran to Janisohn when he fell."

The Manila lieutenant asked, "If you were down here when Janisohn fell, how do you know *that?*"

"Crandon told me they did," she said.

The detective smiled at Sadi Ratan. "You see," he breathed.

Sadi Ratan glared at him. "I shall see more when I talk to Crandon and Foxe."

The coroner said: "If you are finished with the body, I shall have my men remove it, lieutenant."

Sadi Ratan nodded.

When the body had been removed Ratan faced the woman. "You quarreled with The Great Black—why?"

Her red lips trembled. Her eyes went to Jo Gar's. He smiled at her.

"You do not *have* to answer," he said. "But it is within the power of the lieutenant to hold you as a material witness. Perhaps if you are frank with him...."

THE WOMAN looked at Sadi Ratan. "It is personal. Please—if you will send your men away—"

They were sent away. After a few seconds she spoke.

"We quarreled—Hugh and I—because he refused to marry me."

Jo Gar said: "And his reason for not wishing to marry you, princess?"

"My family is of the old regime—I am a princess. Hugh's family—" She moved her lovely hands slightly.

Sadi Ratan said with faint amusement: "But all that, Madame, is ended."

Her voice was precise. "All that, lieutenant, never began for you. You would not understand."

The detective spoke gently. "In any case, Hugh Black left you in anger?"

She said: "In a sort of— quiet anger."

Sadi Ratan cleared his throat. "My men are searching for him. He is necessary, of course, to complete your alibi."

"Alibi?" she asked.

The police lieutenant shrugged. "You are an expert in the art of throwing a dagger, a knife. I myself have witnessed your skill. I myself saw the dead man fall forward. I did not see him struck down, but with the stage lighted as it was, a thrown knife might easily have been missed. I saw few of the knives that you threw at the targets, Madame, until they struck. And with the added deception of mirrors—" He broke off, bowed, his smile sardonic. "The dead man is one Richard Janisohn, posing as The Great Black. If it should be that *he* were hated—"

The woman interrupted. "But *I* did not hate him."

Jo Gar said: "There are other matters. Your men have found no dagger or knife. The two assistants have not been thoroughly questioned. The Princess Vlatchnoff has stated that she was in this room when Janisohn was struck down. *Others* were on the stage behind the man who is now dead."

The police lieutenant moved close to the woman, pointed a brown finger at her. "It is true, is it not, that the one who is now dead was in love with you?"

"Yes!" she said quickly.

Ratan's eyes were small. "And it is true, is it not, that you did not love him?"

Again she spoke swiftly, firmly. "Yes!"

The silence following her answer was broken by the murmur of voices in the corridor beyond the dressing room. A police-uniformed Filipino came into the room. He spoke rapidly to Sadi Ratan in Tagalog.

When he had finished Sadi Ratan hurried through the doorway. The woman turned wide dark eyes to the detective's gray-blue ones.

"I do not understand the language."

"The police have found a knife," said Jo Gar.

"A knife! Where?"

"In the ceiling of the corridor, princess, less than twenty feet from this door."

THE EDGE of a typhoon breeze was gustily slapping the city of Manila as Jo Gar and Sadi Ratan emerged from the Manila Hotel after escorting the princess to her room there.

The police lieutenant halted near his car, frowned at the detective. "Charming liar," he said. "She will do well under guard until I verify my opinion."

"And your opinion is?" Jo Gar asked.

Sadi Ratan shrugged. "Richard Janisohn was in love with her. He would not give her up. Hugh Black, she states, would not marry her because her family was superior to his. That, I think, is a lie. The Great Black would not marry her because he suspected Janisohn. She knew it, and she feared Janisohn. So—"

A gust of typhoon wind rocked both men. Ratan smiled coldly at Jo Gar.

"You have been retained by her, but I do not conceal my thoughts from you. So—she struck Janisohn down with a perfectly thrown knife. Apparently, someone had attempted to murder The Great Black—that was what she wished the police to believe. But she had knowledge that Richard Janisohn was impersonating The Great Black."

"What of her statement that she was in the dressing room with Hugh Black when Janisohn fell? And where is Black?"

Sadi Ratan's voice was positive. "You have a fine reputation, Señor Gar. The princess"—sarcasm crept into the title—"is your client. But I think that *after* the princess threw the knife at the man she knew was impersonating The Great Black she went to Black's dressing room.

I think he had already departed.

"The doorman is an old Filipino by the name of Vincente Lapa. He thinks that The Great Black left the theater just before the pigeons were released—that is because of the applause he heard. The Great Black had left when Lapa heard it. That applause, you recall, was just before Janisohn fell. Almost immediately after that Madame Vlatchnoff threw her knife, unseen; reached the dressing room unseen. Her story that The Great Black was with her there is a lie.

"As for your second question: Where is The Great Black? What does a man do when he has quarreled with the woman he loves? Does he retire to his hotel room? Perhaps. Or perhaps he walks the city, visits drinking places. The police are searching for him, Señor Gar."

"And when you find him?" Jo Gar asked.

Sadi Ratan raised palms to a flurry of warm rain. "You disagree with my theory, but you too have promised your client only that you will seek the murderer of the dead man. Perhaps, then, when we find this Hugh Black, he will not recall having been in the dressing room with Madame Vlatchnoff at the proper time to establish her alibi. Perhaps he will not recall it *in time.*"

"Perhaps," Jo Gar agreed. "Then there was the knife. Since you believe that Princess Vlatchnoff used it in killing a lover she wished to forget—how did it reach the ceiling near the dress room?"

Sadi Ratan's smile became grimmer. "Two men have come to me, Señor Gar. One was seated in the audience in the third row, another in the first. Each of them saw the knife after it had struck. When the assistants pulled the body behind the curtain, the knife remained in the neck."

Jo Gar whistled. "And after that?"

"We found blood on the knife we withdrew from the corridor ceiling."

Jo Gar nodded. "It is so. Yet The Great Black's assistants who lifted Janisohn's' body must have seen the knife."

Sadi Ratan's voice was mocking. "It is so," he replied. "Yet Madame Vlatchnoff is very beautiful, and it is not beyond possibility that they realized Janisohn was only a lover of hers—a past lover—and one who impersonated a great magician for a few minutes."

Jo Gar whistled again. "And thus the knife was returned to the princess, fingerprints removed from the hilt. And it was she who skillfully tossed it against the corridor ceiling."

"And why not, Señor Gar?"

Jo Gar smiled. "I can think of *many* reasons, Lieutenant. But the rain and the wind are for younger men—men like yourself. I seek shelter. *Adios.*"

Surprise was in Sadi Ratan's eyes. "*Adios,* Señor Gar!"

AS JO GAR closed the door of Ling Po's shop, a bell tinkled.

The detective called, "The hour is late, and Jo Gar is regretful."

Ling Po waddled toward Jo Gar, bowing many times. "The hour at which Señor Gar visits me—it is the best," he stated. "You are wet, Señor."

"It does not matter, Ling Po. Tonight I have not come to sip tea and hear wise words. I have come for help. I have been foolish tonight, Ling Po. I have visited many shops. And here in the shop of my good friend—"

His eyes went to a small space on a low shelf holding many objects: dusty Buddhas; fans; strings of wooden beads.

After a few seconds he asked, "Today you sold something from the shelf?"

The wrinkles of Ling Po's yellow skin formed a smile again. "It is as you say Señor," he said. "It was the small lacquer box of very fine workmanship. It brought a good price."

"A lacquer box—and the purchaser did not bargain with you, Ling Po?"

The elderly Chinese looked at the detective with a puzzled expression. "He did not bargain, this one," he stated.

"Some men can afford not to bargain," said Jo Gar. His right hand buried itself in a pocket, withdrew an object, held it beneath Ling Po's eyes. "This is the lacquer box for which the purchaser did not bargain, Ling Po?"

The eyes of the old Chinese widened. He nodded. "It is the box," he muttered. "I do not think that in all Manila there is another—" He stopped. "But Señor Gar, how is it that you—"

Jo Gar smiled and placed the box carefully on a counter. He said, "Please, Ling Po, do not touch the box. You see, there is still dust on a portion of it."

The black eyes of the Chinese held an inscrutable expression. "Since you have not asked me, yet wish to know, Señor Gar—he was a tall one, the purchaser. His shoulders were broad, and he possessed great dignity. His hair was dark and rolling like the China Sea."

Jo Gar smiled. "You perhaps recall the hour of the purchase, Ling Po?"

"It so happens that this one asked me the price of the clock of my ancestors," said Ling Po. "My eyes went to it, and I recall the hour. Within twenty minutes the hour of eleven would strike."

Jo Gar looked at the old clock, glanced at his wrist watch, raised his eyes to the old clock again.

"I told the tall one that the clock was not to be purchased. It has never failed by so much as a minute, Señor Gar. He bowed to me and went away."

The detective nodded. "It is good not to sell things that have served a family well," he said. "And was tonight the first time the purchaser of the lacquer box had come to your shop, Ling Po?"

The elderly Chinese shook his head. "Two mornings ago he visited me, Señor Gar. He did not buy, but he looked at many objects. He asked me then if my shop was open at night, and I answered that my shop was open most hours of the clock and that I slept little."

Jo Gar nodded. "Yet you had been dozing tonight just before the purchaser of the lacquer box entered the shop?"

There was faint surprise in Ling Po's black eyes as he nodded. "It is so. Tonight I was weary. But Señor Gar, how is it that you..." His voice trailed off.

"Tomorrow you shall know many things, Ling Po. But tonight—" Jo Gar lifted the lacquer box from the counter, moved across to the shelf. On the spot where the box had rested there was little dust. Jo

Gar fitted the box at the proper angle on the shelf.

He said: "It is almost two. Long ago I should have been home in bed. Kalaa, my assistant, will be waiting up." His gray-blue eyes smiled. "The box rested there before you sold it to the tall one, Ling Po?"

Ling Po nodded. "For many months, Señor Gar. Then it is purchased, and within a few hours you return it."

The detective removed the lacquer box from the shelf, placed it in a coat pocket. He bowed to Ling Po. "And I go now to return it to the owner, Ling Po. Tomorrow I shall visit you again."

The elderly Chinese bowed low. "Good, Señor Gar, for in mystery there is often danger. I do not seek mystery as you do."

"My profession requires that I seek it," said Jo Gar. "It is so also with the profession of—magician." He went from the shop, closing the door behind him.

The automobile Jo Gar hailed rattled along the Escolta, passing sleepy drivers of *calesas.* When it passed police headquarters the detective called sharply in Tagalog, "Stop! Wait for me here."

Inside the building he went directly to the office of Lieutenant Sadi Ratan.

"You are still up, Señor Gar," the lieutenant observed. "I advise you to return to your house and sleep."

"You are pleased with yourself, Lieutenant—and you offer me advice, May I ask why?"

"It is a pleasure to inform you, Señor Gar. The Great Black left my office only a few minutes ago. His statements did not in any way aid your client, Madame Vlatchnoff. On the contrary, his statements were damaging to her. And he did establish a perfect alibi for himself."

Sadi Ratan was enjoying himself.

"WE HAVE established the exact time that Janisohn fell to the stage, the knife in his neck. It was eighteen minutes to eleven. At that hour the princess states that she was in the dressing room in Hugh Black's arms. And yet, Señor Gar, The Great Black states that he left the theater *before* the applause intended for him and accepted by the dead man, and that at twenty minutes to eleven he was in a shop a half-mile away."

"You have investigated his statement?" Jo Gar asked.

Sadi Ratan shrugged. "Later in the morning, when the shop will be open. But I do not doubt Hugh Black. He came to me of his own accord as soon as he heard of the murder. He tried at first to protect Madame Vlatchnoff. Then, under my questioning, he admitted that he believed she had thrown the knife, knowing Janisohn had taken his place."

"And the reason for the murder?"

"Hugh Black had discovered that she had had an affair with Janisohn. She did not think he knew it. She no longer loved Janisohn and was afraid of him. Black believes it is possible Janisohn was attempting to blackmail her. So"—the police lieutenant shrugged—"she threw the knife, at which she has great skill."

"She lied about being with Hugh Black, thinking that she could reach him before we did, and that he would protect her. Or perhaps she did not think much about Black, believing she would never be suspected. In any case, she murdered Janisohn. I have phoned. She is being brought here now."

Jo Gar glanced at his wristwatch. "How long has Hugh Black been gone from this office?" he asked.

Sadi Ratan said: "About five minutes."

The detective nodded. "You told him you would investigate his statement that he had been in a certain shop at twenty minutes of eleven—after daylight?"

"Yes, Señor Gar."

Jo Gar's voice was soft. "This is the purchase Hugh Black made, Lieutenant." He held the lacquer box toward Sadi Ratan. "The shop was that of Ling Po, who deals in curios of the Orient," Jo Gar went on. "I have talked to Ling Po, and he has said that a man answering the description of the magician purchased this box from him this evening at twenty minutes to eleven. He was aware of the time because the purchaser also questioned him about buying his ancestral clock."

The detective paused. Sadi Ratan was regarding him with suspicion.

"How is it that you possess the box?"

Jo Gar smiled. "It was the only object in Hugh Black's room at the Manila Hotel that had *not* been there before he left for the theater in the evening."

Sadi Ratan frowned. "How do you know that?" he demanded.

"When I accompanied my client and you to the hotel, you recall we went to Hugh Black's room. You talked with the manager outside. The Princess Vlatchnoff informed me that she had left for the theater with Hugh Black and that the box had not been on the table near the window when they departed."

Sadi Ratan continued to frown. "So you took it and traced it to Ling Po's shop. Clever work, Señor Gar!" He laughed nastily. "And all you learned was that Hugh Black was not at the theater at the moment of the crime. In fact, he was merely purchasing the box he placed in his room before we arrived there."

Jo Gar said, "It so happens that I learned more than that." He glanced at his wristwatch again. "Before dawn," he added, "I can turn over to you the murderer of Janisohn."

"The murderess is now under careful guard," Ratan told him.

Jo Gar shook his head. "The princess did *not* murder Janisohn. My reputation is not a small one in the Islands. Will you come with me, Lieutenant?"

"Where do we go?" asked Sadi Ratan.

"To the shop of Ling Po."

THE STREET of the Three Candles was little more than a narrow, curving alley, the entrance to which was almost directly opposite Ling Po's store. Standing in the darkness of the alley, Sadi Ratan whispered impatiently: "We have been here more than thirty minutes, Señor Gar. I am tired. I shall stay with you only ten minutes—"

Jo Gar's fingers gripped Sadi Ratan's wrist in a signal for silence. There had been no sound of footfalls along the street, but now a bent figure came into sight. It paused before the entrance to Ling Po's store. Shadow moved within shadow, and there was the sound of a door closing.

Jo Gar motioned Sadi Ratan to follow him and hurried across the street. In the doorway of the shop the detective's left hand moved to a hip pocket as his right turned the knob of the door. His automatic shifted to his right hand as he entered the store.

Above the counter a light wavered, left the face of Ling Po's ancestral clock. Even as it swung away, Jo Gar saw that the glass covering the clock's face had been hinged to one side.

The beam from the light struck across Jo Gar's face. Then the beam was gone.

Jo Gar said sharply, "Please stand still."

There was a clicking sound—the beam of Sadi Ratan's flashlight shifted high, dropped. Sadi Ratan swore.

The white light shone full on the face of Hugh Black.

Ling Po called sleepily from the rear of the shop, "What is it that happens?"

Jo Gar said grimly: "Remain quiet, Mr. Black. I have in my hand a weapon that is swifter than a knife."

In the flare of the beam Hugh Black's lips were twitching.

Jo Gar called: "Ling Po, it is Señor Gar. Quickly—make a light for us!"

There was silence for several seconds, and then Ling Po pattered into the room. A switch snapped; light from two bulbs whitened the interior.

Jo Gar raised his automatic, walked toward the magician. As he moved he said slowly, "This, Lieutenant Ratan, is the murderer of Janisohn!"

"You lie!" Hugh Black cried fiercely.

Jo Gar halted near the counter. "I do not lie," he said. "The Princess Vlatchnoff loves you more than you love her, Mr. Black. She tried to protect you, even while defending herself. That is why she said you were with her in her dressing room—when Janisohn collapsed on the stage. But you were not with her."

The Great Black stood motionless.

"You murdered Richard Janisohn," the detective went on, "because you discovered he had had an affair with Princess Vlatchnoff. And I think you had come to hate the princess, Mr. Black. Knowing that she would be suspected, being skilled at throwing a knife—"

"You lie!" Hugh Black's voice was hoarse. "I was not in the theater when Janisohn was murdered. I could not throw a knife if I—"

Jo Gar smiled. "You did not *throw* a knife, Mr. Black. You *struck* with it."

"You fool!" The Great Black's words held a smothered fury. "They have told me that he fell in full view of the audience—as he was bowing."

Jo Gar said, "He did not fall in full view of the audience, Mr. Black, It was you who fell! It was *you* who with your magician's skill produced a knife, clutched at it and the back of your neck as you sprawled to the stage!"

"Madre de Dios!" Sadi Ratan's voice was a whisper.

Jo Gar said, "Your two assistants carried your body to one of the illusion cabinets, Janisohn hurried to you, not knowing what had happened. The assistants had left you. It was *then* that you pulled

Janisohn down, Mr. Black. It was *then* that you knifed him!"

The ancestral clock ticked against the heavy breathing of Hugh Black and Sadi Ratan. Ling Po made no sound.

Jo Gar said almost tonelessly: "I did not believe the Princess Vlatchnoff's story that you were with her in the dressing room. The stage-door attendant was not positive of the time he had seen you leave. There was blood on the cabinet base—stains that even the careful Lieutenant Ratan did not see.

"I was not positive that Janisohn had taken the applause for you this evening, Mr. Black. The knife found in the corridor ceiling was a trick to confuse. The princess, having murdered, would not have thrown it there. I think one of your assistants placed it there.

"And then there was the matter of the lacquer box, Mr. Black." He watched The Great Black's eyes widen, as fear came into them. "It puzzled me. The box was not in your room when you left with the princess for the theater. Yet it was there after Janisohn's murder. There was still some dust clinging to the box. It had been handled carefully. I thought perhaps you considered the box—important. I was not wrong. I traced the box to this shop."

THE GREAT BLACK managed a twisted smile. "You are a fool," he breathed. "I have been told that Janisohn fell to the stage at exactly eighteen minutes to eleven. I was just leaving this shop at twenty minutes to eleven."

Ling Po said slowly: "It is as this one says, Señor Gar. It is so."

Jo Gar spoke calmly. "Why did you come here this morning, Mr. Black? You broke into the shop of Ling Po. Why?"

The Great Black laughed. "I wanted to see if I was clever enough to manage an entrance. I wanted to—"

Jo Gar lifted his gun arm. "Knowing Janisohn was murdered, you tell us you wished to test your skill? Play a game?"

The Great Black's eyes were on the detective's weapon.

Jo Gar went on: "We waited for you, Mr. Black. I *knew* that you would come here tonight. You came to Ling Po's shop once before you purchased the lacquer box. You looked around carefully.

"This evening you returned. Ling Po had been dozing. You were in the store when he greeted you. You purchased a lacquer box—and because the box was important to you, it was taken to your room. That was a mistake. You should have kept the box with you.

"You were afraid that the Princess Vlatchnoff might accuse you of the murder of Janisohn, so you sought to establish an alibi, Mr. Black. You saw to it that Ling Po noticed that you departed from his shop at twenty minutes of eleven, but you did *not* depart at twenty minutes of eleven. For while Ling Po was dozing, you had *set back* the large hand of the clock fifteen minutes! It was actually *five* minutes to eleven when you left this shop—and you had already murdered Janisohn."

There was silence in the room. The Great Black was swaying.

Jo Gar spoke gently: "I waited for you because I had noticed that the clock was fifteen minutes slow. I knew you would return. It must be set ahead again. It must be an accurate clock."

There was no color in Hugh Black's face. "The damned—box! I might have—"

Jo Gar turned to Sadi Ratan. "He is your prisoner, Lieutenant Ratan."

As Sadi Ratan moved toward the magician, Jo Gar watched The Great Black's eyes. He could not read the expression in them. A confession to come? A defense? Suicide, perhaps, in a small cell? The detective suddenly felt tired.

Ling Po spoke. "Even at this dark hour, Señor Gar, there is the solace of tea."

Jo Gar nodded and, without looking at The Great Black or Sadi Ratan, went slowly toward the rear of the shop.

A Remembrance of E.R. Hagemann

R.H. Miller

WITH THE passing of E.R. Hagemann in 1994 the world of hardboiled fiction lost one of its best critics and most devoted readers, and I lost a dear friend and valued colleague. Ed and I shared an interest in this exciting school of modern American literature, and he and I talked many hours about Chandler, and especially Hammett, my major interest and one of his, too. My knowledge of the literature of this movement is modest, but his was deep and authoritative. In his career he had lived and taught and studied within the locale of much of the fiction, the state of California, and so smitten was he by the California scene that even after he moved to Kentucky and his permanent post at the University of Louisville he continued to keep all his watches and clocks on Pacific time. It was only one of a number of tics that made Ed a lovable and also at times a frustrating colleague.

His experience and personality fitted him especially to study that literature. He was no stranger to violence, for as a Marine during World War II, and a highly decorated one, he survived some of the most vicious fighting in the Pacific theater, and he recognized the authenticity in hardboiled fiction of the metaphor of violence. In his personal life too Ed was a hard-drinking, irascible guy, who, as one of my colleagues once described him, "often had a thousand gut reactions before his brain went into operation." He and Raymond Chandler were brothers under the skin, so to speak. In temperament as well he seemed a perfect match for this "new fiction" that was to lead directly to the writing and critical thinking of authors like Hemingway and Flannery O'Connor.

Ed's particular interest in this literature was in that ephemeral serial form of publication we have come to know as the "pulps," and he and I were instrumental in getting the university to purchase a large accumulation of pulps that came up for sale in the early '70s.

And within that subcategory he became an expert on Joseph T. Shaw's brainchild, *Black Mask,* and the many writers who passed in parade within the pages of that pioneering publication. A few of those writers caught his critical eye, and we and they are the beneficiaries of his acumen.

Therefore it is especially gratifying to see that his work on one of those writers, Raoul Whitfield, and this eminent publication has been revived. Nothing he did in his scholarly career made him prouder than did his work on *Black Mask,* and I know in life, as in death, he would have been deeply honored to see his efforts once again in print.

R.H. Miller
University of Louisville

R.H. Miller is Professor of English at the University of Louisville, where he specializes in Renaissance literature, particularly manuscripts and early printed books, and modern fiction, especially the author Graham Greene. He has also read papers on detective fiction and recently published two articles on Dashiell Hammett: "Hammett's Physical Falcon, Or, What Exactly Did the Emperor Get?" in Studies in American Culture, *and a note on the Flitcraft episode* (The Maltese Falcon) *in* The Explicator. *His interests also include Raymond Chandler and James M. Cain, and several contemporary authors working in the hardboiled tradition.*

Publication History

WEST OF GUAM by Raoul F. Whitfield, writing as Ramon DeColta. Copyright © 1930 by Pro-Distributors Publishing Company, Inc. Copyright renewed 1958 by Popular Publications, Inc. From *Black Mask* Vol. 12 No. 12 (February 1930).

DEATH IN THE PASIG by Raoul F. Whitfield, writing as Ramon DeColta. Copyright © 1930 by Pro-Distributors Publishing Company, Inc. Copyright renewed 1958 by Popular Publications, Inc. From *Black Mask* Vol. 13 No. 1 (March 1930).

RED HEMP by Raoul F. Whitfield, writing as Ramon DeColta. Copyright © 1930 by Pro-Distributors Publishing Company, Inc. Copyright renewed 1958 by Popular Publications, Inc. From *Black Mask* Vol. 13 No. 2 (April 1930).

SIGNALS OF STORM by Raoul F. Whitfield, writing as Ramon DeColta. Copyright © 1930 by Pro-Distributors Publishing Company, Inc. Copyright renewed 1958 by Popular Publications, Inc. From *Black Mask* Vol. 13 No. 4 (June 1930).

ENOUGH ROPE by Raoul F. Whitfield, writing as Ramon DeColta. Copyright © 1930 by Pro-Distributors Publishing Company, Inc. Copyright renewed 1958 by Popular Publications, Inc. From *Black Mask* Vol. 13 No. 5 (July 1930).

NAGASAKI BOUND by Raoul F. Whitfield, writing as Ramon DeColta. Copyright © 1930 by Pro-Distributors Publishing Company, Inc. Copyright renewed 1958 by Popular Publications, Inc. From *Black Mask* Vol. 13 No. 7 (September 1930).

NAGASAKI KNIVES by Raoul F. Whitfield, writing as Ramon DeColta. Copyright © 1930 by Pro-Distributors Publishing

DeColta. Copyright © 1931 by Pro-Distributors Publishing Company, Inc. Copyright renewed 1959 by Popular Publications, Inc. From *Black Mask* Vol. 14 No. 8 (October 1931).

THE JAVANESE MASK by Raoul F. Whitfield, writing as Ramon DeColta. Copyright © 1931 by Pro-Distributors Publishing Company, Inc. Copyright renewed 1959 by Popular Publications, Inc. From *Black Mask* Vol. 14 No. 10 (December 1931).

THE BLACK SAMPAN by Raoul F. Whitfield, writing as Ramon DeColta. Copyright © 1932 by Pro-Distributors Publishing Company, Inc. Copyright renewed 1960 by Popular Publications, Inc. From *Black Mask* Vol. 15 No. 4 (June 1932).

CHINA MAN by Raoul F. Whitfield, writing as Ramon DeColta. Copyright © 1932 by Pro-Distributors Publishing Company, Inc. Copyright renewed 1960 by Popular Publications, Inc. From *Black Mask* Vol. 15 No. 1 (March 1932).

THE SIAMESE CAT by Raoul F. Whitfield, writing as Ramon DeColta. Copyright © 1932 by Pro-Distributors Publishing Company, Inc. Copyright renewed 1960 by Popular Publications, Inc. From *Black Mask* Vol. 15 No. 2 (April 1932).

CLIMBING DEATH by Raoul F. Whitfield, writing as Ramon DeColta. Copyright © 1932 by Pro-Distributors Publishing Company, Inc. Copyright renewed 1960 by Popular Publications, Inc. From *Black Mask* Vol. 15 No. 5 (July 1932).

THE MAGICIAN MURDER by Raoul F. Whitfield, writing as Ramon DeColta. Copyright © 1932 by Pro-Distributors Publishing Company, Inc. Copyright renewed 1960 by Popular Publications, Inc. From *Black Mask* Vol. 15 No. 9 (November 1932).

THE MAN FROM SHANGHAI by Raoul F. Whitfield, writing as Ramon DeColta. Copyright © 1933 by Pro-Distributors Publishing Company, Inc. Copyright renewed 1961 by Popular Publications, Inc. From *Black Mask* Vol. 16 No. 3 (May 1933).

THE AMBER FAN by Raoul F. Whitfield, writing as Ramon DeColta. Copyright © 1933 by Pro-Distributors Publishing Company, Inc. Copyright renewed 1961 by Popular Publications, Inc. From *Black Mask* Vol. 16 No. 5 (July 1933).